PENGUIN BOOKS

2677

THE WHITE MONKEY

John Galsworthy, the son of a solicitor, was born in 1867 and educated at Harrow and New College, Oxford. He was called to the Bar in 1890; while travelling in the Far East he met Conrad, who became a lifelong friend. In 1897 he published *Four Winds* (short stories) under another name, and later two novels. *The Man of Property* (1906), the first book in *The Forsyte Saga*, together with his first play, *The Silver Box*, established him in the public mind. Other novels and plays followed, but it was not until after the First World War that he completed the first Forsyte trilogy with *In Chancery* (1920) and *To Let* (1921). The complete edition of *The Forsyte Saga*, first published in 1922, has since been through fifty-six impressions. The second Forsyte trilogy, *A Modern Comedy*, appeared in 1929, and the third, *End of the Chapter*, posthumously in 1934. Galsworthy founded the P.E.N. Club, was awarded a Nobel Prize, and received the Order of Merit in 1929. He lived on Dartmoor for many years and afterwards at Bury on the Sussex Downs. He died in 1933. All nine volumes in the three Forsyte trilogies are now in Penguins.

John Galsworthy

THE WHITE MONKEY

✦

BOOK ONE OF

A Modern Comedy

PENGUIN BOOKS

in association with William Heinemann Ltd

Penguin Books Ltd, Harmondsworth, Middlesex, England
Penguin Books Australia Ltd, Ringwood, Victoria, Australia

—

First published by William Heinemann Ltd 1924
Published in Penguin Books 1967
Reprinted 1967, 1968

—

Made and printed in Great Britain
by Hazell Watson & Viney Ltd
Aylesbury, Bucks
Set in Linotype Granjon

—

The White Monkey is Book One of a *Modern Comedy*
which comprises the second three volumes of
The Forsyte Chronicles (nine volumes)

Contents

TO
Max Beerbohm

FORSYTE FAMILY TREE

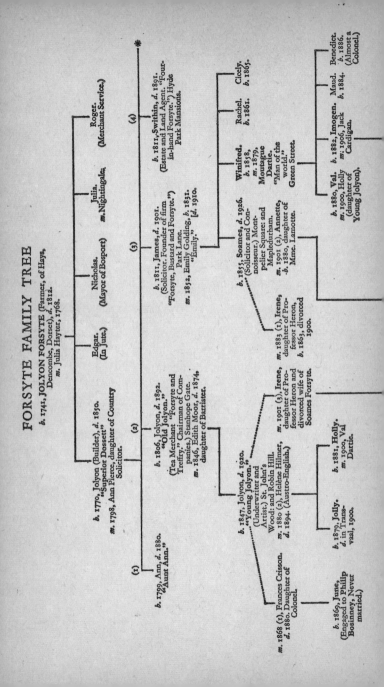

b. 1741, JOLYON FORSYTE (Farmer, of Hays,
Denscombe, Dorset), d. 1812.
m. Julia Hayter, 1768.

b. 1770, Jolyon (Builder), d. 1850.
"Superior Dosset"
m. 1798, Ann Pierce, daughter of Country
Solicitor.

Edgar,
(In Jute.)

Nicholas,
(Mayor of Bosport.)

Julia,
m. Nightingale.

Roger,
(Merchant Service.)

b. 1799, Ann, d. 1880.
"Aunt Ann."

b. 1806, Jolyon, d. 1892.
"Old Jolyon."
(Tea Merchant "Forsyte and
Treffry." Chairman of Companies.) Stanhope Gate.
m. 1846, Edith Moor, d. 1874,
daughter of Barrister.

b. 1811, James, d. 1901.
(Solicitor. Founder of firm
"Forsyte, Bustard and Forsyte."
Park Lane.)
m. 1852, Emily Golding, b. 1831.
"Emily," [d. 1910.]

b. 1814, Swithin, d. 1891.
(Estate and Land Agent. "Four-
in-hand Forsyte.") Hyde
Park Mansions.

m. 1868 (1), Frances Crisson,
d. 1880. Daughter of
Colonel.

b. 1847, Jolyon, d. 1910.
"Young Jolyon."
(Underwriter and
Artist.) St. John's
Wood: and Robin Hill.
m. 1880 (2), Helène Hilmer,
d. 1894. (Austro-English.)

m. 1901 (3), Irene,
daughter of Pro-
fessor Heron and
divorced wife of
Soames Forsyte.

b. 1855, Soames, d. 1926.
(Solicitor and Con-
noisseur.) Mont-
pelier Square: and
Mapledurham.
m. 1901 (2), Annette,
b. 1880, daughter of
Mme. Lamotte.

m. 1883 (1), Irene,
daughter of Profes-
sor Heron,
b. 1863, divorced
1900.

Winifred,
b. 1858,
m. 1879,
Montague
Dartie.
"Man of the
world."
Green Street.

Rachel,
b. 1861.

Cicely,
b. 1865.

b. 1869, June,
(Engaged to Philip
Bosinney, Never
married.)

b. 1879, Jolly,
d. in Trans-
vaal, 1900.

b. 1881, Holly.
m. 1900, Val
Dartie.

b. 1880, Val.
m. 1900, Holly
(daughter of
Young Jolyon).

b. 1882, Imogen.
m. 1906, Jack
Cardigan.

Maud.
b. 1884.

Benedict.
b. 1886.
(Almost a
Colonel.)

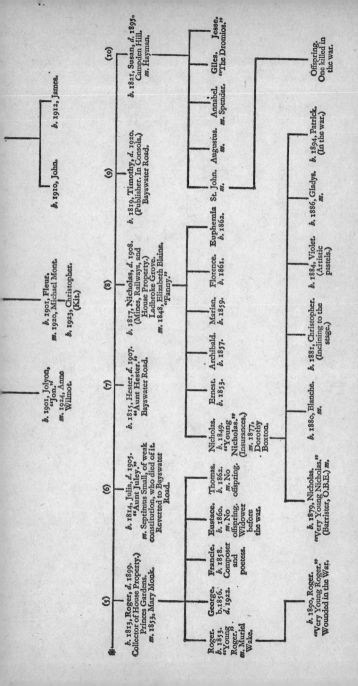

PREFACE

❦

In naming this second part of The Forsyte Chronicles 'A
Modern Comedy' the word comedy is stretched, perhaps, as far
as the word Saga was stretched to cover the first part. And yet,
what but a comedic view can be taken, what but comedic significance gleaned, of so restive a period as that in which we have
lived since the war? An Age which knows not what it wants,
yet is intensely preoccupied with getting it, must evoke a smile,
if rather a sad one.

To render the forms and colours of an epoch is beyond the
powers of any novelist, and very far beyond the powers of this
novelist; but to try and express a little of its spirit was undoubtedly at the back of his mind in penning this trilogy. Like the
Irishman's chicken, our Present runs about so fast that it cannot
be summed up; it can at most be snapshotted while it hurries
looking for its Future without notion where, what, or when
that Future will be.

The England of 1886, when the Forsyte Saga began, also had
no Future, for England then expected its Present to endure, and
rode its bicycle in a sort of dream, disturbed only by two bogles
– Mr Gladstone and the Irish Members.

The England of 1926 – when the Modern Comedy closes –
with one foot in the air and the other in a Morris Oxford, is
going round and round like a kitten after its tail, muttering:
'If one could only see where one wants to stop!'

Everything being now relative, there is no longer absolute
dependence to be placed on God, Free Trade, Marriage, Consols,
Coal, or Caste.

Everywhere being now overcrowded, there is no place where

anyone can stay for long, except the mere depopulated country-side, admittedly too dull, and certainly too unprofitable to dwell in.

Everyone, having been in an earthquake which lasted four years, has lost the habit of standing still.

And yet, the English character has changed very little, if at all. The General Strike of 1926, with which the last part of this trilogy begins, supplied proof of that. We are still a people that cannot be rushed, distrustful of extremes, saved by the grace of our defensive humour, well-tempered, resentful of interference, improvident and wasteful, but endowed with a certain genius for recovery. If we believe in nothing much else, we still believe in ourselves. That salient characteristic of the English will bear thinking about. Why, for instance, do we continually run ourselves down? Simply because we have not got the inferiority complex and are indifferent to what other people think of us. No people in the world seems openly less sure of itself; no people is secretly more sure. Incidentally, it might be worth the while of those who own certain public mouths inclined to blow the British trumpet to remember, that the blowing of one's own trumpet is the insidious beginning of the inferiority complex. Only those strong enough to keep silent about self are strong enough to be sure of self. The epoch we are passing through is one which favours misjudgement of the English character, and of the position of England. There never was a country where real deterioration of human fibre had less chance than in this island, because there is no other country whose climate is so changeable, so tempering to character, so formative of grit, and so basically healthy. What follows in this preface should be read in the light of that remark.

In the present epoch, no Early Victorianism survives. By Early Victorianism is meant that of the old Forsytes, already on the wane in 1886; what has survived, and potently, is the Victorianism of Soames and his generation, more self-conscious, but not sufficiently self-conscious to be either self-destructive or self-forgetful. It is against the background of this more or less fixed quantity that we can best see the shape and colour of the present intensely self-conscious and all-questioning generation. The old Forsytes – Old Jolyon, Swithin and James, Roger, Nicholas and Timothy – lived their lives without ever asking whether life was worth living. They found it interesting, very absorbing from day to day, and even if they had no very intimate belief in a future life, they had very great faith in the progress of their own positions, and in laying up treasure for their children. Then came Young Jolyon and Soames and their contemporaries, who, although they had imbibed, with Darwinism and the 'Varsities, definite doubts about a future life, and sufficient introspection to wonder whether they themselves were progressing, retained their sense of property and their desire to provide for, and to live on in their progeny. The generation which came in when Queen Victoria went out, through new ideas about the treatment of children, because of new modes of locomotion, and owing to the Great War, has decided that everything requires re-valuation. And, since there is, seemingly, very little future before property, and less before life, is determined to live now or never, without bothering about the fate of such offspring as it may chance to have. Not that the present generation is less fond of its children than were past generations – human nature does not change on points so elementary – but when everything is keyed to such a pitch of uncertainty, to secure the future at the expense of the present no longer seems worth while.

This is really the fundamental difference between the present and the past generations. People will not provide against that which they cannot see ahead.

All this, of course, refers only to that tenth or so of the population whose eyes are above the property line; below that line there are no Forsytes, and therefore no need for this preface to dip. What average Englishman, moreover, with less than three hundred a year ever took thought for the future, even in Early Victorian days?

This Modern Comedy, then, is staged against a background of that more or less fixed quantity, Soames, and his co-father-in-law, light weight and ninth baronet, Sir Lawrence Mont, with such subsidiary neo-Victorians as the self-righteous Mr Danby,

Elderson, Mr Blythe, Sir James Foskisson, Wilfred Bentworth, and Hilary Charwell. Pooling their idiosyncrasies, qualities, and mental attitudes, one gets a fairly comprehensive and steady past against which to limn the features of the present — Fleur and Michael, Wilfrid Desert, Aubrey Greene, Marjorie Ferrar, Norah Curfew, Jon, the Rafaelite, and other minor characters. The multiple types and activities of today — even above the Plimsoll line of property — would escape the confines of twenty novels, so that this Modern Comedy is bound to be a gross understatement of the present generation, but not perhaps a libel on it. Symbolism is boring, so let us hope that a certain resemblance between the case of Fleur and that of her generation chasing the serenity of which it has been defrauded may escape notice. The fact remains that for the moment, at least, youth is balancing, twirling on the tiptoes of uncertainty. What is to come? Will contentment yet be caught? How will it all settle down? Will things ever again settle down — who knows? Are there to come fresh wars, and fresh inventions hot-foot on those not yet mastered and digested? Or will Fate decree another pause, like that of Victorian times, during which revaluated life will crystallize, and give property and its brood of definite beliefs a further innings?

But, however much or little 'A Modern Comedy' may be deemed to reflect the spirit of an Age, it continues in the main to relate the tale of life which sprang from the meeting of Soames and Irene in a Bournemouth drawing-room in 1881, a tale which could but end when its spine snapped, and Soames 'took the ferry' forty-five years later.

The chronicler, catechized (as he often is) concerning Soames, knows not precisely what he stands for. Taking him for all in all he was honest, anyway. He lived and moved and had his peculiar being, and now he sleeps. His creator may be pardoned for thinking there was something fitting about his end, for, however far we have travelled from Greek culture and philosophy, there is still truth in the old Greek proverb: 'That which a man most loves shall in the end destroy him.'

JOHN GALSWORTHY

'No retreat, no retreat
They must conquer or die
Who have no retreat!'

Mr Gay

PART ONE

Chapter One

PROMENADE

◄◄‹‹›››

COMING down the steps of 'Snooks' Club, so nicknamed by George Forsyte in the late eighties, on that momentous mid-October afternoon of 1922, Sir Lawrence Mont, ninth baronet, set his fine nose towards the east wind, and moved his thin legs with speed. Political by birth rather than by nature, he reviewed the revolution which had restored his Party to power with a detachment not devoid of humour. Passing the Remove Club, he thought: 'Some sweating into shoes, there! No more confectioned dishes. A woodcock – without trimmings, for a change!'

The captains and the kings had departed from 'Snooks' before he entered it, for he was not of 'that catch-penny crew, now paid off, no sir; fellows who turned their tails on the land the moment the war was over. Pah!' But for an hour he had listened to echoes, and his lively twisting mind, embedded in deposits of the past, sceptical of the present and of all political protestations and pronouncements, had recorded with amusement the confusion of patriotism and personalities left behind by the fateful gathering. Like most landowners, he distrusted doctrine. If he had a political belief, it was a tax on wheat; and so far as he could see, he was now alone in it – but then he was not seeking election; in other words, his principle was not in danger of extinction from the votes of those who had to pay for bread. Principles – he mused – *au fond* were pocket; and he wished the deuce people wouldn't pretend they weren't! Pocket, in the deep sense of that word, of course, self-interest as member of a definite community. And how the devil was this definite community, the English nation, to exist, when all its land was going out of cultivation, and all its ships and docks in danger of

17

destruction by aeroplanes? He had listened that hour past for a single mention of the land. Not one! It was not practical politics! Confound the fellows! They had to wear their breeches out – keeping seats or getting them. No connexion between posteriors and posterity! No, by George! Thus reminded of posterity, it occurred to him rather suddenly that his son's wife showed no signs as yet. Two years! Time they were thinking about children. It was dangerous to get into the habit of not having them, when a title and estate depended. A smile twisted his lips and eyebrows which resembled spinneys of dark pothooks. A pretty young creature, most taking; and knew it, too! Whom was she not getting to know? Lions and tigers, monkeys and cats – her house was becoming quite a menagerie of more or less celebrities. There was a certain unreality about that sort of thing! And opposite a British lion in Trafalgar Square Sir Lawrence thought : 'She'll be getting these to her house next! She's got the collecting habit. Michael must look out – in a collector's house there's always a lumber-room for old junk, and husbands are liable to get into it. That reminds me: I promised her a Chinese Minister. Well, she must wait now till after the General Election.'

Down Whitehall, under the grey easterly sky, the towers of Westminster came for a second into view. 'A certain unreality in that, too,' he thought. 'Michael and his fads! Well, it's the fashion – Socialistic principles and a rich wife. Sacrifice with safety! Peace with plenty! Nostrums – ten a penny!'

Passing the newspaper hubbub of Charing Cross, frenzied by the political crisis, he turned up to the left towards Danby and Winter, publishers, where his son was junior partner. A new theme for a book had just begun to bend a mind which had already produced a *Life of Montrose*, *Far Cathay*, that work of Eastern travel, and a fanciful conversation between the shades of Gladstone, and Disraeli – entitled *A Duet*. With every step taken, from 'Snooks' eastward, his erect thin figure in Astrakhan-collared coat, his thin grey-moustached face, and tortoiseshell rimmed monocle under the lively dark eyebrow, had seemed more rare. It became almost a phenomenon in this dingy back street, where carts stuck like winter flies, and persons went by with books under their arms, as if educated.

He had nearly reached the door of Danby's when he encountered two young men. One of them was clearly his son, better dressed since his marriage, and smoking a cigar – thank goodness – instead of those eternal cigarettes; the other – ah! yes – Michael's sucking poet and best man, head in air, rather a sleek head under a velour hat! He said:

'Ha, Michael!'

'*Hallo*, Bart! You know my governor, Wilfrid? Wilfrid Desert. *Copper Coin* – some poet, Bart, I tell you. You must read him. We're going home. Come along!'

Sir Lawrence went along.

'What happened at "Snooks"?'

'*Le roi est mort*. Labour can start lying, Michael – election next month.'

'Bart was brought up, Wilfrid, in days that knew not Demos.'

'Well, Mr Desert, do *you* find reality in politics now?'

'Do you find reality in anything, sir?'

'In income tax, perhaps.'

Michael grinned.

'Above knighthood,' he said, 'there's no such thing as simple faith.'

'Suppose your friends came into power, Michael – in some ways not a bad thing, help 'em to grow up – what could they do, eh? Could they raise national taste? Abolish the cinema? Teach English people to cook? Prevent other countries from threatening war? Make us grow our own food? Stop the increase of town life? Would they hang dabblers in poison gas? Could they prevent flying in war-time? Could they weaken the possessive instinct – anywhere? Or do anything, in fact, but alter the incidence of possession a little? All party politics are top dressing. We're ruled by the inventors, and human nature; and we live in Queer Street, Mr Desert.'

'Much my sentiments, sir.'

Michael flourished his cigar.

'Bad old men, you two!'

And removing their hats, they passed the Cenotaph.

'Curiously symptomatic – that thing,' said Sir Lawrence; 'monument to the dread of swank – most characteristic. And the dread of swank –'

'Go on, Bart,' said Michael.

'The fine, the large, the florid – all off! No far-sighted views, no big schemes, no great principles, no great religion, or great art – aestheticism in cliques and backwaters, small men in small hats.'

'As panteth the heart after Byron, Wilberforce, and the Nelson Monument. My poor old Bart! What about it, Wilfrid?'

'Yes, Mr Desert – what about it?'

Desert's dark face contracted.

'It's an age of paradox,' he said. 'We all kick up for freedom, and the only institutions gaining strength are Socialism and the Roman Catholic Church. We're frightfully self-conscious about art – and the only art development is the cinema. We're nuts on peace – and all we're doing about it is to perfect poison gas.'

Sir Lawrence glanced sideways at a young man so bitter.

'And how's publishing, Michael?'

'Well, *Copper Coin* is selling like hot cakes; and there's quite a movement in *A Duet*. What about this for a new ad.: "A Duet, by Sir Lawrence Mont, Bart. The most distinguished Conversation ever held between the Dead." That ought to get the psychic. Wilfrid suggested "G.O.M. and Dizzy – broadcasted from Hell." Which do you like best?'

They had come, however, to a policeman holding up his hand against the nose of a van horse, so that everything marked time. The engines of the cars whirred idly, their drivers' faces set towards the space withheld from them; a girl on a bicycle looked vacantly about her, grasping the back of the van, where a youth sat sideways with his legs stretched out towards her. Sir Lawrence glanced again at young Desert. A thin, pale-dark face, good-looking, but a hitch in it, as if not properly timed; nothing *outré* in dress or manner, and yet socially at large; less vivacious than that lively rascal, his own son, but as anchorless, and more sceptical – might feel things pretty deeply, though! The police-man lowered his arm.

'You were in the war, Mr Desert?'

'Oh, yes.'

'Air service?'

'And line. Bit of both.'

'Hard on a poet.'

'Not at all. Poetry's only possible when you may be blown up at any moment, or when you live in Putney.'

Sir Lawrence's eyebrow rose. 'Yes?'

'Tennyson, Browning, Wordsworth, Swinburne – they could turn it out; *ils vivaient, mais si peu.*'

'Is there not a third condition favourable?'

'And that, sir?'

'How shall I express it – a certain cerebral agitation in con-nexion with women?'

Desert's face twitched, and seemed to darken.

Michael put his latchkey into the lock of his front door.

Chapter Two

HOME

◄‹‑›►

THE house in South Square, Westminster, to which the young Monts had come after their Spanish honeymoon two years be-fore, might have been called 'emancipated'. It was the work of an architect whose dream was a new house perfectly old, and an old house perfectly new. It followed therefore, no recognized style or tradition, and was devoid of structural prejudice; but it soaked up the smuts of the metropolis with such special rapidity that its stone already respectably resembled that of Wren. Its windows and doors had gently rounded tops. The high-sloping roof, of a fine sooty pink, was almost Danish, and two 'ducky little windows' looked out of it, giving an impression that very

tall servants lived up there. There were rooms on each side of
the front door, which was wide and set off by bay trees in black
and gold bindings. The house was thick through, and the staircase, of a broad chastity, began at the far end of a hall which
had room for quite a number of hats and coats and cards. There
were four bathrooms; and not even a cellar underneath. The
Forsyte instinct for a house had co-operated in its acquisition.
Soames had picked it up for his daughter, undecorated, at that
psychological moment when the bubble of inflation was pricked,
and the air escaping from the balloon of the world's trade.
Fleur, however, had established immediate contact with the
architect – an element which Soames himself had never quite
got over – and decided not to have more than three styles in
her house: Chinese, Spanish, and her own. The room to the
left of the front door, running the breadth of the house, was
Chinese, with ivory panels, a copper floor, central heating, and
cut-glass lustres. It contained four pictures – all Chinese – the
only school in which her father had not yet dabbled. The fireplace, wide and open, had Chinese dogs with Chinese tiles for
them to stand on. The silk was chiefly of jade green. There were
two wonderful old black tea-chests, picked up with Soames's
money at Jobson's – not a bargain. There was no piano, partly
because pianos were too uncompromisingly occidental, and
partly because it would have taken up much room. Fleur aimed
at space – collecting people rather than furniture or *bibelots*.
The light, admitted by windows at both ends, was unfortunately
not Chinese. She would stand sometimes in the centre of this
room, thinking – how to 'bunch' her guests, how to make her
room more Chinese without making it uncomfortable; how to
seem to know all about literature and politics; how to accept
everything her father gave her, without making him aware
that his taste had no sense of the future; how to keep hold of
Sibley Swan, the new literary star, and to get hold of Gurdon
Minho, the old; or how Wilfrid Desert was getting too fond of
her; of what was really her style in dress; of why Michael had
such funny ears; and sometimes she stood not thinking at all –
just aching a little.

When those three came in she was sitting before a red lacquer tea-table, finishing a very good tea. She always had tea brought in rather early, so that she could have a good quiet preliminary 'tuck-in' all by herself, because she was not quite twenty-one, and this was her hour for remembering her youth. By her side Ting-a-ling was standing on his hind feet, his tawny forepaws on a Chinese foot-stool, his snubbed black and tawny muzzle turned up towards the fruits of his philosophy.

'That'll do, Ting. No more, ducky! *No more!*'

The expression of Ting-a-ling answered:

'Well, then, stop, too! Don't subject me to torture!'

A year and three months old, he had been bought by Michael out of a Bond Street shop window on Fleur's twentieth birthday, eleven months ago.

Two years of married life had not lengthened her short dark chestnut hair; had added a little more decision to her quick lips, a little more allurement to her white-lidded, dark-lashed hazel eyes, a little more poise and swing to her carriage, a little more chest and hip measurement; had taken a little from waist and calf measurement, a little colour from cheeks a little less round, and a little sweetness from a voice a little more caressing.

She stood up behind the tray, holding out her white round arms without a word. She avoided unnecessary greetings or farewells. She would have had to say them so often, and their purpose was better served by look, pressure, and slight inclination of head to one side.

With a circular movement of her squeezed hand, she said:

'Draw up. Cream, sir? Sugar, Wilfrid? Ting has had too much — don't feed him! Hand things, Michael. I've heard all about the meeting at "Snooks". You're not going to canvass for Labour, Michael — canvassing's so silly. If anyone canvassed me, I should vote the other way at once.'

'Yes, darling; but you're not the average elector.'

Fleur looked at him. Very sweetly put! Conscious of Wilfrid biting his lips, of Sir Lawrence taking that in, of the amount of silk leg she was showing, of her black and cream teacups, she adjusted these matters. A flutter of her white lids — Desert ceased to bite his lips; a movement of her silk legs - Sir Lawrence ceased to look at him. Holding out her cups, she said:

'I suppose I'm not modern enough?'

Desert, moving a bright little spoon round in his magpie cup, said without looking up:

'As much more modern than the moderns, as you are more ancient.'

' 'Ware poetry !' said Michael.

But when he had taken his father to see the new cartoons by Aubrey Greene, she said:

'Kindly tell me what you meant, Wilfrid.'

Desert's voice seemed to leap from restraint.

'What does it matter? I don't want to waste time with that.'

'But I want to know. It sounded like a sneer.'

'A sneer? From me? Fleur !'

'Then tell me.'

'I meant that you have all their restlessness and practical get-thereness; but you have what they haven't, Fleur – power to turn one's head. And mine is turned. You know it.'

'How would Michael like that – from *you*, his best man?'

Desert moved quickly to the windows.

Fleur took Ting-a-ling on her lap. Such things had been said to her before; but from Wilfrid it was serious. Nice to think she had his heart, of course ! Only, where on earth could she put it, where it wouldn't be seen except by her? He was incalculable – did strange things ! She was a little afraid – not of him, but of that quality in him. He came back to the hearth, and said:

'Ugly, isn't it? Put that damn' dog down, Fleur; I can't see your face. If you were really fond of Michael – I swear I wouldn't; but you're not, you know.'

Fleur said coldly:

'You know very little; I *am* fond of Michael.'

Desert gave his little jerky laugh.

'Oh yes; not the sort that counts.'

Fleur looked up.

'It counts quite enough to make one safe.'

'A flower that I can't pick.'

Fleur nodded.

'Quite sure, Fleur? Quite, quite sure?'

Fleur stared; her eyes softened a little, her eyelids, so excessively white, drooped over them; she nodded. Desert said slowly:

'The moment I believe that, I shall go East.'

'East?'

'Not so stale as going West, but much the same – you don't come back.'

Fleur thought: 'The East? I should love to know the East! Pity one can't manage that, too. Pity!'

'You won't keep me in your Zoo, my dear. I shan't hang around and feed on crumbs. You know what I feel – it means a smash of some sort.'

'It hasn't been my fault, has it?'

'Yes; you've collected me, as you collect everybody that comes near you.'

'I don't know what you mean.'

Desert bent down, and dragged her hand to his lips.

'Don't be riled with me; I'm too unhappy.'

Fleur let her hand stay against his hot lips.

'Sorry, Wilfrid.'

'All right, dear. I'll go.'

'But you're coming to dinner tomorrow?'

Desert said violently:

'*Tomorrow?* Good God – no! What d'you think I'm made of?'

He flung her hand away.

'I don't like violence, Wilfrid.'

'Well, good-bye; I'd better go.'

The words 'And you'd better not come again' trembled up to her lips, but were not spoken. Part from Wilfrid – life would lose a little warmth! She waved her hand. He was gone. She heard the door closing. Poor Wilfrid? – nice to think of a flame at which to warm her hands! Nice but rather dreadful! And suddenly, dropping Ting-a-ling, she got up and began to walk

about the room. Tomorrow! Second anniversary of her wed-
ding-day! Still an ache when she thought of what it had not
been. But there was little time to think – and she made less. What
good in thinking? Only one life, full of people, of things to do
and have, of things wanted – a life only void of – one thing,
and that – well, if people had it, they never had it long! On
her lids two tears, which had gathered, dried without falling.
Sentimentalism! No! The last thing in the world – the unfor-
givable offence! Whom should she put next whom tomorrow?
And whom should she get in place of Wilfrid, if Wilfrid
wouldn't come – silly boy! One day – one night – what difference? Who should sit on her right, and who on her left?
Was Aubrey Greene more distinguished, or Sibley Swan? Were
they either as distinguished as Walter Nazing or Charles Upshire? Dinner of twelve, exclusively literary and artistic, except
for Michael and Alison Charwell. Ah! Could Alison get her
Gurdon Minho – just one writer of the old school, one glass of
old wine to mellow effervescence? He didn't publish with Danby
and Winter; but he fed out of Alison's hand. She went quickly
to one of the old tea-chests, and opened it. Inside was a telephone.

'Can I speak to Lady Alison – Mrs Michael Mont ... Yes
... That you, Alison? ... Fleur speaking. Wilfrid has fallen
through tomorrow night ... Is there any chance of your bringing Gurdon Minho? I don't know him, of course; but he might
be interested. You'll try? ... That'll be ever so delightful.
Isn't the "Snooks" Club meeting rather exciting? Bart says
they'll eat each other now they've split ... About Mr Minho.
Could you let me know tonight? Thanks – thanks awfully!
... Good-bye!'

Failing Minho, whom? Her mind hovered over the names in
her address book. At so late a minute it must be someone who
didn't stand on ceremony; but except Alison, none of Michael's
relations would be safe from Sibley Swan or Nesta Gorse, and
their subversive shafts; as to the Forsytes – out of the question;
they had their own sub-acid humour (some of them), but they
were not modern, not really modern. Besides, she saw as little

of them as she could – they dated, belonged to the dramatic period, had no sense of life without beginning or end. No! If Gurdon Minho was a frost, it would have to be a musician, whose works were hieroglyphical with a dash of surgery; or, better, perhaps, a psychoanalyst. Her fingers turned the pages till she came to those two categories. Hugo Solstis? A possibility; but suppose he wanted to play them something recent? There was only Michael's upright Grand, and that would mean going to his study. Better Gerald Hanks – he and Nesta Gorse would get off together on dreams; still, if they did, there would be no actual loss of life. Yes, failing Gurdon Minho, Gerald Hanks; he would be free – and put him between Alison and Nesta. She closed the book, and, going back to her jade-green settee, sat gazing at Ting-a-ling. The little dog's prominent round eyes gazed back; bright, black, very old. Fleur thought : 'I *don't* want Wilfrid to drop off.' Among all the crowd who came and went, here, there and everywhere, she cared for nobody. Keep up with them, keep up with everything, of course! It was all frightfully amusing, frightfully necessary! Only – only – what?

Voices! Michael and Bart coming back. Bart had noticed Wilfrid. He *was* a noticing old Bart. She was never very comfortable when he was about – living and twisting, but with something settled and ancestral in him; a little like Ting-a-ling – something judgematic, ever telling her that she was fluttering and new. He was anchored, could only move to the length of his old-fashioned cord, but he could drop on to things disconcertingly. Still, he admired her, she felt – oh ! yes.

Well! What had he thought of the cartoons? Ought Michael to publish them, and with letterpress or without? Didn't he think that the cubic called 'Still Life' – of the Government, too frightfully funny – especially the 'old bean' representing the Prime? For answer she was conscious of a twisting, rapid noise; Sir Lawrence was telling her of his father's collection of electioneering cartoons. She did wish Bart would not tell her about his father; he had been so distinguished, and he must have been so dull, paying all his calls on horseback, with

27

trousers strapped under his boots. He and Lord Charles Cariboo and the Marquis of Forfar had been the last three 'callers' of that sort. If only they hadn't, they'd have been clean forgot. She had that dress to try, and fourteen things to see to, and Hugo's concert began at eight-fifteen! Why did people of the last generation always have so much time? And, suddenly, she looked down. Ting-a-ling was licking the copper floor. She took him up: 'Not that, darling; nasty!' Ah! the spell was broken! Bart was going, reminiscent to the last. She waited at the foot of the stairs till Michael shut the door on him, then flew. Reaching her room, she turned on all the lights. Here was her own style — a bed which did not look like one, and many mirrors. The couch of Ting-a-ling occupied a corner, whence he could see himself in three. She put him down, and said: 'Keep quiet, now!' His attitude to the other dogs in the room had long become indifferent; though of his own breed and precisely his colouring, they had no smell and no licking power in their tongues — nothing to be done with them, imitative creatures, incredibly unresponsive.

Stripping off her dress, Fleur held the new frock under her chin.

'May I kiss you?' said a voice, and there was Michael's image behind her own reflection in the glass.

'My dear boy, there isn't time! Help me with this.' She slipped the frock over her head. 'Do those three top hooks. How do you like it? Oh! and — Michael! Gurdon Minho may be coming to dinner tomorrow — Wilfrid can't. Have you read his things? Sit down and tell me something about them. All novels, aren't they? What sort?'

'Well, he's always had something to say. And his cats are good. He's a bit romantic, of course.'

'Oh! Have I made a gaff?'

'Not a bit; jolly good shot. The vice of our lot is, they say it pretty well, but they've nothing to say. They won't last.'

'But that's just why they will last. They won't date.'

'Won't they? My gum!'

'Wilfrid will last.'

'Ah! Wilfrid has emotions, hates, pities, wants; at least sometimes; when he has, his stuff is jolly good. Otherwise, he just makes a song about nothing – like the rest.'

Fleur tucked in the top of her undergarment.

'But, Michael, if that's so, we – I've got the wrong lot.'

Michael grinned.

'My dear child! The lot of the hour is always right; only you've got to watch it, and change it quick enough.'

'But d'you mean to say that Sibley isn't going to live?'

'Sib? Lord, no!'

'But he's so perfectly sure that almost everybody else is dead or dying. Surely he has critical genius!'

'If I hadn't more judgement than Sib, I'd go out of publishing tomorrow.'

'You – more than Sibley Swan?'

'Of course, I've more judgement than Sib. Why! Sib's judgement is just his opinion of Sib – common or garden impatience of anyone else. He doesn't even read them. He'll read one specimen of every author and say: "Oh! that fellow! He's dull, or he's moral, or he's sentimental, or he dates, or he drivels" – I've heard him dozens of times. That's if they're alive. Of course, if they're dead, it's different. He's always digging up and canonizing the dead; that's how he's got his name. There's always a Sib in literature. He's a standing example of how people can get taken at their own valuation. But as to lasting – of course he won't; he's never creative, even by mistake.'

Fleur had lost the thread. Yes! It suited her – quite a nice line! Off with it! Must write those three notes before she dressed.

Michael had begun again.

'Take my tip, Fleur. The really big people don't talk – and don't bunch – they paddle their own canoes in what seem backwaters. But it's the backwaters that make the main stream. By Jove, that's a *mot*, or is it a bull; and are bulls *mots* or *mots* bulls?'

'Michael, if you were me, would you tell Frederic Wilmer

that he'll be meeting Hubert Marsland at lunch next week? Would it bring him or would it put him off?'

'Marsland's rather an old duck, Wilmer's rather an old goose – I don't know.'

'Oh! do be serious, Michael – you never give me any help in arranging – No! Don't maul my shoulders please.'

'Well, darling, I *don't* know. I've no genius for such things, like you. Marsland paints windmills, cliffs and things – I doubt if he's heard of the future. He's almost a Mathew Maris for keeping out of the swim. If you think he'd like to meet a Vertiginist –'

'I didn't ask you if he'd like to meet Wilmer; I asked you if Wilmer would like to meet him.'

'Wilmer will just say: "I like little Mrs Mont, she gives deuced good grub" – and so you do, ducky. A Vertiginist wants nourishing, you know, or it wouldn't go to his head.'

Fleur's pen resumed its swift strokes, already become slightly illegible. She murmured:

'I think Wilfrid would help – you won't be there; one – two – three. What women?'

'Four painters – pretty and plump; no intellect.'

Fleur said crossly:

'I can't get them plump; they don't go about now.' And her pen flowed on:

DEAR WILFRID – Wednesday – lunch; Wilmer, Hubert Marsland, two other women. Do help me live it down.

Yours ever,
FLEUR

'Michael, your chin is like a bootbrush.'

'Sorry, old thing; your shoulders shouldn't be so smooth. Bart gave Wilfrid a tip as we were coming along.'

Fleur stopped writing. 'Oh!'

'Reminded him that the state of love was a good stunt for poets.'

'*A propos* of what?'

'Wilfrid was complaining that he couldn't turn it out now.'

'Nonsense! His last things are his best.'

'Well, that's what I think. Perhaps he's forestalled the tip. Has he, d'you know?'

Fleur turned her eyes towards the face behind her shoulder. No, it had its native look – frank, irresponsible, slightly faun-like, with its pointed ears, quick lips, and nostrils.

She said slowly,

'If *you* don't know, nobody does.'

A snuffle interrupted Michael's answer. Ting-a-ling, long, low, slightly higher at both ends, was standing between them, with black muzzle upturned. 'My pedigree is long,' he seemed to say : 'but my legs are short – what about it?'

Chapter Three

MUSICAL

-<-->-

ACCORDING to a great and guiding principle, Fleur and Michael Mont attended the Hugo Solstis concert, not because they anticipated pleasure, but because they knew Hugo. They felt, besides, that Solstis, an Englishman of Russo-Dutch ex-traction, was one of those who were restoring English music, giving to it a wide and spacious freedom from melody and rhythm, while investing it with literary and mathematical charms. And one never could go to a concert given by any of this school without using the word 'interesting' as one was coming away. To sleep to this restored English music, too, was impossible. Fleur, a sound sleeper, had never even tried. Michael had, and complained afterwards that it had been like a nap in Liège railway station. On this occasion they occupied those gangway seats in the front row of the dress circle of which Fleur had a sort of natural monopoly. There Hugo and the rest could see her taking her place in the English restoration movement. It was easy, too, to escape into the corridor and exchange the word 'interesting' with side-whiskered cognoscenti; or, slipping out a cigarette from the little gold case, wedding present of Cousin Imogen Cardigan, get a whiff or two's repose. To speak quite honestly, Fleur had a natural sense of rhythm which caused her discomfort during those long and 'interesting' passages which evidenced, as it were, the composer's rise and fall from his bed of thorns. She secretly loved a tune, and the impossibility of ever confessing this without losing hold of Solstis, Baff, Birdigal, MacLewis, Clorane, and other English restoration composers, sometimes taxed to its limits a nature which had its Spartan side. Even to Michael she would not 'confess'; and it was additionally trying when, with his native disrespect of persons, accentuated by life in the trenches and a publisher's office, he would mutter: 'Gad! Get on with it!' or: 'Cripes! Ain't he took bad!' especially as she knew that Michael was really putting up with it better than herself, having a more literary disposition, and a less dancing itch in his toes.

The first movement of the new Solstis composition – 'Phantasmagoria Piémontesque' – to which they had come especially to listen, began with some drawn-out chords.

'What oh!' said Michael's voice in her ear: 'Three pieces of furniture moved simultaneously on a parquet floor!'

In Fleur's involuntary smile was the whole secret of why her marriage had not been intolerable. After all, Michael was a dear! Devotion and mercury – jesting and loyalty – combined, they piqued and touched even a heart given away before it was bestowed on him. 'Touch' without 'pique' would have bored; 'pique' without 'touch' would have irritated. At this moment he was at peculiar advantage! Holding on to his knees, with his ears standing up, eyes glassy from loyalty to Hugo, and tongue in cheek, he was listening to that opening in a way which evoked Fleur's admiration. The piece would be 'interesting' – she fell into the state of outer observation and inner calculation very usual with her nowadays. Over there was L.S.D., the greater dramatist; she didn't know him – yet. He looked rather frightening, his hair stood up so straight. And her eye began picturing him on her copper floor against a Chinese picture. And there – yes! Gurdon Minho! Imagine *his* coming to anything so modern! His profile *was* rather Roman – of the Aurelian period! Passing on from that antique, with the pleased thought that by this time tomorrow she might have collected it, she quartered the assembly face by face – she did not want to miss anyone important.

'The furniture' had come to a sudden standstill.

'Interesting!' said a voice over her shoulder. Aubrey Greene! Illusive, rather moonlit, with his silky fair hair brushed straight back, and his greenish eyes – his smile always made her feel that he was 'getting' at her. But, after all, he was a cartoonist!

'Yes, isn't it?'

He curled away. He might have stayed a little longer – there wouldn't be time for anyone else before those songs of Birdigal's! Here came the singer Charles Powls! How stout and efficient he looked, dragging little Birdigal to the piano.

Charming accompaniment – rippling, melodious!

The stout, efficient man began to sing. How different from the accompaniment! The song hit every note just off the solar plexus, it mathematically prevented her from feeling pleasure. Birdigal must have written it in horror of someone calling it 'vocal'. Vocal! Fleur knew how catching the word was; it would run like a measle round the ring, and Birdigal would be no more! Poor Birdigal! But this was 'interesting'. Only, as Michael was saying: 'O, my Gawd!'

Three songs! Powls was wonderful – so loyal! Never one note hit so that it rang out like music! Her mind fluttered off to Wilfrid. To him, of all the younger poets, people accorded the right to say something; it gave him such a position – made him seem to come out of life, instead of literature. Besides, he had done things in the war, was a son of Lord Mullyon, would get the Mercer Prize probably for *Copper Coin*. If Wilfrid abandoned her, a star would fall from the firmament above her copper floor. He had no right to leave her in the lurch. He must learn not to be violent – not to think physically. No! she couldn't let Wilfrid slip away; nor could she have any more sob-stuff in her life, searing passions, *cul de sacs*, aftermaths. She had tasted of that; a dulled ache still warned her.

Birdigal was bowing, Michael saying: 'Come out for a whiff! The next thing's a dud!' Oh! ah! Beethoven. Poor old Beethoven! So out of date – one did *rather* enjoy him!

The corridor, and refectory beyond, were swarming with the restoration movement. Young men and women with faces and heads of lively and distorted character, were exchanging the word 'interesting'. Men of more massive type, resembling sedentary matadors, blocked all circulation. Fleur and Michael passed a little way along, stood against the wall, and lighted cigarettes. Fleur smoked hers delicately – a very little one in a tiny amber holder. She had the air of admiring blue smoke rather than of making it; there were spheres to consider beyond this sort of crowd – one never knew who might be about! – the sphere, for instance, in which Alison Charwell moved, politico-literary, catholic in taste, but, as Michael always put it: 'Convinced, like a sanitary system, that it's the only sphere in the world; look at the way they all write books of reminiscence about each other!' They might, she always felt, disapprove of women smoking in public halls. Consorting delicately with iconoclasm, Fleur never forgot that her feet were in two worlds at least. Standing there, observant of all to left and right, she noted against the wall one whose face was screened by his programme. 'Wilfrid!' she thought, 'and doesn't mean to see me!' Mortified, as a child from whom a sixpence is filched, she said:

'There's Wilfrid! Fetch him, Michael!'

Michael crossed, and touched his best man's sleeve; Desert's face emerged, frowning. She saw him shrug his shoulders, turn and walk into the throng. Michael came back.

'Wilfrid's got the hump tonight; says he's not fit for human society – queer old son!'

How obtuse men were! Because Wilfrid was his pal, Michael did not see; and that was lucky! So Wilfrid really meant to avoid her! Well, she would see! And she said:

'I'm tired, Michael; let's go home.'

His hand slid round her arm.

'Sorry, old thing; come along!'

They stood a moment in a neglected doorway, watching Woomans, the conductor, launched towards his orchestra.

'Look at him,' said Michael; 'guy hung out of an Italian window, legs and arms all stuffed and flying! And look at the Frapka and her piano – that's a turbulent union!'

There was a strange sound.

'Melody, by George!' said Michael.

An attendant muttered in their ears: 'Now, sir, I'm going to shut the door.' Fleur had a fleeting view of L.S.D. sitting upright as his hair, with closed eyes. The door was shut – they were outside in the hall.

'Wait here, darling; I'll nick a rickshaw.'

Fleur huddled her chin in her fur. It was easterly and cold.

A voice behind her said:

'Well, Fleur, am I going East?'

Wilfrid! His collar up to his ears, a cigarette between his lips, hands in pockets, eyes devouring.

'You're very silly, Wilfrid!'

'Anything you like; am I going East?'

'No; Sunday morning – eleven o'clock at the Tate. We'll talk it out.'

'*Convenu!*' And he was gone.

Alone suddenly, like that, Fleur felt the first shock of reality. Was Wilfrid truly going to be unmanageable? A taxi-cab ground up; Michael beckoned; Fleur stepped in.

Passing a passionately lighted oasis of young ladies displaying to the interested Londoner the acme of Parisian undress, she felt Michael incline towards her. If she were going to keep Wilfrid, she must be nice to Michael. Only:

'You needn't kiss me in Piccadilly Circus, Michael!'

'Sorry, duckie! It's a little previous – I meant to get you opposite the Partheneum.'

Fleur remembered how he had slept on a Spanish sofa for the first fortnight of their honeymoon; how he always insisted that she must not spend anything on him, but must always let him give her what he liked, though she had three thousand a year and he twelve hundred; how jumpy he was when she had a cold – and how he always came home to tea. Yes, he was a dear! But would she break her heart if he went East or West to-morrow?

Snuggled against him, she was surprised at her own cynicism.

A telephone message written out, in the hall, ran: 'Please tell Mrs Mont I've got Mr Gurding Minner. Lady Alisson.'

It was restful. A real antique! She turned on the lights in her room, and stood for a moment admiring it. Truly pretty! A slight snuffle from the corner – Ting-a-ling, tan on a black cushion, lay like a Chinese lion in miniature; pure, remote, fresh from evening communion with the Square railings.

'I see you,' said Fleur.

Ting-a-ling did not stir; his round black eyes watched his mistress undress. When she returned from the bathroom he was curled into a ball. Fleur thought: 'Queer! How does he know Michael won't be coming?' And slipping into her well-warmed bed, she too curled herself up and slept.

But in the night, contrary to her custom, she awoke. A cry – long, weird, trailing, from somewhere – the river – the slums at the back – rousing memory – poignant, aching – of her honeymoon – Granada, its roofs below, jet, ivory, gold; the watchman's cry, the lines in Jon's letter:

> Voice in the night crying, down in the old sleeping
> Spanish City darkened under her white stars.
> What says the voice – its clear, lingering anguish?
> Just the watchman, telling his dateless tale of safety?
> Just a road-man, flinging to the moon his song?
> No! 'Tis one deprived, whose lover's heart is weeping,
> Just his cry: 'How long?'

A cry, or had she dreamed it? Jon, Wilfrid, Michael! No use to have a heart!

Chapter Four

DINING

◄◄•►►

LADY Alison Charwell, born Heathfield, daughter of the first Earl of Campden, and wife to Lionel Charwell, K.C., Michael's somewhat young uncle, was a delightful Englishwoman brought up in a set accepted as the soul of society. Full of brains, energy, taste, money, and tinctured in its politico-legal ancestry by blue blood, this set was linked to, but apart from 'Snooks' and the duller haunts of birth and privilege. It was gay, charming, free-and-easy, and, according to Michael, 'Snobbish, old thing, aesthetically and intellectually, but they'll never see it. They think they're the top notch – quick, healthy, up-to-date, well-bred, intelligent; they simply can't imagine their equals. But you see their imagination is deficient. Their really creative energy would go into a pint pot. Look at their books – they're always *on* something – philosophy, spiritualism, poetry, fishing, themselves; why, even their sonnets dry up before they're twenty-five. They know everything – except mankind outside their own set. Oh! they work – they run the show – they have to; there's no one else with their brains, and energy, and taste. But they run it round and round in their own blooming circle. It's the world to them – and it might be worse. They've patented their own golden age; but it's a trifle fly-blown since the war.'

Alison Charwell – in and of this world, so spryly soulful, debonaire, free, and cosy – lived within a stone's throw of Fleur, in a house pleasant, architecturally, as any in London. Forty years old, she had three children and considerable beauty, wearing a little fine from mental and bodily activity. Something of an enthusiast, she was fond of Michael, in spite of his strange criticisms, so that his matrimonial venture had piqued

37

her from the start. Fleur was dainty, had quick natural intelligence – this new niece was worth cultivation. But, though adaptable and assimilative, Fleur had remained curiously unassimilated; she continued to whet the curiosity of Lady Alison, accustomed to the close borough of choice spirits, and finding a certain poignancy in contact with the New Age on Fleur's copper floor. She met with an irreverence there, which, not taken too seriously, flipped her mind. On that floor she almost felt a back number. It was stimulating.

Receiving Fleur's telephonic inquiry about Gurdon Minho, she had rung up the novelist. She knew him, if not well. Nobody seemed to know him well; amiable, polite, silent, rather dull and austere; but with a disconcerting smile, sometimes ironical, sometimes friendly. His books were now caustic, now sentimental. On both counts it was rather the fashion to run him down, though he still seemed to exist.

She rang him up. Would he come to a dinner tomorrow at her young nephew, Michael Mont's, and meet the younger generation? His answer came, rather high-pitched:

'Rather! Full fig, or dinner jacket?'

'How awfully nice of you! they'll be ever so pleased. Full fig, I believe. It's the second anniversary of their wedding.' She hung up the receiver with the thought: 'He must be writing a book about them!'

Conscious of responsibility, she arrived early.

It was a grand night at her husband's Inn, so that she brought nothing with her but the feeling of adventure, pleasant after a day spent in fluttering over the decision at 'Snooks'. She was received only by Ting-a-ling, who had his back to the fire, and took no notice beyond a stare. Sitting down on the jade green settee, she said:

'Well, you funny little creature, don't you know me after all this time?'

Ting-a-ling's black shiny gaze seemed saying: 'You recur here, I know; most things recur. There is nothing new about the future.'

Lady Alison fell into a train of thought: The new generation! Did she want her own girls to be of it! She would like to talk to Mr Minho about that — they had had a very nice talk down at Beechgroves before the war. Nine years ago — Sybil only six, Joan only four then! Time went, things changed! A new generation! And what was the difference! 'I think we had more tradition!' she said to herself softly.

A slight sound drew her eyes up from contemplation of her feet. Ting-a-ling was moving his tail from side to side on the hearth-rug, as if applauding. Fleur's voice, behind her, said:

'Well, darling, I'm awfully late. It *was* good of you to get me Mr Minho. I do hope they'll all behave. He'll be between you and me, anyway; I'm sticking him at the top, and Michael at the bottom, between Pauline Upshire and Amabel Nazing. You'll have Sibley on your left, and I'll have Aubrey on my right, then Nesta Gorse and Walter Nazing; opposite them Linda Frewe and Charles Upshire. Twelve. You know them all. Oh! and you mustn't mind if the Nazings and Nesta smoke between the courses. Amabel will do it. She comes from Virginia — it's the reaction. I do hope she'll have some clothes on; Michael always says it's a mistake when she has; but having Mr Minho makes one a little nervous. Did you see Nesta's skit in *The Bouquet*? Oh, too frightfully amusing — clearly meant for L.S.D.! Ting, my Ting, are you going to stay and see all these people? Well, then, get up here or you'll be trodden on. Isn't he Chinese? He does so round off the room.'

Ting-a-ling laid his nose on his paws, in the centre of a jade green cushion.

'Mr Gurding Minner!'

The well-known novelist looked pale and composed. Shaking the two extended hands, he gazed at Ting-a-ling, and said:

'How nice! How are *you*, my little man?'

Ting-a-ling did not stir. 'You take me for a common English dog, sir!' his silence seemed to say.

'Mr and Mrs Walter Nazon, Miss Lenda Frow.'

Amabel Nazing came first, clear alabaster from her fair

hair down to the six inches of gleaming back above her waist-line, shrouded alabaster from four inches below the knee to the gleaming toes of her shoes; the eminent novelist mechanically ceased to commune with Ting-a-ling.

Walter Nazing, who followed a long way up above his wife, had a tiny line of collar emergent from swathes of black, and a face, cut a hundred years ago, that slightly resembled Shelley's. His literary productions were sometimes felt to be like the poetry of that bard, and sometimes like the prose of Marcel Proust. 'What oh!' as Michael said.

Linda Frewe, whom Fleur at once introduced to Gurdon Minho, was one about whose work no two people in her draw-ing-room ever agreed. Her works *Trifles* and *The Furious Don* had quite divided all opinion. Genius according to some, drivel according to others, those books always roused an interest-ing debate whether a slight madness enhanced or diminished the value of art. She herself paid little attention to criticism – she produced.

'*The* Mr Minho? How interesting! I've never read anything of yours.'

Fleur gave a little gasp.

'What – don't you know Mr Minho's cats? But they're won-derful. Mr Minho, I do want Mrs Walter Nazing to know you. Amabel – Mr Gurdon Minho.'

'Oh! Mr Minho – how perfectly lovely! I've wanted to know you ever since my cradle.'

Fleur heard the novelist say quietly:

'I could wish it had been longer;' and passed on in doubt to greet Nesta Gorse and Sibley Swan, who came in, as if they lived together, quarrelling over L.S.D., Nesta upholding him because of his 'panache', Sibley maintaining that wit had died with the Restoration; this fellow was alive!

Michael followed with the Upshires and Aubrey Greene, whom he had encountered in the hall. The party was complete.

Fleur loved perfection, and that evening was something of a nightmare. Was it a success? Minho was so clearly the least brilliant person there; even Alison talked better. And yet he had such a fine skull. She did hope he would not go away early. Someone would be almost sure to say 'Dug up!' or 'Thick and bald!' before the door closed behind him. He was pathetically agreeable, as if trying to be liked, or, at least, not despised too much. And there must, of course, be more in him than met the sense of hearing. After the crab soufflé he did seem to be talking to Alison, and all about youth. Fleur listened with one ear.

'Youth feels ... main stream of life ... not giving it what it wants. Past and future getting haloes ... Quite! Contemporary life no earthly just now ... No ... Only comfort for us – we'll be antiquated, some day, like Congreve, Sterne, Defoe ... have our chance again ... *Why?* What *is* driving them out of the main current? Oh! Probably surfeit ... newspapers ... photographs. Don't see life itself, only reports ... reproductions of it; all seems shoddy, lurid, commercial ... Youth says: "Away with it, let's have the past or the future!"'

He took some salted almonds, and Fleur saw his eyes stray to the upper part of Amabel Nazing. Down there the conversation was like Association football – no one kept the ball for more than one kick. It shot from head to head. And after every set of passes someone would reach out and take a cigarette, and blow a blue cloud across the unclothed refectory table. Fleur enjoyed the glow of her Spanish room – its tiled floor, richly coloured fruits in porcelain, its tooled leather, copper articles, and Soames's Goya above a Moorish divan. She headed the ball promptly when it came her way, but initiated nothing. Her gift was to be aware of everything at once. 'Mrs Michael Mont presented' the brilliant irrelevances of Linda Frewe, the pricks and stimulations of Nesta Gorse, the moonlit sliding innuendoes of Aubrey Greene, the upturning strokes of Sibley Swan, Amabel Nazing's little cool American audacities, Charles Upshire's curious bits of lore, Walter Nazing's subversive contradictions, the critical intricacies of Pauline Upshire; Michael's happy-go-lucky slings and arrows, even Alison's knowledgeable quickness, and Gurdon Minho's silences – she presented them all, showed them off, keeping her eyes and ears on the ball of talk lest it should touch earth and rest. Brilliant evening; but – a success?

On the jade green settee, when the last of them had gone and Michael was seeing Alison home, she thought of Minho's 'Youth – not getting what it wants.' No! Things didn't fit. 'They don't fit, do they, Ting!' But Ting-a-ling was tired, only the tip of one ear quivered. Fleur leaned back and sighed. Ting-a-ling uncurled himself, and putting his forepaws on her thigh, looked up in her face. 'Look at me,' he seemed to say, 'I'm all right. I get what I want, and I want what I get. At present I want to go to bed.'

'But I don't,' said Fleur, without moving.

'Just take me up!' said Ting-a-ling.

'Well,' said Fleur, 'I suppose – It's a nice person, but not the right person, Ting.'

Ting-a-ling settled himself on her bare arms.

'It's all right,' he seemed to say. 'There's a great deal too much sentiment and all that, out of China. Come on!'

Chapter Five

EVE

⤚✦⤜

THE Honourable Wilfrid Desert's rooms were opposite a picture gallery off Cork Street. The only male member of the aristocracy writing verse that anyone would print, he had chosen them for seclusion rather than for comfort. His 'junk', however, was not devoid of the taste and luxury which overflows from the greater houses of England. Furniture from the Hampshire seat of the Cornish nobleman, Lord Mullyon, had oozed into two vans, when Wilfrid settled in. He was seldom to be found, however, in his nest, and was felt to be a rare bird, owing his rather unique position among the younger writers partly to his migratory reputation. He himself hardly, perhaps, knew where he spent his time, or did his work, having a sort of mental claustrophobia, a dread of being hemmed in by people. When the war broke out he had just left Eton; when the war was over he was twenty-three, as old a young man as ever turned a stave. His friendship with Michael, begun in hospital, had languished and renewed itself suddenly, when in 1920 Michael joined Danby and Winter, publishers, of Blake Street, Covent Garden. The scattery enthusiasm of the sucking publisher had been roused by Wilfrid's verse. Hob-nobbing lunches over the poems of one in need of literary anchorage, had been capped by the firm's surrender to Michael's insistence. The mutual intoxication of the first book Wilfrid had written and the first book Michael had sponsored was crowned at Michael's wedding. Best man! Since then, so far as Desert could be tied to anything, he had been tied to those two; nor, to do him justice, had he realized till a month ago that the attraction was not Michael, but Fleur. Desert never spoke of the war, it was not possible to learn from his own mouth an effect which he might have summed up thus: 'I lived so long with horror and death; I saw men so in the raw; I put hope of anything out of my mind so utterly, that I can never more have the faintest respect for theories, promises, conventions, moralities, and principles. I have hated too much the men who wallowed in them while I was wallowing in mud and blood. Illusion is off. No religion and no philosophy will satisfy me – words, all words. I have still my senses – no thanks to them; am still capable – I find – of passion; can still grit my teeth and grin; have still some feeling of trench loyalty, but whether real or just a complex, I don't yet know. I am dangerous, but not so dangerous as those who trade in words, principles, theories, and all manner of fanatical idiocy to be worked out in the blood and sweat of other men. The war's done one thing for me – converted life to comedy. Laugh at it – there's nothing else to do!'

Leaving the concert hall on the Friday night, he had walked straight home to his rooms. And lying down full length on a monk's seat of the fifteenth century, restored with down cushions and silk of the twentieth, he crossed his hands behind his head and delivered himself to these thoughts: 'I am not going on like this. She has bewitched me. It doesn't mean anything to her. But it means hell to me. I'll finish with it on Sunday – Persia's a good place. Arabia's a good place – plenty of blood and sand! She's incapable of giving anything up. How has she hooked herself into me! By trick of eyes, and hair, by her walk, by the sound of her voice – by trick of warmth, scent, colour. Fling her cap over the windmill – not she! What then? Am I to hang about her Chinese fireside and her little Chinese dog; and have this ache and this fever because I can't be kissing her? I'd rather be flying again in the middle of Boche whiz-bangs! Sunday! How women like to drag out agonies! It'll be just this afternoon all over again. "How unkind of you to go, when your friendship is so precious to me! Stay, and be my tame cat, Wilfrid!" No, my dear, for once you're up against it! And – so am I, by the Lord! . . .'

When in that gallery which extends asylum to British art, those two young people met so accidentally on Sunday morning in front of Eve smelling at the flowers of the Garden of Eden, there were present also six mechanics in various stages of decomposition, a custodian and a couple from the provinces, none of whom seemed capable of observing anything whatever. And, indeed, that meeting was inexpressive. Two young people, of the disillusioned class, exchanging condemnations of the past. Desert with his off-hand speech, his smile, his well-tailored informality, suggested no aching heart. Of the two Fleur was the paler and more interesting. Desert kept saying to himself: 'No melodrama – that's all it would be!' And Fleur was thinking: 'If I can keep him ordinary like this, I shan't lose him, because he'll never go away without a proper outburst.'

It was not until they found themselves a second time before the Eve, that he said:

'I don't know why you asked me to come, Fleur. It's playing the goat for no earthly reason. I quite understand your feeling. I'm a bit of "Ming" that you don't want to lose. But it's not good enough, my dear; and that's all about it.'

'How horrible of you, Wilfrid!'

'Well! Here we part! Give us your flipper.'

His eyes – rather beautiful – looked dark and tragic above the smile on his lips, and she said stammering:

'Wilfrid – I – I don't know. I want time. I can't bear you to be unhappy. Don't go away! Perhaps I – I shall be unhappy, too; I – I don't know.'

Through Desert passed the bitter thought: 'She *can't* let go – she doesn't know how.' But he said quite softly: 'Cheer up, my child; you'll be over all that in a fortnight. I'll send you something to make up. Why shouldn't I make it China – one place is as good as another? I'll send you a bit of real "Ming", of a better period than this.'

Fleur said passionately:

'You're insulting! Don't!'

'I beg your pardon. I don't want to leave you angry.'

'What is it you want of me?'

'Oh! no – come! This is going over it twice. Besides, since Friday I've been thinking. I want nothing, Fleur, except a blessing and your hand. Give it me! Come on!'

Fleur put her hand behind her back. It was too mortifying! He took her for a cold-blooded, collecting little cat – clutching and playing with mice that she didn't want to eat!

'You think I'm made of ice,' she said, and her teeth caught her upper lip: 'Well, I'm not!'

Desert looked at her; his eyes were very wretched. 'I didn't mean to play up your pride,' he said. 'Let's drop it, Fleur. It isn't any good.'

Fleur turned and fixed her eyes on the Eve – rumbustious-looking female, care-free, avid, taking her fill of flower perfume! Why not be care-free, take anything that came along? Not so much love in the world that one could afford to pass, leaving it unsmelled, unplucked. Run away! Go to the East! Of course, she couldn't do anything extravagant like that! But, perhaps – What did it matter? one man or another, when neither did you really love!

From under her drooped, white, dark-lashed eyelids she saw the expression on his face, and that he was standing stiller than the statues. And suddenly she said: 'You will be a fool to go. Wait!' And without another word or look, she walked away, leaving Desert breathless before the avid Eve.

Chapter Six

'OLD FORSYTE' AND 'OLD MONT'

◄◄◄►►►

M o v i n g away, in the confusion of her mood, Fleur almost trod on the toes of a too-familiar figure standing before an Alma Tadema with a sort of grey anxiety, as if lost in the mutability of market values.

'Father! *You* up in town? Come along to lunch, I have to get home quick.'

Hooking his arm and keeping between him and Eve, she guided him away, thinking: 'Did he see us? Could he have seen us?'

'Have you got enough on?' muttered Soames.

'Heaps!'

'That's what you women always say. East wind, and your neck like that! Well, I don't know.'

'No, dear, but I do.'

The grey eyes appraised her from head to foot.

'What are you doing here?' he said. And Fleur thought: 'Thank God he didn't see. He'd never have asked if he had.' And she answered:

'I take an interest in art, darling, as well as you.'

'Well, I'm staying with your aunt in Green Street. This east wind has touched my liver. How's your – how's Michael?'

'Oh, he's all right – a little cheap. We had a dinner last night.'

Anniversary! The realism of a Forsyte stirred in him, and he looked under her eyes. Thrusting his hand into his overcoat pocket, he said:

'I was bringing you this.'

Fleur saw a flat substance wrapped in pink tissue paper.

'Darling, what is it?'

Soames put it back into his pocket.

'We'll see later. Anybody to lunch?'

'Only Bart.'

'Old Mont! Oh, Lord!'

'Don't you like Bart, dear?'

'Like him? He and I have nothing in common.'

'I thought you fraternized rather over the state of things.'

'He's a reactionary,' said Soames.

'And what are you, ducky?'

'I? What should I be?' With these words he affirmed that policy of non-commitment which, the older he grew, the more he perceived to be the only attitude for a sensible man.

'How is Mother?'

'Looks well. I see nothing of her – she's got her own mother down – they go gadding about.'

He never alluded to Madame Lamotte as Fleur's grandmother – the less his daughter had to do with her French side, the better.

'Oh!' said Fleur. 'There's Ting and a cat!' Ting-a-ling, out for a breath of air, and tethered by a lead in the hands of a maid, was snuffling horribly and trying to climb a railing whereon was perched a black cat, all hunch and eyes.

'Give him to me, Ellen. Come with Mother, darling!'

Ting-a-ling came, indeed, but only because he couldn't go, bristling and snuffling and turning his head back.

'I like to see him natural,' said Fleur.

'Waste of money, a dog like that,' Soames commented. 'You should have had a bull-dog and let him sleep in the hall. No end of burglaries. Your aunt had her knocker stolen.'

'I wouldn't part with Ting for a hundred knockers.'

'One of these days you'll be having *him* stolen – fashionable breed.'

Fleur opened her front door. 'Oh!' she said, 'Bart's here, already!'

A shiny hat was reposing on a marble coffer, present from Soames, intended to hold coats and discourage moth. Placing his hat alongside the other, Soames looked at them. They were too similar for words, tall, high, shiny, and with the same name inside. He had resumed the 'tall hat' habit after the failure of the general and coal strikes in 1921, his instinct having told him that revolution would be at a discount for some considerable period.

'About this thing,' he said, taking out the pink parcel, 'I don't know what you'll do with it, but here it is.'

It was a curiously carved and coloured bit of opal in a ring of tiny brilliants.

'Oh!' Fleur cried: 'What a delicious thing!'

'Venus floating on the waves or something,' murmured Soames. 'Uncommon. You want a strong light on it.'

'But it's lovely. I shall put it on at once.'

Venus! If Dad had known! She put her arms round his neck to disguise her sense of *à propos*. Soames received the rub of her cheek against his own well-shaved face with his usual stillness. Why demonstrate when they were both aware that his affection was double hers?

'Put it on then,' he said, 'and let's see.'

Fleur pinned it at her neck before an old lacquered mirror. 'It's a jewel. Thank you, darling! Yes, your tie is straight. I like that white piping. You ought always to wear it with black. Now, come along!' And she drew him into her Chinese room. It was empty.

'Bart must be up with Michael, talking about his new book.'

'Writing at his age?' said Soames.

'Well, ducky, he's a year younger than you.'

'I don't write. Not such a fool. Got any more new-fangled friends?'

'Just one – Gurdon Minho, the novelist.'

'Another of the new school?'

'Oh, no, dear! Surely you've heard of Gurdon Minho; he's older than the hills.'

48

'They're all alike to me,' muttered Soames. 'Is he well thought of?'

'I should think his income is larger than yours. He's almost a classic – only waiting to die.'

'I'll get one of his books and read it. What name did you say?'

'Get *Big and Little Fishes*, by Gurdon Minho. You can remember that, can't you? Oh! here they are! Michael, look at what Father's given me.'

Taking his hand, she put it up to the opal at her neck. 'Let them both see,' she thought, 'what good terms we're on.' Though her father had not seen her with Wilfrid in the gallery, her conscience still said: 'Strengthen your respectability, you don't quite know how much support you'll need for it in future.'

And out of the corner of her eye she watched those two. The meetings between 'Old Mont' and 'Old Forsyte' – as she knew Bart called her father when speaking of him to Michael – always made her want to laugh, but she never quite knew why. Bart knew everything, but his knowledge was beautifully bound, strictly edited by a mind tethered to the 'eighteenth century'. Her father only knew what was of advantage to him, but the knowledge was unbound, and subject to no editorship. If he *was* late Victorian, he was not above profiting if necessary by even later periods. 'Old Mont' had faith in tradition; 'Old Forsyte' none. Fleur's acuteness had long perceived a difference which favoured her father. Yet 'Old Mont's' talk was so much more up-to-date, rapid, glancing, garrulous, redolent of precise information; and 'Old Forsyte's' was constricted, matter-of-fact. Really impossible to tell which of the two was the better museum specimen; and both so well-preserved!

They did not precisely shake hands; but Soames mentioned the weather. And almost at once they all four sought that Sunday food which by a sustained effort of will Fleur had at last deprived of reference to the British character. They partook, in fact, of lobster cocktails, and a mere risotto of chickens' livers, an omelette *au rhum*, and dessert trying to look as Spanish as it could.

'I've been in the Tate,' Fleur said; 'I do think it's touching.'

'Touching?' queried Soames with a sniff.

'Fleur means, sir, that to see so much old English art together is like looking at a baby show.'

'I don't follow,' said Soames stiffly. 'There's some very good work there.'

'But not grown-up, sir.'

'Ah! You young people mistake all this crazy cleverness for maturity.'

'That's not what Michael means, Father. It's quite true that English painting has no wisdom teeth. You can see the difference in a moment, between it and any Continental painting.'

'And thank God for it!' broke in Sir Lawrence. 'The beauty of this country's art is its innocence. We're the oldest country in the world politically, and the youngest aesthetically. What do you say, Forsyte?'

'Turner is old and wise enough for me,' said Soames curtly. 'Are you coming to the P.P.R.S. Board on Tuesday?'

'Tuesday? We were going to shoot the spinneys, weren't we, Michael?'

Soames grunted. 'I should let them wait,' he said. 'We settle the report.'

It was through 'Old Mont's' influence that he had received a seat on the Board of that flourishing concern, the Providential Premium Reassurance Society, and, truth to tell, he was not sitting very easily in it. Though the law of averages was, perhaps, the most reliable thing in the world, there were circumstances which had begun to cause him disquietude. He looked round his nose. Light weight, this narrow-headed, twisting-eyebrowed baronet of a chap – like his son before him! And he added suddenly: 'I'm not easy. If I'd realized how that chap Elderson ruled the roost, I doubt if I should have come on to that Board.'

One side of 'Old Mont's' face seemed to try to leave the other.

'Elderson!' he said. 'His grandfather was my grandfather's parliamentary agent at the time of the Reform Bill; he put him through the most corrupt election ever fought – bought every vote — used to kiss all the farmer's wives. Great days, Forsyte, great days!'

'And over,' said Soames. 'I don't believe in trusting a man's judgement as far as we trust Elderson's; I don't like this foreign insurance.'

'My dear Forsyte — first-rate head, Elderson; I've known him all my life, we were at Winchester together.'

Soames uttered a deep sound. In that answer of 'Old Mont's' lay much of the reason for his disquietude. On the Board they had all, as it were, been at Winchester together! It was the very deuce! They were all so honourable that they dared not scrutinize each other, or even their own collective policy. Worse than their dread of mistake or fraud was their dread of seeming to distrust each other. And this was natural, for to distrust each other was an immediate evil. And, as Soames knew, immediate evils are those which one avoids. Indeed, only that tendency, inherited from his father, James, to lie awake between the hours of two and four, when the chrysalis of faint misgiving becomes so readily the butterfly of panic, had developed his uneasiness. The P.P.R.S. was so imposing a concern, and he had been connected with it so short a time, that it seemed presumptuous to smell a rat; especially as he would have to leave the Board and the thousand a year he earned on it if he raised smell of rat without rat or reason. But what if there were a rat? That was the trouble! And here sat 'Old Mont' talking of his spinneys and his grandfather. The fellow's head was too small! And visited by the cheerless thought: 'There's nobody here, not even my own daughter, capable of taking a thing seriously,' he kept silence. A sound at his elbow roused him. That marmoset of a dog, on a chair between him and his daughter, was sitting up! Did it expect him to give it something? Its eyes would drop out one of these days. And he said: 'Well, what do *you* want?' The way the little beast stared with those boot-buttons! 'Here,' he said, offering it a salted almond. 'You don't eat these.'

Ting-a-ling did.

'He has a passion for them, Dad. Haven't you, darling?'

Ting-a-ling turned his eyes up at Soames, through whom a

queer sensation passed. 'Believe the little brute likes me,' he
thought, 'he's always looking at me.' He touched the dog's nose
with the tip of his finger. Ting-a-ling gave it a slight lick with
his curly blackish tongue.

'Poor fellow!' muttered Soames involuntarily, and turned to
'Old Mont'.

'Don't mention what I said.'

'My dear Forsyte, what was that?'

Good Heavens! And he was on a Board with a man like this!
What had made him come on, when he didn't want the money,
or any more worries – goodness knew. As soon as he had become a director, Winifred and others of his family had begun to
acquire shares to neutralize their income tax – seven per cent
preference – nine per cent ordinary – instead of the steady five
they ought to be content with. There it was, he couldn't move
without people following him. He had always been so safe, so
perfect a guide in the money maze! To be worried at his time
of life! His eyes sought comfort from the opal at his daughter's
neck – pretty thing, pretty neck! Well! She seemed happy
enough – had forgotten her infatuation of two years ago! That
was something to be thankful for. What she wanted now was a
child to steady her in all this modern scrimmage of twopenny-
ha'penny writers and painters and musicians. A loose lot, but
she had a good little head on her. If she had a child, he would
put another twenty thousand into her settlement. That was one
thing about her mother – steady in money matters, good French
method. And Fleur – so far as he knew – cut her coat according
to her cloth. What was that? The word 'Goya' had caught his
ear. New life of him coming out? H'm! That confirmed his
slowly growing conviction that Goya had reached top point
again.

'Think I shall part with that,' he said, pointing to the picture.
'There's an Argentine over here.'

'Sell your Goya, sir?' It was Michael speaking. 'Think of the
envy with which you're now regarded!'

'One can't have everything,' said Soames.

'That reproduction we've got for *The New Life* has turned

out first-rate. "Property of Soames Forsyte, Esquire." Let's get the book out first, sir, anyway.'

'Shadow or substance, eh, Forsyte?'

Narrow-headed baronet chap – was he mocking?

'*I've* no family place,' he said.

'No, but we have, sir,' murmured Michael; 'you could leave it to Fleur, you know.'

'Well,' said Soames, 'we shall see if that's worth while.' And he looked at his daughter.

Fleur seldom blushed, but she picked up Ting-a-ling and rose from the Spanish table. Michael followed suit. 'Coffee in the other room,' he said. 'Old Forsyte' and 'Old Mont' stood up, wiping their moustaches.

Chapter Seven

'OLD MONT' AND 'OLD FORSYTE'

THE offices of the P.P.R.S. were not far from the College of Arms. Soames, who knew that 'three dexter buckles on a sable ground gules' and a 'pheasant proper' had been obtained there at some expense by his Uncle Swithin in the sixties of the last century, had always pooh-poohed the building, until, about a year ago, he had been struck by the name Golding in a book which he had absently taken up at the Connoisseurs' Club. The affair purported to prove that William Shakespeare was really Edward de Vere, Earl of Oxford. The mother of the earl was a Golding – so was the mother of Soames! The coincidence struck him; and he went on reading. The tome left him with judgement suspended over the main issue, but a distinct curiosity as to whether he was not of the same blood as Shakespeare. Even if the earl were not the bard, he felt that the connexion could only be creditable, though, so far as he could make out, Oxford was a shady fellow. Recently appointed on the Board of the P.P.R.S.,

so that he passed the college every other Tuesday, he had
thought: 'Shan't go spending a lot of money on it, but might
look in one day.' Having looked in, it was astonishing how
taken he had been by the whole thing. Tracing his mother had
been quite like a criminal investigation, nearly as ramified and
fully as expensive. Having begun, the tenacity of a Forsyte could
hardly bear to leave him short of the mother of Shakespeare de
Vere, even though she would be collateral; unfortunately, he
could not get past a certain William Gouldyng, Ingerer – whatever that might be, and he was almost afraid to inquire – of the
time of Oliver Cromwell. There were still four generations to be
unravelled, and he was losing money and the hope of getting
anything for it. This it was which caused him to gaze askance
at the retired building while passing it on his way to the Board
on the Tuesday after the lunch at Fleur's. Two more wakeful
early mornings had screwed him to the pitch of bringing his
doubts to a head and knowing where he stood in the matter of
the P.P.R.S.; and this sudden reminder that he was spending
money here, there and everywhere, when there was a possibility,
however remote, of financial liability somewhere else, sharpened
the edge of a nerve already stropped by misgivings. Neglecting
the lift and walking slowly up the two flights of stairs, he 'went
over' his fellow-directors for the fifteenth time. Old Lord Fontenoy was there for his name, of course; seldom attended, and
was what they called 'a dud' – h'm! – nowadays; the chairman,
Sir Luke Sharman, seemed always to be occupied in not being
taken for a Jew. His nose was straight, but his eyelids gave cause
for doubt. His surname was impeccable, but his Christian
dubious; his voice was reassuringly roughened, but his clothes
had a suspicious tendency towards gloss. Altogether a man who,
though shrewd, could not be trusted – Soames felt – to be giving
his whole mind to other business. As for 'Old Mont' – what was
the good of a ninth baronet on a Board? Guy Meyricke, King's
Counsel, last of the three who had been 'together', was a good
man in court, no doubt, but with no time for business and no
real sense of it! Remained that converted Quaker, old Cuthbert
Mothergill – whose family name had been a by-word for success-

ful integrity throughout the last century, so that people still put Mothergills on to boards almost mechanically – rather deaf, nice clean old chap, and quite bland, but nothing more. A perfectly honest lot, no doubt, but perfunctory. None of them really giving their minds to the thing! In Elderson's pocket, too, except perhaps Sharman, and he on the wobble. And Elderson himself – clever chap, bit of an artist, perhaps; managing director from the start, with everything at his finger-tips! Yes! That was the mischief! Prestige of superior knowledge, and years of success – they all kow-towed to him, and no wonder! Trouble with a man like that was that if he once admitted to having made a mistake he destroyed the legend of his infallibility. Soames had enough infallibility of his own to realize how powerful was its impetus towards admitting nothing. Ten months ago, when he had come on to the Board, everything had seemed in full sail; exchanges had reached bottom, so they all thought – the 're-assurance of foreign contracts' policy, which Elderson had initiated about a year before, had seemed, with rising exchanges, perhaps the brightest feather in the cap of possibility. And now, a twelvemonth later, Soames suspected darkly that they did not know where they were – and the general meeting only six weeks off! Probably not even Elderson knew; or, if he did, he was keeping knowledge which ought to belong to the whole directorate severely to himself.

He entered the board-room without a smile. All there – even Lord Fontenoy and 'Old Mont' – given up his spinneys, had he! Soames took his seat at the end on the fireside. Staring at Elderson, he saw, with sudden clearness, the strength of the fellow's position; and, with equal clearness, the weakness of the P.P.R.S. With this rising and falling currency, they could never know exactly their liability – they were just gambling. Listening to the minutes and other routine business, with his chin clasped in his hand, he let his eyes move from face to face – old Mothergill, Elderson, Mont opposite; Sharman at the head; Fontenoy, Meyricke, back to himself – decisive board of the year. He could not, must not, be placed in any dubious position! At his first general meeting on this concern, he must not face the shareholders without knowing exactly where he stood. He looked again at Elderson — sweetish face, bald head rather like Julius Caesar's, nothing to suggest irregularity or excessive optimism — in fact, somewhat resembling that of old Uncle Nicholas Forsyte, whose affairs had been such an example to the last generation but one. The managing director having completed his exposition, Soames directed his gaze at the pink face of dosey old Mothergill, and said:

'I'm not satisfied that these accounts disclose our true position. I want the Board adjourned to this day week, Mr Chairman, and during the week I want every member of the Board furnished with exact details of the foreign contract commitments which do *not* mature during the present financial year. I notice that those are lumped under a general estimate of liability. I am not satisfied with that. They ought to be separately treated.' Shifting his gaze past Elderson to the face of 'Old Mont', he went on: 'Unless there's a material change for the better on the Continent, which I don't anticipate (quite the contrary), I fully expect those commitments will put us in Queer Street next year.'

The scraping of feet, shifting of legs, clearing of throats which accompany a slight sense of outrage greeted the words 'Queer Street'; and a sort of satisfaction swelled in Soames; he had rattled their complacency, made them feel a touch of the misgiving from which he himself was suffering.

'We have always treated our commitments under one general estimate, Mr Forsyte.'

Plausible chap!

'And to my mind wrongly. This foreign contract business is a new policy. For all I can tell, instead of paying a dividend, we ought to be setting this year's profits against a certain loss next year.'

Again that scrape and rustle.

'My dear sir, absurd!'

The bulldog in Soames snuffled.

'So you say!' he said. 'Am I to have those details?'

'The Board can have what details it likes, of course. But permit me to remark on the general question that it *can* only be a matter of estimate. A conservative basis has always been adopted.'

'That is a matter of opinion,' said Soames; 'and in my view it should be the Board's opinion after very careful discussion of the actual figures.'

'Old Mont' was speaking.

'My dear Forsyte, to go into every contract would take us a week, and then get us no further; we can but average it out.'

'What we have not got in these accounts,' said Soames, 'is the relative proportion of foreign risk to home risk – in the present state of things a vital matter.'

The Chairman spoke.

'There will be no difficulty about that, I imagine, Elderson! But in any case, Mr Forsyte, we should hardly be justified in penalizing the present year for the sake of eventualities which we hope will not arise.'

'I don't know,' said Soames. 'We are here to decide policy according to our common sense, and we must have the fullest opportunity of exercising it. That is my point. We have not enough information.'

That 'plausible chap' was speaking again:

'Mr Forsyte seems to be indicating a lack of confidence in the management.' Taking the bull by the horns – was he?

'Am I to have that information?'

The voice of old Mothergill rose cosy in the silence.

'The Board could be adjourned, perhaps, Mr Chairman; I could come up myself at a pinch. Possibly we could all attend. The times are very peculiar – we mustn't take any unnecessary risks. The policy of foreign contracts is undoubtedly somewhat new to us. We have no reason so far to complain of the results. And I am sure we have the utmost confidence in the judgement of our managing director. Still, as Mr Forsyte has asked for this information, I think perhaps we ought to have it. What do you say, my lord?'

'I can't come up next week. I agree with the chairman that on these accounts we couldn't burke this year's dividend. No good getting the wind up before we must. When do the accounts go out, Elderson?'

'Normally at the end of this week.'

'These are not normal times,' said Soames. 'To be quite plain, unless I have that information I must tender my resignation.' He saw very well what was passing in their minds. A newcomer making himself a nuisance – they would take his resignation readily – only it would look awkward just before a general meeting unless they could announce 'wife's ill-health' or something satisfactory, which he would take very good care they didn't.

The chairman said coldly:

'Well, we will adjourn the Board to this day week; you will be able to get us those figures, Elderson?'

'Certainly.'

Into Soames's mind flashed the thought: 'Ought to ask for an independent scrutiny.' But he looked round. Going too far – perhaps – if he intended to remain on the Board – and he had no wish to resign – after all, it was a big thing, and a thousand a year! No! Mustn't overdo it!

Walking away, he savoured his triumph doubtfully, by no means sure that he had done any good. His attitude had only closed the 'all together' attitude round Elderson. The weakness of his position was that he had nothing to go on, save an uneasiness, which when examined was found to be simply a feeling that he hadn't enough control himself. And yet, there couldn't be two managers – you must trust your manager!

A voice behind him tittupped: 'Well, Forsyte, you gave us quite a shock with your alternative. First time I remember anything of the sort on that Board.'

'Sleepy hollow,' said Soames.

'Yes, I generally have a nap. It gets very hot in there. Wish I'd stuck to my spinneys. They come high, even as early as this.'

Incurably frivolous, this tittupping baronet!

'By the way, Forsyte, I wanted to say: With all this modern birth control and the rest of it, one gets uneasy. We're not the royal family; but don't you feel with me it's time there was a movement in heirs?'

Soames did, but he was not going to confess to anything so indelicate about his own daughter.

'Plenty of time,' he muttered.

'I don't like that dog, Forsyte.'

Soames stared.

'Dog!' he said. 'What's that to do with it?'

'I like a baby to come before a dog. Dogs and poets distract young women. My grandmother had five babies before she was twenty-seven. She was a Montjoy; wonderful breeders, you remember them – the seven Montjoy sisters – all pretty. Old Montjoy had forty-seven grandchildren. You don't get it nowadays, Forsyte.'

'Country's over-populated,' said Soames grimly.

'By the wrong sort – less of them, more of ourselves. It's almost a matter for legislation.'

'Talk to your son,' said Soames.

'Ah! but they think us fogeys, you know. If we could only point to a reason for existence. But it's difficult, Forsyte, it's difficult.'

'They've got everything they want,' said Soames.

'Not enough, my dear Forsyte, not enough; the condition of the world is on the nerves of the young. England's dished, they say, Europe's dished. Heaven's dished, and so is Hell! No future in anything but the air. You can't breed in the air; at least, I doubt it – the difficulties are considerable.'

Soames sniffed.

'If only the journalists would hold their confounded pens,' he said; for, more and more of late, with the decrescendo of scare in the daily Press, he was regaining the old sound Forsyte feeling of security. 'We've only to keep clear of Europe,' he added.

'Keep clear and keep the ring! Forsyte, I believe you've hit it. Good friendly terms with Scandinavia, Holland, Spain, Italy, Turkey – all the outlying countries that we can get at by sea. And let the others dree their weirds. It's an idea!' How the chap rattled on!

'I'm no politician,' said Soames.

'Keep the ring! The new formula. It's what we've been coming

59

to unconsciously! And as to trade – to say we can't do without trading with this country or with that – bunkum, my dear Forsyte. The world's large – we can.'

'I don't know anything about that,' said Soames. 'I only know we must drop this foreign contract assurance.'

'Why not confine it to the ring countries? Instead of "balance of power", "keep the ring"! Really, it's an inspiration!'

Thus charged with inspiration, Soames said hastily:

'I leave you here, I'm going to my daughter's.'

'Ah! I'm going to my son's. Look at these poor devils!'

Down by the Embankment at Blackfriars a band of unemployed were trailing dismally with money-boxes.

'Revolution in the bud! There's one thing that's always forgotten, Forsyte, it's a great pity.'

'What's that?' said Soames, with gloom. The fellow would tittup all the way to Fleur's!

'Wash the working-class, put them in clean, pleasant-coloured jeans, teach 'em to speak like you and me, and there'd be an end of class feeling. It's all a matter of the senses. Wouldn't you rather share a bedroom with a clean, neat-clothed plumber's assistant who spoke and smelled like you than with a profiteer who dropped his aitches and reeked of opoponax? Of course you would.'

'Never tried,' said Soames, 'so don't know.'

'Pragmatist! But believe me, Forsyte – if the working class would concentrate on baths and accent instead of on their political and economic tosh, equality would be here in no time.'

'I don't want equality,' said Soames, taking his ticket to Westminster.

The 'tittupping' voice pursued him entering the tube lift.

'Aesthetic equality, Forsyte, if we had it, would remove the wish for any other. Did you ever catch an impecunious professor wishing he was the King?'

'No,' said Soames, opening his paper.

Chapter Eight

BICKET

❧❦❧

BENEATH its veneer of cheerful irresponsibility, the character of Michael Mont had deepened during two years of anchorage and continuity. He had been obliged to think of others; and his time was occupied. Conscious, from the fall of the flag, that he was on sufferance with Fleur, admitting as whole the half-truth: '*Il y a toujours un qui baise, et l'autre qui tend la joue,*' he had developed real powers of domestic consideration; and yet he did not seem to redress the balance in his public or publishing existence. He found the human side of his business too strong for the monetary. Danby and Winter, however, were bearing up against him, and showed, so far, no signs of the bankruptcy prophesied for them by Soames on being told of the principles which his son-in-law intended to introduce. No more in publishing than in any other walk of life was Michael finding it possible to work too much on principle. The field of action was so strewn with facts – human, vegetable and mineral.

On this same Tuesday afternoon, having long tussled with the price of those vegetable facts, paper and linen, he was listening with his pointed ears to the plaint of a packer discovered with five copies of *Copper Coin* in his overcoat pocket, and the too obvious intention of converting them to his own use.

Mr Danby had 'given him the sack' – he didn't deny that he was going to sell them, but what would Mr Mont have done? He owed rent – and his wife wanted nourishing after pneumonia – wanted it bad. 'Dash it!' thought Michael, 'I'd snoop an edition to nourish Fleur after pneumonia!'

'And I can't live on my wages with prices what they are. I can't, Mr Mont, so help me!'

Michael swivelled. 'But look here, Bicket, if we let you snoop copies, all the packers will snoop copies; and if they do, where are Danby and Winter? In the cart. And, if they're in the cart, where are all of you? In the street. It's better that one of you should be in the street than that all of you should, isn't it?'

'Yes, sir, I quite see your point – it's reason; but I can't live on reason, the least thing knocks you out, when you're on the bread line. Ask Mr Danby to give me another chance.'

'Mr Danby always says that a packer's work is particularly confidential, because it's almost impossible to keep a check on it.'

'Yes, sir, I should feel that in future; but with all this unemployment and no reference, I'll never get another job. What about my wife?'

To Michael it was as if he had said: 'What about Fleur?' He began to pace the room; and the young man Bicket looked at him with large dolorous eyes. Presently he came to a standstill, with his hands deep plunged into his pockets and his shoulders hunched.

'I'll ask him,' he said; 'but I don't believe he will; he'll say it isn't fair on the others. You had five copies; it's pretty stiff, you know – means you've had 'em before, doesn't it? What?'

'Well, Mr Mont, anything that'll give me a chance, I don't mind confessin'. I have 'ad a few previous, and it's just about kept my wife alive. You've no idea what that pneumonia's like for poor people.'

Michael pushed his fingers through his hair.

'How old's your wife?'

'Only a girl – twenty.'

Twenty! Just Fleur's age!

'I'll tell you what I'll do, Bicket; I'll put it up to Mr Desert; if he speaks for you, perhaps it may move Mr Danby.'

'Well, Mr Mont, thank you – you're a gentleman, we all sy that.'

'Oh! hang it! But look here, Bicket, you were reckoning on those five copies. Take this to make up, and get your wife what's necessary. Only for goodness' sake don't tell Mr Danby.'

'Mr Mont, I wouldn't deceive you for the world – I won't sy a word, sir. And my wife – well!'

A sniff, a shuffle – Michael was alone, with his hands plunged deeper, his shoulders hunched higher. And suddenly he laughed. Pity! Pity was pop! It was all dam' funny. Here he was rewarding Bicket for snooping *Copper Coin*. A sudden longing possessed him to follow the little packer and see what he did with the two pounds – see whether 'the pneumonia' was real or a figment of the brain behind those dolorous eyes. Impossible, though! Instead he must ring up Wilfrid and ask him to put in a word with old Danby. His own word was no earthly. He had put it in too often! Bicket! Little one knew of anybody, life was deep and dark, and upside down! What was honesty? Pressure of life *versus* power of resistance – the result of that fight, when the latter won, was honesty! But why resist? Love thy neighbour as thyself – but not more! And wasn't it a darned sight harder for Bicket on two pounds a week to love him, than for him on twenty-four pounds a week to love Bicket? ...

'Hallo! ... That you, Wilfrid? ... Michael speaking. ... One of our packers has been sneaking copies of *Copper Coin*. He's "got the sack" – poor devil! I wondered if you'd mind putting in a word for him – old Dan won't listen to me ... yes, got a wife – Fleur's age; pneumonia, so he says. Won't do it again with yours anyway, insurance by common gratitude – what! ... Thanks, old man, awfully good of you – will you bob in, then? We can go round home together ... Oh! Well! You'll bob in anyway. Aurev!'

Good chap, old Wilfrid! Real good chap – underneath! Underneath – what?

Replacing the receiver, Michael saw a sudden great cloud of sights and scents and sounds, so foreign to the principles of his firm that he was in the habit of rejecting instantaneously every manuscript which dealt with them. The war might be 'off'; but it was still 'on' within Wilfrid, and himself. Taking up a tube, he spoke:

'Mr Danby in his room? Right! If he shows any signs of flitting, let me know at once. ...'

Between Michael and his senior partner a gulf was fixed, not less deep than that between two epochs, though partially filled in by Winter's middle-age and accommodating temperament. Michael had almost nothing against Mr Danby except that he was always right – Philip Norman Danby, of Sky House, Campden Hill, a man of sixty and some family, with a tall forehead, a preponderance of body to leg, and an expression both steady and reflective. His eyes were perhaps rather close together, and his nose rather thin, but he looked a handsome piece in his well-proportioned room. He glanced up from the formation of a correct judgement on a matter of advertisement when Wilfrid Desert came in.

'Well, Mr Desert, what can I do for you? Sit down!'

Desert did not sit down, but looked at the engravings, at his fingers, at Mr Danby, and said:

'Fact is, I want you to let that packer chap off, Mr Danby.'

'Packer chap. Oh! Ah! Bicket. Mont told you, I suppose?'

'Yes; he's got a young wife down with pneumonia.'

'They all go to our friend Mont with some tale or other, Mr Desert – he has a very soft heart. But I'm afraid I can't keep this man. It's a most insidious thing. We've been trying to trace a leak for some time.'

Desert leaned against the mantelpiece and stared into the fire.

'Well, Mr Danby,' he said, 'your generation may like the soft in literature, but you're precious hard in life. Ours won't look at softness in literature, but we're a deuced sight less hard in life.'

'I don't think it's hard,' said Mr Danby, 'only just.'

'Are you a judge of justice?'

'I hope so.'

'Try four years' hell, and have another go.'

'I really don't see the connexion. The experience you've been through, Mr Desert, was bound to be warping.'

Wilfrid turned and stared at him.

'Forgive my saying so, but sitting here and being just is much more warping. Life is pretty good purgatory, to all except about thirty per cent of grown-up people.'

Mr Danby smiled.

'We simply couldn't conduct our business, my dear young

man, without scrupulous honesty in everybody. To make no distinction between honesty and dishonesty would be quite unfair. You know that perfectly well.'

'I don't know anything perfectly well, Mr Danby; and I mistrust those who say they do.'

'Well, let us put it that there are rules of the game which must be observed, if society is to function at all.'

Desert smiled, too: 'Oh! hang rules! Do it as a favour to me. I wrote the rotten book.'

No trace of struggle showed in Mr Danby's face; but his deepset, close-together eyes shone a little.

'I should be only too glad, but it's a matter – well, of conscience, if you like. I'm not prosecuting the man. He must leave – that's all.'

Desert shrugged his shoulders.

'Well, good-bye!' and he went out.

On the mat was Michael in two minds.

'Well?'

'No go. The old blighter's too just.'

Michael stivered his hair.

'Wait in my room five minutes while I let the poor beggar know, then I'll come along.'

'No,' said Desert, 'I'm going the other way.'

Not the fact that Wilfrid was going the other way – he almost always was – but something in the tone of his voice and the look on his face obsessed Michael's imagination while he went downstairs to seek Bicket. Wilfrid was a rum chap – he went 'dark' so suddenly!

In the nether regions he asked:

'Bicket gone?'

'No, sir, there he is.'

There he was, in his shabby overcoat, with his pale narrow face, and his disproportionately large eyes, and his sloping shoulders.

'Sorry, Bicket, Mr Desert has been in, but it's no go.'

'No, sir?'

'Keep your pecker up, you'll get something.'

'I'm afryde not, sir. Well, I thank you very 'eartily; and I thank Mr Desert. Good night, sir; and good-bye!'

Michael watched him down the corridor, saw him waver into the dusky street.

'Jolly!' he said, and laughed. ...

The natural suspicions of Michael and his senior partner that a tale was being pitched were not in fact justified. Neither the wife nor the pneumonia had been exaggerated; and wavering away in the direction of Blackfriars Bridge, Bicket thought not of his turpitude nor of how just Mr Danby had been, but of what he should say to her. He should not, of course, tell her that he had been detected in stealing; he must say he had 'got the sack for cheeking the foreman'; but what would she think of him for doing that, when everything as it were depended on his not cheeking the foreman? This was one of those melancholy cases of such affection that he had been coming to his work day after day feeling as if he had 'left half his guts' behind him in the room where she lay, and when at last the doctor said to him:

'She'll get on now, but it's left her very run down – you must feed her up,' his anxiety had hardened into a resolution to have no more. In the next three weeks he had 'pinched' eighteen *Copper Coins*, including the five found in his overcoat. He had only 'pitched on' Mr Desert's book because it was 'easy sold', and he was sorry now that he hadn't pitched on someone else's. Mr Desert had been very decent. He stopped at the corner of the Strand, and went over his money. With the two pounds given him by Michael and his wages he had seventy-five shillings in the world, and going into the Stores he bought a meat jelly and a tin of Benger's food that could be made with water. With pockets bulging he took a bus, which dropped him at the corner of his little street on the Surrey side. His wife and he occupied the two ground floor rooms, at eight shillings a week, and he owed for three weeks. 'Py that!' he thought, 'and have a roof until she's well.' It would help him over the news, too, to show her a receipt for the rent and some good food. How lucky they had been careful to have no baby! He sought the basement. His landlady was doing the week's washing. She paused, in sheer surprise at such full and voluntary payment, and inquired after his wife.

'Doing nicely, thank you.'

'Well, I'm glad of that, it must be a relief to your mind.'

'It is,' said Bicket.

The landlady thought: 'He's a thread-paper – reminds me of a shrimp before you bile it, with those eyes.'

'Here's your receipt, and thank you. Sorry to 'ave seemed nervous about it, but times are 'ard.'

'They are,' said Bicket. 'So long!'

With the receipt and the meat jelly in his left hand, he opened the door of his front room.

His wife was sitting before a very little fire. Her bobbed black hair, crinkly towards the ends, had grown during her illness; it shook when she turned her head and smiled. To Bicket – not for the first time – that smile seemed queer, 'pathetic-like', mysterious – as if she saw things that one didn't see oneself. Her name was Victorine, and he said: 'Well, Vic? This jelly's a bit of all right, and I've pyde the rent.' He sat on the arm of the chair and she put her hand on his knee – her thin arm emerging blue-white from the dark dressing-gown.

'Well, Tony?'

Her face – thin and pale with those large dark eyes and beautifully formed eyebrows – was one that 'looked at you from somewhere; and when it looked at you – well! it got you right inside!'

It got him now and he said: 'How've you been breathin'?'

'All right – much better. I'll soon be out now.'

Bicket twisted himself round and joined his lips to hers. The kiss lasted some time, because all the feelings which he had not been able to express during the past three weeks to her or to anybody, got into it. He sat up again, 'sort of exhausted', staring at the fire, and said: 'News isn't bright – lost my job, Vic.'

'Oh! Tony! Why?'

Bicket swallowed.

'Fact is, things are slack, and they're reducin'.'

There had surged into his mind the certainty that sooner than tell her the truth he would put his head under the gas!

'Oh! dear! What shall we do, then?'

Bicket's voice hardened.

'Don't you worry – I'll get something;' and he whistled.

'But you liked that job.'

'Did I? I liked some o' the fellers; but as for the job – why, what was it? Wrappin' books up in a bysement all dy long. Let's have something to eat and get to bed early – I feel as if I could sleep for a week, now I'm shut of it.'

Getting their supper ready with her help, he carefully did not look at her face for fear it might 'get him agyne inside!' They had only been married a year, having made acquaintance on a tram, and Bicket often wondered what had made her take to him, eight years her senior and C3 during the war! And yet she must be fond of him, or she'd never look at him as she did.

'Sit down and try this jelly.'

He himself ate bread and margarine and drank cocoa, he seldom had any particular appetite.

'Shall I tell you what I'd like?' he said; 'I'd like Central Austrylia. We had a book in there about it; they sy there's quite a movement. I'd like some sun. I believe if we 'ad sun we'd both be twice the size we are. I'd like to see colour in your cheeks, Vic.'

'How much does it cost to get out there?'

'A lot more than we can ly hands on, that's the trouble. But I've been thinkin'. England's about done. There's too many like me.'

'No,' said Victorine: 'There aren't enough.'

Bicket looked at her face, then quickly at his plate.

'What myde you take a fancy to me?'

'Because you don't think first of yourself, that's why.'

'Used to before I knew you. But I'd do anything for you, Vic.'

'Have some of this jelly, then, it's awful good.'

Bicket shook his head.

68

'If we could wyke up in Central Austrylia,' he said. 'But there's only one thing certain, we'll wyke up in this blighted little room. Never mind, I'll get a job and earn the money yet.'

'Could we win it on a race?'

'Well, I've only got forty-seven bob all told, and if we lose it, where'll you be? You've got to feed up, you know. No, I must get a job.'

'They'll give you a good recommend, won't they?'

Bicket rose and stacked his plate and cup.

'They would, but that job's off – overstocked.'

Tell her the truth? Never! So help him!

In their bed, one of those just too wide for one and just not wide enough for two, he lay, with her hair almost in his mouth, thinking what to say to his Union, and how to go to work to get a job. And in his thoughts as the hours drew on he burned his boats. To draw his unemployment money he would have to tell his Union what the trouble was. Blow the Union! He wasn't going to be accountable to them! *He* knew why he'd pinched the books; but it was nobody else's business, nobody else could understand his feelings, watching her so breathless, pale and thin. Strike out for himself! And a million and a half out o' work! Well, he had a fortnight's keep, and something would turn up – and he might risk a bob or two and win some money, you never knew. She turned in her sleep. 'Yes,' he thought, 'I'd do it agyne ...'

Next day, after some hours on foot, he stood under the grey easterly sky in the grey street, before a plate-glass window protecting an assortment of fruits and sheaves of corn, lumps of metal, and brilliant blue butterflies, in the carefully golden light of advertised Australia. To Bicket, who had never been out of England, not often out of London, it was like standing outside Paradise. The atmosphere within the office itself was not so golden, and the money required considerable; but it brought Paradise nearer to take away pamphlets which almost burned his hands, they were so warm.

Later, he and she, sitting in the one armchair – advantage of being thin – pored over these alchemized pages and inhaled their glamour.

'D'you think it's true, Tony?'

'If it's thirty per cent true it's good enough for me. We just must get there somehow. Kiss me.'

From around the corner in the main road the rumbling of the trams and carts, and the rattling of their window-pane in the draughty dry easterly wind increased their feeling of escape into a gas-lit Paradise.

Chapter Nine

CONFUSION

◄‹·›►

T w o hours behind Bicket, Michael wavered towards home. Old Danby was right as usual – if you couldn't trust your packers, you might shut up shop! Away from Bicket's eyes, he doubted. Perhaps the chap hadn't a wife at all! Then Wilfrid's manner usurped the place of Bicket's morals. Old Wilfrid had been abrupt and queer the last three times of meeting. Was he boiling-up for verse?

He found Ting-a-ling at the foot of the stairs in a conservative attitude. 'I am not going up,' he seemed saying, 'until someone carries me – at the same time it is later than usual!'

'Where's your mistress, you heraldic little beast?'

Ting-a-ling snuffled. 'I could put up with it,' he implied, 'if *you* carried me – these stairs are laborious!'

Michael took him up. 'Let's go and find her.'

Squeezed under an arm harder than his mistress', Ting-a-ling stared as if with black-glass eyes; and the plume of his emergent tail quivered.

In the bedroom Michael dropped him so absent-mindedly that he went to his corner plume pendent, and crouched there in dudgeon.

Nearly dinner time and Fleur not in! Michael went over his sketchy recollection of her plans. Today she had been having Hubert Marsland and that Vertiginist – what was his name? – to lunch. There would have been fumes to clear off. Vertiginists – like milk – made carbonic acid gas in the lungs! Still! Half-past seven! What was happening tonight? Weren't they going to that play of L.S.D.'s? No – that was tomorrow! Was there conceivably nothing? If so, of course she would shorten her unoccupied time as much as possible. He made that reflection humbly. Michael had no illusions, he knew himself to be commonplace, with only a certain redeeming liveliness, and, of course, his affection for her. He even recognized that his affection was a weakness, tempting him to fussy anxieties, which on principle he restrained. To inquire, for instance, of Coaker or Philips – their man and their maid – when she had gone out, would be thoroughly against that principle. The condition of the world was such that Michael constantly wondered if his own affairs were worth paying attention to; but then the condition of the world was also such that sometimes one's own affairs seemed all that were worth paying attention to. And yet his affairs were, practically speaking, Fleur; and if he paid too much attention to them, he was afraid of annoying her.

He went into his dressing-room and undid his waistcoat.

'But no!' he thought; 'if she finds me "dressed" already, it'll put too much point on it.' So he did up his waistcoat and went downstairs again. Coaker was in the hall.

'Mr Forsyte and Sir Lawrence looked in about six, sir. Mrs Mont was out. What time shall I serve dinner?'

'Oh! about a quarter-past eight. I don't think we're going out.'

He went into the drawing-room and passing down its Chinese emptiness, drew aside the curtain. The square looked cold and dark and draughty; and he thought: 'Bicket – pneumonia – I hope she's got her fur coat.' He took out a cigarette and put it back. If she saw him at the window she would think him fussy; and he went up again to see if she had put on her fur!

Ting-a-ling, still couchant, greeted him plume dansetti arrested as at disappointment. Michael opened a wardrobe. She had! Good! He was taking a sniff round, when Ting-a-ling passed him trottant, and her voice said: 'Well, my darling!' Wishing that he was, Michael emerged from behind the wardrobe door. Heaven! She looked pretty, coloured by the wind! He stood rather wistfully silent.

'Hallo, Michael! I'm rather late. Been to the Club and walked home.'

Michael had a quite unaccountable feeling that there was suppression in that statement. He also suppressed, and said: 'I was just looking to see that you'd got your fur, it's beastly cold. Your dad and Bart have been and went away fasting.'

Fleur shed her coat and dropped into a chair. 'I'm tired. Your ears are sticking up so nicely tonight, Michael.'

Michael went on his knees and joined his hands behind her waist. Her eyes had a strange look, a scrutiny which held him in suspense, a little startled.

'If *you* got pneumonia,' he said, 'I should go clean out of curl.'

'Why on earth should I?'

'You don't know the connexion – never mind, it wouldn't interest you. We're not going out, are we?'

'Of course we are. It's Alison's monthly.'

'Oh! Lord! If you're tired we could cut that.'

'My dear! Impos.! She's got all sorts of people coming.'

Stifling a disparagement, he sighed out: 'Right-o! Warpaint?'

'Yes, white waistcoat. I like you in white waistcoats.'

Cunning little wretch? He squeezed her waist and rose. Fleur laid a light stroke on his hand, and he went into his dressing-room comforted. ...

But Fleur sat still for at least five minutes – not precisely 'a prey to conflicting emotions', but the victim of very considerable confusion. *Two* men within the last hour had done this thing – knelt at her knees and joined their fingers behind her waist. Undoubtedly she had been rash to go to Wilfrid's rooms. The moment she got there she had perceived how entirely unprepared she really was to commit herself to what was physical. True he had done no more than Michael. But — Goodness! — she had seen the fire she was playing with, realized what torment he was in. She had strictly forbidden him to say a word to Michael, but intuitively she knew that in his struggle between loyalties she could rely on nothing. Confused, startled, touched, she could not help a pleasant warmth in being so much loved by two men at once, nor an itch of curiosity about the upshot. And she sighed. She had added to her collection of experiences — but how to add further without breaking up the collection, and even perhaps the collector, she could not see.

After her words to Wilfrid before the Eve: 'You will be a fool to go — wait!' she had known he would expect something before long. Often he had asked her to come and pass judgement on his 'junk'. A month, even a week, ago she would have gone without thinking more than twice about it, and discussed his 'junk' with Michael afterwards! But now she thought it over many times, and but for the fumes of lunch, and the feeling, engendered by the society of the 'Vertiginist', of Amabel Nazing, of Linda Frewe, that scruples of any kind were 'stuffy', sensations of all sorts 'the thing', she would probably still have been thinking it over now. When they departed, she had taken a deep breath and her telephone receiver from the Chinese tea-chest.

If Wilfrid were going to be in at half-past five, she would come and see his 'junk'.

His answer: 'My God! Will you?' almost gave her pause. But dismissing hesitation with the thought: 'I will be Parisian — Proust!' she had started for her Club. Three-quarters of an hour, with no more stimulant than three cups of China tea, three back numbers of the *Glass of Fashion*, three back views of country members 'dead in chairs', had sent her forth a careful quarter of an hour behind her time.

On the top floor Wilfrid was standing in his open doorway, pale as a soul in purgatory. He took her hand gently, and drew her in. Fleur thought with a little thrill: 'Is this what it's like?

Du côté de chez Swann!' Freeing her hand, she began at once to flutter round the 'junk', clinging to it piece by piece.

Old English 'junk' rather manorial, with here and there an Eastern or First Empire bit, collected by some bygone Desert, nomadic, or attached to the French court. She was afraid to sit down, for fear that he might begin to follow the authorities; nor did she want to resume the intense talk of the Tate Gallery. 'Junk' was safe, and she only looked at him in those brief intervals when he was not looking at her. She knew she was not playing the game according to 'La Garçonne' and Amabel Nazing; that, indeed, she was in danger of going away without having added to her sensations. And she couldn't help being sorry for Wilfrid; his eyes yearned after her, his lips were bitter to look at. When at last from sheer exhaustion of 'junk' she sat down, he had flung himself at her feet. Half hypnotized, with her knees against his chest, as safe as she could hope for, she really felt the tragedy of it – his horror of himself, his passion for herself. It was painful, deep; it did not fit in with what she had been led to expect; it was not in the period, and how – how was she to get away without more pain to him and to herself? When she *had* got away, with one kiss received but not answered, she realized that she had passed through a quarter of an hour of real life, and was not at all sure that she liked it. ... But now, safe in her own room, undressing for Alison's monthly, she felt curious as to what she would have been feeling if things had gone as far as was proper according to the authorities. Surely she had not experienced one-tenth of the thoughts or sensations that would have been assigned to her in any advanced piece of literature! It had been disillusioning, or else she was deficient, and Fleur could not bear to feel deficient. And, lightly powdering her shoulders, she bent her thoughts towards Alison's monthly.

Though Lady Alison enjoyed an occasional encounter with the younger generation, the Aubrey Greenes and Linda Frewes of this life were not conspicuous by their presence at her gatherings. Nesta Gorse, indeed, had once attended, but one legal and two literary politicos who had been in contact with her, had complained of it afterwards. She had, it seemed, rent little spiked holes in the garments of their self-esteem. Sibley Swan would have been welcome, for his championship of the past, but he seemed, so far, to have turned up his nose and looked down it. So it was not the intelligentsia, but just intellectual society, which was gathered there when Fleur and Michael entered, and the conversation had all the sparkle and all the '*savoir faire*' incidental to talk about art and letters by those who – as Michael put it – 'fortunately had not to *faire*.'

'All the same, these are the guys,' he muttered in Fleur's ear, 'who make the names of artists and writers. What's the stunt, tonight?'

It appeared to be the London *début* of a lady who sang Balkan folk songs. But in a refuge to the right were four tables set out for bridge. They were already filled. Among those who still stood listening, were, here and there, a Gurdon Minho, a society painter and his wife, a sculptor looking for a job. Fleur, wedged between Lady Feynte, the painter's wife, and Gurdon Minho himself, began planning an evasion. There – yes, there was Mr Chalfont! At Lady Alison's, Fleur, an excellent judge of '*milieu*', never wasted her time on artists and writers – she could meet *them* anywhere. Here she intuitively picked out the biggest 'bug', politico-literary, and waited to pin him. Absorbed in the idea of pinning Mr Chalfont, she overlooked a piece of drama passing without.

Michael had clung to the top of the stairway, in no mood for talk and skirmish; and, leaning against the balustrade, wasp-thin in his long white waistcoat, with hands deep thrust into his trousers' pockets, he watched the turns and twists of Fleur's white neck, and listened to the Balkan songs, with a sort of blankness in his brain. The word : 'Mont !' startled him. Wilfrid was standing just below. Mont? He had not been that to Wilfrid for two years !

'Come down here.'

On that half-landing was a bust of Lionel Charwell, K.C., by

Boris Strumolowski, in the genre he had cynically adopted when June Forsyte gave up supporting his authentic but unrewarded genius. It had been almost indistinguishable from any of the other busts in that year's Academy, and was used by the young Charwells to chalk moustaches on.

Beside this object Desert leaned against the wall with his eyes closed. His face was a study to Michael.

'What's wrong, Wilfrid?'

Desert did not move. 'You've got to know – I'm in love with Fleur.'

'What!'

'I'm not going to play the snake. You're up against me. Sorry, but there it is! You can let fly!' His face was death-pale, and its muscles twitched. In Michael, it was the mind, the heart that twitched. What a very horrible, strange, 'too beastly' moment! His best friend – his best man! Instinctively he dived for his cigarette-case – instinctively handed it to Desert. Instinctively they both took cigarettes, and lighted each other's. Then Michael said:

'Fleur – knows?'

Desert nodded: 'She doesn't know I'm telling you – wouldn't have let me. You've nothing against her – yet.' And, still with closed eyes, he added: 'I couldn't help it.'

It was Michael's own subconscious thought! Natural! Natural! Fool not to see how natural! Then something shut-to within him, and he said: 'Decent of you to tell me; but – aren't you going to clear out?'

Desert's shoulders writhed against the wall.

'I thought so; but it seems not.'

'Seems? I don't understand.'

'If I knew for certain I'd no chance – but I don't,' and he suddenly looked at Michael: 'Look here, it's no good keeping gloves on. I'm desperate, and I'll take her from you if I can.'

'Good God!' said Michael. 'It's the limit!'

'Yes! Rub it in! But, I tell you, when I think of you going home with her, and of myself,' he gave a dreadful little laugh, 'I advise you *not* to rub it in.'

'Well,' said Michael, 'as this isn't a Dostoievsky novel, I suppose there's no more to be said.'

Desert moved from the wall and laid his hand on the bust of Lionel Charwell.

'You realize, at least, that I've gone out of my way – perhaps dished myself – by telling you. I've not bombed without declaring war.'

'No,' said Michael dully.

'You can chuck my books over to some other publisher.' Michael shrugged.

'Good night, then,' said Desert. 'Sorry for being so primitive.'

Michael looked straight into his 'best man's' face. There was no mistaking its expression of bitter despair. He made a half-movement with his hand, uttered half the word 'Wilfrid,' and, as Desert went down, he went upstairs.

Back in his place against the balustrade, he tried to realize that life was a laughing matter, and couldn't. His position required a serpent's cunning, a lion's courage, a dove's gentleness: he was not conscious of possessing such proverbial qualities. If Fleur had loved him as he loved her, he would have had for Wilfrid a real compassion. It was so natural to fall in love with Fleur! But she didn't – oh! no, she didn't! Michael had one virtue – if virtue it be – a moderate opinion of himself, a disposition to think highly of his friends. He had thought highly of Desert; and – odd! – he still did not think lowly of him. Here was his friend trying to do him mortal injury, to alienate the affection – more honestly, the toleration – of his wife; and yet he did not think him a cad. Such leniency, he knew, was hopeless; but the doctrines of free-will, and free contract, were not to him mere literary conceptions, they were part of his nature. To apply duress, however desirable, would not be on his cards. And something like despair ravaged the heart of him, watching Fleur's ingratiating little tricks with the great Gerald Chalfont. If she left him for Wilfrid! But surely – no – her father, her house, her dog, her friends, her – her collection of – of – she would not – could not give *them* up? But suppose she kept everything, Wilfrid included! No, no!

She wouldn't! Only for a second did that possibility blur the natural loyalty of his mind.

Well, what to do? Tell her – talk the thing out? Or wait and watch? For what? Without deliberate spying, he could not watch. Desert would come to their house no more. No! Either complete frankness; or complete ignoring – and that meant living with the sword of Damocles above his head! No! Complete frankness! And not do anything that seemed like laying a trap! He passed his hand across a forehead that was wet. If only they were at home, away from that squalling and these cultivated jackanapes! Could he go in and hook her out? Impossible without some reason! Only his brain-storm for a reason! He must just bite on it. The singing ceased. Fleur was looking round. Now she would beckon! On the contrary, she came towards him. He could not help the cynical thought: 'She's hooked old Chalfont!' He loved her, but he knew her little weaknesses. She came up and took hold of his sleeve.

'I've had enough, Michael, let's slip off; d'you mind?'

'Quick!' he said, 'before they spot us!'

In the cold air outside he thought: 'Now? Or in her room?'

'I think,' said Fleur, 'that Mr Chalfont is overrated – he's nothing but a mental yawn. He's coming to lunch tomorrow week.'

Not now – in her room!

'Whom do you think to meet him, besides Alison?'

'Nothing jazzy.'

'Of course not; but it must be somebody intriguing, Michael. Bother! sometimes I think it isn't worth it.'

Michael's heart stood still. Was that a portent – sign of 'the primitive' rising within his adored practitioner of social arts? An hour ago he would have said:

'You're right, my child; it jolly well isn't!' But now – any sign of change was ominous! He slipped his arm in hers.

'Don't worry, we'll snare the just-right cuckoos, somehow.'

'A Chinese Minister would be perfect,' mused Fleur, 'with Minho and Bart – four men – two women – cosy. I'll talk to Bart.'

Michael had opened their front door. She passed him; he lingered to see the stars, the plane trees, a man's figure motionless, collared to the eyes, hatted down to them. 'Wilfrid!' he thought: 'Spain! Why Spain? And all poor devils who are in distress – the heart – oh! darn the heart!' He closed the door.

But soon he had another to open, and never with less enthusiasm. Fleur was sitting on the arm of a chair, in the dim lavender pyjamas she sometimes wore just to keep in with things, staring at the fire. Michael stood, looking at her and at his own reflection beyond in one of the five mirrors – white and black, the pierrot pyjamas she had bought him. 'Figures in a play,' he thought, 'figures in a play! Is it real?' He moved forward and sat on the chair's other arm.

'Hang it!' he muttered. 'Wish I were Antinous!' And he slipped from the arm into the chair, to be behind her face, if she wanted to hide it from him.

'Wilfrid's been telling me,' he said quietly.

Off his chest! What now? He saw the blood come flushing into her neck and cheek.

'Oh! What business – how do you mean "telling you"?'

'Just that he's in love with you – nothing more – there's nothing more to tell, is there?' And drawing his feet up on to the chair, he clasped his hands hard round his knees. Already – already he had asked a question! Bite on it! Bite on it! And he shut his eyes.

'Of course,' said Fleur, very slowly, 'there's nothing more. If Wilfrid chooses to be so silly.'

Chooses! The word seemed unjust to one whose own 'silliness' was so recent – so enduring! And – curious! his heart wouldn't bound. Surely it ought to have bounded at her words!

'Is that the end of Wilfrid, then?'

'The end? I don't know.'

Ah! Who knew anything – when passion was about?

'Well,' he said, holding himself hard together, 'don't forget I love you awfully!'

He saw her eyelids flicker, her shoulders shrugging.

'Am I likely to?'

Bitter, cordial, simple – which? Suddenly her hands came round and took him by the ears. Holding them fast she looked down at him, and laughed. And again his heart *would* not bound. If she did not lead him by the nose, she – ! But he clutched her to him in the chair. Lavender and white and black confused – she returned his kiss. But from the heart? Who knew? Not Michael.

Chapter Ten

PASSING OF A SPORTSMAN

◄◄►►

S O A M E S, disappointed of his daughter, said: 'I'll wait,' and took his seat in the centre of the jade green settee, oblivious of Ting-a-ling before the fire, sleeping off the attentions of Amabel Nazing, who had found him 'just too cunning'. Grey and composed, with one knee over the other, and a line between his eyes, he thought of Elderson and the condition of the world, and of how there was always something. And the more he thought, the more he wondered why he had ever been such a flat as to go on to a Board which had anything to do with foreign contracts. All the old wisdom that in the nineteenth century had consolidated British wealth, all the Forsyte philosophy of attending to one's own business, and taking no risks, the close-fibred national individualism which refused to commit the country to chasing this wild goose or that, held within him silent demonstration. Britain was on the wrong tack politically to try and influence the Continent, and the P.P.R.S. on the wrong tack monetarily to insure business outside Britain. The special instinct of his breed yearned for resumption of the straight and private path. Never meddle with what you couldn't control! 'Old Mont' had said: 'Keep the ring!' Nothing of the sort: Mind one's own business! That was the real 'formula'. He became conscious of his calf – Ting-a-ling was sniffing at his trousers.

'Oh!' said Soames. 'It's you!'

Placing his forepaws against the settee, Ting-a-ling licked the air.

'Pick you up?' said Soames. 'You're too long.' And again he felt that faint warmth of being liked.

'There's something about me that appeals to him,' he thought, taking him by the scruff and lifting him on to a cushion. 'You and I,' the little dog seemed saying with his stare – Chinese little object! The Chinese knew what they were about, they had minded their own business for five thousand years!

'I shall resign,' thought Soames. But what about Winifred, and Imogen, and some of the Rogers and Nicholases who had been putting money into this thing because he was a director? He wished they wouldn't follow him like a lot of sheep! He rose from the settee. It was no good waiting, he would walk on to Green Street and talk to Winifred at once. She would have to sell again, though the shares had dropped a bit. And without taking leave of Ting-a-ling, he went out.

All this last year he had almost enjoyed life. Having somewhere to come and sit and receive a certain sympathy once at least a week, as in old days at Timothy's, was of incalculable advantage to his spirit. In going from home Fleur had taken most of his heart with her; but Soames had found it almost an advantage to visit his heart once a week rather than to have it always about. There were other reasons conducing to light-heartedness. That diabolical foreign chap, Prosper Profond, had long been gone he didn't know where, and his wife had been decidedly less restive and sarcastic ever since. She had taken up a thing they called Coué, and grown stouter. She used the car a great deal. Altogether she was more domestic. Then, too, he had become reconciled to Gauguin – a little slump in that painter had convinced him that he was still worth attention, and he had bought three more. Gauguin would rise again! Soames almost regretted his intuition of that second coming, for he had quite taken to the chap. His colour, once you got used to it, was very attractive. One picture, especially, which meant nothing so far as he could see, had a way of making you keep your eyes on it. He even felt uneasy when he thought of having to part with the thing at an enhanced price. But, most of all, he had been feeling so well, enjoying a recrudescence of youth in regard to Annette, taking more pleasure in what he ate, while his mind dwelt almost complacently on the state of money. The pound going up in value; Labour quiet! And now they had got rid of that Jack-o'-lantern, they might look for some years of solid Conservative administration. And to think, as he did, stepping across St James's Park towards Green Street, that he had gone and put his foot into a concern which he could not control, made him feel – well, as if the devil had been in it!

In Piccadilly he moused along on the Park side, taking his customary look up at the 'Iseeum' Club. The curtains were drawn, and chinks of light glowed, long and cosy. And that reminded him – someone had said George Forsyte was ill. Certainly he had not seen him in the bay window for months past. Well, George had always eaten and drunk too much. He crossed over and passed beneath the Club; and a sudden feeling – he didn't know what – a longing for his own past, a sort of nostalgia – made him stop and mount the steps.

'Mr George Forsyte in the Club?'

The janitor stared, a grey-haired, long-faced chap, whom he had known from away back in the eighties.

'Mr Forsyte, sir,' he said, 'is very ill indeed. They say he won't recover, sir.'

'What?' said Soames. 'Nobody told me that.'

'He's very bad – *very* bad indeed. It's the heart.'

'The heart! Where is he?'

'At his rooms, sir; just round the corner. They say the doctors have given him up. He *will* be missed here. Forty years I've known him. One of the old school, and a wonderful judge of wine and horses. We none of us last for ever, they say, but I never thought to see him out. Bit too full-blooded, sir, and that's a fact.'

With a slight shock Soames realized that he had never known where George lived, so utterly anchored had he seemed to that bay window above.

'Just give me the number of his rooms,' he said.

'Belville Row – No. 11, sir; I'm sure I hope you'll find him better. I shall miss his jokes – I shall, indeed.'

Turning the corner into Belville Row, Soames made a rapid calculation. George was sixty-six, only one year younger than himself! If George was really *in extremis* it would be quite unnatural! 'Comes of not leading a careful life,' he thought; 'always rackety – George! When was it I made his will?' So far as he remembered, George had left his money to his brothers and sisters – no one else to leave it to. The feeling of kinship stirred in Soames, the instinct of family adjustment. George and he had never got on – opposite poles of temperament – still he would have to be buried, and who would see to it if not Soames, who had seen to so many Forsyte burials in his time? He recalled the nickname George had once given him, 'the undertaker'! H'm! Here was poetical justice! Belville Row! Ah! No. 11 – regular bachelor-looking place! And putting his hand up to the bell, he thought: 'Women!' What had George done about women all his life?

His ring was answered by a man in a black cut-away coat with a certain speechless reticence.

'My cousin, Mr George Forsyte? How is he?'

The man compressed his lips.

'Not expected to last the night, sir.'

Soames felt a little clutch beneath his Jaeger vest.

'Conscious?'

'Yes, sir.'

'Could you show him my card? He might possibly like to see me.'

'Will you wait in here, sir?' Soames passed into a low room panelled up to the level of a man's chest, and above that line decorated with prints. George – a collector! Soames had never supposed he had it in him! On those walls, wherever the eye roved, were prints coloured and uncoloured, old and new, depicting the sports of racing and prize-fighting! Hardly an inch of the red wall space visible! About to examine them for marks of value, Soames saw that he was not alone. A woman – age uncertain in the shaded light – was sitting in a very high-backed chair before the fire with her elbow on the arm of it, and a handkerchief held to her face. Soames looked at her, and his nostrils moved in a stealthy sniff. 'Not a lady,' he thought. 'Ten to one but there'll be complications.' The muffled voice of the cut-away man said:

'I'm to take you in, sir.' Soames passed his hand over his face and followed.

The bedroom he now entered was in curious contrast. The whole of one wall was occupied by an immense piece of furniture, all cupboards and drawers. Otherwise there was nothing in the room but a dressing-table with silver accoutrements, an electric radiator alight in the fireplace, and a bed opposite. Over the fireplace was a single picture, at which Soames glanced mechanically. What! Chinese! A large whitish sidelong monkey, holding the rind of a squeezed fruit in its outstretched paw. Its whiskered face looked back at him with brown, almost human eyes. What on earth had made his inartistic cousin buy a thing like that and put it up to face his bed? He turned and looked at the bed's occupant. 'The only sportsman of the lot', as Montague Dartie in his prime had called him, lay with his swollen form outlined beneath a thin quilt. It gave Soames quite a turn to see that familiar beef-coloured face pale and puffy as a moon, with dark corrugated circles round eyes which still had their japing stare. A voice, hoarse and subdued, but with the old Forsyte timbre, said:

'Hallo, Soames! Come to measure me for my coffin?'

Soames put the suggestion away with a movement of his hand; he felt queer looking at that travesty of George. They had never got on, but – !

And in his flat, unemotional voice he said:

'Well, George! You'll pick up yet. You're no age. Is there anything I can do for you?'

A grin twitched George's pallid lips.

'Make me a codicil. You'll find paper in the dressing-table drawer.'

Soames took out a sheet of 'Iseeum' Club notepaper. Standing at the table, he inscribed the opening words of a codicil with his stylographic pen, and looked round at George. The words came with a hoarse relish.

'My three screws to young Val Dartie, because he's the only Forsyte that knows a horse from a donkey.' A throaty chuckle sounded ghastly in the ears of Soames. 'What have you said?'

Soames read: 'I hereby leave my three racehorses to my kinsman, Valerius Dartie, of Wansdon, Sussex, because he has special knowledge of horses.'

Again the throaty chuckle. 'You're a dry file, Soames. Go on. To Milly Moyle, of 12, Claremont Grove, twelve thousand pounds, free of legacy duty.'

Soames paused on the verge of a whistle.

The woman in the next room!

The japing in George's eyes had turned to brooding gloom.

'It's a lot of money,' Soames could not help saying.

George made a faint choleric sound.

'Write it down, or I'll leave her the lot.'

Soames wrote. 'Is that all?'

'Yes. Read it!'

Soames read. Again he heard that throaty chuckle.

'That's a pill. You won't let *that* into the papers. Get that chap in, and you and he can witness.'

Before Soames reached the door, it was opened and the man himself came in.

'The – er – vicar, sir,' he said in a deprecating voice, 'has called. He wants to know if you would like to see him.'

George turned his face, his fleshy grey eyes rolled.

'Give him my compliments,' he said, 'and say I'll see him at the funeral.'

With a bow the man went out, and there was silence.

'Now,' said George, 'get him in again. I don't know when the flag'll fall.'

Soames beckoned the man in. When the codicil was signed and the man gone, George spoke:

'Take it, and see she gets it. I can trust you, that's one thing about you, Soames.'

Soames pocketed the codicil with a very queer sensation.

'Would you like to see her again?' he said.

George stared up at him a long time before he answered.

'No. What's the good? Give me a cigar from that drawer.'

Soames opened the drawer.

'Ought you?' he said.

George grinned. 'Never in my life done what I ought; not going to begin now. Cut it for me.'

Soames nipped the end of the cigar. 'Shan't give him a match,' he thought. 'Can't take the responsibility.' But George did not ask for a match. He lay quite still, the unlighted cigar between his pale lips, the curved lids down over his eyes.

'Good-bye,' he said, 'I'm going to have a snooze.'

'Good-bye,' said Soames. 'I – I hope – you – you'll soon –'

George reopened his eyes – fixed, sad, jesting, they seemed to quench the shams of hope and consolation. Soames turned hastily and went out. He felt bad, and almost unconsciously turned again into the sitting-room. The woman was still in the same attitude; the same florid scent was in the air. Soames took up the umbrella he had left there, and went out.

'This is my telephone number,' he said to the servant waiting in the corridor; 'let me know.'

The man bowed.

Soames turned out of Belville Row. Never had he left George's presence without the sense of being laughed at. Had he been laughed at now? Was that codicil George's last joke? If he had not gone in this afternoon, would George ever have made it, leaving a third of his property away from his family to that florid woman in the high-backed chair? Soames was beset by a sense of mystery. How could a man joke at death's door? It was, in a way, heroic. Where would he be buried? Somebody would know – Francie or Eustace. And what would they think when they came to know about that woman in the chair – twelve thousand pounds! 'If I can get hold of that white monkey, I will,' he thought suddenly. 'It's a good thing.' The monkey's eyes, the squeezed-out fruit – was life all a bitter jest and George deeper than himself? He rang the Green Street bell.

Mrs Dartie was very sorry, but Mrs Cardigan had called for her to dine and make a fourth at the play.

Soames went in to dinner alone. At the polished board below which Montague Dartie had now and again slipped, if not quite slept, he dined and brooded. 'I can trust you, that's one thing about you, Soames.' The words flattered and yet stung him. The depths of that sardonic joke! To give him a family shock and trust him to carry the shock out! George had never cared twelve thousand pounds for a woman who smelled of patchouli. No! It was a final gibe at his family, the Forsytes, at Soames himself! Well! one by one those who had injured or gibed at him – Irene, Bosinney, old and young Jolyon, and now George, had met their fates. Dead, dying, or in British Columbia! He saw again his cousin's eyes above that unlighted cigar, fixed, sad, jesting – poor devil! He got up from the table, and nervously drew aside the curtains. The night was fine and cold. What happened to one – after? George used to say that he had been Charles the Second's cook in a former existence! But reincarnation was all nonsense, weak-minded theorizing! Still, one would be glad to hold on if one could, after one was gone. Hold on, and be near Fleur! What noise was that? Gramophone going in the kitchen! When the cat was away, the mice –! People were all alike – take what they could get, and give as little as they could for it. Well! he would smoke a cigarette. Lighting it at a candle – Winifred dined by candlelight, it was the 'mode' again – he thought: 'Has he still got that cigar between his teeth?' A funny fellow, George – all his days a funny fellow! He watched a ring of smoke he had made without intending to – very blue, he never inhaled! Yes! George had lived too fast, or he would not have been dying twenty years before his time – too fast! Well, there it was, and he wished he had a cat to talk to! He took a little monster off the mantelboard. Picked up by his nephew Benedict in an Eastern bazaar the year after the War, it had green eyes – 'Not emeralds,' thought Soames, 'some cheap stone!'

'The telephone for you, sir.'

He went into the hall and took up the receiver.

'Yes?'

'Mr Forsyte has passed away, sir – in his sleep, the doctor says.'

'Oh!' said Soames: 'Had he a cig –? Many thanks.' He hung up the receiver.

Passed away! And, with a nervous movement, he felt for the codicil in his breast pocket.

Chapter Eleven

VENTURE

◄◄►►

FOR a week Bicket had seen 'the job', slippery as an eel, evasive as a swallow, for ever passing out of reach. A pound for keep, and three shillings invested on a horse, and he was down to twenty-four bob. The weather had turned sou'-westerly and Victorine had gone out for the first time. That was something off his mind, but the cramp of the unemployed sensation, that fearful craving for the means of mere existence, a protesting, agonizing anxiety, was biting into the very flesh of his spirit. If he didn't get a job within a week or two, there would be nothing for it but the work-house, or the gas. 'The gas,' thought Bicket, 'if she will, I will. I'm fed up. After all, what is it? In her arms I wouldn't mind.' Instinct, however, that it was not so easy as all that to put one's head under the gas, gave him a brain-wave that Monday night. Balloons – that chap in Oxford Street to-day! Why not? He still had the capital for a flutter in them, and no hawker's licence needed. His brain, working like a squirrel in the small hours, grasped the great, the incalculable advantage of coloured balloons over all other forms of commerce. You couldn't miss the man who sold them – there he was for every eye to see, with his many radiant circumferences dangling in front of him! Not much profit in them, he had gathered – a penny on a sixpenny globe of coloured air, a penny on every three small twopenny globes; still their salesman was alive, and probably had pitched him a poor tale for fear of making his profession seem too attractive. Over the Bridge, just where the traffic – no, up by St Paul's! He knew a passage where he could stand back a yard or two, like that chap in Oxford Street! But to the girl sleeping beside him he said nothing. No word to her till he had thrown the die. It meant gambling with his last penny. For a bare living he would have to sell – why, three dozen big and four dozen small balloons a day would only be twenty-six shillings a week profit, unless that chap was kidding. Not much towards 'Austrylia' out of that! And not a career – Victorine would have a shock! But it was neck or nothing now – he must try it, and in off hours go on looking for a job.

Our thin capitalist, then, with four dozen big and seven dozen small on a tray, two shillings in his pocket, and little in his stomach, took his stand off St Paul's at two o'clock next day. Slowly he blew up and tied the necks of two large and three small, magenta, green and blue, till they dangled before him. Then with the smell of rubber in his nostrils, and protruding eyes, he stood back on the kerb and watched the stream go by. It gratified him to see that most people turned to look at him. But the first person to address him was a policeman, with:

'I'm not sure you can stand there.'

Bicket did not answer, his throat felt too dry. He had heard of the police. Had he gone the wrong way to work? Suddenly he gulped, and said: 'Give us a chance, constable; I'm right on my bones. If I'm in the way, I'll stand anywhere you like. This is new to me, and two bob's all I've got left in the world besides a wife.'

The constable, a big man, looked him up and down. 'Well, we'll see. I shan't make trouble for you if no one objects.'

Bicket's gaze deepened thankfully.

'I'm much obliged,' he said; 'tyke one for your little girl – to please me.'

'I'll buy one,' said the policeman, 'and give you a start. I go off duty in an hour, you 'ave it ready – a big one, magenta.'

He moved away. Bicket could see him watching. Edging into the gutter, he stood quite still; his large eyes clung to every face that passed; and, now and then, his thin fingers nervously touched his wares. If Victorine could see him! All the spirit within him mounted. By Golly! he would get out of this somehow into the sun, into a life that was a life!

He had been standing there nearly two hours, shifting from foot to unaccustomed foot, and had sold four big and five small – sixpenny worth of profit – when Soames, who had changed his route to spite those fellows who couldn't get past William Gouldyng, Ingerer, came by on his way to the P.P.R.S. board. Startled by a timid murmur: 'Balloon, sir, best quality,' he looked round from that contemplation of St Paul's which had been his lifelong habit, and stopped in sheer surprise.

'Balloon!' he said. 'What should I want with a balloon?'

Bicket smiled. Between those green and blue and orange globes and Soames's grey self-containment there was incongruity which even he could appreciate.

'Children like 'em – no weight, sir, waistcoat pocket.'

'I dare say,' said Soames, 'but I've no children.'

'Grandchildren, sir.'

'Nor any grandchildren.'

'Thank you, sir.'

Soames gave him one of those rapid glances with which he was accustomed to gauge the character of the impecunious. 'A poor, harmless little rat!' he thought. 'Here, give me two – how much?'

'A shilling, sir, and much obliged.'

'You can keep the change,' said Soames hurriedly, and passed on, astonished. Why on earth he had bought the things, and for more than double their price, he could not conceive. He did not recollect such a thing having happened to him before. Extremely peculiar! And suddenly he realized why. The fellow had been humble, mild – to be encouraged, in these days of Communistic bravura. After all, the little chap was – was on the side of Capital, had invested in those balloons! Trade! And, raising his eyes towards St Paul's again, he stuffed the nasty-feeling things down into his overcoat pocket. Somebody would be taking them out, and wondering what was the matter with him! Well, he had other things to think of! ...

Bicket, however, stared after him, elated. Two hundred and fifty odd per cent profit on those two – that was something like. The feeling, that not enough women were passing him here, became less poignant – after all, women knew the value of money, no extra shillings out of them! If only some more of these shiny-hatted old millionaires would come along!

At six o'clock, with a profit of three and eightpence, to which Soames had contributed just half, he began to add the sighs of deflating balloons to his own; untying them with passionate care he watched his coloured hopes one by one collapse, and stored them in the drawer of his tray. Taking it under his arm, he moved his tired legs in the direction of the Bridge. In a full day he might make four to five shillings – Well, it would just keep them alive, and something might turn up! He was his own master, anyway, accountable neither to employer nor to union. That knowledge gave him a curious lightness inside, together with the fact that he had eaten nothing since breakfast.

'Wonder if he was an alderman,' he thought; 'they say those aldermen live on turtle soup.' Nearing home, he considered nervously what to do with the tray? How prevent Victorine from knowing that he had joined the ranks of Capital, and spent his day in the gutter? Ill luck! She was at the window! He must put a good face on it. And he went in whistling.

'What's that, Tony?' she said, pointing to the tray.

'Ah! ha! Great stunt – this! Look 'ere!'

Taking a balloon out from the tray, he blew. He blew with a desperation he had not yet put into the process. They said the

things would swell to five feet in circumference. He felt somehow
that if he could get it to attain those proportions, it would
soften everything. Under his breath the thing blotted out Victorine, and the room, till there was just the globe of coloured
air. Nipping its neck between thumb and finger, he held it up,
and said:

'There you are; not bad value for sixpence, old girl!' and he
peered round it. Lord, she was crying! He let the 'blymed'
thing go; it floated down, the air slowly evaporating till a little
crinkled wreck rested on the dingy carpet. Clasping her heaving
shoulders, he said desperately:

'Cheerio, my dear, don't quarrel with bread and butter. I
shall get a job, this is just to tide us over. I'd do a lot worse
than that for you. Come on, and get my tea, I'm hungry,
blowin' up those things.'

She stopped crying, looked up, said nothing – mysterious
with those big eyes! You'd say she had thoughts! But what
they were Bicket could not tell. Under the stimulus of tea, he
achieved a certain bravado about his new profession. To be
your own master! Go out when you liked, come home when
you liked – lie in bed with Vic if he jolly well pleased. A lot in
that! And there rose in Bicket something truly national, something free and happy-go-lucky, resenting regular work, enjoying a spurt, and a laze-off, craving independence – something
that accounted for the national life, the crowds of little shops, of
middlemen, casual workers, tramps, owning their own souls in
their own good time, and damning the consequences – something inherent in the land, the race, before the Saxons and their
conscience and their industry came in – something that believed
in swelling and collapsing coloured air, demanded pickles and
high flavours without nourishment – yes, all that something
exulted above Bicket's kipper and his tea, good and strong. He
would rather sell balloons than be a packer any day, and don't
let Vic forget it! And when she was able to take a job, they
would get on fine, and not be long before they'd saved enough
to get out of it to where those blue butterflies came from. And
he spoke of Soames. A few more aldermen without children –

say two a day, fifteen bob a week outside legitimate trade. Why, in under a year they'd have the money! And once away, Vic would blow out like one of those balloons; she'd be twice the size, and a colour in her cheeks to lay over that orange and magenta. Bicket became full of air. And the girl, his wife, watched with her large eyes and spoke little; but she did not cry again, or, indeed, throw any water, warm or cold, on him who sold balloons.

Chapter Twelve

FIGURES AND FACTS

WITH the exception of old Fontenoy — in absence as in presence ornamental — the Board was again full; Soames, conscious of special ingratiation in the manner of 'that chap' Elderson, prepared himself for the worst. The figures were before them; a somewhat colourless show, appearing to disclose a state of things which would pass muster, if within the next six months there were further violent disturbances of currency exchange. The proportion of foreign business to home business was duly expressed in terms of two to seven; German business, which constituted the bulk of the foreign, had been lumped — Soames noted — in the middle section, of countries only half bankrupt, and taken at what might be called a conservative estimate.

During the silence which reigned while each member of the Board digested the figures, Soames perceived more clearly than ever the quandary he was in. Certainly, these figures would hardly justify the forgoing of the dividend earned on the past year's business. But suppose there were another Continental crash and they became liable on the great bulk of their foreign business, it might swamp all profits on home business next year, and more besides. And then his uneasiness about Elderson himself – founded he could not tell on what, intuitive, perhaps silly.

'Well, Mr Forsyte,' the chairman was speaking; 'there are the figures. Are you satisfied?'

Soames looked up; he had taken a resolution.

'I will agree to this year's dividend on condition that we drop this foreign business in future, lock, stock and barrel.' The manager's eyes, hard and bright, met his, then turned towards the chairman.

'That appears to savour of the panicky,' he said; 'the foreign business is responsible for a good third of our profit this year.'

The chairman seemed to garner the expressions of his fellow-directors, before he said:

'There is nothing in the foreign situation at the moment, Mr Forsyte, which gives particular cause for alarm. I admit that we should watch it closely –'

'You can't,' interjected Soames. 'Here we are four years from the Armistice, and we know no more where we stand than we did then. If I'd realized our commitment to this policy, I should never have come on the Board. We must drop it.'

'Rather an extreme view. And hardly a matter we can decide in a moment.'

The murmur of assent, the expression, faintly ironical, of 'that chap's' lips, jolted the tenacity in Soames.

'Very well! Unless you're prepared to tell the shareholders in the report that we are dropping foreign business, you drop me. I must be free to raise the question myself at the general meeting.' He did not miss the shift and blink in the manager's eyes. That shot had gone home!

The chairman said:

'You put a pistol to our heads.'

'I am responsible to the shareholders,' said Soames, 'and I shall do my duty by them.'

'So we all are, Mr Forsyte; and I hope we shall all do our duty.'

'Why not confine the foreign business to the small countries – their currency is safe enough?'

'Old Mont,' and his precious 'ring'!

'No,' said Soames, 'we must go back to safety.'

'Splendid isolation, Forsyte?'

'Meddling was all very well in the war, but in peace – politics or business – this half-and-half interference is no good. We can't control the foreign situation.'

He looked around him, and was instantly conscious that with those words he had struck a chord. 'I'm going through with this!' he thought.

'I should be glad, Mr Chairman' – the manager was speaking – 'if I might say a word. The policy was of my initiation, and I think I may claim that it has been of substantial benefit to the Society so far. When, however, a member of the Board takes so strong a view against its continuance, I certainly don't press the Board to continue it. The times *are* uncertain, and a risk, of course, is involved, however conservative our estimates.'

'Now why?' thought Soames: 'What's he ratting for?'

'That's very handsome of you, Elderson; Mr Chairman, I think we may say that is very handsome of our manager.'

Old Dosey Cosey! Handsome! The old woman!

The chairman's rather harsh voice broke a silence.

'This is a very serious point of policy. I should have been glad to have Lord Fontenoy present.'

'If I am to endorse the report,' said Soames shortly, 'it must be decided today. I have made up my mind. But please yourselves.'

He threw in those last three words from a sort of fellow feeling – it was unpleasant to be dragooned! A moment's silence, and then discussion assumed that random volubility which softens a decision already forced on one. A quarter of an hour thus passed before the chairman said:

'We are agreed then, gentlemen, that the report shall contain the announcement that, in view of Continental uncertainty, we are abandoning foreign risks for the present.'

Soames had won. Relieved and puzzled, he walked away alone.

He had shown character; their respect for him had gone up,

he could see; their liking for him down, if they'd ever had any — he didn't know! But why had Elderson veered round? He recalled the shift and blink of the fellow's steely eyes at the idea of the question being raised at the general meeting.

That had done it! But why? Were the figures faked? Surely not! That would be too difficult, in the face of the accountants. If Soames had faith, it was in chartered accountants. Sandis and Jevon were tip-top people. It couldn't be that! He glanced up from the pavement. The dome of St Paul's was dim already in evening sky — nothing to be had out of it! He felt badly in need of someone to talk to; but there was nobody; and he quickened his pace among the hurrying crowd. His hand, driven deep into his overcoat pocket, came into sudden contact with some foreign sticky substance. 'Gracious!' he thought: 'those things!' Should he drop them in the gutter? If only there were a child he could take them home to! He must get Annette to speak to Fleur. He knew what came of bad habits from his own experience of long ago. Why shouldn't he speak to her himself? He was staying the night there! But there came on him a helpless sense of ignorance. These young people! What did they really think and feel? Was old Mont right? Had they given up interest in everything except the moment, abandoned all belief in continuity, and progress? True enough that Europe was in Queer Street. But look at the state of things after the Napoleonic Wars. He couldn't remember his grandfather 'Superior Dosset', the old chap had died five years before he was born, but he perfectly remembered how Aunt Ann, born in 1799, used to talk about 'that dreadful Bonaparte — we used to call him Boney, my dear'; of how her father could get eight or ten per cent for his money; and of what an impression 'those Chartists' had made on Aunts Juley and Hester, and that was long afterwards. Yet, in spite of all that, look at the Victorian era — a golden age, things worth collecting, children worth having! Why not again! Consols had risen almost continuously since Timothy died. Even if Heaven and Hell had gone, they couldn't be the reason; none of his uncles had believed in either, and yet had all made fortunes, and all had families, except Timothy and Swithin. No! It couldn't be the want of Heaven and Hell! What, then, was the reason of the change – if change there really were? And suddenly it was revealed to Soames. They talked too much – too much and too fast! They got to the end of interest in this and that and the other. They ate life and threw away the rind, and – and –. By the way, he must buy that picture of George's! ... Had these young folk more mind than his own generation? And if so – why? Was it diet? That lobster cocktail Fleur had given him the Sunday before last. He had eaten the thing – very nasty! But it hadn't made him want to talk. No! He didn't think it could be diet. Besides – Mind! Where were the minds now that equalled the Victorians – Darwin, Huxley, Dickens, Disraeli, even old Gladstone? Why, he remembered judges and advocates who seemed giants compared with those of the present day, just as he remembered that the judges of James his father's youth had seemed giants to James compared with those of Soames's prime. According to that, mind was steadily declining. It must be something else. There was a thing they called psycho-analysis, which so far as he could understand attributed people's action not to what they ate at breakfast, or the leg they got out of bed with, as in the good old days, but to some shock they had received in the remote past and entirely forgotten. The sub-conscious mind! Fads! Fads and microbes! The fact was this generation had no digestion. His father and his uncles had all complained of liver, but they had never had anything the matter with them – no need of any of these vitamins, false teeth, mental healing, newspapers, psycho-analysis, spiritualism, birth control, osteopathy, broadcasting, and what not. 'Machines!' thought Soames. 'That's it – I shouldn't wonder!' How could you believe in anything when everything was going round so fast? When you couldn't count your chickens – they ran about so? But Fleur had got a good little head on her! 'Yes,' he mused, 'and French teeth, she can digest anything. Two years! I'll speak to her before she gets the habit confirmed. Her mother was quick enough about it!' And perceiving the Connoisseurs' Club in front of him, he went in.

The hall porter came out of his box. A gentleman was waiting.

'What gentleman?' said Soames, sidelong.

'I think he's your nephew, sir, Mr Dartie.'

'Val Dartie! H'm! Where?'

'In the little room, sir.'

The little room – all the accommodation considered worthy of such as were not Connoisseurs – was at the end of a passage, and in no taste at all, as if the Club were saying: 'See what it is not to be one of us!' Soames entered it, and saw Val Dartie smoking a cigarette and gazing with absorption at the only object of interest, his own reflection in the glass above the fire.

He never saw his nephew without wondering when he would say: 'Look here, Uncle Soames, I'm up a stump.' Breeding race-horses! There could only be one end to that!

'Well?' he said, 'how are *you*?'

The face in the glass turned round, and became the back of a clipped sandyish head.

'Oh! bobbish, thanks! *You* look all right, Uncle Soames. I just wanted to ask you: Must I take these screws of old George Forsyte's? They're dashed bad.'

'Gift horse in the mouth?' said Soames.

'Well,' said Val, 'but they're *so* dashed bad; by the time I've paid legacy duty, boxed them to a sale, and sold them, there won't be a sixpence. One of them falls down when you look at it. And the other two are broken-winded. The poor old boy kept them, because he couldn't get rid of them. They're about five hundred years old.'

'Thought you were fond of horses,' said Soames. 'Can't you turn them out?'

'Yes,' said Val, drily; 'but I've got my living to make. I haven't told my wife, for fear she should suggest that. I'm afraid I might see them in my dreams if I sold them. They're only fit for the kennels. Can I write to the executors and say I'm not rich enough to take them?'

'You can,' said Soames, and the words: 'How's your wife?'

98

died unspoken on his lips. She was the daughter of his enemy, young Jolyon. That fellow was dead, but the fact remained.

'I will, then,' said Val. 'How did his funeral go off?'

'Very simple affair – I had nothing to do with it.' The days of funerals were over. No flowers, no horses, no plumes – a motor hearse, a couple of cars or so, was all the attention paid nowadays to the dead. Another sign of the times!

'I'm staying the night at Green Street,' said Val. 'I suppose you're not there, are you?'

'No,' said Soames, and did not miss the relief in his nephew's countenance.

'Oh! by the way, Uncle Soames – do you advise me to buy P.P.R.S. shares?'

'On the contrary. I'm going to advise your mother to sell. Tell her I'm coming in tomorrow.'

'Why? I thought –'

'Never mind my reasons!' said Soames shortly.

'So long, then!'

Exchanging a chilly hand-shake, he watched his nephew withdraw.

So long! An expression, old as the Boer war, that he had never got used to – meant nothing so far as he could see! He entered the reading-room. A number of Connoisseurs were sitting and standing about, and Soames, least clubbable of men, sought the solitude of an embrasured window. He sat there polishing the nail of one forefinger against the back of the other, and chewing the cud of life. After all, what was the point of anything. There was George! He had had an easy life – never done any work! And here was himself, who had done a lot of work! And sooner or later they would bury him too, with a motor hearse probably! And there was his son-in-law, young Mont, full of talk about goodness knew what – and that thin-cheeked chap who had sold him the balloons this afternoon. And old Fontenoy, and that waiter over there; and the out-of-works and the in-works; and those chaps in Parliament, and the parsons in their pulpits – what were they all for? There was the old gardener down at Mapledurham pushing his roller over and over the lawn, week after week, and if he didn't, what would the lawn be like? That was life – gardener rolling lawn! Put it that there was another life – he didn't believe it, but for the sake of argument – that life must be just the same. Rolling lawn – to keep it lawn! What point in lawn? Conscious of pessimism, he rose. He had better be getting back to Fleur's – they dressed for dinner! He supposed there was something in dressing for dinner, but it was like lawn – you came unrolled – undressed again, and so it went on! Over and over and over to keep up to a pitch, that was – ah! what *was* the pitch for?

Turning into South Square, he cannoned into a young man, whose head was craned back as if looking after someone he had parted from. Uncertain whether to apologize or to wait for an apology, Soames stood still.

The young man said abruptly: 'Sorry, sir,' and moved on; dark, neat-looking chap with a hungry look obviously unconnected with his stomach. Murmuring: 'Not at all!' Soames moved forward and rang his daughter's bell. She opened to him herself. She was in hat and furs – just in. The young man recurred to Soames. Had he left her there? What a pretty face it was! He should certainly speak to her. If she once took to gadding about!

He put it off, however, till he was about to say 'Good night' – Michael having gone to the political meeting of a Labour candidate, as if he couldn't find something better to do!

'Now you've been married two years, my child, I suppose you'll be looking towards the future. There's a great deal of nonsense talked about children. The whole thing's much simpler. I hope you feel that.'

Fleur was leaning back among the cushions of the settee, swinging her foot. Her eyes became a little restless, but her colour did not change.

'Of course!' she said; 'only there's no hurry, Dad.'

'Well, I don't know,' Soames murmured. 'The French and the royal family have a very sound habit of getting it over early. There's many a slip and it keeps them out of mischief. You're very attractive, my child – I don't want to see you take too much to gad-about ways. You've got all sorts of friends.'

'Yes,' said Fleur.

'You get on well with Michael, don't you?'

'Oh! yes.'

'Well, then, why not? You must remember that your son will be a what-you-call-it.'

In those words he compromised with his instinctive dislike of titles and flummery of that nature.

'It mightn't be a son,' said Fleur.

'At your age that's easily remedied.'

'Oh, I don't want a lot, Dad. One, perhaps, or two.'

'Well,' said Soames, 'I should almost prefer a daughter, something like – well, something like you.'

Her softened eyes flew, restive, from his face to her foot, to the dog, all over the room.

'I don't know, it's a tie – like digging your own grave in a way.'

'I shouldn't put it as high as that,' murmured Soames, persuasively.

'No man would, Dad.'

'Your mother wouldn't have got on at all without you,' and recollection of how near her mother had been to not getting on at all with her – of how, but for him, she would have made a mess of it, reduced him to silent contemplation of the restive foot.

'Well,' he said, at last, 'I thought I'd mention it. I – I've got your happiness at heart.'

Fleur rose and kissed his forehead.

'I know, Dad,' she said, 'I'm a selfish pig. I'll think about it. In fact, I – I have thought about it.'

'That's right,' said Soames; 'that's right! You've a good head on you – it's a great consolation to me. Good night, my dear!'

And he went up to his bed. If there was point in anything, it was in perpetuation of oneself, though, of course, that begged the question. 'Wonder,' he thought, 'if I ought to have asked her whether that young man –!' But young people were best left alone. The fact was, he didn't understand them. His eye lighted on the paper bag containing those – those things he had bought. He had brought them up from his overcoat to get rid of them – but how? Put into the fire, they would make a smell. He stood at his dressing-table, took one up and looked at it. Good Lord! And, suddenly, rubbing the mouthpiece with his handkerchief, he began to blow the thing up. He blew until his cheeks were tired, and then, nipping the aperture, took a bit of the dental cotton he used on his teeth every night and tied it up. There the thing was! With a pettish gesture he batted the balloon. Off it flew – purple and extravagant, alighting on his bed. H'm! He took up the other, and did the same to it. Purple and green! The deuce! If anyone came in and saw! He threw up the window, batted them, balloon after balloon, into the night, and shut the window down. There they'd be in the dark, floating about. His lips contracted in a nervous grin. People would see them in the morning. Well! What else could you do with things like that?

Chapter Thirteen

TENTERHOOKS

⪡⪡-◦-⪢

MICHAEL had gone to the Labour candidate's meeting partly because he wanted to, and partly out of fellow feeling for 'old Forsyte', whom he was always conscious of having robbed. His father-in-law had been very decent about Fleur, and he liked the 'old man' to have her to himself when he could.

In a constituency which had much casual and no trades-union labour to speak of, the meeting would be one of those which enabled the intellectuals of the Party to get it 'off their chests'. Sentiment being 'slop', and championship mere condescension, one might look for sound economic speeches which left out discredited factors, such as human nature. Michael was accustomed to hearing people disparaged for deprecating change because human nature was constant; he was accustomed to hearing people despised for feeling compassion; he knew that one ought to be purely economic. And anyway that kind of speech was preferable to the tub-thumpings of the North or of the Park, which provoked a nasty underlying class spirit in himself.

The meeting was in full swing when he arrived, the candidate pitilessly exposing the fallacies of a capitalism which, in his view, had brought on the war. For fear that it should bring on another, it must be changed for a system which would ensure that nations should not want anything too much. The individual – said the candidate – was in every respect superior to the nation of which he formed a part; and the problem before them was to secure an economic condition which would enable the individual to function freely in his native superiority. In that way alone, he said, would they lose those mass movements and emotions which imperilled the sanity of the world. He spoke well. Michael listened, purring almost audibly, till he found that he was thinking of himself, Wilfrid and Fleur. Would he ever function so freely in a native superiority that he did not want Fleur too much? And did he wish to? He did not. That seemed to introduce human nature into the speaker's argument. Didn't everybody want something too much? Wasn't it natural? And if so, wouldn't there always be a collective wanting too much – pooling of primary desire, such as the desire of keeping your own head above water? The candidate's argument seemed to him suddenly to leave out heat, to omit friction, to be that of a man in an armchair after a poor lunch. He looked attentively at the speaker's shrewd, dry, doubting face. 'No juice!' he thought. And when 'the chap' sat down, he got up and left the hall.

This Wilfrid business had upset him horribly. Try as he had to put it out of his mind, try as he would to laugh it off, it continued to eat into his sense of security and happiness. Wife and best friend! A hundred times a day he assured himself that he trusted Fleur. Only, Wilfrid was so much more attractive than himself, and Fleur deserved the best of everything. Besides,

Wilfrid was going through torture, and it was not a pleasant thought! How end the thing, restore peace of mind to himself, to him, to her? She had told him nothing; and it simply was impossible to ask. No way even of showing his anxiety! The whole thing was just 'dark', and, so far as he could see, would have to stay so; nothing to be done but screw the lid on tighter, be as nice as he could to her, try not to feel bitter about him. Hades!

He turned down Chelsea Embankment. Here the sky was dark and wide and streaming with stars. The river wide, dark and gleaming with oily rays from the Embankment lamps. The width of it all gave him relief. Dash the dumps! A jolly, queer, muddled, sweet and bitter world; an immensely intriguing game of chance, no matter how the cards were falling at the moment! In the trenches he had thought: 'Get out of this, and I'll never mind anything again!' How seldom now he remembered thinking that! The human body renewed itself – they said – in seven years. In three years' time his body would not be the body of the trenches, but a whole-time peace body with a fading complex. If only Fleur would tell him quite openly what she felt, what she was doing about Wilfrid, for she must be doing something! And Wilfrid's verse? Would his confounded passion – as Bart suggested – flow in poetry? And if so, who would publish it? A miserable business! Well the night was beautiful, and the great thing not to be a pig. Beauty and not being a pig! Nothing much else to it – except laughter – the comic side! Keep one's sense of humour, anyway! And Michael searched, while he strode beneath plane trees half-stripped of leaves and plume-like in the dark, for the fun in his position. He failed to find it. There seemed absolutely nothing funny about love. Possibly he might fall out of love again some day, but not so long as she kept him on her tenterhooks. Did she do it on purpose? Never! Fleur simply could not be like those women who kept their husbands hungry and fed them when they wanted dresses, furs, jewels. Revolting!

He came in sight of Westminster. Only half-past ten! Suppose he took a cab to Wilfrid's rooms, and tried to have it out with him. It would be like trying to make the hands of a clock move backwards to its ticking. What use in saying: 'You love Fleur – well, don't!' or in Wilfrid saying it to him. 'After all, I was first with Fleur,' he thought. Pure chance, perhaps, but fact! Ah! And wasn't that just the danger? He was no longer a novelty to her – nothing unexpected about him now! And he and she had agreed times without number that novelty was the salt of life, the essence of interest and drama. Novelty now lay with Wilfrid! Lord! Lord! Possession appeared far from being nine points of the law! He rounded-in from the Embankment towards home – jolly part of London, jolly Square; everything jolly except just this infernal complication. Something, soft as a large leaf, tapped twice against his ear. He turned, astonished; he was in empty space, no tree near. Floating in the darkness, a round thing – he grabbed, it bobbed. What? A child's balloon! He secured it between his hands, took it beneath a lamp-post – green, he judged. Queer! He looked up. Two windows lighted, one of them Fleur's! Was this the bubble of his own happiness expelled? Morbid! Silly ass! Some gust of wind – a child's plaything lodged and loosened! He held the balloon gingerly. He would take it in and show it to her. He put his latchkey in the door. Dark in the hall – gone up! He mounted, swinging the balloon on his finger. Fleur was standing before a mirror.

'What on earth's that?' she said.

The blood returned to Michael's heart. Curious how he had dreaded its having anything to do with her!

'Don't know, darling; fell on my hat – must belong to heaven.' And he batted it.

The balloon floated, dropped, bounded twice, wobbled and came to rest.

'You *are* a baby, Michael. I believe you bought it.'

Michael came closer, and stood quite still.

'My hat! What a misfortune to be in love!'

'You think so!'

'*Il y a toujours un qui baise, et l'autre qui ne tend pas la joue.*'

'But I do.'

'Fleur !'

Fleur smiled.

'*Baise* away.'

Embracing her, Michael thought: 'She holds me – does with me what she likes; I know nothing of her !'

And there arose a small sound – from Ting-a-ling smelling the balloon.

PART TWO

Chapter One

THE MARK FALLS

THE state of the world had been getting more and more on Soames's nerves ever since the general meeting of the P.P.R.S. It had gone off with that fatuity long associated by him with such gatherings – a watertight rigmarole from the chairman; butter from two reliable shareholders; vinegar from shareholders not so reliable; and the usual 'gup' over the dividend. He had gone there glum, come away glummer. From a notion once taken into his head Soames parted more slowly than a cheese parts from its mites. Two-sevenths of foreign business, nearly all German! And the mark falling! It had begun to fall from the moment that he decided to support the dividend. And why? What was in the wind? Contrary to his custom, he had taken to sniffing closely the political columns of his paper. The French – he had always mistrusted them, especially since his second marriage – the French were going to play old Harry, if he was not greatly mistaken! Their papers, he noticed, never lost a chance of having a dab at English policy; seemed to think they could always call the tune for England to pipe to! And the mark and the franc, and every other sort of money, falling. And, though in Soames was that which rejoiced in the thought that one of his country's bits of paper could buy a great quantity of other countries' bits of paper, there was also that which felt the whole thing silly and unreal, with an ever-growing consciousness that the P.P.R.S. would pay no dividend next year. The P.P.R.S. was a big concern; no dividend would be a sign, no small one, of bad management. Assurance was one of the few things on God's earth which could and should be conducted without real risk. But for that he would never have gone on the Board. And to find assurance had not been so conducted and that by himself, was – well! He had caused Winifred to sell, anyway, though the shares had already fallen slightly. 'I thought it was such a good thing, Soames,' she had said plaintively: 'it's rather a bore, losin' money on these shares.' He had answered without mercy: 'If you don't sell, you'll lose more.' And she had done it. If the Rogers and Nicholases who had followed him into it hadn't sold too – well, it was their look out! He had made Winifred warn them. As for himself, he had nothing but his qualifying shares, and the missing of a dividend or two would not hurt one whose director's fees more than compensated. It was not, therefore, private uneasiness so much as resentment at a state of things connected with foreigners and the slur on his infallibility.

Christmas had gone off quietly at Mapledurham. He abominated Christmas, and only observed it because his wife was French, and her national festival New Year's Day. One could not go so far as to observe that, encouraging a foreign notion. But Christmas with no child about – he still remembered the holly and snapdragons of Park Lane in his own childhood – the family parties; and how disgusted he had been if he got anything symbolic – the thimble, or the ring – instead of the shilling. They had never gone in for Santa Claus at Park Lane, partly because they could see through the old gentleman, and partly because he was not at all a late thing. Emily, his mother, had seen to that. Yes; and, by the way, that William Gouldyng, Ingerer, had so stumped those fellows at the Heralds' College, that Soames had dropped the inquiry – it was just encouraging them to spend his money for a sentimental satisfaction which did not materialize. That narrow-headed chap, 'Old Mont', peacocked about his ancestry; all the more reason for having no ancestry to peacock about. The Forsytes and the Goldings were good English country stock – that was what mattered. And if Fleur and her child, if one came, had French blood in them – well, he couldn't help it now.

In regard to the coming of a grandchild, Soames knew no more than in October. Fleur had spent Christmas with the Monts; she was promised to him, however, before long, and her mother must ask her a question or two!

The weather was extremely mild; Soames had even been out in a punt fishing. In a heavy coat he trailed a line for perch and dace, and caught now and then a roach – precious little good, the servants wouldn't eat them, nowadays! His grey eyes would brood over the grey water under the grey sky; and in his mind the mark would fall. It fell with a bump on that eleventh of January when the French went and occupied the Ruhr. He said to Annette at breakfast: 'Your country's cracked! Look at the mark now!'

'What do I care about the mark?' she had answered over her coffee. 'I care that they shall not come again into my country. I hope they will suffer a little what we have suffered.'

'You,' said Soames; 'you never suffered anything.'

Annette put her hand where Soames sometimes doubted the existence of a heart.

'I have suffered here,' she said.

'I didn't notice it. You never went without butter. What do you suppose Europe's going to be like now for the next thirty years! How about British trade?'

'We French see before our noses,' said Annette with warmth. 'We see that the beaten must be kept the beaten, or he will take revenge. You English are so sloppy.'

'Sloppy, are we?' said Soames. 'You're talking like a child. Could a sloppy people ever have reached our position in the world?'

'That is your selfishness. You are cold and selfish.'

'Cold, selfish and sloppy – they don't go together. Try again.'

'Your slop is in your thought and your talk; it is your instinct that gives you your success, and your English instinct is cold and selfish, Soames. You are a mixture, all of you, of hypocrisy, stupidity and egoism.'

Soames took some marmalade.

'Well,' he said, 'and what are the French? – cynical, avaricious and revengeful. And the Germans are sentimental, heady and brutal. We can all abuse each other. There's nothing for it but to keep clear. And that's what you French won't do.'

Annette's handsome person stiffened.

'When you are tied to a person, as I am tied to you, Soames, or as we French are tied to the Germans, it is necessary to be top dog, or to be bottom dog.'

Soames stayed his toast.

'Do you suppose yourself top dog in this house?'

'Yes, Soames.'

'Oh! Then you can go back to France tomorrow.'

Annette's eyebrows rose quizzically.

'I would wait a little longer, my friend; you are still too young.'

But Soames had already regretted his remark; he did not wish any disturbance at his time of life, and he said more calmly:

'Compromise is the essence of any reasonable existence between individuals or nations. We can't have the fat thrown into the fire every few years.'

'That is so English,' murmured Annette. 'We others never know what you English will do. You always wait to see which way the cat jumps.'

However deeply sympathetic with such a reasonable characteristic, Soames would have denied it at any ordinary moment — to confess to temporizing was not, as it were, done. But, with the mark falling like a cartload of bricks, he was heated to the point of standing by his nature.

'And why shouldn't we? Rushing into things that you'll have to rush out of! I don't want to argue. French and English never did get on, and never will.'

Annette rose. 'You speak the truth, my friend. *Entente, mais pas cordiale*. What are you doing today?'

'Going up to town,' said Soames glumly. 'Your precious Government has put business into Queer Street with a vengeance.'

'Do you stay the night?'

'I don't know.'

'*Adieu*, then, *jusqu'au revoir!*' And she got up.

Soames remained brooding above his marmalade — with the mark falling in his mind — glad to see the last of her handsome figure, having no patience at the moment for French tantrums. An irritable longing to say to somebody 'I told you so' possessed him. He would have to wait, however, till he found some-body to say it to.

A beautiful day, quite warm; and, taking his umbrella as an assurance against change, he set out for the station.

In the carriage going up they were talking about the Ruhr. Averse from discussion in public, Soames listened from behind his paper. The general sentiment was surprisingly like his own. In so far as it was unpleasant for the Huns – all right; in so far as it was unpleasant for British trade – all wrong; in so far as love of British trade was active and hate of Huns now passive – more wrong than right. A Francophil remark that the French were justified in making themselves safe at all cost, was coldly received. At Maidenhead a man got in whom Soames connected automatically with disturbance. He had much grey hair, a san-guine face, lively eyes, twisting eyebrows, and within five min-utes had asked in a breezy voice whether anyone had heard of the League of Nations. Confirmed in his estimate, Soames looked round the corner of his paper. Yes, that chap would get off on some hobby-horse or other! And there he went! The ques-tion – said the newcomer – was not whether the Germans should get one in the eye, the British one in the pocket, or the French one in the heart, but whether the world should get peace and goodwill. Soames lowered his paper. If – this fellow said – they wanted peace, they must sink their individual interests, and think in terms of collective interest. The good of all was the good of one! Soames saw the flaw at once; that might be, but the good of one was not the good of all. He felt that if he did not take care he would be pointing this out. The man was a per-fect stranger to him, and no good ever came of argument. Un-fortunately his silence amid the general opinion that the League of Nations was 'no earthly', seemed to cause the newcomer to regard him as a sympathizer; the fellow kept on throwing his eyebrows at him! To put up his paper again seemed too pointed, and his position was getting more and more false when the train ran in at Paddington. He hastened to a cab. A voice behind him said:

'Hopeless lot, sir, eh! Glad to see *you* saw my point.'

'Quite!' said Soames. 'Taxi!'

'Unless the League of Nations functions, we're all for Gehenna.'

Soames turned the handle of the cab door.

'Quite!' he said again. 'Poultry!' and got in. He was not going to be drawn. The fellow was clearly a firebrand!

In the cab the measure of his disturbance was revealed. He had said 'Poultry', an address that 'Forsyte, Bustard and Forsyte' had abandoned two-and-twenty years ago when, merged with 'Cuthcott, Holliday and Kingson,' they became 'Cuthcott, Kingson and Forsyte'. Rectifying the error, he sat forward, brooding. Fall of the mark! The country was sound about it, yes – but when they failed to pay the next dividend, could they rely on resentment against the French instead of against the directors? Doubtful! The directors ought to have seen it coming! That might be said of the other directors, but not of himself – here was a policy that he personally never would have touched. If only he could discuss the whole thing with someone – but old Gradman would be out of his depth in a matter of this sort. And, on arrival at his office, he gazed with a certain impatience at that changeless old fellow, sitting in his swivel chair.

'Ah! Mr Soames, I was hopin' you might come in this morning. There's a young man been round to see you from the P.P.R.S. Wouldn't give his business, said he wanted to see you privately. Left his number on the phone.'

'Oh!' said Soames.

'Quite a young feller – in the office.'

'What did he look like?'

'Nice, clean young man. I was quite favourably impressed – name of Butterfield.'

'Well, ring him up, and let him know I'm here.' And going over to the window, he stood looking out on to a perfectly blank wall.

Suited to a sleeping partner, his room was at the back, free from disturbance. Young man! The call was somewhat singular! And he said over his shoulder: 'Don't go when he comes, Gradman, I know nothing of him.'

The world changed, people died off, the mark fell, but Gradman was there — embodiment, faithful and grey, of service and integrity — an anchor.

Gradman's voice, grating, ingratiating, rose.

'This French news — it's not nice, Mr Soames. They're a hasty lot. I remember your father, Mr James, coming into the office the morning the Franco-Prussian war was declared — quite in his prime then, hardly more than sixty, I should say. Why, I recall his very words: "There," he said, "I told them so." And here they are — at it still. The fact is, they're cat and dog.'

Soames, who had half turned, resumed his contemplation of a void. Poor old Gradman dated! What would he say when he heard that they had been insuring foreign business? Stimulated by the old-time quality of Gradman's presence, his mind ranged with sudden freedom. He himself had another twenty years, perhaps. What would he see in that time? Where would old England be at the end of it? 'In spite of the papers, we're not such fools as we look,' he thought. 'If only we can steer clear of flibberty-gibberting, and pay our way!'

'Mr Butterfield, sir.' H'm! The young man had been very spry. Covered by Gradman's bluff and greasy greeting, he 'took a lunar', as his Uncle Roger used to call it. The young fellow in a neat suit, a turndown collar, with his hat in his hand, was a medium modest-looking chap. Soames nodded.

'You want to see me?'

'Alone, if I might, sir.'

'Mr Gradman here is my right-hand man.'

Gradman's voice purred gratingly; 'You can state your business. Nothing goes outside these walls, young man.'

'I'm in the office of the P.P.R.S., sir. The fact is, accident has just put some information in my hands, and I'm not easy in my mind. Knowing you to be a solicitor, sir, I preferred to come to you, rather than go to the chairman. As a lawyer, would you tell me: Is my first duty to the Society, being in their employ?'

'Certainly,' said Soames.

'I don't like this job, sir, and I hope you'll understand that

I'm not here for any personal motive – it's just because I feel I ought to.'

Soames regarded him steadily. Though large and rather swimming, the young man's eyes impressed him by their resemblance to a dog's. 'What's it all about?' he said.

The young man moistened his lips.

'The insurance of our German business, sir.'

Soames pricked his ears, already slightly pointed by Nature.

'It's a very serious matter,' the young man went on, 'and I don't know how it'll affect me, but the fact is, this morning I overheard a private conversation.'

'Oh!' said Soames.

'Yes, sir. I quite understand your tone, but the very first words did it. I simply couldn't make myself known after hearing them. I think you'll agree, sir.'

'Who were the speakers?'

'The manager, and a man called Smith – I fancy by his accent his name's a bit more foreign – who's done most of the agenting for the German business.'

'What were the words?' said Soames.

'Well, sir, the manager was speaking, and then this Smith said: "Quite so, Mr Elderson, but we haven't paid you a commission on all this business for nothing; if the mark goes absolutely phut, you will have to see that your Society makes it good for us!"'

The intense longing, which at that moment came on Soames to emit a whistle, was checked by sight of Gradman's face. The old fellow's mouth had opened in the nest of his grizzly short beard; his eyes stared puglike, he uttered a prolonged: 'A-ow!'

'Yes,' said the young man, 'it was a knock-out!'

'Where were you?' asked Soames, sharply.

'In the lobby between the manager's room and the board-room. I'd just come from sorting some papers in the board-room, and the manager's door was open an inch or so. Of course I know the voices well.'

'What after?'

'I heard Mr Elderson say: "H'ssh! Don't talk like that!" and

I slipped back into the board-room. I'd had more than enough, sir, I assure you.'

Suspicion and surmise clogged Soames's thinking apparatus. Was this young fellow speaking the truth? A man like Elderson – the risk was monstrous! And, if true, what was the directors' responsibility? But proof – proof? He stared at the young man, who looked upset and pale enough, but whose eyes did not waver. Shake him if he could! And he said sharply:

'Now mind what you're saying! This is most serious!'

'I know that, sir. If I'd consulted my own interest, I'd never have come here. I'm not a sneak.'

The words rang true, but Soames did not drop his caution.

'Ever had any trouble in the office?'

'No, sir, you can make inquiry. I've nothing against Mr Elderson, and he's nothing against me.'

Soames thought suddenly: 'Good heavens! He's shifted it on to me, and in the presence of a witness. And I supplied the witness!'

'Have you any reason to suppose,' he said, 'that they became aware of your being there?'

'They couldn't have, I think.'

The implications of this news seemed every second more alarming. It was as if Fate, kept at bay all his life by clever wrist-work, had suddenly slipped a thrust under his guard. No good to get rattled, however – must think it out at leisure!

'Are you prepared, if necessary, to repeat this to the Board?'

The young man pressed his hands together.

'Well, sir, I'd much rather have held my tongue; but if you decide it's got to be taken up, I suppose I must go through with it now. I'm sure I hope you'll decide to leave it alone; perhaps it isn't true – only why didn't Mr Elderson say: "You ruddy liar!"?'

Exactly! Why didn't he? Soames gave a grunt of intense discomfort.

'Anything more?' he said.

'No, sir.'

'Very well. You've not told anyone?'

'No, sir.'

'Then don't, and leave it to me.'

'I'll be only too happy to, sir. Good morning!'

'Good morning!'

No – very bad morning! No satisfaction whatever in this sudden fulfilment of his prophetic feeling about Elderson. None!

'What d'you think of that young fellow, Gradman? Is he lying?'

Thus summoned, as it were, from stupor, Gradman thoughtfully rubbed a nose both thick and shining.

'It's one word against another, Mr Soames, unless you get more evidence. But I can't see what the young man has to gain by it.'

'Nor I; but you never know. The trouble will be to get more evidence. Can I act without it?'

'It's delicate,' said Gradman. And Soames knew that he was thrown back on himself. When Gradman said a thing was delicate, it meant that it was the sort of matter on which he was accustomed to wait for orders – presumptuous even to hold opinion! But had he got one? Well, one would never know! The old chap would sit and rub his nose over it till Kingdom Come.

'I shan't act in a hurry,' he said, almost angrily: 'I can't see to the end of this.'

Every hour confirmed that statement. At lunch the tape of his city club showed the mark still falling – to unheard-of depths! How they could talk of golf, with this business on his mind, he could not imagine!

'I must go and see that fellow,' he said to himself. 'I shall be guarded. He may throw some light.' He waited until three o'clock and repaired to the P.P.R.S.

Reaching the office, he sought the board-room. The chairman was there in conference with the manager. Soames sat down quietly to listen; and while he listened he watched that fellow's face. It told him nothing. What nonsense people talked when they said you could tell character from faces! Only a perfect idiot's face could be read like that. And here was a man of experience and culture, one who knew every rope of business life and polite society. The hairless, neat features exhibited no more concern than the natural mortification of one whose policy had met with such a nasty knock. The drop of the mark had already wiped out any possible profit on the next half-year. Unless the wretched thing recovered, they would be carrying a practically dead load of German insurance. Really it was criminal that no limit of liability had been fixed! How on earth could he ever have overlooked that when he came on the Board? But he had only known of it afterwards. And who could have foreseen anything so mad as this Ruhr business, or realized the slack confidence of his colleagues in this confounded fellow? The words 'gross negligence' appeared 'close up' before his eyes. What if an action lay against the Board! Gross negligence! At his age and with his reputation! Why! The thing was plain as a pikestaff; for omitting a limit of liability this chap had got his commission! Ten per cent probably, on all that business – he must have netted thousands! A man must be in Queer Street indeed to take a risk like that! But conscious that his fancy was running on, Soames rose, and turned his back. The action suggested another. Simulate anger, draw some sign from that fellow's self-control! He turned again, and said pettishly: 'What on earth were you about, Mr Manager, when you allowed these contracts to go through without limit of liability? A man of your experience! What was your motive?'

A slight narrowing of the eyes, a slight compression of the lips. He had relied on the word 'motive', but the fellow passed it by.

'For such high premiums as we have been getting, Mr Forsyte, a limited liability was not possible. This is a most outrageous development, and I'm afraid it must be considered just bad luck.'

'Unfortunately,' said Soames, 'there's no such thing as luck in properly regulated assurance, as we shall find, or I'm much mistaken. I shouldn't be surprised if an action lay against the Board for gross negligence!'

That had got the chairman's goat! – Got his goat? What

expressions they used nowadays! Or did it mean the opposite? One never knew! But as for Elderson – he seemed to Soames to be merely counterfeiting a certain flusteration. Futile to attempt to spring anything out of a chap like that. If the thing were true, the fellow must be entirely desperate, prepared for anything and everything. And since from Soames the desperate side of life – the real holes, the impossible positions which demand a gambler's throw – had always been carefully barred by the habits of a prudent nature, he found it now impossible to imagine Elderson's state of mind, or his line of conduct if he were guilty. For all he could tell, the chap might be carrying poison about with him; might be sitting on a revolver like a fellow on the film. The whole thing was too unpleasant, too worrying for words. And without saying any more he went away, taking nothing with him but the knowledge that their total liability on this German business, with the mark valueless, was over two hundred thousand pounds. He hastily reviewed the fortunes of his co-directors. Old Fontenoy was always in low water; the chairman a dark horse; Mont was in land, land right down in value, and mortgaged at that; old Cosey Mothergill had nothing but his name and his director's fees; Meyricke must have a large income, but light come, light go, like most of those big counsel with irons in many fires and the certainty of a judgeship. Not a really substantial man among the lot, except himself! He ploughed his way along, head down. Public companies! Preposterous system! You had to trust somebody, and there you were! It was appalling!

'Balloons, sir – beautiful colours, five feet circumference. Take one, gentleman!'

'Good gad!' said Soames. As if the pricked bubble of German business were not enough!

Chapter Two

VICTORINE

⭅⭆

A L L through December balloons had been slack – hardly any movement about them, even in Christmas week, and from the Bickets Central Australia was as far ever. The girl Victorine, restored to comparative health, had not regained her position in the blouse department of Messrs Boney Blayds & Co. They had given her some odd sewing, but not of late, and she had spent much time trying to get work less uncertain. Her trouble was – had always been – her face. It was unusual. People did not know what to make of a girl who looked like that. Why employ one who without qualification of wealth, rank, fashion, or ability (so far as they knew) made them feel ordinary? For – however essential to such as Fleur and Michael – dramatic interest was not primary in the manufacture or sale of blouses, in the fitting-on of shoes, the addressing of envelopes, making-up of funeral wreaths, or the other ambitions of Victorine. Behind those large dark eyes and silent lips, what went on? It worried Boney Blayds & Co., and the more wholesale firms of commerce. The lurid professions – film-super, or mannequin – did not occur to one, of self-deprecating nature, born in Putney.

When Bicket had gone out of a morning with his tray and his balloons not yet blown up, she would stand biting her finger, as though to gnaw her way to some escape from this hand-to-mouth existence which kept her husband thin as a rail, tired as a rook, shabby as a tailless sparrow, and, at the expense of all caste feeling, brought them in no more than just enough to keep them living under a roof. It had long been clear to them both that there was no future in balloons, just a cadging present. And there smouldered in the silent, passive Victorine a fierce resentment. She wanted better things for herself, for him, chiefly for him.

On the morning when the mark was bumping down, she was putting on her velveteen jacket and toque (best remaining items of her wardrobe), having taken a resolve. Bicket never mentioned his old job, and his wife had subtly divined some cause beyond the ordinary for his loss of it. Why not see if she could get him taken back? He had often said: 'Mr Mont's a gent and a sort o' socialist; been through the war, too; no high-and-mighty about *him*.' If she could 'get at' this phenomenon! With the flush of hope and daring in her sallow cheeks, she took stock of her appearance from the window-glasses of the Strand. Her velveteen of jade-green always pleased one who had an eye for colour, but her black skirt – well, perhaps the wear and tear of it wouldn't show if she kept behind the counter. Had she brass enough to say that she came about a manuscript? And she rehearsed with silent lips, pinching her accent: 'Would you ask Mr Mont, please, if I could see him; it's about a manuscript.' Yes! and then would come the question: 'What name, please?' 'Mrs Bicket?' Never! 'Miss Victorine Collins?' All authoresses had maiden names. Victorine – yes! But Collins! It didn't sound like. And no one would know what her maiden name had been. Why not choose one? They often chose. And she searched. Something Italian, like – like – Hadn't their landlady said to them when they came in: 'Is your wife Eyetalian?' Ah! Manuelli! That was certainly Italian – the ice-cream man in Little Ditch Street had it! She walked on practising beneath her breath. If only she could get to see this Mr Mont!

She entered, trembling. All went exactly as foreseen, even to the pinching of her accent, till she stood waiting for them to bring an answer from the speaking-tube, concealing her hands in their very old gloves. Had Miss Manuelli an appointment? There was no manuscript.

'No,' said Victorine, 'I haven't sent it yet. I wanted to see him first.' The young man at the counter was looking at her hard. He went again to the tube, then spoke.

'Will you wait a minute, please – Mr Mont's lady secretary is coming down.'

Victorine inclined her head towards her sinking heart. A lady secretary! She would never get there now! And there came on her the sudden dread of false pretences. But the thought of Tony standing at his corner, ballooned up to the eyes, as she had spied out more than once, fortified her desperation.

A girl's voice said: 'Miss Manuelli? Mr Mont's secretary, perhaps you could give me a message.'

A fresh-faced young woman's eyes were travelling up and down her. Pinching her accent hard, she said: 'Oh! I'm afraid I couldn't do that.'

The travelling gaze stopped at her face. 'If you'll come with me, I'll see if he can see you.'

Alone in a small waiting-room, Victorine sat without movement, till she saw a young man's face poked through the doorway, and heard the words:

'Will you come in?'

She took a deep breath, and went. Once in the presence, she looked from Michael to his secretary and back again, subtly daring his youth, his chivalry, his sportsmanship, to refuse her a private interview. Through Michael passed at once the thought: 'Money, I suppose. But what an interesting face!' The secretary drew down the corners of her mouth and left the room.

'Well, Miss – er – Manuelli?'

'Not Manuelli, please – Mrs Bicket; my husband used to be here.'

'What!' The chap that had snooped *Copper Coin*! Phew! Bicket's yarn – his wife – pneumonia! She looked as if she might have had it.

'He often spoke of you, sir. And, please, he hasn't any work. Couldn't you find room for him again, sir?'

Michael stood silent. Did this terribly interesting-looking girl know about the snooping?

'He just sells balloons in the street now; I can't bear to see him. Over by St Paul's he stands, and there's no money in it; and we do so want to get out to Australia. I know he's very nervy, and gets wrong with people. But if you *could* take him back here. . . .'

No! she did not know!

'Very sorry, Mrs Bicket. I remember your husband well, but we haven't a place for him. Are *you* all right again?'

'Oh! yes. Except that I can't get work again either.'

What a face for wrappers! Sort of Mona Lisa-ish! Storbert's novel! Ha!

'Well, I'll have a talk with your husband. I suppose you wouldn't like to sit to an artist for a book-wrapper? It might lead to work in that line if you want it. You're just the type for a friend of mine. Do you know Aubrey Greene's work?'

'No, sir.'

'It's pretty good – in fact, very good in a decadent way. You wouldn't mind sitting?'

'I wouldn't mind anything to save some money. But I'd rather you didn't tell my husband I'd been to see you. He might take it amiss.'

'All right! I'll see him by accident. Near St Paul's, you said? But there's no chance here, Mrs Bicket. Besides, he couldn't make two ends meet on this job, he told me.'

'When I was ill, sir.'

'Of course, that makes a difference.'

'Yes, sir.'

'Well, let me write you a note to Mr Greene. Will you sit down a minute?'

He stole a look at her while she sat waiting. Really, her sallow, large-eyed face, with its dead-black, bobbed, frizzy-ended hair, was extraordinarily interesting – a little too refined and anaemic for the public; but, dash it all! the public couldn't always have its Reckitt's blue eyes, corn-coloured hair, and poppy cheeks. 'She's not a peach,' he wrote, 'on the main tree of taste; but so striking in her way that she really might become a type, like Beardsley's or Dana's.'

When she had taken the note and gone, he rang for his secretary.

'No, Miss Perren, she didn't take anything off me. But some type, eh?'

'I thought you'd like to see her. She wasn't an authoress, was she?'

'Far from it.'

'Well, I hope she got what she wanted.'

Michael grinned. 'Partly, Miss Perren – partly. You think I'm an awful fool, don't you?'

'I'm sure I don't; but I think you're too soft-hearted.'

Michael ran his fingers through his hair.

'Would it surprise you to hear that I've done a stroke of business?'

'Yes, Mr Mont.'

'Then I won't tell you what it is. When you've done pouting, go on with that letter to my father about *Duet*: "We are sorry to say that in the present state of the trade we should not be justified in reprinting the dialogue between those two old blighters; we have already lost money by it!" You must translate, of course. Now can we say something to cheer the old boy up? How about this? "When the French have recovered their wits, and the birds begin to sing – in short, when spring comes – we hope to reconsider the matter in the light of – of –" – er – what, Miss Perren?'

' "The experience we shall have gained." Shall I leave out about the French and the birds?'

'Excellent! "Yours faithfully, Danby and Winter." Don't you think it was a scandalous piece of nepotism bringing the book here at all, Miss Perren?'

'What is "nepotism"?'

'Taking advantage of your son. He's never made a sixpence by any of his books.'

'He's a very distinguished writer, Mr Mont.'

'And we pay for the distinction. Well, he's a good old Bart. That's all before lunch, and mind you have a good one. That girl's figure wasn't usual either, was it? She's thin, but she stands up straight. There's a question I always want to ask, Miss Perren: Why do modern girls walk in a curve with their heads poked forward? They can't all be built like that.'

The secretary's cheeks brightened.

'There *is* a reason, Mr Mont.'

'Good! What is it?'

The secretary's cheeks continued to brighten. 'I don't really know whether I can –'

'Oh! sorry. I'll ask my wife. Only she's quite straight herself.'

'Well, Mr Mont, it's this, you see: They aren't supposed to have anything be – behind, and, of course, they have, and they can't get the proper effect unless they curve their chests in and poke their heads forward. It's the fashion-plates and manne-quins that do it.'

'I see,' said Michael; 'thank you, Miss Perren; awfully good of you. It's the limit, isn't it?'

'Yes, I don't hold with it, myself.'

'No, quite!'

The secretary lowered her eyelids and withdrew.

Michael sat down and drew a face on his blotting-paper. It was not Victorine's. . . .

Armed with the note to Aubrey Greene, Victorine had her usual lunch, a cup of coffee and a bit of heavy cake, and took the tube towards Chelsea. She had not succeeded, but the gentleman had been friendly and she felt cheered.

At the studio door was a young man inserting a key – very elegant in smoke-grey Harris tweeds, a sliding young man with no hat, beautifully brushed-back bright hair, and a soft voice.

'Model?' he said.

'Yes, sir, please. I have a note for you from Mr Mont.'

'Michael? Come in.'

Victorine followed him in. It was 'not half' sea-green in there; a high room with rafters and a top light, and lots of pictures and drawings on the walls, and as if they had slipped off on to the floor. A picture on an easel of two ladies with their clothes sliding down troubled Victorine. She became conscious of the gentleman's eyes, sea-green like the walls, sliding up and down her.

'Will you sit for anything?' he asked.

Victorine answered mechanically: 'Yes, sir.'

'Do you mind taking your hat off?'

Victorine took off the toque, and shook out her hair.

'Ah!' said the gentleman. 'I wonder.'

Victorine wondered what.

'Just sit down on the dais, will you?'

Victorine looked about her, uncertain. A smile seemed to fly up his forehead and over his slippery bright hair.

'This is your first shot, then?'

'Yes, sir.'

'All the better.' And he pointed to a small platform.

Victorine sat down on it in a black oak chair.

'You look cold.'

'Yes, sir.'

He went to a cupboard and returned with two small glasses of a brown fluid.

'Have a Grand Marnier?'

She noticed that he tossed his off in one gulp, and did the same. It was sweet, strong, very nice, and made her gasp.

'Take a cigarette.'

Victorine took one from a case he handed, and put it between her lips. He lit it. And again a smile slid up away over the top of his head.

'You draw it in,' he said. 'Where were you born?'

'In Putney, sir.'

'That's very interesting. Just sit still a minute. It's not as bad as having a tooth out, but it takes longer. The great thing is to keep awake.'

'Yes, sir.'

He took a large piece of paper and a bit of dark stuff, and began to draw.

'Tell me,' he said, 'Miss —'

'Collins, sir — Victorine Collins.' Some instinct made her give her maiden name. It seemed somehow more professional.

'Are you at large?' He paused, and again the smile slid up over his bright hair: 'Or have you any other occupation?'

'Not at present, sir. I'm married, but nothing else.'

For some time after that the gentleman was silent. It was interesting to see him, taking a look, making a stroke on the paper, taking another look. Hundreds of looks, hundreds of strokes. At last he said: 'All right! Now we'll have a rest. Heaven sent you here, Miss Collins. Come and get warm.'

Victorine approached the fire.

'Do you know anything about expressionism?'

'No, sir.'

'Well, it means not troubling about the outside except in so far as it expresses the inside. Does that convey anything to you?'

'No, sir.'

'Quite! I think you said you'd sit for the – er – altogether?'

Victorine regarded the bright and sliding gentleman. She did not know what he meant, but she felt that he meant something out of the ordinary.

'Altogether what, sir?'

'Nude.'

'Oh!' She cast her eyes down, then raised them to the sliding clothes of the two ladies. 'Like that?'

'No, I shouldn't be treating you cubistically.'

A slow flush was burning out the sallow in her cheeks. She said slowly:

'Does it mean more money?'

'Yes, half as much again – more perhaps. I don't want you to if you'd rather not. You can think it over and let me know next time.'

She raised her eyes again, and said: 'Thank you, sir.'

'Righto! Only please don't "sir" me.'

Victorine smiled. It was the first time she had achieved this functional disturbance, and it seemed to have a strange effect. He said hurriedly: 'By George! When you smile, Miss Collins, I see you *im*pressionistically. If you've rested, sit up there again.'

Victorine went back.

The gentleman took a fresh piece of paper.

'Can you think of anything that will keep you smiling?'

She shook her head. That was a fact.

'Nothing comic at all? I suppose you're not in love with your husband, for instance?'

'Oh! Yes.'

'Well, try that.'

Victorine tried that, but she could only see Tony selling his balloons.

'That won't do,' said the gentleman. 'Don't think of him! Did you ever see *L'après-midi d'un Faune*?'

'No, sir.'

'Well, I've got an idea. *L'après-midi d'une Dryade*.' About the nude you really needn't mind. It's quite impersonal. Think of art, and fifteen bob a day. Shades of Nijinsky, I see the whole thing!'

All the time that he was talking his eyes were sliding off and on to her, and his pencil off and on to the paper. A sort of infection began to ferment within Victorine. Fifteen shillings a day! Blue butterflies!

There was a profound silence. His eyes and hand slid off and on. A faint smile had come on Victorine's face – she was adding up the money she might earn.

At last his eyes and hand ceased moving, and he stood looking at the paper.

'That's all for today, Miss Collins. I've got to think it out. Will you give me your address?'

Victorine thought rapidly.

'Please, sir, will you write to me at the post office. I don't want my husband to know that I'm – I'm –'

'Affiliated to art? Well! Name of post office?'

Victorine gave it and resumed her hat.

'An hour and a half, five shillings, thank you. And tomorrow, at half-past two, Miss Collins – not "sir".'

'Yes, s–, thank you.'

Waiting for her bus in the cold January air, the altogether appeared to Victorine improbable. To sit in front of a strange gentleman in her skin! If Tony knew! The slow flush again burned up the sallow in her cheeks. She climbed into the bus. But fifteen shillings! Six days a week – why, it would be four pound ten! In four months she could earn their passage out. Judging by the pictures in there, lots must be doing it. Tony must know nothing, not even that she was sitting for her face.

He was all nerves, and that fond of her! He would imagine things; she had heard him say those artists were just like cats. But that gentleman had been very nice, though he did seem as if he were laughing at everything. She wished he had shown her the drawing. Perhaps she would see herself in an exhibition some day. But without – oh! And suddenly she thought: 'If I ate a bit more, I'd look nice like that, too!' And as if to escape from the daring of that thought, she stared up into the face opposite. It had two chins, was calm and smooth and pink, with light eyes staring back at her. People had thoughts, but you couldn't tell what they were! And the smile which Aubrey Greene desired crept out on his model's face.

Chapter Three

MICHAEL WALKS AND TALKS

◄─◄─►►

THE face Michael drew began by being Victorine's, and ended by being Fleur's. If physically Fleur stood up straight, was she morally as erect? This was the speculation for which he continually called himself a cad. He saw no change in her movements, and loyalty refrained from inquiring into the movements he could not see. But his aroused attention made him more and more aware of a certain cynicism, as if she were continually registering the belief that all values were equal and none of much value.

Wilfrid, though still in London, was neither visible nor spoken of. 'Out of sight and hearing, out of mind,' seemed to be the motto. It did not work with Michael – Wilfrid was constantly in his mind. If Wilfrid were not seeing Fleur, how could he bear to stay within such tantalizing reach of her? If Fleur did not want Wilfrid to stay, why had she not sent him away? He was finding it difficult, too, to conceal from others the fact that Desert and he were no longer pals. Often the impetus to go and have it out with him surged up and was beaten back. Either there was nothing beyond what he already knew, or there was something – and Wilfrid would say there wasn't. Michael accepted that without cavil; one did not give a woman away! But he wanted to hear no lies from a war comrade. Between Fleur and himself no word had passed; for words, he felt, would add no knowledge, merely imperil a hold weak enough already. Christmas at the ancestral manor of the Monts had been passed in covert-shooting. Fleur had come and stood with him at the last drive on the second day, holding Ting-a-ling on a lead. The Chinese dog had been extraordinarily excited, climbing the air every time a bird fell, and quite unaffected by the noise of guns. Michael, waiting to miss his birds – he was a poor shot – had watched her eager face emerging from grey fur, her form braced back against Ting-a-ling. Shooting was new to her; and under the stimulus of novelty she was always at her best. He had loved even her 'Oh, Michaels!' when he missed. She had been the success of the gathering, which meant seeing almost nothing of her except a sleepy head on a pillow; but, at least, down there he had not suffered from lurking uneasiness.

Putting a last touch to the bobbed hair on the blotting-paper, he got up. St Paul's, that girl had said. He might stroll up and have a squint at Bicket. Something might occur to him. Tightening the belt of his blue overcoat round his waist, he sallied forth, thin and sprightly, with a little ache in his heart.

Walking east, on that bright, cheerful day, nothing struck him so much as the fact that he was alive, well, and in work. So very many were dead, ill, or out of a job. He entered Covent Garden. Amazing place! A human nature which, decade after decade, could put up with Covent Garden was not in danger of extinction from its many ills. A comforting place – one needn't take anything too seriously after walking through it. On this square island were the vegetables of the earth and the fruits of the world, bounded on the west by publishing, on the east by opera, on the north and south by rivers of mankind. Among discharging carts and litter of paper, straw and men out of drawing, Michael walked and sniffed. Smell of its own, Covent Garden,

earthy and just not rotten! He had never seen – even in the war
– any place that so utterly lacked form. Extraordinarily English!
Nobody looked as if they had anything to do with the soil –
drivers, hangers-on, packers, and the salesmen inside the covered
markets, seemed equally devoid of acquaintanceship with sun,
wind, water, earth or air – town types all! And – Golly! – how
their faces jutted, sloped, sagged and swelled, in every kind of
featural disharmony. What was the English type amongst all
this infinite variety of disproportion? There just wasn't one! He
came on the fruits, glowing piles, still and bright – foreigners
from the land of the sun – globes all the same size and colour.
They made Michael's mouth water. 'Something in the sun,' he
thought; 'there really is.' Look at Italy, at the Arabs, at Australia – the Australians came from England, and see the type now!
Nevertheless – a Cockney for good temper! The more regular
a person's form and features, the more selfish they were! Those
grape-fruit looked horribly self-satisfied, compared with the
potatoes!

He emerged still thinking about the English. Well! They
were now one of the plainest and most distorted races of the
world; and yet was there any race to compare with them for
good temper and for 'guts'? And they needed those in their
smoky towns, and their climate – remarkable instance of adaptation to environment, the modern English character! 'I could
pick out an Englishman anywhere,' he thought, 'and yet,
physically, there's no general type now!' Astounding people! So
ugly in the mass, yet growing such flowers of beauty, and such
strange sprigs – like that little Mrs Bicket; so unimaginative in
bulk, yet with such a blooming lot of poets! How would old
Danby like it, by the way, when Wilfrid took his next volume
to some other firm; or rather what should he – Wilfrid's particular friend! – say to old Danby? Aha! He knew what he should
say:

'Yes, sir, but you should have let that poor blighter off who
snooped the *Copper Coins*. Desert hasn't forgotten your refusal.'
One for old Danby and his eternal in-the-rightness! *Copper
Coin* had done uncommonly well. Its successor would probably

do uncommonly better. The book was a proof of what he – Michael – was always saying: The 'cockyolly-bird period' was passing. People wanted life again. Sibley, Walter Nazing, Linda – all those who had nothing to say except that they were superior to such as had – were already measured for their coffins. Not that they would know when they were in them; not blooming likely! They would continue to wave their noses and look down them!

'*I'm* fed-up with them,' thought Michael. 'If only Fleur would see that looking down your nose is a sure sign of inferiority!' And, suddenly, it came to him that she probably did. Wilfrid was the only one of the whole lot she had ever been thick with; the others were there because – well, because she was Fleur, and had the latest things about her. When, very soon, they were no longer the latest things, she would drop them. But Wilfrid she would not drop. No, he felt sure that she had not dropped, and would not drop Wilfrid.

He looked up. Ludgate Hill! 'Near St Paul's – sells balloons?' And there – sure enough – the poor beggar was!

Bicket was deflating with a view to going off his stand for a cup of cocoa. Remembering that he had come on him by accident, Michael stood for a moment preparing the tones of surprise. Pity the poor chap couldn't blow himself into one of those coloured shapes and float over St Paul's to Peter. Mournful little cuss he looked, squeezing out the air! Memory tapped sharply on his mind. Balloon – in the square – November the first – joyful night! Special! Fleur! Perhaps they brought luck. He moved and said in an astounded voice: '*You*, Bicket? Is this your stunt now?'

The large eyes of Bicket regarded him over a puce-coloured sixpennyworth.

'Mr Mont! Often thought I'd like to see you again, sir.'

'Same here, Bicket. If you're not doing anything, come and have some lunch.'

Bicket completed the globe's collapse, and, closing his tray-lid, said: 'Reelly, sir?'

'Rather! I was just going into a fish place.'

Bicket detached his tray.

'I'll leave this with the crossing-sweeper.' He did so, and followed at Michael's side.

'Any money in it, Bicket?'

'Bare livin', sir.'

'How about this place? We'll have oysters.'

A little saliva at the corner of Bicket's mouth was removed by a pale tongue.

At a small table decorated with a white oilcloth and a cruet stand, Michael sat down.

'Two dozen oysters, and all that; then two good soles, and a bottle of Chablis. Hurry up, please.'

When the white-aproned fellow had gone about it, Bicket said simply:

'My Gawd!'

'Yes, it's a funny world, Bicket.'

'It *is*, and that's a fact. This lunch'll cost you a pound, I shouldn't wonder. If I take twenty-five bob a week, it's all I do.'

'You touch it there, Bicket. I eat my conscience every day.'

Bicket shook his head.

'No, sir, if you've got money, spend it. I would. Be 'appy if you can – there yn't too many that are.'

The white-aproned fellow began blessing them with oysters. He brought them fresh-opened, three at a time. Michael bearded them; Bicket swallowed them whole. Presently above twelve empty shells, he said:

'That's where the Socialists myke their mistyke, sir. Nothing keeps me going but the sight of other people spendin' money. It's what we might all come to with a bit of luck. Reduce the world to a level of a pound a dy – and it won't even run to that, they sy! It's not good enough, sir. I'd rather 'ave less with the 'ope of more. Take awy the gamble, and life's a frost. Here's luck!'

'Almost thou persuadest me to be a capitalist, Bicket.'

A glow had come up in the thin and large-eyed face behind the greenish Chablis glass.

'I wish to Gawd I had my wife here, sir. I told you about her and the pneumonia. She's all right agyne now, only thin. She's the prize I drew. I don't want a world where you can't draw prizes. If it were all bloomin' conscientious an' accordin' to merit, I'd never have got her. See?'

'Me, too,' thought Michael, mentally drawing that face again.

'We've all got our dreams; mine's blue butterflies – Central Austrylia. The Socialists won't 'elp me to get there. Their ideas of 'eaven don't run beyond Europe.'

'Cripes!' said Michael. 'Melted butter, Bicket?'

'Thank you, sir.'

Silence was not broken for some time, but the soles were.

'What made you think of balloons, Bicket?'

'You don't 'ave to advertise, they do it for you.'

'Saw too much of advertising with us, eh?'

'Well, sir, I did use to read the wrappers. Astonished me, I will sy – the number of gryte books.'

Michael ran his hands through his hair.

'Wrappers! The same young woman being kissed by the same young man with the same clean-cut jaw. But what can you do, Bicket? They *will have it*. I tried to make a break only this morning – I shall see what comes of it.' 'And I hope *you* won't!' he thought: 'Fancy coming on Fleur outside a novel!'

'I did notice a tendency just before I left,' said Bicket, 'to 'ave cliffs or landskips and two sort of dolls sittin' on the sand or in the grass lookin' as if they didn't know what to do with each other.'

'Yes,' murmured Michael, 'we tried that. It was supposed not to be vulgar. But we soon exhausted the public's capacity. What'll you have now – cheese?'

'Thank you, sir; I've had too much already, but I won't say "No".'

'Two Stiltons,' said Michael.

'How's Mr Desert, sir?'

Michael reddened.

'Oh! He's all right.'

Bicket had reddened also.

'I wish – I wish you'd let him know that it was quite a – an accident my pitchin' on his book. I've always regretted it.'

'It's usually an accident, I think,' said Michael slowly, 'when we snoop other people's goods. We never *want* to.'

Bicket looked up.

'No, sir, I don't agree. 'Alf mankind's predytory – only, I'm not that sort, meself.'

In Michael loyalty tried to stammer. 'Nor is he.' He handed his cigarette-case to Bicket.

'Thank you, sir, I'm sure.'

His eyes were swimming, and Michael thought: 'Dash it! This is sentimental. Kiss me good-bye and go!' He beckoned up the white-aproned fellow.

'Give us your address, Bicket. If integuments are any good to you, I might have some spare slops.'

Bicket backed the bill with his address and said, hesitating: 'I suppose, sir, Mrs Mont wouldn't 'ave anything to spare. My wife's about my height.'

'I expect she would. We'll send them along.' He saw the 'little snipe's' lips quivering, and reached for his overcoat. 'If anything blows in, I'll remember you. Good-bye, Bicket, and good luck.'

Going east, because Bicket was going west, he repeated to himself the maxim: 'Pity is tripe – pity is tripe!' Then getting on a bus, he was borne back past St Paul's. Cautiously 'taking a lunar' – as old Forsyte put it – he saw Bicket inflating a balloon; little was visible of his face or figure behind that rosy circumference. Nearing Blake Street, he developed an invincible repugnance to work, and was carried on to Trafalgar Square. Bicket had stirred him up. The world was sometimes almost unbearably jolly. Bicket, Wilfrid, and the Ruhr! 'Feeling is tosh! Pity is tripe!' He descended from his bus, and passed the lions towards Pall Mall. Should he go into 'Snooks' and ask for Bart? No use – he would not find Fleur there. That was what he really wanted – to see Fleur in the daytime. But – where? She was everywhere to be found, and that was nowhere.

She was restless. Was that his fault? If he had been Wilfrid –

would she be restless? 'Yes,' he thought stoutly, 'Wilfrid's restless, too.' They were all restless – all the people he knew. At least all the young ones – in life and in letters. Look at their novels! Hardly one in twenty had any repose, any of that quality which made one turn back to a book as a corner of refuge. They dashed and sputtered and skidded and rushed by like motor-cycles – violent, oh! and clever. How tired he was of cleverness! Sometimes he would take a manuscript home to Fleur for her opinion. He remembered her saying once: 'This is exactly like life, Michael, it just rushes – it doesn't dwell on anything long enough to mean anything anywhere. Of course the author didn't mean it for satire, but if you publish it, I advise you to put: "This awful satire on modern life" outside the cover.' And they had. At least, they had put: 'This wonderful satire on modern life.' Fleur *was* like that! She could see the hurry, but, like the author of the wonderful satire, she didn't know that she herself veered and hurried, or – did she know? Was she conscious of kicking at life, like a flame at air?

He had reached Piccadilly, and suddenly he remembered that he had not called on her aunt for ages. That was a possible draw. He bent his steps towards Green Street.

'Mrs Dartie at home?'

'Yes, sir.'

Michael moved his nostrils. Fleur used – but he could catch no scent, except incense. Winifred burnt joss-sticks when she remembered what a distinguished atmosphere they produced.

'What name?'

'Mr Mont. My wife's not here, I suppose?'

'No, sir. Only Mrs Val Dartie.'

Mrs Val Dartie! Yes, he remembered, nice woman – but not a substitute for Fleur! Committed, however, he followed the maid.

In the drawing-room Michael found three people, one of them his father-in-law, who had a grey and brooding aspect, and, from an Empire chair, was staring at blue Australian butterflies' wings under a glass on a round scarlet table. Winifred had jazzed the Empire foundation of her room with a superstructure more suitable to the age. She greeted Michael with fashionable warmth. It was good of him to come when he was so busy with all these young poets. 'I thought *Copper Coin*,' she said – 'what a *nice* title! – such an intriguing little book. I do think Mr Desert is clever! What is he doing now?'

Michael said: 'I don't know,' and dropped on to a settee beside Mrs Val. Ignorant of the Forsyte family feud, he was unable to appreciate the relief he had brought in with him. Soames said something about the French, got up, and went to the window; Winifred joined him – their voices sounded confidential.

'How is Fleur?' said Michael's neighbour.

'Thanks, awfully well.'

'Do you like your house?'

'Oh, fearfully. Won't you come and see it?'

'I don't know whether Fleur would –?'

'Why not?'

'Oh! Well!'

'She's frightfully accessible.'

She seemed to be looking at him with more interest than he deserved, to be trying to make something out from his face, and he added:

'You're a relation – by blood as well as marriage, aren't you?'

'Yes.'

'Then what's the skeleton?'

'Oh! nothing. I'll certainly come. Only – she has so many friends.'

Michael thought: 'I like this woman!' 'As a matter of fact,' he said, 'I came here this afternoon thinking I might find Fleur. I should like her to know you. With all the jazz there is about, she'd appreciate somebody restful.'

'Thank you.'

'You've never lived in London?'

'Not since I was six.'

'I wish she could get a rest – pity there isn't a d-desert handy.' He had stuttered; the word was not pronounced the same – still! He glanced, disconcerted, at the butterflies. 'I've just been talking to a little Cockney whose S.O.S. is "Central Austrylia". But what do you say – Have we got souls to save?'

'I used to think so, but now I'm not so sure – something's struck me lately.'

'What was that?'

'Well, I notice that anyone at all out of proportion, or whose nose is on one side, or whose eyes jut out, or even have a special shining look, always believes in the soul; people who are in proportion, and have no prominent physical features, don't seem to be really interested.'

Michael's ears moved.

'By Jove!' he said; 'some thought! Fleur's beautifully proportioned – *she* doesn't seem to worry. I'm not – and I certainly do. The people in Covent Garden must have lots of soul. You think "the soul's" the result of loose-gearing in the organism – sort of special consciousness from not working in one piece.'

'Yes, rather like that – what's called psychic power is, I'm almost sure.'

'I say, is your life safe? According to your theory, though, we're in a mighty soulful era. I must think over my family. How about yours?'

'The Forsytes! Oh, they're quite too well-proportioned.'

'I agree, they haven't any special juts so far as I've seen. The French, too, are awfully close-knit. It really is an idea, only, of course, most people see it the other way. They'd say the soul produces the disproportion, makes the eyes shine, bends the nose, and all that; where the soul is small, it's not trying to get out of the body, whence the barber's block. I'll think about it. Thanks for the tip. Well, do come and see us. Good-bye! I don't think I'll disturb them in the window. Would you mind saying I had to scoot?' Squeezing a slim, gloved hand, receiving and returning a smiling look, he slid out, thinking: 'Dash the soul, where's her body?'

Chapter Four

FLEUR'S BODY

◄‹─›►

FLEUR's body, indeed, was at the moment in one of those difficult positions which continually threaten the spirit of compromise. It was in fact in Wilfrid's arms; sufficiently, at least, to make her say:

'No, Wilfrid – you promised to be good.'

It was a really remarkable tribute to her powers of skating on thin ice that the word 'good' should still have significance. For eleven weeks exactly this young man had danced on the edge of fulfilment, and was even now divided from her by two clenched hands pressed firmly against his chest, and the word 'good'; and this after not having seen her for a fortnight.

When she said it, he let her go, with a sort of violence, and sat down on a piece of junk. Only the sense of damnable iteration prevented him from saying: 'It can't go on, Fleur.' She knew that! And yet it did! This was what perpetually amazed him. How a poor brute could hang on week after week saying to her and to himself: 'Now or never!' when it wasn't either? Subconsciousness, that, until the word 'now' had been reached, Fleur would not know her own mind, alone had kept him dancing. His own feelings were so intense that he almost hated her for indecision. And he was unjust. It was not exactly indecision. Fleur wanted the added richness and excitement which Wilfrid's affection gave to life, but without danger and without loss. How natural! His frightful passionateness was making all the trouble. Neither by her wish, nor through her fault, was he passionate! And yet – it was both nice and proper to inspire passion; and, of course, she had the lurking sense that she was not 'in the mode' to cavil at a lover, especially since life owed her one.

Released, she smoothed herself and said: 'Talk of something sensible; what have you been writing?'

'This.'

Fleur read. Flushing and biting her lips, she said:

'It's frightfully bitter.'

'It's frightfully true. Does *he* ever ask you now whether you see me?'

'Never.'

'Why?'

'I don't know.'

'What would you answer if he did?'

Fleur shrugged her shoulders.

Desert said quietly: 'Yes, that's your attitude. It can't last, Fleur.' He was standing by the window. She put the sheets down on his desk and moved towards him. Poor Wilfrid! Now that he was quiet she was sorry.

He said suddenly: 'Stop! Don't move! *He's* down there in the street.'

Recoiling, she gasped: 'Michael! Oh! But how – how could he have known?'

Desert said grimly: 'Do you only know him as little as that? Do you suppose he'd be there if he knew you were here?'

Fleur winced.

'Why *is* he there, then?'

'He probably wants to see me. He looks as if he couldn't make up his mind. Don't get the wind up, he won't be let in.'

Fleur sat down; she felt weak in the legs. The ice seemed suddenly of an appalling thinness – the water appallingly cold.

'Has he seen you?' she said.

'No.'

The thought flashed through him: 'If I were a blackguard, I could force her hand, by moving one step and crooking my finger.' Pity one wasn't a blackguard – at all events, not to that point – things would be so much simpler!

'Where is he now?' asked Fleur.

'Going away.'

In profound relief, she sighed out:

'But it's queer, isn't it, Wilfrid?'

'You don't suppose he's easy in his mind, do you?'

Fleur bit her lips. He was jeering, because she didn't or couldn't really love either of them. It was unjust. She *could* have loved – she *had* loved! Wilfrid and Michael – they might go to the deuce!

'I wish I had never come here,' she said suddenly: 'and I'll never come again!'

He went to the door, and held it open.

'You are right.'

Fleur stood quite still, her chin on the collar of her fur, her clear-glancing eyes fixed on his face, her lips set and mutinous.

'You think I'm a heartless beast,' she said slowly. 'So I am – now. Good-bye!'

He neither took her hand nor spoke, he only bowed. His eyes were very tragic. Trembling with mortification, Fleur went out. She heard the door closed, while she was going down the stairs. At the bottom she stood uncertain. Suppose Michael had come back! Almost opposite was that gallery where she had first met him and – Jon. Slip across in there! If he were still hovering round the entrance of the little street, she could tell him with a good conscience where she had been. She peeped. Not in sight! Swiftly she slid across into the doorway opposite. They would be closing in a minute – just on four o'clock! She put down a shilling and slipped in. She must see – in case! She stood revolving – one-man show, the man – Claud Brains! She put down another shilling for a catalogue, and read as she went out. 'No. 7. Woman getting the wind up.' It told her everything; and with a lighter heart she skimmed along, and took a taxi. Get home before Michael! She felt relieved, almost exhilarated. So much for skating on thin ice! It wasn't good enough. Wilfrid must go. Poor Wilfrid! Well, he shouldn't have sneered – what did he know of her? Nobody knew anything of her! She was alone in the world. She slipped her latchkey into the hall door. No Michael. She sat down in the drawing-room before the fire, and took up Walter Nazing's last. She read a page three times. It meant no more with every reading – it meant less; he was the

kind of author who must be read at a gallop, and given away
lest a first impression of wind in the hair be lost in a sensation of
wind lower down; but Wilfrid's eyes came between her and the
words. Pity! Nobody pitied her; why, then, should she pity
them? Besides, pity was 'pop', as Amabel would sây. The situation demanded cast-iron sense. But Wilfrid's eyes! Well – she
wouldn't be seeing them again! Beautiful eyes when theÿ smiled
or when – so much more often – they looked at her with longing, as now between her and the sentence: 'Solemnly and with a
delicious egoism he more than awfully desired her who snug
and rosy in the pink shell of her involuted and so petulant social
periphrasis –' Poor Wilfrid! Pity was 'pop', but there was pride!
Did she choose that he should go away thinking that she had
'played him up' just out of vanity, as Walter Nazing said American women did? Did she? Would it not be more in the mode,
really dramatic – if one 'went over the deep end', as they said,
just once? Would that not be something they could both look
back on – he in the East he was always talking of, she in this
West? The proposition had a momentary popularity in that
organism called Fleur too finely proportioned for a soul according to the theory which Michael was thinking over. Like all
popularities, it did not last. First: Would she like it? She did
not think she would; one man, without love, was quite enough.
Then there was the danger of passing into Wilfrid's power. He
was a gentleman, but he was passionate; the cup once sipped,
would he consent to put it down? But more than all was a physical doubt of the last two or three weeks which awaited verifica-
tion, and which made her feel solemn. She stood up and passed
her hands all over her, with a definite recoil from the thought
of Wilfrid's hands doing the same. No! To have his friendship,
his admiration, but not at that price. She viewed him suddenly,
as a bomb set ón her copper floor; and in fancy ran and seized
and flung him out into the Square – poor Wilfrid! Pity was
'pop'! But one might be sorry for *oneself*, losing him; losing
too that ideal of modern womanhood expounded to her one
evening by Marjorie Ferrar, pet of the 'panjoys', whose red-
gold hair excited so much admiration: 'My ambition – old thing

– is to be the perfect wife of one man, the perfect mistress of another, and the perfect mother of a third, all at once. It's perfectly possible – they do it in France.'

But was it really so perfectly possible – even if pity *was* posh? How be perfect to Michael, when the slightest slip might reveal to him that she was being perfect to Wilfrid; how be perfect to Wilfrid, when every time she was perfect to Michael would be a dagger in Wilfrid's heart? And if – if her physical doubt should mature into certainty, how be perfect mother to the certainty, when she was either torturing two men, or lying to them like a trooperess? Not so perfectly possible as all that! 'If only I were all French!' thought Fleur. . . .

The clicking door startled her – the reason that she was not all French was coming in. He looked very grey, as if he had been thinking too much. He kissed her, and sat down moodily before the fire.

'Have you come for the night, Dad?'

'If I may,' murmured Soames. 'Business.'

'Anything unpleasant, ducky?'

Soames looked up as if startled.

'Unpleasant? Why should it be unpleasant?'

'I only thought from your face.'

Soames grunted. 'This Ruhr!' he said. 'I've brought you a picture. Chinese!'

'Oh, Dad! How jolly!'

'It isn't,' said Soames; 'it's a monkey eating fruit.'

'But that's perfect! Where is it – in the hall?'

Soames nodded.

Stripping the coverings off the picture, Fleur brought it in, and setting it up on the jade-green settee, stood away and looked at it. The large white monkey with its brown haunting eyes, as if she had suddenly wrested its interest from the orange-like fruit in its crisped paw, the grey background, the empty rinds all round – bright splashes in a general ghostliness of colour, impressed her at once.

'But, Dad, it's a masterpiece – I'm sure it's of a frightfully good period.'

'I don't know,' said Soames. 'I must look up the Chinese.'

'But you oughtn't to give it to me, it must be worth any amount. You ought to have it in your collection.'

'They didn't know its value,' said Soames, and a faint smile illumined his features. 'I gave three hundred for it. It'll be safer here.'

'Of course it'll be safe. Only why safer?'

Soames turned towards the picture.

'I can't tell. Anything may come of this.'

'Of what, dear?'

'Is "old Mont" coming in tonight?'

'No, he's at Lippinghall still.'

'Well, it doesn't matter – he's no good.'

Fleur took his hand and gave it a squeeze.

'Tell me!'

Soames's tickled heart quivered. Fancy her wanting to know what was troubling him! But his sense of the becoming, and his fear of giving away his own alarm, forbade response.

'Nothing you'd understand,' he said. 'Where are you going to hang it?'

'There, I think; but we must wait for Michael.'

Soames grumbled out:

'I saw him just now at your aunt's. Is that the way he attends to business?'

'Perhaps,' thought Fleur, 'he was only on his way back to the office. Cork Street *is* more or less between! If he passed the end of it, he would think of Wilfrid, he might have been wanting to see him about books.'

'Oh, here's Ting! Well, darling!'

The Chinese dog, let in, as it were, by Providence, seeing Soames, sat down suddenly with snub upturned eyes brilliant. 'The expression of your face,' he seemed to say, 'pleases me. We belong to the past and could sing hymns together, old man.'

'Funny little chap,' said Soames: 'he always knows me.'

Fleur lifted him. 'Come and see the new monkey, ducky.'

'Don't let him lick it.'

Held rather firmly by his jade-green collar and confronted by an inexplicable piece of silk smelling of the past, Ting-a-ling raised his head higher and higher to correspond with the action of his nostrils, and his little tongue appeared, tentatively savouring the emanation of his country.

'It's a nice monkey, isn't it, darling?'

'No,' said Ting-a-ling, rather clearly. 'Put me down!'

Restored to the floor, he sought a patch where the copper came through between two rugs, and licked it quietly.

'Mr Aubrey Greene, ma'am!'

'H'm!' said Soames.

The painter came gliding and glowing in; his bright hair slipping back, his green eyes sliding off.

'Ah!' he said, pointing to the floor. 'That's what I've come about.'

Fleur followed his finger in amazement.

'Ting!' she said severely, 'stop it! He will lick the copper, Aubrey.'

'But how perfectly Chinese! They do everything we don't.'

'Dad – Aubrey Greene. My father's just brought me this picture, Aubrey – isn't it a gem?'

The painter stood quite still, his eyes ceased sliding off, his hair ceased slipping back.

'Phew!' he said.

Soames rose. He had waited for the flippant; but he recognized in the tone something reverential, if not aghast.

'By George,' said Aubrey Greene, 'those eyes! Where did you pick it up, sir?'

'It belonged to a cousin of mine – a racing man. It was his only picture.'

'Good for him! He must have had taste.'

Soames stared. The idea that George should have had taste almost appalled him.

'No,' he said, with a flash of inspiration: 'What he liked about it was that it makes you feel uncomfortable.'

'Same thing! I don't know where I've seen a more pungent satire on human life.'

'I don't follow,' said Soames dryly.

'Why, it's a perfect allegory, sir! Eat the fruits of life, scatter the rinds, and get copped doing it. When they're still, a monkey's eyes are the human tragedy incarnate. Look at them! He thinks there's something beyond, and he's sad or angry because he can't get at it. That picture ought to be in the British Museum, sir, with the label: "Civilization, caught out." '

'Well, it won't be,' said Fleur. 'It'll be here, labelled "The White Monkey." '

'Same thing.'

'Cynicism,' said Soames abruptly, 'gets you nowhere. If you'd said "*Modernity* caught out"—'

'I do, sir; but why be narrow? You don't seriously suppose this age is worse than any other?'

'Don't I?' said Soames. 'In my belief the world reached its highest point in the eighties, and will never reach it again.'

The painter stared.

'That's frightfully interesting. I wasn't born, and I suppose you were about my age then, sir. You believed in God and drove in *diligences*.'

Diligences! The word awakened in Soames a memory which somehow seemed appropriate.

'Yes,' he said, 'and I can tell you a story of those days that you can't match in these. When I was a youngster in Switzerland with my people, two of my sisters had some black cherries. When they'd eaten about half a dozen they discovered that they all had little maggots in them. An English climber there saw how upset they were, and ate the whole of the rest of the cherries – about two pounds – maggots, stones and all, just to show them. That was the sort of men they were then.'

'Oh! Father!'

'Gee! He must have been gone on them.'

'No,' said Soames, 'not particularly. His name was Powley; he wore side-whiskers.'

'Talking of God and diligences: I saw a hansom yesterday.'

'More to the point if you'd seen God,' thought Soames, but

he did not say so; indeed, the thought surprised him, it was not the sort of thing he had ever seen himself.

'You mayn't know it, sir, but there's more belief now than there was before the war – they've discovered that we're not all body.'

'Oh!' said Fleur. 'That reminds me, Aubrey. Do you know any mediums? Could I get one to come here? On our floor, with Michael outside the door, one would know there couldn't be any hanky. Do the dark *séance* people ever go out? – they're much more thrilling they say.'

'Spiritualism!' said Soames. 'H'mph!' He could not in half an hour have expressed himself more clearly.

Aubrey Greene's eyes slid off to Ting-a-ling. 'I'll see what I can do, if you'll lend me your Peke for an hour or so tomorrow afternoon. I'd bring him back on a lead, and give him every luxury.'

'What do you want him for?'

'Michael sent me a most topping little model today. But, you see, she can't smile.'

'Michael?'

'Yes. Something quite new; and I've got a scheme. Her smile's like sunlight going off an Italian valley; but when you tell her to, she can't. I thought your Peke could make her, perhaps.'

'May I come and see?' said Fleur.

'Yes, bring him tomorrow; but, if I can persuade her, it'll be in the "altogether".'

'Oh! Will you get me a *séance*, if I lend you Ting?'

'I will.'

'H'mph!' said Soames again. *Séances*, Italian sunlight, the 'altogether'! It was time he got back to Elderson, and what was to be done now, and left this fiddling while Rome burned.

'Good-bye, Mr Greene,' he said; 'I've got no time.'

'Quite, sir,' said Aubrey Greene.

'Quite!' mimicked Soames to himself, going out.

Aubrey Greene took his departure a few minutes later, crossing a lady in the hall who was delivering her name to the man-servant.

Alone with her body, Fleur again passed her hands all over it. The 'altogether' – was a reminder of the dangers of dramatic conduct.

Chapter Five

FLEUR'S SOUL

◄◄‹·›►►

'MRS VAL DARTIE, ma'am.'

A name which could not be distorted even by Coaker affected her like a finger applied suddenly to the head of the sciatic nerve. Holly! Not seen since the day when she did not marry Jon. Holly! A flood of remembrance – Wansdon, the Downs, the gravel pit, the apple orchard, the river, the copse at Robin Hill! No! It was not a pleasant sensation – to see Holly, and she said: 'How awfully nice of you to come!'

'I met your husband this afternoon at Green Street; he asked me. What a lovely room!'

'Ting! Come and be introduced! This is Ting-a-ling; isn't he perfect? He's a little upset because of the new monkey. How's Val, and dear Wansdon? It was too wonderfully peaceful.'

'It's a nice backwater. I don't get tired of it.'

'And –' said Fleur, with a little laugh, 'Jon?'

'He's growing peaches in North Carolina. British Columbia didn't do.'

'Oh! Is he married?'

'No.'

'I suppose he'll marry an American.'

'He isn't twenty-two, you know.'

'Good Lord!' said Fleur: 'Am I only twenty-one? I feel forty-eight.'

'That's living in the middle of things and seeing so many people –'

'And getting to know none.'

'But don't you?'

'No, it isn't done. I mean we all call each other by our Christian names; but *après* –'

'I like your husband very much.'

'Oh! yes, Michael's a dear. How's June?'

'I saw her yesterday – she's got a new painter, of course – Claud Brains. I believe he's what they call a Vertiginist.'

Fleur bit her lip.

'Yes, they're quite common. I suppose June thinks he's the only one.'

'Well, she thinks he's a genius.'

'She's wonderful.'

'Yes,' said Holly, 'the most loyal creature in the world while it lasts. It's like poultry farming – once they're hatched. You never saw Boris Strumolowski?'

'No.'

'Well, don't.'

'I know his bust of Michael's uncle. It's rather sane.'

'Yes. June thought it a pot-boiler, and he never forgave her. Of course it was. As soon as her swan makes money, she looks round for another. She's a darling.'

'Yes,' murmured Fleur; 'I liked June.'

Another flood of remembrance – from a tea-shop, from the river, from June's little dining-room, from where in Green Street she had changed her wedding dress under the upward gaze of June's blue eyes. She seized the monkey and held it up.

'Isn't it a picture of "life"?' Would she have said that if Aubrey Greene hadn't? Still it seemed very true at the moment.

'Poor monkey!' said Holly. 'I'm always frightfully sorry for monkeys. But it's marvellous, I think.'

'Yes. I'm going to hang it here. If I can get one more I shall have done in this room; only people have so got on to Chinese things. This was luck – somebody died – George Forsyte, you know, the racing one.'

'Oh!' said Holly softly. She saw again her old kinsman's japing eyes in the church when Fleur was being married, heard his throaty whisper: 'Will she stay the course?' And was she staying it, this pretty filly? 'Wish she could get a rest. If only there were a desert handy!' Well, one couldn't ask a question so personal, and Holly took refuge in a general remark.

'What do all you smart young people feel about life, nowadays, Fleur! when one's not of it and has lived twenty years in South Africa, one still feels out of it.'

'Life! Oh! well, we know it's supposed to be a riddle, but we've given it up. We just want to have a good time because we don't believe anything can last. But I don't think we know how to have it. We just fly on, and hope for it. Of course, there's art, but most of us aren't artists; besides, expressionism – Michael says it's got no inside. We gas about it, but I suppose it hasn't. I see a frightful lot of writers and painters, you know; they're supposed to be amusing.'

Holly listened, amazed. Who would have thought that this girl *saw*? She might be seeing wrong, but anyway she saw!

'Surely,' she said, 'you enjoy yourselves?'

'Well, I like getting hold of nice things, and interesting people; I like seeing everything that's new and worth while, or seems so at the moment. But that's just how it is – nothing lasts. You see, I'm not of the "Pan-joys", nor of the "new-faithfuls".'

'The new-faithfuls?'

'Oh! don't you know – it's a sort of faith-healing done on oneself, not exactly the old "God-good, good-God!" sort; but a kind of mixture of will-power, psycho-analysis, and belief that everything will be all right on the night if you say it will. You must have come across them. They're frightfully in earnest.'

'I know,' said Holly; 'their eyes shine.'

'I dare say. I don't believe in them – I don't believe in anyone; or anything – much. How can one?'

'How about simple people, and hard work?'

Fleur sighed. 'I dare say. I will say for Michael – *he's* not spoiled. Let's have tea? Tea, Ting?' and, turning up the lights, she rang the bell.

When her unexpected visitor had gone, she sat very still before the fire. Today, when she had been so very nearly Wilfrid's!

So Jon was not married! Not that it made any odds! Things did not come round as they were expected to in books. And anyway sentiment was swosh! Cut it out! She tossed back her hair; and, getting hammer and nail, proceeded to hang the white monkey. Between the two tea-chests with their coloured pearl-shell figures, he would look his best. Since she couldn't have Jon, what did it matter – Wilfrid or Michael, or both, or neither? Eat the orange in her hand, and throw away the rind! And suddenly she became aware that Michael was in the room. He had come in very quietly and was standing before the fire behind her. She gave him a quick look and said:

'I've had Aubrey Greene here about a model you sent him, and Holly – Mrs Val Dartie – she said she's seen you. Oh! and father's brought us this. Isn't it perfect?'

Michael did not speak.

'Anything the matter, Michael?'

'No, nothing.' He went up to the monkey. From behind him now Fleur searched his profile. Instinct told her of a change. Had he, after all, seen her going to Wilfrid's – coming away?

'Some monkey!' he said. 'By the way, have you any spare clothes you could give the wife of a poor snipe – nothing too swell?'

She answered mechanically: 'Yes, of course!' while her brain worked furiously.

'Would you put them out, then? I'm going to make up a bunch for him myself – they could go together.'

Yes! He was quite unlike himself, as if the spring in him had run down. A sort of *malaise* overcame her. Michael not cheerful! It was like the fire going out on a cold day. And, perhaps for the first time, she was conscious that his cheerfulness was of real importance to her. She watched him pick up Ting-a-ling and sit down. And going up behind him, she bent over till her hair was against his cheek. Instead of rubbing his cheek on hers, he sat quite still, and her heart misgave her.

'What is it?' she said, coaxing.

'Nothing!'

She took hold of his ears.

'But there is. I suppose you know somehow that I went to see Wilfrid.'

He said stonily: 'Why not?'

She let go, and stood up straight.

'It was only to tell him that I couldn't see him again.'

That half-truth seemed to her the whole.

He suddenly looked up, a quiver went over his face; he took her hand.

'It's all right, Fleur. You must do what you like, you know. That's only fair. I had too much lunch.'

Fleur withdrew to the middle of the room.

'You're rather an angel,' she said slowly, and went out.

Upstairs she looked out garments, confused in her soul.

Chapter Six

MICHAEL GETS 'WHAT-FOR'

AFTER his Green Street quest Michael had wavered back down Piccadilly, and, obeying one of those impulses which make people hang around the centres of disturbance, on to Cork Street. He stood for a minute at the mouth of Wilfrid's backwater.

'No,' he thought at last, 'ten to one he isn't in; and if he is, twenty to one that I get any change except bad change!'

He was moving slowly on to Bond Street, when a little light lady, coming from the backwater, and reading as she went, ran into him from behind.

'Why don't you look where you're going! Oh! You? Aren't you the young man who married Fleur Forsyte? I'm her cousin, June. I thought I saw her just now.' She waved a hand which held a catalogue with a gesture like the flirt of a bird's wing. 'Opposite my gallery. She went into a house, or I should have spoken to her – I'd like to have seen her again.'

Into a house! Michael dived for his cigarette-case. Hard-grasping it, he looked up. The little lady's blue eyes were sweeping from side to side of his face with a searching candour.

'Are you happy together?' she said.

A cold sweat broke out on his forehead. A sense of general derangement afflicted him – hers, and his own.

'I beg your pardon?' he gasped.

'I hope you are. She ought to have married my little brother – but I hope you are. She's a pretty child.'

In the midst of a dull sense of stunning blows, it staggered him that she seemed quite unconscious of inflicting them. He heard his teeth gritting, and said dully: 'Your little brother, who was he?'

'What! Jon – didn't you know Jon? He was too young, of course, and so was she. But they were head over – the family feud stopped that. Well! it's all past. I was at your wedding. I hope you're happy. Have you seen the Claud Brains show at my gallery? He's a genius. I was going to have a bun in here; will you join me? You ought to know his work.'

She had paused at the door of a confectioner's. Michael put his hand on his chest.

'Thank you,' he said, 'I have just had a bun – two, in fact. Excuse me!'

The little lady grasped his other hand.

'Well, good-bye, young man! Glad to have met you. You're not a beauty, but I like your face. Remember me to that child. You should go and see Claud Brains. He's a real genius.'

Stock-still before the door, he watched her turn and enter, with a scattered motion, as of flying, and a disturbance among those seated in the pastry-cook's. Then he moved on, the cigarette unlighted in his mouth, dazed, as a boxer from a blow which knocks him sideways, and another which knocks him straight again.

Fleur visiting Wilfrid – at this moment in his rooms up there – in his arms, perhaps! He groaned. A well-fed young man in a new hat skipped at the sound. Never! He could never stick that! He would have to clear out! He had believed Fleur honest! A double life! The night before last she had smiled on him. Oh! God! He dashed across into Green Park. Why hadn't he stood still and let something go over him? And that lunatic's little brother — John — family feud? Himself — a *pis aller*, then — taken without love at all — a makeshift! He remembered now her saying one night at Mapledurham: 'Come again when I know I can't get my wish.' So that was the wish she couldn't get! A makeshift! 'Jolly,' he thought: 'Oh! jolly!' No wonder, then! What could she care? One man or another! Poor little devil! She had never let him know — never breathed a word! Was that decent of her — or was it treachery? 'No,' he thought, 'if she *had* told me, it wouldn't have made any difference — I'd have taken her at any price. It was decent of her not to tell me.' But how was it he hadn't heard from someone? Family feud? The Forsytes! Except 'Old Forsyte', he never saw them; and 'Old Forsyte' was closer than a fish. Well! he had got what-for! And again he groaned, in the twilight spaces of the Park. Buckingham Palace loomed up unlighted, huge and dreary. Conscious of his cigarette at last, he stopped to strike a match, and drew the smoke deep into his lungs with the first faint sense of comfort.

'You couldn't spare us a cigarette, Mister?'

A shadowy figure with a decent sad face stood beside the statue of Australia, so depressingly abundant!

'Of course!' said Michael; 'take the lot.' He emptied the case into the man's hand. 'Take the case too — "present from Westminster" — you'll get thirty bob for it. Good luck!' He hurried on. A faint: 'Hi, Mister!' pursued him unavailingly. Pity was pulp! Sentiment was bilge! Was he going home to wait till Fleur had — finished and come back? Not he! He turned towards Chelsea, batting along as hard as he could stride. Lighted shops, gloomy great Eaton Square, Chester Square, Sloane Square, the King's Road — along, along! Worse than the trenches — far worse — this whipped and scorpioned sexual jealousy! Yes, and he would have felt even worse, but for that second blow. It made it less painful to know that Fleur had been in love with that cousin, and Wilfrid, too, perhaps, nothing to her. Poor little wretch! 'Well, what's the game now?' he thought. The game of life – in bad weather, in stress? What was it? In the war – what had a fellow done? Somehow managed to feel himself not so dashed important; reached a condition of acquiescence, fatalism, 'Who dies if England live' sort of sob-stuff state. The game of life? Was it different? 'Bloody but unbowed' might be tripe; still – get up when you were knocked down! The whole was big, oneself was little! Passion, jealousy, ought they properly to destroy one's sportsmanship, as Nazing and Sibley and Linda Frewe would have it? Was the word 'gentleman' a dud? Was it? Did one keep one's form, or get down to squealing and kicking in the stomach?

'I don't know,' he thought, 'I don't know what I shall do when I see her – I simply don't know.' Steel-blue of the fallen evening, bare plane trees, wide river, frosty air! He turned towards home. He opened his front door, trembling, and trembling, went into the drawing-room. . . .

When Fleur had gone upstairs and left him with Ting-a-ling he didn't know whether he believed her or not. If she had kept that other thing from him all this time, she could keep anything! Had she understood his words: 'You must do as you like, that's only fair'? He had said them almost mechanically, but they were reasonable. If she had never loved him, even a little, he had never had any right to expect anything; he had been all the time in the position of one to whom she was giving alms. Nothing compelled a person to go on giving alms. And nothing compelled one to go on taking them – except – the ache of want, the ache, the ache!

'You little Djinn! You lucky little toad! Give me some of your complacency – you Chinese atom!' Ting-a-ling turned up his boot-buttons. 'When you have been civilized as long as I,' they seemed to say: 'In the meantime, scratch my chest.'

And scrattling in that yellow fur Michael thought: 'Pull yourself together! Man at the South Pole with the first blizzard doesn't sing "Want to go home! Want to go home!" – he sticks it. Come, get going!' He placed Ting-a-ling on the floor, and made for his study. Here were manuscripts, of which the readers to Danby and Winter had already said : 'No money in this, but a genuine piece of work meriting consideration.' It was Michael's business to give the consideration; Danby's to turn the affair down with the words: 'Write him (or her) a civil letter, say we were greatly interested, regret we do not see our way – hope to have the privilege of considering next effort, and so forth. What !'

He turned up his reading-lamp and pulled out a manuscript he had already begun.

> 'No retreat, no retreat; they must conquer or die who have
> ' no retreat;
> No retreat, no retreat; they must conquer or die who have
> no retreat !'

The black footmen's refrain from *Polly* was all that happened in his mind. Dash it ! He must read the thing ! Somehow he finished the chapter. He remembered now. The manuscript was all about a man who, when he was a boy, had been so greatly impressed by the sight of a maidservant changing her clothes in a room over the way, that his married life was a continual struggle not to be unfaithful with his wife's maids. They had just discovered his complex, and he was going to have it out. The rest of the manuscript no doubt would show how that was done. It went most conscientiously into all those precise bodily details which it was now so timorous and Victorian to leave out. Genuine piece of work, and waste of time to go on with it ! Old Danby – Freud bored him stiff; and for once Michael did not mind old Danby being in the right. He put the thing back into the drawer. Seven o'clock ! Tell Fleur what he had been told about that cousin? Why? Nothing could mend *that* ! If only she were speaking the truth about Wilfrid ! He went to the window – stars above, and stripes below, stripes of courtyard and back garden. 'No retreat, no retreat; they must conquer or die who have no retreat !'

A voice said :

'When will your father be up?'

Old Forsyte ! Lord ! Lord !

'Tomorrow, I believe, sir. Come in! You don't know my den, I think.'

'No,' said Soames. 'Snug! Caricatures. You go in for them – poor stuff!'

'But not modern, sir – a revived art.'

'Queering your neighbours – I never cared for them. They only flourish when the world's in a mess and people have given up looking straight before them.'

'By Jove!' said Michael; 'that's good. Won't you sit down, sir?'

Soames sat down, crossing his knees in his accustomed manner. Slim, grey, close – a sealed book, neatly bound! What was *his* complex? Whatever it was, he had never had it out. One could not even imagine the operation.

'I shan't take away my Goya,' he said very unexpectedly; 'consider it Fleur's. In fact, if I only knew you were interested in the future, I should make more provision. In my opinion death duties will be prohibitive in a few years' time.'

Michael frowned. 'I'd like you to know, sir, once for all, that what you do for Fleur, you do for Fleur. I can be Epicurus whenever I like – bread, and on feast days a little bit of cheese.'

Soames looked up with shrewdness in his glance. 'I know that,' he said, 'I always knew it.'

Michael bowed.

'With this land depression your father's hard hit, I should think.'

'Well, he talks of being on the look-out for soap or cars; but I shouldn't be surprised if he mortgages again and lingers on.'

'A title without a place,' said Soames, 'is not natural. He'd better wait for me to go, if I leave anything, that is. But listen to me: I've been thinking. Aren't you happy together, you two, that you don't have children?'

Michael hesitated.

'I don't think,' he said slowly, 'that we have ever had a scrap, or anything like it. I have been – I am – terribly fond of her, but you have known better than I that I only picked up the pieces.'

'Who told you that?'

'Today – Miss June Forsyte.'

'*That* woman!' said Soames. 'She can't keep her foot out of anything. A boy and girl affair – over months before you married.'

'But deep, sir,' said Michael gently.

'Deep – who knows at that age? Deep?' Soames paused: 'You're a good fellow – I always knew. Be patient – take a long view.'

'Yes, sir,' said Michael, very still in his chair, 'if I can.'

'She's everything to me,' muttered Soames abruptly.

'And to me – which doesn't make it easier.'

The line between Soames's brows deepened.

'Perhaps not. But hold on! As gently as you like, but hold on! She's young. She'll flutter about; there's nothing in it.'

'Does he know about the other thing?' thought Michael.

'I have my own worries,' went on Soames, 'but they're nothing to what I should feel if anything went wrong with her.'

Michael felt a twinge of sympathy, unusual towards that self-contained grey figure.

'I shall try my best,' he said quietly; 'but I'm not naturally Solomon at six stone seven.'

'I'm not so sure,' said Soames, 'I'm not so sure. Anyway, a child – well, a child would be – a – sort of insur–' He baulked, the word was not precisely – !

Michael froze.

'As to that, I can't say anything.'

Soames got up.

'No,' he said wistfully, 'I suppose not. It's time to dress.'

To dress – to dine, and if to dine, to sleep – to sleep, to dream! And then what dreams might come!

On the way to his dressing-room Michael encountered Coaker; the man's face was long.

'What's up, Coaker?'

'The little dog, sir, has been sick in the drawing-room.'

'The deuce he has!'

'Yes, sir; it appears that someone left him there alone. He

makes himself felt, sir. I always say: He's an important little dog. . . .'

During dinner, as if visited by remorse for having given them advice and two pictures worth some thousands of pounds, Soames pitched a tale like those of James in his palmy days. He spoke of the French – the fall of the mark – the rise in Consols – the obstinacy of Dumetrius, the picture-dealer, over a Constable skyscape which Soames wanted and Dumetrius did not, but to which the fellow held on just for the sake of a price which Soames did not mean to pay. He spoke of the trouble which he foresaw with the United States over their precious Prohibition. They were a headstrong lot. They took up a thing and ran their heads against a stone wall. He himself had never drunk anything to speak of, but he liked to feel that he could. The Americans liked to feel that he couldn't, that was tyranny. They were overbearing. He shouldn't be surprised if everybody took to drinking over there. As to the League of Nations, a man that morning had palavered it up. That cock wouldn't fight – spend money, and arrange things which would have arranged themselves, but as for anything important, such as abolishing Bolshevism, or poison gas, they never would, and to pretend it was all-me-eye-and-Betty-Martin. It was almost a record for one habitually taciturn, and deeply useful to two young people only anxious that he should continue to talk, so that they might think of other things. The conduct of Ting-a-ling was the sole other subject of consideration. Fleur thought it due to the copper floor. Soames that he must have picked up something in the Square – dogs were always picking things up. Michael suggested that it was just Chinese – a protest against there being nobody to watch his self-sufficiency. In China there were four hundred million people to watch each other being self-sufficient. What would one expect of a Chinaman suddenly placed in the Gobi Desert? He would certainly be sick.

'No retreat, no retreat; they must conquer or die who have no retreat!'

When Fleur left them, both felt that they could not so soon again bear each other's company, and Soames said:

'I've got some figures to attend to – I'll go to my room.'

Michael stood up. 'Wouldn't you like my den, sir?'

'No,' said Soames, 'I must concentrate. Say good night to Fleur for me.'

Michael remained smoking above the porcelain effigies of Spanish fruits. That white monkey couldn't eat those and throw away the rinds! Would the fruits of his life be porcelain in future? Live in the same house with Fleur, estranged? Live with Fleur as now, feeling a stranger, even an unwelcome stranger? Clear out, and join the Air Force, or the 'Save the Children' corps? Which of the three courses was least to be deplored? The ash of his cigar grew long, dropped incontinent, and grew again; the porcelain fruits mocked him with their sheen and glow; Coaker put his head in and took it away again. (The Governor had got the hump – good sort, the Governor!) Decision waited for him, somewhere, somewhen – Fleur's, not his own. His mind was too miserable and disconcerted to be known; but she would know hers. She had the information which alone made decision possible about Wilfrid, that cousin, her own actions and feelings. Yes, decision would come, and would it matter in a world where pity was punk and only a Chinese philosophy of any use?

But not be sick in the drawing-room, try and keep one's end up, even if there were no one to see one being important! ...

He had been asleep and it was dark, or all but, in his bed-dressing-room. Something white by his bed. A fragrant faint warmth close to him; a voice saying low: 'It's only me. Let me come in your bed, Michael.' Like a child – like a child! Michael reached out his arms. The whiteness and the warmth came into them. Curls smothered his mouth, the voice in his ear: 'I wouldn't have come, would I, if there'd – if there'd been anything?' Michael's heart, wild, confused, beat against hers.

Chapter Seven

'THE ALTOGETHER'

✦✦✦

TONY BICKET, replete, was in vein that fine afternoon; his balloons left him freely, and he started for home in the mood of a conqueror.

Victorine, too, had colour in her cheeks. She requited the story of his afternoon with the story of hers. A false tale for a true — no word of Danby and Winter, the gentleman with the sliding smile, of the Grand Marnier, or 'the altogether'. She had no compunction. It was her secret, her surprise; if, by sitting in or out of 'the altogether', not yet decided, she could make their passage money — well, she should tell him she had won it on a horse. That night she asked:

'Am I so very thin, Tony?' more than once. 'I do so want to get fat.'

Bicket, still troubled that she had not shared that lunch, patted her tenderly, and said he would soon have her as fat as butter — he did not explain how.

They dreamed together of blue butterflies, and awoke to chilly gaslight and a breakfast of cocoa and bread-and-butter. Fog! Bicket was swallowed up before the eyes of Victorine ten yards from the door. She returned to the bedroom with anger in her heart. Who would buy balloons in a fog? She would do anything rather than let Tony go on standing out there all the choking days! Undressing again, she washed herself intensively, in case — ! She had not long finished when her landlady announced the presence of a messenger boy. He bore an enormous parcel entitled 'Mr Bicket.'

There was a note inside. She read:

DEAR BICKET, — Here are the togs. Hope they'll be useful. —
                                        Yours, MICHAEL MONT

In a voice that trembled she said to the boy:

'Thank you, it's O.K. Here's twopence.'

When his rich whistle was heard writhing into the fog, she flung herself down before the 'togs' in ecstasy. The sexes were divided by tissue paper. A blue suit, a velour hat, some brown shoes, three pairs of socks with two holes in them, four shirts only a little frayed at the cuffs, two black-and-white ties, six collars, not too new, some handkerchiefs, two vests beautifully thick, two pairs of pants, and a brown overcoat with a belt and just two or three nice little stains. She held the blue suit up against her arms and legs, the trousers and sleeves would only need taking-in about two inches. She piled them in a pyramid, and turned with awe to the spoil beneath the tissue paper. A brown knitted frock with little clear yellow buttons – unsoiled, uncreased. How could anybody spare a thing like that! A brown velvet toque with a little tuft of goldeny-brown feathers. She put it on. A pair of pink stays ever so little faded, with only three inches of bone above the waist, and five inches of bone below, pink silk ribbons, and suspenders – a perfect dream. She could not resist putting them on also. Two pairs of brown stockings; brown shoes; two combinations, a knitted camisole. A white silk jumper with a hole in one sleeve, a skirt of lilac linen that had gone a little in the wash; a pair of pallid pink silk pants; and underneath them all an almost black-brown coat, long and warm and cosy, with great jet buttons, and in the pocket six small handkerchiefs. She took a deep breath of sweetness – geranium!

Her mind leaped forward. Clothed, trousseaued, fitted out – blue butterflies – the sun! Only the money for the tickets wanting. And suddenly she saw herself with nothing on standing before the gentleman with sliding eyes. Who cared! The money!

For the rest of the morning she worked feverishly, shortening Tony, mending the holes in his socks, turning the fray of his cuffs. She ate a biscuit, drank another cup of cocoa – it was fattening, and went for the hole in the white silk jumper. One o'clock. In panic she stripped once more, put on a new combination, pair of stockings, and the stays, then paused in superstition. No! Her own dress and hat – like yesterday! Keep the rest until –! She hastened to her bus, overcome alternately by heat and cold. Perhaps he would give her another glass of that lovely stuff. If only she could go swimmy and not care for anything!

She reached the studio as two o'clock was striking, and knocked. It was lovely and warm in there, much warmer than yesterday, and the significance of this struck her suddenly. In front of the fire was a lady with a little dog.

'Miss Collins – Mrs Michael Mont; she's lending us her Peke, Miss Collins.'

The lady – only her own age, and ever so pretty – held out her hand. Geranium! This, then, was she whose clothes –!

She took the hand, but could not speak. If this lady was going to stay, it would be utterly impossible. Before her – so pretty, so beautifully covered – oh! no!

'Now, Ting, be good, and as amusing as you can. Good-bye, Aubrey! Good luck to the picture! Good-bye, Miss Collins; it ought to be wonderful.'

Gone! The scent of geranium fading; the little dog snuffling at the door. The sliding gentleman had two glasses in his hands.

'Ah!' thought Victorine, and drank hers at a gulp.

'Now, Miss Collins, you don't mind, do you! You'll find everything in there. It's really nothing. I shall want you lying on your face just here with your elbows on the ground and your head up a little turned this way; your hair as loose as it can be, and your eyes looking at this bone. You must imagine that it's a faun or some other bit of all right. The dog'll help you when he settles down to it. F-a-u-n, you know, not f-a-w-n.'

'Yes,' said Victorine faintly.

'Have another little tot?'

'Oh! please.'

He brought it.

'I quite understand; but you know, really, it's absurd. You wouldn't mind with a doctor. That's right. Look here, I'll put this little cow-bell on the ground. When you're in position, give it a tinkle, and I'll come out. That'll help you.'

Victorine murmured:

'You *are* kind.'

'Not at all – it's natural. Now will you start in? The light won't last for ever. Fifteen bob a day, we said.'

Victorine saw him slide away behind a screen, and looked at the little cow-bell. Fifteen bob! And fifteen bob! And fifteen bob! Many, many, fifteen bobs before –! But not more times of sitting than of Tony's standing from foot to foot, offering balloons. And as if wound up by that thought, she moved like clockwork off the dais, into the model's room. Cosy in there, too; warm, a green silk garment thrown on a chair. She took off her dress. The beauty of the pink stays struck her afresh. Perhaps the gentleman would like – no, that would be even worse –! A noise reached her – from Ting-a-ling complaining of solitude. If she delayed, she never would –! Stripping hastily, she stood looking at herself in a glass. If only that slim, ivory-white image could move out on to the dais and she could stay here! Oh! It was awful – awful! She couldn't – no! she couldn't. She caught up her final garment again. Fifteen bob! But fifteen bob! Before her eyes, wild and mournful, came a vision: Of a huge dome, and a tiny Tony, with little, little balloons in a hand held out! Something cold and steely formed over her heart as icicles form on a window. If that was all they would do for him, she would do better! She dropped the garment; and, confused, numb, stepped forth in 'the altogether'. Ting-a-ling growled at her above his bone. She reached the cow-bell and lay down on her face as she had been told, with feet in the air, crossed. Resting her chin on one hand, she wagged the bell. It made a sound like no bell she had ever heard; and the little dog barked – he did look funny!

'Perfect, Miss Collins! Hold that!'

Fifteen bob! and fifteen bob!

'Just point those left toes a bit more. That's right! The flesh tone's perfect! My God, why must one walk before one runs! Drawing's a bore, Miss Collins; one ought to draw with a brush only; a sculptor draws with a chisel, at least when he's a Michelangelo. How old are you?'

'Twenty-one,' came from lips that seemed to Victorine quite far away.

'I'm thirty-two. They say our generation was born so old that it can never get any older. Without illusions. Well! I never had any beliefs that I can remember. Had you?'

Victorine's wits and senses were astray, but it did not matter, for he was rattling on:

'We don't even believe in our ancestors. All the same, we're beginning to copy them again. D'you know a book called *The Sobbing Turtle* that's made such a fuss? – sheer Sterne, very well done; but sheer Sterne, and the author's tongue in his cheek. That's it in a nutshell, Miss Collins – our tongues are in our cheeks – bad sign. Never mind; I'm going to out-Piero Cosimo with this. Your head an inch higher, and that curl out of your eye, please. Thanks! Hold that! By the way, have you Italian blood? What was your mother's name, for instance?'

'Brown.'

'Ah! You can never tell with Browns. It may have been Brune – or Bruno – but very likely she was Iberian. Probably all the inhabitants of Britain left alive by the Saxons were called Brown. As a fact, that's all tosh, though. Going back to Edward the Confessor, Miss Collins – a mere thirty generations – we each of us have one thousand and seventy-four million, five hundred and seventy-three thousand, nine hundred and eighty-four ancestors, and the population of this island was then well under a million. We're as inbred as race-horses, but not so nice to look at, are we? I assure you, Miss Collins, you're something to be grateful for. So is Mrs Mont. Isn't she pretty? Look at that dog!'

Ting-a-ling, indeed, with forelegs braced, and wrinkled nose, was glaring, as if under the impression that Victorine was another bone.

'He's funny,' she said, and again her voice sounded far away. Would Mrs Mont lie here if he'd asked her? *She* would look pretty! But *she* didn't need the fifteen bob!

'Comfortable in that position?'

In alarm, she murmured:

'Oh! yes, thank you!'

164

'Warm enough?'

'Oh! yes, thank you!'

'That's good. Just a little higher with the head.'

Slowly in Victorine the sense of the dreadfully unusual faded. Tony should never know. If he never knew, he couldn't care. She could lie like this all day – fifteen bob, and fifteen bob! It was easy. She watched the quick, slim fingers moving, the blue smoke from the cigarette. She watched the little dog.

'Like a rest? You left your gown; I'll get it for you.'

In that green silk gown, beautifully padded, she sat up, with her feet on the floor over the dais edge.

'Cigarette? I'm going to make some Turkish coffee. You'd better walk about.'

Victorine obeyed.

'You're out of a dream, Miss Collins. I shall have to do a Mathew Maris of you in that gown.'

The coffee, like none she had ever tasted, gave her a sense of well-being. She said:

'It's not like coffee.'

Aubrey Greene threw up his hands.

'You have said it. The British are a great race – nothing will ever do them in. If they could be destroyed, they must long ago have perished of their coffee. Have some more?'

'Please,' said Victorine. There was such a little in the cup.

'Ready, again?'

She lay down, and let the gown drop off.

'That's right! Leave it there – you're lying in long grass, and the green helps me. Pity it's winter; I'd have hired a glade.'

Lying in long grass – flowers, too, perhaps. She did love flowers. As a little girl she used to lie in the grass, and make daisy-chains, in the field at the back of her grandmother's lodge at Norbiton. Her grandmother kept the lodge. Every year, for a fortnight, she had gone down there – she had liked the country ever so. Only she had always had something on. It would be nicer with nothing. Were there flowers in Central Australia? With butterflies there must be! In the sun – she and Tony – like the Garden of Eden! . . .

'Thank you, that's all for today. Half a day – ten bob. To-morrow morning at eleven. You're a first-rate sitter, Miss Collins.'

Putting on the pink stays, Victorine had a feeling of elation. She had done it! Tony should never know! The thought that he never would gave her pleasure. And once more divested of the 'altogether', she came forth.

Aubrey Greene was standing before his handiwork.

'Not yet, Miss Collins,' he said; 'I don't want to depress you. That hip-bone's too high. We'll put it right tomorrow. Forgive my hand, it's all chalk. *Au revoir!* Eleven o'clock. And we shan't need this chap. No, you don't!'

For Ting-a-ling was showing signs of accompanying the larger bone. Victorine passed out smiling.

Chapter Eight

SOAMES TAKES THE MATTER UP

◄‹–›►

SOAMES had concentrated, sitting before the fire in his bedroom till Big Ben struck twelve. His reflections sum-totalled in a decision to talk it over with 'old Mont' after all. Though light-brained, the fellow was a gentleman, and the matter delicate. He got into bed and slept, but awoke at half-past two. There it was! '*I won't* think of it,' he thought; and instantly began to. In a long life of dealings with money, he had never had such an experience. Perfectly straightforward conformity with the law – itself so often far from perfectly straightforward – had been the *sine qua non* of his career. Honesty, they said, was the best policy. But was it anything else? A normally honest man couldn't keep out of a perfect penitentiary for a week. But then a perfect penitentiary had no relation to prison, or the Bankruptcy Court. The business of working honesty was to keep out of those two institutions. And so far he had never had any difficulty. What, besides the drawing of fees and the drinking of tea, were the duties of a director? That was the point. And how far, if he failed in them, was he liable? It was a director's duty to be perfectly straightforward. But if a director were perfectly straightforward, he couldn't be a director. That was clear. In the first place, he would have to tell his shareholders that he didn't anything like earn his fees. For what did he do on his Boards? Well, he sat and signed his name and talked a little, and passed that which the general trend of business decided must be passed. Did he initiate? Once in a blue moon. Did he calculate? No, he read calculations. Did he check payments out and in? No, the auditors did that. There was policy! A comforting word, but – to be perfectly straightforward – a director's chief business was to let the existing policy alone. Take his own case! If he had done his duty, he would have stopped this foreign insurance business which he had instinctively distrusted the moment he heard of it – within a month of sitting on the Board, or, having failed in doing so, resigned his seat. But he had not. Things had been looking better! It was not the moment, and so forth! If he had done his duty as a perfectly straightforward director, indeed, he would never have become a director of the P.P.R.S., because he would have looked into the policy of the Society much more closely than he had before accepting a position on the Board. But what with the names, and the prestige, and not looking a gift horse too closely in the mouth – there it had been! To be perfectly straightforward, he ought now to be circularizing the shareholders, saying: 'My *laissez-faire* has cost you two hundred odd thousand pounds. I have lodged this amount in the hands of trustees for your benefit, and am suing the rest of the directors for their quotas of the amount.' But he was not proposing to do so, because – well – because it wasn't done, and the other directors wouldn't like it. In sum: You waited till the shareholders found out the mess, and you hoped they wouldn't. In fact, just like a Government, you confused the issues, and made the best case you could for yourselves. With a sense of comfort Soames thought of Ireland: The late Government had let the country in for all that mess in

Ireland, and at the end taken credit for putting an end to what need never have been! The Peace, too, and the Air Force, and Agriculture, and Egypt – the five most important issues they'd had to deal with – they had put the chestnuts into the fire in every case! But had they confessed to it? Not they. One didn't confess. One said: 'The question of policy made it imperative at the time.' Or, better still, one said nothing; and trusted to the British character. With his chin resting on the sheet, Soames felt a momentary relief. The late Government weren't sweating into *their* sheets – not they – he was convinced of it! Fixing his eyes on the dying embers in the grate, he reflected on the inequalities and injustices of existence. Look at the chaps in politics and business, whose whole lives were passed in skating on thin ice, and getting knighted for it. They never turned a hair. And look at himself, for the first time in forty years on thin ice, and suffering confoundedly. There was a perfect cult of hoodwinking the public, a perfect cult of avoiding the consequences of administrative acts; and here was he, a man of the world, a man of the law, ignorant of those cults, and – and glad of it. From engrained caution and a certain pride, which had in it a touch of the fine, Soames shrank from that coarse-grained standard of honesty which conducted the affairs of the British public. In anything that touched money he was, he always had been, stiff-necked, stiff-kneed. Money was money, a pound a pound, and there was no way of pretending it wasn't and keeping your self-respect. He got up, drank some water, took a number of deep breaths, and stamped his feet. Who was it said the other day that nothing had ever lost him five minutes' sleep. The fellow must have the circulation of an ox, or the gift of Baron Munchausen. He took up a book. But his mind would only turn over and over the realizable value of his resources. Apart from his pictures, he decided that he could not be worth less than two hundred and fifty thousand pounds, and there was only Fleur – and she already provided for more or less. His wife had her settlement, and could live on it perfectly well in France. As for himself – what did he care? A room at his club near Fleur – he would be just as happy, perhaps happier! And suddenly he found that he had reached a way out of his disturbance and anxiety. By imagining the far-fetched, by facing the loss of his wealth, he had exorcized the demon. The book, *The Sobbing Turtle*, of which he had not read one word, dropped from his hand; he slept. ...

His meeting with 'old Mont' took place at 'Snooks' directly after lunch. The tape in the hall, at which he glanced on going in, recorded a further heavy drop in the mark. Just as he thought: The thing was getting valueless!

Sitting there, sipping coffee, the baronet looked to Soames almost offensively spry. Two to one he had realized nothing! 'Well!' thought Soames, 'as old Uncle Jolyon used to say, I shall astonish his weak nerves!'

And without preamble he began.

'How are you, Mont? This mark's valueless. You realize we've lost the P.P.R.S. about a quarter of a million by that precious foreign policy of Elderson's. I'm not sure an action won't lie against us for taking unjustifiable risk. But what I've come to see you about is this.' He retailed the interview with the clerk, Butterfield, watching the eyebrows of his listener, and finished with the words: 'What do you say?'

Sir Lawrence, whose foot was jerking his whole body, fixed his monocle.

'Hallucination, my dear Forsyte! I've known Elderson all my life. We were at Winchester together.'

Again! Again! Oh! Lord! Soames said slowly:

'You can't tell from that. A man who was at Marlborough with me ran away with his mess fund and his colonel's wife, and made a fortune in Chile out of canned tomatoes. The point is this: If the young man's story's true, we're in the hands of a bad hat. It won't do, Mont. Will you tackle him, and see what he says to it? You wouldn't like a story of that sort about yourself. Shall we both go?'

'Yes,' said Sir Lawrence, suddenly. 'You're right. We'll both go, Forsyte. I don't like it, but we'll both go. He ought to hear it.'

'Now?'

'Now.'

With solemnity they assumed top hats, and issued.

'I think, Forsyte, we'll take a taxi.'

'Yes,' said Soames.

The cab ground its way slowly past the lions, then dashed on down to the Embankment. Side by side its occupants held their noses steadily before them.

'He was shooting with me a month ago,' said Sir Lawrence. 'Do you know the hymn "O God, our help in ages past"? It's very fine, Forsyte.'

Soames did not answer. The fellow was beginning to tittup!

'We had it that Sunday,' went on Sir Lawrence. 'Elderson used to have a fine voice – sang solos. It's a foghorn now, but a good delivery still.' He gave his little whinnying laugh.

'Is it possible,' thought Soames, 'for this chap to be serious?' and he said:

'If we find this is true of Elderson, and conceal it, we could all be put in the dock.'

Sir Lawrence refixed his monocle. 'The deuce!' he said.

'Will you do the talking,' said Soames, 'or shall I?'

'I think you had better, Forsyte; ought we to have the young man in?'

'Wait and see,' said Soames.

They ascended to the offices of the P.P.R.S. and entered the Board Room. There was no fire, the long table was ungarnished; an old clerk, creeping about like a fly on a pane, was filling inkstands out of a magnum.

Soames addressed him:

'Ask the manager to be so kind as to come and see Sir Lawrence Mont and Mr Forsyte.'

The old clerk blinked, put down the magnum, and went out.

'Now,' said Soames in a low voice, 'we must keep our heads. He'll deny it, of course.'

'I should hope so, Forsyte; I should hope so. Elderson's a gentleman.'

'No liar like a gentleman,' muttered Soames, below his breath.

After that they stood in their overcoats before the empty grate, staring at their top hats placed side by side on the table.

'One minute!' said Soames, suddenly, and crossing the room, he opened a door opposite. There, as the young clerk had said, was a sort of lobby between Board Room and Manager's Room, with a door at the end into the main corridor. He stepped back, closed the door, and, rejoining Sir Lawrence, resumed his contemplation of the hats.

'Geography correct,' he said with gloom.

The entrance of the manager was marked by Sir Lawrence's monocle dropping on to his coat-button with a tinkle. In cut-away black coat, clean-shaven, with grey eyes rather baggy underneath, a pink colour, every hair in place on a rather bald egg-shaped head, and lips alternately pouting, compressed, or smiling, the manager reminded Soames ridiculously of old Uncle Nicholas in his middle period. Uncle Nick was a clever fellow – 'cleverest man in London,' someone had called him – but none had ever impugned his honesty. A pang of doubt and disinclination went through Soames. This seemed a monstrous thing to have to put to a man of his own age and breeding. But young Butterfield's eyes – so honest and dog-like! Invent a thing like that – was it possible? He said abruptly:

'Is that door shut?'

'Yes; do you feel a draught?' said the manager. 'Would you like a fire?'

'No, thank you,' said Soames. 'The fact is, Mr Elderson, a young man in this office came to me yesterday with a very queer story. Mont and I think you should hear it.'

Accustomed to watching people's eyes, Soames had the impression of a film (such as passes over the eyes of parrots) passing over the eyes of the manager. It was gone at once, if, indeed, it had ever been.

'By all means.'

Steadily, with that power he had over his nerves when it came to a point, and almost word for word, Soames repeated a story which he had committed to heart in the watches of the night. He concluded with:

171

'You'd like him in, no doubt. His name is Butterfield.'

During the recital Sir Lawrence had done nothing but scrutinize his finger nails; he now said:

'You had to be told, Elderson.'

'Naturally.'

The manager was crossing to the bell. The pink in his cheeks looked harder; his teeth showed, they had a pouted look.

'Ask Mr Butterfield to come here.'

There followed a minute of elaborate inattention to each other. Then the young man came in, neat, commonplace, with his eyes on the manager's face. Soames had a moment of compunction. This young fellow held his life in his hands, as it were – one of the great army who made their living out of self-suppression and respectability, with a hundred ready to step into his shoes at his first slip. What was that old tag of the provincial actor's declamation – at which old Uncle Jolyon used to cackle so? 'Like a pale martyr with his shirt on fire.'

'So, Mr Butterfield, you have been good enough to exercise your imagination in my regard.'

'No, sir.'

'You stick to this fantastic story of eavesdropping?'

'Yes, sir.'

'We have no further use for your services then. Good morning!'

The young man's eyes, dog-like, sought the face of Soames; a string twitched in his throat, his lips moved without a sound. He turned and went out.

'So much for that,' said the manager's voice; '*he'll* never get another job.'

The venom in those words affected Soames like the smell of Russian fat. At the same moment he had the feeling: This wants thinking out. Only if innocent, or guilty and utterly resolved, would Elderson have been so drastic. Which was he?

The manager went on:

'I thank you for drawing my attention to the matter, gentlemen. I have had my eye on that young man for some time. A bad hat all round.'

Soames said glumly:

'What do you make out he had to gain?'

'Foresaw dismissal, and thought he would get in first.'

'I see,' said Soames. But he did not. His mind was back in his own office with Gradman rubbing his nose, shaking his grey head, and Butterfield's: 'No, sir, I've nothing against Mr Elderson, and he's nothing against me.'

'I shall require to know more about that young man,' he thought.

The manager's voice again cut through.

'I've been thinking over what you said yesterday, Mr Forsyte, about an action lying against the Board for negligence. There's nothing in that; our policy has been fully disclosed to the shareholders at two general meetings, and has passed without comment. The shareholders are just as responsible as the Board.'

'H'm!' said Soames, and took up his hat. 'Are you coming, Mont?'

As if summoned from a long distance, Sir Lawrence galvanitically refixed his monocle.

'It's been very distasteful,' he said; 'you must forgive us, Elderson. You had to be told. I don't think that young man can be quite all there – he had a peculiar look; but we can't have this sort of thing, of course. Good-bye, Elderson.'

Placing their hats on their heads simultaneously the two walked out. They walked some way without speaking. Then Sir Lawrence said:

'Butterfield? My brother-in-law has a head gardener called Butterfield – quite a good fellow. Ought we to look into that young man, Forsyte?'

'Yes,' said Soames, 'leave him to me.'

'I shall be very glad to. The fact is, when one has been at school with a man, one has a feeling, don't you know.'

Soames gave vent to a sudden outburst.

'You can't trust anyone nowadays, it seems to me,' he said. 'It comes of – well, I don't know what it comes of. But I've not done with this matter yet.'

Chapter Nine

SLEUTH

◄◄─►►

THE Hotch-potch Club went back to the eighteen-sixties. Founded by a posse of young sparks, social and political, as a convenient place in which to smoulder, while qualifying for the hearth of 'Snooks', The Remove, The Wayfarers, Burton's, Ostrich Feather, and other more permanent resorts, the club had, chiefly owing to a remarkable chef in its early days, acquired a stability and distinction of its own. It still, however, retained a certain resemblance to its name, and this was its attraction to Michael — all sorts of people belonged. From Walter Nazing, and young semi-writers and patrons of the stage, who went to Venice, and talked of being amorous in gondolas, or of how so-and-so ought to be made love to; from such to bottle-brushed demi-generals, who had sat on courts-martial and shot men out of hand for the momentary weaknesses of human nature; from Wilfrid Desert (who never came there now) to Maurice Elderson, in the card-room, he could meet them all, and take the temperature of modernity. He was doing this in the Hotch-potch smoking-room, the late afternoon but one after Fleur had come into his bed, when he was informed:

'A Mr Forsyte, sir, in the hall for you. Not the member we had here many years before he died; his cousin, I think.'

Conscious that his associates at the moment would not be his father-in-law's 'dream', nor he theirs, Michael went out, and found Soames on the weighing machine.

'I don't vary,' he said, looking up. 'How's Fleur?'

'Very well, thank you, sir.'

'I'm at Green Street. I stayed up about a young man. Have you any vacancy in your office for a clerk — used to figures. I want a job for him.'

'Come in here, sir,' said Michael, entering a small room.

Soames followed and looked round him.

'What do you call this?' he said.

'Well, we call it "the grave"; it's nice and quiet. Will you have a sherry?'

'Sherry!' repeated Soames. 'You young people think you've invented sherry; when I was a boy no one dreamed of dining without a glass of dry sherry with his soup, and a glass of fine old sherry with his sweet. Sherry!'

'I quite believe you, sir. There really is nothing new. Venice, for instance – wasn't that the fashion, too; and knitting, and royalties? It's all cyclic. Has your young man got the sack?'

Soames stared. 'Yes,' he said, 'he has. His name is Butterfield; he wants a job.'

'That's frightfully rife; we get applications every day. I don't want to be swanky, but ours is a rather specialized business. It has to do with books.'

'He strikes me as capable, orderly, and civil; I don't see what more you want in a clerk. He writes a good hand, and, so far as I can see, he tells the truth.'

'That's important, of course,' said Michael; 'but is he a good liar as well? I mean, there's more likely to be something in the travelling line; selling special editions, and that kind of thing. Could you open up about him a bit? Anything human is to the good – I don't say old Danby would appreciate that, but he needn't know.'

'H'm! Well – he – er – did his duty – quite against his interest – in fact, it's ruination for him. He seems to be married and to have two children.'

'Ho, ho! Jolly! If I got him a place, would he – would he be doing his duty again, do you think?'

'I am serious,' said Soames; 'the young man is on my mind.'

'Yes,' said Michael, ruminative, 'the first thing in such a case is to get him on to someone else's, sharp. Could I see him?'

'I told him to step round and see you tonight after dinner. I thought you'd prefer to look him over in private before considering him for your office.'

'Very thoughtful of you, sir! There's just one thing. Don't you think I ought to know the duty he did – in confidence? I don't see how I can avoid putting my foot into my mouth without, do you?'

Soames stared at his son-in-law's face, where the mouth was wide; for the *n*th time it inspired in him a certain liking and confidence; it looked so honest.

'Well,' he said, going to the door and ascertaining that it was opaque, 'this is matter for a criminal slander action, so for your own sake as well as mine you will keep it strictly to yourself', and in a low voice he retailed the facts.

'As I expected,' he ended, 'the young man came to me again this morning. He is naturally upset. I want to keep my hand on him. Without knowing more, I can't make up my mind whether to go further or not. Besides –' Soames hesitated; to claim a good motive was repulsive to him: 'I – it seems hard on him. He's been getting three hundred and fifty.'

'Dashed hard!' said Michael. 'I say, Elderson's a member here.'

Soames looked with renewed suspicion at the door – it still seemed opaque, and he said: 'the deuce he is! Do you know him?'

'I've played bridge with him,' said Michael; 'he's taken some of the best off me – snorting good player.'

'Ah!' said Soames – he never played cards himself. 'I can't take this young man into my own firm for obvious reasons; but I can trust you.'

Michael touched his forelock.

'Frightfully bucked, sir. Protection of the poor – some sleuth, too. I'll see him tonight, and let you know what I can wangle.'

Soames nodded. 'Good Gad!' he thought; 'what jargon! ...'

The interview served Michael the good turn of taking his thoughts off himself. Temperamentally he sided already with the young man Butterfield; and, lighting a cigarette, he went into the card-room. Sitting on the high fender, he was impressed – the room was square, and within it were three square card-tables, set askew to the walls, with three triangles of card players.

'If only,' thought Michael, 'the fourth player sat under the table, the pattern would be complete. It's having the odd player loose that spoils the cubes.' And with something of a thrill he saw that Elderson was a fourth player! Sharp and impassive, he was engaged in applying a knife to the end of a cigar. Gosh! what sealed books faces were! Each with pages and pages of private thoughts, interests, schemes, fancies, passions, hopes and fears; and down came death – splosh! – and a creature wiped out, like a fly on a wall, and nobody any more could see its little close mechanism working away for its own ends, in its own privacy and its own importance; nobody any more could speculate on whether it was a clean or a dirty little bit of work. Hard to tell! They ran in all shapes! Elderson, for instance – was he a nasty mess, or just a lamb of God who didn't look it? 'Somehow,' thought Michael, 'I feel he's a womanizer. Now why?' He spread his hands out behind him to the fire, rubbing them together like a fly that has been in treacle. If one couldn't tell what was passing in the mind of one's own wife in one's own house, how on earth could one tell anything from the face of a stranger, and he one of the closest bits of mechanism in the world – an English gentleman of business! If only life were like *The Idiot* or *The Brothers Karamazov*, and everybody went about turning out their inmost hearts at the tops of their voices! If only club card-rooms had a dash of epilepsy in their composition! But – nothing! Nothing! The world was full of wonderful secrets which everybody kept to themselves without captions or close-ups to give them away!

A footman came in, looked at the fire, stood a moment expressionless as a stork, waiting for an order to ping out, staccato, through the hum, turned and went away.

Mechanism! Everywhere – mechanism! Devices for getting away from life so complete that there seemed no life to get away from.

'It's all,' he thought, 'awfully like a man sending a registered letter to himself. And perhaps it's just as well. Is "life" a good thing – is it? Do I want to see "life" raw again?'

Elderson was seated now, and Michael had a perfect view of the back of his head. It disclosed nothing.

'I'm no sleuth,' he thought; 'there ought to be something in the way he doesn't part his hair behind.' And, getting off the fender, he went home.

At dinner he caught one of his own looks at Fleur and didn't like it. Sleuth! And yet how not try to know what were the real thoughts and feelings of one who held his heart, like an accordion, and made it squeak and groan at pleasure!

'I saw the model you sent Aubrey yesterday,' she said. 'She didn't say anything about the clothes, but she looked ever so! What a face, Michael! Where did you come across her?'

Through Michael sped the thought: 'Could I make her jealous?' And he was shocked at it. A low-down thought – mean and ornery! 'She blew in,' he said. 'Wife of a little packer we had who took to snooping – er – books. He sells balloons now; they want money badly.'

'I see. Did you know that Aubrey's going to paint her in the nude?'

'Phew! No! I thought she'd look good on a wrapper. I say! Ought I to stop that?'

Fleur smiled. 'It's more money and her look-out. It doesn't matter to you, does it?'

Again that thought; again the recoil from it!

'Only,' he said, 'that her husband is a decent little snipe for a snooper, and I don't want to be more sorry for him.'

'She won't tell him, of course.'

She said it so naturally, so simply, that the words disclosed a whole attitude of mind. One didn't tell one's mate what would tease the poor brute! He saw by the flutter of her white eyelids that she also realized the give-away. Should he follow it up, tell her what June Forsyte had told him – have it all out – all out? But with what purpose – to what end? Would it change things, make her love him? Would it do anything but harass her a little more; and give him the sense that he had lost his wicket trying to drive her to the pavilion? No! Better adopt the principle of secrecy she had unwittingly declared her own, bite on it, and grin. He muttered:

'I'm afraid he'll find her rather thin.'

Her eyes were bright and steady; and again he was worried by that low-down thought: 'Could he make her —?'

'I've only seen her once,' he added, 'and then she was dressed.'

'I'm not jealous, Michael.'

'No,' he thought, 'I wish to heaven you were!'

The words: 'A young man called Butterfill to see you, sir,' were like the turning of a key in a cell door.

In the hall the young man 'called Butterfill' was engaged in staring at Ting-a-ling.

'Judging by his eyes,' thought Michael, 'he's more of a dog than that little Djinn!'

'Come up to my study,' he said, 'it's cold down here. My father-in-law tells me you want a job.'

'Yes, sir,' said the young man, following up the stairs.

'Take a pew,' said Michael; 'and a cigarette. Now then! I know all about the turmoil. From your moustache, you were in the war, I suppose, like me! As between fellow-sufferers: Is your story O.K.?'

'God's truth, sir; I only wish it wasn't. I'd nothing to gain and everything to lose. I'd have done better to hold my tongue. It's his word against mine, and here I am in the street. That was my first job since the war, so I can whistle for a reference.'

'Wife and two children, I think?'

'Yes, and I've put them in the cart for the sake of my conscience! It's the last time I'll do that, I know. What did it matter to me, whether the Society was cheated? My wife's quite right, I was a fool, sir.'

'Probably,' said Michael. 'Do you know anything about books?'

'Yes, sir; I'm a good book-keeper.'

'Holy Moses! *Our* job is getting rid of them. My firm are publishers. We were thinking of putting on an extra traveller. Is your tongue persuasive?'

The young man smiled wanly.

'I don't know, sir.'

'Well, look here,' said Michael, carried away by the look in his eyes, 'it's all a question of a certain patter. But, of course, that's got to be learned. I gather that you're not a reader.'

'Well, sir, not a great reader.'

'That, perhaps, is fortunate. What you would have to do is to impress on the poor brutes who sell books that every one of the books on your list – say about thirty-five – is necessary in large numbers to his business. It's lucky you've just chucked your conscience, because, as a matter of fact, most of them won't be. I'm afraid there's nowhere you could go to to get lessons in persuasion, but you can imagine the sort of thing, and if you like to come here for an hour or two this week, I'll put you wise about our authors, and ready you up to go before Peter.'

'Before Peter, sir?'

'The Johnny with the keys; luckily it's Mr Winter, not Mr Danby; I believe I could get him to let you in for a month's trial.'

'Sir, I'll try my very best. My wife knows about books, she could help me a lot. I can't tell you what I think of your kindness. The fact is, being out of a job has put the wind up me properly. I've not been able to save with two children; it's like the end of the world.'

'Right-o, then! Come here tomorrow evening at nine, and I'll stuff you. I believe you've got the face for the job, if you can get the patter. Only one book in twenty is a necessity really, the rest are luxuries. Your stunt will be to make them believe the nineteen are necessaries, and the twentieth a luxury that they need. It's like food or clothes, or anything else in civilization.'

'Yes, sir, I quite understand.'

'All right, then. Good night, and good luck!'

Michael stood up and held out his hand. The young man took it with a queer reverential little bow. A minute later he was out in the street; and Michael in the hall was thinking: 'Pity is tripe! Clean forgot I was a sleuth!'

Chapter Ten

FACE

◄-‹-›-►

WHEN Michael rose from the refectory table, Fleur had risen, too. Two days and more since she left Wilfrid's rooms, and she had not recovered zest. The rifling of the oyster Life, the garlanding of London's rarer flowers which kept colour in her cheeks, seemed stale, unprofitable. Those three hours, when from shock off Cork Street she came straight to shocks in her own drawing-room, had dislocated her so that she had settled to nothing since. The wound re-opened by Holly had nearly healed again. Dead lion beside live donkey cuts but dim figure. But she could not get hold again of – what? That was the trouble: What? For two whole days she had been trying. Michael was still strange, Wilfrid still lost, Jon still buried alive, and nothing seemed novel under the sun. The only object that gave her satisfaction during those two dreary, disillusioned days was the new white monkey. The more she looked at it, the more Chinese it seemed. It summed up the satirical truth of which she was perhaps subconscious, that all her little modern veerings and flutterings and rushings after the future showed that she believed in nothing but the past. The age had overdone it and must go back to ancestry for faith. Like a little bright fish out of a warm bay, making a splash in chill, strange waters, Fleur felt a subtle nostalgia.

In her Spanish room, alone with her own feelings, she stared at the porcelain fruits. They glowed, cold, uneatable! She took one up. Meant for a passion fruit? Alas! Poor passion! She dropped it with a dull clink on to the pyramid, and shuddered a little. Had she blinded Michael with her kisses? Blinded him to – what? To her incapacity for passion?

'But I'm not incapable,' she thought; 'I'm not. Some day I'll

show him; I'll show them all.' She looked up at 'the Goya'
hanging opposite. What gripping determination in the painting
– what intensity of life in the black eyes of a rather raddled
dame! *She* would know what she wanted, and get it, too! No
compromise and uncertainty there – no capering round life,
wondering what it meant, and whether it was worth while,
nothing but hard living for the sake of living!

Fleur put her hands where her flesh ended, and her dress
began. Wasn't she as warm and firm – yes, and ten times as
pretty, as that fine and evil-looking Spanish dame, with the
black eyes and the wonderful lace? And, turning her back on
the picture, she went into the hall. Michael's voice and another's! They were coming down! She slipped across into the
drawing-room and took up the manuscript of a book of poems,
on which she was to give Michael her opinion. She sat, not reading, wondering if he were coming in. She heard the front door
close. No! He had gone out! A relief, yet chilling! Michael not
warm and cheerful in the house – if it were to go on, it would
be wearing. She curled herself up and tried to read. Dreary
poems – free verse, blank introspective, all about the author's
inside! No lift, no lilt! Duds! She seemed to have read them a
dozen times before. She lay quite still – listening to the click and
flutter of the burning logs! If the light were out she might go
to sleep. She turned it off, and came back to the settee. She could
see herself sitting there, a picture in the firelight; see how lonely
she looked, pretty, pathetic, with everything she wished for, and
– nothing! Her lip curled. She could even see her own spoiled-
child ingratitude. And what was worse, she could see herself
seeing it – a triple-distilled modern, so subtly arranged in life-
tight compartments that she could not be submerged. If only
something would blow in out of the unkempt cold, out of the
waste and wilderness of a London whose flowers she plucked.
The firelight – soft, uncertain – searched out spots and corners
of her Chinese room, as on a stage in one of those scenes, seduc-
tive and mysterious, where one waited, to the sound of tam-
bourines, for the next moment of the plot. She reached out and
took a cigarette. She could see herself lighting it, blowing out

the smoke – her own half-curled fingers, her parted lips, her white rounded arm. She was decorative! Well, and wasn't that all that mattered? To be decorative, and make little decorations; to be pretty in a world that wasn't pretty! In *Copper Coin* there was a poem of a flicker-lit room, and a spoiled Columbine before the fire, and a Harlequin hovering without, like 'the spectre of the rose'. And suddenly, without warning, Fleur's heart ached. It ached definitely, rather horribly, and, slipping down on to the floor before the fire, she snuggled her face against Ting-a-ling. The Chinese dog raised his head – his black eyes lurid in the glow.

He licked her cheek, and turned his nose away. Huf! Powder! But Fleur lay like the dead. And she saw herself lying – the curve of her hip, the chestnut glow in her short hair; she heard the steady beat of her heart. Get up! Go out! Do something! But what – what was worth doing? What had any meaning in it? She saw herself doing – extravagant things; nursing sick women; tending pale babies; making a speech in Parliament; riding a steeplechase; hoeing turnips in knickerbockers – decorative. And she lay perfectly still, bound by the filaments of her self-vision. So long as she saw herself she would do nothing – she knew it – for nothing would be worth doing! And it seemed to her, lying there so still, that not to see herself would be worse than anything. And she felt that to feel this was to acknowledge herself caged for ever.

Ting-a-ling growled, turning his nose towards the windows. 'In here,' he seemed to say, 'we are cosy; we think of the past. We have no use for anything outside. Kindly go away – whoever it is out there!' And again he growled – a low, continuous sound.

'What is it, Ting?'

Ting-a-ling rose on his fore-legs, with muzzle pointed at the window.

'Do you want your walk?'

'No,' said the growl.

Fleur picked him up. 'Don't be so silly!' And she went to the window. The curtains were closely drawn; rich, Chinese lined, they excluded the night. Fleur made a chink with one hand, and started back. Against the pane was a face, the forehead pressed against the glass, the eyes closed, as if it had been there a long time. In the dark it seemed featureless, vaguely pale. She felt the dog's body stiffen under her arm – she felt his silence. Her heart pumped. It was ghastly – face without body.

Suddenly the forehead was withdrawn, the eyes opened. She saw – the face of Wilfrid. Could he see in – see her peering out from the darkened room? Quivering all over, she let the curtains fall to. Beckon? Let him in? Go out to him? Wave him away? Her heart beat furiously. How long had he been out there – like a ghost? What did he want of her? She dropped Ting-a-ling with a flump, and pressed her hands to her forehead, trying to clear confusion from her brain. And suddenly she stepped forward and flung the curtains apart. No face! Nothing! He was gone! The dark, draughty square – not a soul in it! Had he ever been – or was the face her fancy? But Ting-a-ling! Dogs had no fancies. He had gone back to the fire and settled down again.

'It's not my fault,' she thought passionately. 'It's not! I didn't want him to love me. I only wanted his – his –!' Again she sank down before the fire. 'Oh! Ting, have a feeling heart!' But the Chinese dog, mindful of the flump, made no response. . . .

Chapter Eleven

COCKED HAT

━◄━►━

AFTER missing his vocation with the young man Butterfield, Michael had hesitated in the hall. At last he had not gone upstairs again, but quietly out. He walked past the Houses of Parliament and up Whitehall. In Trafalgar Square, it occurred to him that he had a father. Bart might be at 'Snooks', The

Coffee House, The Aeroplane; and, with the thought, 'He'd be restful,' he sought the most modern of the three.

'Yes, Sir Lawrence Mont is in the lounge, sir.'

He was sitting with knees crossed, and a cigar between his fingertips, waiting for someone to talk to.

'Ah! Michael! Can you tell me why I come here?'

'To wait for the end of the world, sir?'

Sir Lawrence sniggered. 'An idea,' he said. 'When the skies are wrecking civilization, this will be the best-informed tape in London. The wish to be in at the death is perhaps the strongest of our passions, Michael. I should very much dislike being blown up, especially after dinner; but I should still more dislike missing the next show if it's to be a really good one. The air-raids were great fun, after all.'

Michael sighed.

'Yes,' he said, 'the war got us used to thinking of the millennium, and then it went and stopped, and left the millennium hanging over us. Now we shall never be happy till we get it. Can I take one of your cigars, sir?'

'My dear fellow! I've been reading Frazer again. Extraordinary how remote all superstition seems, now that we've reached the ultimate truth: That enlightenment never can prevail.'

Michael stopped the lighting of his cigar.

'Do you really think that, sir?'

'What else can one think? Who can have any reasonable doubt now that with the aid of mechanics the head-strong part of man must do him in? It's an unavoidable conclusion from all recent facts. "*Per ardua ad astra*," "Through hard knocks we shall see stars."'

'But it's always been like that, sir, and here we are alive?'

'They say so, but I doubt it. I fancy we're really dead, Michael. I fancy we're only living in the past. I don't think – no, I don't think we can be said to expect a future. We talk of it, but I hardly think we hope for one. Underneath our protestations we subconsciously deduce. From the mess we've made of it these last ten years, we can feel the far greater mess we shall make of it in the next thirty. Human nature can argue the hind legs off a donkey, but the donkey will be four-legged at the end of the discussion.'

Michael sat down suddenly and said:

'You're a bad, bold Bart.'

Sir Lawrence smiled.

'I should be glad to think that men really believed in humanity, and all that, but you know they don't – they believe in novelty and getting their own way. With rare exceptions they're still monkeys, especially the scientific variety; and when you put gunpowder and a lighted match into the paws of monkeys, they blow themselves up to see the fun. Monkeys are only safe when deprived of means to be otherwise.'

'Lively, that!' said Michael.

'Not livelier than the occasion warrants, my dear boy. I've been thinking. We've got a member here who knows a trick worth twenty of any played in the war – an extraordinarily valuable fellow. The Government have got their eye on him. He'll help the other valuable fellows in France and Germany and America and Russia to make history. Between them, they'll do something really proud – something that'll knock all the other achievements of man into a cocked hat. By the way, Michael, new device of "*Homo sapiens*" – the cocked hat.'

'Well,' said Michael, 'what are you going to do about it?'

Sir Lawrence's eyebrow sought his hair.

'Do, my dear fellow? What should I do? Can I go out and grab him and the Government by the slack of their breeches; yes, and all the valuable fellows and Governments of the other countries? No! All I can do is to smoke my cigar and say: "God rest you, merry gentlemen, let nothing you dismay!" By hook or crook, they will come into their own, Michael; but in the normal course of things I shall be dead before they do.'

'I shan't,' said Michael.

'No, my dear; but think of the explosions, the sights, the smells. By Jove, you've got something to live for, yet. Sometimes I wish I were your age. And sometimes,' Sir Lawrence relighted his cigar, 'I don't. Sometimes I think I've had enough of our pretences, and that there's nothing left but to die like gentle-men.'

'Some Jeremiad, Dad!'

'Well,' said Sir Lawrence, with a twirl of his little grizzled moustache, 'I hope I'm wrong. But we're driving fast to a condition of things when millions can be killed by the pressing of a few buttons. What reason is there to suppose that our bumps of benevolence will increase in time to stop our using these great new toys of destruction, Michael!'

' "Where you know little, place terrors." '

'Very nice; where did you get that?'

'Out of a life of Christopher Columbus.'

'Old C.C.! I could bring myself to wish sometimes that he hadn't been so deucedly inquisitive. We were snugger in the dark ages. There were something to be said for not discovering the Yanks.'

'Well,' said Michael, '*I* think we shall pedal through, yet. By the way, about this Elderson stunt: I've just seen the clerk – he doesn't look to me the sort that would have made that up.'

'Ah! That! But if Elderson could do such a thing, well – really, anything might happen. It's a complete stumper. He was such a pretty bat, always went in first wicket down. He and I put on fifty-four against Eton. I suppose old Forsyte told you?'

'Yes, he wanted me to find the chap a job.'

'Butterfield. Ask him if he's related to old Butterfield the gardener! It would be something to go on. D'you find old Forsyte rather trying?'

Loyal to Fleur, Michael concealed his lips. 'No, I get on very well with him.'

'He's straight, I admit that.'

'Yes,' said Michael, 'very straight.'

'But somewhat reticent.'

'Yes,' said Michael.

On this conclusion they were silent, as though terrors had been placed beyond it. And soon Michael rose.

'Past ten, I'd better go home.'

Returning the way he came, he could think of nothing but
Wilfrid. What wouldn't he give to hear him say: 'It's all right,
old man; I've got over it!' – to wring him by the hand again.
Why should one catch this fatal disease called love? Why should
one be driven half crazy by it? They said love was Nature's
provision against Bart's terrors, against the valuable fellows. An
insistent urge – lest the race die out. Prosaic, if true! Not that
he cared whether Fleur had children. Queer how Nature camouflaged her schemes – leery old bird! But over-reaching herself a
bit, wasn't she? Children might yet go clean out of fashion if
Bart was right. A very little more would do it; who would have
children for the mere pleasure of seeing them blown up,
poisoned, starved to death? A few fanatics would hold on, the
rest of the world go barren. The cocked hat! Instinctively
Michael straightened his own, ready for crossing under Big
Ben. He had reached the centre of Parliament Square, when a
figure coming towards him swerved suddenly to its left and
made in the direction of Victoria. Tall, with a swing in its
walk. Wilfrid! Michael stood still. Coming from – South
Square! And suddenly he gave chase. He did not run, but he
walked his hardest. The blood beat in his temples, and he felt
confused to a pitch past bearing. Wilfrid must have seen him,
or he wouldn't have swerved, wouldn't be legging it away like
a demon. Black! – black! He was not gaining, Wilfrid had
the legs of him – to overtake him, he must run! But there
rose in Michael a sort of exaltation. His best friend – his wife!
There was a limit. One might be too proud to fight that. Let
him go his ways! He stood still, watched the swift figure disappear, and slowly, head down under the now cocked hat,
turned towards home. He walked quite quietly, and with a
sense of finality. No use making a song about it! No fuss, but
no retreat! In the few hundred yards before he reached his
Square he was chiefly conscious of the tallness of houses, the
shortness of men. Such midgets to have made this monstrous
pile, lighted it so that it shone in an enormous glittering heap
whose glow blurred the colour of the sky! What a vast business
this midget activity! Absurd to think that his love for another

midget mattered! He turned his key in the lock, took off his cocked hat and went into the drawing-room. Unlighted – empty? No. She and Ting-a-ling were on the floor before the fire! He sat down on the settee, and was abruptly conscious that he was trembling and sweating as if he had smoked a too strong cigar. Fleur had raised herself, cross-legged, and was staring up at him. He waited to get the better of his trembling. Why didn't she speak? Why was she sitting there, in the dark? 'She knows'; he thought: 'we both know this is the end. O God, let me at least be a sport!' He took a cushion, put it behind him, crossed his legs, and leaned back. His voice surprised him suddenly:

'May I ask you something, Fleur? And will you please answer me quite truly?'

'Yes.'

'It's this: I know you didn't love me when you married me. I don't think you love me now. Do you want me to clear out?'

A long time seemed to pass.

'No.'

'Do you mean that?'

'Yes.'

'Why?'

'Because I don't.'

Michael got up.

'Will you answer one thing more?'

'Yes.'

'Was Wilfrid here tonight?'

'Yes – no. That is –'

His hands clutched each other; he saw her eyes fix on them, and kept them still.

'Fleur, don't!'

'I'm not. He came to the window there. I saw his face – that's all. His face – it – Oh! Michael, don't be unkind tonight!'

Unkind! Unkind! Michael's heart swelled at that strange word.

'It's all right,' he stammered: 'So long as you tell me what it is you want.'

Fleur said, without moving :

'I want to be comforted.'

Ah ! She knew exactly what to say, how to say it ! And going on his knees, he began to comfort her.

Chapter Twelve

GOING EAST

-<-->-

HE had not been on his knees many minutes before they suffered from reaction. To kneel there comforting Fleur brought him a growing discomfort. He believed her tonight, as he had not believed her for months past. But what was Wilfrid doing? Where wandering? The face at the window – face without voice, without attempt to reach her ! Michael ached in that illegitimate organ the heart. Withdrawing his arms, he stood up.

'Would you like me to have a look for him? If it's all over – he might – I might –'

Fleur, too, stood up. She was calm enough now.

'Yes, I'll go to bed.' With Ting-a-ling in her arms, she went to the door; her face, between the dog's chestnut fur and her own, was very pale, very still.

'By the way,' she said, 'this is my second no go, Michael; I suppose it means –'

Michael gasped. Currents of emotion, welling, ebbing, swirling, rendered him incapable of speech.

'The night of the balloon,' she said : 'Do you mind?'

'Mind? Good God ! Mind !'

'That's all right, then. *I* don't. Good night !'

She was gone. Without reason, Michael thought : 'In the beginning was the Word, and the Word was with God, and the Word was God.' And he stood, as if congealed, overcome by an uncontrollable sense of solidity. A child coming ! It was as though the barque of his being, tossed and drifted, suddenly rode tethered – anchor down. He turned and tore at the curtains. Night of stars! Wonderful world! Jolly – jolly! And – Wilfrid! He flattened his face against the glass. Outside there Wilfrid's had been flattened. He could see it if he shut his eyes. Not fair! Dog lost – man lost! S.O.S. He went into the hall, and from the mothless marble coffer rived his thickest coat. He took the first taxi that came by.

'Cork Street! Get along!' Needle in bundle of hay! Quarter-past eleven by Big Ben! The intense relief of his whole being in that jolting cab seemed to him brutal. Salvation! It *was* – he had a strange certainty of that as though he saw Fleur suddenly 'close up' in a very strong light, concrete beneath her graceful veerings. Family! Continuation! He had been unable to anchor her, for he was not of her! But her child could and would! And, perhaps, he would yet come in with the milk. Why did he love her so – it was not done! Wilfrid and he were donkeys – out of touch, out of tune with the times!

'Here you are, sir – what number?'

'All right! Cool your heels and wait for me! Have a cigarette!'

With one between his own lips which felt so dry, he went down the backwater.

A light in Wilfrid's rooms! He rang the bell. The door was opened, the face of Wilfrid's man looked forth.

'Yes, sir?'

'Mr Desert in?'

'No, sir. Mr Desert has just started for the East. His ship sails tomorrow.'

'Oh!' said Michael blankly. 'Where from?'

'Plymouth, sir. His train leaves Paddington at midnight. You might catch him yet.'

'It's very sudden,' said Michael, 'he never –'

'No, sir. Mr Desert is a sudden gentleman.'

'Well, thanks; I'll try and catch him.'

Back in the cab with the words: 'Paddington – flick her along!' he thought: 'A sudden gentleman!' Perfect! He remembered the utter suddenness of that little interview beside the bust of Lionel Charwell. Sudden their friendship, sudden its end – sudden even Wilfrid's poems – offspring of a sudden soul! Staring from window to window in that jolting, rattling cab, Michael suffered from St Vitus's dance. Was he a fool? Could he not let well alone? Pity was posh! And yet! With Wilfrid would go a bit of his heart, and in spite of all he would like him to know that. Upper Brook Street, Park Lane! Emptying streets, cold night, stark plane trees painted-up by the lamps against a bluish dark. And Michael thought: 'We wander! What's the end – the goal? To do one's bit, and not worry! But what is my bit? What's Wilfrid's? Where will he end up, now?'

The cab rattled down the station slope and drew up under cover. Ten minutes to twelve, and a long heavy train on platform one!

'What shall I do?' thought Michael: 'It's so darned crude! Must I go down – carriage by carriage? "Couldn't let you go, old man, without" – blurb!'

Bluejackets! If not drunk – as near as made no matter. Eight minutes still! He began slowly walking along the train. He had not passed four windows before he saw his quarry. Desert was sitting back to the engine in the near corner of an empty first. An unlighted cigarette was in his mouth, his fur collar turned up to his eyes, and his eyes fixed on an unopened paper on his lap. He sat without movement; Michael stood looking at him. His heart beat fast. He struck a match, took two steps, and said:

'Light, old boy?'

Desert stared up at him.

'Thanks,' he said, and took the match. By its flare his face was dark, thin, drawn; his eyes dark, deep, tired. Michael leaned in the window. Neither spoke.

'Take your seat, if you're going, sir.'

'I'm not,' said Michael. His whole inside seemed turning over.

'Where are you going, old man?' he said suddenly.

'Jericho.'

'God, Wilfrid, I'm sorry!'

Desert smiled.

'Cut it out!'

'Yes, I know! Shake hands?'

Desert held out his hand.

Michael squeezed it hard.

A whistle sounded.

Desert rose suddenly and turned to the rack above him. He took a parcel from a bag. 'Here,' he said, 'these wretched things! Publish them if you like.'

Something clicked in Michael's throat.

'Thanks, old man! That's great! Good-bye!'

A sort of beauty came into Desert's face.

'So long!' he said.

The train moved. Michael withdrew his elbows; quite still, he stared at the motionless figure slowly borne along, away. Carriage after carriage went by him, full of bluejackets leaning out, clamouring, singing, waving handkerchiefs and bottles. Guard's van now – the tail light – all spread – a crimson blur – setting East – going – going – gone!

And that was all – was it? He thrust the parcel into his coat pocket. Back to Fleur, now! Way of the world – one man's meat, another's poison! He passed his hand over his eyes. The dashed things were full of – blurb!

PART THREE

Chapter One

BANK HOLIDAY

→←→←

Whitsuntide Bank Holiday was producing its seasonal invasion of Hampstead Heath, and among the ascending swarm were two who meant to make money in the morning and spend it in the afternoon.

Tony Bicket, with balloons and wife, embarked early on the Hampstead Tube.

'You'll see,' he said, 'I'll sell the bloomin' lot by twelve o'clock, and we'll go on the bust.'

Squeezing his arm, Victorine fingered, through her dress, a slight swelling just above her right knee. It was caused by fifty-four pounds fastened in the top of her stocking. She had little feeling, now, against balloons. They afforded temporary nourishment, till she had the few more pounds needful for their passage-money. Tony still believed he was going to screw salvation out of his blessed balloons: he was 'that hopeful – Tony', though their heads were only just above water on his takings. And she smiled. With her secret she could afford to be indifferent now to the stigma of gutter hawking. She had her story pat. From the evening paper, and from communion on buses with those interested in the national pastime, she had acquired the necessary information about racing. She even talked of it with Tony, who had street-corner knowledge. Already she had prepared chapter and verse of two imaginary coups; a sovereign made out of stitching imaginary blouses, invested on the winner of the Two Thousand Guineas, and the result on the dead-heater for the Jubilee at nice odds; this with a third winner, still to be selected, would bring her imaginary winnings up to the needed sixty pounds odd she would so soon have saved now out of 'the altogether'. This tale she would pitch to Tony in a week or two, reeling off by heart the wonderful luck she had kept from him until she had the whole of the money. She would slip her forehead against his eyes if he looked at her too hard, and kiss his lips till his head was no longer clear. And in the morning they would wake up and take their passages. Such was the plan of Victorine, with five ten-pound and four one-pound notes in her stocking, attached to the pink silk stays.

Afternoon of a Dryad had long been finished, and was on exhibition at the Dumetrius Gallery, with other works of Aubrey Greene. Victorine had paid a shilling to see it; had stood some furtive minutes gazing at that white body glimmering from among grass and spikey flowers, at the face, turned as if saying: 'I know a secret!'

'Bit of a genius, Aubrey Greene — that face is jolly good!' Scared, and hiding the face, Victorine had slipped away.

From the very day when she had stood shivering outside the studio of Aubrey Greene she had been in full work. He had painted her three times – always nice, always polite, quite the gentleman! And he had given her introductions. Some had painted her in clothes, some half-draped, some in that 'altogether', which no longer troubled her, with the money swelling her stocking and Tony without suspicion. Not everyone had been 'nice'; advances had been made to her, but she had nipped them in the bud. It would have meant the money quicker, but – Tony! In a fortnight now she could snap her fingers at it all. And often on the way home she stood by that plate-glass window, before the fruits, and the corn, and the blue butterflies. . . .

In the packed railway carriage they sat side by side, Bicket with tray on knee, debating where he had best stand.

'I favour the mokes,' he said at last, 'up by the pond. People'll have more money than when they get down among the swings and coconuts; and you can go and sit in a chair by the pond, like the seaside – I don't want you with me not till I've sold out.'

Victorine pressed his arm.

Along the top and over on to the heath to north and south

the holiday swarms surged, in perfect humour, carrying paper bags. Round the pond, children with thin, grey-white, spindly legs, were paddling and shrilly chattering, too content to smile. Elderly couples crawled slowly by, with jutting stomachs, and faces discoloured by the unaccustomed climb. Girls and young men were few, for they were dispersed already on the heath, in search of a madder merriment. On benches, in chairs of green canvas or painted wood, hundreds were sitting, contemplating their feet, as if imagining the waves of the sea. Now and again three donkeys would start, urged from behind, and slowly tittup their burdens along the pond's margin. Hawkers cried goods. Fat dark women told fortunes. Policemen stood cynically near them. A man talked and talked and took his hat round.

Tony Bicket unslung his tray. His cockney voice, wheedling and a little husky, offered his coloured airs without intermission. This was something like! It was brisk! And now and again he gazed through the throng away across the pond, to where Victorine would be seated in a canvas chair, looking different from everyone – he knew.

'Fine balloons – fine balloons! Six for a bob! Big one, Madam? Only sixpence. See the size! Buy, buy! Tyke one for the little boy!'

No 'aldermen' up here, but plenty in the mood to spend their money on a bit of brightness!

At five minutes before noon he snapped his tray to – not a bally balloon left! With six Bank Holidays a week he would make his fortune! Tray under arm, he began to tour the pond. The kiddies were all right, but – good Lord – how thin and pale! If he and Vic had a kid – but not they – not till they got out there! A fat brown kid, chysin' blue butterflies, and the sun oozin' out of him! Rounding the end of the pond, he walked slowly along the chairs. Lying back, elegant, with legs crossed, in brown stockings showing to the knees, and neat brown shoes with the flaps over – My! she looked a treat – in a world of her own, like that! Something caught Bicket by the throat. Gosh! He wanted things for her!

'Well, Vic! Penny!'

'I was thinkin' of Australia.'

'Ah! It's a gaudy long wait. Never mind – I've sold the bally lot. Which shall we do, go down among the trees, or get to the swings, at once?'

'The swings,' said Victorine.

The Vale of Health was in rhapsodic mood. The crowd flowed here in a slow, speechless stream, to the cries of the booth-keepers, and the owners of swings and coconuts. 'Roll – bowl – or pitch! Now for the milky ones! Penny a shy! ... Who's for the swings? ... Ices ... Ices ... Fine bananas!'

On the giant merry-go-round under its vast umbrella the thirty chain-hung seats were filled with girls and men. Round to the music – slowly – faster – whirling out to the full extent of the chain, bodies bent back, legs stuck forward, laughter and speech dying, faces solemn, a little lost, hands gripping the chains hard. Faster, faster; slowing, slowing to a standstill, and the music silent.

'My word!' murmured Victorine. 'Come on, Tony!'

They entered the enclosure and took their seats. Victorine, on the outside, locked her feet, instinctively, one over the other, and tightening her clasp on the chains, curved her body to the motion. Her lips parted:

'Lor, Tony!'

Faster, faster – every nerve and sense given to that motion! O-o-h! It *was* a feeling – flying round like that above the world! Faster – faster! Slower – slow, and the descent to earth.

'Tony, it's 'eaven!'

'Queer feelin' in yer inside, when you're swung right out!'

'I'd like it level with the top. Let's go once more!'

'Right-o!'

Twice more they went – half his profit on balloons! But who cared? He liked to see her face. After that, six shies at the milky ones without a hit, an ice apiece: then arm-in-arm to find a place to eat their lunch. That was the time Bicket enjoyed most, after the ginger-beer and sandwiches; smoking his fag, with his head on her lap, and the sky blue. A long time like that; till at last she stirred.

'Let's go and see the dancin'!'

In the grass enclosure ringed by the running path, some two dozen couples were jigging to a band.

Victorine pulled at his arm. 'I *would* love a turn!'

'Well, let's 'ave a go,' said Bicket. 'This one-legged bloke'll 'old my tray.'

They entered the ring.

'Hold me tighter, Tony!'

Bicket obeyed. Nothing he liked better; and slowly their feet moved – to this side and that. They made little way, revolving, keeping time, oblivious of appearances.

'You dance all right, Tony.'

'*You* dance a treat!' gasped Bicket.

In the intervals, panting, they watched ever the one-legged man; then to it again, till the band ceased for good.

'My word!' said Victorine. 'They dance on board ship, Tony!'

Bicket squeezed her waist.

'I'll do the trick yet, if I 'ave to rob the Bank. There's nothin' I wouldn't do for you, Vic.'

But Victorine smiled. She had done the trick already.

The crowd with parti-coloured faces, tired, good-humoured, frowsily scented, strolled over a battlefield thick-strewn with paper bags, banana peel, and newspapers.

'Let's 'ave tea, and one more swing,' said Bicket; 'then we'll get over on the other side among the trees.'

Away over on the far side were many couples. The sun went very slowly down. Those two sat under a bush and watched it go. A faint breeze swung and rustled the birch leaves. There was little human sound out here. All seemed to have come for silence, to be waiting for darkness in the hush. Now and then some stealthy spy would pass and scrutinize.

'Foxes!' said Bicket. 'Gawd! I'd like to rub their noses in it!'

Victorine sighed, pressing closer to him.

Someone was playing on a banjo now; a voice singing. It grew dusk, but a moon was somewhere rising, for little shadows stole out along the ground.

They spoke in whispers. It seemed wrong to raise the voice, as though the grove were under a spell. Even their whisperings were scarce. Dew fell, but they paid no heed to it. With hands locked, and cheeks together, they sat very still. Bicket had a thought. This was poetry – this was! Darkness now, with a sort of faint and silvery glow, a sound of drunken singing on the Spaniard's Road, the whirr of belated cars returning from the north – and suddenly an owl hooted.

'My!' murmured Victorine, shivering. 'An owl! Fancy! I used to hear one at Norbiton. I 'ope it's not bad luck!'

Bicket rose and stretched himself.

'Come on!' he said: 'we've 'ad a dy. Don't you go catchin' cold!'

Arm-in-arm, slowly, through the darkness of the birch-grove, they made their way upwards – glad of the lamps, and the street, and the crowded station, as though they had taken an overdose of solitude.

Huddled in their carriage on the Tube, Bicket idly turned the pages of a derelict paper. But Victorine sat thinking of so much, that it was as if she thought of nothing. The swings and the grove in the darkness, and the money in her stocking. She wondered Tony hadn't noticed when it crackled – there wasn't a safe place to keep it in! What was he looking at, with his eyes so fixed? She peered, and read: '*Afternoon of a Dryad*. The striking picture by Aubrey Greene, on exhibition at the Dumetrius Gallery.'

Her heart stopped beating.

'Cripes!' said Bicket. 'Ain't that like you?'

'Like me? No!'

Bicket held the paper closer. 'It *is*. It's like you all over. I'll cut that out. I'd like to see that picture.'

The colour came up in her cheeks, released from a heart beating too fast now.

''Tisn't decent,' she said.

'Dunno about that; but it's awful like you. It's even got your smile.'

Folding the paper, he began to tear the sheet. Victorine's little finger pressed the notes beneath her stocking.

'Funny,' she said slowly, 'to think there's people in the world so like each other.'

'I never thought there could be one like you. Charin' Cross; we gotta change.'

Hurrying along the rat-runs of the Tube, she slipped her hand into his pocket, and soon some scraps of torn paper fluttered down behind her following him in the crush. If only he didn't remember where the picture was!

Awake in the night, she thought:

'I don't care; I'm going to get the rest of the money – that's all about it.'

But her heart moved queerly within her, like that of one whose feet have trodden suddenly the quaking edge of a bog.

Chapter Two

OFFICE WORK

MICHAEL sat correcting the proofs of *Counterfeits* – the book left by Wilfrid behind him.

'Can you see Butterfield, sir?'

'I can.'

In Michael the word Butterfield excited an uneasy pride. The young man fulfilled with increasing success the function for which he had been engaged, on trial, four months ago. The head traveller had even called him 'a find'. Next to *Copper Coin* he was the finest feather in Michael's cap. The Trade were not buying, yet Butterfield was selling books, or so it was reported; he appeared to have a natural gift of inspiring confidence where it was not justified. Danby and Winter had even entrusted to him the private marketing of the vellum-bound 'Limited' of *A Duet*, by which they were hoping to recoup their losses on the ordinary edition. He was now engaged in working through a list of names considered likely to patronize the little masterpiece. This method of private approach had been suggested by himself.

'You see, sir,' he had said to Michael: 'I know a bit about Coué. Well, you can't work that on the Trade – they've got no capacity for faith. What can you expect? Every day they buy all sorts of stuff, always basing themselves on past sales. You can't find one in twenty that'll back the future. But with private gentlemen, and especially private ladies, you can leave a thought with them like Coué does – put it into them again and again that day by day in every way the author's gettin' better and better; and ten to one when you go round next, it's got into their subconscious, especially if you take 'em just after lunch or dinner, when they're a bit drowsy. Let me take my own time, sir, and I'll put that edition over for you.'

'Well,' Michael had answered, 'if you can inspire confidence in the future of my governor, Butterfield, you'll deserve more than your ten per cent.'

'I can do it, sir; it's just a question of faith.'

'But you haven't any, have you?'

'Well, not, so to speak, in the author – but I've got faith that I can give *them* faith in him; that's the real point.'

'I see – the three-card stunt; inspire the faith you haven't got, that the card is there, and they'll take it. Well, the disillusion is not immediate – you'll probably always get out of the room in time. Go ahead, then!'

The young man Butterfield had smiled. . . .

The uneasy part of the pride inspired in Michael now by the name was due to old Forsyte's continually saying to him that he didn't know – he couldn't tell – there was that young man and his story about Elderson, and they got no further. . . .

'Good morning, sir. Can you spare me five minutes?'

'Come in, Butterfield. Bunkered with *Duet*?'

'No, sir. I've placed forty already. It's another matter.' Glancing at the shut door, the young man came closer.

'I'm working my list alphabetically. Yesterday I was in the E's.' His voice dropped. 'Mr Elderson.'

'Phew!' said Michael. 'You can give *him* the go-by.'

'As a fact, sir, I haven't.'

'What! Been over the top?'

'Yes, sir. Last night.'

'Good for you, Butterfield! What happened?'

'I didn't send my name in, sir – just the firm's card.'

Michael was conscious of a very human malice in the young man's voice and face.

'Well?'

'Mr Elderson, sir, was at his wine. I'd thought it out, and I began as if I'd never seen him before. What struck me was – he took my cue!'

'Didn't kick you out?'

'Far from it, sir. He said at once: "Put my name down for two copies."'

Michael grinned. 'You both had a nerve.'

'No, sir; that's just it. Mr Elderson got it between wind and water. He didn't like it a little bit.'

'I don't twig,' said Michael.

'My being in this firm's employ, sir. He knows you're a partner here, and Mr Forsyte's son-in-law, doesn't he?'

'He does.'

'Well, sir, you see the connexion – two directors believing me – not *him*. That's why I didn't miss him out. I fancied it'd shake him up. I happened to see his face in the sideboard glass as I went out. *He's* got the wind up all right.'

Michael bit his forefinger, conscious of a twinge of sympathy with Elderson, as for a fly with the first strand of cobweb round his hind leg.

'Thank you, Butterfield,' he said.

When the young man was gone, he sat stabbing his blotting-paper with a paper-knife. What curious 'class' sensation was this? Or was it merely fellow-feeling with the hunted, a tremor

at the way things found one out? For, surely, this was real
evidence, and he would have to pass it on to his father, and
'Old Forsyte'. Elderson's nerve must have gone phut, or he'd
have said: 'You impudent young scoundrel – get out of here!'
That, clearly, was the only right greeting from an innocent,
and the only advisable greeting from a guilty man. Well! Nerve
did fail sometimes – even the best. Witness the very proof-sheet
he had just corrected:

THE COURT MARTIAL

'See 'ere! I'm myde o' nerves and blood
　　The syme as you, not meant to be
Froze stiff up to me ribs in mud.
　　You try it, like I 'ave, an' see!

'Aye, you snug beauty brass hat, when
　　You stick what I stuck out that d'y,
An' keep yer ruddy 'earts up – then
　　You'll learn, maybe, the right to s'y:

'Take aht an' shoot 'im in the snow,
　　Shoot 'im for cowardice! 'E who serves
His King and Country's got to know
　　There's no such bloody thing as nerves.'

Good old Wilfrid!
'Yes, Miss Perren?'
'The letter to Sir James Foggart, Mr Mont; you told me to
remind you. And will you see Miss Manuelli?'
'Miss Manu– Oh! Ah! Yes.'
Bicket's girl wife, whose face they had used on Storbert's
novel, the model for Aubrey Greene's – Michael rose, for the
girl was in the room already.
'I remember that dress!' he thought: 'Fleur never liked it.'
'What can I do for you, Mrs Bicket? How's Bicket, by the
way?'
'Fairly, sir, thank you.'
'Still in balloons?'
'Yes.'

'Well, we all are, Mrs Bicket.'

'Beg pardon?'

'In the air – don't you think? But you didn't come to tell me that?'

'No, sir.'

A slight flush in those sallow cheeks, fingers concerned with the tips of the worn gloves, lips uncertain; but the eyes steady – really an uncommon girl!

'You remember givin' me a note to Mr Greene, sir?'

'I do; and I've seen the result; it's topping, Mrs Bicket.'

'Yes. But it's got into the papers – my husband saw it there last night; and of course, he doesn't know about me.'

Phew! For what had he let this girl in?

'I've made a lot of money at it, sir – almost enough for our passage to Australia; but now I'm frightened. "Isn't it like you?" he said to me. I tore the paper up, but suppose he remembers the name of the Gallery and goes to see the picture! That's even much more like me! He might go on to Mr Greene. So would you mind, sir, speaking to Mr Greene, and beggin' him to say it was someone else, in case Tony did go?'

'Not a bit,' said Michael. 'But do you think Bicket would mind so very much, considering what it's done for you? It can be quite a respectable profession.'

Victorine's hands moved up to her breast.

'Yes,' she said, simply. 'I have been quite respectable. And I only did it because we do so want to get away, and I couldn't bear seein' him standin' in the gutter there sellin' those balloons in the fogs. But I'm ever so scared, sir, now.'

Michael stared.

'My God!' he said; 'money's an evil thing!'

Victorine smiled faintly. 'The want of it is, I know.'

'How much more do you need, Mrs Bicket?'

'Only another ten pound, about, sir.'

'I can let you have that.'

'Oh! thank you; but it's not that – I can easy earn it – I've got used to it; a few more days don't matter.'

'But how are you going to account for having the money?'

'Say I won it bettin'.'

'*Thin!*' said Michael. 'Look here! Say you came to me and I advanced it. If Bicket repays it from Australia, I can always put it to your credit again at a bank out there. I've got you into a hole, in a way, and I'd like to get you out of it.'

'Oh! no, sir; you did me a service. I don't want to put you about, telling falsehoods for me.'

'It won't worry me a bit, Mrs Bicket. I can lie to the um-teenth when there's no harm in it. The great thing for you is to get away sharp. Are there many other pictures of you?'

'Oh! yes, a lot – not that you'd recognize them, I think, they're so square and funny.'

'Ah! well – Aubrey Greene has got you to the life!'

'Yes; it's like me all over, Tony says.'

'Quite. Well, I'll speak to Aubrey, I shall be seeing him at lunch. Here's the ten pounds! That's agreed then? You came to me today – see? Say you had a brain-wave. I quite understand the whole thing. You'd do a lot for him; and he'd do a lot for you. It's all right – don't cry!'

Victorine swallowed violently. Her hand in the worn glove returned his squeeze.

'I'd tell him tonight, if I were you,' said Michael, 'and I'll get ready.'

When she had gone he thought: 'Hope Bicket won't think I received value for that sixty pounds!' And, pressing his bell, he resumed the stabbing of his blotting-paper.

'Yes, Mr Mont?'

'Now let's get on with it, Miss Perren.

'DEAR SIR JAMES FOGGART, — We have given the utmost consideration to your very interesting – er – production. While we are of opinion that the views so well expressed on the present condition of Britain in relation to the rest of the world are of great value to all – er – thinking persons, we do not feel that there are enough – er – thinking persons to make it possible to publish the book, except at a loss. The – er – thesis that Britain should now look for salvation through adjustment of markets, population, supply and demand, within the Empire, put with such exceedingly plain speech, will, we are afraid, get the goat of all the political parties; nor do we feel that your plan of emigrating boys and girls in large quantities before they are spoiled by British town life, can do otherwise than irritate a working-class which knows nothing of conditions outside its own country, and is notably averse to giving its children a chance in any other.'

'Am I to put that, Mr Mont?'

'Yes; but tone it in a bit. Er –

'Finally, your view that the land should be used to grow food is so very unusual in these days, that we feel your book would have a hostile Press except from the Old Guard and the Die-hard, and a few folk with vision.'

'Yes, Mr Mont?'

' "In a period of veering – er – transitions" – keep that, Miss Perren – "and the airy unreality of hopes that have gone up the spout" – almost keep that – "any scheme that looks forward and defers harvest for twenty years, must be extraordinarily un-popular. For all these reasons you will see how necessary it is for you to – er – seek another publisher. In short, we are not taking any.

' "With – er –" what you like – "dear Sir James Foggart,

' "We are your obedient servants,

DANBY AND WINTER." '

'When you've translated that, Miss Perren, bring it in, and I'll sign it.'

'Yes. Only, Mr Mont – I thought you were a Socialist. This almost seems – forgive my asking?'

'Miss Perren, it's struck me lately that labels are "off". How can a man be anything at a time when everything's in the air? Look at the Liberals. They can't see the situation whole because of Free Trade; nor can the Labour Party because of their Capital levy; nor can the Tories because of Protection; they're all hag-ridden by catch-words! Old Sir James Foggart's jolly well right, but nobody's going to listen to him. His book will be waste paper if anybody ever publishes it. The world's unreal just now, Miss Perren; and of all countries we're the most un-real.'

'Why, Mr Mont?'

'Why? Because with the most stickfast of all the national temperaments, we're holding on to what's gone more bust for us than for any other country. Anyway, Mr Danby shouldn't have left the letter to me, if he didn't mean me to enjoy myself. Oh! and while we're about it – I've got to refuse Harold Master's new book. It's a mistake, but they won't have it.'

'Why not, Mr Mont? *The Sobbing Turtle* was such a success!'

'Well, in this new thing Master's got hold of an idea which absolutely forces him to say something. Winter says those who hailed *The Sobbing Turtle* as such a work of art, are certain to be down on this for that; and Mr Danby calls the book an outrage on human nature. So there's nothing for it. Let's have a shot:

'MY DEAR MASTER, – In the exhilaration of your subject it has obviously not occurred to you that you've bust up the show. In *The Sobbing Turtle* you were absolutely in tune with half the orchestra, and that – er – the noisiest half. You were charmingly archaic, and securely cold-blooded. But now, what have you gone and done? Taken the last Marquesan islander for your hero and put him down in London town! This thing's a searching satire, a real criticism of life. I'm sure you didn't mean to be contemporary, or want to burrow into reality; but your subject has run off with you. Cold acid and cold blood are very different things, you know, to say nothing of your having had to drop the archaic. Personally, of course, I think this new thing miles better than *The Sobbing Turtle*, which was a nice little affair, but nothing to make a song about. But I'm not the public, and I'm not the critics. The young and thin will be aggrieved by your lack of modernity, they'll say you're moralizing; the old and fat will call you bitter and destructive; and the ordinary public will take your Marquesan seriously, and resent your making him superior to themselves. The prospects, you see, are not gaudy. How d'you think we're going to "get away" with such a book? Well, we're not! Such is the fiat of the firm. I don't agree with it. I'd publish it tomorrow; but needs must when Danby and Winter drive. So, with every personal regret, I return what is really a masterpiece.

Always yours,

MICHAEL MONT.'

'D'you know, Miss Perren, I don't think you need translate that?'

'I'm afraid it would be difficult.'

'Right-o, then; but do the other, please. I'm going to take my wife out to see a picture; back by four. Oh! and if a little chap called Bicket, that we used to have here, calls any time and asks to see me, he's to come up; but I want warning first. Will you let them know downstairs?'

'Yes, Mr Mont. Oh! didn't – wasn't that Miss Manuelli the model for the wrapper on Mr Storbert's novel?'

'She was, Miss Perren; alone I found her.'

'She's very interesting-looking, isn't she?'

'She's unique, I'm afraid.'

'She needn't mind that, I should think.'

'That depends,' said Michael; and stabbed his blotting-paper.

Chapter Three

'AFTERNOON OF A DRYAD'

◄◄·►►

FLEUR was still gracefully concealing most of what Michael called 'the eleventh baronet', now due in about two months' time. She seemed to be adapting herself, in mind and body, to the quiet and persistent collection of the heir. Michael knew that, from the first, following the instructions of her mother, she had been influencing his sex, repeating to herself, every evening before falling asleep, and every morning on waking the words: 'Day by day, in every way, he is getting more and more male,' to infect the subconscious which, everybody now said, controlled the course of events; and that she was abstaining from the words; 'I *will* have a boy,' for this, setting up a reaction, everybody said, was liable to produce a girl. Michael noted that she turned more and more to her mother, as if the French, or more naturalistic, side of her, had taken charge of a process which

209

had to do with the body. She was frequently at Mapledurham, going down in Soames's car, and her mother was frequently in South Square. Annette's handsome presence, with its tendency to black lace was always pleasing to Michael, who had never forgotten her espousal of his suit in days when it was a forlorn hope. Though he still felt only on the threshold of Fleur's heart, and was preparing to play second fiddle to 'the eleventh baronet', he was infinitely easier in mind since Wilfrid had been gone. And he watched, with a sort of amused adoration, the way in which she focused her collecting powers on an object that had no epoch, a process that did not date.

Personally conducted by Aubrey Greene, the expedition to view his show at the Dumetrius Gallery left South Square after an early lunch.

'Your Dryad came to me this morning, Aubrey,' said Michael in the cab. 'She wanted me to ask you to put up a barrage if by any chance her husband blows round to accuse you of painting his wife. It seems he's seen a reproduction of the picture.'

'Umm!' murmured the painter: 'Shall I, Fleur?'

'Of course you must, Aubrey!'

Aubrey Greene's smile slid from her to Michael.

'Well, what's his name?'

'Bicket.'

Aubrey Greene fixed his eyes on space, and murmured slowly:

> 'An angry young husband called Bicket
> Said: "Turn yourself round and I'll kick it;
>   You have painted my wife
>   In the nude to the life.
> Do you think, Mr Greene, it was cricket?'

'Oh! Aubrey!'

'Chuck it!' said Michael, 'I'm serious. She's a most plucky little creature. She's made the money they wanted, and remained respectable.'

'So far as I'm concerned, certainly.'

'Well, I should think so.'

'Why, Fleur?'

'You're not a vamp, Aubrey!'

'As a matter of fact, she excited my aesthetic sense.'

'Much that'd save her from some aesthetes!' muttered Michael.

'Also, she comes from Putney.'

'There you have a real reason. Then, you *will* put up a barrage if Bicket blows in?'

Aubrey Greene laid his hand on his heart. 'And there we are!'

For the convenience of the eleventh baronet Michael had chosen the hour when the proper patrons of Aubrey Greene would still be lunching. A shock-headed young man and three pale-green girls alone wandered among the pictures. The painter led the way at once to his masterpiece; and for some minutes they stood before it in a suitable paralysis. To speak too soon in praise would never do; to speak too late would be equally tactless; to speak too fulsomely would jar; to mutter coldly: 'Very nice – very nice indeed!' would blight. To say bluntly: 'Well, old man, to tell you the truth, I don't like it a little bit!' would get his goat.

At last Michael pinched Fleur gently, and she said:

'It really is charming, Aubrey; and awfully like – at least –'

'So far as one can tell. But really, old man, you've done it in once. I'm afraid Bicket will think so, anyway.'

'Dash that!' muttered the painter. 'How do you find the colour values?'

'Jolly fine; especially the flesh; don't you think so, Fleur?'

'Yes; only I should have liked that shadow down the side a little deeper.'

'Yes?' murmured the painter: 'Perhaps!'

'You've caught the spirit,' said Michael. 'But I tell you what, old man, you're for it – the thing's got meaning. I don't know what the critics will do to you.'

Aubrey Greene smiled. 'That was the worst of her. She led me on. To get an idea's fatal.'

'Personally, I don't agree to that; do you, Fleur?'

'Of course not; only one doesn't say so.'

'Time we did, instead of kow-towing to the Café C'rillon. I say, the hair's all right, and so are the toes – they curl as you look at 'em.'

'And it *is* a relief not to get legs painted in streaky cubes. The asphodels rather remind one of the flowers in Leonardo's *Virgin of the Rocks*, Aubrey.'

'The whole thing's just a bit Leonardoish, old man. You'll have to live that down.'

'Oh! Aubrey, my father's seen it. I believe he's biting. Something you said impressed him – about our white monkey, d'you remember?'

Aubrey Greene threw up his hands. 'Ah! That white monkey – to have painted that! Eat the fruit and chuck the rinds around, and ask with your eyes what it's all about.'

'A moral!' said Michael: 'Take care, old man! Well! Our taxi's running up. Come along, Fleur; we'll leave Aubrey to his conscience.'

Once more in the cab, he took her arm.

'That poor little snipe, Bicket! Suppose I'd come on *you* as he'll come on his wife!'

'I shouldn't have looked so nice.'

'Oh! yes; much nicer; though she looks nice enough, I must say.'

'Then why should Bicket mind, in these days of emancipation?'

'Why? Good Lord, ducky! you don't suppose Bicket –! I mean, we emancipated people have got into the habit of thinking we're the world – well! we aren't; we're an excrescence, small, and noisy. We talk as if all the old values and prejudices had gone; but they've no more gone, really, you know, than the rows of villas and little grey houses.'

'Why this outburst, Michael?'

'Well, darling, I'm a bit fed-up with the attitude of our crowd. If emancipation were true, one could stick it; but it's not. There isn't ten per cent difference between now and thirty years ago.'

'How do you know? You weren't alive.'

'No; but I read the papers, and talk to the man in the street, and look at people's faces. Our lot think they're the tablecloth, but they're only the fringe. D'you know, only one hundred and fifty thousand people in this country have ever heard a Beethoven Symphony? How many, do you suppose, think old B. a back number? Five thousand, perhaps, out of forty-two millions. How's that for emancipation?'

He stopped, observing that her eyelids had drooped.

'I was thinking, Michael, that I should like to change my bedroom curtains to blue. I saw the exact colour yesterday at Harton's. They say blue has an effect on the mind – the present curtains really are too jazzy.'

The eleventh baronet!

'Anything you like, darling. Have a blue ceiling if it helps.'

'Oh, no! But I think I'll change the carpet, too; there's a lovely powder blue at Harton's.'

'Then get it. Would you like to go there now? I can take the Tube back to the office.'

'Yes, I think I'd better. I might miss it.'

Michael put his head out of the window. 'Harton's, please!' And, replacing his hat, he looked at her. Emancipated! Phew!

Chapter Four

AFTERNOON OF A BICKET

JUST about that moment Bicket re-entered his sitting-room and deposited his tray. All the morning under the shadow of St Paul's he had re-lived Bank Holiday. Exceptionally tired in feet and legs, he was also itching mentally. He had promised himself a refreshing look from time to time at what was almost like a photo of Vic herself. And he had lost the picture! Yet he had taken nothing out of his pockets – just hung his coat up. Had it jogged out in the crush at the station, or had he missed his pocket opening and dropped it in the carriage? And he had wanted to see the original, too. He remembered that the Gallery began with a 'D', and at lunch-time squandered a penny-half-penny to look up the names. Foreign, he was sure – the picture being naked. 'Dumetrius?' Ah!

Back at his post, he had a bit of luck. 'That alderman', whom he had not seen for months, came by. Intuition made him say at once: 'Hope I see you well sir. Never forgotten your kindness.'

The 'alderman', who had been staring up as if he saw a magpie on the dome of St Paul's, stopped as though attacked by cramp.

'Kindness?' he said; 'what kindness? Oh! Balloons! They were no good to me!'

'No, sir, I'm sure,' said Bicket humbly.

'Well, here you are!' muttered the 'alderman'; 'don't expect it again.'

Half a crown! A whole half-crown! Bicket's eyes pursued the hastening form. 'Good luck!' he said softly to himself, and began putting up his tray. 'I'll go home and rest my feet, and tyke Vic to see that picture. It'll be funny lookin' at it together.'

But she was not in. He sat down and smoked a fag. He felt aggrieved that she was out, this the first afternoon he had taken off. Of course she couldn't stay in all day! Still –! He waited twenty minutes, then put on Michael's suit and shoes.

'I'll go and see it alone,' he thought. 'It'll cost half as much. They charge you sixpence, I expect.'

They charged him a shilling – a shilling! One fourth of his day's earnings, to see a picture! He entered bashfully. There were ladies who smelled of scent and had drawling voices but not a patch on Vic for looks. One of them, behind him, said:

'See! There's Aubrey Greene himself! And that's the picture they're talking of – *Afternoon of a Dryad*.'

They passed him and moved on. Bicket followed. At the end of the room, between their draperies and catalogues, he glimpsed the picture. A slight sweat broke out on his forehead. Almost life-size, among the flowers and spiky grasses, the face smiled round at him – very image of Vic! Could someone in the world be as like her as all that? The thought offended him, as a collector is offended finding the duplicate of a unique possession.

'It's a wonderful picture, Mr Greene. What a type!'

A young man without hat, and fair hair sliding back, answered:

'A find, wasn't she?'

'Oh! perfect! the very spirit of a wood-nymph; so mysterious!'

The word that belonged to Vic! It was unholy. There she lay for all to look at, just because some beastly woman was made like her! A kind of rage invaded Bicket's throat, caused his cheeks to burn; and with it came a queer physical jealousy. That painter! What business had he to paint a woman so like Vic as that – a woman that didn't mind lyin' like that! They and their talk about cahryscuro and paganism, and a bloke called Leneardo! Blast their drawling and their tricks! He tried to move away, and could not, fascinated by that effigy, so uncannily resembling what he had thought belonged to himself alone. Silly to feel so bad over a 'coincidence', but he felt like smashing the glass and cutting the body up into little bits. The ladies and the painter passed on, leaving him alone before the picture. Alone, he did not mind so much. The face was mournful-like, and lonely, and – and teasing, with its smile. It sort of haunted you – it did! 'Well!' thought Bicket, 'I'll get home to Vic. Glad I didn't bring her, after all, to see herself-like. If I was an alderman, I'd buy the blinkin' thing, and burn it!'

And there, in the entrance-lobby, talking to a 'dago', stood – his very own 'alderman'! Bicket paused in sheer amazement.

'It's a rithing name, Mr Forthyte,' he heard the Dago say: 'hith prithes are going up.'

'That's all very well, Dumetrius, but it's not everybody's money in these days – too highly-finished, altogether!'

'Well, Mr Forthyte, to *you* I take off ten per thent.'

'Take off twenty and I'll buy it.'

That Dago's shoulders mounted above his hairy ears – they did; and what a smile!

'Mithter Forthyte! Fifteen, thir!'

'Well, you're doing me; but send it round to my daughter's in South Square – you know the number. When do you close?'

'Day after tomorrow, thir.'

So! The counterfeit of Vic had gone to that 'alderman', had it? Bicket uttered a savage little sound, and slunk out.

He walked with a queer feeling. Had he got unnecessary wind up? After all, it wasn't her. But to know that another woman could smile that way, have frizzy-ended short black hair, and be all curved the same! And at every woman's passing face he looked – so different, so utterly unlike Vic's!

When he reached home she was standing in the middle of the room, with her lips to a balloon. All around her, on the floor, chairs, table, mantelpiece, were the blown-out shapes of his stock; one by one they had floated from her lips and selected their own resting-places: puce, green, orange, purple, blue, enlivening with their colour the dingy little space. All his balloons blown up! And there, in her best clothes, she stood, smiling, queer, excited.

'What in thunder!' said Bicket.

Raising her dress, she took some crackling notes from the top of her stocking, and held them out to him.

'See! Sixty-four pounds, Tony! I've got it all. We can go.'

'*What!*'

'I had a brain-wave – went to that Mr Mont who gave us the clothes, and he's advanced it. We can pay it back, some day. Isn't it a marvel?'

Bicket's eyes, startled like a rabbit's, took in her smile, her excited flush, and a strange feeling shot through all his body, as if *they* were taking *him* in! She wasn't like Vic! No! Suddenly he felt her arms round him, felt her moist lips on his. She clung so tight, he could not move. His head went round.

'At last! At last! Isn't it fine? Kiss me, Tony!'

Bicket kissed; his vertigo was real, but behind it, for the moment stifled, what sense of unreality! ...

Was it before night, or in the night, that the doubt first came – ghostly, tapping, fluttering, haunting – then, in the dawn, jabbing through his soul, turning him rigid. The money – the picture – the lost paper – that sense of unreality! This story she had told him! Were such things possible? Why should Mr Mont advance that money? She had seen him – that was certain; the room, the secretary – you couldn't mistake her description of that Miss Perren. Why, then, feel this jabbing doubt? The money – such a lot of money! Not with Mr Mont – never – he was a gent! Oh! Swine that he was, to have a thought like that – of Vic! He turned his back to her and tried to sleep. But once you got a thought like that – sleep? No! Her face among the balloons, the way she had smothered his eyes and turned his head – so that he couldn't think, couldn't go into it and ask her questions! A prey to dim doubts, achings, uncertainty, thrills of hope, and visions of 'Austrylia', Bicket arose haggard.

'Well,' he said, over their cocoa and margarined bread: 'I must see Mr Mont, that's certain.' And suddenly he added: 'Vic?' looking straight into her face.

She answered his look – straight, yes, straight. Oh! he was a proper swine! ...

When he had left the house Victorine stood quite still, with hands pressed against her chest. She had slept less than he. Still as a mouse, she had turned and turned the thought: 'Did I take him in? Did I?' And if not – what? She took out the notes which had bought – or sold? – their happiness, and counted them once more. And the sense of injustice burned within her. Had she wanted to stand like that before men? Hadn't she been properly through it about that? Why, she could have had the sixty pounds three months ago from that sculptor, who was wild about her; or – so he said! But she had stuck it; yes, she had. Tony had nothing against her really – even if he knew it all. She had done it for him – Well! mostly – for him selling those balloons day after day in all weathers! But for her, they would still be stuck, and another winter coming, and unemployment – so they said in the paper – to be worse and worse! Stuck in the fogs and the cold, again! Ugh! Her chest was still funny sometimes; and he always hoarse. And this poky little room, and the bed so small that she couldn't stir without waking him. Why should Tony doubt her? For he did – she had felt it, heard it in his 'Vic?' Would Mr Mont convince him? Tony was sharp! Her head drooped. The unfairness of it all! Some had everything to their hand, like that pretty wife of Mr Mont's! And if one tried to find a way and get out to a new chance – then – then – this! She flung her hair back. Tony *must* believe – he should! If he wouldn't, let him look out. She had done nothing to be ashamed of! No, indeed! And with the longing to go in front and lead her happiness along, she got out her old tin trunk, and began with careful method to put things into it.

Chapter Five

MICHAEL GIVES ADVICE

MICHAEL still sat, correcting the proofs of *Counterfeits*. Save 'Jericho', there had been no address to send them to. The East was wide, and Wilfrid had made no sign. Did Fleur ever think of Wilfrid – well, probably he was forgetting her already. Even passion required a little sustenance.

'A Mr Forsyte to see you, sir.'

Apparition in bookland!

'Ah! Show him in.'

Soames entered with an air of suspicion.

'This your place?' he said. 'I've looked in to tell you that I've bought that picture of young Greene's. Have you anywhere to hang it?'

'I should think we had,' said Michael. 'Jolly good, sir, isn't it?'

'Well,' muttered Soames, 'for these days, yes. He'll make a name.'

'He's an intense admirer of that White Monkey you gave us.'

'Ah! I've been looking into the Chinese. If I go on buying –'
Soames paused.

'They *are* a bit of an antidote, aren't they, sir?' That "Earthly
Paradise"! And those geese – they don't seem to mind your
counting their feathers, do they?'

Soames made no reply; he was evidently thinking: 'How on
earth I missed those things when they first came on the market!'
Then, raising his umbrella, and pointing it as if at the book
trade, he asked:

'Young Butterfield – how's he doing?'

'Ah! I was going to let you know, sir. He came in yesterday
and told me that he saw Elderson two days ago. He went to sell
him a copy of my father's "Limited"; Elderson said nothing and
bought two.'

'The deuce he did!'

'Butterfield got the impression that his visit put the wind up
him. Elderson knows, of course, that I'm in this firm, and your
son-in-law.'

Soames frowned. 'I'm not sure,' he said, 'that sleeping
dogs –! Well, I'm on my way there now.'

'Mention the book, sir, and see how Elderson takes it. Would
you like one yourself? You're on the list. E, F – Butterfield
should be reaching you today. It'll save you a refusal. Here it is
– nice get-up. One guinea.'

'*A Duet*,' read Soames. 'What's it about? Musical?'

'Not precisely. A sort of cat-calling between the ghosts of the
G.O.M. and Dizzy!'

'I'm not a reader,' said Soames. He pulled out a note. 'Why
didn't you make it a pound? Here's the shilling.'

'Thanks awfully, sir; I'm sure my father'll be frightfully
bucked to think you've got one.'

'Will he?' said Soames, with a faint smile. 'D'you ever do any
work here?'

'Well, we try to turn a doubtful penny.'

'What d'you make at it?'

'Personally, about five hundred a year.'

'That all?'

'Yes, but I doubt if I'm worth more than three.'

'H'm! I thought you'd got over your Socialism.'

'I fancy I have, sir. It didn't seem to go with my position.'

'No,' said Soames. 'Fleur seems well.'

'Yes, she's splendid. She does the Coué stunt, you know.'

Soames stared. 'That's her mother,' he said; 'I can't tell. Good-bye! Oh! I want to know; what's the meaning of that expression "got his goat"?'

'"Got his goat"? Oh, raised his dander, if you know what that means, it was before my time.'

'I see,' said Soames; 'I had it right, then. Well!' He turned. His back was very neat and real. It vanished through the doorway, and with it seemed to go the sense of definition.

Michael took up the proofs, and read two poems. Bitter as quinine! The unrest in them – the yearning behind the words! Nothing Chinese there! After all, the ancients – like Old Forsyte, and his father in a very different way – had an anchor down. 'What is it?' thought Michael. 'What's wrong with us? We're quick, and clever, cocksure, and dissatisfied. If only something would enthuse us, or get *our* goats! We've chucked religion, tradition, property, pity; and in their place we put – what? Beauty? Gosh! See Walter Nazing, and the Café C'rillon! and yet – we must be after something! Better world? Doesn't look like it. Future life? Suppose I ought to "look into" spiritualism, as Old Forsyte would say. But – half in this world, half in that – deuced odd if spirits are less restive than we are!'

To what – to what, then, was it all moving?

'Dash it!' thought Michael, getting up, 'I'll try dictating an advertisement!'

'Will you come in, please, Miss Perren? For the new Desert volume – Trade Journals: "Danby and Winter will shortly issue *Counterfeits*, by the author of *Copper Coin*, the outstanding success of the last publishing season." I wonder how many publishers have claimed that, Miss Perren, for how many books this year? "These poems show all the brilliancy of mood, and more than the technical accomplishment of the young author's first volume." How's that?'

'Brilliancy of mood, Mr Mont? Do you think?'

'No. But what am I to say? "All the pangs and pessimism"?'

'Oh, no! But possibly: "All the brilliancy of diction. The strangeness and variety of mood." '

'Good. But it'll cost more. Say: "All the brilliant strangeness"; that'll ring their bells in once. We're nuts on "the strange", but we're not getting it – the *outré*, yes, but not the strange.'

'Surely Mr Desert gets –'

'Yes, sometimes; but hardly anyone else. To be strange, you've got to have guts, if you'll excuse the phrase, Miss Perren.'

'Certainly, Mr Mont. That young man Bicket is waiting to see you.'

'He is, is he?' said Michael, taking out a cigarette. 'Give me time to tighten my belt, Miss Perren, and ask him up.'

'The lie benevolent,' he thought; 'now for it!'

The entrance of Bicket into a room where his last appearance had been so painful, was accomplished with a certain stolidity. Michael stood, back to the hearth, smoking; Bicket, back to a pile of modern novels, with the words 'This great new novel' on it. Michael nodded.

'Hallo, Bicket!'

Bicket nodded.

'Hope you're keeping well, sir?'

'Frightfully well, thank you.' And there was silence.

'Well,' said Michael at last, 'I suppose you've come about that little advance to your wife. It's quite all right; no hurry whatever.'

While saying this he had become conscious that the 'little snipe' was dreadfully disturbed. His eyes had a most peculiar look, those large, shrimp-like eyes which seemed, as it were, in advance of the rest of him. He hastened on:

'I believe in Australia myself. I think you're perfectly right, Bicket, and the sooner you go, the better. She doesn't look too strong.'

Bicket swallowed.

'Sir,' he said, 'you've been a gent to me, and it's hard to say things.'

'Then don't.'

Bicket's cheeks became suffused with blood: queer effect in that pale, haggard face.

'It isn't what you think,' he said: 'I've come to ask you to tell me the truth.' Suddenly he whipped from his pocket what Michael perceived to be a crumpled novel-wrapper.

'I took this from a book on the counter as I came by, downstairs. There! Is that my wife?' He stretched it out.

Michael beheld with consternation the wrapper of Storbert's novel. One thing to tell the lie benevolent already determined on — quite another to deny this!

Bicket gave him little time.

'I see it is, from your fyce,' he said. 'What's it all mean? I want the truth — I must 'ave it! I'm gettin' wild over all this. If that's 'er fyce there, then that's 'er body in the Gallery — Aubrey Greene; it's the syme nyme. What's it all mean?' His face had become almost formidable; his cockney accent very broad. 'What gyme 'as she been plyin'? You gotta tell me before I go aht of 'ere.'

Michael's heels came together. He said quietly:

'Steady, Bicket.'

'Steady! You'd be steady if *your* wife — ! All that money! *You* never advanced it — you never give it 'er — never! Don't tell me you did!'

Michael had taken his line. No lies!

'I lent her ten pounds to make a round sum of it — that's all; the rest she earned — honourably; and you ought to be proud of her.'

Bicket's mouth fell open.

'Proud? And how's she earned it? Proud! My Gawd!'

Michael said coldly:

'As a model. I myself gave her the introduction to my friend, Mr Greene, the day you had lunch with me. You've heard of models, I suppose?'

Bicket's hands tore the wrapper, and the pieces fell to the floor. 'Models!' he said: 'Pynters – yes, I've 'eard of 'em – Swines!'

'No more swine than you are, Bicket. Be kind enough not to insult my friend. Pull yourself together, man, and take a cigarette.'

Bicket dashed the proffered case aside.

'I – I – was stuck on her,' he said passionately, 'and she's put this up on me!' A sort of sob came out of his lungs.

'You were stuck on her,' said Michael; his voice had sting in it. 'And when she does her best for you, you turn her down – is that it? Do you suppose she liked it?'

Bicket covered his face suddenly.

'What should I know?' he muttered from behind his hands. A wave of pity flooded up in Michael. Pity! Blurb!

He said dryly: 'When you've quite done, Bicket. D'you happen to remember what *you* did for *her*?'

Bicket uncovered his face and stared wildly. 'You've never told her that?'

'No; but I jolly well will if you don't pull yourself together.'

'What do I care if you do, now – lyin' like that, for all the men in the world! Sixty pounds! Honourably! D'you think I believe that?' His voice had desolation in it.

'Ah!' said Michael. 'You don't believe simply because you're ignorant, as ignorant as the swine you talk of. A girl can do what she did and be perfectly honest, as I haven't the faintest doubt she is. You've only to look at her, and hear the way she speaks of it. She did it because she couldn't bear to see you selling those balloons. She did it to get you out of the gutter, and give you both a chance. And now you've got the chance, you kick up like this. Dash it all, Bicket, be a sport! Suppose I tell her what you did for her – d'you think she's going to squirm and squeal? Not she! It was damned human of you, and it was damned human of her; and don't you forget it!'

Bicket swallowed violently again.

'It's all very well,' he said sullenly; 'it 'asn't 'appened to you.'

Michael was afflicted at once. No! It hadn't happened to him! And all his doubts of Fleur in the days of Wilfrid came hitting him.

'Look here, Bicket,' he said, 'do you doubt your wife's affection? The whole thing is there. I've only seen her twice, but I don't see how you can. If she weren't fond of you, why should she want to go to Australia, when she knows she can make good money here, and enjoy herself if she wants? I can vouch for my friend Greene. He's dashed decent, and I *know* he's played cricket.'

But, searching Bicket's face, he wondered: Were all the others she had sat to as dashed decent?

'Look here, Bicket! We all get up against it sometimes; and that's the test of us. You've just *got* to believe in her; there's nothing else to it.'

'To myke a show of herself for all the world to see!' The words seemed to struggle from the skinny throat. 'I saw that picture bought yesterday by a ruddy alderman.'

Michael could not conceal a grin at this description of 'Old Forsyte'.

'As a matter of fact,' he said, 'it was bought by my own father-in-law as a present to us, to hang in our house. And, mind you, Bicket, it's a fine thing.'

'Ah!' cried Bicket, 'it *is* a fine thing! Money! It's money bought her. Money'll buy anything. It'll buy the 'eart out of your chest.'

And Michael thought: 'I can't get away with it a bit! What price emancipation? He's never heard of the Greeks! And if he had, they'd seem to him a lot of loose-living foreigners. I must quit.' And, suddenly, he saw tears come out of those shrimp's eyes, and trickle down the hollowed cheeks.

Very disturbed, he said hastily:

'When you get out there, you'll never think of it again. Hang it all, Bicket, be a man! She did it for the best. If I were you, I'd never let on to her that I knew. That's what she'd do if I told her how you snooped those *Copper Coins*.'

Bicket clenched his fists – the action went curiously with the tears; then, without a word, he turned and shuffled out.

'Well,' thought Michael, 'giving advice is clearly not my stunt! Poor little snipe!'

Chapter Six

QUITTANCE

◄–‹–›–►

BICKET stumbled, half-blind, along the Strand. Naturally good-tempered, such a nerve-storm made him feel ill, and bruised in the brain. Sunlight and motion slowly restored some power of thought. He had got the truth. But was it the whole and nothing but the truth? Could she have made all that money without –? If he could believe that, then, perhaps – out of this country where people could see her naked for a shilling – he might forget. But – all that money! And even if all earned 'honourable', as Mr Mont had put it, in how many days, exposed to the eyes of how many men? He groaned aloud in the street. The thought of going home to her – of a scene, of what he might learn if there *were* a scene, was just about unbearable. And yet – must do it, he supposed. He could have borne it better under St Paul's, standing in the gutter, offering his balloons. A man of leisure for the first time in his life, a blooming 'alderman' with nothing to do but step in and take a ticket to the ruddy butterflies! And he owed that leisure to what a man with nothing to take his thoughts off simply could not bear! He would rather have snaffled the money out of a shop till. Better that on his soul, than the jab of this dark fiendish sexual jealousy. 'Be a man!' Easy said! 'Pull yourself together! She did it for you!' He would a hundred times rather she had not. Blackfriars Bridge! A dive, and an end in the mud down there? But you had to rise three times; they would fish you out alive, and run you in for it – and nothing gained – not even the pleasure of thinking that Vic would see what she had done, when she came to identify the body. Dead was dead, anyway, and he would never know what she felt post-mortem! He trudged across the bridge, keeping his eyes before him. Little Ditch Street – how he used to scuttle down it, back to her, when she had pneumonia! Would he never feel like that again? He strode past the window, and went in.

Victorine was still bending over the brown tin trunk. She straightened herself, and on her face came a cold, tired look.

'Well,' she said, 'I see you know.'

Bicket had but two steps to take in that small room. He took them, and put his hands on her shoulders. His face was close, his eyes, so large and strained, searched hers.

'I know you've myde a show of yourself for all London to see; what I want to know is – the rest!'

Victorine stared back at him.

'The rest!' she said – it was not a question, just a repetition, in a voice that seemed to mean nothing.

'Ah!' said Bicket hoarsely; 'the rest – Well?'

'If you think there's a "rest", that's enough.'

Bicket jerked his hands away.

'Aoh! for the land's sake, daon't be mysterious. I'm 'alf orf me nut!'

'I see that,' said Victorine; 'and I see this: You aren't what I thought you. D'you think I liked doing it?' She raised her dress and took out the notes. 'There you are! You can go to Australia without me.'

Bicket cried hoarsely: 'And leave you to the blasted pynters?'

'And leave me to meself. Take them!'

But Bicket recoiled against the door, staring at the notes with horror. 'Not me!'

'Well, *I* can't keep 'em. I earned them to get you out of this.'

There was a long silence, while the notes lay between them on the table, still crisp if a little greasy – the long-desired, the dreamed-of means of release, of happiness together in the sunshine. There they lay; neither would take them! What then?

'Vic,' said Bicket at last, in a hoarse whisper, 'swear you never let 'em touch you!'

'Yes, I can swear that.'

And she could smile, too, saying it – that smile of hers! How believe her – living all these months, keeping it from him, telling him a lie about it in the end! He sank into a chair by the table and laid his head on his arms.

Victorine turned and began pulling an old cord round the trunk. He raised his head at the tiny sound. Then she really meant to go away! He saw his life devastated, empty as a coconut on Hampstead Heath; and all defence ran melted out of his cockney spirit. Tears rolled from his eyes.

'When you were ill,' he said, 'I stole for you. I got the sack for it.'

She spun round. 'Tony – you never told me! What did you steal?'

'Books. All your extra feedin' was books.'

For a long minute she stood looking at him, then stretched out her hands without a word. Bicket seized them.

'I don't care about anything,' he gasped, 'so 'elp me, so long as you're fond of me, Vic!'

'And I don't neither. Oh! let's get out of this, Tony! this awful little room, this awful country. Let's get out of it all!'

'Yes,' said Bicket; and put her hands to his eyes.

Chapter Seven

LOOKING INTO ELDERSON

◄‹–›►

SOAMES had left Danby and Winter divided in thought between Elderson and the White Monkey. As Fleur surmised, he had never forgotten Aubrey Greene's words concerning that bit of salvage from the wreck of George Forsyte. 'Eat the fruits of life, scatter the rinds, and get copped doing it.' His application of them tended towards the field of business.

The country was still living on its capital. With the collapse

of the carrying trade and European markets, they were import-
ing food they couldn't afford to pay for. In his opinion they
would get copped doing it, and that before long. British credit
was all very well, the wonder of the world and that, but you
couldn't live indefinitely on wonder. With shipping idle, concerns making a loss all over the place, and the unemployed in
swarms, it was a pretty pair of shoes! Even insurance must
suffer before long. Perhaps that chap Elderson had foreseen
this already, and was simply feathering his nest in time. If one
was to be copped in any case, why bother to be honest? This was
cynicism so patent, that all the Forsyte in Soames rejected it;
and yet it would keep coming back. In a general bankruptcy,
why trouble with thrift, far-sightedness, integrity? Even the
Conservatives were refusing to call themselves Conservatives
again, as if there were something ridiculous about the word, and
they knew there was really nothing left to conserve. 'Eat the
fruit, scatter the rinds and get copped doing it.' That young
painter had said a clever thing – yes, and his picture was clever,
though Dumetrius had done one over the price – as usual!
Where would Fleur hang it? In the hall, he shouldn't be surprised – good light there; and the sort of people they knew
wouldn't jib at the nude. Curious – where all the nudes went to!
You never saw a nude – no more than you saw the proverbial
dead donkey! Soames had a momentary vision of dying donkeys
laden with pictures of the nude, stepping off the edge of the
world. Refusing its extravagance, he raised his eyes, just in time
to see St Paul's, as large as life. That little beggar with his balloons wasn't there today! Well – he'd nothing for him! At a
tangent his thoughts turned towards the object of his pilgrimage
– the P.P.R.S. and its half-year's accounts. At his suggestion,
they were writing off that German business wholesale – a dead
loss of two hundred and thirty thousand pounds. There would
be no interim dividend, and even then they would be carrying
forward a debit towards the next half-year. Well! better have a
rotten tooth out at once and done with; the shareholders would
have six months to get used to the gap before the general meeting. He himself had got used to it already, and so would they in

time. Shareholders were seldom nasty unless startled – a long-suffering lot!

In the board-room the old clerk was still filling his ink-pots from the magnum.

'Manager in?'

'Yes, sir.'

'Say I'm here, will you?'

The old clerk withdrew. Soames looked at the clock. Twelve! A little shaft of sunlight slanted down the wainscotting and floor. There was nothing else alive in the room save a bluebottle and the tick of the clock; not even a daily paper. Soames watched the bluebottle. He remembered how, as a boy, he had preferred bluebottles and greenbottles to the ordinary fly, because of their bright colour. It was a lesson. The showy things, the brilliant people, were the dangerous. Witness the Kaiser, and that precious Italian poet – what was his name! And this Jack-o'-lantern of their own! He shouldn't be surprised if Elderson were brilliant in private life. Why didn't the chap come? Was that encounter with young Butterfield giving him pause? The bluebottle crawled up the pane, buzzed down, crawled up again; the sunlight stole inward along the floor. All was vacuous in the board-room, as though embodying the principle of insurance: 'Keep things as they are.'

'Can't kick my heels here for ever,' thought Soames, and moved to the window. In that wide street leading to the river, sunshine illumined a few pedestrians and a brewer's dray, but along the main artery at the end the traffic streamed and rattled. London! A monstrous place! And all insured! 'What'll it be like thirty years hence?' he thought. To think that there would be London, without himself to see it! He felt sorry for the place, sorry for himself. Even old Gradman would be gone. He supposed the insurance societies would look after it, but he didn't know. And suddenly he became aware of Elderson. The fellow looked quite jaunty, in a suit of dittoes and a carnation.

'Contemplating the future, Mr Forsyte?'

'No,' said Soames. How had the fellow guessed his thoughts? 'I'm glad you've come in. It gives me a chance to say how grateful I am for the interest you take in the concern. It's rare. A manager has a lonely job.'

Was he mocking? He seemed altogether very spry and uppish. Light-heartedness always made Soames suspicious – there was generally some reason for it.

'If every director were as conscientious as you, one would sleep in one's bed. I don't mind telling you that the amount of help I got from the Board before you came on it was – well – negligible.'

Flattery! The fellow must be leading up to something!

Elderson went on:

'I can say to you what I couldn't say to any of the others: I'm not at all happy about business, Mr Forsyte. England is just about to discover the state she's really in.'

Faced with this startling confirmation of his own thoughts, Soames reacted.

'No good crying out before we're hurt,' he said; 'the pound's still high. We're good stayers.'

'In the soup, I'm afraid. If something drastic isn't done – we *shall* stay there. And anything drastic, as you know, means disorganization and lean years before you reap reward.'

How could the fellow talk like this, and look as bright and pink as a new penny? It confirmed the theory that he didn't care what happened. And, suddenly, Soames resolved to try a shot.

'Talking of lean years – I came in to say that I think we must call a meeting of the shareholders over this dead loss of the German business.' He said it to the floor, and looked quickly up. The result was disappointing. The manager's light-grey eyes met his without a blink.

'I've been expecting that from you,' he said.

'The deuce you have!' thought Soames, for it had but that moment come into his mind.

'By all means call one,' went on the manager; 'but I'm afraid the Board won't like it.'

Soames refrained from saying: 'Nor do I.'

'Nor the shareholders, Mr Forsyte. In a long experience I've found that the less you rub their noses in anything unpleasant, the better for everyone.'

'That may be,' said Soames, stiffening in contrariety; 'but it's all a part of the vice of not facing things.'

'I don't think, Mr Forsyte, that you will accuse *me* of not facing things, in the time to come.'

Time to come! Now, what on earth did the fellow mean by that?

'Well, I shall moot it at the next Board,' he said.

'Quite!' said the manager. 'Nothing like bringing things to a head, is there?'

Again that indefinable mockery, as if he had something up his sleeve. Soames looked mechanically at the fellow's cuffs – beautifully laundered, with a blue stripe; at his holland waistcoat, and his bird's-eye tie – a regular dandy. He would give him a second barrel!

'By the way,' he said, 'Mont's written a book. I've taken a copy.'

Not a blink! A little more show of teeth, perhaps – false, no doubt!

'I've taken two – poor, dear Mont!'

Soames had a sense of defeat. This chap was armoured like a crab, varnished like a Spanish table.

'Well,' he said, 'I must go.'

The manager held out his hand.

'Good-bye, Mr Forsyte. I'm so grateful to you.'

The fellow was actually squeezing his hand. Soames went out confused. To have his hand squeezed was so rare! It undermined him. And yet, it might be the crown of a consummate bit of acting. He couldn't tell. He had, however, less intention even than before of moving for a meeting of the shareholders. No, no! That had just been a shot to get a rise; and it had failed. But the Butterfield shot had gone home, surely! If innocent, Elderson must certainly have alluded to the impudence of the young man's call. And yet such a cool card was capable of failing to rise, just to tease you! No! nothing doing – as they said nowadays. He was as far as ever from a proof of guilt; and to speak truth, glad of it. Such a scandal could serve no purpose save that of blackening the whole concern, directors and all. People were so careless, they never stopped to think, or apportion blame where it was due. Keep a sharp eye open, and go on as they were! No good stirring hornets' nests! He had got so far in thought and progress, when a voice said:

'Well met, Forsyte! Are you going my way?'

'Old Mont', coming down the steps of 'Snooks'!

'I don't know,' said Soames.

'I'm off to the Aeroplane for lunch.'

'That new-fangled place?'

'Rising, you know, Forsyte – rising.'

'I've just been seeing Elderson. He's bought two copies of your book.'

'Dear me! Poor fellow!'

Soames smiled faintly. 'That's what he said of you! And who d'you think sold them to him? Young Butterfield.'

'Is he still alive?'

'He was this morning.'

Sir Lawrence's face took on a twist:

'I've been thinking, Forsyte. They tell me Elderson keeps two women.'

Soames stared. The idea was attractive; would account for everything.

'My wife says it's one too many, Forsyte. What do you say?'

'I?' said Soames. 'I only know the chap's as cool as a cucumber. I'm going in here. Good-bye!'

One could get no help from that baronet fellow; he couldn't take anything seriously. Two women! At Elderson's age! What a life! There were always men like that, not content with one thing at a time – living dangerously. It was mysterious to him. You might look and look into chaps like that, and see nothing. And yet, there they were! He crossed the hall, and went into the room where connoisseurs were lunching. Taking down the menu at the service table, he ordered himself a dozen oysters; but, suddenly remembering that the month contained no 'r', changed them to a fried sole.

Chapter Eight

LEVANTED

❁

'No, dear heart, Nature's "off"!'

'How d'you mean, Michael?'

'Well, look at the Nature novels we get. Sedulous stuff pitched on Cornish cliffs or Yorkshire moors – ever been on a Yorkshire moor? – it comes off on you; and the Dartmoor brand. Gosh! Dartmoor, where the passions come from – ever been on Dartmoor? Well, they don't, you know. And the South Sea bunch! Oh, la la! And the poets, the splash-and-splutter school don't get within miles of Nature. The village idiot school is a bit better, certainly. After all, old Wordsworth made Nature, and she's a bromide. Of course, there's raw nature with the small "n"; but if you come up against that, it takes you all your time to keep alive – the Nature we gas about is licensed, nicely blended and bottled. She's not modern enough for contemporary style.'

'Oh! well, let's go on the river, anyway, Michael. We can have tea at "The Shelter".'

They were just reaching what Michael always called 'this desirable residence', when Fleur leaned forward, and, touching his knee, said:

'I'm not half as nice to you as you deserve, Michael.'

'Good Lord, darling! I thought you were.'

'I know I'm selfish; especially just now.'

'It's only the eleventh baronet.'

'Yes; it's a great responsibility. I only hope he'll be like you.'

Michael slid in to the landing-stage, shipped his sculls, and sat down beside her.

'If he's like me, I shall disown him. But sons take after their mothers.'

'I meant in character. I want him frightfully to be cheerful and not restless, and have the feeling that life's worth while.'

Michael stared at her lips – they were quivering; at her cheek, slightly browned by the afternoon's sunning; and, bending sideways, he put his own against it.

'He'll be a sunny little cuss, I'm certain.'

Fleur shook her head.

'I don't want him greedy and self-centred; it's in my blood, you know. I can see it's ugly, but I can't help it. How do you manage not to be?'

Michael ruffled his hair with his free hand.

'The sun isn't too hot for you, is it, ducky?'

'No. Seriously, Michael – how?'

'But I *am*. Look at the way I want you. Nothing will cure me of that.'

A slight pressure of her cheek on his own was heartening, and he said:

'Do you remember coming down the garden one night, and finding me in a boat just here? When you'd gone, I stood on my head, to cool it. I was on my uppers; I didn't think I'd got an earthly –' He stopped. No! He would not remind her, but that was the night when she said: 'Come again when I know I can't get my wish!' The unknown cousin!

Fleur said quietly:

'I was a pig to you, Michael, but I was awfully unhappy. That's gone. It's gone at last; there's nothing wrong now, except my own nature.'

Conscious that his feelings betrayed the period, Michael said:

'Oh! if that's all! What price tea?'

They went up the lawn arm-in-arm. Nobody was at home – Soames in London, Annette at a garden party.

'We'll have tea on the verandah, please,' said Fleur.

Sitting there, happier than he ever remembered being, Michael conceded a certain value to Nature, to the sunshine stealing down, the scent of pinks and roses, the sighing in the aspens. Annette's pet doves were cooing; and, beyond the quietly-flowing river, the spires of poplar trees rose along the further bank. But, after all, he was only enjoying them because of the girl beside him, whom he loved to touch and look at, and because, for the first time, he felt as if she did not want to get up and flutter off to someone or something else. Curious that there could be, outside oneself, a being who completely robbed the world of its importance, 'snooped', as it were, the whole 'bag of tricks' – and she one's own wife! Very curious, considering what one was! He heard her say:

'Of course, mother's a Catholic; only, living with father down here, she left off practising. She didn't even bother me much. I've been thinking, Michael – what shall we do about *him*?'

'Let him rip.'

'I don't know. He must be taught something, because of going to school. The Catholics, you know, really do get things out of their religion.'

'Yes; they go it blind; it's the only logical way now.'

'I think having no religion makes one feel that nothing matters.'

Michael suppressed the words: 'We could bring him up as a sun-worshipper,' and said, instead:

'It seems to me that whatever he's taught will only last till he can think for himself; then he'll settle down to what suits him.'

'But what do *you* think about things, Michael? You're as good as anyone I know.'

'Gosh!' murmured Michael, strangely flattered: 'Is that so?'

'What *do* you think? Be serious!'

'Well, darling, doctrinally nothing – which means, of course, that I haven't got religion. I believe one has to play the game – but that's ethics.'

'But surely it's a handicap not to be able to rely on anything but oneself? If there's something to be had out of any form of belief, one might as well have it.'

Michael smiled, but not on the surface.

'You're going to do just as you like about the eleventh baronet, and I'm going to abet you. But considering his breeding – I fancy he'll be a bit of a sceptic.'

'But I don't *want* him to be. I'd rather he were snug, and convinced and all that. Scepticism only makes one restless.'

'No white monkey in him? Ah! I wonder! It's in the air, I guess. The only thing will be to teach him a sense of other people, as young as possible, with a slipper, if necessary.'

Fleur gave him a clear look, and laughed.

'Yes,' she said: 'Mother used to try, but Father wouldn't let her.'

They did not reach home till past eight o'clock.

'Either your father's here, or mine,' said Michael, in the hall; 'there's a prehistoric hat.'

'It's Dad's. His is grey inside. Bart's is buff.'

In the Chinese room Soames indeed was discovered, with an opened letter, and Ting-a-ling at his feet. He held the letter out to Michael, without a word.

There was no date, and no address; Michael read:

DEAR MR FORSYTE. — Perhaps you will be good enough to tell the Board at the meeting on Tuesday that I am on my way to immunity from the consequences of any peccadillo I may have been guilty of. By the time you receive this, I shall be there. I have always held that the secret of life, no less than that of business, is to know when not to stop. It will be no use to proceed against me, for my person will not be attachable, as I believe you call it in the law, and I have left no property behind. If your object was to corner me, I cannot congratulate you on your tactics. If, on the other hand, you inspired that young man's visit as a warning that you were still pursuing the matter, I should like to add new thanks to those which I expressed when I saw you a few days ago.

Believe me, dear Mr Forsyte,
Faithfully yours,
ROBERT ELDERSON.

Michael said cheerfully:

'Happy release! Now you'll feel safer, sir.'

Soames passed his hand over his face, evidently wiping off its expression. 'We'll discuss it later,' he said. 'This dog's been keeping me company.'

Michael admired him at that moment. He was obviously swallowing his 'grief', to save Fleur.

'Fleur's a bit tired,' he said. 'We've been on the river, and had tea at "The Shelter"; Madame wasn't in. Let's have dinner at once, Fleur.'

Fleur had picked up Ting-a-ling, and was holding her face out of reach of his avid tongue.

'Sorry you've had to wait, Dad,' she murmured, behind the yellow fur; 'I'm just going to wash; shan't change.'

When she had gone, Soames reached for the letter.

'A pretty kettle of fish!' he muttered. 'Where it'll end, I can't tell!'

'But isn't this the end, sir?'

Soames stared. These young people! Here he was, faced with a public scandal, which might lead to he didn't know what – the loss of his name in the city, the loss of his fortune, perhaps; and they took it as if –! They had no sense of responsibility – none! All his father's power of seeing the worst, all James' nervous pessimism, had come to the fore in him during the hour since, at the Connoisseur's Club, he had been handed that letter. Only the extra 'form' of the generation that succeeded James saved him, now that Fleur was out of the room, from making an exhibition of his fears.

'Your father in town?'

'I believe so, sir.'

'Good!' Not that he felt relief. That baronet chap was just as irresponsible – getting him to go on that Board! It all came of mixing with people brought up in a sort of incurable levity, with no real feeling for money.

'Now that Elderson's levanted,' he said, 'the whole thing must come out. Here's his confession in my hand –'

'Why not tear it up, sir, and say Elderson has developed consumption?'

The impossibility of getting anything serious from this young man afflicted Soames like the eating of heavy pudding.

'You think that would be honourable?' he said grimly.

'Sorry, sir!' said Michael, sobered. 'Can I help at all?'

'Yes; by dropping your levity, and taking care to keep wind of this matter away from Fleur.'

'I will,' said Michael earnestly: 'I promise you. I'll Dutch-oyster the whole thing. What's your line going to be?'

'We shall have to call the shareholders together and explain this dicky-dealing. They'll very likely take it in bad part.'

'I can't see why they should. How could you have helped it?'

Soames sniffed.

'There's no connexion in life between reward and your deserts. If the war hasn't taught you that, nothing will.'

'Well,' said Michael, 'Fleur will be down directly. If you'll excuse me a minute; we'll continue it in our next.'

Their next did not occur till Fleur had gone to bed.

'Now, sir,' said Michael, 'I expect my governor's at the Aeroplane. He goes there and meditates on the end of the world. Would you like me to ring him up, if your Board meeting's to-morrow?'

Soames nodded. He himself would not sleep a wink – why should 'Old Mont'?

Michael went to the Chinese tea-chest.

'Bart? This is Michael. Old For– my father-in-law is here; he's had a pill. ... No; Elderson. Could you blow in by any chance and hear? ... He's coming, sir. Shall we stay down, or go up to my study?'

'Down,' muttered Soames, whose eyes were fixed on the white monkey. 'I don't know what we're all coming to,' he added, suddenly.

'If we did, sir, we should die of boredom.'

'Speak for yourself. All this unreliability! I can't tell where it's leading.'

'Perhaps there's somewhere, sir, that's neither heaven nor hell.'

'A man of *his* age!'

'Same age as my dad; it was a bad vintage, I expect. If you'd been in the war, sir, it would have cheered you up no end.'

'Indeed!' said Soames.

'It took the linch-pins out of the cart – admitted; but, my

238

Lord! it did give you an idea of the grit there is about, when it comes to being up against it.'

Soames stared. Was this young fellow reading him a lesson against pessimism?

'Look at young Butterfield, the other day,' Michael went on, 'going over the top, to Elderson! Look at the girl who sat for "the altogether" in that picture you bought us! She's the wife of a packer we had, who got hoofed for snooping books. She made quite a lot of money by standing for the nude, and never lost her wicket. They're going to Australia on it. Yes, and look at that little snooper himself; he snooped to keep her alive after pneumonia, and came down to selling balloons.'

'I don't know what you're talking about,' said Soames.

'Only grit, sir. You said you didn't know what we were coming to. Well, look at the unemployed! Is there a country in the world where they stick it as they do here? I get awfully bucked at being English every now and then. Don't you?'

The words stirred something deep in Soames; but far from giving it away, he continued to gaze at the white monkey. The restless, inhuman, and yet so human, angry sadness of the creature's eyes! 'No whites to them!' thought Soames: 'that's what does it, I expect!' And George had liked that picture to hang opposite his bed! Well, George had grit – joked with his last breath: very English, George! Very English, all the Forsytes! Old Uncle Jolyon, and his way with shareholders; Swithin, upright, puffy, huge in a too little armchair at Timothy's: 'All these small fry!' he seemed to hear the words again; and Uncle Nicholas, whom that chap Elderson reproduced as it were unworthily, spry and all-there, and pretty sensual, but quite above suspicion of dishonesty. And old Roger, with his crankiness, and German mutton! And his own father, James – how he had hung on, long and frail as a reed, hung on and on! And Timothy, preserved in Consols, dying at a hundred! Grit and body in those old English boys, in spite of their funny ways. And there stirred in Soames a sort of atavistic will-power. He would see, and they would see – and that was all about it!

The grinding of a taxi's wheels brought him back from

reverie. Here came 'Old Mont', tittuppy, and light in the head as ever, no doubt. And, instead of his hand, Soames held out Elderson's letter.

'Your precious schoolfellow's levanted,' he said.

Sir Lawrence read it through, and whistled.

'What do you think, Forsyte – Constantinople?'

'More likely Monte Carlo,' said Soames gloomily. 'Secret commission – it's not an extraditable offence.'

The odd contortions of that baronet's face were giving him some pleasure – the fellow seemed to be feeling it, after all.

'I should think he's really gone to escape his women, Forsyte.'

The chap was incorrigible! Soames shrugged his shoulders almost violently.

'You'd better realize,' he said, 'that the fat is in the fire.'

'But surely, my dear Forsyte, it's been there ever since the French occupied the Ruhr. Elderson has cut his lucky; we appoint someone else. What more is there to it?'

Soames had the peculiar feeling of having overdone his own honesty. If an honourable man, a ninth baronet, couldn't see the implications of Elderson's confession, were they really there? Was any fuss and scandal necessary? Goodness knew, *he* didn't want it! He said heavily:

'We now have conclusive evidence of a fraud; we *know* Elderson was illegally paid for putting through business by which the shareholders have suffered a dead loss. How can we keep this knowledge from them?'

'But the mischief's done, Forsyte. How will the knowledge help them?'

Soames frowned.

'We're in a fiduciary position. I'm not prepared to run the risks of concealment. If we conceal, we're accessory after the fact. The thing might come out at any time.' If that was caution, not honesty, he couldn't help it.

'I should be glad to spare Elderson's name. We were at –'

'I'm aware of that,' said Soames, drily.

'But what risk is there of its coming out, Forsyte? Elderson won't mention it; nor young Butterfield, if you tell him not to.

Those who paid the commission certainly won't. And beyond us three here, no one else knows. It's not as if we profited in any way.'

Soames was silent. The argument was specious. Entirely unjust, of course, that he should be penalized for what Elderson had done!

'No,' he said, suddenly, 'it won't do. Depart from the law, and you can't tell where it'll end. The shareholders have suffered this loss and they have the right to all the facts within the directors' knowledge. There might be some means of restitution they could avail themselves of. We can't judge. It may be they've a remedy against ourselves.'

'If that's so, Forsyte, I'm with you.'

Soames felt disgust. Mont had no business to put it with a sort of gallantry that didn't count the cost; when the cost, if cost there were, would fall, not on Mont, whose land was heavily mortgaged, but on himself, whose property was singularly realizable.

'Well,' he said, coldly, 'remember that tomorrow. I'm going to bed.'

At his open window upstairs he felt no sense of virtue, but he enjoyed a sort of peace. He had taken his line, and there it was!

Chapter Nine

SOAMES DOESN'T GIVE A DAMN

◄‹◦›►

DURING the month following the receipt of Elderson's letter, Soames aged more than thirty days. He had forced his policy of disclosure on a doubting Board, the special meeting had been called, and, just as, twenty-three years ago, pursuing divorce from Irene, he had to face the public eye, so now he suffered day and night in dread of that undiscriminating optic. The French had a proverb: *'Les absents ont toujours tort!'* but

Soames had grave doubts about it. Elderson would be absent from that meeting of the shareholders, but – unless he was much mistaken – he himself, who would be present, would come in for the blame. The French were not to be relied on. What with his anxiety about Fleur, and his misgiving about the public eye, he was sleeping badly, eating little, and feeling below par. Annette had recommended him to see a doctor. That was probably why he did not. Soames had faith in doctors for other people; but they had never – he would say – done anything for *him*, possibly because, so far, there had not been anything to do.

Failing in her suggestion, and finding him every day less sociable, Annette had given him a book on Coué. After running it through, he had meant to leave it in the train, but the theory, however extravagant, had somehow clung to him. After all, Fleur was doing it; and the thing cost you nothing : there might be something in it ! There was. After telling himself that night twenty-five times that he was getting better and better, he slept so soundly that Annette, in the next room, hardly slept at all.

'Do you know, my friend,' she said at breakfast, 'you were snoring last night so that I could not hear the cock crow.'

'Why should you want to?' said Soames.

'Well, never mind – if you had a good night. Was it my little Coué who gave you that nice dream?'

Partly from fear of encouraging Coué, and partly from fear of encouraging her, Soames avoided a reply; but he had a curious sense of power, as if he did not care what people said of him.

'I'll do it again tonight,' he thought.

'You know,' Annette went on, 'you are just the temperament for Coué, Soames. When you cure yourself of worrying, you will get quite fat.'

'Fat !' said Soames, looking at her curves. 'I'd as soon grow a beard.'

Fatness and beards were associated with the French. He would have to keep an eye on himself if he went on with this – er – what was one to call it? Tomfoolery was hardly the word to conciliate the process, even if it did require you to tie twenty-five knots in a bit of string : very French, that, like telling your beads! He himself had merely counted on his fingers. The sense of power lasted all the way up to London; he had the conviction that he could sit in a draught if he wanted to, that Fleur would have her boy all right; and as to the P.P.R.S. – ten to one he wouldn't be mentioned by name in any report of the proceedings.

After an early lunch and twenty-five more assurances over his coffee, he set out for the city.

This Board, held just a week before the special meeting of the shareholders, was in the nature of a dress rehearsal. The details of confrontation had to be arranged, and Soames was chiefly concerned with seeing that a certain impersonality should be preserved. He was entirely against disclosure of the fact that young Butterfield's story and Elderson's letter had been confided to himself. The phrase to be used should be a 'member of the Board'. He saw no need for anything further. As for explanations, they would fall, of course, to the chairman and the senior director, Lord Fontenoy. He found, however, that the Board thought he himself was the right person to bring the matter forward. No one else – they said – could supply the personal touch, the necessary conviction; the chairman should introduce the matter briefly, then call on Soames to give the evidence within his knowledge. Lord Fontenoy was emphatic.

'It's up to you, Mr Forsyte. If it hadn't been for you, Elderson would be sitting there today. From beginning to end you put the wind up him; and I wish the deuce you hadn't. The whole thing's a confounded nuisance. He was a very clever fellow, and we shall miss him. Our new man isn't a patch on him. If he did take a few thou. under the rose, he took 'em off the Huns.'

Old guinea-pig! Soames replied, acidly:

'And the quarter of a million he's lost the shareholders, for the sake of those few thou.? Bagatelle, I suppose?'

'Well, it might have turned out a winner; for the first year it did. We all back losers sometimes.'

Soames looked from face to face. They did not support this blatant attitude, but in them all, except perhaps 'Old Mont's', he felt a grudge against himself. Their expressions seemed to say:

'Nothing of this sort ever happened till you came on the Board.' He had disturbed their comfort, and they disliked him for it. They were an unjust lot! He said doggedly:

'You leave it to me, do you? Very well!'

What he meant to convey – or whether he meant to convey anything, he did not know; but even that 'old guinea-pig' was more civil afterwards. He came away from the Board, however, without any sense of power at all. There he would be on Tuesday next, bang in the public eye.

After calling to inquire after Fleur, who was lying down rather poorly, he returned home with a feeling of having been betrayed. It seemed that he could not rely, after all, on this fellow with his twenty-five knots. However much better he might become, his daughter, his reputation, and possibly his fortune, were not apparently at the disposition of his subconscious self. He was silent at dinner, and went up afterwards to his picture gallery, to think things over. For half an hour he stood at the open window, alone with the summer evening; and the longer he stood there, the more clearly he perceived that the three were really one. Except for his daughter's sake, what did he care for his reputation or his fortune? His reputation! Lot of fools – if they couldn't see that he was careful and honest so far as had lain within his reach – so much the worse for them! His fortune – well, he had better make another settlement on Fleur and her child at once, in case of accidents; another fifty thousand. Ah! if she were only through her trouble! It was time Annette went up to her for good; and there was a thing they called twilight sleep. To have her suffering was not to be thought of!

The evening lingered out; the sun went down behind familiar trees; Soames's hands, grasping the window-ledge, felt damp with dew; sweetness of grass and river stole up into his nostrils. The sky had paled, and now began to darken; a scatter of stars came out. He had lived here a long time, through all Fleur's childhood – best years of his life; still, it wouldn't break his heart to sell. His heart was up in London. Sell? That was to run before the hounds with a vengeance. No – no! – it wouldn't come to *that*! He left the window and, turning up the lights, began the thousand and first tour of his pictures. He had made some good purchases since Fleur's marriage, and without wasting his money on fashionable favourites. He had made some good sales, too. The pictures in this gallery, if he didn't mistake, were worth from seventy to a hundred thousand pounds; and, with the profits on his sales from time to time, they stood him in at no more than five-and-twenty thousand – not a bad result from a life's hobby, to say nothing of the pleasure! Of course, he might have taken up something – butterflies, photography, archaeology, or first editions; some other sport in which you backed your judgement against the field, and collected the results; but he had never regretted choosing pictures. Not he! More to show for your money, more kudos, more profit, and more risk! The thought startled him a little; had he really taken to pictures because of the risk? A risk had never appealed to him; at least, he hadn't realized it, so far. Had his 'subconscious' some part in the matter? He suddenly sat down and closed his eyes. Try the thing once more; very pleasant feeling, that morning, of not 'giving a damn'; he never remembered having it before! He had always felt it necessary to worry – kind of insurance against the worst; but worry was wearing, no doubt about it, wearing. Turn out the light! They said in that book, you had to relax. In the now dim and shadowy room, with the starlight, through many windows, dusted over its reality, Soames, in his easy chair, sat very still. A faint drone rose on the words: 'fatter and fatter' through his moving lips. 'No, no,' he thought: 'that's wrong!' And he began the drone again. The tips of his fingers ticked it off; on and on – he would give it a good chance. If only one needn't worry! On and on – 'better and better!' If only –! His lips stopped moving; his grey head fell forward into the subconscious. And the stealing starlight dusted over him, too, a little unreality.

Chapter Ten

BUT TAKES NO CHANCES

❯❮❯❯

MICHAEL knew nothing of the City; and, in the spirit of the old cartographers: 'Where you know nothing, place terrors', made his way through the purlieus of the Poultry, towards that holy of holies, the offices of Cuthcott, Kingson and Forsyte. His mood was attuned to meditation, for he had been lunching with Sibley Swan at the Café C'rillon. He had known all the guests — seven chaps even more modern than old Sib — save only a Russian so modern that he knew no French and nobody could talk to him. Michael had watched them demolish everything, and the Russian closing his eyes, like a sick baby, at mention of any living name. ... 'Carry on!' he thought, several of his favourites having gone down in the *mêlée*. 'Stab and bludge! Importance awaits you at the end of the alley.' But he had restrained his irreverence till the moment of departure.

'Sib,' he said, rising, 'all these chaps here are dead — ought they to be about in this hot weather?'

'What's that?' ejaculated Sibley Swan, amidst the almost painful silence of the chaps.

'I mean — they're alive — so they *must* be damned!' And avoiding a thrown chocolate which hit the Russian, he sought the door.

Outside, he mused: 'Good chaps, really! Not half so darned superior as they think they are. Quite a human touch — getting that Russian on the boko. Phew! It's hot!'

On that first day of the Eton and Harrow match all the forfeited heat of a chilly summer had gathered and shimmered over Michael, on the top of his Bank bus; shimmered over straw hats, and pale, perspiring faces, over endless other buses, businessmen, policemen, shopmen at their doors, sellers of newspapers, laces, jumping toys, endless carts and cabs, letterings and wires, all the confusion of the greatest conglomeration in the world – adjusted almost to a hair's-breadth, by an unseen instinct. Michael stared and doubted. Was it possible that, with everyone pursuing his own business, absorbed in his own job, the thing could work out? An ant-heap was not busier, or more seemingly confused. Live wires crossed and crossed and crossed – inextricable entanglement, you'd say; and yet, life, the order needful to life, somehow surviving! 'No slouch of a miracle!' he thought, 'modern town life!' And suddenly it seemed to cease, as if demolished by the ruthless dispensation of some super Sibley Swan; for he was staring down a *cul-de-sac*. On both sides, flat houses, recently re-buffed, extraordinarily alike; at the end, a flat buff house, even more alike, and down to it, grey virgin pavement, unstained by horses or petrol; no cars, cats, carts, policemen, hawkers, flies, or bees. No sign of human life, except the names of legal firms to right and left of each open doorway.

' "Cuthcott, Kingson and Forsyte, Commissioners for Oaths: First Floor." '

'Rule Britannia!' thought Michael, ascending wide stone steps.

Entering the room to which he had been ushered, he saw an old and pug-faced fellow with a round grizzled beard, a black alpaca coat, and a roomy holland waistcoat round his roomy middle, who rose from a swivel chair.

'Aoh!' he said, 'Mr Michael Mont, I think. I've been expecting you. We shan't be long about it, after Mr Forsyte comes. He's just stepped round the corner. Mrs Michael well, I hope?'

'Thanks; as well as –'

'Ye-es; it makes you anxious. Take a seat. Perhaps you'd like to read the draft?'

Thus prescribed for, Michael took some foolscap from a pudgy hand, and sat down opposite. With one eye on the old fellow, and the other on the foolscap, he read steadily.

'It seems to mean something,' he said at last.

He saw a gape, as a frog at a fly, settle in the beard; and hastened to repair his error.

'Calculating what's going to happen if something else doesn't, must be rather like being a bookmaker.'

He felt at once that he had not succeeded. There was a grumpy mutter:

'We don't waste our time 'ere. Excuse me, I'm busy.'

Michael sat, compunctious, watching him tick down a long page of entries. He was like one of those old dogs which lie outside front doors, keeping people off the premises, and notifying their fleas. After less than five minutes of that perfect silence Soames came in.

'You're here, then?' he said.

'Yes, sir; I thought it best to come at the time you mentioned. What a nice cool room!'

'Have you read this?' asked Soames, pointing to the draft.

Michael nodded.

'Did you understand it?'

'Up to a point, I think.'

'The interest on *this* fifty thousand,' said Soames, 'is Fleur's until her eldest child, if it's a boy, attains the age of twenty-one, when the capital becomes his absolutely. If it's a girl, Fleur retains half the income for life, the rest of the income becomes payable to the girl when she attains the age of twenty-one or marries, and the capital of that half goes to her child or children lawfully begotten, at majority or marriage, in equal shares. The other half of the capital falls into Fleur's estate, and is disposable by her will, or follows the laws of intestacy.'

'You make it wonderfully clear,' said Michael.

'Wait!' said Soames. 'If Fleur has no children –'

Michael started.

'Anything is possible,' said Soames gravely, 'and my experience is that the contingencies not provided for are those which happen. In such a case the income of the whole is hers for life, and the capital hers at death to do as she likes with. Failing that, it goes to the next of kin. There are provisions against anticipation and so forth.'

'Ought she to make a fresh will?' asked Michael, conscious of sweat on his forehead.

'Not unless she likes. Her present will covers it.'

'Have I to do anything?'

'No. I wanted you to understand the purport before I sign; that's all. Give me the deed, Gradman, and get Wickson in, will you?'

Michael saw the old chap produce from a drawer a fine piece of parchment covered with copperplate writing and seals, look at it lovingly, and place it before Soames. When he had left the room, Soames said in a low voice:

'This meeting on Tuesday – I can't tell! But, whatever happens, so far as I can see, this ought to stand.'

'It's awfully good of you, sir.'

Soames nodded, testing a pen.

'I'm afraid I've got wrong with your old clerk,' said Michael; 'I like the look of him frightfully, but I accidentally compared him to a bookmaker.'

Soames smiled. 'Gradman,' he said, 'is a "character". There aren't many, nowadays.'

Michael was wondering: Could one be a 'character' under the age of sixty? – when the 'character' returned, with a pale man in dark clothes.

Lifting his nose sideways, Soames said at once:

'This is a post-nuptial settlement on my daughter. I deliver this as my act and deed.'

He wrote his name, and got up.

The pale person and Gradman wrote theirs, and the former left the room. There was a silence as of repletion.

'Do you want me any more?' asked Michael.

'Yes. I want you to see me deposit it at the bank with the marriage settlement. Shan't come back, Gradman!'

'Good-bye, Mr Gradman.'

Michael heard the old fellow mutter through his beard half buried in a drawer to which he was returning the draft, and followed Soames out.

'Here's where I used to be,' said Soames as they went along the Poultry; 'and my father before me.'

'More genial, perhaps,' said Michael.

'The trustees are meeting us at the bank; you remember them?'

'Cousins of Fleur's, weren't they, sir?'

'Second cousins; young Roger's eldest, and young Nicholas'. I chose them youngish. Very young Roger was wounded in the war – he does nothing. Very young Nicholas is at the Bar.'

Michael's ears stood up. 'What about the next lot, sir? Very, very young Roger would be almost insulting, wouldn't it?'

'There won't be one,' said Soames, 'with taxation where it is. He can't afford it; he's a steady chap. What are you going to call your boy, if it *is* one?'

'We think Christopher, because of St Paul's and Columbus. Fleur wants him solid, and I want him inquiring.'

'H'm. And if it's a girl?'

'Oh! – if it's a girl – Anne.'

'Yes,' said Soames: 'very neat. Here they are!'

They had reached the bank, and in the entrance Michael saw two Forsytes between thirty and forty, whose chinny faces he dimly remembered. Escorted by a man with bright buttons down his front, they all went to a room, where a man without buttons produced a japanned box. One of the Forsytes opened it with a key; Soames muttered an incantation, and deposited the deed. When he and the chinnier Forsyte had exchanged a few remarks with the manager on the question of the bank rate, they all went back to the lobby and parted with the words: 'Well, good-bye.'

'Now,' said Soames, in the din and hustle of the street, 'he's provided for, so far as I can see. When exactly do you expect it?'

'It should be just a fortnight.'

'Do you believe in this – this twilight sleep?'

'I should like to,' said Michael, conscious again of sweat on his forehead. 'Fleur's wonderfully calm; she does Coué night and morning.'

'That!' said Soames. He did not mention that he himself was doing it, thus giving away the state of his nerves. 'If you're going home, I'll come, too.'

'Good!'

He found Fleur lying down with Ting-a-ling on the foot of the sofa.

'Your father's here, darling. He's been anointing the future with another fifty thou. I expect he'd like to tell you all about it.'

Fleur moved restlessly.

'Presently. If it's going on as hot as this, it'll be rather a bore, Michael.'

'Oh! but it won't, ducky. Three days and a thunder-storm.'

Taking Ting-a-ling by the chin, he turned his face up.

'And how on earth is your nose going to be put out of joint, old man? There's no joint to put.'

'He knows there's something up.'

'He's a wise little brute, aren't you, old son?'

Ting-a-ling sniffed.

'Michael!'

'Yes, darling?'

'I don't seem to care about anything now – it's a funny feeling.'

'That's the heat.'

'No. I think it's because the whole business is too long. Everything's ready, and now it all seems rather stupid. One more person in the world or one more out of it – what does it matter?'

'Don't! It matters frightfully!'

'One more gnat to dance, one more ant to run about!'

Anguished, Michael said again:

'Don't, Fleur! That's just a mood.'

'Is Wilfrid's book out?'

'It comes out to-morrow.'

'I'm sorry I gave you such a bad time, there. I only didn't want to lose him.'

Michael took her hand.

'Nor did I – goodness knows!' he said.

'He's never written, I suppose?'

'No.'

'Well, I expect he's all right by now. Nothing lasts.'

Michael put her hand to his cheek.

'*I* do, I'm afraid,' he said.

The hand slipped round over his lips.

'Give Dad my love, and tell him I'll be down to tea. Oh! I'm so hot!'

Michael hovered a moment, and went out. Damn the heat, upsetting her like this!

He found Soames standing in front of the white monkey.

'I should take this down, if I were you,' he muttered, 'until it's over.'

'Why, sir?' asked Michael, in surprise.

Soames frowned.

'Those eyes!'

Michael went up to the picture. Yes! He was a haunting kind of brute!

'But it's such top-hole work, sir.'

Soames nodded.

'Artistically, yes. But at such times you can't be too careful what she sees.'

'I believe you're right. Let's have him down.'

'I'll hold him,' said Soames, taking hold of the bottom of the picture.

'Got him tight? Right-o. Now!'

'You can say I wanted an opinion on his period,' said Soames, when the picture had been lowered to the floor.

'There can hardly be a doubt of that, sir – the present!'

Soames stared. 'What? Oh! You mean –? Ah! H'm! Don't let her know he's in the house.'

'No. I'll lock him up.' Michael lifted the picture. 'D'you mind opening the door, sir?'

'I'll come back at tea-time,' said Soames. 'That'll look as if I'd taken him off. You can hang him again, later.'

'Yes. Poor brute!' said Michael, bearing the monkey off to limbo.

Chapter Eleven

WITH A SMALL 'n'

❧❧❧

ON the night of the Monday following, after Fleur had gone to bed, Michael and Soames sat listening to the mutter of London coming through the windows of the Chinese room opened to the brooding heat.

'They say the war killed sentiment,' said Soames suddenly: 'Is that true?'

'In a way, yes, sir. We had so much reality that we don't want any more.'

'I don't follow you.'

'I meant that only reality really makes you feel. So if you pretend there *is* no reality, you don't have to feel. It answers awfully well, up to a point.'

'Ah!' said Soames. 'Her mother comes up tomorrow morning, to stay. This P.P.R.S. meeting of mine is at half-past two. Good night!'

Michael, at the window, watched the heat gathered black over the Square. A few tepid drops fell on his outstretched hand. A cat stole by under a lamp-post, and vanished into a shadow so thick that it seemed uncivilized.

Queer question of 'Old Forsyte's' about sentiment; odd that he should ask it! 'Up to a point! But don't we all get past that point?' he thought. Look at Wilfrid, and himself — after the war they had deemed it blasphemous to admit that anything mattered except eating and drinking, for tomorrow they died; even fellows like Nazing, and Master, who were never in the war, had felt like that ever since. Well, Wilfrid had got it in the neck; and he himself had got it in the wind; and he would bet that — barring one here and there whose blood was made of ink — they would all get it in the neck or wind soon or late. Why, he

253

would cheerfully bear Fleur's pain and risk, instead of her! But if nothing mattered, why should he feel like that?

Turning from the window, he leaned against the lacquered back of the jade-green settee, and stared at the wall space between the Chinese tea-chests. Jolly thoughtful of the 'old man' to have that white monkey down! The brute was potent – symbolic of the world's mood: beliefs cancelled, faiths withdrawn! And, dash it! not only the young – but the old – were in that temper! 'Old Forsyte', or he would never have been scared by that monkey's eyes; yes, and his own governor, and Elderson, and all the rest. Young and old – no real belief in anything! And yet – revolt sprang up in Michael, with a whirr, like a covey of partridges. It *did* matter that some person or some principle outside oneself should be more precious than oneself – it dashed well did! Sentiment, then, wasn't dead – nor faith, nor belief, which were the same things. They were only shedding shells, working through chrysalis, into – butterflies, perhaps. Faith, sentiment, belief, had gone underground, possibly, but they were there, even in 'Old Forsyte' and himself. He had a good mind to put the monkey up again. No use exaggerating his importance! ... By George! Some flare! A jagged streak of vivid light had stripped darkness off the night. Michael crossed, to close the windows. A shattering peal of thunder blundered overhead; and down came the rain, slashing and sluicing. He saw a man running, black, like a shadow across a dark-blue screen; saw him by the light of another flash, suddenly made lurid and full of small meaning, with face of cheerful anxiety, as if he were saying: 'Hang it, I'm getting wet!' Another frantic crash!

'Fleur!' thought Michael; and clanging the last window down, he ran upstairs.

She was sitting up in bed, with a face all round, and young, and startled.

'Brutes!' he thought – guns and the heavens confounded in his mind: 'They've waked her up!'

'It's all right, darling! Just another little summer kick-up! Were you asleep?'

'I was dreaming!' He felt her hand clutching within his own, saw a sudden pinched look on her face, with a sort of rage. What infernal luck!

'Where's Ting?'

No dog was in the corner.

'Under the bed – you bet! Would you like him up?'

'No. Let him stay; he hates it.'

She put her head against his arm, and Michael curled his hand round her other ear.

'I never liked thunder much!' said Fleur, 'and now it – it hurts!'

High above her hair Michael's face underwent the contortions of an overwhelming tenderness. One of those crashes which seem just overhead sent her face burrowing against his chest, and, sitting on the bed, he gathered her in, close.

'I wish it were over,' came, smothered, from her lips.

'It will be directly, darling; it came on so suddenly!' But he knew she didn't mean the storm.

'If I come through, I'm going to be quite different to you, Michael.'

Anxiety was the natural accompaniment of such events, but the words: 'If I come through' turned Michael's heart right over. Incredible that one so young and pretty should be in even the remotest danger of extinction; incredibly painful that she should be in fear of it! He hadn't realized. She had been so calm, so matter-of-fact about it all.

'Don't!' he mumbled; 'of course you'll come through.'

'I'm afraid.'

The sound was small and smothered, but the words hurt horribly. Nature, with the small 'n', forcing fear into this girl he loved so awfully! Nature kicking up this godless din above her poor little head!

'Ducky, you'll have twilight sleep and know nothing about it; and be as right as rain in no time.'

Fleur freed her hand.

'Not if it's not good for him. Is it?'

'I expect so, sweetheart; I'll find out. What makes you think – ?'

'Only that it's not natural. I want to do it properly. Hold my hand hard, Michael. I – I'm not going to be a fool. Oh! Someone's knocking – go and see.'

Michael opened the door a crack. Soames was there – unnatural – in a blue dressing-gown and scarlet slippers!

'Is she all right?' he whispered.

'Yes, yes.'

'In this bobbery she oughtn't to be left.'

'No, sir, of course not. I shall sleep on the sofa.'

'Call me, if anything's wanted.'

'I will.'

Soames's eyes slid past, peering into the room. A string worked in his throat, as if he had things to say which did not emerge. He shook his head, and turned. His slim figure, longer than usual, in its gown, receded down the corridor, past the Japanese prints which he had given them. Closing the door again, Michael stood looking at the bed. Fleur had settled down; her eyes were closed, her lips moving. He stole back on tiptoe. The thunder, travelling away south, blundered and growled as if regretfully. Michael saw her eyelids quiver, her lips stop, then move again. 'Coué!' he thought.

He lay down on the sofa at the foot of the bed, whence, without sound, he could raise himself and see her. Many times he raised himself. She had dropped off, was breathing quietly. The thunder was faint now, the flashes imperceptible. Michael closed his eyes.

A faint last mutter roused him to look at her once more, high on her pillows by the carefully shaded light. Young – young! Colourless, like a flower in wax! No scheme in her brain, no dread – peaceful! If only she could stay like that and wake up with it all over! He looked away. And there she was at the far end, dim, reflected in a glass; and there to the right, again. She lay, as it were, all round him in the pretty room, the inhabiting spirit – of his heart.

It was quite still now. Through a chink in those powder-blue curtains he could see some stars. Big Ben chimed one.

He had slept, perhaps, dozed at least, dreamed a little. A

small sound woke him. A very little dog, tail down, yellow, low and unimportant, was passing down the room, trailing across it to the far corner. 'Ah!' thought Michael, closing his eyes again: 'You!'

Chapter Twelve

ORDEAL BY SHAREHOLDER

◄‹·›►

REPAIRING, next day, to the Aeroplane Club, where, notably spruce, Sir Lawrence was waiting in the lounge, Michael thought: 'Good old Bart! he's got himself up for the guillotine all right!'

'That white piping will show the blood!' he said. 'Old Forsyte's neat this morning, but not so gaudy.'

'Ah! How is "Old Forsyte"? In good heart?'

'One doesn't ask him, sir. How do you feel yourself?'

'Exactly as I used to before the Eton and Winchester match. I think I shall have shandy-gaff at lunch.'

When they had taken their seats, Sir Lawrence went on:

'I remember seeing a man tried for murder in Colombo; the poor fellow was positively blue. I think my favourite moment in the past, Michael, is Walter Raleigh asking for a second shirt. By the way, it's never been properly settled yet whether the courtiers of that day were lousy. What are you going to have, my dear fellow?'

'Cold beef, pickled walnuts, and gooseberry-tart.'

'Excellent for the character. I shall have curry; they give you a very good Bombay duck here. I rather fancy we shall be fired, Michael. "*Nous sommes trahis!*" used to be the prerogative of the French, but I'm afraid we're getting the attitude, too. The Yellow Press has made a difference.'

Michael shook his head.

'We say it, but we don't act on it; the climate's too uncertain.'

'That sounds deep. This looks very good curry — will you change your mind? Old Fontenoy sometimes comes in here; he has no inside. It'll be serious for him if we're shown the door.'

'Deuced rum,' said Michael suddenly, 'how titles still go down. There can't be any belief in their business capacity.'

'Character, my dear fellow — the good old English gentleman. After all, there's something in it.'

'I fancy, sir, it's more a case of complex in the shareholders. Their parents show them a lord when they're young.'

'Shareholders,' said Sir Lawrence; 'the word is comprehensive. Who are they, what are they, when are they?'

'This afternoon,' said Michael, 'and I shall have a good look at them.'

'They won't let you in, my dear.'

'No?'

'Certainly not.'

Michael frowned.

'What paper,' he said, 'is sure not to be represented?'

Sir Lawrence gave his whinnying laugh.

'*The Field*,' he said; '*The Horse and Hound; The Gardener's Weekly.*'

'I'll slide in on them.'

'You'll see us die game, I hope,' said Sir Lawrence, with sudden gravity.

They took a cab together to the meeting, but separated before reaching the door of the hotel.

Michael had thought better of the Press, and took up a position in the passage, whence he could watch for a chance. Stout men, in dark suits, with a palpable look of having lunched off turbot, joints, and cheese, kept passing him. He noticed that each handed the janitor a paper. 'I'll hand him a paper, too,' he thought, 'and scoot in.' Watching for some even stouter men, he took cover between two of them, and approached the door, with an announcement of *Counterfeits* in his left hand. Handing it across a neighbouring importance, he was quickly into a seat. He saw the janitor's face poked round the door. 'No, my friend,' thought Michael, 'if you could tell duds from share-holders, you wouldn't be in that job!'

He found a report before him, and holding it up, looked at other things. The room seemed to him to have been got by a concert-hall out of a station waiting-room. It had a platform with a long table, behind which were seven empty chairs, and seven inkpots, with seven quill pens upright in them. 'Quills!' thought Michael; 'symbolic, I suppose – they'll all use fountain-pens!'

Back-centre of the platform was a door, and in front, below it, a table, where four men were sitting, fiddling with note-books. 'Orchestra,' thought Michael. He turned his attention to the eight or ten rows of shareholders. They looked what they were, but he could not tell why. Their faces were cast in an infinity of moulds, but all had the air of waiting for something they knew they would not get. What sort of lives did they lead, or did their lives lead them? Nearly all wore moustaches. His neighbours to right and left were the same stout shareholders between whom he had slipped in; they both had thick lobes to their ears, and necks even broader than the straight broad backs of their heads. He was a good deal impressed. Dotted here and there he noticed a woman, or a parson. There was practically no conversation, from which he surmised that no one knew his neighbour. He had a feeling that a dog somewhere would have humanized the occasion. He was musing on the colour scheme of green picked out with chocolate and chased with gold, when the door behind the platform was thrown open, and seven men in black coats filed in, and with little bows took their seats behind the quills. They reminded him of people getting up on horses, or about to play the piano – full of small adjustments. That – on the chairman's right – would be old Fontenoy, with a face entirely composed of features. Michael had an odd conceit: a little thing in a white top-hat sat inside the brain, driving the features eight-in-hand. Then came a face straight from a picture of Her Majesty's Government in 1850, round and pink, with a high nose, a small mouth, and little white whiskers; while at the end on the right was a countenance whose jaw and eyes seemed boring into a conundrum beyond the wall at Michael's back. 'Legal!' he thought. His scrutiny passed back to the chairman. Chosen? Was he – or was he not? A bearded man, a little behind on the chairman's left, was already reading from a book, in a rapid monotonous voice. That must be the secretary letting off his minute guns. And in front of him was clearly the new manager, on whose left Michael observed his own father. The dark pothooks over Sir Lawrence's right eye were slightly raised, and his mouth was puckered under the cut line of his small moustache. He looked almost Oriental, quick but still. His left hand held his tortoise-shell-rimmed monocle between thumb and finger. 'Not quite in the scene!' thought Michael; 'poor old Bart!' He had come now to the last of the row. 'Old Forsyte' was sitting precisely as if alone in the world; with one corner of his mouth just drawn down, and one nostril just drawn up, he seemed to Michael quite fascinatingly detached; and yet not out of the picture. Within that still neat figure, whereof only one patent-leather boot seemed with a slight movement to be living, was intense concentration, entire respect for the proceedings, and yet, a queer contempt for them; he was like a statue of reality, by one who had seen that there was precious little reality in it. 'He chills my soup,' thought Michael, 'but – dash it! – I can't help half admiring him!'

The chairman had now risen. 'He *is*' – thought Michael; 'no, he isn't – yes – no – I can't tell!' He could hardly attend to what the chairman said, for wondering whether he was chosen or not, though well aware that it did not matter at all. The chairman kept steadily on. Distracted, Michael caught words and words: 'European situation – misguided policy – French – totally unexpected – position disclosed – manager – unfortunate circumstances shortly to be explained to you – future of this great concern – no reason to doubt –'

'Oil,' thought Michael, 'he is – and yet –!'

'I will now ask one of your directors, Mr Forsyte, to give you at first hand an account of this painful matter.'

Michael saw Soames, pale and deliberate, take a piece of paper from his breast-pocket, and rise. Was it to the occasion?

'I will give you the facts shortly,' he said in a voice which reminded Michael of a dry, made-up wine. 'On the eleventh of January last I was visited by a clerk in the employ of the Society –'

Familiar with these details, Michael paid them little attention, watching the shareholders for signs of reaction. He saw none, and it was suddenly borne in on him why they wore moustaches: They could not trust their mouths! Character was in the mouth. Moustaches had come in when people no longer went about, like the old Duke, saying: 'Think what you damned well like of my character!' Mouths had tried to come in again, of course, before the war; but what with majors, shareholders, and the working classes, they now had little or no chance! He heard Soames say: 'In these circumstances we came to the conclusion that there was nothing for it but to wait and see.' Michael saw a sudden quiver pass over the moustaches, as might wind over grass.

'Wrong phrase,' he thought; 'we all do it, but we can't bear being reminded of it.'

'Six weeks ago, however,' he heard Soames intone, 'an accidental incident seems to have warned your late manager that Sir Lawrence and I still entertained suspicions, for I received a letter from him practically admitting that he had taken this secret commission on the German business, and asking me to inform the Board that he had gone abroad and left no property behind him. This statement we have been at pains to verify. In these circumstances we had no alternative but to call you together, and lay the facts before you.'

The voice, which had not varied an iota, ceased its recital; and Michael saw his father-in-law return to his detachment – stork on one leg, about to apply beak to parasite, could have inspired no greater sense of loneliness. 'Too like the first account of the battle of Jutland!' he thought: 'He mentioned all the losses, and never once struck the human note.'

A pause ensued, such as occurs before an awkward fence, till somebody has found a gate. Michael rapidly reviewed the faces of the Board. Only one showed any animation. It was concealed in a handkerchief. The sound of the blown nose broke the spell. Two shareholders rose to their feet at once — one of them Michael's neighbour on the right.

'Mr Sawdry,' said the chairman, and the other shareholder sat down.

With a sonorous clearing of the throat, Michael's neighbour turned his blunt red face towards Soames.

'I wish to ask you, sir, why you didn't inform the Board when you first 'eard of this?'

Soames rose slightly.

'You are aware, I presume, that such an accusation, unless it can be fully substantiated, is a matter for criminal proceedings?'

'No; it would ha' been privileged.'

'As between members of the Board, perhaps; but any leakage would have rendered us liable. It was a mere case of word against word.'

'Perhaps Sir Lawrence Mont will give us 'is view of that?'

Michael's heart began to beat. There was an air of sprightliness about his father's standing figure.

'You must remember, sir,' he said, 'that Mr Elderson had enjoyed our complete confidence for many years; he was a gentleman, and, speaking for myself, an old school-fellow of his, I preferred, in common loyalty, to give his word preference, while – er – keeping the matter in mind.'

'Oh!' said Michael's neighbour: 'What's the chairman got to say about bein' kept in the dark?'

'We are all perfectly satisfied, sir, with the attitude of our co-directors, in a very delicate situation. You will kindly note that the mischief was already done over this unfortunate assurance, so that there was no need for undue haste.'

Michael saw his neighbour's neck grow redder.

'I don't agree,' he said. ' "Wait and see" – We might have 'ad that commission out of him, if he'd been tackled promptly.' And he sat down.

He had not reached mahogany before the thwarted shareholder had started up.

'Mr Botterill,' said the chairman.

Michael saw a lean and narrow head, with two hollows in a hairy neck, above a back slightly bent forward, as of a doctor listening to a chest.

'I take it from you, then, sir,' he said, 'that these two directors represent the general attitude of the Board, and that the Board were content to allow a suspected person to remain manager. The gentleman on your extreme left – Mr Forsyte, I think – spoke of an accidental incident. But for that, apparently, we should still be in the hands of an unscrupulous individual. The symptoms in this case are very disquieting. There appears to have been gross over-confidence; a recent instance of the sort must be in all our minds. The policy of assuring foreign business was evidently initiated by the manager for his own ends. We have made a severe loss by it. And the question for us shareholders would seem to be whether a Board who placed confidence in such a person, and continued it after their suspicions were aroused, are the right people to direct this important concern.'

Throughout this speech Michael had grown very hot. ' "Old Forsyte" was right,' he thought; 'they're on their uppers, after all.'

There was a sudden creak from his neighbour on the left.

'Mr Tolby,' said the chairman.

'It's a serious matter, this, gentlemen. I propose that the Board withdraw, an' leave us to discuss it.'

'I second that,' said Michael's neighbour on the right.

Searching the vista of the Board, Michael saw recognition gleam for a second in the lonely face at the end, and grinned a greeting.

The chairman was speaking.

'If that is your wish, gentlemen, we shall be happy to comply with it. Will those who favour the motion hold up their hands?'

All hands were held up, with the exception of Michael's, of two women whose eager colloquy had not permitted them to hear the request, and of one shareholder, just in front of Michael, so motionless that he seemed to be dead.

'Carried,' said the chairman, and rose from his seat.

Michael saw his father smiling, and speaking to 'Old Forsyte' as they both stood up. They all filed out, and the door was closed.

'Whatever happens,' Michael thought, 'I've got to keep my head shut, or I shall be dropping a brick.'

'Perhaps the Press will kindly withdraw, too,' he heard someone say.

With a general chinny movement, as if inquiring their rights of no one in particular, the four Pressmen could be seen to clasp their notebooks. When their pale reluctance had vanished, there was a stir among the shareholders, like that of ducks when a dog comes up behind. Michael saw why at once. They had their backs to each other. A shareholder said:

'Perhaps Mr Tolby, who proposed the withdrawal, will act as chairman.'

Michael's left-hand neighbour began breathing heavily.

'Right-o!' he said. 'Anyone who wants to speak, kindly ketch my eye.'

Everyone now began talking to his neighbour, as though to get at once a quiet sense of proportion, before speaking. Mr Tolby was breathing so heavily that Michael felt a positive draught.

''Ere, gentlemen,' he said suddenly, 'this won't do! We don't want to be too formal, but we must preserve some order. I'll open the discussion myself. Now, I didn't want to 'urt the feelin's of the Board by plain speakin' in their presence. But, as Mr What's-'is-name there, said: The public 'as got to protect itself against sharpers, and against slackness. We all know what 'appened the other day, and what'll 'appen again in other concerns, unless we shareholders look after ourselves. In the first place, then, what I say is: They ought never to 'ave touched anything to do with the 'Uns. In the second place, I saw they showed bad judgement. And in the third place I saw they were too thick together. In my opinion, we should propose a vote of no confidence.'

Cries of: 'Hear, hear!' mixed with indeterminate sounds, were broken sharply by a loud: 'No!' from the shareholder who had seemed dead. Michael's heart went out to him, the more so as he still seemed dead. The negative was followed by the rising of a thin, polished-looking shareholder, with a small grey moustache.

'If you'll forgive my saying so, sir,' he began, 'your proposal seems to me very rough-and-ready justice. I should be interested to know how you would have handled such a situation if you had been on the Board. It is extremely easy to condemn other people!'

'Hear, hear!' said Michael, astonished at his own voice.

'It is all very well,' the polished shareholder went on, 'when anything of this sort happens, to blame a directorate, but, speaking as a director myself, I should be glad to know whom one is to trust, if not one's manager. As to the policy of foreign insurance, it has been before us at two general meetings; and we have pocketed the profit from it for nearly two years. Have we raised a voice against it?'

The dead shareholder uttered a 'No!' so loud that Michael almost patted his head.

The shareholder, whose neck and back were like a doctor's, rose to answer.

'I differ from the last speaker in his diagnosis of the case. Let us admit all he says, and look at the thing more widely. The proof of pudding is in the eating. When a Government makes a bad mistake of judgement, the electorate turns against it as soon as it feels the effects. This is a very sound check on administration; it may be rough and ready, but it is the less of two evils. A Board backs its judgement; when it loses, it should pay. I think, perhaps, Mr Tolby, being our informal chairman, was out of order in proposing a vote of no confidence; if that be so, I should be happy to do so, myself.'

The dead shareholder's 'No!' was so resounding this time that there was a pause for him to speak; he remained, however, without motion. Both of Michael's neighbours were on their feet. They bobbed at each other over Michael's head, and Mr Tolby sat down.

'Mr Sawdry,' he said.

'Look 'ere gentlemen,' said Mr Sawdry, 'and ladies, this

seems to me a case for compromise. The directors that knew about the manager ought to go; but we might stop at that. The gentleman in front of me keeps on saying "No." Let 'im give us 'is views.'

'No,' said the dead shareholder, but less loudly.

'If a man can't give 'is views,' went on Mr Sawdry, nearly sitting down on Michael, ''e shouldn't interrupt, in my opinion.'

A shareholder in the front row now turned completely round so that he faced the meeting.

'I think,' he said, 'that to prolong this discussion is to waste time; we are evidently in two, if not three, minds. The whole of the business of this country is now conducted on a system of delegated trust; it may be good, it may be bad – but there it is. You've got to trust somebody. Now, as to this particular case, we've had no reason to distrust the Board, so far; and, as I take it, the Board had no previous reason to distrust the late manager. I think it's going too far, at present, to propose anything definite like a vote of no confidence; it seems to me that we should call the Board in and hear what assurances they have to give us against a repetition of anything of the sort in the future.'

The sounds which greeted this moderate speech were so inextricable that Michael could not get the sense of them. Not so with the speech which followed. It came from a shareholder on the right, with reddish hair, light eyelashes, a clipped moustache, and a scraped colour.

'I have no objection whatever to having the Board in,' he said in a rather jeering voice, 'and passing a vote of no confidence in their presence. There is a question, which no one has touched on, of how far, if we turn them out, we could make them liable for this loss. The matter is not clear, but there is a good sporting chance, if we like to take it. Whereas, if we don't turn them out, it's obvious we can't take it, even if we wish.'

The impression made by this speech was of quite a different order from any of the others. It was followed by a hush, as though something important had been said at last. Michael stared at Mr Tolby. The stout man's round, light, rather prominent eyes were extraordinarily reflective. 'Trout must look like that,' thought Michael, 'when they see a mayfly.' Mr Tolby suddenly stood up.

'All right,' he said, ' 'ave 'em in!'

'Yes,' said the dead shareholder. There was no dissent. Michael saw someone rise and ascend the platform.

'Let the Press know!' said Mr Tolby.

Chapter Thirteen

SOAMES AT BAY

━◄•►━

WHEN the door had closed behind the departing directors, Soames sought a window as far as possible from the lunch eaten before the meeting.

'Funeral baked meats, eh, Forsyte?' said a voice in his ear. 'Our number's up, I think. Poor old Mothergill's looking very blue. I think he ought to ask for a second shirt!'

Soames's tenacity began wriggling within him.

'The thing wants tackling,' he grumbled; 'the chairman's not the man for the job!' Shades of old Uncle Jolyon! He would have made short work of this! It wanted a masterful hand.

'Warning to us all, Forsyte, against loyalty! It's not in the period. Ah! Fontenoy!'

Soames became conscious of features rather above the level of his own.

'Well, Mr Forsyte, hope you're satisfied? A pretty damned mess! If I'd been the chairman, I'd never have withdrawn. Always keep hounds under your eye, Mont. Take it off, and they'll go for you! Wish I could get among 'em with a whip; I'd give it those two heavy pug-faced chaps – they mean business! Unless you've got something up your sleeve, Mr Forsyte, we're dished.'

'What should I have up my sleeve?' said Soames coldly.

'Damn it, sir, you put the chestnuts in the fire, it's up to you to pull 'em out. I can't afford to lose these fees!'

Soames heard Sir Lawrence murmur: 'Crude, my dear Fontenoy!' and said with malice:

'You may lose more than your fees!'

'Can't! They may have Eaglescourt tomorrow, and take a loss off my hands.' A gleam of feeling burned up suddenly in the old eyes: 'The country drives you to the wall, skins you to the bone, and expects you to give 'em public service gratis. Can't be done, Mont – can't be done!'

Soames turned away; he had an utter disinclination for talk, like one standing before an open grave, watching a coffin slowly lowered. Here was his infallibility going – going! He had no illusions. It would all be in the papers, and his reputation for sound judgement gone for ever! Bitter! No more would the Forsytes say: 'Soames says –' No more would old Gradman follow him with eyes like an old dog's, grudging sometimes, but ever submitting to infallibility. It would be a nasty jar for the old fellow. His business acquaintances – after all, they were not many, now! – would no longer stare with envious respect. He wondered if the reverberations would reach Dumetrius, and the picture market! The sole comfort was: Fleur needn't know. Fleur! Ah! If only her business were safely over! For a moment his mind became empty of all else. Then with a rush the present filled it up again. Why were they all talking as if there were a corpse in the room? Well! There was – the corpse of his infallibility! As for monetary loss – that seemed secondary, remote, incredible – like a future life. Mont had said something about loyalty. He didn't know what loyalty had to do with it! But if they thought he was going to show any white feather, they were extremely mistaken. Acid courage welled up into his brain. Shareholders, directors – they might howl and shake their fists; he was not going to be dictated to. He heard a voice say:

'Will you come in, please, gentlemen?'

Taking his seat again before his unused quill, he noticed the silence – shareholders waiting for directors, directors for shareholders. 'Wish I could get among 'em with a whip!' Extravagant words of that 'old guinea-pig', but expressive, somehow!

At last the chairman, whose voice always reminded Soames of a raw salad with oil poured over it, said ironically:

'Well, gentlemen, we await your pleasure.'

That stout, red-faced fellow, next to Michael, stood up, opening his pug's mouth.

'To put it shortly, Mr Chairman, we're not at all satisfied; but before we take any resolution, we want to 'ear what you've got to say.'

Just below Soames, someone jumped up and added:

'We'd like to know, sir, what assurances you can offer us against anything of this sort in the future.'

Soames saw the chairman smile – no real backbone in that fellow!

'In the nature of things, sir,' he said, 'none whatever! You can hardly suppose that if we had known our manager was not worthy of our confidence, we should have continued him in the post for a moment!'

Soames thought: 'That won't do – he's gone back on himself!' Yes, and that other pug-faced chap had seen it!

'That's just the point, sir,' he was saying: 'Two of you *did* know, and yet, there the fellow was for months afterwards, playin' 'is own 'and, cheatin' the Society for all he was worth, I shouldn't wonder.'

One after another, they were yelping now:

'What about your own words?'

'You admitted collective responsibility.'

'You said you were perfectly satisfied with the attitude of your co-directors in the matter.' Regular pack!

Soames saw the chairman incline his head as if he wanted to shake it; old Fontenoy muttering, old Mothergill blowing his nose, Meyricke shrugged his sharp shoulders. Suddenly he was cut off from view of them – Sir Lawrence was standing up between.

'Allow me a word! Speaking for myself, I find it impossible to accept the generous attempt of the chairman to shoulder a responsibility which clearly rests on me. If I made a mistake of judgement in not disclosing our suspicions, I must pay the penalty; and I think it will clear the – er – situation if I tender my resignation to the meeting.'

Soames saw him give a little bow, place his monocle in his eye, and sit down.

A murmur greeted the words – approval, surprise, deprecation, admiration? It had been gallantly done. Soames distrusted gallantry – there was always a dash of the peacock about it. He felt curiously savage.

'I, apparently,' he said, rising, 'am the other incriminated director. Very good! I am not conscious of having done anything but my duty from beginning to end of this affair. I am confident that I made no mistake of judgement. And I consider it entirely unjust that I should be penalized. I have had worry and anxiety enough, without being made a scapegoat by shareholders who accepted this policy without a murmur, before ever I came on the Board, and are now angry because they have lost by it. You owe it to me that the policy has been dropped: you owe it to me that you have no longer a fraudulent person for a manager. And you owe it to me that you were called together today to pass judgement on the matter. I have no intention whatever of singing small. But there is another aspect to this affair. I am not prepared to go on giving my services to people who don't value them. I have no patience with the attitude displayed this afternoon. If anyone here thinks he has a grievance against me, let him bring an action. I shall be happy to carry it to the House of Lords, if necessary. I have been familiar with the City all my life, and I have not been in the habit of meeting with suspicions and ingratitude. If this is an instance of present manners, I have been familiar with the City long enough. I do not tender my resignation to the meeting; I resign.'

Bowing to the chairman, and pushing back his chair, he walked doggedly to the door, opened it and passed through.

He sought his hat. He had not the slightest doubt but that he had astonished their weak nerves! Those pug-faced fellows had their mouths open! He would have liked to see what he had left behind, but it was hardly consistent with dignity to open the door again. He took a sandwich instead, and began to eat it with his back to the door and his hat on. He felt better than he had for months. A voice said:

'"And the subsequent proceedings interested him no more!" I'd no idea, Forsyte, you were such an orator! You gave it 'em between the eyes! Never saw a meeting so knocked out! Well, you've saved the Board by focusing their resentment entirely on yourself. It was very gallant, Forsyte!'

Soames growled through his sandwich:

'Nothing of the sort! Are you out, too?'

'Yes. I pressed my resignation. That red-faced fellow was proposing a vote of confidence in the Board when I left – and they'll pass it, Forsyte – they'll pass it! Something was said about financial liability, by the way!'

'Was there?' said Soames, with a grim smile: 'That cock won't fight. Their only chance was to claim against the Board for initiating foreign assurance *ultra vires*; if they're re-affirming the Board, after the question's been raised in open meeting, they're dished. Nothing'll lie against you and me, for not disclosing our suspicions – that's certain.'

'A relief, I confess,' said Sir Lawrence, with a sigh. 'It was the speech of your life, Forsyte!'

Perfectly well aware of that, Soames shook his head. Apart from the horror of seeing himself in print, he was beginning to feel that he had been extravagant. It was always a mistake to lose your temper! A bitter little smile came on his lips. Nobody, not even Mont, would see how unjustly he had been treated.

'Well,' he said, 'I shall go.'

'I think I shall wait, Forsyte, and hear the upshot.'

'Upshot? They'll appoint two other fools, and slaver over each other. Shareholders! Good-bye!' He moved to the door.

Passing the Bank of England, he had a feeling of walking away from his own life. His acumen, his judgement, his manner of dealing with affairs – aspersed! They didn't like it; well – he would leave it! Catch him meddling, in future! It was all of a piece with the modern state of things. Hand to mouth, and the steady men pushed to the wall! The men to whom a pound was a pound, and not a mess of chance and paper. The men who knew that the good of the country was the strict, straight conduct of their own affairs. They were not wanted. One by one, they would get the go-by – as he had got it – in favour of Jack-o'-lanterns, revolutionaries, restless chaps, or clever, unscrupulous fellows, like Elderson. It was in the air. No amount of eating your cake and wanting to have it could take the place of common honesty.

He turned into the Poultry before he knew why he had come there. Well, he might as well tell Gradman at once that he must exercise his own judgement in the future. At the mouth of the backwater he paused for a second, as if to print its buffness on his brain. He would resign his trusts, private and all! He had no notion of being sneered at in the family. But a sudden wave of remembrance almost washed his heart into his boots. What a tale of trust deeds executed, leases renewed, houses sold, investments decided on – in that back room up there; what a mint of quiet satisfaction in estates well managed! Ah! well! He would continue to manage his own. As for the others, they must look out for themselves, now. And a precious time they'd have of it, in face of the spirit there was about!

He mounted the stone steps slowly.

In the repository of Forsyte affairs, he was faced by the unusual – not Gradman, but, on the large ripe table, a large ripe melon alongside a straw bag. Soames sniffed. The thing smelled delicious. He held it to the light. Its greeny yellow tinge, its network of threads – quite Chinese! Was old Gradman going to throw its rind about, like that white monkey?

He was still holding it when a voice said:

'Aoh! I wasn't expecting you today, Mr Soames. I was going early; my wife's got a little party.'

'So I see!' said Soames, restoring the melon to the table. 'There's nothing for you to do at the moment, but I came in to tell you to draw my resignation from the Forsyte trusts.'

The old chap's face was such a study that he could not help a smile.

'You can keep me in Timothy's; but the rest must go. Young Roger can attend to them. He's got nothing to do.'

A gruff and deprecating: 'Dear me! They won't like it!' irritated Soames.

'Then they must lump it! I want a rest.'

He did not mean to enter into the reason – Gradman could read it for himself in the *Financial News*, or whatever he took in.

'Then I shan't be seeing you so often, Mr Soames; there's never anything in Mr Timothy's. Dear me! I'm quite upset. Won't you keep your sister's?'

Soames looked at the old fellow, and compunction stirred within him – as ever, at any sign that he was appreciated.

'Well,' he said, 'keep me in hers; I shall be in about my own affairs, of course. Good afternoon, Gradman. That's a fine melon.'

He waited for no more words. The old chap! *He* couldn't last much longer, anyway, sturdy as he looked! Well, they would find it hard to match him!

On reaching the Poultry, he decided to go to Green Street and see Winifred – queerly and suddenly home-sick for the proximity of Park Lane, for the old secure days, the efflorescent privacy of his youth under the wings of James and Emily. Winifred alone represented for him now, the past; her solid nature never varied, however much she kept up with the fashions.

He found her, a little youthful in costume, drinking China tea, which she did not like – but what could one do, other teas were 'common'! She had taken to a parrot. Parrots were coming in again. The bird made a dreadful noise. Whether under its influence or that of the China tea – which, made in the English way, of a brand the Chinese grew for foreign stomachs, always upset him – he was soon telling her the whole story.

When he had finished, Winifred said comfortably:

'Well, Soames, I think you did splendidly; it serves them right!'

273

Conscious that his narrative must have presented the truth as it would not appear to the public, Soames muttered:

'That's all very well; you'll find a very different version in the financial papers.'

'Oh! but nobody reads them. I shouldn't worry. Do you do Coué? Such a comfortable little man, Soames; I went to hear him. It's rather a bore sometimes, but it's quite the latest thing.'

Soames became inaudible – he never confessed a weakness.

'And how,' asked Winifred, 'is Fleur's little affair?'

'"Little affair!"' echoed a voice above his head. That bird! It was clinging to the brocade curtains, moving its neck up and down.

'Polly!' said Winifred: 'don't be naughty!'

'Soames!' said the bird.

'I've taught him that. Isn't he rather sweet?'

'No,' said Soames. 'I should shut him up; he'll spoil your curtains.'

The vexation of the afternoon had revived within him suddenly. What was life, but parrotry? What did people see of the real truth? They just repeated each other, like a lot of shareholders, or got their precious sentiments out of *The Daily Liar*. For one person who took a line, a hundred followed on, like sheep!

'You'll stay and dine, dear boy!' said Winifred.

Yes! he would dine. Had she a melon, by any chance? He'd no inclination to go and sit opposite his wife at South Square. Ten to one Fleur would not be down. And as to young Michael – the fellow had been there that afternoon and witnessed the whole thing; he'd no wish to go over it again.

He was washing his hands for dinner, when a maid, outside, said:

'You're wanted on the phone, sir.'

Michael's voice came over the wire, strained and husky:

'That you, sir?'

'Yes. What is it?'

'Fleur. It began this afternoon at three. I've been trying to reach you.'

'What?' cried Soames. 'How? Quick!'

'They say it's all normal. But it's so awful. They say quite soon, now.' The voice broke off.

'My God!' said Soames. 'My hat!'

By the front door the maid was asking: 'Shall you be back to dinner, sir?'

'Dinner!' muttered Soames, and was gone.

He hurried along, almost running, his eyes searching for a cab. None to be had, of course! None to be had! Opposite the 'Iseeum' Club he got one, open in the fine weather after last night's storm. That storm! He might have known. Ten days before her time. Why on earth hadn't he gone straight back, or at least telephoned where he would be? All that he had been through that afternoon was gone like smoke. Poor child! Poor little thing! And what about twilight sleep? Why hadn't he been there? He might have – nature! Damn it! Nature – as if it couldn't leave even her alone!

'Get on!' he said, leaning out: 'Double fare!'

Past the Connoisseurs, and the Palace, and Whitehall; past all preserves whence nature was excluded, deep in the waters of primitive emotion Soames sat, grey, breathless. Past Big Ben – eight o'clock! Five hours! Five hours of it!

'Let it be over!' he muttered aloud: 'Let it be over, God!'

Chapter Fourteen

ON THE RACK

WHEN his father-in-law bowed to the chairman and withdrew, Michael had restrained a strong desire to shout: 'Bravo!' Who'd have thought the 'old man' could let fly like that? He had 'got their goats' with a vengeance. Quite an interval of fine mixed vociferation followed, before his neighbour, Mr Sawdry, made himself heard at last.

'Now that the director implicated has resigned, I shall 'ave pleasure in proposing a vote of confidence in the rest of the Board.'

Michael saw his father rise, a little finicky and smiling, and bow to the chairman. 'I take my resignation as accepted also; if you permit me, I will join Mr Forsyte in retirement.'

Someone was saying:

'I shall be glad to second that vote of confidence.'

And brushing past the knees of Mr Sawdry, Michael sought the door. From there he could see that nearly every hand was raised in favour of the vote of confidence; and with the thought: 'Thrown to the shareholders!' he made his way out of the hotel. Delicacy prevented him from seeking out those two. They had saved their dignity; but the dogs had had the rest.

Hurrying west, he reflected on the rough ways of justice. The shareholders had a grievance, of course; and someone had to get it in the neck to satisfy their sense of equity. They had pitched on Old Forsyte, who, of all, was least to blame; for if Bart had only held his tongue, they would certainly have lumped him into the vote of confidence. All very natural and illogical; and four o'clock already!

Counterfeits! The old feeling for Wilfrid was strong in him this day of publication. One must do everything one could for his book – poor old son! There simply must not be a frost.

After calling in at two big booksellers, he made for his club, and closeted himself in the telephone booth. In old days they 'took cabs and went about'. Ringing-up was quicker – was it? With endless vexations, he tracked down Sibley, Nazing, Upshire, Master, and half a dozen others of the elect. He struck a considered note likely to move them, the book – he said – was bound to 'get the goat of the old guard and the duds generally'; it would want a bit of drum-beating from the cognoscenti. To each of them he appealed as the only one whose praise really mattered. 'If you haven't reviewed the book, old chap, will you? It's you who count, of course.' And to each he added: 'I don't care two straws whether it sells, but I do want old Wilfrid to get his due.' And he meant it. The publisher in Michael was dead during that hour in the telephone booth, the friend alive and kicking hard. He came out with sweat running down his forehead, quite exhausted; and it was half-past five.

'Cup of tea – and home!' he thought. He reached his door at six. Ting-a-ling, absolutely unimportant, was cowering in the far corner of the hall.

'What's the matter, old man?'

A sound from above, which made his blood run cold, answered – a long, low moaning.

'Oh, God!' he rasped, and ran upstairs.

Annette met him at the door. He was conscious of her speaking in French, of being called '*mon cher*', of the words '*vers trois heures*. . . . The doctor says one must not worry – all goes for the best.' Again that moan, and the door shut in his face; she was gone. Michael remained standing on the rug with perfectly cold sweat oozing from him, and his nails dug deep into his palms.

'This is how one becomes a father!' he thought: 'This is how I became a son!' That moaning! He could not bear to stay there, and he could not bear to go away. It might be hours, yet! He kept repeating to himself: 'One must not worry – must not worry!' How easily said! How meaningless! His brain, his heart, ranging for relief, lighted on the strangest relief which could possibly have come to him. Suppose this child being born, had not been his – had been – been Wilfrid's; how would he have been feeling, here, outside this door? It might – it might so easily have been – since nothing was sacred, now! Nothing except – yes, just that which was dearer than oneself – just that which was in there, moaning. He could not bear it on the rug, and went downstairs. Across and across the copper floor, a cigar in his mouth, he strode in vague, rebellious agony. Why should birth be like this? And the answer was: It isn't – not in China! To have the creed that nothing mattered – and then run into it like this! Something born at such a cost, must matter, should matter. One must see to that! Speculation ceased in Michael's brain; he stood, listening terribly. Nothing! He could not bear it down there, and went up again. No sound at first, and then another moan! This time he fled into his study, and ranged round the room, looking at the cartoons of Aubrey Greene. He did not see a single one, and suddenly bethought him of 'Old Forsyte'. He ought to be told! He rang up the 'Connoisseurs', the 'Remove', and his own father's clubs, in case they might have gone there together after the meeting. He drew blank everywhere. It was half-past seven. How much longer was this going on? He went back to the bedroom door; could hear nothing. Then down again to the hall. Ting-a-ling was lying by the front door, now. 'Fed-up!' thought Michael, stroking his back, and mechanically clearing the letter-box. Just one letter – Wilfrid's writing! He took it to the foot of the stairs and read it with half his brain, the other half wondering – wandering up there.

DEAR MONT, – I start tomorrow to try and cross Arabia. I thought you might like a line in case Arabia crosses me. I have recovered my senses. The air here is too clear for sentiment of any kind; and passion in exile soon becomes sickly. I am sorry I made you so much disturbance. It was a mistake for me to go back to England after the war, and hang about writing drivel for smart young women and inky folk to read. Poor old England – she's in for a bad time. Give her my love; the same to yourselves.

Yours ever,

WILFRID DESERT

P.S. – If you've published the things I left behind, send any royalties to me care of my governor. – W.D.

Half Michael's brain thought: 'Well, that's that! And the book coming out today!' Queer! Was Wilfrid right – was it all a blooming gaff – the inky stream? Was one just helping on England's sickness? Ought they all to get on camels and ride the sun down? And yet, in books were comfort and diversion; and they were wanted! England had to go on – go on! 'No retreat, no retreat, they must conquer or die who have no retreat! ...' God! There it was again! Back he flew upstairs, with his ears covered and his eyes wild. The sounds ceased; Annette came out to him.

'Her father, *mon cher*; try to find her father!'

'I have – I can't,' gasped Michael.

'Try Green Street – Mrs Dartie. *Courage!* All is normal – it will be quite soon, now.'

When he had rung up Green Street and been answered at last, he sat with the door of his study open, waiting for 'Old Forsyte' to come. Half his sight remarked a round hole burnt in his trouser leg – he hadn't even noticed the smell; hadn't even realized that he had been smoking. He must pull himself together for the 'old man'. He heard the bell ring, and ran down to open.

'Well?' said Soames.

'Not yet, sir. Come up to my study. It's nearer.'

They went up side by side. That trim grey head, with the deep furrow between the eyes, and those eyes staring as if at pain behind them, steadied Michael. Poor old chap! He was 'for it', too! They were both on 'their uppers'!

'Have a peg, sir? I've got brandy here.'

'Yes,' said Soames. 'Anything.'

With the brandies in their hands, half-raised, they listened – jerked their hands up, drank. They were automatic, like two doll figures worked by the same string.

'Cigarette, sir?' said Michael.

Soames nodded.

With the lighted cigarettes just not in their mouths, they listened, put them in, took them out, puffed smoke. Michael had his right arm across his chest. Soames his left. They formed a pattern, thus, side by side.

'Bad to stick, sir. Sorry!'

Soames nodded. His teeth were clenched. Suddenly his hand relaxed.

'Listen!' he said. Sounds – different – confused!

Michael's hand seized something, gripped it hard; it was cold, thin – the hand of Soames. They sat thus, hand in hand, staring at the doorway, for how long neither knew.

Suddenly that doorway darkened; a figure in grey stood there – Annette!

'It is all r-right! A son!'

Chapter Fifteen

CALM

ON waking from deep sleep next morning, Michael's first thought was: 'Fleur is back!' He then remembered.

To his: 'O.K.?' whispered at her door, he received an emphatic nod from the nurse.

In the midst of excited expectation he retained enough modernity to think: 'No more blurb! Go and eat your breakfast quietly!'

In the dining-room Soames was despising the broken egg before him. He looked up as Michael entered, and buried his face in his cup. Michael understood perfectly; they had sat hand in hand! He saw, too, that the journal opened by his plate was of a financial nature.

'Anything about the meeting, sir? Your speech must read like one o'clock!'

With a queer little sound Soames held out the paper. The headlines ran: 'Stormy meeting – resignation of two directors – a vote of confidence.' Michael skimmed down till he came to:

'Mr Forsyte, the director involved, in a speech of some length, said he had no intention of singing small. He deprecated the behaviour of the shareholders; he had not been accustomed to meet with suspicions. He tendered his resignation.'

Michael dropped the sheet.

'By Jove!' he said – '"Involved – suspicions". They've given it a turn, as though –!'

'The papers!' said Soames, and resumed his egg.

Michael sat down, and stripped the skin off a banana. '"Nothing became him like his death",' he thought: 'Poor old boy!'

'Well, sir,' he said, 'I was there, and all I can say is: You and my father were the only two people who excited my re-spect.'

'That!' said Soames, putting down his spoon.

Michael perceived that he wished to be alone, and swallowing the banana, went to his study. Waiting for his summons, he rang up his father.

'None the worse for yesterday, sir?'

Sir Lawrence's voice came clear and thin, rather high.

'Poorer and wiser. What's the bulletin?'

'Top-hole.'

'Our love to both. Your mother wants to know if he has any hair?'

'Haven't seen him yet. I'm just going.'

Annette, indeed, was beckoning from the doorway.

'She wants you to bring the little dog, *mon cher*.'

With Ting-a-ling under his arm, and treading on tiptoe, Michael entered. The eleventh baronet! He did not seem to amount to much, beneath her head bent over him. And surely her hair was darker! He walked up to the bed, and touched it reverently.

Fleur raised her head, and revealed the baby sucking vigorously at her little finger. 'Isn't he a monkey?' said her faint voice.

Michael nodded. A monkey clearly – but whether white – that was the question!

'And you, sweetheart?'

'All right now, but it was –' She drew her breath in, and her eyes darkened: 'Ting, look!'

The Chinese dog, with nostrils delicately moving, drew back-ward under Michael's arm. His whole demeanour displayed a knowing criticism. 'Puppies,' he seemed to say, 'we do it in China. Judgement reserved!'

'What eyes!' said Michael: 'We needn't tell *him* that this was brought from Chelsea by the doctor.'

Fleur gave the tiniest laugh.

'Put him down, Michael.'

Michael put him down, and he went to his corner.

'I mustn't talk,' said Fleur, 'but I want to, frightfully; as if I'd been dumb for months.'

'Just as I felt,' thought Michael, 'she's been away, away somewhere, utterly away.'

'It was like being held down, Michael. Months of not being yourself.'

Michael said softly: 'Yes! the process *is* behind the times! Has he got any hair? My mother wants to know.'

Fleur revealed the head of the eleventh baronet, covered with dark down.

'Like my grandmother's; but it'll get lighter. His eyes are going to be grey. Oh! and, Michael, about godparents? Alison, of course – but men?'

Michael dwelled a little before answering:

'I had a letter from Wilfrid yesterday. Would you like him? He's still out there, but I could hold the sponge for him in church.'

'Is he all right again?'

'He says so.'

He could not read the expression of her eyes, but her lips were pouted slightly.

'Yes,' she said: 'and I think one's enough, don't you? Mine never gave me anything.'

'One of mine gave me a Bible, and the other gave me a wigging. Wilfrid, then.' And he bent over her.

Her eyes seemed to make him a little ironic apology. He kissed her hair, and moved hurriedly away.

By the door Soames was standing, awaiting his turn.

'Just a minute only, sir,' the nurse was saying.

Soames walked up to the bedside, and stood looking at his daughter.

'Dad, dear!' Michael heard her say.

Soames just touched her hand, nodded, as if implying approval of the baby, and came walking back, but, in a mirror, Michael saw his lips quivering.

On the ground floor once more, he had the most intense desire to sing. It would not do; and, entering the Chinese room, he stood staring out into the sunlit square. Gosh! It was good to be alive! Say what you liked, you couldn't beat it! They might turn their noses up at life, and look down them at it; they might bolster up the future and the past, but – give him the present!

'I'll have that white monkey up again!' he thought. 'I'll see the brute further before he shall depress me!'

He went out to a closet under the stairs, and, from beneath four pairs of curtains done up in moth-preserver and brown paper, took out the picture. He held it away from him in the dim light. The creature's eyes! It was all in those eyes!

'Never mind, old son!' he said: 'Up you go!' And he carried it into the Chinese room.

Soames was there.

'I'm going to put him up again, sir.'

Soames nodded.

'Would you hold him, while I hook the wire?'

Soames held the picture.

Returning to the copper floor, Michael said:

'All right, sir!' and stood back.

Soames joined him. Side by side they contemplated the white monkey.

'He won't be happy till he gets it,' said Michael at last: 'The only thing is, you see, he doesn't know what *it* is.'

MORE ABOUT PENGUINS

If you have enjoyed reading this book you may wish to know that *Penguin Book News* appears every month. It is an attractively illustrated magazine containing a complete list of books published by Penguins and still in print, together with details of the month's new books. A specimen copy will be sent free on request.

Penguin Book News is obtainable from most bookshops; but you may prefer to become a regular subscriber at 3s. for twelve issues. Just write to Dept EP, Penguin Books Ltd, Harmondsworth, Middlesex, enclosing a cheque or postal order, and you will be put on the mailing list.

Some other books published by Penguins are described on the following pages.

Note : *Penguin Book News* is not
available in the U.S.A., Canada or Australia

John Galsworthy

TO LET

1920: the old Forsytes are dead except Timothy, now a centenarian reverting to petulant babyhood, and the Forsytes are split into two camps: those of Soames, the tight-lipped lawyer; and of Jolyon, his opposite in temperament. When Soames's daughter, Fleur, and Jolyon's son, Jon, fall in love, the Forsyte armistice is over, and old wounds are mercilessly reopened.

Also in the Forsyte Saga available in Penguins

THE MAN OF PROPERTY

IN CHANCERY

NOT FOR SALE IN THE U.S.A. OR CANADA

Two other Forsyte novels by John Galsworthy

THE SILVER SPOON

When Soames Forsyte hears his daughter Fleur described as a snob and a nobody in her own house, he orders the speaker, fast-living Marjorie Ferrar, to leave. In the following weeks, brittle social niceties collapse as tension gathers ... and fashionable London watches as events move towards a courtroom climax, a head-on collision between Forsyte standards and the morals of a new generation.

SWAN SONG

The General Strike of 1926 finds Fleur Mont running a railway canteen; across the counter she catches her first sight in seven years of Jon Forsyte, her first and only love. Both have since married but current loyalties are soon held to ransom by re-awakened passion. Fleur's father, Soames, is drawn into the conflict and discovers, too late, the truth of the old proverb: 'That which a man most loves shall in the end destroy him.'

ROSEM... FOR REMEM...RANCE

Susan Sallis

CORGI BOOKS

ROSEMARY FOR REMEMBRANCE

A CORGI BOOK   0 552 13136 9

First publication in Great Britain

PRINTING HISTORY

Corgi edition published 1987
Corgi edition reprinted 1987
Corgi edition reprinted 1988
Corgi edition reprinted 1990

Copyright © Susan Sallis 1987

This book is set in 10/11pt Palatino

Corgi Books are published by Transworld Publishers Ltd.,
61–63 Uxbridge Road, Ealing, London W5 5SA,
in Australia by Transworld Publishers (Australia) Pty. Ltd.,
15–23 Helles Avenue, Moorebank, NSW 2170, and in New
Zealand by Transworld Publishers (N.Z.) Ltd., Cnr. Moselle
and Waipareira Avenues, Henderson, Auckland.

Reproduced, printed and bound in Great Britain by
BPCC Hazell Books
Aylesbury, Bucks, England
Member of BPCC Ltd.

One

IT was the first real Alert since war had been declared, and the three women herded the children together hastily and ran down the garden to the air raid shelter clutching Thermoses, gas masks, baby bottles and torches. They should have known the drill; there had been practices galore and they had entertained the children with dramatic constructions of how they would stand under the throbbing night sky, shaking their fists upward, defying old Hitler to do his worst. But the real thing robbed them of their wits. They were like a gaggle of geese making for a pond and finally falling into it.

It was the time of the phoney war. They had gathered at the big house in Bedford Close while their husbands attended a meeting about fire-fighting. It was almost like old times; they became the three Rising girls again, acknowledged beauties, and with something added. War was terrible and two of their children were in it up to their necks, but it was a catastrophe they could share; it bound them; it gave them something outside . . something legitimate . . . to fear and to fight. Those other things which split them in the past, inner demons, were temporarily defeated.

The sisters, March, May and April, had settled themselves before one of March's enormous fires — because coal shortage or no, she always had a big fire — and talked as they had always done. Inconsequential, mean-ingless chat which sometimes held such significance that it was years later before they realized their own prescience.

March Luker, ramrod-straight at forty-seven, sat next to her favourite niece, Davina Daker. May Gould, suspiciously golden-haired at forty-six, definitely plump, nursed her second child, eighteen-month-old Gretta; her surprise baby, born eighteen years after her son, Victor. Flora, April's second daughter, leaned over the baby, examining closely the sweep of golden lashes on the cheek. April herself leaned back, gloriously relaxed and warm, thinking that if David got back in time, the four of them could cycle home to Winterditch Lane in time to put up the blackout shutters for Aunt Sylv. Aunt Sylv, deep into her seventies, could cope with the heavy bombazine curtains in the kitchen, but the shutters, made by David with roofing felt on a frame of battens, were too much for her.

Out of the blue March said suddenly, 'I think Albert might try to come home for your fourteenth birthday, darling.' She spoke to Davina and though the girl did not move from her position on the floor, she became alert. Her blue eyes, unfocused on the fire caverns, sharpened frowningly, and her throat moved as she swallowed.

'Why . . . what makes you think . . . have you had a letter?'

'No.' March did not enlarge for a long moment, and April, knowing how much it hurt her sister that Albert, her only child, remained stubbornly incommunicado, said softly, 'Look at Gretta, Davie. She looks like a little angel, doesn't she?'

Davie glanced obediently at the sleeping baby and smiled. She was indeed pleased that another fair baby had been born into the family. She and Albert were both colourless compared with the vivid dark intelligence of Victor and Flo. Now Gretta swung the balance in their favour. She was beautiful; and surely if she was beautiful

8

then Davina herself couldn't possibly be as nondescript as her mirror constantly insisted.

May laughed, wonderfully happy in spite of the Siegfried Line and old Hitler and Victor being in the Bloody Infantry which was bloody ridiculous when he was a talented artist. How could she help being happy when she was so fully and satisfyingly self-conscious? Conscious of herself, that was; conscious of herself as a mature, beautiful, complete woman. Loved . . . no, idolized . . . by her handsome Monty, a mother — triumphantly a mother for the second time — at forty-four, and with a talented, good-looking son who suitably worshipped from afar.

She gurgled, 'Darlings, has it occurred to you that we're perpetuating ourselves? The three Rising girls. Now there are three more. Davie, Flo and Gretta.' She put her free arm around her nine-year-old niece. 'Darling Flo, do you mind following in our footsteps? It's been quite good fun, you know.'

April smiled too but said quickly, 'History never repeats itself. Not really. Similarities perhaps—'

Flora said, 'The war. There was the Great War, Mummy. When you were little girls.'

March laughed. 'I was twenty-two when *that* little lot happened. I can remember Pa reading out Mr Asquith's speech to us.'

'We were rescuing Belgium then,' May said. 'Now we're rescuing Poland. A great many similarities, April.'

Surprisingly March nodded; she so rarely agreed with May. But she was remembering her brother Albert and her deep, never-forgotten love for him. Soon after his death at Mons, her own son, Albert Frederick had been conceived. And for years now she had nursed the hope that he and his cousin Davina would somehow live out her own dead love. It wasn't *exactly* history repeating itself, of course; they were cousins, not brother and sister; but it was near enough.

She said, 'As a matter of fact Davie, when Victor wrote

9

to tell us that Albert was stationed in this country but that he'd promised to keep his whereabouts dark, Uncle Fred pulled a few strings and found out just where. He won't tell me where it is, but he's going to see him and see if this whole sorry business can be forgotten now.'

Davie said nothing. She had moved away from her aunt's knees and was clutching her own very tightly. April and May smiled uncertainly. Albert's flight was two years old now, and should have been forgotten. As far as anyone knew he had had some trouble with a girl in Birmingham when he was doing his mechanics course at the Austin works. He'd gone to Spain to fight with the International Brigade and when he got in touch with Victor to say he'd returned to England to join the Royal Air Force, they'd all expected him to come home. He had not done so.

April said tentatively, 'That's good of Fred. Very good, March.'

March nodded. She and Fred Luker had had their ups and downs, but for the last two years they had drawn close. She said with typical brevity, 'Yes.'

Davina came to life. 'Look, Aunt March. Uncle Fred mustn't *ask* Albert to come home for my birthday. I mean it sounds as if — I mean — I don't want Albert to feel he has to do anything which might . . . which might . . .'

March understood so well. She leaned down and wrapped her long arms around the tight narrow shoulders.

'Darling, he won't. Believe me. But when he gives Albert all the family news . . . well, I just think that he will want to come home and your birthday will be the ideal time to do it.'

May said sentimentally, 'Talk about history repeating itself. D'you remember when our Albert came home on leave — just before your birthday it was, March—' And then she stopped, remembering that when he had gone back from that leave he had been killed.

April was still casting about for a suitably diverting

10

subject when Chattie knocked on the door and came in pushing the tea trolley.

'Dark already,' she commented. 'And you sitting 'ere with no blackout!' She bustled over to the tall French doors and began pulling at the heavy velvet curtains.

April stood up and took over the trolley.

'No lights though, Chattie,' she pointed out.

'That there fire 'll cast a glow to light the way for 'Itler's Luffty Waffy.' Chattie marched back to the door and switched on the light. Everyone squinted and blinked and May put a shading hand over Gretta's sleeping face.

Chattie surveyed them all, her disapproval fading into a sentimental smile. She had been with March and Fred Luker for only five years, but she was one of the family now. She had suffered with them when Master Albert left for Spain and she had wept loyal tears when Fred had taken a mistress. If she had her way the whole family would move in together and fortify the house against attackers.

She said, 'I put a pinch of that reconstituted egg in them there scones. They're nice though I says it as shouldn't. And that man came with the logs and 'e's stacked 'em quite neat and nice along the side of the garage. 'E wanted to put 'em in the air raid shelter — says as we might as well use it for summat. But I said no because our girls like to play house there.'

Flo said, 'Good old Chattie.'

April said, 'Don't be cheeky to Chattie, Flo.'

And, unexpectedly, Davie laughed.

It was so unusual that Chattie waited for an explanation. When none came, she too laughed just to keep Davie company and went back to the kitchen to skin the rabbit which Mr Luker had brought in from Robinswood Hill that very afternoon. March, May and April knew why Davie had laughed and all in their way were apprehensive about it. March because she wanted to see her son and her niece eventually united and her personal hopes never seemed to bear fruit. May because

11

she thought that Albert had skedaddled off to Spain to escape from a very difficult intense relationship with Davie. And April . . . April simply prayed silently: 'Don't let him hurt her again. Not again.'

Then, with the teapot poised over the first cup, the siren began its anguished wail.

At first they did not take it seriously. They found that night's *Citizen* and searched it for some notice of a practice raid. Davie said, 'Did we leave the gas masks in Aunt March's room with our coats?'

May gave a small groan because the enormous respirator specially constructed for babies was sitting on her kitchen table in Chichester Street.

April said, 'It's not a genuine raid. It can't be. The ARP would have had some warning of aircraft in the area and the warden would have come to tell us. And David, Fred and Monty would have come home straightaway.'

The door burst open and Chattie stood there.

'The dentist and his wife over the road, Mrs Luker . . . they've gone down to their shelter. And someone's doin' a rattle somewhere up the Barnwood Road.'

'Oh dear God,' gasped May because rattles warned of gas bombs.

'We'd best go down the garden.' Chattie began pulling cushions off the chairs. Davie and April ran for the coats. Flo held the baby while March and May went to the kitchen for the Thermos flasks. Somehow they got themselves down the dark path, their shaded torches useless. Already searchlights struck at the sky, the ack-ack guns over on the greyhound track thundered out and the garden was lit luridly by their flashes. The tennis court on their left was spotlit: with its high wire fence it looked like a prison compound. Ahead of them was the dark hole of the shelter.

April shouted, 'Get down quickly. Shrapnel.'

They practically fell down the shelter steps and into the deckchairs which were neatly arranged around its edge.

The baby was sobbing hysterically and in the intervals when she drew breath, May's soothing 'There, there . . .' sounded over-loud. No-one else spoke. April and March began feeling their way around. Chattie lit the old storm lantern; they distributed cushions, coats and gas masks. Gretta began to hiccough on her sobs and her weeping turned to a grizzle.

'So long as those blasted guns don't go off again, she'll be all right,' May said in a curiously sing-song voice meant to be reassuring. 'My God, that was enough to stop anyone's heart.'

March said, 'Look May, if there is a gas warning, I've got a spare respirator — Fred didn't take his.'

'Sis, babies have great big things. They go inside them.'

'I know. But if the worst comes to the worst—'

Flo said in a wobbly voice, 'Chattie was right. We guided the German planes right to Gloucester. It's our fault.'

'We did no such thing.' April managed to sound as if the whole thing was a joke. 'Haven't you noticed something? Or rather, not noticed something?'

'Oh Mummy. Is it one of your riddles?'

'There are no planes. D'you remember Daddy telling us the sort of noise German planes make? A sort of coming-and-going noise? Well there's no noise like that. In fact, since the guns went off there's no noise at all except from us!'

'We shot them all down!' Flora crowed.

Gretta woke from her weep-induced coma and gurgled at her cousin. May laughed, kissing her ear and holding the precious body to her in an excess of love.

'Perhaps it was a practice after all.'

March said, 'If it was, I shall write to the mayor about it. We could have fallen and broken something. Or had heart attacks like you said, May!'

'Let us string up old Adolf on his Siegfried Line . . .' May bounced Gretta in time to the jingle, heart attacks and respirators forgotten in sudden euphoria. It was as if they'd gone into battle and won.

13

Flora took up the chorus. 'Watch him swing and hear him sing his little tune.'

They all sang raucously, 'Oh, let us string up old Adolf on his Siegfried line . . .'

And from the mouth of the shelter, Monty's unmistakable tenor continued, 'And just listen to that croon.' And Fred called, 'What is this? You girls having a party down there?' And David — April was so thankful David was with them — just laughed and laughed.

They trooped out, helped and hindered by the men, and as they straggled back up the garden path, the searchlights disappeared and the All Clear wailed its constant note over bewildered Gloucester.

They had left the back door unlocked and no guard around the fire.

'Once burglars latch on to what is happening they'll love it when there's an Alert,' Fred commented gloomily, crouching before the fire to lift and lighten it for the shivering women.

Chattie mourned, ''Tis all my fault, Mr Luker. It just took my wits.'

'It took all our wits. Make another pot of tea, Chattie, and butter some more scones, there's a dear.' March, who might have snapped at Fred two years ago, passed behind him and touched his head lightly. His pale straw-coloured hair was thin now and liberally salted with white: it was also pearled with mist.

'Where is your cap?' she asked in her old sharp voice. 'I've told you you mustn't go out without a cap this treacherous weather!'

And he, who might have met her aggression with steely indifference in the past, caught at the hand, pulled himself up and held her for a moment to his side.

'We were issued with our tin hats,' he grinned. 'They fell off on the way home so we carried them.'

Monty produced his and stuck it on his Brylcreemed head. 'Underneath the spreading chestnut tree, Mr

Chamberlain said to me, if you want to have your tin hat free, you must join the ARP.' He grabbed the baby and paraded around the grand piano, the image of Max Miller. Flora crowed with laughter and even Davie permitted herself a smile.

'Idiot,' commented May fondly.

David explained properly.

'The meeting was at the top of Northgate Mansions where the Observer Corps have their HQ. So we heard about the stray Heinkel before the siren went. Everyone with families just left immediately. We were at the top of the pitch when the siren went.'

April said nothing: they must have run all the way and David's groin was still full of shrapnel from 1916. Davie got up and sat on the arm of her father's chair.

'So what's happening? Is there to be another meeting?' March opened the door for Chattie and took over the trolley. The clatter of cups, odd notes on the piano picked out by Gretta, the gentle hissing of fresh logs on the fire were like an orchestra tuning up.

Fred grinned. 'Don't think so. It's a right pig's dinner, but we did sort out some kind of training programme for fire-watching and fighting. What it amounts to is that each street has its warden and the warden is responsible for blackout, getting people into shelters, checking on gas masks. There are to be two fire-watchers on duty all through the hours of darkness.'

'My God,' March said blankly; she had considered fire-watching.

'You won't have to watch all that time, Marcie,' Fred reassured her. 'Only when there's an Alert. I've got a tin hat for you.' He grinned again. 'I reckon it'll suit you too.'

They all tried on the tin hats in between eating scones and drinking tea. Chattie, scurrying to and fro replenishing the pot, heating more scones, making certain no-one was dropping dead from starvation, pronouncd that Flora and Davie could do a music-hall turn in theirs. Immediately the two girls fell into plans for a Christmas concert they were putting on in aid of the Spitfire Fund.

Eventually April said, 'I think we should go home, darlings. Aunt Sylv will be worried sick.'

They donned coats and scarves again and went out to switch on their shaded bicycle lamps. Davie hung back and got Fred to herself.

'Uncle Fred . . .'

He watched her, as he always did, which made her very wary of him. Albie had always loathed his stepfather and that was reason enough for Davie to treat him with suspicion.

'Uncle Fred, Aunt March says you are going to see Albert soon.'

She tried to meet the cold grey stare and was surprised when he was the first to look away. The little nerve that sometimes ticked away at the top of his jaw was very obvious.

He said curtly, 'I had thought of it.'

She gathered all her courage. 'I wondered . . . would you give him a message from me?'

He stood up and leaned on the mantelpiece, gazing into the fire.

'I'll give him messages from all of us, of course. I shall tell him how well your singing lessons are going, how proud we arc of you.'

Fred often told her that the family were proud of her. She was glad, of course; her voice compensated a little for her utter plainness. But it wasn't what she wanted to tell Albert.

She said, 'I meant . . . would you ask him to write to me please, Uncle Fred?'

'I don't think . . . I'm sure he would have written to you already, Davina, if he thought it was right.'

She looked at the back of his jacket; there were leather patches at the elbows and two openings in the seams which made it very fashionable. Uncle Fred was rich and powerful and could do almost anything. Except bring Albert back home.

She asked suddenly, surprising herself, 'Were you glad when he ran off to Spain to find Uncle Tolly?'

He stiffened and did not answer immediately. Then he said in a tired voice, 'No. No, I wasn't glad, Davie,'

'You could have got him back. You could have gone there and found him and brought him back.'

'There was a war over there, darling.'

'Yes. But Tolly got over there. Albert got over there. You could have done it easily if you'd wanted to.'

There was a little silence; he rested his head on his arm as if it were too heavy to hold up.

'I could have gone there, yes. He wouldn't have come back with me.'

Doubt hardened into suspicion.

'Did you make him go? Did you tell him never to write to me again? Never to see me again?'

She couldn't believe he would have done that; and if he'd tried she couldn't believe that Albert would have obeyed him. But when he was still silent it became an appalling possibility.

She repeated sharply, '*Did* you?'

He said, 'I did not tell him to go to Spain, my darling. I had no idea . . . can't you remember how I scoured London for him? It's only two years ago, Davie. Can't you remember that?'

'But something must have happened. Something really terrible.'

'I thought Victor explained. Albert wrote to Victor and I understood—'

'But that was two *years* ago!'

She remembered Victor's words that frightful day in the bluebell woods when he told her that he had had a letter from Albert. '*Davie, darling Davie, he won't come back to you. I'm sorry, so sorry. But he won't.*' She hadn't believed him; not with her whole self. Only with her brain.

She repeated, 'That was two years ago. I know there was another girl.' She took a deep breath and clenched

17

her hands at her side until the nails bit into her palms. 'I . . . I suppose she had a baby. That's what happens, isn't it? It's terrible, I know that. But I don't care!' Embarrassment almost choked her; no-one spoke of such things. But she had to make it crystal clear that whatever Albert had done made no difference to her.

Fred was embarrassed too. He said levelly, 'Listen Davie, please be sensible. We love you very much and when this happened we had to watch you being hurt. And that is not easy. But time has gone on and you're interested in your singing and . . . please leave things as they are, my dear. If Albert had wanted . . . don't you think . . . wouldn't he have let you know?'

She hung on to her courage physically, cutting deeper and deeper into her palms. She had never been able to voice her feelings except to Victor that day in the woods. If she were ever to be honest, this was the time.

'You mean that he got tired of his little girl cousin loving him? Following him around like a puppy? You mean he doesn't want that to happen again?'

'Not quite so . . .' He turned and held out his arms, his face twisted with pain.

She stepped back. 'No. You don't understand at all.' She picked up her gas mask and slung it over her neck and one arm. It wouldn't matter how honest she was, no-one would ever understand. 'It wasn't like that. I was his sister and he was my brother. He could have told me anything.'

Fred's arms dropped to his side.

'What do you mean?' He sounded stupid.

She said dismissively, 'It doesn't matter. It's no good talking about it. Just tell him that I won't bother him. But that whatever he has done, he can tell me.' She gestured. 'He knows that anyway.'

She swung out of the sitting-room and along the darkened passage. David was returning to find her.

'Come on, little apple.' He held out his hand to her and she took it between hers and held it tightly. Perhaps she

18

had been wrong when she thought no-one understood. Her father and she never spoke of Albert, but sometimes she thought he understood everything. Everything in the whole world.

She said, 'Daddy, I wish you wouldn't call me little apple. I'm five foot two and I'm going to be gigantic!'

He raised his brows comically.

'I'm sorry darling. But you see, you're so darned *edible*!' And they went into the night laughing together.

March, returning shivering to the warmth of the sitting-room, found Fred staring blankly into the fire with an expression she had come to dread. She knelt by his chair and took his face in her hands.

'Early night, Freddie?' she asked softly, kissing his nose and eyes.

He tried to respond. 'Vamp.' But then he said, 'I wish you hadn't told Davie I'm going to see Albert. It's raised her hopes again.'

March stood up and took a cigarette from the mantelpiece. It was almost the only issue these days on which they still disagreed.

'And why not? All that upset two years ago . . . he should be over that by now. I really cannot see why — eventually — those two can't make a match of it. They're ideally suited.'

He closed his eyes. 'Marcie. When I told Albert that I was his father, it did something to him.'

She refused to think back, to imagine it. That was a part of her life she had sectioned off for ever; Fred's leave from France, her consequent pregnancy and hasty marriage to her elderly uncle. It was terrible, frightful, that her darling Albert Frederick now knew the truth. She accepted that it had made a permanent rift between them. But Davie could heal that breach; Davie could make everything almost all right again.

She laughed lightly. 'Obviously. He couldn't face us. He went away and he's never come back.' She inhaled

19

fiercely. 'Obviously it did something to him. I had noticed.'

He squeezed his eyes tightly as if with sudden pain, but his voice was calm enough when he spoke.

'More than that, darling. It put him off . . . marriage.'

She looked down at him through her cigarette smoke, wishing for the millionth time that he hadn't told Albert the truth. Then she leaned down and kissed him again.

'I know what you mean, Freddie. I know. You mean sex. And especially sex with someone like Davie, someone innocent and sweet.' She stroked his jaw, feeling the slight twitch beneath her fingers, trying to smooth it out. 'Darling, of all people in the world, don't you think I understand that?'

He permitted himself a small smile. So much of their marriage had been frigid. That March could now admit it, could talk so freely, was wonderful. He cupped her chin and held her mouth with his for a long time.'

When Chattie knocked and came in for the trolley ten minutes later, they were on the rug in front of the fire and she retreated hastily, her face red, but smiling. She had thought — not very long ago — that they could never bear to touch each other again.

Fred whispered, 'That was Chattie.'

'Oh dear, was it? Should we stop?'

'We can't, can we?'

'No.'

But afterwards he said, 'Marcie, my darling. Can you forgive me?'

She said drowsily, 'Why do you always say that, Freddie? You know I forgave you a long time ago. You know it's all right between us now.'

But Fred had long ago accepted that there was no such thing as certainty. He snapped on his braces and buttoned his trousers and called through the door to Chattie. And as she marched in, still red-faced, eyes turned away from March's déshabillé, he thought suddenly of Albert with great and enormous relief. Albert hated him, hated him

20

for himself and for being his father. But Albert knew the whole truth. He would be able to talk to Albert, giving and taking pain, but with complete honesty.

Two

ALBERT TOMMS looked around the Mess at his fellow pilots and thought that if he indulged in much laughter these days, he might well crease up with it right now. There were seasoned fliers here, at least two of them instructors from the Navigation School at Prestwick, others civilian pilots with many hours of flying behind them; but they were so totally innocent. Albert had returned to England soon after the Munich Pact last year, and had gained his treasured wings just before Hitler entered Poland, but of all the men here, he alone knew what he had let himself in for. He had vivid memories of the crack Fascist squadron — the Condors — coming at him out of the sun. He had seen cities bomb-devastated and had gone into ruins to pull human remains into the daylight. He was frightened. It did not show; among the assembled men he seemed the least nervous, the most natural; his lack of banter and his calm appraising look gave him an assurance which belied any inner fears.

Jack Doswell, fresh from the Auxiliary Air Force, said to him, 'I say Tomms old man, have you heard about Bussie Mayhew pranging the Spit after patrol today? It was killing. They plotted a Heinkel lurking around the convoy, and three of us went after it and Bussie was in the cannon Spit so of course he got it. We followed it inland and when it crash-landed, he went down after it. Next thing we knew, he'd turned over and the Jerries had to pull

22

him out! It was the funniest thing I've seen since the war began!'

Albert looked at him straightly and shrugged. 'I suppose so. But it was the only Spit we'd got with cannon.'

It finished the exchange. Albert found that a great many conversations died a similar death. He was the same age as his fellow fliers, but his experience put him at a distance from them. He was the only sober guest at a wild party.

He looked round the Mess again, noting objectively the eager faces, listening to the hoarse laughter, and thinking as he always thought, of Davina Daker; then of Davina's mother, his once-adored Aunt April, who had two-timed Uncle David so cruelly; then of Bridget Hall, Uncle Tolly's wife, who had done the same thing to Tolly; and lastly of his own mother, March Luker, who had two-timed her elderly husband Edwin Tomms. Sometimes he thought he hated all women. Every one of them. Except Davina, who was innocent, and who was — as he was himself — a victim of the others.

'Hey, Tomms old chap.' It was Jack Doswell again. Jack had tried to attach himself to Albert from the moment they assembled here on 30th August. 'Come back from wherever you've gone! Tarragona, was it?' So word had got around that he'd been with the Comintern Brigade. He fixed Jack with his bleak, pale blue gaze, and wondered what the boy would say if he knew just what that meant. 'Boy'? Jack Doswell had been in the Auxiliary Air Force since leaving school in 1934. It really *was* laughable.

He made an effort and said lightly, 'Not quite so far as Tarragona. Matter of fact I was thinking of Gloucester. My home.' He mustered a grin. 'First bridgehead of the Severn, don't y'know.'

Jack grinned back gratefully. 'Very old hat. I recall from dust-moted school afternoons—' he donned a pseudo-pedantic air — 'the Domesday Book was compiled there. And nothing much happened after.'

'Little do you know, sonny-boy.'

It was so easy really. Albert wondered how on earth he could have forgotten the knack of meaningless repartee; he had been taught by an expert after all. Yes, cousin Victor could knock spots off all these would-be men-of-the-world.

Jack's grin stretched from ear to ear at this unlooked-for response from his hero.

'Well, if you don't mind old man, I won't climb on your knee at this precise moment. But—' he went down, arms spread à la Jolson, '—not quite from heaven, dear old Dad, but near enough for you—' he gave up and rose to his feet to dust off his uniform trousers. 'In other words, you've got a visitor. From Gloucester I should guess by the vowel sounds.'

'What?' Albert sprang to his feet, convinced it was Victor. The way his cousin had come to mind just then was typical of all their old telepathy. 'By all that's holy — where is he?'

Jack paused, hardly believing his ears and eyes. Ever since he'd met Albert Tomms last August, he had admired his complete self-containment which no-one else on the station possessed. In spite of his comic name, his lack of decent schooling, his absurd absorption with the inside of his aircraft as well as the actual flying of it, Albert Tomms was someone Jack knew instinctively could be relied on. Jack sensed, though could not name, his own insubstantiality, the insubstantiality of everyone else here. No-one ever knew what was happening. When they were sent after a 'plot' it usually turned out to be a fishing boat or a reconnaissance plane. When they'd found that Heinkel, the triumph of Bussie's 'bag' had ended absurdly. There was constantly a feeling that the whole war-thing might turn out to be a joke. Until you looked into the eyes of Albert Tomms.

And now, here was the tempered steel springing into a life of its own. He watched Albert practically gallop out of the Mess, the draught from his going sweeping

24

someone's cards from the table. Jack grinned. He was glad he'd been the one to bring news of Tommy's visitor. Perhaps that's what it was, poor old Tommy was homesick just like everyone else. Except, of course, he'd cleared off to Spain in '37 and apparently hadn't seen anyone from home since then.

Fred had had a long and complicated train journey to reach Tangmere. The Wolseley had been fitted with a gas bag which meant it could not muster more than thirty miles an hour. Even on the train he could see each station, its name-board carefully blacked out, bearing the poster 'Is your journey really necessary?' It was enough that troops had to be moved around the country; if the civilian population went too far too often it was difficult to keep tabs on them, to provide them with their rations, to make certain they weren't spies. Even so, the compartment was packed, and people stood in the corridors. No-one spoke. The short message next to the seaside poster above the seats telling them to 'Be like Dad, Keep Mum' was totally unnecessary. This was England. Fred almost grinned to imagine a German spy trying to find anything out on an English train. Poor sod.

In order to avoid London, Fred had changed at Swindon and come through Westbury to Salisbury, then waited there for a stopping train to Portsmouth where he had managed to get a taxi to Chichester. The driver told him that the six-oh-nine squadron were all billeted at Goodwood, but when he'd made enquiries there, it seemed they were being kept in readiness in their Mess at the airfield.

He had left the Great Western Railway station at Gloucester at seven in the morning and arrived at Tangmere at three in the afternoon. He was hungry, tired, and very anxious. The last time he had seen his son was in a plush restaurant in Birmingham two years previously. A lot had happened to them both since then.

The young Flying Officer who took his message seemed

a nice enough lad. Fair like Albert, and with Albert's quality of fresh-faced enthusiasm too. They were doubtless all like that; the war was still a game to them and to be among aircraft each and every day must be a delight.

Fred expected another delay after the young man left. Obviously when told of his visitor, Albert would be cautious. He wouldn't be able to send Fred away; after all, there might be a message from Davie. But he'd have to prepare himself — arm himself almost — for this contact with his father. So, when barely five minutes after Jack Doswell had left the tiny wooden office next to the control tower, the door flew open and Albert bounded inside, Fred forgot his weariness and rose delightedly to greet such eagerness.

And so, for a split second, the two men who were so alike, who were tied by a relationship which must remain secret to all but a very few, looked into each other's faces with openness permitting entry, as it were. In that second, Fred imagined he had been right and that Albert was still the keen young mechanic of two years ago. But then the shutter came down visibly. The blue eyes blinked and were wintry, the mouth hardened into a straight line and the jaw became more prominent.

'I thought it was Victor,' Albert said flatly. And, ignoring the outstretched hand, turned to the window. 'There should be a Waaf on duty.'

Fred tightened his own face and body and said levelly, 'She's gone for a cup of tea for me. I've been on the road since dawn.'

'I didn't see the car.'

'No. Railway.'

'Ah, I see.'

Fred made a gigantic effort to relax; he sat down on the folding wooden chair with a deep sigh. 'Could have done it in three or four hours in the car. Even with the gas bag.'

'You can't get hold of any petrol?'

'Not unless you've got a damned good reason.'

26

'Surprised you didn't think of one.'

There was a little silence then Fred said, 'I reckon I had one, don't you? But who would believe it?'

Albert turned and stared down at him; Fred knew there was a time when he couldn't have done that. There was a time too when Fred could have met those bleak eyes without flinching, when Fred had been master of his own conscience. That time was gone; just as he had been forced to look away from Davina's accusing gaze, so he turned from Albert's.

The boy said, 'No-one probably. That you could father me *and* Davina is hard to believe. I still find myself thinking it's some kind of nightmare.'

Fred did not feel the relief he had expected at this complete frankness. Perhaps he had let himself believe, as March had, that two years would make all the difference between hatred and forgiveness.

He said quickly, 'God, if I could change things . . . I tried to tell you how it was. Christamighty Albert, it's wartime again, can't you understand how it was for us? Your mother had just lost her brother and, believe me, she loved him like you love Davie — yes, she did, don't look like that. She turned to me—'

'Made all the running, did she?'

Fred dropped his head at that. The Albert he had known was incapable of sarcasm. And Albert himself might have felt some shame because he made a gesture of dismissal with the flat of his hand. 'Oh yes. Yes, I suppose I can . . . though you hurt her time and time again—'

'I know. Oh God, I know. It seemed — at the time — but things are better now, son. I wanted you to know.'

'Don't call me son, please. And don't tell me anything about your life with my mother. Please. I'm simply not interested.'

Fred looked up again, wondering whether he dared hope. The sarcasm had been a sudden burst of fury and though Albert's hatred was still there between them, he was able to speak with his old simplicity. Fred could admire that; the plea for independence — a separation — from the parents who had cheated him for so long, *was* comprehensible. It was probably the only way the boy could cope with such a situation. Fred had always understood that. It was why he had never tried to find Albert, never tried to persuade him to come home again. Not even for March's sake. Especially not for Davina's.

He said with unaccustomed humility, 'Very well, Albert. I won't call you son and I won't speak of your mother or myself. But you must understand that when we heard you were in England I had to find out where and come to see you. If I hadn't done so your mother would have gone mad.'

Albert was silent, apparently accepting this. He hooked the other chair away from the typewriter and straddled it. 'How did you know where I was?'

'I had my sources.'

'Not Victor?'

'No.'

'Good. It's nice to have someone in the family to trust.'

Fred turned his hands palm up. 'Please, Albert. We must know where you are. We . . . we're your next of kin.'

'So you are.' The wintry smile appeared again. He looked older than his twenty-one years. He reminded Fred of someone. Could it be the first Albert who had died in 1917?

Fred said, 'Look old man, I don't know what Victor has told you about everyone at home — I gather he's written fairly regularly over the past two years.'

'Yes.'

'You know your Aunt May has had a baby — a little girl?'

'Yes.' Albert shifted on his chair and Fred realized the economy of his movements since he'd entered the office. He held himself so rigidly in control most of the time. Just like . . . who was it?

'Has he mentioned Bridget Hall to you?'

Albert held on to the back of the chair.

'No.'

28

There was another small silence. Fred gnawed his bottom lip with his top teeth. Albert had spent a lot of time with Tolly in Spain; did he know why Tolly had left Bridget?

'She asked me to enquire whether you had any news of Tolly.'

Albert did not reply. He stared levelly at Fred for a long moment then he took a breath.

'All right. Aunt May, Bridget Hall . . . what have you really come to tell me? You've not come to beg me to return home — that's the last thing on earth you want. So what is it? It's Davie, isn't it? You haven't come all this way for a chat about the family and friends. Christ — you always were a sadist! What has happened to Davie?'

Fred was shocked at the intensity of Albert's voice. Suddenly the iron control had slipped; there was still very little movement, but the hands holding the back of the chair were white at the knuckles.

'Nothing. She is fine, Albert. Fine.'

'Then why have you come?'

'Christamighty, do I have to have a reason? Well, I have a reason of course, but I've just promised not to talk of it!' Fred stood up again and paced the small office. 'It was time . . . time to establish contact as you people call it.' The pathetic attempt at humour fell flat. 'And actually . . . she asked me to tell you to write to her.'

Albert watched him carefully in silence for a long time. Then he dropped his gaze to the floor and said, 'Victor reckons she is all right. He says she is well and working hard at school and taking singing lessons. He says she is all right.'

'She is all those things. She started singing lessons this time last year.' Fred suddenly wanted to put his hand on his son's shoulder and give him some gesture of comfort.

'She could always sing.' Albert's voice lifted slightly in reminiscence. 'I remember when she was just a little girl she would sing for Grandma Rising.' He took another

29

long breath and let it out slowly. 'Victor says you are paying for the lessons.'

'Yes . . . I . . . we wanted to. Your mother and I. She is very close to Davie.'

Albert said deliberately, 'And you, of course, are her father. So you've a right to pay for her singing lessons!' He gave a sort of laugh. 'Does David know?'

'Albert—'

'No, of course not. You'd be dead if he knew.' The cold eyes turned upwards and surveyed Fred. 'What about my mother?'

'March? What do you mean?'

'Does my mother know that you fathered Davie as well as me?'

Fred forced himself not to answer; forced himself to take the full impact of the pale blue stare.

Albert shook his head, answering his own question. 'I only wondered whether you'd broken down and confessed all. But you're still living together Victor says, so you couldn't have done much confessing because, knowing Mother, she wouldn't be with you now if she knew what we both know. Would she?'

Again Fred did not reply. In a strange way he welcomed this outburst; it was like being flayed alive. Surely after it he would have expiated some of his sin.

Albert narrowed his eyes, then removed his gaze contemptuously.

'When you told me first I think I hated Aunt April and Mother more than you. I expected anything of you. But they . . . I loved them. And April especially — she was married to Uncle David, she professed to be in love with him since she was four years old! Then she went off with you!'

Fred could no longer keep silent. He said wearily, 'I tried to explain to you, Albert. She did what she did *for* David. He was going mad thinking he was impotent, no good to her. They'd had a row and he'd thrown her out . . . just believe me, Davina is living proof of April's love for David. Nothing more.'

30

'Yes, yes. I know. In any case it makes no difference to the facts, does it? Davie and I are made for each other and can never have each other.' Albert stood up suddenly and the flimsy chair crashed to the ground. He looked at it, shocked for a moment out of his bitterness.

Fred picked it up and put it back in front of the typewriter.

'She's all right, Albert. Really. She's young and she'll forget and find someone else and—'

Albert said in his old level voice, 'No. No, no, no, no. She's not all right. And she's not that young, not in the way you mean. And she'll never find anyone else.' He went to the window. 'At least I know why we can't see each other again. At least I can talk like this to you —' he cast his half-smile at Fred again and this time it did contain a glimmer of amusement. 'Strange, but there is a sort of relief in being completely honest with someone, even you. Davie cannot have that relief. She has no idea why I left her or why I went to find Tolly in Spain. I know what Victor told her — that I'd got a Birmingham girl into trouble and couldn't face her again. But she wouldn't care about that. Not Davie. So whatever Victor tells me, whatever you tell me, I know the truth. I know that Davie is unhappy. She won't show it to anyone, but I know.'

It was the longest speech Fred had heard his son make. To refute it with superficial reassurance would have been insulting. He stood still for a long moment, then moved to the window and stood next to Albert, staring at the long length of runway, lined with oil drums.

He said, 'All right. She is unhappy. She is living for the day when you come home or write to her, or let her have an address where she can write to you. When she knew I was coming she begged me . . .' he took a breath. 'Listen Albert, if you want to . . . I mean after the war if you and she decided . . . I wouldn't interfere again. I wouldn't say anything to anyone.'

'Am I supposed to thank you for that?' Albert's quick glance was not cold any more, it sparked with anger. 'If you feel like that you should never have told me! D'you think . . . Besides, Victor knows. And you told me Aunt Sylv knew too.'

'They'd keep quiet. They love you. And Davie.'

'Victor's probably told half-a-dozen of his cronies already. Makes a good story doncha know!' Albert went to the door. 'And Aunt Sylv would protect Davie with her life if need be.' He shook his head. 'And anyway, I know. I know because you bloody well told me!'

Fred said desperately, 'There's something you could do to make it easier for yourself. And for Davie too.'

Albert's frosty smile returned.

'Let myself be killed, d'you mean?' He turned the handle of the door and opened it a few inches. Across the runway from the Mess a young Waaf came cautiously, holding a cup with a saucer over its top. 'I thought of that. In Spain. But then I didn't want to. I'm not very brave.'

'I didn't mean . . . you know I didn't mean that!'

The Waaf paused and looked skywards. It was raining.

'I meant, you could find another girl. Get married.'

'Like you did?'

'Albert—'

'Oh forget it!'

Albert pulled the door wide and went out, nearly cannoning into the Waaf. She held on to her cap, looked at him doubtfully as he strode towards the Mess, then came up the steps into the office.

'I hoped he might be able to get a couple of hours off after you've had such a journey to see him.' She pushed the typewriter aside and placed the saucer, then the cup, on to the table. 'There's quite a decent little hotel on the Chichester Road where you should get a bed all right. And perhaps tomorrow Sergeant Tomms will have more time to spare.'

Fred sipped his tea gratefully.

'I don't think I'll be staying. Thanks all the same.'

It was at Kemble that Fred realized suddenly whom Albert resembled. As the 'Cotswold Cads' — the old

32

Gloucester name for the landed gentry who lived on their big estates in the hills — descended carefully on to the ill-lit platform a woman ran forward and embraced one of them. Man and woman relaxed their stiff upper lips for just a moment, smiled into each other's eyes and kissed with a kind of gratitude. Then they resumed their roles. 'Have you got the car, darling?' 'Sorry, absolutely no petrol. I've resurrected the governess cart—'. 'I *say* darling—' they were gone. Two peas in a pod. Just like Albert and Davina. Tightly buttoned against the whole world, but opening out for one another.

Fred frowned fiercely to control what must be an incipient cold. Albert was right. He should never have told anyone the truth. He should have let the relationship blossom into whatever it wanted.

Then he remembered that canny old Aunt Sylv had discovered the truth for herself.

He adjusted the blind on the window and grabbed at the strap as the train lurched into motion again. Unbidden into his mind came the old and terrible words of the second commandment: 'For I the Lord thy God am a jealous God, and visit the sins of the fathers upon the children unto the third and fourth generation of them that hate me. . . .'

Three

AUNT SYLV, the last of her generation of Risings, moved her bulk to a more comfortable position on the kitchen chair, and surveyed Bridget Hall above her spectacles.

'I knowed your mother-in-law a long time afore you did, my girl. Kitty Hall wet-nursed our Teddy along 'a your Tolly and were a good friend to Florence Rising, and that's good enough for me. I don't want to sit 'ere and listen to anything agenst 'er.' She turned to April who was pouring water from kettle to teapot. 'Why dun't you and young Bridie go and sit in the front room while I start on the sprouts?'

They were in the kitchen of Longmeadow, April and David's home in Winterditch Lane; it was a working afternoon, and the three of them were about to tackle the Christmas Brussels sprouts.

Bridget grinned, unaffected by Aunt Sylv's censure.

'Young Bridie, eh? I'm forty next year I'll have you know, Sylvia Rising.'

'Sylvia Turpin if you please, Bridie.'

'Oh sorry, sorry. You're so bloody touchy about your marital status!'

'Marital status be blowed. I en't 'aving my Dick's existence forgotten, that's all. 'E might 'a bin a deserter in the last war, 'e might 'a spent a lot o' time in prison . . . but 'e were the only man what married me. An' I'm never goin' to forget 'im!'

34

April and Bridget stared in amazement at this uncharacteristic outburst. Bridget grinned, but April put down the teapot and came to the table to hug her aunt.

'We'll never forget Uncle Dick, darling.' She kissed the balding pate lovingly. 'Any more than we'll forget Mother and Dad. Or Teddy and Albert. Or any of them.' She sat down and smiled into the blue Rising eyes. 'D'you know, sometimes I think how exciting it's going to be to die.' She laughed at Bridget's disgusted exclamation. 'No, honestly Bridie. I don't mean in a religious way at all. I mean what fun it will be to see them all again. To talk and just . . . be together.' She patted Sylvia's lumpy hand. 'Anyway Mrs Turpin, we'd much rather stay out here in the warm with you if you don't mind. It's cold in the sitting-room and the view of the army convoys grinding up to the camp is not exactly elevating!' She shot Bridget a look. 'Bridie will make no more — not one — sniffy remark about dear Kitty. And we can all do the sprouts and drink tea and be happy and chatty.'

She stood up and dragged a huge net of sprouts to the table while Bridget took over the teapot and grumbled self-righteously.

'If I can't let my hair down with my oldest friend it's a poor look-out. My God, every daughter-in-law has to grouch sometimes. I'm the first to admit that I couldn't have got through the last few years without Kitty. I adore the woman. The fact remains that she is being absolutely pig-headed about Tolly. And she's not the only one. Olga and Natasha are even worse.'

April distributed knives and spread newspaper.

'What do you expect, Bridie? He is their father, after all. While there's no news of him, they naturally hope against hope that he's still alive.'

'Look here, April, you know the whole story, and I daresay the wise old monkey over there with the sprouts has put two and two together, so let's be honest. Tolly left me. He knew Barty couldn't be his child, so he left me. All that business about him going to fight in Spain for his

35

ideals was so much tarrydiddle. All right, I've accepted it. But in leaving me, he also left his five daughters. Why can't *they* accept it as I have? We've simply got to start living properly again, and the only way to do that is to have him presumed dead!'

Aunt Sylv made a sound like a camel with croup. April tried to laugh. 'Well, you were always known for your devastating frankness, Bridie dear. But I hope it's just for us. If you talk like this in front of the girls—'

'Don't be an idiot, April. Good God, you are the only person in the whole world . . . not even Barty's real father knows!' She shot Aunt Sylv a look. 'I trust you two to the grave and beyond. All right, Mrs Turpin, I know you don't approve of me swearing and smoking and driving my car on black market petrol, but you'd still do a murder for me so—'

Aunt Sylv made another horrendous noise and then found her real voice. 'I allus presumed my 'usband was *alive!* Still do, in spite o' not seeing 'im for over twenty year! 'Ow long since young Tolly left the country? No more 'n three year I'll be bound—'

'When the king abdicated. The tenth of this month three years ago. Yes.' Bridget looked woodenly at the mound of sprouts on the table. 'D'you think I've forgotten him, Aunt Sylv? He's in my blood — I'll never forget Tolly Hall. I never forgot Teddy Rising either. I was eight years old when Teddy died and I tried to drown myself. Did you know that? But then I bundled up all the feeling I had for Teddy and gave it to Tolly. Since I was eight years old I knew I would marry Tolly. He *is* me — just as Teddy is me. Nothing can change that. But this — this presumption of death — it's a legality. That's all.' She sighed and picked up her knife. 'I wish I could make Kitty and the girls understand that. I'm not trying to kill Tolly. It's just a legality.'

There was a silence broken only by the fall of coal in the grate and knives cutting the sprouts. April kept her eyes on her work. She knew that unless she was given proof she would never 'presume' Tolly Hall was dead; but to go against Bridie was difficult. When Bridie had told her just why Tolly had gone to join the International Brigade, she had been unable to condemn her old school friend. How could she condemn any woman in those circumstances when every day she looked at Davina and saw Fred Luker's eyes looking back at her?

Eventually it was Aunt Sylv who spoke, and it was obvious she was making a real effort to be fair.

'I thought as 'ow our Fred was goin' to ask Albert whether 'e'd 'ad any news from Tolly? What came of that?'

Bridget shrugged, already bored with the subject. April said, 'I don't think anything could have come of it. Fred had very little to say except that Albert looked well and older.'

Bridget put down her knife and picked up her tea cup. 'Ridiculous man. What did he expect. How Fred Luker has got where he is beats me. At times he can be positively retarded. When I think of May's gorgeous Monty — and your David, April — I simply cannot understand . . . I mean did he think for one moment that "well and older" would satisfy Davie? How did she take it, for God's sake?'

'Very calmly. What he actually said to her was "Albert has changed, he is now a man." I think she understood perfectly.'

'Oh God. Poor kid. Trouble is, she's the loyal kind. With her voice and that calm angelic face of hers she could have anyone. Robin Adair called round the other day with some books for Olga. My poor daughter thought he was interested in her but he only wanted to pump her about Davie.'

'Keep that Robin Adair away from Olga, Bridie,' said Aunt Sylv suddenly. ''E's a wrong 'un.'

'You're like the voice of doom. I think I know the Adairs better than you do, Aunt Sylv.'

The old lady's face flushed. 'I doubt that, my girl. I don't say things just to listen to me own voice. Not like you, all wind and no shit.'

37

'Aunty!' April tried to look outraged then collapsed with laughter over her colander of sprouts. Bridie tightened her mouth against a smile and the door opened with a crash as Flora flung herself inside.

'Mummy, it's snowing! It's actually snowing right now! Look, can you see?' The nine-year-old held out her gas mask on which lay a film of fast-melting snow. Bridie got up and closed the door hastily. Flora looked from her to April and then to Aunt Sylv whose walnut face was stretched unwillingly. 'Why is everyone laughing? What has happened? Have we won the war?'

That seemed to set them off properly. And because Aunt Sylv's infrequent laughter always reminded Flora of the donkey on Porthmeor beach at St Ives who brayed whenever he saw her, she too started to laugh.

'It's nearly, nearly Christmas!' she carolled. 'And we've nearly, nearly won the war!'

Kitty Hall was waiting up for Bridget when she got home that night. There were many things about her daughter-in-law of which Kitty disapproved, but her contact with the three Rising sisters was not one of them. And of all the sisters April seemed to Kitty to be most like her mother, Florence Rising. Not in looks; March was the only one to have her mother's colouring; but in her gentle ways and fair-minded dealings, April was another Florence. Kitty still wept when she thought of her old friend. There would never be another one like her; she always had one foot in the next world even when she lived in this one. Thin, fastidious, with the true aristocrat's sense of democracy, the whole business of human reproduction had been foreign to her. Yet she had had five children with all their problems, and a straying husband whom she had loved devotedly.

'Ah Flo . . . Flo . . .' Kitty murmured aloud as she hurried downstairs to open the front door to Bridget. 'You'd be proud of your girls now. Proud you'd be.' And she wished she could feel the same about Bridget as she came in out of the dark, looking much too smart for wartime with real silk stockings and a red felt hat over one eye, her fur coat pearled with snowflakes. Not for the first time Kitty wondered where she got her clothes and petrol and the limitless coal supplies. But then Bridget was not *her* girl, strictly speaking; and she was proud enough of Olga, Natasha, Beatrice, Catherine, and Svetlana.

'How I hate this blackout,' Bridget grumbled, standing beneath the dim light in the hall to get rid of her outdoor things. 'The bus from Winterditch was like a hearse, all blue lights.' She grinned at her mother-in-law, suddenly thankful for her presence which made the tall Brunswick Road house into a decent, old-fashioned home. 'Kitty, did you know that those blue lights don't show up false teeth?'

'What on earth d'you mean?' Kitty took the fur coat and shook it lightly before putting it on a padded hanger. 'Fancy wearing high heels out when it's snowing! You'll have to stuff them with newspaper and keep them away from the fire. And where's your gas mask?'

'In here.' Bridget waved her handbag. 'It's a new idea. See? Gas mask in front and handbag behind. Let's go upstairs, Kitty. I can't face the kitchen. Been sitting in April's all afternoon and evening doing sprouts! Honestly!'

Kitty hid a smile as she followed the high heels up to the first-floor sitting-room which jutted out above Brunswick Road.

'We've kept some cocoa for you in the Thermos,' she said. 'And Olga says now that this new butter rationing has started you can have hers and she'll have marge. It's going to be part of her war effort.'

'Goody-goody,' Bridget commented, going across to the window and peering through in spite of blackout regulations. 'Are they all in bed, Kitty?'

'Ah. I didn't have to do a thing. Nashie read to Barty. Beattie saw to Catherine and Lana.'

'And Olga did without her butter,' Bridie said drily.

39

'You know she mustn't lug the children about,' Kitty defended quickly. 'Not with her back.'

'If she'd carried on with Tolly's exercises like I told her to, she wouldn't be round-shouldered. That's all it is.' She turned and saw the look on Kitty's face. 'You should have come with me, darling,' she said with sudden warmth. 'You're feeling like I feel — obsolete. That's the word now, did you know? All those old guns and railings and saucepans they collect . . . obsolete.' She flopped into an armchair by the fire and kicked off her shoes. 'Never mind, Kitty. The guns and railings and saucepans are made into something else. Munitions probably. We'll turn ourselves into something else. If we're not needed to look after the children, then we . . . we'll show 'em.'

Kitty did not reply. She wanted to move the shoes from the fireside, but knew it would irritate Bridie if she did so. It occurred to her that Bridie had spent her whole life trying to 'show 'em'. She had been born an exhibitionist and somehow other people had suffered because of it. When the six-year-old Bridie had thought it was a good idea to swing from an apple bough in Chichester Street, it had been Teddy Rising who had fallen and broken his arm. Kitty let her thoughts go on and on: cause and effect . . . cause and effect . . . until she came up to the present.

'Bridie . . .' her voice was slow, thinking as it spoke. 'Bridie, are you planning to get married again?'

Kitty did not look at her daugher-in-law; she watched the shoes begin to steam. If there was nothing in that final couplet of 'cause and effect' Bridie would jump or laugh or display obvious signs of intense irritation.

She did none of those things. She stayed very very still, as if she were holding herself against any give-away sign whatsoever. Then she said lazily, 'Well, you come up with some peculiar things sometimes, mother-in-law. But really, what in God's name gave you this one?'

The shoes were real leather; they would go very hard and take a lot of gentle work with Cherry Blossom.

Kitty said, 'This business of presuming Tolly's death.

40

There would be no reason for it if you weren't considering getting married again.'

'Oh, is that all?' Bridget laughed. 'How many times have I got to tell you, it's just a legality.'

'Did you tell April it was just a legality?'

'Well yes, it did come up as a matter of fact. So I did tell her that. Yes.'

'What did she say?'

'Nothing much. But I think she understood my point of view. Which is more than can be said for my own family.'

'And Sylvia? What did *she* say?'

Bridie laughed. 'Oh Kitty, you're cannier than people realize, aren't you? You know very well that April would say nothing, but that Sylvia would come straight out with it.' She rolled off the armchair on to her knees and picked up her shoes. 'Here, where shall I put these? Is that last night's *Citizen?*' She began to rip the newspaper and tuck it into the shoes. Looking at her, Kitty could see again the outrageous flapper who had claimed her son's heart whether he offered it or not. There were moments when Bridie was infinitely lovable. She leaned back now on Kitty's knees with the same proprietary air.

'My God,' she mused aloud. 'It was at your house that poor old Sylvia first set eyes on her knight in shining armour, wasn't it?'

Kitty knew she was being wooed, but the invitation to reminisce was irresistible.

'Outside the cottage it was. In Prison Lane. Poor old Dick was in chains — my Barty was taking a line of them up the river to Bristol. Dick looked up and saw Sylvia staring at him and that was that. If Flo had been able to nurse baby Teddy, it wouldn't have happened. One thing happens, Bridie, and the rest just has to follow after. There's nothing we can do about it.'

Bridie stopped tearing paper and stared sombrely into the heart of the fire, doing her own reminiscing.

'Yes. Yes, you're right there.'

Kitty looked down at the glossy brown hair parted in

41

the middle and drawn back à la Mrs Simpson.

She said slowly, 'Remember it then. Think what you might be starting if you try to presume Tolly is dead.'

'Oh *Mother!*' Bridget flung the shoes from her and stood up almost as lithely as someone half her age. 'Wouldn't you think I'd be finishing something rather than starting it?'

At the sight of Kitty's suddenly contracted face, she leaned down contritely and kissed her. 'Stop it Kitty, stop it! I said to April today — and I say it to you — I'll never forget Tolly, never! He is part of me — part of the girls!' She drew back and stood up, flexing her back. 'Let's have some cocoa and talk about something else, for goodness sake.' She went to the low table where a Thermos jug and thin china cups and saucers were neatly arranged on a tray. 'It's quite true about the false teeth, you know. Apparently this special blue light doesn't reflect from them. Isn't it a scream? Can't you just imagine going out with somebody who looks like Errol Flynn and at midnight they give you a smile and —' she enacted horror for Kitty's amusement. Then, as she carried the cups to the fire, she said seriously, 'Kitty, you wouldn't ever leave, would you?'

'What? Leave Olga and Nashie and Lana and—'

Bridget put one of the cups down so that the cocoa slopped into the saucer.

'No. Quite. And I do wish you wouldn't shorten their names, Mother! It's bad enough that Tolly christened them with such outlandish monikers, but when you bastardize them—'

'Bridie! Language!'

'Oh God.' Bridie sighed mightily and crouched again by the fire. 'What a life. What a damned awful life.'

'Count your blessings, dear. You've got the girls and a lovely little boy.'

'Sorry. I meant the place. Gloucester. It's such an utter dump. Nothing ever happens. If only we lived in London or somewhere.'

42

'London? Now? People are getting out of London as fast as they can, my girl. Gloucester is a safe area, that's why we've got all the evacuees—'

'Exactly. Safe. Boring. Dull.' Bridget pulled her handbag and gas mask case towards her and rummaged inside for a hanky. A letter came with it. Kitty noticed how quickly she replaced it in the bag. Kitty was long-sighted but did not recognize the handwriting. However, she did notice it had a London postmark.

At the outbreak of war, the Girls High School in Gloucester shared their accommodation with girls from the Kings Norton Grammar School in Birmingham. The girls never met during school hours; the home population used the school in the morning, the visitors in the afternoon, but here and there contacts were made. Some of the Birmingham girls were billeted in the homes of High School pupils. Others left notes in their desks. It was a game, a joke; I'm hiding, come and find me.

The next afternoon, after a lunch of macaroni cheese, alias slimy string, served in the dining-room at the top of the red brick building in Denmark Road, Davina Daker and her cousins, Olga and Natasha Hall, cycled slowly to St Catherine's Hall for French conversation with Madame Courbiere, alias the old crow. Natasha was in her most aggravating mood, teasing Olga unmercifully about her 'boy friend', pedalling her bicycle between the two older girls and snatching at their velour hats so that they snapped on their elastics. Olga slapped irritably backwards with her gloved hand, but made no attempt to stop the flow of coy innuendoes. She chose, rather, to draw attention to them.

'Just listen to her!' she said to Davina, who seemed as usual to be in a world of her own. 'The way she is keeping on about poor Robin anyone would think he'd asked me to marry him or something!'

Surprisingly, that remark brought Davina back to the present. She looked sideways at her cousin with startled awareness and repeated, 'Marry you? Robin Adair?'

'It's just Nash being silly,' Olga said hastily, imagining reports reaching her mother's ears. 'Robin's been engaged about eight times. And there was all that scandal about the girl in the Forest of Dean.'

Davie knew nothing of that and cared less. She asked curiously, 'Would you get married to him if he asked you, Olga?'

Olga giggled insanely but Natasha said much too loudly from behind, 'Rather! Olga would do anything to get away. She hates everyone at home — everyone!'

'Well, I certainly hate you!' Olga spat over her shoulder. 'But as a matter of fact I don't hate Barty. And I don't hate Grandma. So you've not got your facts *quite* right, have you? As per usual!'

Davie smiled. 'You're such idiots, pretending to loathe each other all the time. D'you know, Mother told me once that Aunt Bridie was very lonely when she was a little girl and always wanted a big family. So that none of you would be lonely ever. I think that's lovely.'

'Well, you would. Flora's no trouble. And your father is home. And your mother doesn't want to get rid of him and marry someone else.'

Davie was shocked completely out of her constant inner questioning and scheming. She turned slightly on her saddle and gave a meaning frown in Natasha's direction.

Olga said impatiently, 'Oh she agrees with me, don't worry. That's the one thing we don't argue about!'

Natasha stopped plaguing the older girls and accelerated past them and into the churchyard.

'The only thing we don't know,' she announced carelessly, 'is . . . who has Mother got her eye on.' She flung her bike against the church wall and added to her sister, 'It could be Robin's father, you know. So if you want to marry Robin you'd better be quick about it. He might be your stepbrother before long!'

'Shut up you little twerp,' advised Olga.

'You're not allowed to say twerp.'

'Max Miller says twerp on the wireless.'

'What Max Miller says is one thing, what you say . . .' chanted Natasha.

Davie put her bicycle carefully alongside Olga's and said thoughtfully, 'Poor Aunt Bridie. I hadn't really thought before . . . poor Aunt Bridie.'

The girls filed into the hall and Natasha joined her own cronies. Olga said quietly in Davie's ear, 'If you're thinking that my mother feels about Father like you feel about Albert, you're quite wrong, you know. She did something terrible and he could never forgive her. That's why I hate her. She drove him away.'

Davie watched her cousin as she took her place on one of the few chairs, allotted to her because of her back. She could say no more, but she wondered why Olga did not realize that when you loved someone you went on loving them whatever happened. It was of course obvious to her that Albert had done something very shameful and could not bear to face her. But she knew, and Uncle Tolly and Aunt Bridie must know too, that it made no difference. She slid her hand inside her striped blouse and felt the real engagement ring Albert had given her when she was only eleven years old. Nothing had changed since then. If only someone — Uncle Fred or Victor — would give her Albert's address, she would go and see him, just as she had done when she was still a little girl, and everything would be all right.

Madame de Courbiere was holding a conversation with Melissa Franks who was bilingual anyway, so Davina opened her satchel and found the letter left by the Kings Norton girl who occupied her desk in the afternoons.

'Dear Davina Daker,' it said. 'Thank you for your letter. I am writing this in history which is the most boring subject in the world. Yes, I know West Heath well as it is very near Kings Norton. I remember seeing the Austin apprentices when they used to do their hikes on Sundays. My father let me caddy for him on the golf

45

course and they would often walk across. I rather like your idea of becoming a detective. It won't be easy because after two years the trail will be rather cold, but next time I go home, I will instigate enquiries. If your cousin did something awful like stealing, or even murder, do you really want to know about it? Yours sincerely, Audrey Merriman.'

Davina pushed the letter back and pressed her hand again to her chest.

''Ave you a penn, Davina?' enquired the old crow.

'A pen, madame?'

'*Penn*, child. In your boo-soom.'

There were titters all round. Davina blushed demurely.

'Not really, madame. I have a weak chest and this foggy weather . . .'

'Gloucester is ze most un'ealthy. You will please to tell me why. En français.'

Gillian Smith, the clown of the Upper Fourth, said, 'Parce que le Severn runs through it.'

Even the old crow had to join in the laughter. All these young ladies were so innocent, so sweet, on the brink of womanhood, as yet, untouched . . .

May was rather sorry the snow had gone. The crisp cold weather was so much better for Gretta than the usual foggy Gloucester variety. She knew she should have stayed indoors that afternoon, but Hettie Luker had knocked to say that Fearis' had some fancy cakes in and the queue wasn't too bad. May was unable to resist the lure of rich food. She had long ago resigned herself to her ample curves, indeed had made them an asset. She put on Gretta's new fur-trimmed bonnet and wrapped her into the pram and bounced it down the step of number thirty-three Chichester Street with a sudden sense of excitement. It was Christmas weather. Already beginning to darken. And she had been born in Chichester Street. Memories of other winters joined with this present moment, and she felt again that childhood certainty that something wonderful was just around the corner.

The street itself had hardly changed. Chichester House, where Will Rising had taken his family for a few years when they had indeed been 'rising', was now a nurses' home and the caped figures which hurried down the street to the City General Hospital in Great Western Road, helped to merge past and present. When the Risings had lived in the House, the wounded soldiers from the hospital had found their way there to call on March and May, and to play lexicon and dominoes with the young schoolgirl, April. Nurses had trundled invalid chairs under the railway bridge and called for their charges at the unholy hour of nine o'clock.

The two terraces facing each other across what had been the drive to the House were as shabby as ever, each with its bootscraper and metal-covered coal chute. Most of the front windows still sported an aspidistra in a pot; but where Will had advertised his tailoring business in frosted glass, May had a clear window, unadorned by the usual Nottingham lace, at the moment pretty with a small Christmas tree. Goodrich's dairy and the Lamb and Flag still guarded opposite corners where Chichester Street met London Road, but the midwife, Snotty Lotty, was long gone, and the livery stables owned by the Lukers at number nineteen contained obsolete cars. Fred had taken the transport business into London Road and left his parents to enjoy the old house like two old pigs in a sty. Even Gladys and Henry, the last of the big Luker family, had moved out into digs in town. Hettie and Alf snuffled and snorted their days away, visited sometimes, usually surreptitiously, by their successfully wayward daughter, Sibbie.

These thoughts flitted through May's mind as she turned into London Road and went beneath the railway bridge.

'Woo . . . hoo . . .' she called so that Gretta could hear the echo, then, 'Choo . . . choo . . . choo . . .' as a train

47

went overhead. The child screwed up her face with delicious laughter, and May simply had to stop the pram outside the Catholic church and lean into it to kiss the tiny nose. There was no-one about, so she did it again, then straightened to say aloud, 'Oh Mother . . . Dad . . . I'm so lucky. So terribly, terribly lucky!'

An armoured car, leading a convoy of troop carriers, rumbled down George Street and turned right into London Road. May stood still, watching them. The transport had obviously just met a train and were taking personnel to the camp in Winterditch Lane. The men were packed in like cattle and looked frozen and miserable. May's heart went out to them. She leaned over the pram and adjured Gretta to wave to the 'brave soldiers'. Mother and child lifted gloved hands, smiling encouragingly. As the lorries ground slowly beneath the bridge some of the men gave a hoarse cheer. The next moment it was taken up along the line. May could picture it so clearly from their viewpoint. An elegantly attractive older woman with her small child, patriotically encouraging the fighting forces as they arrived in her home town. Tears filled her eyes. She must get April to hold a few soirees at Longmeadow. Officers, of course. Just three or four at a time. Herself at the piano. Davina could sing. It would be really nice.

The last of the lorries disappeared into the murk and she continued into Northgate Street, smiling happily. The queue at Fearis' was quite long by now, but Madame Helen, who had been May's employer at the hair salon, was second from the front. Normally May would have merely smiled and gone to the end of the line, but she felt today was her lucky day.

'Madame! How marvellous to see you!'

She stood alongside the older woman, noting the sagging jawline and crumpled neck. Poor old soul, she must be nearly sixty by now and still having to slog into that ghastly little shop each day and pretend to be French. May remembered the dreadful day Madame had given

48

her the sack and smiled right at her. Madame Helen owed her something.

'Why if it isn't Miss May!'

The older woman made a space for her, acknowledging the ages-long debt, and May tucked herself into the queue.

'It must be such a job to get out to the shops with the baby,' she gushed for the benefit of the woman behind. 'I'm sure no-one will mind. And how is Monty, my dear? And your gallant son protecting us all from those dreadful Germans?'

That disposed of any objections, and the conversation pattered on till they were at the counter.

'Two eclairs and three cream horns I think,' May dimpled. 'I don't want to take more than my fair share.'

May watched her old employer trotting off on her high heels towards the salon and felt a pang of guilt towards everyone who wasn't May Gould. Poor Madame Helen . . . and the poor little schoolgirl at the end of the queue who certainly wouldn't get any cakes and was probably buying for her family. May opened her paper bags and did a little discreet juggling of the contents, then went back to the queue.

'I think I bought more than my fair share.' She smiled charmingly. 'Do take these — a cream horn and an eclair.' She walked quickly away, dismissing the girl's stammered thanks. She felt really marvellous, the incidents of the cheering soldiers and Madame Helen and the grateful schoolgirl boosting her morale sky-high. She decided to go round to King's Street and call into the office of Williams' Auctioneers. Monty might well be out, she couldn't remember what his itinerary was this week, but his work had doubled since the War Office took over some of the old Cotswold manors. Monty had slid automatically into Tolly Hall's position as head of the book department, and many of the old Gloucestershire families were entrusting him with their libraries 'for the duration'.

She left the pram on the narrow pavement and opened

the office door cautiously. Where March had once pounded a typewriter behind the small pigeon-hole in the wall, a turbaned head now appeared. Girls came and went in this job now, gaining 'office experience' and going on into well-paid clerical jobs in the Forces.

May said doubtfully, 'Marian, is it?'

'Margaret actually, Mrs Gould. Mr Gould is in his office if you want to go up.'

She opened the door next to the pigeon-hole and May went inside the office to the stairs. There was a letter in the three-bank Oliver typewriter which began 'My darling dream-boy'. She smiled again and as she went up the ancient wooden stairs, she reflected that Hitler had made life quite a bit more interesting for some people.

She opened the door to Monty's room, brimming with love and good feeling, then stopped dead. Monty was sitting at his enormous desk as usual, surrounded by piles of books and papers beneath pitted brass paperweights, but, wedged between his waistcoat and the edge of his desk — in fact sitting squarely on his lap — was a woman. Her back was towards May, but her light brown hair, drawn back like Wallis Simpson's, looked very like Sibbie's. May knew in that instant that if it *was* Sibbie Williams, née Luker, sitting on Monty's lap, she could not bear it. Once before when she had caught Sibbie with Monty, she had had raging hysterics. Already she could feel the screams gathering in her throat.

Then Monty felt the draught from the door, and turned, and the woman turned with him. It was Bridget Hall.

'Good God—' completely unabashed, she grinned at May, put her arms around Monty's neck and sank back against his shoulder. 'Caught in the act!' She extricated herself without haste and stood up. 'Darling May. I do wish you'd knock before you open the door. I might have had time to take off my fur coat and rumple my hair slightly!'

May felt herself relax. Bridie had been an enfant terrible

50

and still enjoyed shocking everyone. Monty's neck was bright red above his starched collar and he did indeed look shocked. May refused to join him.

'Bridie, you are incorrigible. Unhand my husband this instant and both of you come downstairs and see Gretta in her new bonnet.'

They trooped back down, Monty leaping ahead to open doors, Bridie patently bored with their besotted baby-worship. She hardly looked at Gretta before turning away.

'You're not that clever. I've got to get back to my little wonder,' she said. She waved and went off down King's Street on her high heels.

May turned to Monty.

'Fancies for tea, darling. I came up to stand in Fearis' queue. Aren't I wonderful?'

'A few cakes aren't worth risking Gretta in this fog,' Monty protested, thinking all was well.

May's smile disappeared as Bridie turned the corner into Eastgate Street.

'What on earth was going on just now? Just as well I came out in the fog, it seems. Gretta certainly won't come to any harm. I'm not so sure about you!'

'Don't be ridiculous, May. You know what Bridget is. She came to see what the book department is doing, and of course declined a chair—'

'How often does she have to see how the book department is doing?'

'About once a month. In a way she's my boss now that Tolly's out of the picture.'

'Ah, I see. And you have to sit your "boss" on your knee, I suppose.'

'May, for God's sake—'

May snapped, 'It's not Bridie I'm worried about. I know Bridie — that sort of thing means nothing to her. But if Bridie is your boss, what about Sibbie? She is the wife of the owner. What if she comes in to keep an eye on things?'

'You didn't think for one moment—'

51

'It crossed my mind. Yes. The fur coat. The hairstyle. yes, it did just cross my mind.'

Monty laughed. 'Well, we both know that Sibbie would never sit on *my* knee, don't we?' He leaned across the handle of the pram and right there in the street he kissed her. Properly. 'May, you're not jealous of *Sibbie*, are you?'

She felt herself being cajoled like a child, and smiled unwillingly. 'How could I be? I think that particular boot should be on your foot, my darling.'

They both remembered that horrific night when Sibbie had finally declared her true love for May, and thereby lost May for ever. In the triumph of that moment had sprung a new, grateful love between husband and wife; and, of course, Gretta.

Their thoughts ran side by side and at the same moment they both turned and smiled at the beautiful child in the pram. May said again, 'We're so lucky. So very lucky.'

'Get her home and in the warm, Mummy,' Monty said dotingly. 'I shan't be far behind you. Nearly four o'clock already.' He kissed them both and went back inside the office and May turned and walked across King's Square and past the Bon Marché to Northgate Street. It was completely dark beneath London Road railway bridge, and the fog was rasping on the chest. Her euphoria began to evaporate and she tried to recapture it by saying aloud — 'We're so lucky . . .' but she spoke without her previous conviction. She frowned, remembering Bridget Hall's oddly single state. Remembering too that once before after an almight row with Tolly, Bridget had turned to Monty for comfort.

Audrey Merriman let herself into the house in Quedgeley with her own key. One of the good things about living with the Adairs was that they all 'lived their own lives'. This actually meant that Mrs Adair did very little cooking and cleaning and spent a lot of time in a nice bottle-green uniform, drving around on special petrol allowance doing all sorts of things like taking people to hospital or packing huge parcels of 'comforts for the troops'. In between assignments she could be seen lunching or dining in good hotels all over the county with various older men in officers' uniforms. Mr Adair still did some farming, but his interests seemed to lie primarily in running the Observer Corps. He wore a navy-blue uniform and carried binoculars around his neck even when he put on his Noel Coward dressing-gown in the evenings. He talked a lot about 'plots' . . . 'The R.A.F. Spits at Kemble followed one of our plots today . . .' So far all his plots had been false alarms, but his keenness was unblunted.

Robin Adair, twenty-one, world-weary and cynical, had funny feet and was doing his war work in the Records Office at Quedgeley. He was very handsome and Audrey wished very much that she was four years older and did not need glasses.

She too lived her own life at Quedgeley Lodge and waited eagerly for Friday afternoons when the school staff took it in turns to escort the girls back home for the weekend. No-one could see an end to the phoney war, and Audrey's parents were among the many who were suggesting that the school should return to its proper quarters.

As she walked down the parquet hallway that murky December afternoon, she knew she wasn't alone in the house. She hoped Mrs Adair was in the kitchen, perhaps even making something for tea. If it was Mr Adair or Robin, she'd have to give away one of her precious cakes. And Mr Adair would insist on kissing her for it.

It was Robin. He was in the dining-room crouched before the radiogram, trying to tune in to an elusive station. As she went past the door, sudden caterwauling atmsopherics made her give a little scream. He guffawed.

'That you, kid? Thought we'd have a little dance music. Come on in — come on, don't be shy.'

'I've got homework to do, Robin. I think I'll go to my room.'

He fiddled with the tuner, grumbling as he did so.

'Talk about a bluestocking. You're worse than Olga Hall. Come to think of it you're like Olga in a lot of ways and she must be your age. She goes to Denmark Road. D'you know her?'

'No.' He had asked her this before. He could not think of anything to say to her. 'We don't see any of the Gloucester girls. I know one girl by name, that's all. We write notes to each other.'

'What's her name?' Robin suddenly got perfect reception and Ambrose's band blared out 'Mr Franklin De Roosevelt Jones'.

Audrey said in a low voice and well beneath the cover of the music, 'Daker.' She started back down the hall. 'I'm going to make some tea and take it up to my room, Robin. Would you like a cup?'

Robin stood up slowly. He wasn't very tall but in his grey pinstriped suit and black Oxfords he looked smart and a bit like Don Ameche. Audrey felt her heart skip a beat.

He warbled into an imaginary microphone, 'What a name, and how he knows it . . . what a smile and how he shows it . . .' He held out his arms. 'Come on Audrey — it's a quickstep. You ought to learn. Part of your education.'

She backed away. 'No, I—'

He leapt at her, flung aside her satchel and the greasy paper bag and took her in his arms. They shuffled around the dining-room with much arm-pumping.

'You're good. You're damned good, kid! Let's try a quarter turn, slow, quick, quick, quick . . . let yourself go . . . what sort of notes? You tell each about your boy friends I'll be bound. I bet you boast that I'm crazy about you, don't you? Eh?'

'No. Of course not. She doesn't even know where I'm billeted. Nothing like that.' Audrey could hardly breathe but she had to keep talking. 'She asks me things. About Birmingham. People I might know. At home.'

'Does she? And do you know anyone at home that she might know too?' He was laughing, making fun of her, pressing her hard against his jacket and sort of bending her back like Fred Astaire did with Ginger Rogers.

She panted, 'I might do. I'm going to make enquiries this weekend and tell her.'

'Like a detective?'

Those had been Davina Daker's words too. Audrey hated the way she was telling him everything. The notes were strictly confidential.

She blurted out desperately, 'Robin, a nice lady came up to me in a cake queue this afternoon and gave me a chocolate eclair and a cream horn. Which would you like?'

For some reason that amused him very much. He stopped dancing and leaned on the sideboard, laughing his head off. Then he cupped her face, kissed her briefly and said, 'We'll have half each. How's that? You're a darling, Audrey — did you know? A little darling!'

He quickstepped around the room, holding an imaginary partner. Audrey knew her father would probably call him a gigolo, but she couldn't help feeling terribly excited and happy. He switched off the radiogram and they went into the kitchen together.

Four

THE first Christmas of the war came and went, and it was Davie's fourteenth birthday and the first day of 1940. A new decade beginning. April finished pressing Flora's party dress and put it carefully on a hanger suspended from the picture rail. In the clear grey light reflected from the snowy garden, the three party dresses looked insubstantial and cobwebby. There was a blue silk designed by David for their trip to Italy in '36; the material was swathed cleverly so that it seemed to come entirely from the left hip. It had been an instant success with the American friends they had made in Venice; David had made copies for Miranda and for many of her friends. Next to it, Flo's frock was one of Davie's, modelled on a dress worn by Princess Margaret with big puff sleeves and a wide sash. Beside its deep rose colour, Davie's dress was definitely insipid. She had chosen it, ready-made, from the Bon Marché last year when she had been particularly withdrawn and reserved. It was the colour of old parchment and took away what little colour Davie possessed. April sighed and mentally ran through her itsy-bitsy drawer which contained scarves, gloves, artificial flowers and belts. Maybe a bright sash with flowers pinned to the ends? She bit her lip, knowing that Davie would turn down any suggestions for making her the belle of her own ball.

There was an enormous knock at the front door and

she peered through and saw the postman with a pile of packages. Flora got there first, closely followed by Davie and Aunt Sylv. One of the parcels was from America, perfectly timed by Henry and Miranda to arrive on the first of January.

David appeared behind the postman. He had been in the motor house testing the gas bag Fred had fitted on to the Rover. They would go to Davie's party in style today, but first there was the January Sales. Dakers' Gowns would not become a bargain basement like many Gloucester shops, but there would be a few 'genuine bargains'.

David pulled off his gloves and cap and stamped about in front of the kitchen fire. April watched him, smiling; there had been a time when to stamp like that would have made his leg ache unbearably where the shrapnel still moved sluggishly and griped and moved again. Now for long periods he could be almost free of pain. She no longer tried to work out why this was; he was better. He was happy too. They were both happy.

He said below the level of the excited chatter around the table, 'Why are you smiling, Primrose? Have I got an icicle on my nose?'

She shook her head at him. 'I just love you,' she said simply.

Aunt Sylv rescued the last of the string and began to wind it carefully into a ball. She glanced up at them and caught one of their special looks; she made her camel noise.

'What's up, Sylvia?' David grinned at her aggravatingly. Their old relationship had been by way of being an armed truce; that time had long gone.

'You two.' Aunt Sylv pretended disgust. 'Never met such a pair. Still, at least you don't maul each other about in public like our May and 'er Monty.'

'What do we do instead, Sylv?' teased David.

'Oh, 'tis all words with you two.' She screwed up her face and spoke in a falsetto voice. 'If you're 'appy then I'm

57

'appy. And if I'm 'appy then you're 'appy!'

Flora screamed with laughter and Davie, succumbing to the pleasures of a birthday, sng in her clear soprano, 'I can be happy with you . . . If you can be happy with me . . .'

Aunt Sylv snorted again.

'Mad. All o' you. Should be in an asylum!'

Flora shrieked, 'Oh look! It's a dress — a new dress, Davie! Oh, it's lovely — it's beautiful — oh, it's better than anything the princesses have got!'

It was indeed a fairytale dress. For one thing, it was right down to the ground and had a net overskirt which made the peacock-blue satin look like the clear moving sea in Cornwall where Davie and Albert had first recognised their love for each other. She took it reverently from its bed of tissue and held it aloft. Miranda had never met Davie, but she had seen photographs and listened when April and David spoke of her. The dress had dignity; the sleeves were elbow-length and the neckline was what was call 'sweetheart'.

'It's like the dress Snow White wore at the pictures,' Flora breathed.

'It's better than that,' Davie said, similarly awestruck.

Aunt Sylv shook her head. 'Pity you didn't 'ire the Cadena like we wanted. It's a real proper dance dress that.'

Davie shook her head emphatically. 'I couldn't have worn it to the Cadena. But I can wear it to Aunt May's.' She smiled at her parents. 'It reminds me of my first birthday party at Chichester Street when Grandma and Grandpa made me a fairy dress from crêpe paper.'

April smiled against the sudden tears. When they had begged Davie to have a birthday party this year, she had said, 'Can I have it at Chichester Street? Will Aunt May mind? Only that's the only place for a birthday party really.'

And now they knew why.

Just like that first party when Davie had been four

years old, they congregated at three o'clock in the front sitting-room. Then it had been Will's work room and his cutting-table had taken up most of the floor space. Now, with Victor's pictures on the white walls and the Christmas tree still in the window, it could have been in a different house, except for the firescreen in one corner. When Will had died Florence had had his engraved window taken out and made into the firescreen. Brass-framed, it was his special memorial. 'W. Rising' it said in clear letters against the frosted glass. 'Bespoke Tailoring'. Davie touched it gently while Aunt May collected the outdoor things and took them into the hall. She could remember Grandpa Rising faintly, but his memory was just part of the enormous legacy left her by Grandma Rising. In that tiny wasted figure and tranquil face had been stored all the Rising roots. Grandpa of course, and Uncle Teddy and Uncle Albert whom Davie had never seen; old Mrs Daker and young Mrs Goodrich. And aspects of Great Grandma Rising which were missed out of Aunt Sylv's descriptions.

'Happy birthday Davie!'

It was Aunt March and Uncle Fred arriving. Uncle Fred went to work only when he felt like it these days. Uncle Monty would arrive later, as would Daddy.

Davie did not look at Uncle Fred.

'Thank you kindly,' she said demurely, dropping a curtsey. March was overwhelmed.

'Davie! You look simply splendid!'

And then, from upstairs, came the sound of the piano.

April said, 'Just like before. You wouldn't remember but Aunt May played a polka for you when you were four years old.'

'Oh, I remember very well. And Victor asked me to dance. And you danced with Albert.'

Everyone laughed delightedly to cover the sudden thought that neither Victor nor Albert would be here for Davie's fourteenth birthday party. Neither would Will. Nor Tolly Hall.

59

Just then, Bridie arrived with her brood and summed up the general feeling.

'So many *women!*' She took off Barty's coat and passed him to Davie. 'Here you are darling. I've got a present in my bag, but this is much better. He can take you in to the dance.'

Little Barty, so unlike his pale, earnest sisters, squirmed with delight to be in the arms of this story-book princess. Davie twirled till he screamed with laughter and then planted a kiss on his nose.

'Will you take me to the ball, Prince Charming?'

'Yes. Yes. Yes. Yes . . .'

They all trooped up the stairs to the big back room which had been christened by Florence many years ago as the bandy room. It contained the piano with its brass candle sconces, Will's banjo and an old-fashioned gramophone with a handle and a horn. The door was open, the candles already lit, and May sat there in one of her strangely Edwardian dresses, her white-blonde hair piled in a myriad curls to the front of her head, her carefully contrived rose-petal complexion flattered by the soft light, her blue eyes shining as she slipped into the song they'd sung in the shelter not so long ago. 'Let us string up old Adolf on his Siegfried Line, let him swing and hear him sing his little tune . . .' And there, behind the piano, laughing, teeth white in his dark face, was . . . Victor!

Davie stopped dead while everyone crowded into the room around her. Flora ran screaming to her cousin and was picked up and kissed heartily and put down again. May rattled away on the piano and the Hall girls came into the room smiling awkwardly because Victor was so terribly handsome and so terribly talented and they weren't real cousins so had never been able to take him for granted like Davie and Flo did.

Only Barty was not enjoying this sudden apparition. He sensed that his special place had been taken away from him. One of his honorary aunts took him off Davina and he began to cry. But then the aunt carried him to the piano and said, 'Oh May . . . how did you keep it secret? Oh Victor — darling — how marvellous to see you.' And he decided to be interested in other things.

Victor said, 'All right Mother. Let's have the dancing now and the talking afterwards!' He went forward and held out his arms to Davie. 'Princess Davina, I believe. May I wish you many happy returns and ask you for the first dance?'

Davie felt her heart melt with affection. It was only three months since they'd seen Victor and she hadn't realised how much she'd missed him. His charm was facile and meant nothing; yet everything. It *was* Victor, or at any rate, his essence.

She took his hand and went into a deep curtsey. And then they polka'd. Just as they'd done ten years before. Fred took Olga, Bridie swept prim March across the room and April took Barty on one arm and swung Svetlana with her spare hand. The party was going to be an enormous success.

Kitty had cried off; she was in her mid-sixties and since the housekeeper had left the Brunswick Road house, Kitty had taken on the main cooking and cleaning. The girls were marvellous and Bridie had someone in to do the rough and the laundry, but still a great deal of work was claimed by Kitty. She loved to be needed and she felt she was standing in for Tolly as far as the children were concerned. But sometimes she was so tired she hardly knew what to do with herself. The oportunity for having the house to herself was too good to miss. She retired to the first-floor sitting-room, made up the fire and lay on the sofa feeling like Clara Bow in an old silent movie.

'Silence is golden,' she murmured to herself. 'Silent films. Silent reading. Silent night . . .' she knew she was rambling and she smiled at herself. 'Talking to yourself, Kitty — first sign . . .' She sighed. 'Ah. You knew the value of silence, didn't you Tolly? What a quiet one you were. What went on in that head of yours, I wonder. You kept surprising everyone, even your old mother. Going off to France like that when you were only sixteen . . . my Lord, if Olga decides to do something like that in a couple of years time, we'll all have forty fits!' She shook her head. 'Then marrying Bridie and having all these children. Joining the Communist Party. I was frightened to death when you went to them Olympic Games in Germany, my lad — you've given your old mother many a scare. I knew you were up to something — when it all came out about you helping them poor Jews to escape, I weren't a bit surprised. But now . . . oh Tolly, where are you now? Hurry up and come home, lad — she wants a man. Who's to blame her? She needs someone and she'll have you presumed dead and—'

The knocker thumped on the front door and poor Kitty jumped guiltily and swung her feet off the sofa and put a hand to her heart. It thumped again. Seven o'clock — they couldn't be back yet. Was it Sylvia Rising come to sit with her? But Sylvia hardly left Longmeadow these days.

Kitty stood up with difficulty and went to the oriel window overhanging Brunswick Road. Beneath her, half-hidden by the porch, was a heavily overcoated and hatted figure. A man. David Daker? It was the same build and height. But David Daker would have leaned on the wall to take the weight off his leg; and his shoulders were straight; these were bent.

The figure backed out of the porch and looked up at the window. Kitty recoiled sharply. Even in the dim winter light she recognised him now. He had called before to bring news of Tolly. His name was Emmanuel Stein.

She made a staying gesture, got off the oriel seat and hurried downstairs. She hadn't cared for Mr Stein; his part in the escape plot had seemed to her to be very suspect. He had taken money to conduct half a dozen refugees from Berlin to England, but in the end it had been Tolly's bravado that had got them over the frontier safely. Nevertheless, this unlikely arrival must mean . . .

62

something. Her heart was pounding when she reached the door. He had come to tell them one of two things; either Tolly was alive or he was dead. And she had never ever believed he could be dead. She would know. She was his mother and something would have happened inside her body if her only child had died.

She flung open the door, but he slid in sideways as if the habit of furtiveness was ingrained in him.

She said, 'Mr Stein?' on an inward breath. He swung the door shut against the light and stood where she could see his face. She stared and stared, hope dying slowly. Then she collapsed in a heap on the hall floor.

Monty arrived at Daker's Gowns at five o'clock as arranged. The showroom, usually so tranquilly luxurious, was ravaged. Mrs Porchester who had recently moved from Denton's Furs to manage the shop, was dealing with an elderly woman who was trying on one of David's new 'military' costumes. She handed over to one of the girls and came across to Monty.

'Mr Daker is packing — yes, it's been all hands to the wheel!' She tried to laugh and her voice cracked with tiredness. 'D'you know Mr Gould, on the Continent before the war, January the first was a general holiday! And here it's the busiest day of the year!'

Monty turned on the charm with something of an effort. 'Well, hard work certainly seems to suit you, Mrs Porchester. You look younger every time I see you.'

'Go along with you, Mr Gould!' but she blushed and did in fact look instantly rejuvenated. Monty reflected, not for the first time, that he should have been a doctor. Or a lawyer. Or a parson. He grinned to himself; as an actor he had been all three, and even now he acted the part of book expert for Edward Williams. But it was too long a performance, and he was, once again, thoroughly bored. He waited by the all-glass counter with its inlaid brass measuring rod. 'Come home Tolly, all is forgiven,' he murmured as Mrs Porchester bustled off to find David, and the old girl in the Air Force blue two-piece left the shop well satisfied. Monty watched the girls clearing up the aftermath of the sale and reflected on the oddness of life. Here he was, calling for David Daker, whom he'd heartily disliked twenty years ago, going to meet Fred Luker who had been completely beyond the pale in those days, to celebrate his niece's birthday in the old Rising house which he had thought of once as a hovel. Life was . . . unexpected. It was churlish of him to feel boredom when something could be just around the corner. He grinned, remembering Bridie Hall the other day. She was as brazen as Sibbie Luker had been in the old days, but because she had a bit of class she got away with it. She would be there this afternoon. His grin widened.

David joined him, his limp back again.

'Ghastly day,' he grunted, shouldering into his coat with some difficulty. 'After the blasted clothes have left the drawing-board I'm not interested.'

'Unless April's wearing them,' Monty reminded him, still grinning. 'My God, you used to deck her out and parade her in front of everyone like a proud papa. And you were almost old enough to be her pa too — no wonder poor old Will disapproved of the match.'

David could not have taken this from anyone but the insouciant Monty. He grunted again. 'Don't remind me, for God's sake. I must have been unbearable, how the hell did she put up with me?'

'There's been one man for April Rising. And that's you, you old son of a gun!' Monty's charm was different for David but it worked just as well. David grinned unwillingly as he turned his collar up against the fog. The two men walked the length of the Northgate and turned into Chichester Stree by the Lamb and Flag. Trains rattled constantly over the railway bridge. 'Lot of troop movement going on,' David commented. 'They're pouring men over to France. Getting them up to the Ardennes, I suppose.'

Monty, who knew very little of the real details of the

campaign, said, 'What about the good old Maginot Line?'

'It peters out up there. They rely on the terrain to hold back the Jerries. The hills and woods. It's the weak spot. That's where they'll get us.'

'Christamighty David, you're cheerful?'

'I'm realistic, Monty. Look at the way the Nazis went into Austria and Czechoslovakia, then Poland. The war hasn't started yet.'

Monty put the big old key into the lock at number thirty-three. 'I hope it finishes before they send Victor out there,' he said.

'So do I.' The two men stood in the narrow passage, getting out of their coats and finding places for them in the pile on the hall stand. David held the wall and tried to find a comfortable position for his leg to fit into its hip socket. 'I'd like to talk to Tolly about it all. Wish to heaven he'd come back home.'

But Monty was looking up the stairs.

'Good God! It's our Victor! He's here — Good God!'

David hung back and watched smilingly as father and son clasped each other unashamedly. They were so alike, their dark good looks making them look like a pair of matinee idols, their feelings always on show.

'Uncle David — isn't this marvellous? Getting leave for Davie's birthday?'

They shook hands. Victor's eyes did not smile so David knew this was embarkation leave.

Tea over, Svetlana said, 'Can we play real proper games now? Can we play hide-and-seek all over the house?'

Natasha said, 'You're such a baby, Lana.'

Flo said, 'But it would be fun, Nash. And afterwards we can dance again. I'll ask Victor if he will dance with you if you like.'

Bridie said, 'The food was marvellous, May. How did you manage all this and cope with Gretta?'

'Oh, April did it all. And Fred brought it round in the

65

car. It is rather pre-war isn't it? Listen. Victor is here for ten whole days. Shall we go to Cheltenham and walk along the Prom-prom-prom? And go to Robinswood? It might snow and we could make a snowman.' May was like a girl again; Victor always made her feel young.

April said, 'Darling, I can see your leg is painful. Go on home and get Aunt Sylv to make you a poultice.'
'Certainly not. I don't intend to miss my daughter's party.' He smiled into her blue eyes. 'Oh Primrose, I do love you. Thank God we haven't got a son.'
They linked hands beneath the loaded dining-table and felt, as always, the empathy-flow between them.

Olga said, 'He came round again last night. He calls regularly you know, Davie.'
Davie smiled, knowing what Olga wanted her to say. 'He must be in love with you, Olga. He *must* be.'
Olga went unattractively red. 'You see, he's got such a frightful name since there was all that business with the Forest girl. But he never tries to get fresh with me. He respects me, Davie. That's important, isn't it?'
'Yes. Yes, it is.'
'And it doesn't matter to me how many girls he's got in the family way. *You* understand that, don't you?'
It was Davie's turn to blush, but she nodded again.
'He does things to get in my good books too,' Olga boasted more confidently. 'Like this business with Albert.'
Davie became alert. 'Albert? D'you mean our Albert?'
'Yes. That was why he came round last night. He knows how you feel about Albert — he says he understands what true love is. That means something, doesn't it?'
'Yes, but what did he say — what did he say about Albert?'
'Well. You know he practically runs the Records Office in Eastern Avenue? Just because he's not medically fit to fight doesn't mean he's not doing his bit. He's got terrific responsibilities there, Davie. He was telling me last week

. . . anyway, he found Albert's file. He's a pilot now, did you know?

'Yes, Uncle Fred said. But he wouldn't tell me where he was. He wouldn't tell me anything. And I've been asking Victor, but he's promised not to tell either. Did Robin really tell you where Albert is stationed?'

'No.' Olga looked slightly annoyed. 'No, he wouldn't do that. He said it was practically a traitorous act. He had to sign something — just like taking the king's shilling it was. He mustn't divulge . . . anyway he did say if you would meet him some time he'd try to let you know where Albert is stationed without actually telling you.'

Davie frowned. 'It sounds rather silly, Olga. Either he tells me or he doesn't.'

'There are ways and means, April. But of course if you don't want to know it doesn't matter.'

'Of course I want to know. I want to know more than anything else! But . . .' Davie wanted to say she did not really trust a young man of twenty-one who paid attentions to schoolgirls of fourteen. However it was impossible to say this because Albert had been eighteen when he had given her their engagement ring, and she had been only eleven. But of course, that was different. Everything about Albert and herself was different.

After the games there was more dancing in the bandy room. Then March took over at the piano and she and Davie sang their 'party piece', a duet about rooks flying westward. Then, as it was close to Christmas, there were carols and Auld Lang Syne. It was eight-thirty, very late for the small children. Coats were brought and a last drink made for the grown-ups.

Victor took Davie upstairs to show her the work he had brought home with him from Wiltshire. The attic room next to his bedroom was his studio, and a portfolio of drawings was just inside the door. He pulled the blind carefully and put on the light.

'It's beautiful country all around the camp, Davie,' he said. 'This is Warminster — a charcoal sketch. And this is Westbury . . . you'd love it.'

'I expect David loves it. Did he come with you when you did these?' Davie asked innocently.

'No.' Victor removed several caricatures from the portfolio and spread them on the floor. 'No, he didn't come with me. And no, he isn't in Wiltshire.' He kept his eyes off the tall slim figure of his cousin. Ever since he had learned the truth about her two years before she had become increasingly fascinating to him. He had always assumed she was all April with just a dash of David in her artistic inclinations. Now he knew she was Fred's daughter, he saw very clearly the steely, obstinate quality she had inherited from her real father. And he saw too that the white-blonde hair and pale blue eyes that had made her albino-plain as a child, were deepening into the kind of allure that her Aunt Sibbie had had in her heyday. Victor bit his lip. If Albert had fallen in love with her when she was a child, what would he think of her now, on the edge of adulthood? And in that fancy flouncy American outfit she looked so much like Greta Garbo it was almost shocking.

He said, following his own thought-line, 'Did you know Mother and Dad named Gretta for Greta Garbo? They spelled it with two t's so that no-one would be able to mispronounce it.'

'Yes. Yes I knew. And I know you're trying to change the subject.'

'Not at all. Sorry. These are sketches of some of the chaps in the camp. This is one of Herbert Atkins — of course we call him Tommy. And this is Jim Jameson from Newcastle—'

'I'll give you one last chance, Victor. Tell me where Albert is stationed. Now.'

He let himself look at her. Her colour was high and her eyes flashed. Her straight hair hung down to her ears then bent under. He was reminded of an article in the *Citizen* many years ago when his mother and her two sisters had been described as the 'daffodil girls'. Davie, too, was like a daffodil.

He tried to grin at her. 'And if I don't tell you now, you'll never ask me again?'

'No. No, I won't. Never again. And whatever happens will be your fault!'

Her mouth was set and hard. Like Albert's when he had said, 'If you ever tell her where I am, I'll kill you, d'you hear me Victor?' God what a pair they would make; both were such balanced combinations of the Rising softness and the Luker drive.

Together they might accomplish anything. For a moment Victor felt himself wavering. Why not? Why not tell her everything and let her make up her own mind? He knew what her decision would be. And again . . . why not? Stupid convention, that's all it was. And he liked to think he was the most unconventional person on earth.

He swallowed then said quietly, 'So be it, Davie. I've promised Albert I won't tell you, and I'm not going to break my promise.' He came over and put his arms round her. 'I'm sorry, coz. Truly sorry.'

For a moment she was stiff and furious, then she leaned on his tunic buttons. He was the only one who knew truly how she felt. It was good to be with him again. They embraced.

Then he said into her ear, 'Davie. They don't know yet. This is an embarkation leave. I go to France on the tenth.'

She said nothing. Her arms tightened around his waist. He waited for the tears and prepared his own words of comfort.

Then she broke away and said bracingly, 'You'd just better come back safely, Victor Gould. Otherwise I'll never speak to you again.'

They were laughing together when the door-knocker beat a rapid tattoo two floors below. Victor flicked off the light and raised the blind, then the window. Together they leaned out over the street and tried to make out who it could be.

David and April opened the door to Mannie Stein. He

had been David's best man at their wedding, but since then his presence had been an omen of much misery between them. And Mannie Stein hated them; they both recognized that. The sight of him standing on the doorway like a funeral crow was shocking and more terrifying than an air raid.

His white face did not smile.

'I have come for Mrs Hall.' The slightly accented voice was unnecessarily loud. Bridie crowded forward.

'Why, Mannie! I didn't expect you for a while!' Her words caused David and April to exchange a glance. 'What on earth happened?' Her hand went to her throat. 'Is it Tolly? You said you would get news of Tolly! Is it Tolly?'

The others packed in behind Bridie. Nobody considered asking Mannie Stein to come inside.

'Yes. Yes, I have news of your husband. But before I could give it to old Mrs Hall, she collapsed.' There was a sharp edge to his voice, like triumph. He was pleased to be bringing this news. 'I went straight to Brunswick Road from the train. I thought it kinder to bring the news in person rather than telephone it to you, my dear. Your husband's mother opened the door and I went inside. Whether she knew from my face . . . she fell at my feet and by the time the doctor arrived, she was dead.'

'*Dead*? Kitty . . . dead?' Bridie's face was suddenly completely open, completely vulnerable. 'She can't be. Not Tolly's mother! Not Kitty!'

'I am afraid so. And my news of your husband is the same. He is dead, Mrs Hall. And so is his mother.'

Bridie let out a long wail, put her hands to her ears, turned and saw Monty.

'Monty — oh Monty darling. What shall I do? I'm really alone now — really alone!' And she cast herself on to his chest.

Five

As a child March Rising had been known for her sudden and terrible outbursts of temper. Later these had vented themselves in the long-standing and bitter feud with Fred Luker, but since the disappearance of their son over two years ago, she appeared to have changed. Faced with the complete breakdown of her husband, the stormy passionate feeling between them had mellowed. March had discovered a talent for cherishing; it was a completely new one for her. She had never cherished her son, nor her first husband, and certainly not her second. But she knew how it was done. She had been taught by her saintly mother and by her love-starved aunt. In an effort to salvage something from the debacle of Albert's desertion, she used this knowledge and found it worked.

But beneath her new gentleness, shreds of the old March still lurked. Fred and Victor knew where Albert was stationed and refused to tell her. She had respected Fred's silence initially, because she had been certain that when Victor came home she would be able to elicit the necessary — vital — information from him. But then Victor did come home, and it seemed, had given his word to Albert that he too would keep his counsel.

March put up with it for a while. There was the awfulness of Mannie Stein's news to contend with first of all. Bridie turned to her three friends, weeping and keening and not knowing what to do and how to cope.

They took it in turns to sit with her and March even lent Chattie for a while. It wasn't easy. March's store of natural sympathy was not deep. By her third visit it was nearly all gone.

'I mean, we can't even have a funeral!' Bridie cried despairingly ten days after Davie's party. 'If his name was on the roll of honour, or if there was a grave — oh God — oh God — how can I bear it!'

March could not bring herself to pat the heaving shoulders, but she made soothing sounds and suggested that Kitty's funeral had been partly in memory of dear Tolly too. And in any case Mannie Stein could easily be wrong, official records often were, so surely the kind of information he had — word-of-mouth only, remember — was unreliable to say the least.

Bridie refused all suggestions. Kitty was Kitty and Tolly was Tolly. And Mannie Stein's sources of information were a bloody sight better than the government's. It had been Mannie who told her she had better get the legal side sorted out otherwise she might be gypped out of Tolly's share of the business. And it had been Mannie who got her silk stockings. No, not the petrol. Charles Adair had got her the petrol from his Observer Corps allowance.

March said, tight lipped, 'You seem to have done very nicely for yourself, Bridie. What has Monty been getting for you?'

Bridget wailed anew at that. 'Monty has been wonderful to me! He discusses the book department with me so that I know exactly what Tolly would need to know when . . . if . . . and now he won't come back! Oh my God . . . my God . . . what shall I do?'

'You haven't had Tolly since '36, Bridie, and you've done pretty well for yourself!' March snapped suddenly, her patience disappearing. 'I can quite understand that you will miss Kitty very much indeed. But Chattie will stay with you till you find someone else for the girls. It shouldn't be too difficult. Probably your father has some elderly relative who—'

72

'You know very *well* I haven't had anything to do with my father since he married Sibbie Luker, March! You're being deliberately aggravating!' Bridget's voice soared into top key and she flung herself on to the sofa in complete despair.

Chattie came in with the tea things and sighed gustily. She would do anything for Mr and Mrs Luker, but she hoped they would not ask her stay in Brunswick Road for long. She wasn't used to young children and the Hall girls did nothing but squabble all day long.

'Mr Stein is in the dining-room, madam. Shall I show him up?' she said to Bridget's heaving shoulders.

The shoulders steadied and jerked themselves upright. Bridget plucked a handkerchief from her sleeve and dabbed frantically.

'Mannie? I thought he went back to London after Kitty's funeral. Oh God, what do I look like? Pass me that hand mirror, Chattie. And my bag, dear. Where on earth is the rouge?'

March stood up smartly.

'Well, if you've got a caller, I'm off,' she said. 'April said she'd be round tomorrow. And May the day after. And really Bridie, for the children's sake, you must try to pull yourself together.' She laid a sympathetic hand on Chattie's as she passed her, but left Bridie to it. Mannie Stein could pat her shoulder if need be.

She seethed all the way home, certain that most of Bridie's histrionics were hypocritical. Snow was thick on the ground and the buses had been cancelled so she had to walk. Thank goodness Davie had had her special day; but it was typical that when the girl was happy something would happen to eclipse her happiness. March tramped past Chichester Street, tempted to go in and talk to May, then knowing that May would irritate her still further with her white-faced anxiety about Victor. London Road stretched endlessly ahead. She drew level with the almshouses and wondered what it would be like to end one's days there, cajoled if not quite bullied by a matron and a procession of 'kind ladies'. Thank God it hadn't happened to Mother or Father. Please God it wouldn't happen to anyone else she knew. Yet Albert was alone, young though he was. And he would be grieving for Tolly too; he would grieve far more than Bridie. Why had he turned to Tolly in his extremity? And *why* had Fred told him the truth about his parentage? What must Albert have thought of *her*? Had he tried to picture his actual conception? Had he felt sick at the thought of his mother in a stable with Fred Luker?

She reached the top of Wotton Pitch and started down the other side. So many questions, all never to be answered. Her whole life seemed composed of unanswered questions; infuriating, stupid, degrading questions. Right from the start when she had said to her brother Albert, 'How much do you love me? More than May? More than Mother? How much?' Until he had had to tell her that he loved her enough to die for her. And, in time, he had in fact died for her. She started to run as if she could escape her thoughts; it was slippery on the snow and she almost went when down when she reached the bottom of the pitch. There were public gardens here along the banks of the brook. She clung to the boundary wall for a moment, getting her breath. It was almost dark and no-one was about, no traffic, no convoys of lorries trundling their way to Winterditch camp; the whole world was deserted except for her. It was like one of her nightmares. Then she saw two silhouettes walking beneath the trees in the gardens. She stood upright and began to move herself towards Bedford Close. For a moment she thought one of the figures might be Davie, but then she changed her mind. Davie would still be at school now.

The house, too, was deserted. She was going to miss Chattie, not only for her hard work but for her persistent optimism. Besides, March tried not to lose her temper when Chattie was around. The girl idolised her and Fred and it was something to live up to.

explain it, but if you hadn't gone over Victor wouldn't

She reached inside the big Westinghouse fridge for the milk and started making the tea. The fire in the breakfast room was damped down. She stirred it with the poker and spread the cloth over the table. When Fred came in from the garage she had made toast and put some of Chattie's damson jam in a pretty dish. But in spite of her efforts, she looked at Fred without any of her hard-won compassion. If he'd kept his mouth shut Albie would still be with them now.

Davie said patiently, 'Look. It's very awkward to skip out of school like this—'

'Oh come off it, Davina! I may call you Davina, mayn't I? I feel I know you so well — your cousins and I used to play cricket you know. When I was at Cheltenham Coll.'

Olga had arranged their meeting as soon as was decent after the party. She hadn't liked it. She felt she was losing Robin before she really had him. And just when she needed him most too. The loss of Tolly had hit her hard.

Davie said, not quite so patiently, 'Yes, of course I know. I wouldn't have agreed to meet you otherwise. But when Olga said three-thirty—'

'Well, I was off at three today. You didn't want to keep me hanging about, did you? You're only up at the church hall, dammitall. I thought if I arranged down here, on your way home — I did it for your convenience, my dear. Not mine.'

'We don't finish till three-forty. I had to pretend to feel ill. Doc Moore will probably ask my parents about it next time there's anything on at school.'

Robin did not answer. He was furious with her for arguing the toss with him, Christ, she was only a kid when all was said and done. But he'd get his own back. He kicked at a stone on the gravel path and thought of Albert Tomms and how exceedingly he disliked him.

He said at last, 'Well, you're here now. And we're going to talk about one of your cousins, aren't we?'

She wasn't a sop like Olga Hall. He knew Tomms had a

crush on her and she had one on him, but she wasn't going to grovel about it evidently. Her voice was tart when she replied.

'I hope so. Olga had an idea that you might be able to tell me where he is stationed without actually committing a traitorous act!' She made it sound pretty ridiculous and he felt his anger mounting again.

'Olga . . . dear Olga. Such a romantic child.'

She did not reply. He wanted to grab her and shake her until her teeth rattled, but then it would be over. His revenge against Tomms, which was also his revenge against Tomms' ghastly stepfather Fred Luker, was going to be long, and very, very sweet.

He said, 'Well now. You want to know about Albert, do you?'

'Yes.'

'No please or thank you? You're not a very well brought-up little girl, are you?'

'Look here, Robin. If you've got something to tell me then please tell me. Otherwise I'm going back for my bike and I'm going home. It's jolly cold.'

It was. He could smell the brook and compared with the snow, it smelled almost warm.

He said, 'Gosh, I'm sorry, Davie. Here, let me warm you up.' He got an arm around her and pinned her to his side. She tried to push away and when she couldn't she continued to walk very stiffly and faster than before.

He laughed in his throat.

'Didn't Albert ever give you a cuddle, darling? I'm sure he would do if he were here now.'

She rebelled violently and they scuffled on the snow until he released her. He was still laughing.

She said, 'I see. It's just a nasty joke is it? Well, goodbye.'

She moved so fast she was a shadow against the snow before he could grab her again. He let her go. Her bicycle was just inside the wall of the gardens. He watched the dim lights go on then stepped in front of her as she began to pedal back towards him. They both crashed into the bank and he pinned her down amid the spinning wheels and sharp pedals. She became pantingly still.

He said in a low voice, 'I know exactly where Albert Tomms is stationed, Davie. Exactly. And I know he doesn't want you to find out. So why should I tell you?'

She said nothing and after a while of savouring her closeness, of smelling her hair and inside the collar of her gaberdine raincoat, he said in the same tone, 'He wants to be rid of you, Davie. Can't you accept that? He enjoyed your running after him like a little dog — like a little bitch in fact — for a long time. Then he met other girls. Big girls. Women. And he didn't want his little bitch any more.'

She jerked convulsively and he dug his knee into her stomach.

'I know how he feels, darling. I understand so well. Olga has the same effect on me. Those cow eyes. And the way she droops. God . . .' Experimentally he opened his mouth against her cheek. She turned her head into the snow.

'Ah now . . . that won't do, Davie. If I'm going to break my oath of allegiance to King and Country, I shall need some payment.'

She did not move and he wondered if she might suffocate down there. He rolled off her and stood up; she was still motionless. He reached down and pulled her to her feet. She was as limp as a doll and he felt a sudden stab of fear. Had the fall broken something?

He let her go and she did not fall down. So he pulled the bike upright. The lights were still on.

'Here. You'd better get on home now,' he said brusquely. 'Think about what I said. If you're nice to me I'll tell you where Albert is stationed. Not all that far actually. I might even get hold of some petrol and run you down there one Sunday. Yes, that would be rather something, wouldn't it? Me turning up with ex-girl friend.' He laughed at the thought. Then repeated, 'If you're nice to me, of course.'

He thrust the bike at her and she took it and stood there holding it like a dummy. He walked back towards Barnwood Road, and at the gateway — the gate had been removed towards the war effort — he looked back. She was a darker silhouette against the darkness, still where he'd left her. But after a few moments she wheeled her bike into the road and got on it. He watched the red glow of her rear light until it was out of sight, then he turned and trudged up the pitch towards the city. On the whole he wasn't displeased with the encounter.

Fred watched March clear away the tea things and knew with awful certainty that she was going to start nagging him about Albert's whereabouts again. He opened the night's *Citizen* and got behind it. There was a headline about Lord Woolton clothing the Army and another about Hore-Belisha and Field Marshall Ironside. He gave his wintry grin; it was hard to imagine those two characters working in harness and he guessed one of them would have to go. He put his money on Ironside.

March said in a brittle voice, 'Please don't bother to get up and help me clear away. I can manage perfectly well alone.'

Fred came from a family where what little housework was done was always done by the womenfolk. He knew that had not been the case with the Risings, and probably Monty and David also gave a hand.

He said, 'I've been at work all day, March.'

'Oh I am sorry. I forgot. I've been round to sit with Bridie you see, so I didn't notice.'

'For God's sake, Marcie . . . two cups and saucers and two plates!'

'It's the *principle!*' she said loudly.

'Look, I pay Chattie to help in the house—'

'And Chattie's not here. She's helping Bridie out, if you recall.'

He shrugged. 'That's your fault. You shouldn't have

78

offered. I bet Chattie didn't want to go.'

The truth of this was too much for March. She slammed the saucers together a little too fiercely, and they broke neatly in half. Fred did not emerge from the *Citizen* so she picked up the four pieces and hurled them with all her might at the floor. As the breakfast room at Bedford Close was carpeted they did not shatter satisfyingly, and she was practically forced to stamp on them.

Fred folded the paper neatly in half and laid it on the table. March had not behaved like this for a long time.

He said, 'What has happened? Did Bridget Hall say something?'

She flared round at him. 'What d'you mean by that? Is there some gossip I don't know? Have you been seeing Tilly Adair *again?*'

'Of course not. Don't be ridiculous, Marcie. You know all that . . . it's over.'

She stooped and began to pick up the pieces of china. Quite deliberately she gripped one of the broken edges and watched with a certain satisfaction as blood welled over her fingers. Fred whipped out his handkerchief.

'Come here.'

'No. I won't come here. I won't be bullied by you any more, Fred Luker. I've been your doormat for long enough. I've got rights . . . my God, poor old Bridie might have lost her husband and mother-in-law, but she's still got that Mannie Stein at her beck and call!' She encouraged the blood to trickle down her wrist and continued to clear up angrily with her other hand.

Fred said, 'Mannie Stein was there today?'

'Oh yes. Probably with a parcel of stockings or something for Bridie!'

Fred frowned, wondering what Stein was up to and how it would affect April. March sensed she had lost his attention and rounded on him again.

'All I want to know is — where is Albert? In the name of God, Fred, where is my son?'

'Our son, Marcie.'

79

'I want to write to him! That's all. I'm not going to pester him — I've promised I won't tell Davie—'

'Write a letter and I will see he gets it.'

'It's a conspiracy! You and Victor — you both know where he is and you won't say!'

'My dearest girl, we have promised him, can't you understand that?' He held out a hand. 'Now come here and let me bind that cut.' He smiled at her. 'Come on, Marcie. Don't be angry any more. I can't tell you where the boy is — I've cheated him so often, this time I have to keep faith. Perhaps if I'm honest with him from now on there might come a time when he can stop hating me.'

She moved towards him on her knees very slowly and held out her cut hand. Gently he staunched the blood and bound it. She watched his work-blunted fingers; they were very like Albert's, very capable. Suddenly she bent over them and touched them with her lips.

'I want to see him. I want to see him so much, Freddie.'

For a split second he wavered. Then he imagined how she would feel if Albert's blue eyes stared at her with the same dislike they'd shown him.

'One day perhaps he'll forgive us, Marcie,' he said steadily. He bent his own head to kiss her, but she jerked up again suddenly and cracked her forehead on his chin.

She gave a cry and held her eyes.

'It's all your fault!'

He tried to gather her into his arms, but she beat at him and staggered back on to a chair.

'You shouldn't have told him — you did it to punish me, I know that — he hated you already and you thought he should hate me too!'

'March, it wasn't like that — I've tried to explain — and to ask your—'

'Damn you!' With the bloodstained handkerchief held to her head she looked mortally wounded. 'Damn you, Fred Luker! You've been a curse to me all my life — all my life!'

He stood up and came towards her and she sprang to

her feet and got the other side of the table.

'Keep away from me. I'll never forget the way you blacked Tilly Adair's eye — and now you're trying to do the same to me! Keep away!'

Suddenly he couldn't make the effort to get through to her. He simply could not be bothered.

'By all means.' He relapsed into his chair again and picked up the paper. 'Take your time, March.'

She said, 'I'm going to bed. And I don't want any company. You can sleep in Albert's room like you did before!' She looked at the table. '*And* you can wash up!'

She stormed out of the room.

Mannie Stein took Bridget to dinner at the New County, where, in spite of wartime shortages, they still served a three-course meal starting with brown Windsor and ending with three biscuits and a small square of cheese. In between there were beef croissants, which turned out to be rissoles, with mashed swede, mashed potatoes and cauliflower. Grief did not interfere with Bridget's appetite, and though Mannie might look like an undertaker he had been wonderfully good to her in the last eighteen months. She knew that April loathed him, in fact was frightened of him, and that lent piquancy to his companionship. Tolly had been safe and predictable, ignoring her flirtations and most of her whims until she finally went too far. She had honestly thought he would eventually came to terms with Barty and her infidelity. But now he was dead and she had to look out for herself. Mannie Stein had already proved supportive and the dangerous quality in him made him interesting.

He leaned across the table to pour her coffee and said softly, 'You realize, of course, that I know a great deal of your affairs. The business for instance of your father marrying the Luker girl.'

She shrugged. 'Everyone knows that, Mannie. It was the talk of Gloucester at one time. Pa was an idiot. It was one thing to sleep with Sibbie Luker, quite another to marry her.' She stirred her coffee. 'When you advised me to keep an eye on Tolly's old department at the firm, were you thinking of that marriage?'

He too shrugged. 'It does no harm to familiarise oneself with the business which one day *should* be yours.'

'Oh Mannie, you are good to me. All the advice you have given me . . . and I have taken it, my dear. I've got Monty to show me all the catalogues.' She smiled into his hooded eyes. 'In fact, Mannie, I could take over that job tomorrow. And do it a darned sight better than Monty Gould does it!'

'Good girl!' His smile was genuine. Bridget's forthrightness had always amused him. In so many ways she reminded him of April Daker. And at the thought of April, the smile disappeared and he put a tentative hand over Bridget's. 'I also know that you have had nothing to do with your father since his marriage. Is that wise?'

She did not remove her hand.

'I know what you mean, of course. Sibbie might get the whole shebang when poor old Daddy dies.' She sighed. 'I don't think so. Tolly was the son he never had, you see. He told me — when he married Sibbie — that she would have the house and an income, but Tolly would have the business. And Daddy still pays me an allowance as well as Tolly's salary. A very good allowance.'

Mannie turned her hand over very carefully and clasped it. 'But my darling girl . . . Tolly is dead.'

She returned the clasp.

'I am still here. And Tolly's daughters.'

He hooded his eyes again. 'And Tolly's son, of course.'

'Well. Yes. Barty. Of course.'

This time his smile seemed to be directed inwards. He said gently, 'Supposing your father tied up any bequests so that only the children inherited. How would you feel about that?'

Her hand tightened.

'He wouldn't do that.'

'It depends.'

'On what?'

'On how much Sibbie dislikes you and on how much influence she has with your father.'

'Oh, she dislikes me all right. She hates me for never speaking to Daddy since their marriage. And even more she absolutely loathes the Rising girls, and of course I'm practically a Rising myself. I used to escape from the Barnwood Road house as often as I could and rush down to Chichester Street. I dressed like them and talked like them . . . you know how children are.'

His thumb moved slightly, massaging the inside of her wrist. 'Yes. Yes, Bridie dear. I always think of you as a Rising. One of the family as it were.' He sighed. 'Except that if you were truly a Rising you would not be sitting here with me now, holding hands.'

She laughed and tried to withdraw her fingers from his; he would not release her.

She said lightly, 'Oh rubbish, Mannie — some old quarrel long forgotten.'

He said, 'The quarrel was not on my side, Bridie — please know that. They did not like my Jewishness.'

'Now that really *is* rubbish. Why, David is Jewish himself!' She pulled harder and he had to let her go. His hand stayed where it was, half turned up as if pleading with her.

He said, 'That was what brought us together. Then David realised the drawbacks of being Jewish. And it drove us apart.' He lifted heavy lids and stared at her. 'You too, Bridie?'

Quickly she reached across the table and took his hand again and held it tightly.

'If you go on like that, Mannie, I'm likely to hit you! My God, what should I have done without you during the last year? Half the stuff in the refrigerator is what you've brought down! And coming with me like you did to register the deaths — that deposition you had from the soldier who fought by Tolly in Spain — our wedding ring—' Suddenly and unexpectedly a spasm of grief

83

shook her body. That deposition and their wedding ring had made it so final. The years stretched ahead of her, completely empty, no goal in sight. She lowered her head and squeezed her eyes tight shut.

Mannie said, 'Ah Bridie, Bridie, don't, my darling. How can I comfort you in a public place like this?'

'I have no-one . . . no-one . . .'

'Dearest girl, you still have your family. And . . . dare I say this . . . you have me, Bridget. I know I must seem an old man to you—'

She said quickly, 'You're not much older than David.'

'Quite. It's just that, in spite of being a mother six times over, you seem such a child.'

That pleased her. She had retained her looks after all. She hadn't gone to fat like May and she wasn't dehydrating like April. She managed a small, brave smile.

He said, 'Bridie, I wasn't going to say anything yet. It's too soon and I'm afraid you might send me away.'

She whispered, 'I would never do that, Mannie.'

He smiled again, knowing full well he had made himself indispensable; silk stockings and underwear were a necessity to Bridie.

'I might have to send myself away,' he warned her. 'If you . . . I'm going to say it, Bridie. Will you — one day — consider a marriage between us? You need not love me madly, my darling, it can be any kind of marriage you want. I am lonely, you are lonely. We can help each other.'

She gripped his hand hard as if she were drowning and her whisper was even fainter. 'Is it . . . would it be . . . just because of loneliness, Mannie? Do you have not the smallest affection for me?'

He reached out with his other hand and took hers. 'You do not know me very well yet, Bridie. I am madly in love with you. I do not want to frighten you with talk of passion.'

But she gave a small smile of satisfaction. She could crook her finger and summon Charles Adair any time she wanted. But he had Tilly and could never marry her. Mannie Stein could offer everything Charles could, and more. He was a man of considerable, if mysterious, power. She rather fancied him in the role of doting sugar-daddy.

She said, 'You don't frighten me, Mannie. But of course you're right, it is too soon. I am still in a state of grief and shock.'

'I understand, Bridie. Put it out of your mind for now, my dear. Right out of your mind. Let us have some more coffee.''

He poured and she drank.

'I say . . .' she began to giggle. 'It would make April sit up and think, wouldn't it?'

He smiled back at her. 'It certainly would,' he agreed.

It was David's night on warden duty, and he came in at ten-thirty looking tired and drawn. April waited up for him and showed her anxiety by divesting him of overcoat, tin hat and gas mask almost before his eyes had become accustomed to the living-room light. He did not protest, knowing her need to help him was more important than his need for independence. But after she had put his stuff away in the hall he held her still, hands clamped to her sides, and kissed her gently.

'No, I don't want any supper,' he murmured before she could ask. 'And yes, I would like some cocoa. Thank you kindly, Primrose Sweet.'

She had to laugh. 'Oh David Daker. I've got thick pea soup and some of Aunt Sylv's faggots, and—'

'Spare me! When you went to St. Ives with the girls that time, Aunt Sylv force-fed me her faggots, her brawn and her neck of mutton until they came out of my ears!'

'No-one can force you to do anything you don't want to, David! You thoroughly enjoyed them — she told me so herself!'

He released her, looking sheepish. 'I couldn't hurt her feelings, could I?' He went to the fire and rubbed his

85

hands. 'You've been sitting over that sewing machine all evening, April. I told you to rest. Doc Green has also told you to rest. Anaemia is not something that goes away for ever, you know.'

'I wanted to finish the skirts.' April skimmed through to the kitchen and came back with a jug of steaming cocoa. 'The skirts are so straightforward. It's the military trimmings on the jackets that take the time.' She poured and placed two mugs on the high mantelpiece, then stood with him gazing into the fire. 'Actually I had an idea when I looked at your sketches. What about a hat with a peak? It would complete the ensemble perfectly. I meant to tell you — when we went to the Hippodrome last week, there were some pictures from America on the Movietone News. Something about lend-lease. And Mrs Roosevelt was wearing a hat which looked rather like an officer's and I thought then—'

David's chuckle made her stop with raised brows.

'Sorry, Primrose. Everyone else is sweating blood about lend-lease and you notice what the President's wife is wearing on her head! Why is it that if May did that, or Bridget — or anyone else in the world — it would drive me mad? But when you do it, it makes me laugh.'

'Because you know what a truly deep and intellectual person I am underneath my hat,' April said with deliberate smugness as she pushed him into a chair and handed him his cocoa. 'Now drink this and then tell me about your day.'

'Well, something unusual. But first, how are all the girls? And I include Sylvia in that.'

'Flora can take the scholarship this year if we agree. Sylvia finished her hundredth sock for the Forces.' She frowned. 'Poor old Davie came a cropper off her bike on the way home. She's covered in bruises.'

He looked up, dark eyes concerned. 'Nothing more?'

'No. But she's so quiet and reserved. She went to bed at half-past seven.' She sighed deeply. 'This crush on Albert is not abating at all, David. In fact his silence is making it worse. I can understand that. When you sent me packing, it had no effect on me and I was the same age as she is. If only Albert would write to her and explain.'

He said slowly, 'If you're drawing analogies between us, darling, consider this. I spent all my youth thinking I was in love with May. It took some years to realize that I had made her into a romantic princess and fallen in love with that image. Not the real May at all. Then I had to come to terms with the fact that I was in love with a girl-child. May's sister.' He reached for her hand. 'Supposing it's been slightly different for Albert? Supposing he imagined himself in love with his girl-cousin. Then one day — either because he fell for someone else, or simply woke up and realized it — he has to accept that it was the idea he loved. Not the real person. How can he explain that to our Davie?' He sighed. 'You see, darling, he probably still *loves* her. He cannot bear to hurt her. He's waiting and praying she will find someone else and release him.'

She nodded. 'I know. It's the obvious answer. I just don't believe it.'

'Well, don't push it. March is pushing it all the time. Keeping the idea alive in Davie's mind. May still thinks it's awfully sweet and romantic and beautiful. We mustn't have an opinion at all. We must be here, just here. For Davie to lean on.'

She sat on the arm of his chair and looked at him. 'Oh David, you are so . . . *wise*. You used to be just clever and not very wise at all. But now—' she kissed him, then leaned back quickly. 'Not yet,' she commanded. 'You haven't told me your unusual news.'

He grinned up at her. 'Cruel woman.' He picked up her hand and put it to his face. 'And you don't have to stop kissing me because you think I'm too tired to make love to you.' His grin widened at her expression. 'I'm not a bit wise, Primrose, but I can read you like a book.' He turned his head and kissed her palm and felt her instant response. He kissed the beating pulse inside her wrist and spoke in between kisses. 'I have been asked to turn over the business to making uniforms. A government contract.' He held on to her hand by force as she tried to sit up. 'Worthwhile war work at last, April. Next to food, clothing is a necessity.' He pushed up her cardigan sleeve with his nose and nibbled at the inside of her elbow. 'A consignment of white cloth will arrive next week—'

She managed to get enough breath to squeak, 'White?'

'We're sending men over to Norway. White clothing will provide camouflage against the now.'

'*David!*' The squeak was higher than ever. She lay back across his lap and stared up at him with big eyes. 'Darling, how marvellous! It's exactly what you want — your own special line of war work! Oh darling, I'm so pleased. Tell me everything. Let me sit up. Oh David!'

'I've told you. And we're not going to sit up half the night discussing it. When I know more, then we can talk. Meanwhile—' He put his mouth very carefully and gently over hers. For a moment she stayed alert, her mind still grappling with his news. Then she succumbed with a laugh that sounded like a sob. Her hands went to his head, so familiar under her searching fingers. The brittle dry curls at the nape of his neck, the velvety ear. She pressed him to her with sudden passion.

Six

THAT long winter of the phoney war dragged on until the Germans made their spring push through the Ardennes at the northern end of the Maginot Line. All the enormous forts linked by miles of underground corridors were suddenly abandoned as the grand retreat began. The storm-troopers pushed into France in concentrated drives like the tines of a fork, isolating pockets of the Allies, encircling them, cutting them off from their supply routes. It was impossible to know where the Front actually was any more. Victor, stumbling back to his bivouac from the latrines one pearly morning, spotted the misty outline of a tank surrounded by its crew poring over a map. He froze where he was and began to back away. As soon as they were swallowed in fog he ran like a hare in the other direction. Another hefty silhouette took form ahead of him, this time an armoured car with the swastika'd flags on its wings showing it contained a high-ranking officer. He dropped to the ground and tried to think. He had no wish to spend a long time in a prisoner of war camp without his painting materials. On the other hand, he did not wish to be shot. His outstretched fingers felt an edge to the rough grass. He slid sideways and found a shell-hole and got into it. He felt sick yet hungry; he was cold in spite of his greatcoat. Supposing they thought he was a spy? He wasn't wearing full uniform; at five o'clock in the morning a trip to the lats had not warranted more than a greatcoat over shirt and trousers. They shot spies.

At six o'clock the sun melted the mist in five minutes flat and the shooting and shouting began. He looked over the lip of the shell-hole and saw soldiers with Bren guns and pistols firing fruitlessly at a line of advancing tanks. He recognized Dusty Miller trying to set up the anti-tank gun just as the left-hand tank swung round and annihilated him. The noise was incredible and he waited to die. The tanks were going to grind him bloodily into the earth. There was something satisfying about that, 'earth to earth', dead and buried without any fuss. Probably painless. Someone was running towards him, not seeing him, just running. Then not running. Flat and covered in blood. The tanks would go over him first; Victor would be able to watch it and know what his own end would look like.

He crawled out of the hole and ran too, bent double, towards the prone figure. It was a man he didn't like very much, a corporal, William Ferdinand. He had red hair to match his red legs. Victor caught hold of the hair and started to pull him back to the shell-hole. The tanks came inexorably on. He backed into the hole, pulling Ferdinand on top of him. The next minute the sky disappeared. The foremost tank caterpillared its way above them, its twin tracks neatly straddling the pit in which they lay. The sky reappeared. Ferdinand was heavy and odorous on him, an exhausted lover. Was he dead? Victor could not move. The infantry would be behind the tanks, they would come along to do the mopping-up. If Ferdy wasn't already dead they would shoot him. Then they might shoot Victor or they might yell at him to surrender. He lay still, warm now because of Ferdy's body, strangely, tremblingly relaxed after the jangling tension of the past two hours. At some time he felt warmth between his legs and knew he had urinated. The sun climbed high into a cloudless sky. There were no groans outside; he could hear distant firing and felt the ground shake occasionally at the impact of a shell.

At midday the flies arrived. Big bluebottles, walking over his clasping hands to reach whatever they wanted on Ferdy. They tried to crawl into his eyes and he blinked them away so that he could go on looking at the grass blowing gently on the lip of his particular crater. It was very beautiful and he wished he could paint it. The way the light caught it and made each blade wonderfully individual, yet the same. Like men. He wanted his painting things very badly. Also a drink.

Eventually he decided he would rather be shot than lie there any longer; so he eased himself away from his companion and stuck his head above the surface of the earth. It was immediately obvious that no-one was alive. The tanks had rolled over a couple of tents containing most of his squad. Presumably they were dead and decently shrouded; there was nothing he could do about that. He stumbled around among the others who had put up futile resistance. Some of them were not recognizable as being human and the flies were having a field day.

He leaned back into the crater and heaved Ferdy out and got him around his neck like a scarf. He began to walk. He had no idea where he was going; he just walked. He had probably gone no further than a quarter of a mile from his shell-hole, when he was spotted by a sortieing Spitfire who radioed a message to his ground command. An ambulance diverted, and Victor was discovered walking determinedly towards the enemy lines. He was taken to the field hospital at Sedan and a bullet removed from his shoulder. As there were no enemy field arms used during the attack, the bullet must have been a 'friendly' one. He felt pretty sick about it; it all seemed tamely unheroic in the event. However, as luck would have it, Corporal Ferdinand was just alive, and Victor had most definitely saved his life.

His nurse, resplendent in the flapping headgear of the Queen Alexandra's, said, 'This will mean a medal, Private. Yes, a D.S.O. at least, I should think.'

Victor said, 'Bugger the D.S.O. What about getting out

of here? The bloody Jerries are everywhere.'

She tucked in her chin. 'No need to panic, Private. A temporary setback, that is all.'

Albert, temporarily based at Sedan, landed right after Jack Doswell and went into a huddle with his ground crew. He had taken a hit in his tailplane but had got the Messerschmidt that did it and managed to plot half a dozen British infantrymen who had been cut off from their units.

Jack Doswell ran over to exchange news.

'I'd have had my lot this time, Tommy, if it weren't for the mirrors.'

Albert smiled briefly. It had been his idea to fit rear-view mirrors in the Spits so that there was no need to turn and twist during a dogfight in order to keep the enemy in view. He had also adapted several of the craft in his squadron so that the undercarriage lever was on the right instead of the left of the pilot. Even experienced pilots could roll the fighters on landing because of that awkwardly-placed lever. He listened to Jack now and at the same time ran an exploring hand over the bullet-holes in the tailplane. He needed to touch his machines; in the old days at the Austin works he had been unable to put his ideas on to paper, but given an actual engine he left the other apprentices standing.

'I kin 'ave her airworthy in a coupla hours,' grunted the mechanic following him around the machine.

'Make it an hour and I'll buy you a beer,' Albert offered.

'Call this French swill beer?' the man grunted. 'But you're on.'

Albert and Jack walked to the crew dispersal hut on the field that had belonged to a private flying club not long ago. The runway was lined with enormous oil drums used to light it at night, and it was surrounded by the wooded foothills of the Ardennes. Along the edge of the wood, the airmen themselves had cleared small areas for dispersing the Spitfires; more aircraft were lost on the ground in bombing raids than in the air.

Jack was agog with the latest gossip, plus news from home.

'We're being sent to Westhampnett — it's practically official. Tubby Morrison had it from the Waaf on the field telephone. The Boche have definitely broken through the Line and we shall be needed to look after the old fort.' Jack clapped Albert's shoulder. 'We're sure to get some leave, old man, and if you're not going back to Gloucester, you might as well come home with me. Elizabeth has finished her training and is in a hospital in Dorchester. I've just had a letter. We can get up to London and do some shows. You'll like her.'

Elizabeth was Jack's sister and had joined the Q.A.R.A.N.C. just after Christmas. Jack was inordinately proud of her.

'I might do that. Thanks a lot, old man. That is, of course, if we are sent back and if we do get leave.' Albert made a face. 'Let's hope you're wrong about that.' Because if he wasn't wrong it meant France was going to capitulate. And with Russia grabbing part of Poland and all of Finland, that would mean Britain would stand alone.

He hardly heard Jack as they walked together to the crew room. For the first time he saw that it was possible that Britain might lose the war. And in that kind of maelstrom, what would it matter if a brother and sister loved each other?

Victor was taken by truck the 'long way round' to the coast. Corporal Ferdinand was with him, still alive but unknowing of the terror of that drive. In a small village east of Paris they snatched a few hours sleep in a tiny inn, and it was there they learned that Reynaud had resigned and Pétain was Prime Minister of France.

Victor took his arm from its sling and crashed his fist on the table.

93

'Damanblastit!' he said so loudly the innkeeper's wife spilt the coffee she was pouring.

The young driver from the A.T.S. pursed her lips disapprovingly. 'Honestly, Private Gould. I didn't think you were like that. Swearing in front of ladies.'

'Sorry Gladys. It's just that after all that's happened we're still not going to get back to Blighty.'

'My name is *not* Gladys!'

'It's not that I mind P.O.W. camp. It's just that I haven't got any paints.'

She took her coffee and smiled up at the Frenchwoman proffering cream. The French might be on the losing side, but they still had more in the way of food than the poor old British.

'You an artist then, Private?' she said without much interest.

He said gloomily, 'I was. A long time ago. Blood tears toil and sweat indeed. The French are the sensible ones.'

'Now then, Private.'

He made a ghastly face at her and mimicked, 'Now then, Gladys.'

'My name is *not*—'

A despatch rider on a very noisy motor-bike roared into the yard. Gladys went to meet him and brought back a flimsy which they pored over together. Evacuation was being organised from the port of Dunkirk and they were asked to be there by 28th May. The next day.

Victor said, 'Pop upstairs, Glad, and see if the orderly thinks we can move Ferdie. If so, we'll get going.'

'I'm not driving through these country roads at night and that's flat,' Gladys protested.

'How d'you fancy a baby farm just outside Berlin?' Victor asked brutally.

The girl, not much older than Davina, left the room hurriedly.

Charles Adair had a smart cruiser on the Gloucester canal. When preparations for the Dunkirk evacuation

94

began, he used some of his buckshee petrol and commandeered a van to tow it across country to Weymouth. Robin was no hero and would have pleaded commitment to his work at Records, but he thought it was possible Davina might think more of him if he went with his father. She now allowed him to kiss her whenever they met, but there was never the slightest response from those schoolgirl lips. Sometimes he wished she would fight him as she had done that night in Estcourt Road gardens. At least there had been some kind of passion then.

He met her from school that afternoon, lurking along Lansdown Road so that Olga would not see him. The Birmingham girls had at last returned home, bored by the phoney war, and the High School playing-field was lumpy with air raid shelters which gave him useful cover. Her velour hat had been replaced by a straw panama and she wore a blazer over her blue poplin uniform dress. She stood on the pedals of her bike to give her a start up the steep pitch from the school, and he saw the length of her honey-coloured leg as her skirt caught on her saddle. Robin Adair was unable to define beauty when he saw it, but he said aloud, 'That is some girl. That really is some girl.' Then he whizzed his own bicycle out of Lansdown Road and pedalled parallel with her.

'Oh. Hello Robin,' she said with noticeable lack of enthusiasm.

'Hi there babe.' He put on an American twang but she did not smile. 'How are things?' He laid a proprietary hand on her shoulder.

'All right. What do you want?'

'You, of course, What else?'

'Oh do stop it, Robin. I'm not going to meet you tonight. Or any other night. You've no intention of telling me anything about my cousin—'

'Darling, I'm going to rescue your cousin probably. Or one of them.' He whinnied a laugh. 'Ah. That's surprised you, hasn't it? Haven't you heard about the Dunkirk evacuation?'

She wobbled ominously and he propelled her to the top of the pitch and then gave her a shove to start her down the other side. They careered at breakneck speed to the roundabout and tore around it to the Estcourt Road gardens.

'Over here!' he called into the wind. 'Our special place.'

He had already forgotten the unpleasantness of that first night and thought of it as 'their place'. She swerved across the road and stopped by the gate.

'Robin . . . I don't want to . . . what did you mean?'

She was out of breath. He watched fascinated as the front of her dress went up and down. Sometimes he thought of Davina Daker without clothes on and sweated. He propped his bike, then took hers from her and locked them together.

'Come on. I'll tell you all about it.'

Her reluctance meant little to him; he was not a sensitive young man. He put his arm around her and walked her along the gravel path where they had gone before. The willows drooped their branches to the ground and he led her inside one of the natural arbours and immediately began to kiss her.

'Robin, I just told you—' she struggled free. 'Listen! I have to be home in ten minutes. If you've got something to say please say it and let me go!'

He laughed. 'You drive me crazy, darling. And you know it, don't you?' He held out his hands. 'All right, all right. I'll tell you.' He turned away from her and held on to the willow's trunk, gazing down into the slow-moving stream. Suddenly he was horribly frightened. The pater expected him to go, and at the office they expected him to go. If only Davina would beg him not to. He said, 'They're getting all the British Expeditionary chaps assembled on some beach in France. Everyone with a seaworthy boat is going over. You know we've got the *Gremlin*—'

'The *Gremlin*?' Davie could see the long fingers whiten on the smooth willow bark.

'Our boat, you idiot. You know. You must have seen it on the canal.'

'We don't go down that way much.'

'Well, it's a decent enough little cabin cruiser. The pater and me — we're taking it across country to Weymouth tomorrow. Going over with the others to pick up as many as we can.'

Davina said slowly, 'You think Victor might be one of them?'

'Who knows? I doubt if we shall be asking their names.'

'You won't be able to bring many. In a cabin cruiser.'

'Exactly. That's what I told Pater. He wouldn't listen. He wants to be a hero. It's ridiculous.' He turned suddenly and took her by the shoulders. 'Listen. Davie. If you ask me not to go, I won't go. I don't care if he calls me a coward — I don't care what they say at the office — if you don't want me to go, then —'

'Don't be silly, Robin. Of course I want you to go. I simply meant that it's a pity you haven't got a bigger boat.' She disengaged herself without the usual difficulty. 'I think it's marvellous of you and your father. Really marvellous.' She smiled at him properly for the first time and he drew a quick breath. 'You might be able to make two or three trips. Or tow back a life-raft. Or . . . something.'

He felt a hardening of his stomach muscles. Where they had shaken and griped, they stilled as if waiting for something. He said, 'Probably. Yes, quite probably.' His spine stiffened next. 'I say, it would be rather a hoot if Victor *was* there, wouldn't it?'

She smiled again. 'He'd probably say — nice meeting you again, young Robin.'

'Yes. He's not bad, is Gould.' He snickered. 'I suppose if I rescued him, you'd be eternally grateful to me.'

Davina opened her eyes very wide. 'Oh, I would. I would, Robin.' She held him in her enormous cornflower-blue gaze. 'Will it . . . will it be very dangerous?'

The spine and stomach slackened slightly.

'Of course it will, you little idiot.'

'Oh Robin,' she breathed.

'Would you care then? If I didn't come back?'

Behind her back, her hands clenched hard. She whispered again, 'Oh Robin.' Then she turned away. 'But of course you will, and I shall be so proud of you.'

He grabbed at her shoulder and twisted her to face him again. 'Will you go out with me? Properly?'

She did not fight him. 'I should have to see Albert first.'

He thrust her from him. 'Oh, so that's what it's all about still, is it? You little twister.'

'You've never understood, have you, Robin? I'm engaged to Albert. I have to see him to break it off properly before I can go out with anyone else.'

'You and Tomms, engaged?' He tried to laugh. 'You were only a kid! As if that meant anything.'

She shrugged. 'It meant something to me. I've got to settle it with Albert first. I've got to be above board with him. And that's that.'

There was a long pause. Robin knew that part of her enormous attraction was her loyalty. If she ever went with him, that would be it — for life. He licked his lips.

'And when I come back — if I tell you where Albert is . . .'

She shrugged. 'If you come back. Yes.'

'Well, if I don't, it won't matter, will it?'

She began to walk back up the path. 'It's up to you, Robin. Entirely up to you. Good luck for tomorrow.'

He hurried after her. 'Oh dammit, Davie, you always get your own bloody way, don't you? He's at Tangmere. Or will be. At the moment he's at an airfield in France, and I can't bloody well tell you where *that* is! Now, are you satisfied?'

'Perfectly.'

She waited while he unlocked the bicycles, then she suddenly drew him back to the brook and beneath the veil of the willow, she kissed him voluntarily. It was a kiss of gratitude, but to Robin it was the most romantic thing that had ever happened to him. His sexual adventures had been many, but they had been clumsy and soon over. This kiss left him weak and breathless. He watched as she mounted her bicycle and rode away, still smiling and waving. He wanted to hate her and couldn't. He told himself she had used him. But then there was that kiss and the way she had stood within his arms, pliant and responsive at last. And when she smiled at him with those blue eyes, he could melt with love. The thought of the physical contact between herself and her bicycle saddle made him want to fall to the ground. And as she disappeared around the bend of Oxstalls Lane he felt again the old Agincourt stiffening of his sinews. She was going to be proud of him. She *was* going to be proud of him. She was going to be *proud* of him. He had taken up with Davina Daker in the first place to wreak some kind of revenge on the hateful Albert Tomms. But now he was deliriously, besottedly, marvellously, in love.

Fred Luker — Filthy Luker to his many enemies — was a godsend to the Local Defence Volunteers. He had commanded a machine-gun nest in the 'first lot' and had spent eighteen months as a prisoner in Silesia. But his first-hand experience of war with the bloody Jerries was only one of his advantages. The bigger one, by far, was his enormous influence in Gloucester affairs, his ability to manipulate people, his apparently limitless money. A retired general came down specially from the War Office and gave him the honorary rank of captain. He was allocated a miniscule budget, a hall just off Barrack Square near the prison, a consignment of rifles and uniforms; and he was told to get on with it. Hand to hand pitchforks on the Cross if necessary. But until the Hun actually landed, it would be patrol jobs. Liaison with fire watchers and Observer Corps. Exercises. Keep the men busy; busy men were keen men.

Fred listened to this jingoism with a jaundiced ear. Nevertheless he took the job, mainly because he knew he was the best man to do it. If the Jerries really did arrive, he would be able to negotiate the very best terms with the Gloucester Gauleiter, whoever he might be. Poor old Quisling and Pétain were Judas names with the British at the moment, but maybe they had the right idea. And if the worst came to the worst, he was capable of putting an end to his whole family and finishing himself off afterwards.

He talked it over with David and Monty that same evening when they congregated at Chichester Street to celebrate May's birthday. That in itself was the complete turn-up; he wondered as they sat around in May's white-walled sitting-room what old Will Rising would make of their many family get-togethers. It would please Florence of course; but Will? Will would know from personal experience that their family closeness depended on more than mere liking. Old Will, simple tailor of Gloucester though he'd been, knew all about the ties of passion and fear and even hatred. He might not be able to work out the relationships that bound his family tighter than they had ever been, but he would see that the three sisters and their three husbands and their five children could quite easily asphyxiate one another in the future.

Fred half grinned at the thought and caught David's eye in a moment of sympathy. That was strange too. David Daker had not interested him one iota until that night in 1925 when he had practically kicked April into the street because he'd found her naked with Mannie Stein. David Daker had seemed to him an unsatisfactory husband, effete with his dress-designing and evening classes and peculiar political leanings. Then, through April and her intense, burning love for the man, Fred had learned more about David. And when Fred married March, he had set himself to understand, even to like, his new relatives. He had wanted to take Will's place as head of the Rising family. Dammit, he had fathered two of the children, it was about time he stopped being an outsider.

Yes, he had a lot in common with David Daker now.

100

Two years in France for one thing. April Rising for another. Fred listened to the girls talking soberly about Dunkirk one minute, the awful threat of clothes rationing the next, and wondered again about David. How much did he know? Davina had always been 'Daddy's girl'. His 'little apple'. Could he have any inkling that the child was not his? At one time Fred knew he had suspected Mannie Stein of being the true father; he had told April that he would accept that. His love for April and for Davina could overcome the hateful fact. April had denied it and left it there. But David was as devious as Fred himself. And at the time of Davina's conception he had been practically impotent. Unless Flora's conception and birth had convinced him otherwise, of course. There was no end to the way a man could fool himself when he really wanted. Fred let his cynical gaze slide across to March; yes, he had fooled himself for years that she really loved him. Loved him as April loved David. But March was as superficial as May. She could be aroused to heights of passion akin to her tearing tempers. And she could feel pity. But in between those two extremes of emotions, there was a large empty space.

Monty said, 'Don't worry, old man, it might never happen.'

'What's that, old man?' Fred thought Monty Gould was a weak idiot who was lucky enough to come up smelling of roses each time he fell in the muck.

'Clothes rationing of course. What else?' Monty grinned his male collusion with the other two, and David grinned back — another strange anomaly; David actually liked Monty Gould.

He said now, cutting through Monty's apparent triviality, 'Funny isn't it? Listen to us all. As if it's just another of May's birthday parties. I suppose it's a relief in a way. Them and us.' He grinned again. 'Get the B.E.F. back from France and we shall do it. I haven't got the remotest idea how. But we shall do it.'

Fred felt a twinge of annoyance that he hadn't cottoned

on to Monty's non sequitur and David had. It proved Monty wasn't the idiot he so often seemed, and David was deep rather than devious. For a moment Fred felt an outsider again and growled illogically, 'Bloody Russians.'

David was not to be drawn; his grin inverted itself ruefully. May chipped in eagerly.

'We shall get them back all right, David. I've got absolute faith in the Navy, absolute and complete faith. Victor will be in this house — sitting here — in less than a week.'

She spoke as if her own conviction could make it happen and Fred's annoyance turned to compassion. If Albert were over there instead of Victor, he'd feel the same. As if he could bring the boy back by sheer force of will.

Monty said jovially, 'Oh of course Victor will be all right. He's like me, no-one can finish us off!'

David, March and April echoed their reassurances with a supreme confidence belied by April's hands clenched prayerfully in her lap. May might have noticed them too because she give her sister a special smile.

'I was talking to Charles Adair today,' she confided. 'And he is taking the *Gremlin* across country tonight to Weymouth. He promised he'd look out for Victor.'

It was so crazy it made Fred want to laugh out loud, but everyone else seemed to think that confirmed Victor's rescue. Except Monty. His cheeky Max Miller grin disappeared.

'You were talking to Charles Adair?' he said disbelievingly. 'I didn't think you'd ever speak to that bastard again.'

'Language dear,' May remonstrated quickly, flicking her eyes at Davie and Flora who were doing an enormous wooden jigsaw with Gretta.

'Well . . . Christamighty May . . .'

Fred recalled vaguely that there had been a would-be seduction between Charles Adair and May two or three years ago. March had hardly been able to tell him for laughing. Apparently they grappled on the floor, and May had kneed Adair quite painfully. Fred knew that Monty was right anyway; Charles Adair was a bastard.

May leaned forward and kissed Monty in a way that would have made old Grandmother Rising throw up her hands with cries of 'hussy'.

'I taught him his lesson, darling boy. And it doesn't pay to make enemies. If he speaks to me in town, then I am polite.' She kissed him again. 'Distant, but polite.'

He looked into her eyes and laughed unwillingly.

'You . . . minx!'

Davie suddenly got up from the floor and went to sit by her father. 'I heard about that too, Aunt May. Robin told me. I made him promise he'd bring Victor home with him.'

David encircled her with his arm. 'Then it'll be up to Fred and his Local Defence Volunteers,' he said like a rallying call.

That was when Fred began to talk over his immediate plans. He wanted Monty and David as sergeants of the two platoons. The unit was going to supervise the dismantling and storing of the great east window at the cathedral; they would back up the fire-watchers there; they would provide patrols around the barrage balloon emplacements and the ack-ack guns at the greyhound track; he wanted them to specialise in boat patrols along the river and the canal.

May brought paper and pen for March to make notes. She began importantly, 'In the event of paratroop landings, the Volunteers will be deployed as follows . . .'

It helped to keep their minds off Albert and Victor if nothing else.

At half-past seven Gretta went to bed and they had supper in the kitchen: cocoa and cheese sandwiches with pickled cabbage. Flora mashed her cheese into the red vinegar and cut it into sections, and Davie gave half of hers to her father. At nine o'clock they listened to Stewart Hibberd who said that the British troops were making an orderly retreat towards the Channel where the Royal Navy were waiting to bring them home.

'Sounds like a day trip to Boulogne,' Monty commented.

'They'll have gone through France in less than a week,' David marvelled. 'I saw in the paper it's called the space and gap tactic.'

'It's the strafing that does it,' Fred put in from his own knowledge. 'Those Stuka dive-bombers open up a space, or make a gap, and the bloody Jerry tanks fill it. Why they haven't put the Air Force to good use I'll never know.'

He noticed Davie staring at him narrow-eyed and added quickly, 'They know what they are doing, of course.' He met her gaze squarely. 'So you're quite friendly with Robin Adair then, Davie. Your boy friend, is he?'

She flushed angrily. 'He's Olga's boy friend,' she corrected and turned away.

Fred glanced at David, but of course the Dakers knew nothing about the Adairs. They might have heard from March that Tilly Adair had been his mistress at one time, but that wouldn't colour their opinion of Robin. He desperately wanted Davie to find someone else to love and admire, someone other than Albert. But not Robin Adair, please not Robin Adair.

Support came from March who knew Robin through Albert.

'I shouldn't get too friendly with him, darling. He's not a very nice young man. Albert never liked him.'

Well, that was that. She'd drop young Adair like a hot cake now, and cling to her image of Albert with March's encouragement. Damn March. She had a talent for doing the right thing and putting her foot in it knee-deep.

They did not go home till nearly ten o'clock. British Double Summertime meant that it would be light till nearly midnight; there was no need for lights on their bicycles. Davie and Flora went ahead of their parents, linking hands and swinging each other forward and back

104

across the empty roads. Davie thought of Mr Adair and Robin driving in a lorry across England towards the coast nearest to France. She imagined Victor waiting on a beach and the *Gremlin* moving sedately towards him. She thought of Albert back in Tangmere and was glad that France had fallen because it was bringing both her cousins home again. And then she thought of the letter that had been waiting for her with the afternoon post from Audrey Merriman in Birmingham. The sum of her thoughts made her smile her painfully wide smile.

Flora said, 'What's up, Sis? You've been excited all evening.'

Davie swung ahead of her sister and looked over her shoulder. Flo was not at all like her; dark with clear tea-brown eyes and a straight fringe emphasising the breadth of her forehead, she looked a bit like pictures of nuns in the Religious Knowledge books at school. It was a pity she was so young really because if she'd understood, Davie could have told her everything. She could keep secrets and she didn't say silly things and she loved Albert too; moreover she was entirely without the conniving streak which Davie knew was in her and which she disliked but could not eradicate. Flo might well have kissed Robin Adair this afternoon in gratitude, but she would never have let him kiss and fondle her in advance payment for information. Davie reviewed her behaviour over the past five months, and though she hated it, she knew she would do it all again if there was the faintest chance it would lead her to Albert. She remembered how she had run off to Birmingham to see him when she was only eleven, catching the train by herself and finding her own way up to West Heath where he lived. She felt suddenly strong; mistress of her own fate. She would find him, she would show him that whatever he had done, it didn't matter.

'I'm just happy,' she answered Flora truthfully. 'I don't know why. The Germans are winning and it's all awful, but I'm happy.'

Flora swung level with her and said solemnly, 'I expect you're proud to be British. After what Mr Churchill said you can't help being proud to be British, can you?'

'Oh Flo . . .' Davie manoeuvred her bicycle close to her sister's in spite of warning shouts from her mother. 'Oh Flo, you are sweet. Don't ever abandon me, will you? Whatever I do, however horrible I might seem.'

Flora obviously thought she was teasing. *Abandon Ship* had been one of the films they'd seen recently at the Picturedrome, and 'abandon' had been Flo's favourite word ever since. Davie joined in the torrent of giggles and wondered at her own words. As if . . .

When she got home she went to bed immediately without the cocoa which Aunt Sylv had ready. And she read Audrey's letter again, sitting by the window which looked out over fields towards the cathedral spires.

'Dear Davina Daker,' it began, because the two girls had never met face to face. 'I haven't been to school since returning home last month as I am not very well. But it has given me time to do some detective work myself on your behalf. I went to the address you gave me in West Heath, and found Mrs Potter to be very talkative about your cousin, so I did not have to ask questions. It is still a mystery why he left the Austin works so suddenly. He had been behaving normally and there was no trouble that she knew about. Then his stepfather came to see him. They went out together. He must have come back to his lodgings about half-past two. He left the landlady a note. That was all she knew. Then at three o'clock the stepfather arrived. He did not seem surprised that your cousin had disappeared. Mrs Potter says he never saw any young ladies and there was never any trouble with him and he was a very gentlemanly young man. Does this help you at all? I miss Gloucester terribly. It was awful at first there, and then I became friendly with someone and it was marvellous. That was why I went to West Heath. I expect you feel as I feel now. I might write and ask you to do some detective work for me! With kindest regards from your pen friend. Audrey Merriman.'

Davina folded the letter and put it in her old desk among her poetry and story books. It was Uncle Fred's doing. She had always known it. Somehow he had threatened Albert and made him go away and never come home again.

After Chichester Street's cosiness, the house in Bedford Close seemed too big and empty. The dinner dishes were still in the sink and the breakfast room where they sat most of the time now seemed full of overflowing ashtrays.

Fred said, 'Christamighty, March. When the hell is Chattie coming back? It's been six months now.'

'Five months actually. January, February, March—'

'Oh do shut up. If you don't want to say anything to Bridget Hall, I will. She's just a selfish cow.'

'Kindly don't use that kind of language to me, Fred. And you're welcome to try to talk to Bridie. She spends most of her time in London these days and someone has to be with all those children. It's Chattie I feel sorry for.'

Fred emptied ashtrays viciously. 'She's probably better off there. The three older girls will help her and she's got the shops right outside the door. God, don't you ever do *anything* round here any more?' He picked up a cup and saucer from the side of an armchair and held it out to her. She ignored it, went to the window and deliberately took her time extracting a cigarette from her silver case.

He watched her tapping it against the lid, then put the cup and saucer back where he'd found it. He said, 'I don't think I've ever met anyone quite so selfish as you, March,'

The bodice of her flowered summer dress rose and fell quickly, but her voice was very calm when she spoke.

'Even Tilly Adair?'

'Even Tilly Adair,' he agreed.

He expected her to fly off the handle and planned to use her temper to force her into another kind of passion. It had happened before. It seemed the only way to bring them together.

Her voice became lower. 'How can you say that, Fred, after the last three years.'

'Yes, those years fooled me too. But think about it, March. You'd lost your son. You thought you were going to lose me — a nervous breakdown don't they call it? You looked after me — loved me then — for your own sake. Didn't you? I was all you had left. It was self-preservation — that's all. Admit it.'

She drew deeply on her cigarette and he realized she was not angry, not really angry. She seemed to be thinking.

At last she said, 'I don't know, I was worried about you, yes. Otherwise I couldn't have forgiven you for telling Albert that he was illegitimate. Now . . .' She drew again on her cigarette, lifted her head and exhaled fiercely through her nose. 'Now I cannot believe that I accepted your — your cruel stupidity so easily. My God, you did the one thing you had promised never to do. You turned Albert against me. If he'd died in Spain it would have been your fault. Yet I nursed you — that's what it amounted to — I looked after you as if you were a child — for two years.' She found an ashtray on the window ledge and stubbed out the cigarette. 'I really don't know why I did it, Fred. Perhaps it *was* self-preservation.' She shrugged. 'Anyway, your refusal to let me go to see Albert now, has finished that. So it doesn't really matter, does it?' She went to the door. 'I'm off to bed. Actually I'd be very grateful if you would speak to Bridie about Chattie. I'm not very interested in looking after this house and cooking your meals, I'm afraid.'

She went out, closing the door carefully behind her. After a long moment, Fred reached inside his jacket and got out the notes she had made for the Volunteers. He spread them on the dusty table and went to the bureau for a map of the city. He might as well do something properly.

The ambulance, its canvas red cross shivering in the

108

morning breeze off the Channel, lined up with others full of wounded. Most of the casualties could walk, like Victor himself; the severely injured had been left in French hospitals to the undeniably efficient mercies of the German medics. Victor had refused to leave Ferdy. 'I'll carry the poor bugger again if necessary,' he said aggressively to the young subaltern who had stopped them on the road from Arras. The ambulances were unloaded behind the sand dunes as dawn paled the sky in pink stripes. 'Red at dawning, shepherd's warning,' Victor murmured, remembering Grandpa Rising's adage as he helped the orderly with Ferdy's stretcher. The poor blighter started moaning and jerking immediately. He'd never make it. And if he did he'd be just the same as he'd been before, a pain in the neck. Was it worth it?

There were boats and rafts bobbing towards them like toys, ready to take them to the first of the destroyers before it was light enough for the Stukas to start shooting up the whole beach.

'Thank God for the Royal Navy,' Gladys sobbed, stumbling in the sand, holding the canvas stretcher sides in an effort to keep the wind off Ferdy's twitching body. Victor plunged into the shallows and bellowed, 'Hearts of Oak are our ships, Hearts of Oak are our men!' And the song was taken up immediately on all sides as men scrambled on to whatever was floating near them and the toy flotilla started back to the looming mass of iron ships in the mist.

'We're ready boys, ready!'

'Steady . . . boys . . . steady . . .'

As the voices dipped low on that bottom note, a whine could be heard in the distance. A whine like a mosquito looking for blood. Then the sky was speckled with dots in the north-east; the dots materialized rapidly into fifty or more fighter aircraft. The men in the boats fell silent, and even the sweating sailors forgot to grunt as they pulled on their oars. Most of them bent their heads away from the terror to come, but Victor could not. Sight was his main

109

perception. He must see. Everything.

From where they had come, the beach was already glowing yellow in the climbing sun above the tidemark. Beyond the level the colour deepened and shifted from pale sienna to burnt umber. Weatherbeaten faces; khaki uniforms, brown boots, beige kitbags . . . they jostled like the constantly moving atom. In the dunes the ambulances offered a splash of colour, and somewhere in the middle, the morning sunshine sparked off a bugle and the shining chrome of a side drum. Victor narrowed his eyes to bring it all together in one moving, glinting brown mass, then there was the familiar crump of bomb hitting earth, and the colours were torn apart to make room for a rosette of crimson. The next instant the Stukas were directly above them and the sea was spitting as bullets ricocheted across its surface.

After the initial attack, it seemed at first as though the same silence reigned as after the tank attack at Sedan. The sudden cessation of screaming engines and staccato fire made the alternative sounds negligible. Human screams were muted and soon stifled, curses and shouts for help were puny. Then eardrums recovered from the shock and the noise engulfed Victor He had cowered before the Stukas, but the human sounds afterwards were what made him want to jump into the sea.

'Gladys' the ambulance driver was dead and silent, hanging face up over the edge of the liberty boat. Fresh blood pumped from Ferdy — his arm this time — and one of the oarsmen bent groaning over a shattered wrist. Two of the boats were upended and the water was full of struggling figures. What was so terrifying was that the Stukas were wheeling on the horizon and making an enormous sweep across the sky to attack again. Two of the sailors tipped Gladys unceremoniously overboard and lugged two people in to replace her. Victor ripped off his sling and made a makeshift tourniquet above the spurting red pump in Ferdy's arm. He thought, 'In a minute, when there's time, I'll be sick. Not now. They're

110

coming back. Not now. Oh Christ.'

It happened all over again. Ahead of them a fire broke out on the destroyer and into its red pathway they tipped other bodies.

'They won't come again,' someone said. But they were coming again. 'Back to the beach!' shouted the young naval lieutenant in charge of the boats. A hand reached over the gunwale and took hold of Victor's shoulder. As the drowning man hoisted himself up, so he pulled Victor out of the boat. Slowly, almost gracefully, they changed places. Victor hung on to one of the rubber fenders and let the water wash into his mouth, but not even the salt helped him to be sick.

He considered letting go and drifting into the cleanness of the Channel. The Stukas were going to land on his head anyway. He looked up as one of them banked above him, and saw the pilot quite distinctly. For a split second, brown English eyes looked into blue German ones. Then the fighter was gone, and the water spurted around Victor and above him in the boat someone shouted and pointed. Victor looked up again. Six Spitfires were screaming after the Stukas. Machine guns were rattling. He thought frantically, 'I mustn't forget it — the sky, the planes ripping it up like paper — and a human being — an actual human being — in one of them. My enemy. My *enemy*!' And the water closed over his head.

They pulled him up on the beach and put Ferdy in his arms and waited for the dogfight to end. Before it did, a launch arrived and took them off to another destroyer where Ferdy was removed and a cup of cocoa put in Victor's hands instead. They thought he was suffering from shock; he was too absorbed in looking to contradict them. The Spitfires didn't stand a chance; outnumbered six to one, they harried and nibbled at the Stukas like Jack Russell terriers at the postman's heels. They kept the German planes so busy there was time to load the destroyer to capacity and get under way. And then, with the engine-room bell ringing like a knell, one of the Spits,

111

a little too daring for its own good, bought it. A Stuka engaged it on the port side and on the starboard — in spite of its wing mirrors — another Stuka got a direct hit into the engine. It went down in a plume of smoke which effectively screened any attempt the pilot might have made to escape. Victor stopped being objective.

'That could be Albert,' he said aloud. 'Christamighty, that could be Albert.' And at last he vomited.

Seven

STRANGELY, Victor arrived home before the Adairs. As he disembarked from the destroyer at Dover, walking close to Ferdy's stretcher, the Pathe News cameras were waiting on the quay. He put up his thumb and gave an imitation of his father's cheerful cockney grin, and by the time he'd made sure Ferdy was settled and had been given his official leave pass, his face had been seen by everyone in Gloucester and he was hailed as a hero. Monty and May loved it. The old Victor would have revelled in it too. Now he could not. He stayed in the house, playing with Gretta and refusing to see Beryl Langham, his erstwhile girl friend, or even Davina. Both girls called, declaring they wanted to talk to him 'urgently'. Davina would want to know about Albert, of course. Beryl would see his flesh wound and his very narrow escape as an excuse to fuss over him and get him into one of her 'situations' when it was impossible not to make love to her. But he didn't love her. He'd told her so a dozen times and she still thought that the passion she could induce in him would lead to something deeper. Poor Beryl. He couldn't get Gladys' dead face out of his head. He had to paint. He must do some work. But not the kind he had done before. Not his schoolboy nudes of Beryl and his Constable landscapes. How did you paint death? How did you paint war?

On his third day home, David called in with a message from April. Ever since Albert had confided the full story of Davie's conception, Victor had been intrigued by his aunt and uncle. He had always respected David's cleverness; suddenly he recognized his immense wisdom. Because surely, surely, David knew . . . he must know. And April, beautiful April, who had been Gloucester's special flapper what had she suffered for her David Daker? Yes, it was fascinating, and Victor was glad in a distant sort of way to see David and talk to him a little.

David said, 'I thought this war might be slightly less hellish than the last. Apparently not.'

Victor had not been born when David Daker was invalided out of the army in 1917 with a groin full of shrapnel, but his precocious ears had heard tales.

'How did *you* cope with it?' he asked bluntly.

David held out a finger and Gretta grasped it and pulled herself to her feet, smiling beatifically at him.

'With difficulty. April wanted to help me, but she was a child and I could not let her. Even so, her innocence was like a beacon.' He looked inward, smiling slightly. 'She was fourteen. And she knew so much. And forgave everything.'

Victor said with a sense of revelation, 'That is what is so difficult. The forgiving.'

David gave him Gretta's hand.

'You're doing the right thing. This little sister of yours will help. Original sin . . . I'm never certain about that. But original innocence is something we can see and touch.' he smiled. 'Don't fight it too hard. I turned to drink and it got me nowhere. It's all experience and it will help your work eventually.' He had hit the nail on the head and was rewarded by a responsive smile. He watched as Victor picked up Gretta and took her to the window. Then he said, 'D'you remember at the end of *War and Peace* where Pierre finds the ultimate answer at the bedsides of his children? Old Tolstoy knew what he was talking about. Remember that.'

So Victor clung to Gretta — to May's delight — and even knelt with her to say her prayers in the evening. And as she lisped, 'Gentle Jesus meek and mild . . .' so he

114

muttered, 'Let it not be Albert. Let Albert be safe.'

Robin too was changed by the enormity of Dunkirk. Although he passed nearly three days in a state of blue funk he actually went through the motions, obeying Charles' orders when they were given, lugging men aboard, taking the tiller, upending cans of fuel into the small but beautifully-kept engine. Once they were strafed, but they had escaped a direct hit miraculously, and the bombers were more interested in the big shipping than in the flotilla of small boats plying back and forth with their half-dozen passengers. Yet, in total they had brought home over fifty men; fifty men who would be in enemy hands if there had been no *Gremlin*, no Charles and Robin Adair. It was something to be proud of, something to justify the ignominy of his 'reserved occupation' in the Records Office. He enjoyed being put to bed by his mother as if he were a small boy. Decent meals were brought up to him, and when the *Citizen* did a whole article about their venture, his mother insisted on reading it out to him as if his eyes were affected. However when she went downstairs, he picked it up again and saw the front-page picture of Victor Gould arriving at Dover. In spite of the newspaper dots, it was possible to see that Victor was not in a blue funk at all. Robin gnawed his chapped lips and thought how typical it was of the Goulds to upstage everyone around. The father was some kind of music-hall has-been after all, and Victor had played to the gallery in the old days of their cricket matches at Cheltenham.

As soon as Charles and Tilly returned to their normal way of life — his father to the Observer Corps, his mother to her socialising — he donned a pair of kid gloves to hide his blistered hands, and cycled round to Winterditch Lane. He could call on Davina openly now; he had news for her and he was a hero.

He timed his call for just before her arrival home from school, thinking to ingratiate himself with April beforehand, but April and David were being taken over the cathedral by the verger preparatory to beginning fire-watching duties there that night. Robin was greeted by dour Aunt Sylv and kept under her eagle eye in the kitchen while she prepared tea for her girls. Robin was not sure how much Sylvia Turpin knew about him. She had lived on the edge of the Forest of Dean as a girl and gossip about his adventures down there might have reached her ears. However she too had read the *Citizen*, and he did not give her a chance to voice any kind of disapproval. He did not think his monologue came close to bragging and hardly noticed her thinning lips; she was one of those old ladies who forget to put her teeth in anyway. But he was glad when the door flew open and Davina entered.

'Aunty — have you seen the *Citizen* — it's all over school about Victor and—' she spotted Robin and gave a squeak. 'Robin! You're back! I've been round to see Victor twice and he won't see me and I didn't know what had happened to you until I saw the *Citizen* and . . .' she drew a breath at last, '. . . and you did it, Robin! You did it!'

It was as if she knew about his terror and was genuinely pleased for him. It was the best thing that had happened to him in his life. He could have fallen on the floor and kissed her feet. She wore brown sandals that were dusty from her ride home. And white ankle socks. He wondered whether her feet smelled feety. There was something so special about the smell of schoolgirls. He thought of the ones he had known: Gertie Danvers from Lydney; Olga Hall; Audrey Merriman. But this one was different; this one he adored. He said, 'Hello, Davie.'

It was the best thing he could have said. He had got his bragging off his chest to Sylvia and he was stunned by Davie's beauty into a simplicity that warmed her heart.

She said, 'I told you it was worth it. Fifty-three survivors — it's marvellous, Robin. Marvellous.'

He grinned. 'I missed your Victor, though.'

'Oh Robin . . . he got through because of you. I can't explain it, but if you hadn't gone over Victor wouldn't

116

have been picked up. You didn't have to do it *personally—'* she laughed. 'Oh I know it sounds silly.'

'It certainly does,' Aunt Sylv said tartly. 'Now I'll thank you to go upstairs and get yourself washed before tea-time. Flo will be in directly and she'll be half starved as usual.' Her non-invitation to Robin was so obvious that Davina was embarrassed.

'You'll stay to tea, Robin,' she said looking meaningfully at Aunt Sylv. 'Come on, you can wash first. I'll show you where the bathroom is.'

They went upstairs together, much to Sylvia's annoyance. She began to lay an extra place at the table while she rehearsed grimly what she would say to Davina when she got her alone.

Robin said, 'Actually Davie, I can't wash my hands. They're rather cut up.' He laughed. 'Ropes and so on. You know.'

'Oh, how awful — how dreadful. Let me see. Oh Robin, I'm so sorry. I didn't know.'

The gloves, carefully removed, revealed hands which, unused to manual work, had blistered very quickly. Davina lifted them on her own palms and kissed them gently. Robin felt tears run down his face.

She said, 'Robin, what is it? Did I hurt you?'

He gasped, 'No. It's just that . . . I did it for you. Oh Davie, I love you. I love you so much. I'm sorry for what . . . I love you. I've never felt like this before.'

She did not fight him off when he took her in his arms, how could she? He kissed her over and over again, passion mounting to fever pitch.

'I want to touch you,' he groaned.

She said reluctantly, 'Well, all right. If that's all you want. Really.'

He sobbed, 'I can't. My hands don't feel . . . oh God.'

'Robin, please. It's all right. Don't get so upset, please.' She began to weep herself, half frightened by his desperation. Half flattered too.

117

He reached between them for a moment and undid his trousers. 'Please darling. Hold me. Just for a moment. Don't be frightened.'

Davie wasn't frightened. She had been brought up with just a sister, certainly, but there had been a time when Victor painted only nudes; male and female. Then, four years ago, in Cornwall, a poor simple-minded man had exposed himself to her. She had reacted hysterically, screaming for Albert, frightening the man away. And he had been killed. She had always felt responsible for his death . . . if she hadn't screamed, he wouldn't have run . . .'

She said reproachfully, 'Oh Robin.'

But he was past caring. He sobbed and pleaded with her and at last she slid her hand down and took hold of the soft and hard mass she found there.

And it was then that Flora, sent upstairs by the outraged Aunt Sylv, arrived at the bathroom door. She looked at them both with her wide brown eyes and said blankly, 'Whatever *are* you doing, you two?'

They all went down ten minutes later. And Robin did not stay to tea.

Chattie went back to Bedford Close the very next day, and life there returned to what passed for normal. During the week after Dunkirk there was a state of controlled panic in Gloucester. Fred was frantically busy at the garage and every evening he had his duties with the Volunteers. April as well as David was roped into all this activity; she was on the fire-watching rota at the cathedral and was undergoing an intensive course in fire-fighting. May was kept at home with Gretta and Victor. Bridie decided that Chattie's return to her home was tantamount to desertion in the face of the enemy and cut off her relations with the Lukers. March was lonely and at a loose end. Victor refused to see anyone; the gall of bitterness ate into her soul.

Then came the War Office telegram.

118

It never occurred to her that it could be about Albert. His severance from his family had been so complete and so lengthy she had assumed it had gone the whole way and he would never dream of entering her name as his next of kin on any official form or document. Yet it seemed he had. The telegram was to inform her that her son had suffered an injury during an engagement with the enemy and was in a military hospital outside Haslemere.

March stared at the flimsy piece of yellow paper with its embossed seal, and at last raised her eyes to the frightened telegraph boy.

'It's all right,' she said automatically. 'He's not dead.' She reached behind her for her bag and there was Chattie, white-faced and shaking. She said again, 'It's all right, Chattie, Master Albert is alive.'

She managed to press sixpence into the boy's hand, then the two women fell into each other's arms weeping. Chattie was still frightened because her idol was in hospital, but March was ecstatic. Albert had acknowledged her as his mother. She knew where he was. She could visit him.

As soon as they had had some tea, found a map and plotted a route to Haslemere, March went upstairs to pack. She was absolutely determined she would see Albert without Fred. Twice Fred had had his son to himself; once when he told the sordid truth about the boy's parentage, and once when he'd gone to see him at Tangmere. Both times he had alienated Albert. This time March would see her son on her own.

She closed her case and stood looking out of the window, frowning slightly and playing with a tendril of her hair. It was going to be hard; this first contact with her son since he had known that she had done . . . what she had done. They had never been very good at communicating at the best of times; it would be much worse now. She needed someone to go with her; someone who knew Albert as she knew him, and loved him as she loved him.

119

She picked up her case and went downstairs and into the garage. Chattie was already there loading two Thermoses, some of their strawberries, some flowers, and his favourite book on model railways.

'Oh Mrs Luker, give him my love. Please tell him to get better quickly and come and have some of Chattie's nice dinners.'

March rested her hand on the small plump one of her faithful retainer. She had few blessings, but Chattie was one of them, and she was so thankful that the girl had been back with her when that telegram came.

'I'm going round to see if Davina will come with me,' she said. 'Tell Mr Luker all that has happened and ask him to explain to Mr and Mrs Daker. Will you, Chattie?'

The car, with its ridiculous gas bag sitting on top like a clown's hat, chugged out of the garage. Fred had done the adaptation himself, but it did not like running on gas. She wouldn't get more than thirty out of it, if that.

March knew that Davina was at home. There had been some quarrel between her and Flora a couple of days ago and yesterday both girls had been thoroughly upset and bilious after it. April had called after fire-watching practice last night to tell March not to expect Davie to drop in after school as she occasionally did. The quarrel between the two sisters was inexplicable; they rarely disagreed and when they did Flo would always give in. She adored Davie and understood her better than anyone. April was rather bothered about it and March had promised to go round that afternoon and talk to the girls. Which she was doing. Except that it was still morning and her talk was akin to bursting a bomb under their noses. In a way it was lucky that April would be out on her course, because Aunt Sylv wasn't up to putting up many coherent objections these days. In the event she was in the garden picking the first of the blackcurrants to bottle for next winter, and did not know what was happening.

'If we're to get back tonight there's not a moment to be

lost,' March said rapidly to the two girls who were washing kilner jars in the kitchen. 'Don't you agree Flo, that Davie should come with me? If Albert is injured he will want to see us — surely at last he *will* want to see us? What do you think, darlings?'

If March hoped to seal the breach between the sisters, she had her wish. Flora was absolutely and wholeheartedly with the idea. Strangely it was Davie now who stared at her aunt in a state of shock, and seemed unable to reach a decision.

'Mother won't like it,' she prevaricated helplessly.

Flora clasped her hands in front of her pleadingly. 'I'll explain to her, Davie. I'll tell her how terribly important it is for Albert to open his eyes and see you and Aunt March standing at his bedside—'

'This isn't a film at the Picturedrome you know, Flo!' Davie said, a sharp note entering her voice.

'Oh I know, I know!' Flora moved from one foot to the other. 'Davie, please go. You know Albert is the one — he's always been the one.'

March did not smile. Flo might sound melodramatic, but what she said was true. 'I didn't think I'd have to persuade you to come with me, Davie,' she said with gentle reproach.

'I'm sorry, Aunt March. Of course I'll come. It's just that . . .' she wanted to explain what a waste of time it had been with Robin Adair all these months, when now, at the end, the War Office had informed them where Albert was and Aunt March was giving her a lift right up to his hospital bed.

'I know. Your mother. But you're not deceiving her, darling. I've rushed you off your feet — she'll understand that. Shall I go and explain to Aunt Sylv?'

Flora said quickly, 'No. I'll do that. You go. It's already half-past ten.'

So they left, the gas bag undulating gently in the June sunshine, the engine labouring already.

It was five days since Chattie had left Brunswick Road and in that time Bridie had got through two maids-of-all-work. She looked at the third applicant and felt mildly hopeful. Marlene wore thick pebble glasses which meant she couldn't get into the women's forces or work at the aircraft factory. She loved children — Barty seemed to have taken to her on sight — and the reference from the headmaster of her recently-left school described her as 'honest and industrious'.

'I realize the money isn't as much as you'd get at a factory,' Bridie admitted. 'But obviously with a living-in job everything you earn is pocket money.'

'Not for me, miss. Me mum has my money.'

'Madam. You will call me madam. Or Mrs Hall. And do I gather you had a job before this? You spoke then as if you had paid your wages to your mother before.'

'Oh yes miss. I thought Mum told you. I worked for Parson Jones at the manse out Tuffley way. Me mum visited and said I didn't ought to sit on 'is knee. So when she 'eard you was looking for someone and there weren't no man in the 'ouse, she thought it'd be ideal.'

'Ah yes. I see.' Bridie pursed her lips consideringly, though she had already decided that Marlene was 'ideal' too. Mannie wanted her to go to town next week to do a show. There had to be someone here to see to things. But she didn't want Marlene to think she was over-eager.

In the hall the telephone rang, and Bridie excused herself. She hoped it was March apologising for her selfishness, or maybe Mannie telling her to be on an earlier train so that they could shop together. Or . . . Incredibly, it was Sibbie Luker. Or rather Sibbie Edwards, her stepmother. Stepmother. Six years older than she was herself and the one-time scarlet woman of Gloucester. Bridie felt her hackles rise as she recognized the voice. And then immediately afterwards she knew that there was only one reason why Sibbie would telephone her.

The well-remembered voice said huskily, 'I'm sorry Bridie . . . oh God, I'm sorry.'

122

Bridget said blankly, 'Daddy? He hasn't *gone*? He's ill — you're ringing to tell me he's ill and he wants me to come to see him. He hasn't *gone*?' She had so often envisaged her father's death. The reconciliation scene. All stubbornness would melt away on her side; and on his there would be repentance and remorse. 'I know I was a fool, Bridie . . . no fool like an old fool . . .' and there would be days together when they could recall the past. He had loved her. Until Sibbie, he had loved her more than anyone on earth. Much more than his first wife. They were the same; they could laugh at the same things. They would remember the terrible time after Teddy Rising's death when they had been so close. And the three-wheeled Morgan sports car he had bought her when she went to teacher training college. Oh God, she couldn't be deprived of those memories. They were her life. If he had died without sharing them again he had taken most of her past with him.

Sibbie said, 'He went in his sleep, Bridie. So peacefully. When I woke up this morning I didn't even realize . . . I took him his breakfast tray as usual at nine o'clock—' Bridie didn't want to hear this. The intimate details of her father's domestic bliss were unwelcome to her ears. His real life was the one which connected him to his daughter; not to Sibbie Luker. But Sibbie needed to talk about it. 'I called the doctor of course. He came as soon as he could. He's still here. He wants to give me a sedative, but I said I had to ring you first. Oh Bridie . . . what shall I do?'

What should *Sibbie* do? She'd had him until last night . . . she'd talked to him . . . there had been no ten-year rift between them which would go for ever unhealed. Bridie put her head against the mouthpiece of the telephone and pressed very hard. She said aloud, 'I can't take this. I can't take it. Daddy . . . Daddy . . .' Sibbie couldn't hear her, of course. She took the phone away from her head and said, 'If Tolly were here he'd know what to do.'

Sibbie sobbed suddenly, 'We're in the same boat, Bridie. No men. No-one to protect either of us now.'

123

That wasn't strictly true for Bridie. She held the phone and listened to Sibbie gabbling about 'arrangements' and knew that she could now make her own personal decision. She had Mannie. She could marry Mannie and he would protect her all right. Protect her from vultures like Sibbie and Monty who would now both be grabbing whatever they could from her father's estate.

Eventually she put down the phone and went back to Marlene and Barty.

'Oh miss, you got a great bruise on your forehead!' exclaimed the girl.

Bridie went to the mirror and rubbed at her head with her fingers. After all, Marlene had showed concern for her new mistress and maybe the 'miss' was a compliment.

She said, 'Marlene, I've just had some very bad news and I have to go out for the rest of the day. Will you be all right here? Olga and Natasha will be in from school at four and they will help you.' She leaned down suddenly and took Barty in her arms. 'Granddad has gone to live with Jesus, darling.' Tears suddenly rolled down her face.

Barty did not know his granddad, but he had just said goodby to Grandma Hall who had gone to live with Jesus. And his mother's tears were enough to start his too. They wept bitterly and Marlene wept with them. It was as if they were sealing some unwritten contract.

The last real town they chugged through was Haslemere and the clock on the dashboard said five past three. They had stopped once for some tea from one of the Thermoses and half a sandwich each. They were neither of them hungry; when March said, 'Another half-hour should do it,' Davie suddenly wanted a lavatory. She tightened the muscles in her buttocks fiercely and stared through the dusty windscreen, trying consciously to imprint the route and the countryside on her memory. She had managed to push the thought of Robin Adair and Flo and the past five months to the back of her mind. She *must* feel optimistic. There was no hope for this meeting if

124

she couldn't carry her own optimism with her. It had been so sudden; Aunt March's arrival and announcement and their departure without even saying goodbye to Aunt Sylv. But she'd had over four hours since then to take it all in. To forget that all her connivings had been for nothing; her dignity lost for nothing; her closeness with her little sister Flo gone for nothing.

Flo knew it all now. Davie had told her everything after the debacle two days ago. She explained just why she'd been 'tickling' Robin Adair, why she'd been so friendly with him in the first place. And Flo had understood and forgiven. But now Flo also knew that it was all for nothing.

Davie dragged her mind back to the present yet again and said brightly, 'It's a lovely summer. All the cow parsley is so pretty.'

Aunt March forced a smile. 'Yes dear. And the roads are so narrow that we'll be powdered all over with blossom by the time we get there.'

'Like confetti,' Davie said without thinking. And then could have torn out her tongue. But of course Aunt March understood and her smile became more natural.

'Just like confetti,' she agreed.

The manor house had been requisitioned from its owners for the duration, and turned into a hospital for officers. Its ancient grey walls were ivy-covered, nature's camouflage. It was in a direct line between Germany and London if Hitler did start his blitzkrieg, but so far he seemed to be intent on his take-over of France, and the house and gardens looked the picture of eternal peace. They drove to the stable yard at the back where two ambulances looked incongruous parked next to an old pump. Geraniums, stocks, snapdragons and lupins were everywhere, apparently growing wild. Behind the house as they emerged from the car, they could see well-kept kitchen gardens and fruit enclosures. There were several men working there and one of them came forward when he spotted the civilian females. He showed them a side door where they would be able to see the matron when she returned from her afternoon rounds. He told them that as the men recuperated they could work in the gardens if they were able. March told him Albert's name and he smiled.

'Tommy's one of those quiet, determined ones,' he said. 'He can't wait to start gardening, reckons it's in his blood.'

'Tommy.' It sounded so odd. Davie had never called him anything but Albert or Albie. For the first time it struck her as an old-fashioned name. But then he'd been named for his uncle.

'I will show you where he is if you like,' offered their guide. 'No need to wait for Matron. It's visiting time all afternoon officially, though of course being out in the wilds we don't get many visitors.'

Aunt March murmured, 'That would be nice,' and Davie felt herself flush to the roots of her hair, then go very cold. She would have preferred a stiff, starchy matron to superintend their first visit. She trailed after the other two and tried to swallow sudden bile in her mouth. She was frightened.

The stairs were wide and shallow but the young man escorting them trod each step separately, and hung on to the bannisters with both hands. Then there was a long landing with a row of doors one side and mullioned windows the other looking on to the gardens. The windows were open to the afternoon sunshine and the scent of flowers was everywhere.

They stopped by a numbered door. Nineteen. Davie knew she would remember it because it was the number of Hettie and Alf Luker's house in Chichester Street where Uncle Fred had been born. The young man smiled briefly at them, tapped and retreated.

'See you later,' he promised. 'I'll fix some tea for you in the garden if you like.'

'How kind.' Aunt March's hand was trembling as she turned the door handle.

'Come in!' Albert shouted from within. She turned and

stared at Davie and let go of the handle.

'It was him!' Her whisper sounded shocked, as if she had expected a stranger to be inside the room. 'It . . . it's Albie! Oh my God!'

She wilted against the door jamb, apparently unable to move. Davie felt quite differently. She stared at Aunt March, exchanging disbelief for conviction. Yes, it *was* Albie. How could she have been frightened or nervous? He would be changed, she accepted that, but underneath it was still Albie.

She pushed at the open door, let it swing wide and stepped past her aunt and into the oak-panelled room.

He was sitting in an armchair by a window overlooking yet another vista of trees and rolling countryside. A newspaper was spread on a table pushed across his knees, and he held a pencil and seemed to be doing a crossword. He did not look up.

'Put it by the bed, Sister,' he said. 'I'll be getting back in a minute.'

Davie stood three feet from him and for the fraction of a second before he lifted his head interrogatively, she caught up on their three years of separation. At first she thought he was the same. In 1937 he had been nineteen and adult. Now he was twenty-two and adult. His hair was the same pale straw colour, his shoulders broad and bony, his hands short-fingered and intensely practical. Then he looked up and she saw he had changed. His mouth was no longer full and sensitive, his eyes were smaller, and there was a slight tic at the top of his jawbone rather like Uncle Fred's.

He showed two signs of shock and two only. His eyes narrowed still further and he drew a long shuddering breath. Then he said, 'Mother brought you?'

March surged forward. Somehow she was on her knees by his chair, though how she got there Davie did not know. She gave a strangled cry then said, 'Albert. Albert. Can you ever forgive me?'

Davie did not understand. She stayed where she was,

wishing she'd changed from her cotton frock and ankle socks into something more grown-up. He must realize that she was grown-up now. Not the little puppy who had followed him everywhere. Certainly not young enough to harbour any schoolgirl crushes any more.

He made no attempt to put his arms around Aunt March as he would have done in the old days. His head went back against the chair as if he were unutterably weary, and he said, 'Of course. I forgive everyone. What else is there to do?'

Aunt March looked at him imploringly and Davie could see tears all over her face.

'It was wartime, darling. Like now. If only you could know — if only we could talk — you would understand, I know you would.'

'But we've never been able to talk, Mother.'

His hands were gripping the sides of the chair now and Davie realised with a horrible shock that he was in the most awful pain. That was why his head had been down over the paper, why he hadn't looked up when he thought the sister was bringing his tea. He was hanging on to his self-control desperately.

She said, 'Aunt March, Albert's not well. Shall we come back in a moment when he's had his tea?'

Aunt March did not seem to hear her. She put her forehead on Albert's white hand and let her tears flow over his knuckles.

'Albert, I did it for you. Everything I have ever done has been for you.'

'Aunt March, please. I think he's going to faint. Please come away now.'

'*He* told you — in order to punish me, Albert. It's the sort of thing he does — you know that—'

Davie turned and ran from the room and down the sun-filled landing. A door at the end was open and a bevy of starched nurses were bending over a bed.

'Please — please come quickly!' she gasped. 'My cousin — Albert Tomms — he's very ill. Please come.'

They flapped gently like white butterflies, then two of them left the rest and followed her back to number nineteen. One of them was not like a butterfly. She was like a ship in full sail.

She took in the situation instantly and brushed March away as if she were a fly. The table and the newspaper went too, and some pills were shaken from a bottle and presented to Albert with a glass of water. It was the last Davie saw of him. The matron — for there was no doubt it was the matron — whisked her outside with March and the newspapers.

'Nobody sees anyone here without my express permission,' she said icily, and shut the door in their faces.

March was completely undone. She leaned against the wall, her head in her hand, silent sobs shaking her thin shoulders. Davie put her arms around her and felt as if she were holding them both together. It was hard to understand what was happening. They had shocked Albert, that was certain. And he had then become very ill. But there was more than that. Much more.

After a while the matron came out and took them both in hand. They went downstairs and into a small side garden where there were tables and chairs set out on a lawn. Tea was brought and she talked to them about Albert. He had spent a long time in the sea and was severely shocked. But more than that; the bullet which had ripped his Spitfire in half had spent itself in his thigh. They had been unable to extract it so far. Another operation was scheduled when he was stronger, but until then the pain sometimes became unendurable.

March said pitifully, 'We did not know. The telegram simply said he was wounded.'

The matron relaxed slightly. 'That is why it is so important for all visitors to see me first. The shock of seeing relatives can do more harm than good. Your son must rest and let the sedatives do their work. Then, if he is strong enough, you may see him again.'

They waited. The matron went away and their erstwhile guide appeared.

'Thanks for not letting on.' He was grinning like a schoolboy. He probably was a schoolboy, or almost. He said his name was William.

'Call me Bill. Everyone does. Even Matron when she's telling me off. She's always telling me off.'

Davie waited for Aunt March to make a comment and when she did not she swallowed the lump in her throat and said, 'Don't you mind?'

'Good lord no. She does it because she . . . well, she thinks a lot of us. You know.'

'Yes. Yes, I suppose it's all part of her job really.'

'Oh, it's more than a job for her.'

Aunt March seemed incapable of taking any part in the conversation and Davie continued to give 'Bill' his answers. It transpired that Albert had visitors from his squadron. Someone called Jack Doswell came regularly and his sister too had put in an appearance. She was a nurse in a hospital in Dorset. Tommy was a lucky chap.

'Is she very pretty then?' Davie asked, realizing that as a cousin and wearing ankle socks, she was seen as no competition whatever.

'Bit like Jessie Matthews.'

'Oh. I see.'

Aunt March said suddenly, 'Will the sedative put Albert to sleep, d'you think?'

Bill said, 'Oh, he had a sedative, did he? No, it probably won't send him right off. They save the big doses until bedtime. It'll ease off the pain a bit.'

Davie burst out, 'How can he talk of working in the garden when he's in so much pain?'

Bill looked at his feet. 'You'd be surprised. Once they can locate the bullet in his groin and whip it out, he'll be up and doing in no time.'

Davie swallowed again. She realized suddenly that Bill's left shoe was quite different from his right one. He had an artificial leg.

130

March said, 'His groin? Matron said the thigh. She said the bullet went into his thigh.'

'Well, thereabouts. Sorry.'

'No. It's all right.' March looked pitifully at Davie. 'You see? History is repeating itself. Your father still has shrapnel in his groin from the Great War. Oh Davie.'

Bill said, 'Look, I'll get you something stronger than tea. You've had a helluva shock. I shouldn't have taken you straight up like that — thought you knew—'

'It's all right. Honestly.' Davie went to sit by her aunt. 'As soon as Matron says we can see Albert again, everything will be all right. It's not your fault.'

But he disappeared anyway and came back with a small, leather-covered flask. Aunt March drank some of the contents without demur and seemed a little better afterwards. Bill had to go and take a bath; Davie did not dare think about the mechanics of that. They continued to wait, while the glorious afternoon ripened into evening. March said raggedly, 'We shall be home about midnight at this rate. They'll be worried.'

'No. Not when we're together. Perhaps we could telephone Uncle Fred and he will go round and tell Mother?'

March reached for Davie's hand and they sat numbly still again.

Then at last Matron came back. Her severe manner was lessened this time by something else: embarrassment. She sat down opposite them, waving a wash-wrinkled hand at a skein of midges, and offered more tea.

March found her voice. 'No. Thank you, Matron, once we've seen Albert we shall have to leave. I promise you we won't upset him this time. Just ten minutes to reassure him and we'll be on our way.'

The matron stretched her neck out of her uniform and took a breath which swelled her considerable bosom. She looked like a pigeon.

'Yes. Well actually Mrs Tomms, I'm afraid your son is not in any condition—'

131

March said eagerly, 'Five minutes — two. We promise . . . we've come so far.'

It was strange to hear Aunt March called Mrs Tomms. Davie had been four when she heard it last.

Matron linked her hands.

'I'm afraid not. Try to understand. We have to keep him very quiet and he—'

Davie said suddenly, 'He won't see us, will he? He's told you not to let us come up again. Hasn't he?'

The woman's eyes, blue, compassionate eyes, looked at Davina. For a long moment she seemed to consider. Then she nodded her head.

'I'm afraid so, my dear. I have no wish to pry into your family affairs, but he is adamant. He refuses to see either of you. He has asked me to tell you not to visit him again.' She looked back at March. 'Perhaps there is some reason for this. Perhaps when he is stronger he will change his mind. But at the moment I have to respect his wishes, and I think you will want to also.'

March was white to the lips. She nodded dumbly. Davina said in the same strong voice, 'He's a coward! That's what he is. A coward!'

'Please, Davie—' Aunt March stood up and took charge at last. 'Matron, this has been unbearable for . . . I must apologise . . . we will . . .'

Davie heard her voice rise. 'He can't face me! He might be able to fight the Germans, but he can't face me! I'm not his enemy — tell him that — I'm not! If he thinks — if he thinks—'

'Davie!' March's voice rose too, rose above Davie's and flattened it. She took one of Davie's arms which, unaccountably, was raised above her head, and dragged it through her own. 'Come. We are leaving now.' She turned to the matron. 'I trust you will write to me if there is any change in his condition.'

'Certainly. Of course. And his attitude will change. Many of them, when they think they are going to be incapacitated for life, turn against their families. I assure you it is not an unusual symptom.'

'Quite.' March's grip did not slacken on Davie's arm. She picked up her bag and walked around the small tables and across a gravel drive to the stable yard. Davie began to cry. March whispered fiercely, 'Don't you dare to show anyone your feelings, Davie. Never show your feelings. You are a Rising. Hold your head high.'

So they walked past the pump to the safety of the Wolseley. Davie slid on to the leather seat, hot in the sunshine.

'I wish we'd never come,' she gasped, fighting her sobs. 'I hate him — why won't he let us help him, Aunt March?'

And March said, 'Wait till we're on the road, darling. And I'll tell you.'

She told Davie what she knew. It was very difficult for her and Davie realized this. She was confessing her past to a fourteen-year-old schoolgirl who had always admired and respected and loved her. She did it in the spirit of an ascetic taking to his bed of nails. As if, after Albert's terrible rejection of them, she could cleanse her soul.

'I think . . .' her voice was very low. 'I think when your Uncle Fred told Albert the truth, it made him distrust all women, darling. And now . . . you realize what the matron was saying?'

'She said he would change his mind. When he was stronger.'

'She said he might be incapacitated for life. Don't you understand, Davie? It's the same as your poor father. He and your mother were married seven years before you came along.'

Davie could not quite follow this. She put it to the back of her mind for future thought. Aunt March was weeping, and it made her weep again too. Their tears united them.

'Poor Albert,' sobbed March. And Davie nodded.

'I'll never forgive Fred,' March wept.

Davie did not nod and she said nothing. But she had known for some time that it was all Uncle Fred's fault.

Eight

'BILL' was quite right. Once Albert was strong enough for an operation the result was amazing. His leg was saved, he would walk with a limp for years perhaps, but the frightful pain was eased to an intermittent ache. Like his Uncle David he was going to know the weather by the state of his right leg.

He was desperate to get back to the war, mainly because he knew that it was the only way to banish the thought of Davie standing beside him, white-faced and anguished. He had dreamed of her so often and when he'd looked up that terrible afternoon, he'd thought at first she was another dream. Then he saw that she was different. For one thing she was stunningly beautiful. For another she was in pain; a pain he had inflicted on her.

For two weeks he lived in a tortured half-world, then, as he felt physically better, he knew what to do. The calm voice of Stewart Hibberd on the wireless belied the frantic preparations under way to defend Britain against the expected invasion. The Local Defence Volunteers were renamed the Home Guard and were issued with extra equipment. Fighter Command brought squadrons from the north of the country to defend the vulnerable south, barrage balloons blossomed in the sky against the Stuka and Heinkel dive-bombers. Victor wrote that the great east window of the cathedral — the largest stained-glass window in the whole of Europe — had been safely stowed piece by piece in the crypt.

Amazingly he did not receive any letter from Davina, but one came from Flo. It started with a couplet from a poem she had written: 'The west window stands and guards o'er the nave. Now that east window lies in its grave.' Then went on to describe the fire-watching arrangements in the cathedral. Albert tried to read between the lines of the curiously formal letter, but could not get very far. It obviously meant that Davina was not going to write to him; it might mean that Davina was so hurt by his rebuff she now hated him and Flo felt bound to offer sympathy. It might mean that Davina had *asked* Flo to write to him.

A short note came from his mother.

'My dear boy. I relied on your understanding and forgiveness, but realize neither can be given. However it is beyond my understanding that you have cut yourself off from your cousin too. You must know she has a special affection for you and is deeply wounded by your attitude. I do not expect to hear from you, but please — please Albert — write to Davina. With all my love, your anxious mother.'

At the end of June it was suggested he should spend a few days at a convalescent home in the Cotswolds. It was too near Gloucester and he turned it down. Jack and Elizabeth Doswell were visiting him that day, and when they heard they exchanged significant glances. Albert was still on his best behaviour with Elizabeth but he did say sourly to Jack, 'What are you smirking about?'

Jack gave his open smile. 'Aha. Just that Lizzie and I were talking about something on the way here which fits rather well with the subject of convalescing.'

Albert shook his head. 'I know what you're going to say. But your parents are busy farmers, Jack. They don't want a semi-invalid plonked on them just at hay-making time. No. I shall go back to the billets and take it steady for a few days — there's a decent little stream where I can try for some fish—'

Elizabeth interrupted gently. 'Listen, Tommy. You haven't heard our plan yet. It's quite true that the parents are up to their eyes. But you see I've got a leave. Ten days. I've got to go home — they expect it — but it's not much fun for me these days. All my old friends are doing war work . . . well, you know how it is. You'd be marvellous company for me. And after all, I am a nurse so you'd be safe enough.'

Jack made a face and made some comments about his sister's nursing expertise, and for a few seconds while Albert sorted out the pros and cons in his mind, there was the bedlam of friendly bickering. At first he did not know what to do. The Doswell farm held enormous attractions for him. Mainly because it would be a sanctuary, ungetatable by his family. And country life always appealed to him. But what obligation would he then have to Jack and Elizabeth? It was so obvious what was at the back of Jack's mind. Elizabeth was petite, darkly pretty, with sparkling eyes and a ready laugh. She was completely unmysterious. She was also intensely practical: a typical nurse.

She finished her family argument by slapping Jack in the solar plexus, then turned to Albert and gave a feminine interpretation of her brother's frank grin.

'Listen, Tommy—' most of her remarks began with 'Listen'. 'If you're worried I'll compromise you, forget it. I know you're practically engaged to your cousin back home and she can come and visit you too. You know how it is with nurses, they can give an alcohol rub and think about what's for dinner.'

'Rump steak?' grunted Jack vulgarly, and was again attacked physically.

Perhaps it was her reassurance that decided Albert. The visit from March and Davina had had one positive result; he knew that he wanted some female company. But he wanted it without any emotional strings. He wanted to be with someone like Elizabeth Doswell.

He said to Jack, 'How did you know about my cousin?

136

I've never mentioned her to you.'

Jack looked uncomfortable.

'When I came to see you first you were a bit under the weather, old man. Doollally, to put it mildly. You kept telling a bloke called Dave to chuck away your ring. I had to say something to you, so I asked who'd got your ring. First of all you said it was your sister. Then you said your cousin.' He pulled a ghastly face. 'Sorry, old man. You're so damned close about your family I felt as if I was prying. But you didn't give much away.'

Albert said briefly, 'It was rubbish actually. When I was a kid I gave a ring to my cousin. That's all. Didn't mean a thing.' He grinned at Elizabeth. 'I'd quite enjoy having an alcohol rub. Thanks. Thanks, both of you.'

Doswell's farm was right outside his experience. Once his grandfather had taken him to the labourer's cottage outside Newent where Grampa Rising, Aunt Sylv, Aunt Vi, Uncle Jack and Uncle Wallie had all been born. It was little more than a shed. His mother told him the sort of life they had lived there and how she had hated it. Grampa must have hated it too because he'd been so eager to leave it and become apprenticed as a tailor in Gloucester. But his mother had also told him that his Uncle Albert had adored going to Kempley. She could not understand it, but she reported faithfully his joy when he had accompanied Grampa there in the horse and trap. There was a phrase he used to describe the uncaring life they all lived in that filthy hovel. 'Happy as pigs in shit.'

There was shit at Doswell's farm of course, but it was kept well under control. Mr Doswell had recently installed one of the new milking machines and the cowsheds were painted white and looked like laboratories. In the fields the corn was cut and bundled by machine and a pair of Land Army girls put the stooks into small wigwams which would dry in the sun. There was a cherry orchard; a plum orchard; an apple orchard. Most days members of the local Women's Institute — Mrs

Doswell was their president — would collect in the farm kitchen to jam and bottle the glut of blackcurrants, strawberries and raspberries. It was like living in the middle of an enormous harvest festival. He could see that Elizabeth might well be lonely. There were a dozen jobs which her practical hands could have done, but her parents were determined she shouldn't. 'This is your leave Lizzie!' one or other of them would exclaim. 'You are not to do a thing!.

Albert and she walked every morning, sometimes taking the trap to nearby beauty spots. They went to Corfe Castle one day, then to Swanage. Barbed wire rolls were being laid along the beach, and concrete tank traps were jutting like teeth from the promenade. The sight of the war had a deflating effect on both of them. Albert's limp worsened and Elizabeth's chatter dried up. He realized how much effort she was making for his sake.

'Let's have lunch here,' he suggested, taking the initiative for the first time. 'There's a decent enough pub where we left Judy and they won't miss us at home.'

She smiled faintly, pleased he had called the farm 'home'.

'That would be nice,' They turned and retraced their steps against the slight breeze. 'Listen Tommy, stop being independent. Lean on me. Look, I'm just the right height for a crutch.'

So he put his arm over her shoulders and let her take some of his weight and they timed their strides as if it was a three-legged race. It marked the beginning of a closer relationship. Before she had been his nurse, after the trip to Swanage, she was his companion.

In the afternoons he rested. Sometimes in his room, sometimes in the hammock slung between two trees in the apple orchard. On Victor's recommendation he was reading *War and Peace* but it was hard going and usually ended up flat on his chest after half an hour. He did not know what Elizabeth did with that time, talked to her parents presumably. Contentment seemed to drop out of the trees on to his closed eyes. How could he be content? None of his problems were solved or ever could be, there was a terrible war raging which Britain might well lose . . . yet he was content. Surrounded by busy people whose work was ruled by sun and rain, light and dark, he felt at ease.

One afternoon, half-asleep, he heard a distant dogfight going on in the sky and did not even open his eyes to look for it. Yet when the note of the tractor altered, then ceased, he became awake instantly and listened for it to recommence with such intensity his ears hummed.

Eventually Elizabeth arrived apologetically, bearing a cup of tea.

'Listen Tommy. I know it's awful of me but I've offered your services. The tractor has broken down and Dad is hauling hay bales along to the barn. The weather forecast is a bit dicey for tonight, he ought to get it finished.' She stirred the tea and held it for him as if he were completely helpless. But he sipped anyway. 'Jack is always on about your way with engines. Do you think you could have a look at it? Dad's sent for the rep but heaven knows what time he will get there.'

He grinned at her. Her face was four inches from his and her skin looked like one of the apples above his head.

'If I can't hold a cup of tea I don't really see how I can hold a spanner, do you?'

She laughed with relief and helped him to sit up. She was wearing overalls and her hair was in a bandeau. Thank God she never, ever, in the slightest way, reminded him of Davie. She took him through the orchard to the hayfield where her father, his cowman and the two land girls were bending over the engine of the tractor. It was familiar to Albert; as a 'mechanical student' at Austin's, he had worked on all kinds of engines. This one, made by Listers in Dursley, was a gem of engineering. He rolled up his shirtsleeves and rammed the tail of his shirt firmly into his flannels, then he put his square, short-fingered hands on the engine casing and began to feel his way around.

139

At supper that night everyone acted as if he'd sprouted wings. Mrs Doswell wondered whether her Goblin vacuum cleaner might be made to work again; Albert had a look at it, cleaned the brushes and it whirred into life. Suddenly he was one of the family. His routine did not change, but he was no longer a convalescent visitor. He had a place in this particular scheme of things — he could mend engines. George Doswell shook his hand: 'Always a place for you, Tommy — after this lot's over!'

He began to learn about Jack and Elizabeth from another angle. Ellen Doswell produced family photograph albums; Jack at boarding-school, Lizzie as Brownie pack leader.

Wandering through Dorchester one day, he said to Elizabeth, 'You think a lot of Jack, don't you?'

'Of course. We're slightly related!'

He leaned on her shoulder now as a matter of course. He was beginning to know the scent of her hair, the shape of her shoulderblade.

He said, 'It's something new to me. Not having a sister. Chap I knew in Spain . . . didn't know he had a sister and he met her as a stranger. It was difficult for him. He fell in love with her.'

She laughed. 'You're joking, Tommy.'

'No. He told me about it. He'd joined the Brigade to get away from her actually. She didn't know, you see. She loved him too.'

'Good lord. Sorry, I can't imagine that. I mean . . . I'm sure I'd know Jack was my brother. Well, I might not realize . . . but I certainly wouldn't fall in love with him.' Her laughter pealed out at the mere thought and after a bit he joined in.

They did Ellen Doswell's shopping for her and went back to Judy and the trap. Suddenly she said, 'Listen, Tommy. D'you fancy going to see Hardy's cottage?'

'Hardy?'

'Thomas Hardy the writer. Haven't you read *Return of the Native*? Or *Far From the Madding Crowd*?'

'I don't think so. My cousin will have.'

'The one you were engaged to?'

'No. Victor. The one in the army. He reads all the time when he's not painting.' He told her about Victor while they jogged along quiet country lanes towards Bockhampton, and she told him about Thomas Hardy. When they arrived the cottage was empty and the caretaker opened up specially for them. Inside everything was dappled green, a mixture of sunshine and leaf-shadow, incredibly romantic. Outside, the garden was overgrown with lush vegetation; it seemed a microcosm of rural England — enduring, even everlasting. Feeling its archetypal roots pulling at him, Albert knew full well why Elizabeth had brought him here. When she turned to him, he wasn't surprised. But he did not kiss her. In a flash of unusual vision, he knew that he would always like Elizabeth, he might even love her; but it would be with his head, not with his heart. And Thomas Hardy spoke entirely to his heart.

She waited for a moment, her face upturned to his. Then she turned almost naturally to look at the cottage. 'It's like a fairy tale,' she said prosaically.

'Yes.' He wished she hadn't fallen for him; their relationship would now have to be changed again. 'Yes, untrue.'

She was very still. 'Perhaps that's what this leave is? A fairy tale.'

He did not reply and she led the way back to the trap without offering her shoulder. Then on the way home when the atmosphere began to build up tangibly, they saw a squadron of Heinkels overhead, flying in perfect formation as if the sky and the country beneath it belonged to them.

Elizabeth cowered against his shoulder. 'Can they see us?'

'Of course. But they're not interested in us.'

'Where are they going, d'you suppose?'

'East. London I expect. Or one of the airfields.'

141

She was quiet again until the Heinkels had disappeared over the horizon. Then she said weakly, 'I know how you feel, Tommy. No commitments. Not till after the war . . . a lot of my patients feel like that. But we have to go on living normally. Whatever happens.'

'I know. And that's what we've done, haven't we? Oh Lizzie, it's been a marvellous day. Thank you so much.'

'Yes but . . . you're dying to get back to the squadron, aren't you?'

They drew up in the farmyard and she leapt out, not waiting for an answer. He got down carefully and watched her carry the tack into the stable. Her face was bright red. She was like an apple. David called Davina his little apple, but it was the complete misnomer. Davina was a daffodil. Lizzie was an apple. Her cheeks were round, so were her breasts and buttocks. She was tiny and slim but she was also very round and womanly.

A voice behind hailed him, and he turned as quickly as his leg would allow.

'By all that's holy.'

It was Victor. Victor standing by the kitchen door in his awful old painting trousers and open-necked shirt, his hair straggling wildly out of its Army cut. Albert could hardly believe it. Victor had written to him in hospital telling him about his narrow escape from Dunkirk, but Albert had assumed he would be back with his unit by now.

The cousins shook hands painfully for a long time, grinning from ear to ear. Then Elizabeth had to be introduced and Mrs Doswell called that supper was ready. Victor had already met the Doswells and the land girls and even the cowman. He seemed to know them as well as Albert, who had been here a whole week.

'So how's the arm?' Albert managed to ask at last.

'Fine. But it's going to be a bit tricky carrying a rifle.' He accepted another small trout with fervour. 'I say, this is marvellous . . . anyway. Yes. I'm now in the Reconnaissance Corps, old man. I imagine

142

congratulations are in order.'

Everyone duly congratulated him. One of the land girls, Elsie, asked what it actually meant.

'Well, I'm going on a course to do with photography. And I have to do things like maps and sketches.'

'Have you done any painting lately?' Albert asked.

'Yes. Quite a bit. When you get home you must go to Chichester Street and see what I've done.'

There was a silence.

Then it was milking time, time to clear away the meal, time to disperse. Victor was staying the night and Albert went upstairs with him to show him the bathroom and the views from the attic windows. Victor stared out at the country scene as if imprinting it on his brain. Then he said quietly, 'What an absolute crazy mess it all is, isn't it?'

Albert did not know whether he meant the war or his own complicated relationship to Davie. He said nothing.

Victor said, 'All my paintings — fifteen of them in twenty days — have been of a girl's face.'

Albert was still silent.

'The same girl. I called her Gladys. She was an ambulance driver in France. Killed in the liberty boat when we were getting away.'

'Oh God. You loved her?'

'No. She was a silly little thing. Petty. I didn't love her.'

Albert looked at the back of Victor's head. He remembered fights they had had; schooldays; picnics by the river at Rodley; cricket matches. He said wonderingly, 'But you love everything, old man. Every thing and every one. That's why you keep painting it.'

Victor was still for a long minute, then he turned and stared at his cousin who was annoyingly practical and unimaginative, yet had this habit of putting his finger right on the heart of things.

He smiled. The sunset was still in his eyes and it was a blind smile. He could no longer see and record; his smile was one of recognition for a truth. To paint, he must love. And he must know that he loved. His observations must always be compassionate.

He said at last, 'Albie, old man. I'm being sent to Greece. The Italians are sitting there ready to go in and there's a few of us who are going to try to rally some resistance. Otherwise it'll be another Norway, only hot.' His blinding smile softened to a grin. 'I'm not supposed to tell you, so keep mum.'

Albert clapped him on the shoulder. It was no good asking how dangerous it was. He himself would be living dangerously again soon, if the two lots of Heinkels he'd seen were anything to go by. Victor read his thoughts as usual and said, 'Might see you next learning the harp, eh, old man?'

'For God's sake, Victor—'

'Probably, yes. The sort of caterwauling you'll make, He's the only one who'll put up with it.'

Albert had to laugh. They went again to the window and watched the land girls walking across the yard to their quarters, giggling and shoving each other. They glanced back at the house then quickly away, and Albert knew that they were 'gone' on Victor. He had that instant effect on all girls.

'D'you remember that bloody Imps dance at the Corn Exchange when Beryl Langham nearly threw herself at your feet?'

Victor said nothing; the incident had been the start of a long and hideous quarrel between them. He let his thoughts run on like a film until they reached the place where ten-year-old Davie had used him quite deliberately to make Albert jealous.

He said, 'Davie was pretty devastated by her visit to you in hospital, old man. Couldn't you write to her or something?'

Albert did not ask what he was talking about. His progression from Beryl Langham to Davina Daker was absolutely logical to them both.

After a while he said, 'When I wrote to you and told you about Davina and me being brother and sister, I said

144

we would never speak of it.'

Victor shrugged impatiently. 'I know. But it's so ridiculous, Albert. All these hurt feelings everywhere. Unnecessary. All you have to do is tell the girl.'

'Have *you* told her? Is that what you're trying to say?'

'Of course I've not told her. Oh, it's crossed my mind. I've come damned near to it. But I haven't said a word. That's your job.'

'What do you think it would do to Davie to know her father was Fred Luker and her mother—'

'All right. I know. Sorry. I tend to forget the background. Seeing you two tearing yourselves to bits, I get my facts out of order sometimes.' Victor sighed gustily to cover his own feelings, then said, 'But I still don't see why you can't put pen to paper and tell her something. Anything. Until she hears from you, she can't rest, you know.'

'Whatever I said would be wrong, Victor. It's so hard to explain. Davie and me . . . we go beyond words. She'd know I was lying. The only thing that will eventually convince her is my absolute silence . . . my coldness.'

'You're wrong, old man.' Victor leaned forward and began to doodle on the window with his forefinger. 'So long as you don't say anything, don't do anything, she will wait.' He turned his head to one side so that the sun threw up his fingermark in sharp relief. 'I wasn't going to mention this, but perhaps it will give you some idea of her state of mind. Flo came to see me last week. That kid knows parts of Davie that no-one else will ever know. Bit like you and me. Strange that. The same sort of physical differences too, she's dark and Davie is so fair . . . Anyway.' He drew in a sharp breath and made some more marks on the glass. 'She told me Davie was ill again—'

'Ill?' Albert's voice sharpened.

'She meant that Davie had gone into the Slough of Despond again. She does that when she's missing you very badly.'

'Oh God. I know.'

Albert thought of the past week here; the unexpected contentment; the visit to Hardy's cottage that very afternoon and his awareness of Elizabeth Doswell. He said again, 'Oh God.'

Victor said, 'Quite. Flo said it was because it had all been such a waste. I wasn't taking her quite seriously, she looks a bit like Grandma Rising when she's being very solemn, that nun quality.'

'Well, what *did* she mean?'

'Apparently Robin Adair had access to your file. He works at the Records Offices in Eastern Avenue, you know. He promised Davie he'd tell her where you were if she granted him little favours.'

'*Christ!*'

'It's okay, old man. I thought that. But it was just kisses. Davie always had the upper hand. But Flo was worried about it. She thinks Davie might turn to Robin Adair or someone. I don't know. But it wouldn't hurt to write to Davie and put her straight.

'She'd never . . . oh my God, Victor. *You* know what Adair's like. Christ, when we knew him first he came to dinner with his parents. Fred was trying to get them to sell some land or something. He was boasting then about his conquests.'

Victor grinned. 'I remember you telling me. You hit him, didn't you?'

'I did. He said something about April . . . I didn't know then of course.' He smacked his fist into the wall. 'Davie couldn't — wouldn't —'

'Of course she wouldn't, you idiot. She had a reason — the reason's gone now. But you can see how she must feel. Not only ignored by you, but the whole episode with Adair making her feel humiliated.'

There was a long silence. Victor finished his doodle and stepped back. The sun dipped behind a line of elms which bordered the cornfield, and the farm was bathed in lurid orange light. From the direction of Dorchester came the wail of the siren and, minutes later, the intermittent

146

engine-note of a horde of German bombers. Both men ignored everything, apparently locked in their own thoughts.

Then Victor said quietly, 'D'you see what I've drawn? Come this side of the window — can you see? It's Gladys again. I didn't even know I was doing it.'

Albert surveyed the doodle through narrowed eyes. A girl's head, tilted backwards, mouth open in a scream. He put out a hand and gripped Victor's shoulder.

'I'll write to her. I'll write to her tomorrow night. That's a promise.'

Victor left early the next morning. Albert drove him to Westbury in the trap and he caught the London train to report to his new unit. From there he was leaving for 'destination unknown'. Albert watched the train's tail-lamp out of sight and limped back to the now-familiar Judy. He missed Elizabeth's shoulder. Inconsequentially he reflected that Davie would be too tall to be of much help to him in that way. Then he tried to think of all Davie's disadvantages compared with Elizabeth. He started with her age — she was a girl and Elizabeth was a woman. Then her lack of qualifications — Elizabeth was a trained nurse and Davie was pretty helpless in times of emergency. And of course Davie would want to go in for voice training or whatever singers did, whereas Elizabeth was a natural home-maker. And Elizabeth . .. Elizabeth Doswell was not tied to him by blood and bone.

He flicked the reins on Judy's back and suddenly cursed aloud. What did he imagine he was doing? What puerile, foolish exercise was this? If Elizabeth was an angel and Davie a devil, it would make no difference. Davie was . . . of himself. Elizabeth was a separate entity.

Breakfast was under way when he arrived back at Doswells'. The early milking had been done and the land girls were scoffing bread and butter as if their lives depended on it. Mrs Doswell dished up his bacon and eggs straight from the frying-pan while she recounted her plans for the day.

'Fire-fighting this morning. Jamming again this afternoon. Bread and cheese for lunch and supper will be late, so make yourselves tea when you're ready. Cake in the crock. Lizzie darling, can you see to things here?'

'Of course, Mummy.'

'George, don't forget the Food Office man is coming. I've done the paperwork, it's in the office.'

'Righto, darling.'

'Tommy, we were wondering whether you'd be up to driving the tractor for an hour this afternoon while George sees to the Ministry man?

It was obvious who was the organizer at Doswells'. Albert grinned and nodded. He knew he'd be unable to lie in the hammock today with Victor on his way to Greece or wherever. And Mrs Doswell knew it too.

So that day was purposely busy. He did not see much of Elizabeth. In the morning he walked along footpaths she had shown him, to a local beauty spot called Tyler's Tump. From there he could see most of the farm; the window where he and Victor had watched last night's sunset, the old tithe barn, the green of the cow-bitten pastures fading in the heat of this wonderful summer. Although he had always lived in towns, he knew that somewhere in his past he was linked with the country, and this piece of country was the first he had been able to know well. It was almost as if he recognized it; it represented England for him far better than the old grey cityscape of Gloucester.

He sat crossed-legged and stared.

'I could easily love her,' he said aloud. 'This is her place and I love that already so . . .' He picked a daisy and twirled it in his fingers, not taking his eyes from the view beneath him, yet knowing exactly how that small flower would look, seeing it with his fingers. He said 'She might not have me. She has known me for a week, that is all.' But he spoke without conviction. She had tried to tell him at Hardy's cottage that she would have him. He knew she would have him.

He dropped his head and surveyed the daisy.

'I don't . . . not really . . . but I've got to show you that it's no good, my darling. I've got to finish it for good and all. You must look round for something else . . . someone else. You've got plenty of time and I'm wasting that time.' He remembered with indifference that it had been Fred's solution. Fred had said, 'You could find another girl. Get married.' Trust Fred to be right in the end.

He stood up at last and dropped the daisy on to the Tump. Then he started to limp back to the house and bread and cheese for lunch. It was good to get inside the kitchen. Good to be with these congenial people.

It was as if she knew of his decision. She watched him from the corner of her eye as she hacked a cottage loaf into wedges. She did not ask him about his morning or how he was feeling, or whether he was tired. She said, 'Daddy won't be long. When he relieves you on the tractor, come in for some tea. You won't feel like the hammock this afternoon.'

How did she know about his feelings? Or was she giving instructions as her mother did? Either way it was all right by him. He said, 'Righto,' just like her father did. Then he smiled and added, 'Thanks, Lizzie.'

The land girls were at the sink, their backs to the table. She leaned over it and brushed her mouth across his. Then she went bright red and bustled off to the larder for pickles and tomatoes. He cut off some cheese and smiled slightly. He couldn't help being flattered. Girls didn't go for him, not like they did for Victor. And she was so pretty and wholesome and nice. Dammitall, why shouldn't he feel flattered?

George Doswell came in and went to the sink.

'Mother get off to Snooks' Farm all right?'

'Yes Daddy.'

'Good. Dig into that loaf, Tommy. You won't get bread like that when you leave here. National loaf my foot! National sawdust most like!'

Albert's smile widened and he hacked at the loaf again. He felt right here. With Davie he could have roamed the world and felt right. But if he couldn't have Davie then this was a good second best. And Elizabeth was his passport to Doswell's Farm.

His decision made, he enjoyed the hour driving the tractor up and down the field, waiting while the girls unloaded and driving off again. The sun was hot and there were no sirens. He kept his mind on the sights and smells around him and what he had to do next. The feel of a motor beneath his hand was good. He wished time would stand still at now.

But when it was supper and Ellen Doswell was reporting on the jamming at Snooks', he was glad it had not stopped. Elizabeth had cooked an enormous toad-in-the-hole with home-made sausages, and there were new potatoes and peas, and rhubarb fool to follow. He remembered Tolly saying once, the ordinary everyday happenings of life were what made it good; the extraordinary poisoned it. How Tolly would love all this. His clever, closed-up face would open with a smile as he looked at all these people leading decent ordinary lives, somehow shutting out the extraordinary events happening all around them. Yet they were not heartless; they did not, could not, ignore what was going on. Jack was doubtless being scrambled right at this moment as the sun set and the bombers arrived from Germany. Next week Elizabeth would be back in hospital nursing young men crippled for life. This afternoon George had coped with someone from the Food Office; Ellen had been making jam for next winter. Somehow their goodness ran alongside the horrors. If there was enough of it, it might even nullify the war.

Albert was not a thinker; he knew he was out of his depth, so he abandoned his ephemeral ideas and concentrated on enjoying the moment. When the clearing-up was done he suggested a walk without any

150

premonition of burning his boats. Elizabeth's shoulder presented itself by his elbow and he leaned on it gratefully.

'I missed you this morning,' he said.

She replied tranquilly, 'Good.'

'I walked to the Tump. The farm looked so safe. So self-contained.'

'It's done you good being here, Tommy. You're fatter and you've got a colour at last.'

'Thanks. How much fatter?'

'Well . . . I can still stand your weight.'

There was a little silence while they both realized that her words could contain innuendo. Then she added hastily, 'You've got a long way to go before you beat Oliver Hardy.'

'I should hope so.'

They trudged around the barn. There was a bench against the old stone wall, possibly put there for people to sit and admire the sunset. They sat.

'It's hurting today, Tommy, isn't it?'

'I told you. I've missed you.'

'Was it the tractor? Honestly now.'

'No. I just think it might rain tomorrow.'

'Oh . . . you . . .'

He had kept his arm on her shoulders, now he hugged her to his side. He said: 'Lizzie. Lizzie Doswell. You're what my Aunt Sylv would call posh, d'you know that?'

'Me? Posh? Don't be silly, Tommy. No-one could possibly call me posh.'

'You went to a posh school. You talk posh.'

'You can see we're ordinary people. Your Aunt whatever-you-call-her would see that too.'

'No. She was born in the country, you see. Six in one room. The hens came in too sometimes. And apparently if you wanted to sit down you had to turn the odd pig out of a chair.'

'Oh Tommy!'

'True. I never saw it. But she's told me.'

151

'Well probably if I went back a couple of generations . . . oh stop this, Tommy. You and Victor were talking about your old school last night. It sounded very progressive to me.'

'I'm just trying to point out that we — you and me — we're very different.'

'So. You like my family. You like the farm.'

'You wouldn't like *my* family. I wouldn't want you to meet them. If we . . . get married . . . I'd want to cut us right off from my family. Would you be willing to do that?'

She said faintly, 'Do what, Tommy.?'

'Firstly. Get married.'

'Yes. Yes. I'd like to marry you, Tommy dear.'

'And hold you only unto me? Not my relations, just me?'

'Oh Tommy, do stop it. Kiss me or something.'

He kissed her. It was very enjoyable. He consciously enjoyed it. He did it again and it was still very nearly marvellous. He would not let himself remember the kiss he had shared with Davina on the cliff path at St. Ives. Everything in the universe had come together for that kiss. But this one was . . . most enjoyable.

She murmured, 'I'll always be grateful to your cousin.'

He was startled. 'My cousin?'

'Victor. He must have said something — done something—'

'Oh, *Victor*. He's the one member of the family you are allowed to like!'

Much later he went up to his room and found notepaper and envelopes. And began his letter to Davina.

152

Nine

FOR Davie, those weeks between Robin's return on 3rd June, and the arrival of Albert's letter on 30th June were a blur of complete misery. First the ignominy of being seen by Flo doing . . . what she had been doing . . . haunted her and sometimes she would push the thought away physically, her hands going to her ears and small moans escaping her closed lips. Then the promise of salvation with the arrival of Aunt March waving her yellow telegram; and the agony of futher rejection at Haslemere.

Then Aunt March's 'confession'.

Davie did not know what to make of that. For one thing it was simply impossible to imagine Aunt March as a young and beautiful girl, heartbroken by the death of her favourite brother, letting Uncle Fred . . . no, it was not possible. But the subsequent events were even more unlikely. Aunt March had told her of the holiday in Weymouth when Aunt Sylv had correctly diagnosed her 'illness' and of the plans she had made secretly and frantically. Because, by this time, Uncle Fred had been reported missing believed dead. To get married to Uncle Edwin — old enough to be her grandfather — actually to get married to him and to fool him until his death . . . it was like a story from one of the penny dreadfuls Natasha Hall smuggled around school And no-one ever knew. Except Uncle Fred and Aunt Sylv, then later, Albert, and now . . . herself.

She cried a great deal through that month in 1940. April and David were worried stiff and called in Doctor Green, but he said it was her age and the war and the strain of studying for her School Certificate, and she must get plenty of rest and eat all the fruit she could.

Aunt Sylv snapped, 'The child is going into a decline, Doctor. I've seen it before.' But he shook his head, smiling. 'That was the euphemistic way of saying someone had tuberculosis, Mrs Turpin. I can assure you Davie has no such illness. And she is not anaemic. She is very worried and tense, and if she stays quietly at home with her family, she will recover. I promise you.'

Aunt Sylv showed him the door, grumbling beneath her breath that his father knew better. Doctor Green smiled gently. He and his father between them had treated the Risings since 1890 and he could give a diagnosis by looking at them. His father would have described Davina's condition as 'lovesick'. But young Doctor Green was certain that love, requited or not, could not make you sick.

So Davie ate all the strawberries that were going in that strawberry-summer, she drank hot blackcurrant tea when the temperatures were in the high seventies, she took gentle walks and lay in the deckchair in the garden in the afternoons. Unknowingly, her routine echoed Albert's. But as he slowly recovered and regained his strength, so hers trickled away from her. On the day of Edward Williams' funeral, she shivered and shook like a leaf in her afternoon sleep. When April gently roused her with a cup of tea, she clapped her hands to her head and shouted 'No! No!'

'Darling, please. Just half a cup,' April said, holding her close, wishing she had not left her to go to the farce of poor Edward's funeral.

'Oh . . . oh Mummy. I was dreaming. It was only a dream.' Davie clung to her mother's thin shoulders gratefully. For the first time since 3rd June she could find something to be thankful for. Her own mother was so good, she had never done anything shameful in her life; she and Daddy were like twin rocks in this terrifying new world.

'You must have that dream often, my love.' April put a cushion behind Davie's head and propped her higher in the deckchair so that she could drink the tea. 'I've seen you cover your ears like that before. Are you sure you've no pain there? Not a touch of earache.?'

'Nothing Mummy, honestly. What time is it?'

'Three o'clock. Daddy went straight to the shop after the funeral. But he'll be home early tonight.' April guessed rightly that Davie needed them both. She chatted on, consciously trying to create a safe atmosphere. 'Flo will be in soon and we can have tea out here, I think. I'll make tomato and cucumber sandwiches and we'll put the tea in a Thermos and pretend it's a picnic, shall we?'

'Oh Mummy, I do love you.' Tears of weakness came into Davie's eyes. 'You and Daddy and Flo, and dear old Aunt Sylv . . .Flo says she's like an old, old ox. And she is, isn't she? Not in a horrid way. In a kind, furry way.'

April laughed and nodded as Aunt Sylv lumbered slowly down the garden path towards them. She tried to work out Sylvia's age. She must be seventy.

'Well?' The big body lowered itself with difficulty into a third deckchair. 'Well, how did it go?'

April shot warning glances at her but Aunt Sylv was impervious to all but the most ham-handed hints. She went on comfortably, 'Nothing like a nice funeral. A proper send-off. I suppose all the councillors were there? And how did Sibbie and Bridie get along? Losing poor old Edward Willaims seems to have brought them together, doesn't it?'

April nodded. 'I'll tell you about it later, dear. How are you today?' Aunt Sylv had taken to getting up after the family had sorted themselves out in the morning and consequently had not seen April till now.

Davie said, 'Go on Mummy, tell us about Mr Williams' funeral. I'm not going to cry or anything silly like that. I

155

didn't know him. Anyway he must have been about a hundred.'

Aunt Sylv said, 'He was the same age as me, young lady, so none of your cheek!' She grinned. 'It was marrying young Sibbie Luker what wore 'im out!'

Because Davie seemed so much better, April did talk about the funeral. In fact not many of his fellow councillors had come — Edward had been forced to resign when he married Sibbie — but there had been a decent enough turnout. May and Monty — Victor had stayed at home to look after Gretta — March and Fred — Edward had helped Fred with many of his deals in the past. And the Lukers had come in force. Hetty and Alf, conspicuous in their rusty black, Gladys with her goitre decently covered by a grey scarf, even the disreputable Henry. Sibbie's marriage had been advantageous to them all and they were grateful to Edward Williams and sorry he had to go.

Afterwards at the big house in Barnwood Road, they had eaten until they could barely move. May and Sibbie had not spoken a word to each other, though May watched Sibbie with a smile on her face and Sibbie flushed uncomfortably every time she saw it. April knew there had been some frightful quarrel before Gretta was born, but had no idea what it was all about and found May's behaviour rather embarrassing in the circumstances. Bridie and Sibbie, the two chief protagonists at the occasion, were very silent. Not that party chat was in order, but knowing both of them so well April was surprised that they did not make the most of being 'on stage'. Bridie especially; after all, she had not seen her father for over ten years so she could hardly be prostrate with grief.

May, showing April the dining-room and boasting that in fact she had designed it, said, 'Oh, we shall see the fox among the chickens now, April! Sibbie might be silent and sad and Bridie eaten up with remorse at the moment. But just wait till the solicitors read the will. I'm ready to bet you that whatever poor old Edward has said in it, there'll be a grand free-for-all.'

April shook her head remonstratingly. 'Oh May, how can you speculate like that? It'll all be perfectly legal and above board. Mr Williams was a businessman, after all.'

'And Sibbie will have made quite certain he looked after her, don't worry. And whatever Bridie is saying and doing now, she has loathed Sibbie for marrying her father and she will fight every inch of the way to make sure Sibbie knows who's boss.'

'May! Really!'

April repeated none of this to Davie and Aunt Sylv that afternoon. Her expurgated version of the service and following funeral meats was as light as she could make it. Davie was not well, and Aunt Sylv . . . well, she was the same age as Edward Williams apparently, and whatever she said he'd had life easy compared with her.

Then Flo came charging through the gate with one of the awful Byard girls from the top of the lane, and April went to the kitchen to make their picnic tea. She wondered again about Bridie and Sibbie and wished for the millionth time that Tolly was still alive.

And so the days went carefully by. Sometimes the siren would wail over the cathedral spires when it became dark, but no bombs dropped on Gloucester. Flo concocted an all-embracing prayer which she gabbled when she heard the German engines overhead. 'Dear God, keep us all safe through this night. Let us go to sleep quickly and wake up refreshed and let us win the war very quickly for thy name's sake Amen.' Davie agreed it was a good prayer, but Flo knew she did not say it herself. She knew that Davie was praying for Albert all the time, day and night.

On July the first his letter arrived. It came by the first post when they were all — except Aunt Sylv — at breakfast. April was going into the city with David that morning; she was helping the WVS with their 'evacuee visiting'. She recognized the writing on the envelope and handed it over to Davie without a word, but immediately planning to run to the phone box at the end of the lane and cancel her morning's work. However, the child opened the letter with absolute composure and read it through without a change of expression. It was a short letter and she looked up after less than two minutes and caught the family waiting goggled-eyed.

She smiled slightly.

'He's all right. He's sorry he was horrid to Aunt March and me at the hospital. It was his leg hurting. Now he's all right again and convalescing at a farm in Dorset. It sounds lovely.'

There was a pause, then David said calmly, 'And is he coming home now? Is he really all right?'

Davie turned her sky-blue eyes on to her beloved father. She said, 'No. He can't do that. He can't come home again.'

David frowned slightly. 'What are you saying, my little apple? He'll come back one day.'

Davie stood up. 'Not if he can help it, Daddy.' She tucked her chair neatly back beneath the table. 'I think I'll go back to school today. I'll slip and change into my uniform.'

She got to the door and April said hoarsely, 'Davie, what has happened? What does Albert say?'

Davie turned. 'He's getting married, Mummy. To a nurse. She's called Elizabeth Doswell and she's very nice he says.'

She went quietly out of the kitchen and they heard her climb the stairs. Flo said blankly, 'He can't. He's engaged to Davie.'

April said with wavering voice, 'What is he *thinking* of — to write to her like that — I could kill him!'

And David took a deep breath. 'Let her go to school. She knows she's got to make a fresh start now. Perhaps Albert knows best. Perhaps he's done the right thing.'

So Davie went back to school and deliberately threw herself into her childhood again. There was a list of names on the notice board; girls who had volunteered to go fruit-picking during the summer holidays. She wrote her name in. There were groups who shinned up ropes on to the roof and learned how to put out various kinds of incendiary bombs. She joined one of them. When Olga Hall commiserated with her on 'losing' Robin Adair, she listened without protests. It seemed he'd gone back to Olga, his passion regenerated. Olga wanted to tell her all about it. Wasn't she just the tiniest little bit jealous?

'Of course not, Olga. I'm glad . . . really, I'm very glad. Really.'

Olga hugged Davie's arm to her side. 'I'm so *happy*, Davie. I know I shouldn't be with the war and Grampa dying and everything, but I can't help it. Daddy always said that women and men are equal, but he was wrong. Robin is far above me. He's wonderful. He's brave and strong and masterful. I worship him. I absolutely worship him.'

'Oh good,' Davie said doubtfully. From the depths of her misery a thought arose; she had never *worshipped* Albert. They had been like Uncle Tolly must have meant men and women to be. Equal. Equal in love and happiness and sadness. She put a hand to her head.

'Have you got a headache, Davie? You're always holding your head now.'

'No. It's just a habit. Mother says I do it all the time.'

'Well, that's good.' Olga laughed affectedly. 'I thought for a dreadful moment I might be boring you!'

'Oh no. No, not at all.'

'His father is doing a field course this weekend, Davie. And his mother is staying with friends. So I'm going round there. He asked me if I'd go and look after him. Cook and everything. So I said yes."

'Is that all right?'

'Of course. He *asked* me, silly.'

'Yes, but it's not the thing is it? To stay with a man unchaperoned.'

'My God, you sound like Queen Victoria! Honestly

Davie — Winterditch Lane must be like the ark! What about the old King and Mrs Simpson? He just wants me to *cook* for him! That's all!'

'What does your mother say?'

'She's gone to London again. She goes every weekend and leaves us with that ghastly Marlene girl. So while the cat's away . . .'

'Olga. You shouldn't talk like that. And I don't think you should go either.'

'You're jealous. You're just pretending to be all sweet and nice as per usual. You're jealous. Robin never asked you to come and look after him, did he? Ha-ha!'

'Oh Olga . . . just be careful, that's all.

That night after school, Davie's form mistress asked her to report to the headmistress's office. Davie went in fear and trembling. Nobody was summoned by Doc Moore for anything but a severe reprimand. She stood on the square of carpet just outside the door and surveyed the half-tiled walls. They looked like the corned beef you could get off ration, pinky-red with white fat streaks running through. Was it possible, was it *possible*, that Dr Moore had found out about Robin Adair? How could she? But Davie hadn't cheated or lost a library book or anything else.

The office was more like a very pleasant sitting-room. There were chintz-covered armchairs either side of the deep window which overlooked the front garden, and the desk looked more like a sideboard because it was edged with silver cups and the House shields. Doc Moore was sitting behind it, writing, but she stopped when Davie closed the door and came round to shake hands as if Davie was another person instead of one of her pupils.

'I so rarely meet you girls on a personal basis . . .' She smiled and indicated one of the armchairs. Davie fidgeted by it until the headmistress took one, then she sat on the very edge of the chintz-covered cushion. Doc Moore's lisle-clad legs crossed themselves at the ankle and her hands clasped each other loosely on her tweed lap. Davie tried doing likewise and caught the buckle of her sandal in her ankle sock.

The indulgent smile widened. 'Naughty girls, brilliant girls . . but the in-between ones don't come my way.'

'Oh . . . No. I suppose not.'

'Not that you are an also-ran, Davina. Far from it. Miss Cyril gives me glowing reports of your singing.'

Davie made a deprecating noise in her throat and finished with a cough.

'Steady on. I understand you've been ill for quite a while. Was it a cough?'

'Well, yes. And other things. But I'm all right now.'

'Good.' The tone became bracing 'Well, I have good news for you and your family. Twenty-five girls were being awarded scholarships to the school this year.'

'Yes.' Davie looked at the Indian rug laid on the glowing parquet and hoped it would not slip away from her when she stood up. They had all been only mildly disappointed by Flo's failure to gain a place this year. She was only ten and would have another chance when she was eleven.

'Twenty-four girls have accepted their scholarships. The twenty-fifth is being sent to America for the duration of hostilities. That means that her place will be offered to the next on the list. Your sister. Flora Daker. I am delighted that she will have an extra year here as I expect your family will be. You may take the news home with you this evening.'

A month ago Davie would have been more delighted than she was now. She could partially forget her shame when she was at school, but if Flo was to be there as well the shame would probably be there too. However it was a great honour and Flo would be overjoyed.

'That is wonderful,' she said politely.

'I think so. And perhaps the competition will spur you to greater academic efforts, my dear.' Here came the bitter pill beneath the sugar. 'You have to set your sights firmly on the School Certificate now, Davina. We are all proud of your voice of course, but that talent must wait for full fruition. Your duty to your parents, to your country and to yourself, is to get a really good result in your Cambridge and to go on to the Higher Certificate, a State Scholarship and a place at university.'

Davie felt her eyes open wide. Did Doc Moore really think she was capable of all that studying? Davie herself knew she was not, but she still murmured, 'Yes, Dr Moore.'

'That's the spirit. That's what our young men are fighting for. That's the way my girls must show their patriotism.'

'Yes, Dr Moore.'

Monica Cresswell was waiting outside on the square carpet, studying the corned-beef tiles. She had tried to wipe away the lipstick on her mouth but it was obvious to Davie that it had been there. Monica, sixteen and strapping, was literally on the carpet.

Edward Williams had made a new will soon after his marriage to Sibbie Luker. Divested of its legal jargon it meant that Sibbie had the house for her lifetime, together with an annuity of £3,000. The family business of Williams and Son, Auctioneers and Valuers was to be split between her and 'my daughter and her husband'. Bridget was to continue to receive the very generous allowance she had enjoyed through her marriage. The children had handsome legacies held in trust until they came of age. On Sibbie's death the house and contents were to be sold and the proceeds divided between the children again.

Bridget said privately to April, 'My god, Sibbie's done well out of our family. The house. Three thousand a year. And a share in the firm. I resent that, April. Daddy hasn't been near the office for years. Tolly built it up to what it is today and Monty has kept it ticking over . . . it's nothing at all to do with Sibbie.'

'Darling, why quarrel about it? You've got more than enough to last you if you have a spending spree every day of the week.' April had done her fire-watching stint at the cathedral the previous night and was dead tired. She lacked her usual sympathy. 'It's obvious that your father knew Sibbie only too well. If she is hard-up or bored she will go back to her old ways. So he's left her plenty of cash and an interest in life. What could be more sensible than that?'

A week after the will was read, the solicitors concerned wrote to Bridie. She opened the letter after the girls had gone to school; Barty was downstairs with Marlene. It seemed that Mrs Williams had pointed out that the wording of the will could mean that the firm was to be split three ways, a third for her, a third for Mr Bartholomew Hall, and a third for Mrs Bartholomew Hall. If that were the case, Mr Bartholomew Hall's third would be in dispute and she was contending that as the next of kin it should come to her.

Bridie thought she might faint. Two-thirds of Williams' to Sibbie Luker? In other words, the firm controlled by Sibbie Luker? Bridie had already had a new desk installed in the office above Monty's and had spent two days there, transferring a great deal of the work to herself. She was certain that eventually she could run her grandfather's business herself; she rather fancied the idea. She would wear severe navy-blue suits and white blouses with a bow at the throat. Perhaps she would stand for the Council as her father and grandfather had before her.

But now . . .

She ripped the letter neatly down the middle and put it in the waste-paper basket behind the firescreen. Then she paced up and down the sitting-room from oriel to door and back again, nibbling furiously at her thumbnail and trying to think what the hell to do. April didn't care, that was obvious. May had quarrelled with Sibbie and never saw her now, but the way she kept smiling at her during the funeral made Bridie wonder how deep the quarrel went. She wasn't going to risk telling May and seeing that smile again.

As for March: March had never had any patience with Bridie Williams. The very first time Bridie had gone to tea with the Risings, March had been cross with her. She had been in a state of irritation with her ever since.

What was Sibbie *thinking* of? How *dared she*? She was an interloper, when all was said and done. Bridie knelt on the oriel seat and stared down Brunswick Road. Fred Luker's Wolseley, gas bag breathing gently, came raggedly beneath her window. Bridie had not yet forgiven Fred for taking Chattie away summarily, but she leaned out and waved anyway. Fred was Sibbie's sister and they got on fairly well. Fred might be willing to talk some sense into her.

But he didn't see her. The car jogged on to the Spa Pump Rooms and disappeared from her view.

'Blast and dammit,' she said loudly and withdrew her head. Then she went to the empty fireplace and fished behind the screen for the two pieces of her letter. She smoothed them out on the carpet and crouched on hands and knees to read the letter again. Tolly's name was not mentioned. 'My daughter and her husband' — that's all it said.

She folded the two pieces of paper carefully and put them in her handbag. Then she went downstairs to the hall and the telephone. Marlene was singing in the kitchen; 'The White Cliffs of Dover'. Bridie could just about recognize it. She got hold of 'trunks' and asked for a London number. There were the usual clicks and clacks. She removed the phone and rubbed her ear. 'Marlene!'

'Yes miss?'

'Just shut up, will you?'

'Sorry miss. I'm mincing.'

'What's that got to do with anything?'

'I always sing when I'm mincing, miss. It makes the rissoles taste nicer.'

'Oh for God's . . . Mannie? Is that you darling? What are you doing, can you talk for a moment?' She banished Marlene with an impatient wave and stood very close to

the mouthpiece. 'It's Bridie. Yes. I know it's early, darling.
The post has just been and brought something interesting.
I want to talk to you about it straightaway.' She realized
that the silence from the kitchen was now a listening one.
She turned round and yelled. 'You can go on singing now
Marlene!'

'Righty-ho miss.'

'Nothing, Mannie. Just that idiot girl. Listen my dear,
Sibbie Luker is contesting the will. What? I can't hear you
. . . Sibbie what? Oh well, if you must be so precise, yes,
Sibbie Williams. Well, I don't know how good a case she's
got. Surely she must have *some* case, otherwise the
solicitors wouldn't be taking her seriously. I mean, it's
absolutely ludicrous, but you know the law is an ass, and
there's always a chance she might win.' She stopped
talking and listened. 'You know you're welcome at any
time, my dear. It's just that the girls are so insanely
jealous. Yes, I could do that, of course. Book you into the
Bell, shall I? A single room with bath if possible — how
many nights? Well, that's marvellous, Mannie. Are you
sure you can spare . . . oh, you're such a flatterer!' She
listened, her tense face gradually relaxing into a
Chsehire-cat smile. After a while she gave a laugh. 'Well,
if you must know, I'm wearing blue silk, the one you
bought for me. Yes, it's next to my skin in places — I'm
wearing a waist slip. Do you *have* to know that? Mannie,
you're terrible. Really. Satin. White satin.' She laughed
again then said, 'Shall I meet you at the station? You'll
come straight here, will you? Yes, we'll go out for dinner if
you don't mind. I can't stand looking at Olga's face much
longer. Silent accusation does not suit her!' Another
laugh, then she made a kissing sound and replaced the
receiver.

'. . . and joy ever after, tomorrow, when the world is
free . . .'

'Oh Marlene, do shut up!' she shouted. And dialled the
number of the Bell hotel. As she waited for them to reply
she reflected that if only Mannie would wear something

besides black and perhaps change his name by deed poll to Stone, he wouldn't be such a bad catch at all.

After prayers that morning, the Lower and Upper Fifth forms were asked to stay behind for a special announcement. The orchestra played the dispersal march and the rest of the school filed out, wide-eyed and curious. Dr Moore descended the steps of the dais and stood among the remaining girls.

'Please sit,' she said quietly and waited while they did so, her arms folded inside her gown, her mortarboard nodding slightly as she looked at them.

'Girls, I have something tragic to report. I considered whether I should tell you at all, then realized it was my duty to protect you and the only way I could do that was to acquaint you with the facts.'

She paused. Olga turned her head and met Davie's eyes. It could only be a another death; the brother or father of one of their number. Davie clenched her hands on her lap.

'For some months last year and into this year too, you will remember we shared our school with another. We rarely met but I think you will agree that we acted as hostesses to the girls from Birmingham.' She waited and one or two braver souls nodded agreement. 'Quite. Hostesses. And hostesses have a great responsibility to their guests. They protect them. They guard them. They care for them. Would you not agree with that also?' A few more nods this time. Davie began to relax. Nothing to do with the armed forces, obviously. Dr Moore dropped her head almost to her pigeon chest. 'I'm sorry to have to tell you, girls, that we failed in that duty. We permitted one of these girls to become embroiled with a man. A ne'er-do-well. You can imagine with what result.'

There was a moment for the imagination. Most of the girls looked puzzled.

Dr Moore said, 'Naturally that girl is disgraced for ever. Her life is ruined. She should have known better, but evidently she did not. And in view of the terrible danger

166

of such ignorance . . .' the voice became familiarly brisk. 'The staff and I have decided that beginning in September, there will be an additional subject on the curriculum. Miss Lilybrook will incorporate this into her human biology lessons. But there will be a time for questions. If you find direct questioning something of an embarrassment, as I have no doubt you will, you may drop anonymous question papers into a box provided and she will deal with them one by one. We want you to be frank, girls. We cannot have this sort of thing happening again. Not ever.' She took a short walk up and down the line of violin stands. Then looked up. 'Very well. That is all.' And she left them.

Wild surmise was kept in check until they reached their formrooms, then it ran rife. Miss Miller, Davie's form mistress, gave her charges ten minutes to themselves, then walked purposefully to her desk. She was a short, dry woman, but before the war, at Heidelberg University, she had fallen in love.

She said, 'I think many of you are puzzled. Let me tell you the facts. One of the Birmingham girls was seduced by a young man while she was resident in Gloucester. Since returning home it has been discovered that she is expecting a baby.' She looked around. 'I think we will not talk about this any more. If you wish to know anything relevant to the case, you may come to me privately and ask me.'

Nobody went to her. It was too ghastly to talk about, too ghastly to contemplate. Davie lifted her desk lid and wondered whether Audrey Merriman knew the poor girl concerned.

Fred turned the Wolseley left at Spa Road and drove down to Southgate Street, then into the Bristol Road. The gas bag did not allow much speeding and there was plenty of time to consider what he would say to Charles Adair. Charles practically ran the Observer Corps and Fred the Home Guard. In spite of past differences, it was necessary

167

for them to get together, but it was not going to be easy. Fred had acquired a great deal of the Adair holdings when he had discovered that they belonged to Mrs Tilly Adair; he had done so by the tried and trusted method of seducing her right under her husband's nose. He had then sold the land to the City Council for building a new outer circle road at considerable profit to himself. When Tilly had become tiresome, he had blackmailed Charles into getting her off his back. The enmity between them went very deep indeed and it was going to be difficult to find some kind of working relationship. Luckily these days Charles Adair was something of a local hero, so with pride well restored he might be more approachable. When Fred had telephoned him at the Corps headquarters in Northgate Mansions half an hour previously, Adair had sounded jovial enough.

'Come straight out to the house, Luker, can you? I've done a night duty and I'm packing up here now. I can give you an hour before I flake out. Will that do?'

'Certainly. Thanks.'

There was a short pause then Adair said in the same jovial tone, 'Tilly won't be there. You're quite safe.'

Fred braked at the level crossing and waited while a goods train loaded with tanks chugged across. He tightened his mouth against an unwilling grin; he had to admit he was glad Adair was going to be out-in-the-open frank with him about the past. He was sick to death of the innuendoes, the veiled looks, the ill-hidden dislike which was the atmosphere created by March these days. The rows and bad temper had been masked when Chattie returned to Bedford Close. March did her best to preserve an outward appearance of congeniality for the girl's sake, but beneath the veneer she swung from irritation to anger, from coldness to contempt.

He turned into Quedgeley and found the house strangely different from how he remembered it. Weeds grew up in the gravel drive, and the modern metal window frames were rusting through their white paint. Also the Adairs' Rover, run on black market petrol, was not outside. Fred cursed and sat back to wait.

He was just reaching for cigarettes in the map pocket, when the front door opened and Tilly Adair emerged. He cursed again. What the hell had happened. This would be extremely embarrassing.

But Tilly did not look at all embarrassed. She was dressed smartly, in her green WVS uniform, no hat, her short hair curling girlishly around her ears without a trace of grey. He remembered the last time he had seen her when he blacked her eye. He waited for the scathing comment.

She came round the car to the driver's side. She was smiling; actually smiling.

'Well, this is a surprise, Fred. I'd just got in from canteen duties and the phone rang and Charles warned me — told me to behave myself!' She laughed. She had always laughed a lot for not much reason. He waited for it to get on his nerves, but it didn't. He hadn't heard much laugher lately.

'He said you wouldn't be here.'

'Well, he should know my itinerary by now. Anyway he said he would be late and would I get you a drink and behave myself.' She laughed again, throwing back her head and showing a long line of throat above her collar and tie. She stopped laughing and crouched by the window. 'Aren't you pleased to see me, Fred, after all these years? I'm terribly pleased to see you.'

Christ, was it all going to begin again? Was she that much of a fool after what had happened between them? What the hell was going on? Fred forced a grin and got out of the car and let himself be led inside. If Adair had planned this . . . If he'd got the idea he would break in on a love scene and kill them both . . . it was too silly for words.

She went down the hall into the kitchen. The whole place was a mess, the sink piled high with crocks, dirty cups and strewn cutlery covering every surface. Fred had

169

lived like this as a boy, and one of the joys of his marriage to March had been her high standard of cleanliness; these days he was more fastidious than she was herself. His nose wrinkled. Tilly threw up her hands.

'Darling, I'd forgotten you were such a fusspot. Into the sitting-room with you while I get the drinkies. Go on — off — off —' she shooed him out, laughing inanely and he went if only to avoid physical contact with her. The sitting-room was no better, if you substituted overflowing ashtrays for tableware. It smelled stale and he opened French windows into the overgrown garden and stood breathing in the summer air.

Tilly came in behind him, a bottle tucked under one arm, wet glasses and a damp towel on a tray. She plonked everything down on a side table and began to rub at the glasses. She hadn't changed after all. She had gone right back to the 'silly Tilly' she'd been before she became enslaved by him. He remembered that at first there had been attractions. Only when she had followed him around, weeping and wailing that she loved him, had she become unbearable.

Following his line of thought he said, 'What happened to your dog?'

'Buster Keaton? Charles got fed up when he became incontinent and we had him put down. You can still smell him sometimes when it gets hot.' She sniffed luxuriously. 'I loved that dog.'

'Yes. I remember.'

She handed him a drink and laughed again. 'What about that first time, Fred. D'you remember you had to feed the poor old Buster our lunch before he'd let you get into bed with me?'

He glanced at the door, practically waiting for Charles to make his appearance. 'That's enough, Tilly,' he said lamely.

'Oh I know it was. For you.' She sipped her drink, still smiling. 'You're the kind of man who only wants women when the chase is on. Now if I'd played my cards right —'

'Tilly, it was wonderful. It's over. It's been over for three years now. You know that.'

She nodded with amazing equanimity. 'I had to learn that the hard way, didn't I?'

Was she getting at him? That last scene back in '37 had been terrible; he realized how near he had come to killing her. He swallowed. 'Look . . . I'm sorry.'

'Don't be.' She moved away and sat down in one of the enormous armchairs. 'I'm all right now, Fred. Probably I'm much better.' She gave that laugh again. 'In fact I know I'm much better. My boy friend is very flattering.' She fluffed at her girlish curls. 'I had a good teacher.'

She was telling him he wasn't the only pebble on the beach and she had gone on to better things. He accepted this and relaxed slightly, taking the chair opposite hers and sipping at his drink. He'd hear Adair's car anyway.

Tilly wanted to boast. 'He's Polish actually. Came over and joined the RAF when old Adolf went into his country. He's a count.' She spoke airily, sipping at her drink between sentences. It was good whisky; Adair must have contacts all over the place.

He said, 'Good for you. And . . . how is Robin these days? I take it he and his father have got over the evacuation business?'

'Well . . . Charles certainly has. He revelled in it. But Robin — you know how delicate he's always been, Fred. He's been terribly peaky since then. He's picking up slightly now but for two or three weeks . . . That friend of yours, is it Mrs Hall? Her daughter has always been a staunch supporter of Robin's'. Again the laugh but with a trace of anxiety this time. 'She is quite a little helpmate at the moment.'

'Olga? She's only fourteen you know, Tilly.' He had successfully steered the conversation away from her conquests, but he had forgotten that she was a besotted mother.

'Yes, I know. But the girls these days mature so quickly and Robin has a charmingly young streak in him. They

171

get on famously. I expect he can help her with her homework.'

'Probably.' Thank God a similar friendship with Davina had been only temporary.

Tilly upended her glass, then said, 'Actually, Charles is on a field course this weekend and I'm going to show my Polish friend how lovely the Cotswolds are at this time of year.' Another giggle. 'I nearly cancelled it when I realized Robin would be alone here, but he was most insistent that I should go. He is completely unselfish, that boy. Completely.'

Gravel crunched outside and a car door slammed. Tilly made no move to compromise Fred and when Charles appeared they were both sitting back with empty glasses. However Charles did not appear to be disappointed.

'Hello Luker. Sorry about this. Delayed at the last minute.' He took Tilly's glass and poured himself a whisky. She said automatically, 'Don't ask me if I want another,' and he, with an equal lack of resentment replied, 'You've had enough already.' Then he took the bottle over to Fred and filled his glass. 'Why the hell are you tanking around with that gas bag, Luker? Not your style is it?'

Fred nodded thanks for the drink and waited while Charles downed his in one gulp.

'No petrol,' he explained.

'Don't give me that, old man. If I can get the stuff, you can.'

'Yes. I daresay I could. But how would it look to my customers? A garage owner has to be very careful indeed.'

Adair drank and scoffed again. 'Garage owner my foot. You'll have me in tears next.'

'Officially I run Rising and Luker's. That's my job.' Fred felt at a disadvantage in the low chair and struggled to his feet. 'I wanted to talk to you about liaison between the Corps and the Home Guard. Obviously we need notification of enemy movements—'

Charles guffawed. 'Expecting landing craft up the river

are you, old man? You'll be the first to know — that I promise!'

Fred wandered through the French windows and Charles followed perforce. 'Thanks, old man.' Fred's voice was as dry as dust. 'What about aircraft?'

Charles moved across the knee-high lawn and pretended to sniff a rose. 'No instructions about informing the Home Guard of any plots we make, old man. Air raid wardens, yes. Home Guard, no.' A thorn caught in his jacket sleeve and he pulled away irritably. 'Damnd garden going to seed for want of attention. You'd think Tilly . . . other women seem to find time . . .'

'I was thinking of paratroop landings.'

Charles guffawed again. 'I think I can safely promise you a quick phone call when they start coming down, Luker. Or you might even spot them yourselves.'

Fred had known it wasn't going to be easy. He had lost his taste for this sort of manoeuvring and suddenly wanted to hit Adair very hard.

He said, 'You're right, the garden could do with a bit of attention. How about Robin? Or is he busy elsewhere?' Charles became still. Fred could see his eyes flicking unseeingly over the wilderness of roses and knew that unwittingly he had found a weak spot. Robin had been up to something again. Surely to Christ not with Olga Hall? Bridget would personally dismember him if there was anything like that.

Charles said at last, 'So you know do you? Trust you. My God, they promised me they'd keep it quiet for the sake of the girl.'

'No-one else knows,' Fred assured him with perfect truth.

'Then how the hell did you—'

Fred contented himself with a shrug.

'I suppose when the bloody headmistress at Denmark Road gave it out, the girls put two and two together.' Charles let his breath go in an explosive sigh and kicked at the rose roots. They were old and gnarled and he

173

winced. 'You haven't changed, Luker. Threats, blackmail, women, you usually get what you want.'

Fred said mildly, 'In this case it's only a telephone call when you have a plot. It doesn't seem much to ask in wartime, old man.' He grinned. 'And you haven't changed much yourself. Throwing Tilly at my head like that.'

Charles looked up, suddenly more affable. 'No. No, perhaps you're right. I must admit when you rang this morning I wondered if it might be a chance to get this bloody Polish count out of my hair!, He laughed. 'What between a randy wife and a randy son—'

'You're not so pure yourself, are you?'

That pleased him. His guffaw rang around the garden. They went back inside and had another drink, and Charles became maudlin and talked about 'your beautiful sister-in-law'. For a moment Fred thought he was referring to April and very nearly smashed his glass in the smug face. But then he realized it was May. There had been that business between May and Adair before Gretta came along. For a moment he wondered about Gretta, then recalled her likeness to Monty. He must ask March exactly what had happened. Or perhaps not.

He left when Charles fell asleep in his chair. Tilly came to the door with him, still smiling reminiscently. He got into the car and grinned back at her, and she rushed across the gravel, leaned in through his open window, and planted a kiss on his mouth.

He drove home thoughtfully. There was, after all, a great deal to think about.

Ten

THE wedding was arranged for the last Saturday in August. Mrs Doswell wanted a full-scale affair. The church was to be decorated early for Harvest Festival, so would be a bower of flowers and fruit. The Women's Institute were pressed into doing the reception and the village hall booked well in advance. She wanted George to be in grey topper and tails. Naturally he rebelled.

'I'm not going to eclipse our Lizzie,' he said fondly. 'It's her day, hers and Tommy's. He and Jack will be in full regalia I take it, and she'll have your white dress—'

'No Daddy.' Elizabeth was unexpectedly firm about this. 'I'm thrilled about the church and the hall and everything. But I shall be married in uniform too. It's wartime and I'm a nurse.'

Albert felt a pang of pride in her. She was everything he could possibly wish for in a wife. He must never forget it. It was as if he was marrying her family and the farm, not just Lizzie. He had to remind himself sometimes that they would live alone together, not at the farm. The farm would belong to Jack.

Ellen Doswell sat with pen poised above a pile of invitations.

'Tommy, I cannot believe you're serious when you say you want no guests. There must be someone.' She looked at him directly. 'You cannot leave your mother out, Tommy. You simply cannot.'

He returned her look. 'I'm sorry, Mrs Doswell. You see if I ask my mother, my stepfather will come too. And I cannot . . . if you and George are there, then I have family enough.

She gave an inverted smile that was near to tears and eventually accepted it. It was obvious to them both that the family quarrel must go very deep if Tommy had left England in '37 because of it. George Doswell thumped him on the back.

'So be it, Tommy my boy. Just remember that — even when we get on your nerves. We're family. All right?'

It *was* all right. It reinforced the feeling he'd had all along of a composite marriage. He read the Solemnisation of Matrimony in the prayer book and thought that the phrase 'keep thee only unto her' was perhaps a little too exclusive in the circumstances.

Elizabeth must have felt the same.

'Tommy, . . . darling Tommy. You've been part of the family from the moment you arrived here. You need never feel an orphan while you're with us.

He had never felt an orphan before. In Spain he had been one of many outcasts, but not orphaned. Now, he supposed that was what he had been.

He went back to active duty with a completely different attitude. For one thing the squadron was well and truly 'blooded' and there was no longer a gulf between him and his fellow fliers. The three months in Sedan had bound them together. The RAF had not been popular at the time of Dunkirk, the Army had considered they had been let down by their flying men; the 'Brylcreem boys' had it easy when they were sweating in the mud. But men like Albert who had been shot down trying to provide a respite for the evacuation, had done much to heal the breach; and now with the Battle of Britain well under way, the RAF were seen to be the guardians of the narrow moat between the fortress of Britain and the marauding barbarians who were laying siege to her. Air Vice Marshal Keith Park came down to Westhampnett to pin on three Distinguished Flying Crosses, one of which went to Albert. Park had flown a Hurricane over the French coast observing the combined tactics of Air Force, Army and Navy, and had actually seen Albert's Spitfire go into the sea.

In hospital Albert had thought the decoration would mean less than nothing to him. In the event he discovered that the honour was enormous. He caught sight of George and Ellen among the audience; Elizabeth was on duty and could not attend the ceremony. The Doswells had brought with them a copy *Tess of the D'Urbevilles* inscribed 'To Tommy with all my love and congratulations'. As he lay uncomfortably in an armchair in the readiness room, waiting to be scrambled, he began to read it.

On 16th August, the squadron were scrambled four times. The ground crew worked frantically to keep the Spitfires going. The first time up it was to defend a convoy in the Solent from a Dornier attack. The second time Messerschmidts appeared above the airfield and destroyed three aircraft before they could become airborne. The third time they were sent up to try to intercept the raid on Brize Norton, and the fourth time was when Jack Doswell was killed.

With Stukas screaming at them like klaxons the Spitfires took off all over the airfield. The pressing urgent need to get off the ground before they were blown up superseded all other considerations. Albert, keeping low over the trees, easing his stick towards his chest, caught a glimpse of Jack in his mirror, the six red hearts on his fuselage identifying him instantly. They climbed into the air as if strung together with invisible wire, and both banked to come in on the airfield with the sun behind them. Albert got the wingspan of a Stuka within the semi-circle of his sights and pressed the firing button. The enemy aeroplane belched black smoke and nose-dived. Albert jinked his Spit above the hangar and banked again. Behind him Jack was completing his circuit too, and appeared to have missed his quarry. But they weren't the only ones to use the setting sun for cover.

There was a saying in the readiness room, 'Beware the Hun in the Sun'. In Albert's mirror, very clearly, appeared the reflection of a Stuka on Jack's tail. There was nothing he could do. If Jack saw it there was not much he could do either. His wing became ragged as bullets tore into it. Then the Spitfire disintegrated in a ball of fire. Albert watched it happening, unable to take his eyes away from the mirror, his hand automatically pulling the stick towards him to climb away from the airfield, his feet on the rudder pedals taking him into a wide banking turn so that he could return to the attack. He could not believe the evidence of his eyes. Many of his fellow pilots had been killed, but Jack was a member of his new family. Jack and he were more than fellow pilots; they were brothers.

He completed his turn and climbed vertically this time, his eyes on the killer Stuka. It was heading out towards sea, making for home. He kept after it. The radar aerials at Ventnor flashed beneath him; he was south of Worthy Down and still going. The Stuka was beginning to turn. It was making for the landfall of Portland, then straight across the Channel to the airport at Cherbourg. Albert got beneath and closed the distance. They crossed the coast. The sea seemed to be flicking at the belly of the Spitfire. The whole sky was red with sunset. Beneath his starboard wing the enormous bow of Chesil Beach swooped away.

He remembered Jack's schoolboy grin; the way he had so obviously manoeuvred the meeting with Elizabeth, his pleasure when Albert asked him to be best man at the wedding. The Spitfire was beneath the Stuka and climbing up towards the soft underbelly. In approximately three seconds the nose of the Spit would gouge a hole between the two black crosses. Albert pressed his firing button, not bothering to sight the guns. It didn't matter any more. He wanted to die.

178

But it was not his time. The Stuka blew up and fell beneath him instantaneously. He screamed over the flaming wreckage, climbed, banked, watched it settle into the sea. No trace of pilot, parachute, life-jacket. It was over. An eye for an eye.

He headed for home, his face wet with tears.

It was on that same Friday in August that Emmanuel Stein and Bridget Hall were married in Gloucester Registrar's Office. They were attended by five very sulky girls and one sprightly boy. Marlene and Monty Gould were witnesses.

Bridget had taken an invitation to April, knowing full well what the answer would be. Then she chose to be piqued by the expected reaction.

'I thought you were my best friend,' she wailed as she watched the colour drain from April's thin cheeks. 'You could at least pretend to be happy for me!'

People rarely passed on gossip to April these days and she had had no idea of the furtive courtship going on between Bridget and Mannie Stein. She remembered that last autumn Bridget had been anxious to find a way of proving poor Tolly's death, but when that had been finally legalised, she had heard no more.

She said, 'You know how I feel about Mannie Stein, Bridie. He fills me with horror. You cannot do this thing. You simply cannot.'

The small malicious spark of pleasure Bridie had felt at bursting her bombshell, disappeared in the face of April's appalled concern.

'Darling, I am going to do it. My God, all the fuss. You assured me ages ago that the rift between you and Mannie Stein had been solely to do with David's business. He and Mannie were partners — David became insanely jealous of Mannie because he looked sideways at you — and he wasn't the only man in Gloucester to do that, after all — they had a blazing row and split up! That was sixteen years ago, April. Sixteen *years*.

179

'He hasn't changed,' April said whitely. 'D'you remember when he brought you news that Tolly was safe? When was that — four years ago? He threatened David then.'

'Rubbish. He's told me about that. He came on an errand of mercy and David imagined he'd come after you. I'm sorry, April, but David is neurotic about the man and he's made you the same.'

'He tried to spread a rumour that Davie was his child, Bridie! You know that — you told me yourself!'

'*He* said no such thing. That was Charles Adair's little bit of gossip.'

'Bridie, *please*! He's only doing this thing for his own ends. Believe me.'

April had gone too far. Bridget drew a deep and offended breath. 'I suppose we all get married because we want to, my dear. If that is doing something for our own ends, then so be it. I am afraid that David's obsession against poor Mannie has infected you. You cannot honestly believe he is marrying me so that he can look at you every day, can you? Honestly darling —' her tone became cruelly light, '— tempus has been fugiting, you know. You will be forty soon, April. And you haven't looked after yourself like I have. Take a look in the mirror my dear and . . . relax!'

Bridie felt tears pricking her eyes. She loved April. Her thinness, her fading golden hair, the roughness of her long-fingered hands . . . they were precious to Bridie. And she hated herself for deriding them.

She turned abruptly.

'I want you to come. I want your blessing. But if I can have neither of those things then I am still going to marry Mannie. So that's that.'

She left, thinking that the whole family would follow April's example. Strangely, May did not.

'I'm stuck with Gretta,' she explained in a letter. 'But if Monty can snatch an hour from the office he will be there to represent all of us.'

Bridie was touched. She had always enjoyed a flirtatious relationship with May's actor husband; his warmth and sympathy had helped her more than once in the past. She could guess that May and Monty were worried about the future of Williams and Sons, and were doubtless influenced by such considerations, but even so . . .

March and Fred, of course, possessed a telephone. March rang the Brunswick Road house immediately she received her invitation.

'You're a damned fool,' she told Bridie bluntly. 'You've got money and your freedom. Why tie yourself to an underhand—'

'I suppose for the same reason that you married Fred, March dear,' Bridget interrupted her. 'They're not dissimilar really, are they?'

March put the phone down.

After the marriage there was a meal at the New Inn. Catherine, the youngest of the Hall girls, found an earwig in the famous courtyard, secreted it in her pocket and introduced it into Mannie's lettuce leaf. When the meal began he discovered the earwig and lifted it, lettuce and all, on to Olga's plate.

'Yours I believe, daughter?' he said with his unmistakable accent.

She flushed puce. There was no point in denying it, and in any case by watching Catherine's act without protesting she had become part of it. Catherine giggled happily and jogged her sister's elbow when the wine was poured so that two glasses went flying.

'Oh Olga, honestly!' Bridie said, bored by the silent thunder coming from the children.

Monty saved the day by pretending to suck the wine from the tablecloth. Then he proceeded to get tipsy and at the end of the meal stood up to make a speech which began unfortunately, 'Let bygones be bygones. Let the dead bury their dead. Let the . . .'

181

The siren went and the party broke up hurriedly and repaired to the cellars. Reports came from someone who knew someone in the Observer Corps that there was a raid somewhere near Oxford, perhaps the training school at Brize Norton. They emerged, flurried and still drunk, into a golden afternoon. 'Well, we had better be on our way, wife,' Mannie said, arranging Bridie's silver fox a little lower on her shoulders in view of the heat. He bent and kissed her exposed neck. 'The carriage awaits.'

He had of course got petrol and a car. They were going to Weston-super-Mare for the weekend. London was out of the question now, and Bridie had wanted to be by the sea.

'Goodbye darlings.' Bridie kissed them all, wanting them to cry. They did not. Tears ran down her own cheeks. 'Oh Mannie darling—'

He got her into the car and went round the other side. 'Goodbye my children.' He slid in by Bridget and enfolded her in his arms. He made the kiss very long and possessive. Only Monty responded with a loud war whoop. Marlene looked at her charges and her mouth turned down.

'Well, at least Marlene shed a tear when I left,' Bridie said as they drove over the deserted Cross. 'The girls . . . even Barty . . . they're heartless. Heartless, Mannie.'

'They need a father, wife. Now they have one.'

Mannie smiled as he drove into the sun.

Back home Olga went straight to the phone and dialled the number of the Quedgeley house. Luckily Robin answered.

'Oh Robin, he's awful!' she wept. 'He calls me daughter and he keeps calling her wife, and I know he hates us all. I know it!'

'Baby . . . baby . . . just calm down. Tell your Robin all about it and he'll understand.'

'Robin, I'm so glad I've got you, what would I *do* without you now? Oh Robin, I can't say much, someone will be sure to hear. But you know. *You* know, don't you. Oh Robin . . .'

'See you tomorrow, baby. They'll both be gone by midday and you'll be waiting behind the hedge as usual, won't you?'

'Oh yes, Robin.'

It was a long walk to Quedgeley and at first she had felt degraded that she had to lurk among the laurels until Robin's parents had departed. But now she would walk a hundred times as far and lurk for days if it meant she could have him all to herself. Someone of her very own. Like her father had been.

Albert thought they should postpone the wedding. The memorial service for Jack was on the 24th and all the village came, besides the enormous offshoots of the Doswell family. It seemed indecent that just one week later they should all turn up again for a wedding. Elizabeth was stunned. Her feminine roundness seemed to shrink, her Jessie Matthews vitality was dimmed. To whatever was suggested she nodded agreement.

But George and Ellen were adamant. Ellen said strongly, 'He would want it to go through as planned. Jack was so happy about you and Lizzie . . . he would want it.'

And George put a heavy hand on Albert's shoulder.

'We've lost a son. We want another, Tommy. The sooner the better. Please.'

Albert, taught how to be undemonstrative by his mother, suddenly put his arms around the older man. He had never had a father. He closed his mind to Fred.

He said, 'You've still got a son. When you came to that ceremony — that was when you became my father.'

The night before he was married he finished reading *Tess of the D'Urbevilles*. He closed the book and put it on the table by the side of his bed and lay looking at the white walls of his room at Doswells'. He knew he was tired to the bone. Only two weeks ago he had seen his friend killed and had killed his killer in return. Since then he had been scrambled at least twice a day and had had no time to think. The juxtaposition of violence and peace — the violence of the incessant dogfights and the peace of the place — was echoed in the book he had just finished. But there was something else in its pages which was just eluding him.

In spite of his exhaustion, he lay watching the daylight fade slowly in the dormer window, trying to discover what it was. As he slid into sleep at last, it came to him. Tess . . . Tess had a quality which reminded him of Davina.

Perhaps because of Jack's death, the wedding of his sister and his best friend was more significant than it would have been. Albert had accepted from the beginning that Elizabeth was not his first love; sometimes he was certain she knew that too. What might have been a pretty country wedding, sealing a very suitable match, became sweetly poignant. But it was also emphasised again that Albert was taking on much more than a wife. His fervent entry into the Doswell family had a spiritual quality of dedication that made Elizabeth a small part of it. And in her nurse's uniform, her billowing cap, the red ribbons crossed on her breast, she was a completely untraditional bride. She seemed to be giving herself to much more than a human marriage. Afterwards in the dust-moted village hall she did not smile demurely when the village wag shouted the traditional toast, 'May all your troubles be little ones.' She looked straight at Albert and lifted her glass solemnly. And when George and Ellen escorted them that evening to the tiny labourer's cottage which had been decked out for their one night together, George said with agricultural bluntness, 'Give us some grandchildren, Tommy. Let the house be filled with youngsters again. Then you'll see Ellen and Lizzie come back to life.'

They knew what was expected of them; they were not

shocked or put off by the fact that the hundred or so people at the wedding that day knew exactly where they were and what they were doing. They were more than stallion and mare; they were the future; England's hope.

But it was no good.

Elizabeth said anxiously, 'Is it your leg, my darling? D'you think they removed everything properly?'

'I don't know.' Albert felt all the bitterness of the last two weeks turn to gall in his stomach. 'Perhaps it's just tiredness . . . I don't know.'

'Don't worry, Tommy. Don't worry.' She lay on her side by him kissing and caressing him. She might have said, 'There's plenty of time.' But who could tell? Perhaps tonight would be all they would ever have. She breathed, 'You have done it before, haven't you, sweetheart?'

'In Spain there was a time . . . yes.'

'That's all right then. Wait a while. Just wait.'

He wasn't shocked by her acceptance of his fornication. There was no need to explain the circumstances, the way Tolly had shrugged — 'It might help to forget Davie for a couple of hours . . .' She wasn't interested. She had just wanted to check that he was aware of the mechanics of copulation.

In the end he might have managed something. He didn't quite know what happened. He was so tired he felt sick, and when Elizabeth whispered, 'Oh darling, I think it's all right. Oh darling . . . well done,' he just rolled away from her and dropped into an abyss of sleep.

During the previous winter and spring, when Bridie had spent so many weekends in London, she had slept with Mannie and knew that they were well suited in bed. After their marriage, the streak of cruelty which he had hidden so well, lent a certain spice to their passion at first. He would make her gasp and even scream, but she never pushed him away. One night in September when the throbbing of enemy bombers was everywhere, she gave him some of his own medicine. The next moment she was on the floor, her head singing from the swipe he had given her.

She clutched at her ear, sobbing furiously.

'Why the hell did you do that? My God, my head is ringing!'

He leaned casually on one elbow looking down at her, his black eyes glinting.

'If you ever try anything like that again, Birdy Stein, I will put you in hospital. Do you hear me?'

'But I only did what you do! I thought you would like it.' She sobbed and dragged at one of the sheets to cover herself. He pulled it away from her.

'I am the man. I am in control, always. You must understand that, my dear.'

'Tolly wasn't like that.'

'No. I am not Tolly. I am Emmanuel Stein. You are my wife. My little Birdy. Your children are now my children.'

She said angrily, 'And my house is your house. And my father's business is your business.' She waited for him to deny it, but he did not.

'Quite so. That is your law as well as mine, Birdy. That is why I forbade Olga to leave the house this weekend. That is why I go into the office each day—'

'And visit Sibbie at least once a week?' she cried bitterly.

'That too. In one year, perhaps two, your father's and grandfather's business will be yours once more, Birdy. Entirely yours. That I promise.'

She tried again to pull the sheet over her nakedness and was again baulked.

'Entirely mine . . . you mean entirely yours, surely?'

He shrugged. 'What is mine is yours, Birdy. You did not listen very hard to the marriage service, did you?'

She said nothing. The ack-ack guns by the greyhound track suddenly thumped into life. Mannie said idly, 'London is having a full basin tonight. Nearly a thousand people killed last week. Hitler knows what he is doing.'

She shivered at his indifference.

'I'm cold,' she whimpered.

'Then come back to bed, Birdy. I will keep you warm. Just as I will keep you rich and well-fed and well-clothed and a respected woman in Gloucester.'

'I don't think I want to sleep with you, Mannie Stein,' but there was a trace of coquetry in her voice.

'Then lie there where I can see you, Birdy. It gives me great pleasure. How old are you now — forty-two? Many women look old at forty-two, and after six children you should look old, babushka. But you do not look old. It must reassure you to think that I am fourteen years your senior. So you are truly an old man's darling. You like that, hein?'

'Oh Mannie. You're incorrigible. If I am your darling, how can you leave me here without my covers? I am prone to bronchitis you know — and that can lead to pneumonia.'

'I am waiting, Birdy. You will come to me in a moment.'

There was a massive earth-tremoring crunch and from above came Marlene's screams and a skittering sound as the girls got out of bed. Bridie leapt up and flung herself into Mannie's waiting arms. The next moment Olga was rattling the doorknob.

'Come on down to the cellar, Mummy, quick! That bomb fell somewhere by the park — come quickly!'

Bridie began to move but Mannie held on to her firmly.

'Mummy and I do not move from German bombs, daughter! he called. 'Go with Marlene. We are too busy just now to join you.'

There was a silence from outside the door, then Olga could be heard telling Marlene to shut up and bring Barty downstairs.

'That will thoroughly upset her!' Bridie hissed indignantly. 'Come on this instant!'

He held her. 'They must learn too, my Birdy. They must learn too.'

She groaned, but this time she made no mistakes.

The next day Gloucester — designated a safe area — counted the cost. Two tall houses almost opposite the memorial to the First War, were blackened shells. Glass was scattered far and wide. Another house had been sliced in half and a cast iron fireplace on the third floor still boasted two candlesticks on its mantelpiece, though it hung at a crazy angle.

It was Saturday and many of the city's children wandered past to look wide-eyed at the craters. Davie and Flo cycled from Winterditch Lane and joined Natasha and Beatrice Hall in Montpellier Road. Beatrice and Flora had started at the High School that month, Beatrice as a fee-paying girl, Flora as the youngest scholarship girl ever. They held hands across Flora's bike, a thing they had never done before. When Davie called to them sharply to come away, they obeyed without the usual protest, and followed the two older girls along Spa Road towards the play area in the park.

Fallen leaves were everywhere, and they scuffed through them, heads down, avoiding looking at the white marble memorial, though they could not have said why. Natasha called back, 'Cheer up chickens!' But Davie said, 'Let them be, Nash.' One of the bombed houses had been the home of the Midwinter ladies who had run the Midland Road School. Bridie and April had attended the school together, and later April had taught there. The house had been something of a monument for the Daker and Hall girls. 'Let them be,' Davie repeated.

Along by the swings were a batch of air raid shelters. Flora and Davie propped their bikes and scrambled on top of the grassy mounds to watch the trains going down to the docks. Natasha and Beatrice took the chains of the giant-stride and lolloped around after each other.

'Let's hide from them, Davie,' Flo whispered. 'Let's go into one of the shelters when they're not looking.'

Davie wasn't keen. Dirty old men sometimes urinated in the privacy of unoccupied air raid shelters; even worse, lovers would take up residence. But Flo was having a hard

188

time at school and last night's raid had terrified her. If this was a way of cheering her up then it was worth risking germs and embarrassment.

They slid down the blind side of the shelter and crept round to its mouth. Flo would have gone in first, but Davie held her back and went down the concrete steps with questing wrinkled nose and ears open for sounds of love. Both sense organs were immediate assailed. The smell was putrid, the sounds unmistakable, especially since the new human biology lessons from Miss Lillybrook (which had enlightened even that erudite lady, as well as her pupils).

Davie turned and stumbled back up shoving Flo ahead of her. As she was silhouetted against the daylight, a hoarse agonised voice from behind called, 'Davie! Oh God . . . Davie, is that you?

She pushed Flo out, but turned herself and looked down the tunnel of the shelter. A shape detached itself from the darkness and came towards her. It became grey and recognisable. It was Robin Adair.

'Davie, I swear to you — were you looking for me — oh my love. I've tried to reach you — take no notice of this — I've never stopped loving you, but your aunt said—'

A pitiful voice interrupted him. 'Robin! You said you loved *me*!'

Davie waited no longer. It was Olga's voice.

The Sunday post brought her a letter from Birmingham. After a silence of nearly five months, Audrey Merriman had written again.

'Dear Davina Daker,' the letter began in its usual formal way. 'I expect you have heard what happened to me. As you were in love with your cousin perhaps you will understand. Do you remember I said once I might ask you to do something for me? I am writing to ask you to contact my true love and tell him that he has a beautiful baby boy. I cannot write to him because if it gets out, he might be put in prison. But I would like him to know that

189

in spite of everything, I still love him and am proud to be the mother of his son. I realize it will be an embarrassing errand for you, but hope that you can find the courage to do it. He lives at Quedgeley House and his name is Robin Adair. With kindest regards. Your sincerely, Audrey Merriman. Will you tell him that I have called the baby Robert Alan so that he will have the same initials as his father? Thank you.'

Davina read and re-read the letter. Then she folded it over and over again until it was the size of a postage stamp, and put it in her handkerchief box next to the few she had received from Albert.

The following weeks, the blitz on London continued unabated. Bristol and Yeovil were attacked, but unsuccessfully. Everywhere people talked about the war, in the food queues, outside cinemas, in camouflaged public houses. In lowered voices in case a German spy was listening they discussed the latest news, the latest raid, the latest triumph for the RAF.

It was easy for Olga to avoid talking personally to her cousin. More lists were going up, this time for potato-planting, and when Davina said outright, 'Olga, I've got to see you about something terribly important,' Olga said desperately, 'In a minute Davie — I must get my name on the dig-for-victory list.'

And then David and April took the two girls to the Plaza picture house and there on the Movietone News was Albert. It put everything else out of Davie's head. It was simply a shot of a group of pilots on stand-by — 'our marvellous fliers taking a brief respite'. He was lying back in a wooden-armed chair, gazing open-eyed at the ceiling, a book lying face-down on his stretched legs. He looked terribly lonely, yet she knew he must be married by now, and anyway the comradeship of the RAF was well-known.

She went on staring at the screen long after the thin curtains had rippled across it and the lights were put up.

Then she glanced at her father. He nodded.

'Yes, it was Albie,' he said. 'And that book, it was one of Hardy's. I couldn't see which one, could you?'

'No.'

April said, 'Are you sure it was him, darling? Of course I haven't seen him for a long time I know, but his face looked . . . different.'

Flo said, 'It was him.' She sighed. 'The book was *Tess of the D'Urbevilles*. It's the saddest book in the whole world.'

April was sharply surprised. 'You haven't read *Tess*, Flo! It's much too old for you.'

David smiled. 'I lent it to her when she felt unhappy last summer.'

'Daddy told me that if I was going to be miserable I might as well be properly unhappy about something fictitious!' Flo explained to her mother.

David said wryly, 'She was worse than ever after.'

Flo nodded and Davie laughed with everyone else, knowing that Flo was deliberately taking the limelight away from her older sister. Last summer was when Flo had come on Robin and herself in the bathroom. Was that why she had been miserable?

By the time she had borrowed a copy of *Tess* from the library and read it, October was almost over. At last she managed to corner Olga in a deserted gymnasium and tell her about Audrey Merriman.

'You're lying!' Olga gasped, expecting something quite different, shocked out of any pretence she might have put up. 'He wouldn't . . . he loves me. Oh, I know you think you've got him where you want him, but that's just because you — you're so unattainable! Or you pretend to be! He thinks you're some ice maiden and only he can melt you! But I've told him about Albert and he realizes now that I'm the only one who really cares for him. As for the Birmingham evacuee — she's lying.'

'We can't both be liars, Olga!' Davie expostulated,

hating the whole thing so much she felt physically ill. 'Surely you remember Doc Moore's voice of doom last July? She must have heard about it then — can't you put two and two together for once? Robin Adair is no good! This is the second time — and both times it's been girls of our age! Don't be such an idiot, Olga — d'you want to be the third?'

Olga stared at her, round shoulders held determinedly back, short-sighted eyes squinting in the cavernous gym. She took a deep breath.

'Yes,' she said in a high voice. 'Yes. I would be honoured to be the third! So take your nasty little mind somewhere else, Davina Daker! You hate me and Robin because you can't have Albert Tomms! That's all it is — I know!'

She rushed off and Davina stood still, staring after her, sick to the heart in case she was right.

She wondered whether to tell her father. But what could he do? And her mother did two nights every week fire-watching at the cathedral and two days helping the billeting officer. Everyone was so terribly busy these days. Except Aunt Bridie. She no longer went into Williams and Sons' offices as she used to. Her new husband considered that wives should stay at home and look afer the house and the children. Davina did not want to tell Aunt Bridie; it was nearly tale-bearing. But after a week of worrying about it there seemed nothing else to do. Of course she could do that — nothing. But then how would she feel when Olga had to go through the same terrible disgrace as Audrey? Miss Lillybrook had made it quite clear what happened when the 'final act' took place.

Davina waited until a Saturday when her mother was to leave the house at three o'clock in the afternoon to mount guard in the cloister. Flo had gone to tea with Steffie Johnson who had moved into the lane when her father was stationed at the Winterditch camp, and Davie asked if she could cycle into Gloucester with her mother and come back home with her father. April was doubtful.

'It's cold and it's raining and it'll be dark soon,' she objected.

'Daddy would be so pleased to see me in the shop,' Davie wheedled. 'And when we cycle home together we always sing and he's so happy.' She knew that would persuade her mother. The thought of Daddy singing as he cycled home in the dark would be enough for her.

'Oh . . . all right!' April hugged her daughter to her. 'Hey. D'you realize you're nearly as tall as I am? And I was the tallest girl in Gloucester in my day!'

Davie pulled her mouth down. She hated being tall for herself; but Albert had never minded.

She left her mother at the Northgate Street end of St. John's Lane. Supposedly she was going straight over the road to Daker's Gowns. However as soon as April's rear mudguard had disappeared past the gas-lit second-hand shop, she scooted off up to the Cross and turned into Eastgate Street, then right at Brunswick Road. It was foggy and almost dark. The clock on the Co-op building was glimmeringly lit: four o'clock. Aunt Bridie might be in the kitchen getting tea for everyone. Davie wondered whether she could avoid the girls by going around the back. Olga wasn't there, she'd gone up to Quedgeley yet again. But when Aunt Bridie forbade her to see Robin, Natasha would report on Davie's visit and she would guess the rest.

Davie propped her bike at the side of the house and clambered over the padlocked side gate. The blackout hadn't been done yet and she could look in the top half of the kitchen door and see Marlene sawing away with the bread knife at a cottage loaf. On the table behind her was a big bowl of watercress, a dish of jam and some swiss rolls. Davie thought of the kippers which she knew Aunt Sylv had for their high tea and felt sympathy with the Hall girls.

She tapped on the glass and Marlene jumped a mile, then clucked towards her.

'You frit me to death, Miss Davie,' she said, patting her

193

bibbed front dramatically. 'An' if you'm after Miss Olga, you'm unlucky, 'cos she's gone to stay with a school friend for the weekend. An' Mrs Stein 'as gone out to look for a new dress for Christmas so—'

The door opened behind her and to Davie's horror Mr Stein appeared. Nothing had ever been said about Mr Stein by her family, but she knew in her bones that her father detested him, and that was enough for her. She turned to flee.

Mannie's voice was silky-smooth.

'Afraid, young lady? I thought the Dakers were supposed to be courageous?'

It was highly embarrassing. Obviously he knew how her father felt about him; after all, Uncle Monty had been the only one in the whole family to go to the wedding.

She turned slowly.

'I beg your pardon, Mr Stein. I came to see Olga, and Marlene says she's not in, so I thought I'd better go.'

'Not at all. If you'd given yourself time to see Olga, then you will have time on your hands. Come. We will have a cup of tea, Marlene. Upstairs in the sitting-room if you please. Davina . . . it is Davina, is it not? She will enjoy sitting in the oriel window and watching darkness come to the city.'

His slightly foreign phraseology was fascinating. And his manners so . . . impeccable. She knew instantly what her father disliked about him: his air of insincerity. But then those exquisitely Continental manners did seem insincere. And he was Olga's stepfather after all. She felt bound to be polite to him.

She had always loved the oriel room at the Brunswick Road house, but she had invariably had to share it with the horde of Hall girls, so that her turn at the window was limited to a few minutes. Mr Stein piled cushions in the deep seat and bowed towards it, and she sat sideways with her knees drawn up and her skirt over her ankles. Aunt Sylv had knitted her what was known as a pixie hood, and she let it drop back on the collar of her coat.

She felt very . . . Russian.

Mr Stein said, 'You are very much like your mother, Davina. Beautiful. Aristocratic. I have met you before but never tête-à-tête like this.'

She flushed to her pale hair roots, and ducked her head so that the hair swung to hide her face. She wondered why he laughed at that. Then Marlene came in with a tray and banged about putting it on the piano and standing the hot-water jug in the grate. He moved to the tray and busied himself with the cups, giving her time to cool down and look out at the traffic and decide on her course of behaviour.

'Thank you so much.' She took the cup and saucer with aplomb and held it at chest level. 'How simply fascinating it is to watch everything from so high up.'

'Quite. Like God. It is a good condition to practise.'

'Like God?' She was startled out of her assurance.

'Objectivity. It is not just the oriel, you know. It is a state of mind.'

She was genuinely interested and hardly noticed when he brought his own tea and sat beside her. There was barely room for two people on the window seat, and he held his tea with one hand while the other gently lifted her knees and tucked his own beneath them. Close up he looked very old, too old for Aunt Bridie really. His stubble was silver-white, a bit like Grandad's had been. She couldn't understand why Olga loathed him so much. It wasn't as if he was an evil man like Uncle Fred.

Her cup clattered in its saucer as she remembered it was about an evil man she had come here in the first place.

He said quietly, 'What is the matter, Lady Davina? Can you not tell an older gentleman like myself?' He gave that small laugh again. 'After all, we are practically related.'

She shook her head. 'Nothing is the matter Mr Stein. And actually, Aunt Bridie isn't really my aunt, you know. She and Mummy were great friends when they were children. That is all.'

'Ah . . . but may I tell you a secret, Lady Davina?'

195

She could not control the blushes again. 'Well . . .'

'A long, long time ago, before you were born, I was terribly in love with your mother. So you see if she hadn't been passionately in love with your father, it is just possible we might have been related. Do you understand?'

She understood. It was very romantic. It made her father's dislike of this man a little clearer too.

She stammered, 'I didn't know. I'm sorry. Were you . . . unhappy?'

'Terribly. Sometimes I am still. Can you understand that too?'

'Oh yes.' She was fervent. 'Oh yes . . . yes, I understand.'

'So if there is something troubling you — something you were going to ask Olga — I would deem it an honour if you could confide in me.'

'I — well — actually, I didn't really want to see Olga at all. In fact I knew she wasn't at home.'

'Then it was Natasha.'

'No. I thought I might . . . just . . . have a word with Aunt Bridie.'

'And she is not here. Aaaah. No wonder you turned to flee. Only a woman could hear what you have to say, yes? It is doubtless something about your mother and you are worried. She is ill?'

Davie began to feel extremely harassed and extremely warm. Her pixie hood seemed to contain a hot water bottle. She stammered, 'No — ' and began to explain that her mother was fire-watching at the cathedral. He interrupted, 'She is unhappy then? There is trouble between her and David?'

'No. Really . . .' Somehow she had to turn the conversation away from her mother; his eyes were burning with concern and obviously if he still loved her he was frantic with worry. 'No. It was about Olga. I'm terribly worried about Olga, Mr Stein.' After all, why not tell the truth? He might be able to help her more than Aunt Bridie, more than anyone.

He seemed almost disappointed. 'Aaaah. Olga. You are worried about Olga. What has she been saying at school? Tales about her new papa?'

This was worse and worse. If he guessed at some of the things Olga said. . . Davina gulped at some tea and coughed. He took her cup and patted her gently on the back. He smelled foreign. Like comfits. She blurted, 'I've had a letter from my friend in Birmingham. She was evacuated to Gloucester with her school and she stayed with the Adairs in Quedgeley. She has had a baby boy. And she says that Robin Adair is the father.' It came out in gasps between choking fits. She took a deep breath and concluded, 'That was what I came to tell Aunt Bridie.'

He said nothing for a long time. His hands, still on her shoulders, suddenly cupped her face, and he stared into her eyes as if he was about to eat her. She breathed fast and got her legs ready to shoot her off the window seat and halfway down the sitting-room.

Then he said, 'Are you worried about Olga then, liebchen? Yes, that is it. Before I came here to live, Olga had a great friend in Robin Adair. Now she visits a school friend nearly each weekend. Hein?'

Davie could not look at him any more. She dropped her head again and felt his hands dig into her cheek muscles. He released her slowly; his fingers slid over her shoulders and down her coat sleeves, and he picked up her hands and held them lightly.

'I think I understand your concern, Lady Davina. I thank you for having the courage to tell me this. You need worry no more.' He slid his legs adroitly from under hers and stood up, drawing her with him. She was conscious of feeling graceful and cherished. He pulled one of her hands into his elbow and walked her slowly down the long room. 'You are very close to your father, my dear, is that not so?'

Davie thought of David and his silent, loving concern for her. She whispered against sudden tears, 'Yes.'

'And you realize of course, that he is, like me, a Jewish man?'

Of course she knew, but he wasn't like Mr Stein, not a bit.

'Jewish fathers have a reputation for being very close to their daughters, Lady Davina. I am very close to Olga. There will be no more Robin Adair for her. That I promise you.

Davie made a sound. She wished she could forget Olga's agonised voice when she spoke of her love for Robin.

Mr Stein went on in his reassuring, stilted English. 'It was ordained that you should come here today and at this hour. When my wife and daughers were all out of the house and I was here alone.' They were outside the door and he preceded her down the stairs, then waited at the bottom to hand her off the last one as if she were made of china. 'Always it is the head of the house who must protect and guard the family. You understand this?'

It wasn't quite like that at home of course. The three adults, Aunt Sylv, Mummy and Daddy had kind of meetings about things. Very often she and Flo were called in as well to help make decisions. But the idea of Mr Stein shouldering all poor Aunt Bridie's worries and looking after her huge family, was rather nice. It was a bit like Victorian times. She nodded.

'You are a good girl as well as beautiful and aristocratic. One day you will make a wonderful wife and mother.'

That made her feel fluttery too. For the first time she thought about bearing Albert's children.

He opened the front door and came out with her to wheel her bike to the kerb and switch on her lights. Then, belive it or not, he kissed the back of her hand and waited while she cycled away. She turned into Eastgate Street again and then stopped to put on her woollen gloves. Of course, with Albert married to Elizabeth Doswell, it made everything impossible. Not that marriage had much to do with producing children, as Miss Lillybrook kept pointing out. Davie considered having a baby outside wedlock. It didn't sound as though Audrey Merriman minded much. And Olga had said she would be honoured. Davina felt her stomach flutter again. She knew she was being sinful just thinking about it. But it was better than thinking about Olga and how she had just told her precious secret to the stepfather she hated.

She left her bike beneath the fire escape in Northgate street and began the long climb to the rooms at the top where her father worked on his cutting. He opened the door to her special knock, his face alight with pleasure at the sight of her. She threw herself at him.

'Oh, I'm so pleased to see you — so pleased!' she told him.

He held her close, his chin just able to sit on the top of her pixie hood. His dark eyes, looking at the long table covered in bolts of Air Force blue serge, were unfathomable.

Eleven

BRIDIE was never to forget her arrival home that winter night. For once, she had taken all the children out with her. There was a special tea at the Bon Marché to celebrate the commencement of Lend-Lease, and Bridie had wanted Mannie to take them. When he had told her smoothly that he must spend an hour with Mrs Williams 'going over the books' she was furious, though she knew better than to show it.

'That's all right,' she said airily. 'I'll take them. It's too good to miss. There will be crackers and American waffles. Marlene can come to look after Barty.'

'No, Birdy. Marlene will be busy preparing tea. She will stay at home.'

Bridie drew a breath. 'I've just told you, dear. We'll be having our tea at the Bon.'

He made one of his foreign sounds of dismissal. 'An English afternoon tea! Not good enough for any of you. Marlene will prepare tea as usual. Besides, I need Marlene to get *my* tea. You can surely manage, dearest? Natasha and Beatrice are quite old enough to help with the little ones.' He kissed her affectionately. 'Dear little Birdy. Enjoy your Christmas shopping. And hurry back to your husband.'

She did not hurry back. None of them wanted to hurry back. For three hours it was almost like it had been when Kitty was alive. There was a proper orchestra at the Lend-Lease tea, and they played American tunes. One of them was 'Mr Franklin De Roosevelt Jones'. Charles Adair looked in for half an hour in between his duties with the Observer Corps, and he quickstepped Natasha around the floor; then Bridie.

'You've finished with me then?' he asked, pulling a comic face at her. 'My silk stockings and petrol weren't good enough. You had to find someone to make an honest woman of you.'

'Oh Charles . . .' she tried to laugh but the sudden recollection of her life before her second marriage, when Charles had spent time and money on trying to get her to bed again, and Monty Gould had flirted with her, and she had gone to the office and felt she was going on with Tolly's work, was almost too much for her. She leaned her cheek against his and closed her eyes. The trouble was, she had a very passionate nature, and Mannie could satisfy her physically. More than satisfy her sometimes.

'Regrets?' Charles whispered into her ear. 'I'm always here, you know. When Tilly goes off with her Pole at weekends we could use the house.' He snickered. 'At least we could use it with your Olga's permission.'

Bridie jerked away from him. 'Olga? What are you talking about, Chas?'

'Oh Christ. Have I put my foot in it? You know that Olga is Robin's latest?'

Bridie was genuinely horrified. 'Of course I didn't know. She is supposed to be with the Cresswell girl. D'you mean to tell me she's been spending weekends with Robin at your house?' She stared into his eyes. 'Charles . . . Charles, you should know better than to allow that! She is still fifteen! Fif*teen!*'

'And Robin's record is fairly poor,' he agreed, nodding. 'But darling, we're modern. I've told him what to do and he does it now. And the girl's mad for him — never gives him any peace—'

'Oh my God. Oh my poor Olga!'

'Come on Bridie! How old were you when you seduced Tolly?'

201

She did not protest. 'But Olga is so . . . different. She's like her father — introspective.' She let him put her into a reverse turn. 'Oh Charles. Does Robin really love her?'

He squeezed her very tightly. 'Like I love you, my darling. Like I love you.'

In many ways Bridie was a realist and she knew what that meant. They finished the dance in silence and he led Beatrice on to the floor.

'Mummy, this is such fun!' Natasha's eyes were brighter than they'd been since her grandmother died. 'Fancy Mr Adair turning up when he should be on duty!'

'Yes. Fancy.' Bridie refused to let her new knowledge spoil the afternoon for the girls. She took Natasha for a polka, and even Barty was whirled around between them for the Valeta. Then she danced with Charles again.

She said urgently, 'Chas, you must do something for me. Please. Take your car — now — immediately, and fetch Olga for me. Don't go inside the house, Mannie might be back by now. But make sure she goes in. Tell her I'll see her when I get home.'

'Darling . . . best will in the world . . . am on war work y'know . . .'

'Charles, if you don't do this for me I'll never speak to you again.'

'Not much chance of that anyway, old girl.'

'And I shall go out to your house myself and kick up such a stink—'

'Enough said. Message received loud and clear.' He wasn't taking any of it very seriously. He aimed a kiss at her nose and met Barty's silky head instead. 'Y'know, at one time I thought this little nipper might be something to do with me!' He laughed uproariously. 'God knows what happened after you left me that night, Bridie. I suppose there was an almighty row with Tolly and you made it up to him in your usual fashion?'

Bridie was so worried about Olga she hardly noticed the additional pang of remembering that night. If it had never happened, Tolly would still be with her now.

She timed her arrival back for six o'clock, giving Charles plenty of time to fetch Olga and leave her at the front door. She tried not to imagine the girl's shame at being discovered with Robin. She wouldn't be too hard on her. Just tell her that it must never happen again. Perhaps it would do her good in many ways; stop her being such a little prig.

She let Natasha and Beattie swing Barty between them down Brunswick Road, though it was no way to behave; but it was dark anyway. She held the two small girls, Svetlana and Catherine, by the hand. They were still young enough to enjoy twisting their heads into the fur sleeve of her coat now and then and snuffling like puppies. Brunswick Road was as dark as a tunnel and completely empty. The big Co-op department store was closed and the restaurant had long ceased serving evening meals. The Hall family seemed to fill the night with noise and life; but in between their chatter, Bridie though she heard a kitten crying.

'Hush a moment, children.' They hadn't had a cat since Tolly left them; if there was a stray it would be impossible for Mannie to turn it away. It would be something for Olga. 'I think I heard a cat.'

The girls stopped breathing. Barty said, 'What?' and was immediately shut up. Everyone listened. Clearly from the tall, three-storied house, there came a cry.

Natasha said, 'That's not a cat! That's Marlene crying again. Honestly, she does nothing but cry. Every time she opens one of those little books she reads, the tears just—'

The cry escalated into a piercing scream of pain and terror.

Svetlana whimpered, 'Mummy—' And Bridie said, 'Oh no. Oh my God. Please no.' And Beattie quavered, 'Mummy, that's Olga.' And Barty started to blubber.

Bridie pounded at the front door just once, and it was torn open by a frantic Marlene. They all crowded into the hall.

'It's Olga, miss.' Marlene's eyes were half out of her

head. 'She kem 'ome about 'alf an hour ago, and the master just grabbed her and took her to her room and locked the door!' She gave a terrified sob. 'I tried to get in. I dunno what 'e's doin' to 'er, but she bin screaming like that for over—' Another scream cut off her words.

Bridie did not stop to take off coat or hat. She raced upstairs and flung herself at Olga's door like someone possessed.

'Open this door, Mannie!' She tried to shout, but her voice cracked helplessly because she was completely breathless. 'Open up this instant, d'you hear me?'

The only reply she got was another scream from Olga. She pounded desperately on the door panels and one of them splintered slightly. Olga was sobbing now. 'Please . . . please . . . Mummy . . .'

Bridie shouted, 'If you don't let me in I'll call the police — d'you hear me!'

The door clicked and opened and Mannie's hand came out, took hold of the coat and dragged her inside the room. The door was slammed and locked. She stood still, staring in horror.

Olga's hands were bound at the wrists and then tied to the bottom of her bed. She was stripped to vest and navy school knickers, but both garments were in tatters. Her face was cupped by her upper arms, and she was sobbing hysterically. Mannie was standing by her, apparently perfectly relaxed. In his hand was a whippy sort of cane she'd never seen before.

She said, 'What the *hell* is going on, Mannie?'

'I am chastising my daughter, wife,' he replied calmly. 'She is a whore. She has very nearly brought disgrace on our family. I am going to make very certain she never does it again.'

Bridie choked, 'How *dare* you touch her! She is *not* your daughter and you have no right—'

'I am her legal guardian, wife. Just as I am yours. I do not choose to bandy words with you at the moment. You will take the family into the kitchen and commence tea. It is all ready for you. I will join you when I have finished here. One hundred strokes is the punishment.'

He raised the cane and brought it smartly down on Olga's buttocks. She screamed again, and Bridie pounced. She was like a tigress and wrested the cane easily from Manny's hand. But the fur coat hampered her. She tried to snap the cane across a raised knee and succeeded only in bending it double. Then Mannie's hand hit her across the face. She reeled back, her hand to her cheek, and he followed up. Two more stinging blows across the face, then his hands went round her throat. She tried to bring up her knee, but the coat was in the way and her gloved hands could not get a grip on his clothes or arms. Her head ached and her eyes could not focus. She made ghastly noises and her legs buckled beneath her. He let her fall and lie where she was.

'I am becoming very impatient with you, Birdy,' he commented sternly, stepping over her to retrieve the cane. 'I am doing my best to weld us into a family who can face the world without shame. And you are doing nothing to help me.' He sliced the cane through the air and Olga screamed. 'This girl — I will not shirk responsibility, I will still call her daughter — has been indulging in the sin of fornication. If she is pregnant she will be sent away from here. If she is not, she will be watched very carefully in future. She will be kept away from her sisters and her brother.' Each sentence was punctuated by the descent of the cane and Olga's sobbing response. 'And she will never be allowed to forget this day.'

Bridie sat up with difficulty. She held her head in her hands. Her dress and coat were rucked up and showed her suspenders. Her hat was over one eye.

She said, 'I shall never forgive you for this. We are not going to stay with you — you must know that—'

He leaned down and hit her again, and she fell on one side.

'I know no such thing, wife. I warn you if you try to defy me in any way, the whole of Gloucester will learn who Barty's true father is. Also that your eldest daughter is a whore like her mother. Is that clear?'

Bridie choked on a scream. No-one knew about Barty . . . no-one. Except April. Oh God . . . her best friend.

She drew breath to make a denial, but the words that emerged from her swollen mouth were: 'Not in front of . . . oh please Mannie . . . Olga . . .'

'Then behave yourself. Stand up and adjust your clothes. Go downstairs and assemble the children around the tea table. Do your duty as I am doing mine.'

The cane whistled; it seemed for the last time. He threw it on the bed and flexed his neck and hand, then with the old-fashioned courtesy which had so impressed Davie, he helped Bridie to her feet and brushed her down solicitously.

'Ah Birdy . . . Birdy . . . how long it is taking you to learn . . .' he sounded genuinely grieved. He indicated Olga who had now sunk to her knees and was blubbering with relief. 'Do you really want this child to grow into someone like Mrs Williams? When I lived in Gloucester before, she was known throughout the city. Is that what you wish for Olga? No, I know it is not.' He cupped Bridie's face and kissed it. 'Ah, the poor lips are swollen . . .' he kissed them gently. 'But the other blows were cushioned by your hat and your hair. Just as Olga's were cushioned by her underclothes.' He smiled. 'There will be no marks, Birdy. Your mouth? Ah, you have a cold. So many colds this winter, hein?'

She sobbed and stood very still, half afraid of him, half wanting to be comforted and reassured. He extracted a handkerchief from his pocket and dabbed at her eyes. 'My beautiful wife no longer looks beautiful when she is angry and raucous. We must make her beautiful again.' He kissed and dabbed. She could not believe she was permitting him to do this, but her legs were like jelly and her head ached so much. Then, as if she were delaying him, he turned from her to Olga.

'Now wife, I have to see to our daughter.' He reached

for a jar of ointment obviously brought in for this very purpose. Later his cold foresight was to chill Bridie as much as his violence. He unscrewed the lid and went over to the sobbing heap of rags on the floor. Expertly he stripped off vest and knickers. Olga whimpered but made no attempt to move. Her rounded shoulders looked pathetic under the electric light, her vertebrae separately defined. Mannie palmed some of the ointment and began to smear it on.

'There,' he murmured. 'There, it will no longer hurt. In two minutes, only the memory will remain. And that *must* remain.'

Bridie watched, horrified but unmoving, while he massaged her daughter's buttocks and the red welts gradually disappeared into a general glowing mass as the blood came to the surface. Olga was still tied to the bed, but the sobbing was less frequent now and she took her weight on her knees and lifted her head occasionally. Her face told more of her agony than her back. It was raw and open and twisted in a grimace of complete despair. Bridie shivered in spite of her fur coat. Olga was so much Tolly's child and Tolly had been capable of that kind of abnegation.

Still talking, Mannie finished his anointing and went familiarly to Olga's dressing-table drawer for clean underwear.

Bridie protested at last. 'She can do it — let her do it!' she said.

But he leaned down and fitted the kneeling legs into clean knickers and wriggled them up to her waist as if she were a baby. Only then did he untie her hands and raise her to his level. She stood in front of him, head down like a beaten horse. Very gently he put on her nightdress. Bridie thought she might faint; she leaned against the wall.

'There.' He took Olga's hands and led her to the bed, flipped back the covers and sat her down. 'There, you will lie down now, Olga. You will not sleep. You will think about what you have done and the public disgrace you might have brought on your family. You will remember your beating, but you will feel no physical pain. Your pain will all be here.' He touched her head. Then he knelt by the bed and lifted her legs inside it and covered her. At last he stood and moved away. Bridie was quite certain that one more second of seeing him in contact with Olga would have deprived her of her senses.

He said, 'Come Birdy. We will go downstairs together.' He unlocked the door and propelled her outside. 'Good night, daughter.' He snapped off the light and closed the door on the girl inside.

'I did not speak to her. Mannie, I must go in and—'

'You will do as *I* say, Birdy. We go downstairs together. To see our children.'

March was no longer listed as Albert's next of kin, but Elizabeth let her know immediately she received her own telegram from the War Office. Her wire read simply: 'Safe but wounded stop please tel Croker four two stop Elizabeth Tomms.' It took March several seconds to connect Elizabeth with Albert and then to realize that he must have been wounded again. She looked at the telegram. It was addressed simply to Bedford Close. Elizabeth — her own daughter-in-law — did not even know her name.

She telephoned immediately and George Doswell answered. March had no way of knowing whether he was father or son. She said loudly above the crackling on the line, 'Mr Doswell . . . this is March Luker here. I am Albert's mother.'

'Ah. Mrs Luker. Of course. I am so sorry. You have received Lizzie's wire then?'

'Yes.' March blocked her free ear. Was it his Dorset accent that made her practically unintelligible? 'What has happened?'

'Tommy was shot down again. Yesterday. Intercepting last night's raid on Plymouth.'

'Tommy? Oh . . . Albert.' The strain of listening then shouting brought tears to March's eyes. She fumbled in her sleeve for a handkerchief and dabbed, then replaced her hand to her ear. 'How . . . what . . . is he . . ?'

Elizabeth's father said something which March could not hear. Then something else.

She said numbly, 'You mean he will lose his *arm?* Oh God. Not his *arm!* He's a mechanic — he mustn't lose his arm!'

George Doswell, who had lost his son, said sturdily, 'He will manage, Mrs Luker. He is *alive*, that is what matters. And he loves the farm. One day it will be his. And there are plenty of one-armed farmers!' He chuckled. To March he sounded completely heartless.

She said, 'I must see him. Is it the same hospital as before?'

'No. He has a bed where Elizabeth nurses. And . . .' Hesitation built into embarrassment. 'Just at the moment medical opinion is that he must be kept very quiet at—'

'At all costs.' March finished bitterly. 'At all costs to his famiiy. Yes We understand perfectly.'

'I'm sure later on—'

'How much later on, would you think?'

'Mrs Luker, this will probably mean that Tommy will be invalided out of the Air Force. He will be at home. At peace. The first peace he has known since he went to Spain.'

'Invalided out? They'll find him a desk job surely?'

'Probably not. He will be far more use on the farm. It is war work, after all.'

'Oh.' She dabbed again at her face.

'Take heart, Mrs Luker. We will keep in touch.'

She managed to thank him before she put the phone down. As before, Chattie was standing behind her. She turned and put her arms around the girl.

'It's his arm, Chattie. There dear, don't cry. See, I am not crying. His father-in-law says he will be invalided out and will live on their farm.'

'But he can't work with engines no more, Mrs Luker,' Chattie wailed. 'And he loves his engines.'

March said hardily, 'Maybe this is a judgement on him for marrying a stranger and ignoring Davie. I'm not going to shed tears over him. He'll be all right with those Doswells.'

'Oh Mrs Luker.'

'I know, Chattie. But I've grieved and worried over Albert for too long. He is married and he is settled and he is now as safe as any of us. I am not going to waste any more time over any men.' She looked over the top of the girl's head. 'I am going to do some war work. Chattie, I am going to London to drive an ambulance.'

'Mrs Luker!'

'I'm a good driver. They need good drivers in London now. No-one needs me here. You will look after Mr Luker and keep the house in order. And Davie is my example. She has given Albert up and turned her attention to living her own life. I must do the same.'

'Oh madam. What about Mrs Daker and Mrs Gould?'

March kept her arm around the girl and began to walk her to the kitchen.

'May is thoroughly absorbed in Gretta. And she has Monty to help her with her anxiety about Victor. And April is very busy. I am the only one who has nothing to do.' March smiled. In spite of the tearstains on her face she looked happier than she had looked for some time. 'Go and make us a cup of tea now, dear. I am going to telephone Mrs Peplow about joining the Red Cross.'

Carrie watched her mistress walk back to the telephone and recognised well her mood of complete determination. She went into the pristine kitchen and assembled tea things on a tray. 'Poor Mr Luker,' she said aloud. And she wept again for all of them.

Surprisingly, Fred did not argue with March's decision. Even more surprisingly perhaps, he took the whole miserable business down to Barnwood Road to discuss it with his sister, Sibbie.

Sibbie's position since Edward Williams' death was a peculiar one. There were many men in Gloucester who would have married her after so many years of respectability, but Sibbie had genuinely loved her older husband and could not consider marriage again. She had outgrown her family too; for many years she had visited her mother surreptitiously, and even though her father officially refused her entry into the Chichester Street house, he still accepted her generosity. It would have been easy to heal all the breaches now, but Sibbie dare not go to Chichester Street in case she might meet May, and she would prefer to keep her disreputable parents out of sight of her present neighbours. Only Fred was really welcome at Barnwood. And she welcomed him with literally open arms that cold day in November 1940, and he hugged her too. He was usually undemonstrative, but suddenly she reminded him of the days when he had plotted and schemed and enjoyed the devious way he got to the top. Besides, she smelled nice.

She took him into the room that had been Edward's study. She had made it into a tiny sitting room easily heated and as it looked over the back of the house at the sweep of green fields climbing to Chosen Hill it was a very pleasant place.

'Darling Fred. I'm so pleased to see you. Are you all right there — cushion? I feel closer to Edward in this room. Really I might as well close the rest of the house, it's much too big for me.' She opened the door and called into the hall. 'I've managed to get hold of a couple of school girls from the village. They come in at weekends and after school. But I need someone to do the rough. I wish Ma wasn't past it.'

'Why don't you move Sib? A flat in town would be your line I'd have thought.'

'No. I need a bolt hole. All my old clients would come knocking at the door if I was too available. And this is Edward's home.' She flopped into a chair and reached for

211

the cigarette box. 'Christ Fred. I do miss him. I didn't think I would but . . .'

'Poor old Sib. Never mind, you made him as happy as a king. No regrets, eh?'

'None. He was the only man who gave me more than I gave him. Sorry, I was forgetting Will Rising. Will and Edward, they loved me. I've been very lucky.' Tea arrived on a chrome trolley. Fred noted the school girl who brought it, tall, gangly, anxious to please. Trust Sibbie to milk the only labour market available at the moment.

As soon as she'd gone he said bluntly, 'Well, you've been luckier than me, Sib. March is leaving at last.'

'What?' Sibbie almost dropped the teapot. 'After what she's put up with? I thought everything was all right again now? Christ, you haven't been messing about again, Fred?'

'No.' He thought of Tilly Adair. He hadn't been messing about again. 'Albert's lost an arm. He'll be living on his wife's farm from now on. Settled. Apparently all right — as all right as he'll ever be with one arm. I think March feels she's hung around long enough.'

'Poor Albert!' Sibbie closed her eyes for a long moment, then opened them and continued to dispense tea. As she passed the cup to Fred she said, 'I don't get it. If Albert is all right, why leave you? How do the two things connect.'

'It's too difficult to explain, Sib, and I don't think you'd understand in a hundred years. March thought I was going to die. She thought Albert might be killed. Neither of those things have happened. She isn't . . . needed any more.'

Sibbie put his tea on a stool near his hand. The way she looked after men was second nature to her; Fred felt himself beginning to relax slightly.

She sat back herself and picked up her cigarette from the ashtray. 'Are you saying you don't want her?'

He looked into the fire for a long moment.

'I don't know, Sib. I'm tired of fighting March. I've been tired for years. She softened for a time, but now she is

212

angry again and I cannot . . . I simply cannot do a thing about it.'

'You don't care enough?'

'Perhaps that's it. I don't know.'

'What is she going to do? Where is she going?'

'London apparently. She phoned Marjorie Peplow — d'you remember Edward and I bought land from Arthur Peplow in that ring-road deal? His wife is queen bee of the local Red Cross. She has told March what to do. March knows they are desperate for ambulance drivers during the blitz. And she's a damned good driver.' He grinned faintly. 'I taught her myself when we were kids.'

'I remember.' Sibbie drew on the last of her cigarette and exhaled slowly. 'You were always meant for each other, Fred. If she goes now she might not come back. Ever.'

'Quite.'

'Christ, Fred. Forbid her to go.'

'Don't be an idiot. You know March.'

'Mannie Stein wouldn't let Bridie leav.. him, whatever he had to do to keep her. He'd tie her up first.'

Fred grinned again. 'I'd like to see him tie March up. She'd slip arsenic in his next meal.'

'Not if she . . . oh never mind.'

Fred picked up his tea. 'What does this mean, Sib? That Bridie has found her master at last? Dammit, Tolly could never tame her. How is Mannie Stein doing it?'

Sibbie did not look at him. 'He can be very persuasive when he likes, my dear.'

Fred's grin vanished. 'Surely the rumour I heard from Monty isn't true? You haven't had him here, have you?' He looked at her. 'You damned fool, Sib. He's after your share of the business! Surely you can see that?'

'He comes about the business, yes. And I suppose I do know that. But he has charm, Fred. I know you've never seen it. April and David have turned you against him. He's protective and kind. And other things.'

Fred said brutally, 'He's good in bed you mean? Oh

Christ, Sib, you haven't changed. Edward . . . Will Rising . . . but the leopard never changes his spots.'

She said, 'I need him, Fred. To prove I can still . . . you know. Besides, he keeps it no secret from Bridie and that girl deserves everything she gets, I promise you that!' She turned her mouth down mockingly. 'You're just the same, Freddiekins. I'll lay you odds that within a month of March going to London you'll have found some woman.'

He thought again of Tilly and was silent on that score, but before he left, he warned her again about Mannie Stein. 'He married Bridie for the business, Sib. And maybe something else . . . maybe to get close to April. Or Davina.'

'Really. That's too far-fetched for words, Fred!'

'Look Sis, do me a favour will you? If you're going to insist on seeing him, keep your ears open and report to me.'

'About the firm, d'you mean?'

'About anything. Anything at all, my dear. A look . . . any indication of what particular pies he is dabbling those long fingers in.'

In November Coventry 'bought it'. In Winterditch Lane the Daker family, minus April, ventured out of the cupboard beneath the stairs and went up to the attic to watch in awe as the sky to the north-west reflected a burning city. They had no idea where the terrible raid was taking place; David thought Birmingham, and Davie said 'Poor Audrey'; Aunt Sylv thought it was nearer, Evesham or Stratford-upon-Avon.

'Nothing much there for them to bomb, Sylv,' David said, his arms tightly around his daughters. 'There's plenty of military targets in Brum.' They gazed in silent agony for another ten minutes, then turned away by mutual consent. It was indecent to watch such slaughter even at long distance. 'So long as they don't unload any bombs on their way back,' David murmured in aside to Sylvia as they climbed down the narrow stairs. 'God. I wish April would give up this fire-watching caper.'

214

April had turned in at midnight in the chapter house as usual. The first routine of the evening was for all the fire-watchers to patrol the cathedral thoroughly to check for intruders. They worked in pairs, and April was with Mr Dark, one of the vergers. She led the way along the whispering gallery and across the nave to the Lady Chapel, then on to the roof to survey the gardens.

Mr Dark said quietly, 'No raids tonight. We'll turn in early and get a proper sleep for once.'

April was fond of the old boy; sometimes in the mornings he looked like death warmed up; even so, they were supposed to stay awake until midnight and patrol again immediately the siren sounded.

She said, 'What makes you so certain we shall have a quiet night, Mr Dark?'

'No moon. And plenty of cloud. Much too dark for any raids tonight.'

April sighed. 'It's hard to imagine, isn't it? So peaceful. Whereas in London and Bristol . . .' She turned and went inside again. 'My sister has volunteered to drive an ambulance in London.'

Mr Dark made clicking noises with his tongue which, translated, probably meant that though such a course was admirable he personally considered a woman's place was in her own home at any time, particularly wartime.

'Permit me to go first, Mrs Daker.' He preceded April down the winding stone staircase with his usual little joke. 'If you should fall you will then have what the R.A.F. call a soft landing.'

And April obediently chuckled.

At just past midnight, when she had found a fairly comfortable position on the camp bed at one end of the chapter house, while Mr Dark's snores had just started up at the other end, the Alert wailed its message over the city. She rolled out on to the coconut matting which was spread over the flags for warmth, and dragged her coat over her arms. Mr Dark handed her a long-handled shovel as she reached him. Around them the other firewatchers were groaning and shuffling about, getting into their heavy winter coats and picking up their shovels. April had one of her moments of vision when it seemed that they became monks of the Middle Ages turning out for Midnight Mass or compline. Gloucester might be escaping this war lightly so far, but the city was battle-scarred from countless hordes in the past and was used to donning armour.

She led the way along their route: out on to the roof of the nave, along the narrow walkway, the lead catching at unwary ankles, the stonecoping, waist-high but suddenly much too low, on the right. After the first circuit they heard approaching aircraft: many aircraft. After the second, the whole world seemed full of their intermittent throb. Searchlights stabbed at the low cloud and were reflected back; futilely the ack-ack guns pounded away; the German attack was indefatigable. Doggedly Mr Dark and April patrolled the roof. On turrets and in the main tower, the others showed a glimmer of torchlight occasionally. A sense of terrible helplessness settled over the city like atmospheric pressure. A lot of people were going to be killed and there was nothing they could do about it.

On the sixth circuit Mr Dark caught up with April. The noise was lessening; even so he had to put his mouth close to her ear for her to hear his voice.

'There's someone in the cloisters. I saw a torch just now.'

April said, 'Hubert Bohannum, the railway clerk. He does the cloisters.' Hubert had no head for heights.

'He was sick earlier. He went home.'

'Oh.' April was nonplussed but not unduly alarmed. They were after incendiaries, not spies. 'Someone else then.'

'I think I will investigate.'

'Let me go.' April was desperate to get off the roof and have a definite errand. 'It'll be a message from the air raid warden.' She made her voice light. 'I can run faster than you.'

216

She was gone before he could argue. Down the stairs to the whispering gallery and across the nave to the organ loft, then down again into the nave and a fast but respectful walk past the tomb of Edward II to the small door in the wall leading to the cloisters. She reached above it for the key and fitted it with difficulty by the jumping light from her shaded torch, then she was down the steps and into the living quarters of the monks themselves.

There was no sign of anyone. Mr Dark had imagined the light. Or someone had got lost walking through the gardens and found their way in and then out of the quadrangle. But at least the enemy armada had passed overhead. She tried to believe that somewhere out there in the darkness, the night fighters from Brize Norton would be lying in wait for them.

At the far end of the cloister, something moved. April swallowed and flashed her torch to the fan-vaulted ceiling. She knew how oddly sound travelled in this ancient place and hoped, though feared, she had disturbed a bat. But if not, then Mr Dark would see her torch and start down towards her.

Nothing moved.

She called, 'Is anyone there? This is the fire-watcher. If you have a message please walk towards my torch. There is no obstruction, you are perfectly safe.'

Immediately a shadow pulled away from the ancient lavatorium and hurried towards her. She shone the torch on her own face.

A voice said, 'April. I thought you would be here. Davina told me how to find you. My dear girl, are you all right?'

She felt the hair on the nape of her neck rise. This man had a frightening effect on her; she had no idea why it was quite so devastating. When she had first taken him on to the roof of the Cadena during her wedding reception and shown him Gloucester as a hostess shows a stranger her own town, she had felt his power through her delirious happiness. When he had listened to a private conversation between herself and David six months later, she had felt unclean. And when he had tried to force himself on her, insisting that she had encouraged him, her distress had been overwhelming. Whatever Bridie said, April knew Mannie Stein was an evil man.

She hung on to the rough stone of the arched window and managed to croak, 'Davina?'

Mannie, his black suit shrouded by a black greatcoat, did not make the mistake of touching her. He stood three feet away, head thrust forward, peering.

'I have talked to her lately. Hasn't she told you?'

'I — I don't believe you.'

He gave an impatient gesture. 'Why should I lie? She came to me last month. She needed a confidant.'

'I warn you, if any harm comes to Davina—'

He interrupted brusquely. 'April, stop that hysterical talk. Davina came to see Olga and stayed to talk to me. I told her how I have always felt about you. She understood. In many ways she is older than her years.'

'How dare you talk to her like that!'

'I told her the truth. I told her I wanted to be friends again. She told me when you were on duty here. That is all.'

She said, 'Get *out!* Get out and keep away from Davina! D'you hear me — d'you understand? If I tell David of this he will — he will —'

'But you won't tell David, my dear. You know it will upset him and you are always trying to spare him, aren't you?' She was silent and he laughed. 'Had you forgotten that I know about you and David, my dear?'

She said again, 'Get out! The others will arrive at any moment and you will be turned out then. Go now.'

'My dear. Can't we put an end to this silly enmity here and now? Let us meet for tea and talk as we used to do.'

'You fool. Do you honestly think I would meet you anywhere?'

'April, April, April . . .' his voice became weary. 'You

are intelligent. You must have known that one of the reasons for marrying Bridie was to secure a place for myself in Gloucester again. So that I could see you. I have never given up hope, April. Never.'

She turned to flee and at last he put a hand on her. She became shudderingly still.

He whispered, 'Perhaps if I tell you something . . . interesting . . . you will feel more kindly towards me. Did you know, my darling, that your sister March married Edwin Tomms for one reason only, April? To give a name to her unborn child. You see my darling, the man who had fathered that child had been reported missing in France. Did you never guess? Albert Tomms is Fred Luker's son.'

April heard her breath whistle in her nostrils. She knew he was waiting to be asked where he had come upon such information, but she said nothing. It was as if she had known the truth for some time and been unable to face it. Albert's face on the flickering screen at the Plaza had been a replica of Fred's. And Davie sometimes, when she was tired and washed out, had the unmistakable look of the Lukers. She waited, holding herself rigid in his grip, knowing that he was now going to tell her that he had also found out about Davie's true father.

But he did not.

He said softly, 'I can tell you are surprised, my dear, and I can hear someone coming. I think when you have had time to consider what I've just told you, you might well feel you can be friends again.'

And he was gone.

At the end of that terrible night, when the enemy planes had returned and reports were brought by the wardens of the devastation in Coventry, April climbed again to the roof of the nave and looked over her city. Dawn was still some hours away, but the moon had broken through a patch of cloud and lit the huddle of houses and streets beneath her in a murky grey light. Gloucester looked tired, and very, very old. Once again, the enemy was in its midst.

And in the midst of one of its families too. April hung on to the coping and released the shuddering which she had kept under control for so long.

For over fifteen years, April had had to live with the terrible knowledge that her elder daughter was not David's. The reasons for this cruel fact no longer mattered; David was no longer impotent — Flora was living proof of this. Like Davina, April knew the bitter gall of forestalling events needlessly. She had succumbed to Fred Luker's inexorable logic that day they had gone to the Forest of Dean. Fred had said, 'I will be a donor, nothing more, David will always be the father.' And she had cheated her husband and lied to him ever since.

Sometimes her secret had been easy to bear; David had made it easy to bear, by his love and understanding. At other times, it was not easy, and for years she had avoided Fred like the plague and could not listen to the name of Mannie Stein because he had been — unknowingly — the start of it all.

And now she learned that Albert was also Fred's son, and she began to understand some of the heartbreak suffered by Albert and Davie. Her own predicament seemed small in comparison. Mannie Stein seemed smaller still.

She lifted her head to the shrouded moon and said aloud, 'Mother . . . Dad . . .'

She waited and then looked down towards their old home in Chichester Street. Of course, their heaven would be there; neither of them had cared for heights.

'Oh Mother. Poor Albert Frederick. And poor Davie. And March. There's nothing to be done, is there? Forgive me, Mama. Help the children somehow. Please help them.'

She asked no help for herself. She wanted none. In a way perhaps she hoped that damnation for herself might buy redemption for Albert and Davie. It was April's way; she had always bargained for those she loved most.

Twelve

CHRISTMAS came and went, followed by 1941 and Davie's fifteenth birthday. It was the coldest winter she could remember. At weekends she and Flo would go to the Winterditch pond and slide across it underneath the petrified brambles and between the tufts of frozen weed which broke the steely surface. The cycle rides to school though hazardous, were an awesome experience. The barbed wire entanglements, inches deep in frost, became exquisite; the static water tanks were enormous iced wedding cakes, dustbin lids wore fur hats often set at ridiculous angles. The girls were allowed to wear knitted pixie hoods in the school colours, or navy-blue berets pulled down around their ears. Coal was desperately short and there were days when the school furnaces could not be stoked. Then they kept their gaberdines on over their cardigans and even wore gloves when they weren't actually writing.

At home Aunt Sylv kept a fire going somehow in the range; to her a fire was more important than food. She lumbered around the garden picking out the wood from the blanket of snow and stacking it to dry in the fender; sometimes, with the addition of steaming gloves and wellingtons, it was only just possible to see that a fire burned somewhere behind the barricade. On top of the range she kept a pot of soupy stew mixture bubbling constantly. Sometimes it consisted of boiled vegetables only, with a meat cube thrown in for flavouring. At other times she would add some precious scrag-end of mutton, and the house would be permeated with a wonderful aroma, delicate and substantial at the same time. Sylv would grin toothlessly at the loud appreciation from her family and say, 'Takes me back to Kempley it does. Our mam used to allus 'ave a sheep's 'ead a-bobbin' away in the pot.' This did not put anyone off their food. Sylv's tales were apocryphal by now.

It was February that the Director of Public Prosecutions decided there was a case against Robin Adair of Quedgeley Lodge, Gloucestershire. He was arrested, granted bail, and kept very much to himself. It was explained carefully to a tearful Audrey Merriman that it was her duty to be honest and open about the birth of Robert Alan. Robin Adair had never contacted her again, and other young girls were in serious danger from him. Miserably she nodded. She had no idea how the information had reached the ears of the police and wondered about her friend from Gloucester, Davina Daker. Olga, white-faced and still desperate, chose to suspect Davina, though she must have known who the real informer was. The case was heard in camera and no reporters were present, but rumours got about and Tilly Adair told Fred that she could never hold up her head again. Robin was sent to Hortham Prison in Bristol for two years.

By the end of March the snow had gone and the spring vegetables were beginning to show in the school gardens. Dinner had just been cleared away in the big dining-room at the top of the building, when the siren wailed dismally over the city. The girls filed reluctantly into the shelters. At first it had been one way of wasting time, now it was so boring that double maths was preferable. The Lower Fifth crowded sulkily into the back of Shelter Two and Miss Miller took charge of the iron rations and drinking water. Outside it was cloudy and rain threatened; but inside it was dank and stuffy, the slatted seats were hard and the duckboards squelched under fifty pairs of feet.

'Now girls!' Miss Miller called down the mutinous tunnel. 'Let's have a song. How about "Muss i' den?" We'll sing it as a round.'

Obediently if sullenly, the girls split into groups and sang the German folk song with ill grace. It was obvious no German planes were within miles of the city. Davina, sitting next to Olga, felt the usual tremor from the stick-thin arms as they braced on the seat to support the weak back.

'Lean on me, Olga,' she whispered. 'Put your legs sideways and lean on my shoulder.'

'No thank you.'

It was shocking to hear the dislike in Olga's voice. Davie swallowed and tried again.

'Are you going to pick up the early potatoes at Easter? Gillian Smith says we can all go out to her place. Her mother will let us eat our sandwiches in the barn.'

'Are you going?'

'Yes.'

'Then I'm not.'

'Oh . . . Olga.'

'Stop trying to suck up to me all the time, Davina Daker. If I hadn't told you about Robin you wouldn't have been able to sneak on him. You betrayed me.'

Davina said nothing. She remembered that day she had gone to see Mr Stein and he had been so charming to her and called her Lady Davina. It must have been him. But of course Olga was right; indirectly it was all her fault. She felt an unexpected tear roll down her cheek and hoped it would not fall on Olga's hand.

Miss Miller said, 'Girls, girls! Conversation is one thing. Gabble is another. Let us have silence.'

Olga said suddenly and with a malicious note in her voice, 'Why don't we ask Davina Daker to sing for us, Miss Miller?'

Miss Miller examined the idea and could not find a

flaw. 'Why not indeed? Davina, would you care to entertain us?'

Davina knew it was a command, not a request, and her stomach knotted itself. Olga was very aware of her reluctance to sing in front of her fellows.

Olga said now, 'Oh do sing that one that's on the wireless, Davie. The one about the White Cliffs of Dover.'

Before Miss Miller could question the choice at least thirty voices were applauding it. Davie swallowed her tears, pressed her thumbs hard into the knots in her abdomen and expanded her diaphragm. There was a silence. Into it, clear and true, poured Davie's soprano.

After the first few bars she forgot her nerves. She had sung the song often in the bath; it was the one beloved of Marlene, and Olga had hoped it would sound as ludicrous in the blackness of the shelter as it did in the Brunswick Road kitchen. But it didn't. The treacly sentiment became sincere, the nostalgia, poignant. Miss Miller did not interrupt it though she realized that Olga and Davina had pulled a fast one. She had had no idea that the tall quiet girl with the colourless hair and very blue eyes had this sort of voice. It was a voice that might well be lost in a concert hall, but was intimate and heart-moving in a smaller space. The song came to an end and there was some spontaneous clapping and encouraging cries of 'Come on Davie. Let's have another one. What about "Wish Me Luck as You Wave Me Goodbye?" 'That had been a song sung by Gracie Fields; Miss Miller knew that.

'I think not.' She had no wish to be accused in the staff-room of wallowing in radio rubbish. She clapped her hands. 'Was that the All Clear?'

It was not, but Dr Moore came down the steps to say that as it was three forty-five the girls who lived within five minutes of the school might go home.

'No sign of any enemy action,' she announced. 'But walk quickly, girls, and be ready to go into the nearest house if need be.' She let three girls go past her. 'Everyone else may take some exercise on the field.'

Olga went ahead of Davina; she was one of the girls going home. Davie caught her up by the bicycle shed.

'Why don't you just leave me alone, Davina!' Olga sounded vicious. 'You think you're marvellous, don't you? Singing as if you're on the wireless! But you can't ever have Albert. Not ever. And I can have Robin. I shall wait for him, you see. And when I'm seventeen we shall get married. So who's going to be the winner in the end?'

She jumped on her bicycle and rode quickly away. Down Oxford Street she went. Then through the town as if she was going to the cemetery. Nobody knew why she passed Brunswick Road and kept going. Nobody knew why she turned into Derby Road. But when the Junkers appeared over the city, harried by fighters and attacked by flak, she was just turning left. The enemy plane unloaded a stick of four bombs to lighten itself. Her bicycle was found inside the actual crater, strangely undamaged. Her body, very much damaged, was thirty yards away. But her uniform was recognizable and the Warden on duty sent a policeman to the school to inform Dr Moore what had happened. Completely stunned, the headmistress gathered the rest of the girls in the hall and broke the news as gently as she could, adding 'I shall never forgive myself.' Davie wanted to echo that sentiment. She knew that, somehow, it was all her fault.

She and Flo hardly spoke a word on the ride home. Luckily Aunt Sylv and April were both in the kitchen getting tea and were able to take the brunt of the girls' grief. And then April got her own bicycle out of the garage and cycled in to see Bridie.

The house in Brunswick Road was unusually silent. Marlene opened the door, dry-eyed and shocked; there was no sign of the children.

'They're all in the sitting-room, miss,' Marlene whispered. 'The vicar and 'is missis is with them. She and 'im —' her mouth tightened against a spasm,'— they're up in the bedroom. I'll just go an' —'

'No.' April shook her head definitely. 'You go on

getting some tea, Marlene dear. They'll need it later. I know where Bridie's room is. I'll go on up.'

'Master won't like it, miss.'

'I'll go on up all the same.'

She swept upstairs before second thoughts could detain her. Mannie answered her light tap and actually smiled with satisfaction to see her.

'I knew you'd come. Eventually,' he said with a kind of smugness.

She pushed past him. Bridie was sitting by the window staring into the walled garden where Tolly had put the girls through their Swedish exercises. She wore a satin negligee over her nightdress. April frowned; it was not yet six o'clock.

Mannie said, 'We're just going to tuck her up in bed with a nice cup of tea. She's had a shock.'

April felt her face widen with indredulity, but Bridie, looking away from the window at last, smiled gently.

'Mannie looks after me like a mother hen.'

April gave a choking sob and crouched by her childhood friend, enfolding her as best she could. The negligee was slippery and beneath it she could feel the shoulder bones, as sharp as Olga's had been. She held on as if they were both drowning.

Bridie touched April's fading golden hair.

'Darling . . . don't grieve,' she said in a low voice. 'It's all right. Olga is safe now.'

'Oh Bridie.' April had come to offer comfort and was being given it. 'My dear, I am so sorry. So sorry.'

'Yes. Yes, I know. But she wasn't happy, April. She was her father's girl always and when he went . . . she stopped being happy. Now they are together.'

April gabbled the usual words. 'It was instantaneous, darling. She felt nothing — knew nothing.'

'I know. I know.' They clung together, remembering Olga's short life. Bridie's shoulders moved convulsively.

Don't be afraid to cry, darling,' April whispered. 'Don't—'

Mannie moved swiftly forward and put a hand on

227

Bridie's head. 'My wife is very tired, April. The doctor has given her a sedative and she should go to bed.'

'I'll be ten minutes only.' April did not look up but her arms tightened protectively. 'Perhaps you could fetch Bridie's tea.'

There was a brief silence; April was conscious that Mannie was stroking Bridie's head. Then Bridie said in a low voice, 'Mannie is right, darling, I am tired. Come to see me tomorrow.'

'No, dearest. We must register the death tomorrow. And there will be all the arrangements to be made. I will telephone April when she may come.'

April said stonily, 'We are not on the telephone. I will call round—'

He went on as if she had not spoken, 'You will need to know the time of the funeral, of course.' He moved away and April heard him open the bedroom door. 'Perhaps Bridie will be strong enough to come to see you and make those arrangements, April.'

Her hands tightened on Bridie's shoulders; he would have to remove her by force.

Then Bridie whispered, 'Please darling. Go now. It is for the best,' and drew away. April stared at her disbelievingly. Bridie was smiling. She repeated her first words, 'Olga is safe now.' Then she leaned back in her chair and closed her eyes dismissively. April felt the satin slip away from her fingers. She stood up reluctantly, then at last turned to face Mannie. He was standing holding the door, his tall figure stooped as usual. He followed her down the stairs.

'I think it is best if she is quiet now, April. Tomorrow we shall be busy. The day after I shall look after her again. Then perhaps if I put her on the bus, she might be able to come to see you.'

'My sisters will want to call. The headmistress of the school—'

'I will see them. I know what is best for my wife, April. And my children.'

The house was still so quiet. Was it entirely because of this shocking bereavement? Or was it always like this when Mannie was at home?

He opened the front door and smiled at her.

'It has taken a tragedy to bring you to me, April, but I knew something would. Don't worry, we will meet again.'

April stared at him, horrified anew. Could Bridie have meant that Olga was not 'safe' from him? She remembered those thin shoulders beneath the expensive satin and anger boiled in her. It was almost seven o'clock. Three hours ago Olga had been alive. And this man was still here.

She turned. 'Mannie. If I had told Fred Luker what you said to me in the cloisters last winter, you would now be dead. Perhaps Olga would be alive.' She paused and watched her words at last piercing his enormous satisfaction. She went on tensely, 'I did not tell him because I wanted the evil to stop there — right there in the cloisters. But I will say this to you now — since I have seen Bridie and realize what has been going on in this house — I regret I did not make sure that you left this earth!'

She was shaking. She went outside. Lying in the small front area were several bunches of flowers that had not been there when she arrived. Daffodils. The first from Newent. She bent to look at the labels. 'To Olga from Davie'. 'To Olga from Flo'. 'To Olga from Gillian Smith and Winnie Cresswell'. They must be somewhere near.

She began to weep as she cycled down Brunswick Road. And when she turned into Clarence Street and saw them all waiting for her, she almost fell off her bike to gather them closely. They sobbed against her almost desperately. The deaths they had known had been from 'natural causes' and they had not associated them with evil before. Now, it was as if they had come face to face with Adolf himself.

Two days later Bridie arrived at Longmeadow as Mannie had promised. When she asked Davie if she would sing at the funeral April knew immediately who had made the suggestion and said swiftly, 'No. It is too much for her, Bridie — I'm not going to let her answer you. Forgive me, but no.'

Bridie said nothing. She was sitting at the kitchen table where she had sat just over a year ago, doing sprouts and talking outrageously. Now she stared at her gloved hands as if she had never seen them before.

Aunt Sylv put a cup of steaming tea in front of her. 'Come on now Bridie love, 'ave a cup of this. Life's got to go on, and your little 'un is with her gran now.'

Bridie looked up with a quick smile. 'Oh I know, Sylv. It is such a relief to me, you simply can't imagine.' She glanced almost covertly at Davie. 'It's just that Olga's friend, Gillian, came to see us and told us that Olga asked Davie to sing. In the shelter that afternoon. And we thought, Mannie and I, that it would be Olga's wish — but I do understand that it would be a frightful ordeal and I shouldn't have asked in the first place.'

'I'll do it,' Davie said suddenly. She shook her head at her mother. 'No, honestly Mummy. I want to do it.'

'It's . . . upsetting. You know how a single voice — in a church —' April put her hand over Bridie's. 'It's not a good idea, darling, really.'

Apparently Bridie did not hear. 'Mannie thought —' she was looking at Davie eagerly. 'Mannie thought Ave Maria.'

April flinched, but Davie just swallowed and nodded.

When David arrived home Bridie managed to smile and reply to him with a vestige of her old spirit. He said afterwards to April, 'I know she's lost a great deal of weight Primrose, but haven't we all? In the ghastly circumstances I thought she was bearing up with enormous courage.'

'That's just it! She shouldn't be. She's thankful that

230

Olga is out of it. He must have hated the girl — Nash said something once that made me wonder — and I think he's behind this idea of Davie singing a solo in church.'

'What motive could he have?'

'He hopes she'll break down. He hopes everyone will break down. He'll be magnanimous and even gentle—'

'She won't break down, April.' He put an arm around her shoulders. 'Darling, haven't you noticed? Davie is growing up. She won't break down. It'll be her tribute to Olga. You'll see.'

'She was heartbroken the other night. She told me they'd had a quarrel.'

'That is why she must do this.' He kissed her. 'She is so like you, Primrose. Put yourself in her position and you will know that she has to sing for Olga.'

April said no more.

He was right, Davie did not break down. Her voice had the effortless quality of a chorister's: it did not shake and as it climbed to the heights of the church on Gloucester's Cross, the congregation relaxed visibly as if it took their grief and horror with it and offered everything to God. The final amen was broken by a fit of coughing from Mannie Stein, but far from ruining Davie's tribute it enabled everyone to return from that rarefield world of the spirit under the cover of someone else's emotion. The pall-bearers lifted the coffin on to their shoulders; everyone stood, umbrellas were knocked over and righted again, Sibbie Williams leaned forward and hit Mannie on the back with her fist. He stopped coughing abruptly.

The mourners shuffled out and got into cars. March had not been able to take time off to come home and Charles Adair was on duty, so it was sensible that Tilly should get into Fred's Wolseley with the Dakers. It was a bit of a squash but they managed. They began the long crawl along Barton Street to the cemetery. At the level crossing they waited for a troop train to chug across and sat silently looking at the hearse in front of them, the back window framing Bridie's black hat and Mannie's homburg. It began to rain.

Chattie had been roped in to help Marlene with the funeral meal, so after Fred had dropped the Dakers he took Tilly back with him to Bedford Close.

'My place is empty nearly all the time now, Freddie,' she reminded him, glancing nervously across the road at the dentist's house. 'I don't want any trouble like last time.'

Fred said frankly, 'I couldn't. Not in all that mess and muddle!' He let her in through the back door and grinned wryly. 'I don't know whether I can here actually, Tilly. It's been a long time. And I'm not used to being unfaithful any more.'

She led the way into the breakfast room. Fred lived in this small room all the time now and there was one of the new electric fires in the hearth that looked like real burning coals. She squealed with delight and switched it on.

'Oh darling, I always did like your house. And we can be *warm*! I'm hardly ever warm these days. Let's do it here.'

She went into his arms and began to kiss him with an insouciant passion that took away any sense of ghastly betrayal and brought the whole episode down to the level of necking in the one-and-ninepennies at the old Picturedrome. She went on kissing him even as she peeled off her clothes and started on his. By the time she'd finished she was giggling helplessly. They collapsed in a heap on the rug and he found it very easy; very easy indeed.

It was afterwards it became suddenly awful. As they lay looking into the ersatz fire, there was a sensation of . . . it was hard to put a word to it . . . disintegration. As if his whole life, so carefully and tortuously constructed, was under a giant hammer. He'd had it under his own control until . . . until when? He couldn't even remember that. He

232

knew it was no longer under his control.

Tilly leaned on one elbow and began to kiss him again. Then she raised her head.

'Christ, Freddie. Are you crying?'

He forced a laugh. 'Oh yes. Like a baby.' He pushed her down and began to bite her neck. She shrieked with laughter and wriggled about and he made growling noises at her. It helped to create an illusion of mastery. And shut out the fear. Yes, by God. He was frightened.

At Easter Davie went to Gillian Smith's farm to pick up the early potatoes. The tubers were turned on top of the earth by machine and the girls worked in a line, walking along the rows putting the small potatoes into bags. It was back-breaking work and after so much rain the earth clung to potatoes and boots, reluctant to let go of anything. Conversation was perforce laboured and sporadic. Gillian Smith's sister was getting married in June and Gillian described her bridesmaid's dress gaspingly and without elation.

'It's been altered from something Mummy had before the war!' she panted. 'Honestly. You never saw anything like it. There's a great scorch mark on the shoulder which we're embroidering over.'

'You could borrow my party frock if you like, Gill.' Davie thought of the lovely American dress hanging under dust sheets in her wardrobe. It would be too short for her to wear full length now anyway. 'It's blue satin with a net over the top.'

'Satin? where did you get a satin frock from?' Gill stopped work and stared wide-eyed.

'My aunt sent it from America. She's not really my aunt, but she sends us all sorts of things. Food parcels and things.' Davie straightened. 'It'll be all right on you, you're miles shorter than me.'

Gillian was enthusiastic. She came home with Davie that very night and tried on the dress. She must have

233

talked a lot about Davie when she got back home with it. The next week came a letter from Mrs Smith inviting the whole family to the wedding and asking whether Davie would sing in the church while the register was being signed. Davie sang 'O Perfect Love' and afterwards everyone said it was the most delightful rendering they'd heard.

In August she sang at a Forces concert in the Shire Hall. Two weeks later a letter arrived from an unknown firm in London who described themselves as 'Theatrical Agents'. The letter was signed by Henry Biggins and suggested that Davie might like to sing at a concert being held in Cheltenham for the Russian Relief Fund. A fee was named which surprised them all. David said, 'I can remember Henry Biggins. He was a music-hall chap. Monty might know something about him.'

Aunt Sylv shook her head. 'We don't want our girl on the stage. Not proper.'

Flo said, 'Oh it would be lovely. She might be another Forces' Sweetheart when she's older and all the girls at school would know I was her sister.'

April said, 'I agree with Aunt Sylv. She's too young and there's the School Certificate next year.'

David laughed. 'Stop jumping the gun, everybody. This Henry whatsit is offering to pay Davie to sing at the town hall. What does she say?'

Davie thought of the enormous town hall filled with people, and she quailed. Then she thought of the five pounds less ten percent.

'I could buy a new bike,' she said.

Monty knew Henry Biggins from the old music-hall days and said he was a decent chap.

'Don't forget your old uncle when you're world famous, will you, Davie?' He got on one knee and made sheep's eyes at her. 'I could be your manager. Arrange all the bookings. Keep the wolves from the door.'

April shortened the American dress to mid-calf and

234

dyed her own white satin wedding shoes a pale blue to match. May offered to perm Davie's hair for the occasion, but then it was decided that her 'Veronica Lake' style suited her better. May provided some blue net gloves and March sent money for a corsage. On the morning of the concert an enormous sheaf of roses arrived from Fred.

The town hall at Cheltenham had been built when the Spa drew as many visitors as Bath; it was not unlike the school hall at Denmark Road, high-ceilinged with galleries running around its perimeter wall. The platform was a bower of foliage and crowded with the orchestra and a grand piano, Davie had had a single rehearsal that afternoon with a piano accompaniment only. She was to sing 'Fairest Isle'.

Mr Biggins had come down personally and he and Monty stood either side of her in the corridor leading to the wings and reminisced about their days in music hall. They both knew someone called Maud Davenport who had recently got a contract at the BBC. Monty was thrilled to bits about it, but — Davie could tell — also jealous. He said, 'Good for Maud. Marvellous.' Then — 'Bit long in the tooth now though, surely, old man.' And Mr Biggins said, 'Shows what I can do for people, Monty. If ever you want to tread the boards again just get in touch.' Davie wondered if she could smell her own sweat and when she sniffed experimentally the dust in the corridor made her sneeze. Uncle Monty patted her quickly. 'Enough of that, young lady. Come on. Stand straight. Expand the—'

Mr Biggins said, 'It's you now. Go to it, girl.'

And Davie was edging between the piano and the evergreens and the conductor was tapping his baton and she couldn't see her parents anywhere.

Immediately the orchestra struck up, she knew it wasn't going to be any good. Her voice could not compete with an organ in church, let alone twenty-five people all playing instruments at once.

'Fairest Isle, all i-i--sles excelling . . .'

The only audible bits were during the crescendos. In between, her voice might have reached the front row and the first half of the first gallery. She struggled gamely on, her nerves forgotten in the sheer hard work of singing. She felt anger too; she wanted to turn around and tell the conductor to shut up. She *wanted* to be heard. Now she was out here facing everyone, the least she could was to sing audibly for them.

The applause was kind, but not enormous. As she sank into a curtsey she saw her parents clapping madly, her mother's eyes suspiciously bright. Then, behind Flo, a face detached itself from the mass. It was Mr Stein. He was smiling. She turned to walk off and Uncle Monty yelled 'Encore!' It was so typical of him and very embarrassing in the circumstances. But he kept shouting it and making pushing motions with his hands. The conductor took her arm and led her back to centre stage.

'I would like to sing "The White Cliffs of Dover",' she said tremulously. 'And, if you don't mind awfully, I would like to sing unaccompanied.'

There was a ripple of laughter from the front stalls. It was sympathetic; she sensed that. The conductor bowed and retreated and she clasped May's blue net gloves in front of her and raised her 'top half from her bottom half' as her singing teacher always told her. Then she looked deliberately at Mannie Stein for just an instant and after that she thought only of Olga.

She sang as she had sung that awful afternoon in March. Her voice was still not strong enough to fill the big hall, but its fragility was now part of its charm. It suited the sentimentality of the popular song. The performers who sang it over the air had powerful, resonant voices. Davie's spoke of the frailty of human love in war, yet its indestructibility. At the end there was a pause, then she received an ovation.

Henry Biggins was ecstatic. Monty took most of the credit — 'Never let them die on you darling, if there's the slightest chance of resuscitation!' May hugged her over and over again and said, 'You're launched, Davie — you're well and truly launched!' April and David and Flo stood slightly back from the others, smiling and smiling, with their faces tremulous in the harsh light of the greenroom. The young solo pianist was weeping in the corner; the comedy duo who had done "Gert and Daisy" peeled off their wigs to reveal a pair of elderly gentlemen; the dancing-school girls giggled and showed off atrociously, refusing to change back into their everyday clothes. It was bedlam but exciting bedlam. Davie, shy and retiring, knew that this was what she wanted. If anything could fill the void of Albert's absence in her life, of Olga's death and of her own part in that betrayal, then it was this. 'Public performance' Mr Biggins was calling it. 'Get in as many public performances as you can, girl. Experience — that's what you need. Experience. I'll get you local engagements till you've finished school. Then . . . we'll see.'

Much later that night April and David lay in the big double bed at home, and relived the whole evening.

'Did you see her face when Mr Biggins as good as told her she had a future?' April hugged David's arm to her side. 'I never thought she'd be able to do it. Church, yes. And that Shire Hall do was just like a big party. But she was actually paid for this! And when she stood there and said she'd sing unaccompanied—'

'I knew she'd pull it off somehow,' David maintained stoutly. 'Just for a few minutes I admit she was a bit shaky—'

'*She* was shaky! You were trembling like a leaf!'

'It was because I was holding on to you and you were vibrating the whole time!'

'Oh David —' she laughed helplessly and kissed him and they clung together, conscious as so often of the tenuousness of their relationship; of all relationships.

He whispered, 'I'm so thankful she's . . . got something.'

April's eyes opened and stared into the darkness.

'Yes. I know.'

'But?'

'Nothing, my darling.'

'But you wish there was someone special for Davie. Someone like Albert.'

She stopped breathing, wondering, as so often before, how much David knew. Really knew.

He kissed her hair. 'You really want something for our girls like we have.' His hand came up and cupped her face. 'Primrose, it doesn't have to be the same. Perhaps Albert and Davie had it, perhaps not. But someone else will come along and another bond will be forged. And perhaps it will be even stronger. Who knows?'

She breathed again and closed her eyes. He did not know. For a moment relief flooded her, then aching disappointment. If only he knew everything, if only he could share with her the anguish of her knowledge.

She whispered, 'I'm sure you're right, darling.' She lifted her face. 'Oh David, sometimes I wish I didn't love you quite so much.'

He understood that too. Their love had never been entirely without pain.

Thirteen

NINETEEN forty-one seemed to fly by as if Davina's emergence from the chrysalis might have been precipitated by world events. American lend-lease swung into action. Then there was old Hitler's sudden vicious attack on Russia. Then Italy's invasion of Greece. And to finish the year the disasters and triumphs of Pearl Harbour and Stalingrad.

Victor came home hurriedly as Mussolini and Hitler between them over-ran Greece and Yugoslavia. Officially his work had been done with camera, but he had sketches that spoke more than any photograph. For a month he had lived with the guerrillas of Crete, and his charcoal had perfectly captured their hollow, burning eyes, sunken faces, veiled aggression. In January of the New Year, he was given three weeks leave, and he spent most of it in his attic studio at Chichester Street working on a massive canvas into which he worked his sketches.

On his first Sunday back, the Dakers came to lunch to welcome him home officially. Fred was invited but was otherwise engaged. May had got hold of a home-bred rabbit and had stuffed and roast it like a chicken. The meat was as white, and with bread sauce and some of David's home-grown sprouts it was as good as Christmas.

'Welcome home son,' Monty lifted one of Florence's special glasses containing some of Aunt Sylv's home-brewed wine. Everyone followed suit with great solemnity, except Gretta, who, at three and a half was as precocious as her brother had been.

'He's not weally home,' she objected, shaking her head petulantly as her mother proffered ginger beer. 'He's upstairs all the time. An' he never brought me a present. An' he won't draw me any more. An' he won't do jigsaws with me. An'—'

'And he's going rapidly off his beastly little sister,' Victor finished without a lot of humour.

'Oh darling!' May protested, hugging Gretta consolingly. 'She's been dying to see you after all.'

Flora said, 'I'll do a puzzle with you this afternoon Gretta.'

Victor said, 'I've got three weeks in which to do three years' work, Mother.'

Monty said, 'No need to snap your mother's head off, old man.'

'I wasn't snapping anyone's—'

April said, 'This is simply delicious, May. You were always a marvellous cook but you've surpassed yourself today.'

'Pity about the bones — rabbit bones are so small. I have to be very careful when I give Gretta any.'

'I don't like wabbit anyway.'

Victor said pleasantly, 'How would you like to have to eat rats and mice? Or simply go without for a few days.' He surveyed her. 'Wouldn't hurt you. You're as fat as a butterball.'

'Victor!' protested May.

Gretta, prompted by her mother's tone, began to wail. Her ginger beer was somehow swept on to Monty's lap and he leapt up with streaming trousers and flicked at her head with his napkin. She screamed in earnest.

'Oh Christ.' Victor stood up too. 'I'll skip pudding if you don't mind, mother. Mustn't waste the light.'

'Victor!' May said yet again.

'Don't make a drama Mama! It'll be dark by four — I'll

be down then and do a puzzle with Ghastly Gretta.' He ruffled the fair hair and the child could only just hide a reciprocal smile.

David said, 'Go to it, Victor. We're proud of you.'

'Thanks, David. Thanks.'

Victor paused by the door. 'Any chance of some proper coffee? Davie could bring it up, Mother. To save your poor old legs.'

May looked up, trying unsuccessfully to be annoyed; then she put out her tongue. Everyone laughed.

Davie studied Victor's painting from all possible angles while he crouched on an upturned box, sipping his coffee with great relish.

'Well? Aren't you going to say anything?' he asked at last.

'They're like . . . embers,' she replied tentatively. 'I mean they look all banked down. As if they're beaten. But you know they're not. I mean you've put something there, in them. There's still a fire burning right underneath. I don't know. I'm hopeless at art.'

'No you're not. You can't work it out, but you feel it all right. Embers. I like that.' He sipped and looked and considered. 'Yes. That's how they are, Davie. A match, a bit of kindling, and they'll flare up again. Thanks, old girl. Thanks.'

'I like this one better than the one you did ages ago. After Dunkirk. That dead girl. I didn't like that.'

'This is just as grim. Worse if anything. She'd escaped the old mortal coil. These poor blighters are being strangled by it but they're still alive.'

She said flatly, 'I can't bear death. Everything is over. You can't say sorry. You can't do anything.' She went close to the painting. 'These people . . . there's hope for them.' He was silent for a while, remembering. Finally he sighed sharply and said, 'If I couldn't paint, I'd go mad.' He brought himself back to the present. 'I paint. You sing. Strange, isn't it, Davie?'

She moved away from the canvas and went to the window. Outside, the sky was full of snow, but none had fallen yet.

She said, 'I don't really *sing*. Not like you paint.'

He said, 'Come off it. Monty's told me about the do at the town hall. You sing all right.

'It's funny. You calling your father Monty.' She laughed uncomfortably. 'It wasn't the singing so much. I can't explain. It's doing something frightening. Making them listen. *Conq*uering something.'

'Well?' He came and stood by her. 'I have to make people *see*.'

'No you don't. You're painting it's . . . sort of . . . out of yourself. I mean you're up here all by yourself. I don't want to sing by myself. It's only when people want me to sing and I don't want to and I make myself.'

He waited for further explanations, but none came. He turned and balanced his buttocks on the narrow window ledge so that he wasn't looking at her.

'And does that make it better for you, Davie?'

'A bit. Perhaps. I think . . . I hope it might later on.'

He said flatly, 'I don't get it.' He made his voice like James Cagney's and she giggled. Then sobered.

'I don't either. Not really. It's just that so much bad has happened. Somehow, it must be — partly — my fault —' He exclaimed and turned to her but she ducked away. 'No, I don't mean the war, though I don't see why not. It can't have been made by Hilter all on his own. I was thinking of Audrey Merriman and Robin Adair and Olga. And Albert getting wounded and marrying Elizabeth Doswell.'

'Oh God. Davie. You're too bright to think any of that is your *fault*, surely? Hitler was definitely responsible for Olga. As for that swine Adair . . . Albert and I used to play cricket against him when we were at school. He was a swine then, and he's till a swine.'

She said stubbornly, 'We're all responsible — a bit — for everything that happens. That's all I mean.'

She walked behind his easel and peered round at the

picture as if she hoped to catch it unawares. Then she went back to the window ledge and tackled a piece of loose paint with her thumbnail.

'No, it's not the same. You've always had to paint. I haven't had to sing. It's more than just doing something difficult. It's . . .'

'Go on. You must try to explain.'

'I'm trying. It's a sort of . . . payment.'

'Oh God. A penance? A propitiation to the gods?'

'I suppose so.'

He did not look at her; he closed his eyes for a long moment. Then he opened them and said, 'Davie, when this bloody war is over, let's get married. We understand each other more than most married couples.'

She laughed. 'You don't have to rescue me you know, Victor.'

'Oh Christ. Listen, Davie. Albert is *married*. She's a nice girl. Are you making all these offerings to the gods in the hope that they'll strike her dead and give you another chance?'

A small drift of paint flakes floated to the floor of the attic. She said in a low voice, 'You shouldn't have said that.'

'Davie, I'm sorry. Forgive me. Come here and—'

'But since you have . . . are you going to see them before you go back to your unit?'

'No.'

'Please, Victor.'

'I haven't been asked, Davie.'

'You don't have to wait for an invitation. Not you.'

'Hells Bells. What good will it do?'

'I want to know how he is.'

'A medical report? How Albert Tomms copes with one arm?'

She swallowed and started on the rusted paint on the catch. 'Yes. And more than that. How he *is*. And . . .'

'Go on,' he said mercilessly.

'Nothing.'

243

'How Elizabeth is? How their marriage is? How they get on in bed? Would you like me to sneak up the stairs after lights out and listen at their door?'

Her nail broke and she flinched.

He put his arms around her and forced to her to stand still within them.

'You damned fool, Davie. If only you knew . . . . Christ, if only you knew. Of course I'll go. Next weekend.'

She sobbed once into his neck.

'Even if it snows?'

'Even if it snows.'

'Thanks, Victor. I just want to know. I must be in contact with him somehow. I'm sorry.'

'Shut up. And keep asking me things and telling me things, d'you hear?' He held her away, shaking her fairly hard. 'D'you hear me? I'm the only one who understands. The only one.'

She knew of course that that wasn't true, but she smiled obediently and nodded. 'All right, Victor. All right.'

Albert opened his mail inexpertly with his left hand; there was some information about combine harvesting which was interesting; a new treatment for liver fluke in sheep which he pushed straight into the waste-paper basket because they had no sheep at Doswells'. Finally there was a letter from Victor. He spread the single sheet with splayed fingers. It was the sixth letter he'd had from old Victor; for that reason alone he should practice more often writing with his left hand.

'Lizzie!' He called through to the lean-to kitchen where Elizabeth, on leave from her hospital, was making a cake. 'Lizzie — Victor's coming! You remember Victor? My cousin from Gloucester. He's on leave, three whole weeks, lucky devil. He'll stay a night. We can't put him up here, have to move back to the farm.'

Elizabeth appeared in the doorway. She had never looked girlish; now, after eighteen months of marriage and nursing, a resignation was added to her previous maturity. She had not given up trying to attain some kind of happiness, but with the death of her brother she might well have realized that her youthful dreams of pastoral bliss should be confined between the covers of Thomas Hardy's novels. Already the resemblance between her mother and herself was marked. When she was at home she wanted to be in command. To do this effectively she moved them out of the farmhouse and into their honeymoon cottage. Everyone chose to see this as a romantic escape; in fact it was much more practical; she wanted her own kitchen and she wanted her husband to herself. She thought her mother did too much for Albert. Some of her patients were more handicapped than he was, yet far more independent.

For that reason she said now, 'Oh, we can manage here. After all, this is our home. He can sleep on the sofa in this room.'

Albert said mildly, 'But why, darling.? It's awfully primitive here and it will be hard work for you.

'Not if you help,' she replied lightly but with a glance towards the languishing fire. 'And Victor's not entirely helpless, if I recall.'

He gave her his usual sweet smile. 'If that's what you want, Lizzie.'

She felt suddenly perverse. 'It's not what I *want*, Tommy. It's what I think would be best. It seems odd to me to move back to my parents' house when we have a guest.'

'But I never think of Doswell Farm as your parents' house. It's surely the family's house?' He got up from the table and went to the coal hod. Immediately she felt consumed with guilt. 'And anyway they wouldn't mind in the slightest.' He began to throw coal on piece by piece.

'Let me do that, Tommy.' She lifted the hod and hurled coal. The fire went black and dead. She straightened and dusted her hands together. 'I know they wouldn't mind, dear. That's not quite the point.' She turned her back on the sulky grate. 'Anyway, it's warmer here.'

'Yes. It's fine for us of course. But . . . there's no privacy.'

Suddenly she was angry. 'Are you afraid Victor will hear us in the bedroom?'

There was a small silence while they both appeared to hold their breath. Then he said quietly, 'I was referring to the lavatory.'

'Yes. Yes, I know.' She moved away from him and leaned on the table. Victor Gould's writing was enormous, he had got no more than a dozen words on to his single page. She blinked. 'Tommy darling. I'm sorry.'

'No. You're right of course. Victor must take us as he finds us. This is our home.'

'No darling. *You're* right. The farm is our home too and Mummy and Daddy will adore to have us all under one roof for once.'

'Lizzie. Please. You don't have to—'

'It'll be better. I'm tired. It will be a rest for me too.' She blundered towards the door to the stairs. 'I'll go and throw a few things together. We might as well walk over before lunch.'

'But your cake—'

'I'll take it with me. Mummy's oven is much better.' She coughed as she started up the stairs.

Albert stared after her. Then he went into the kitchen and looked at the mixing-bowl. Strange how losing an arm affected the balance; he was always barging into things, especially in this tiny cottage. Over at the farm, Ellen made sure there was plenty of space for him when he was on the move. Ellen and George were good to him, they made no demands, they expected nothing of him. Not that Lizzie exactly expected him to take on the world.

He pushed the mixing-bowl against a biscuit tin and pinioned it there with his stomach; then he held the wooden spoon in his left hand and made laborious orbits around the bowl. It was like that silly game where you rubbed your stomach with one hand and patted your head with the other. It simply wouldn't work properly. He

246

went back to the table and read Victor's letter again. It would be good to see Victor. He might be able to talk to him.

The snow came the following Saturday. Gloucestershire, Wiltshire and Dorset became anonymous beneath six inches of it. Victor insisted on building an enormous snowman in the garden of the farmhouse. Davie, Flora and Gretta had a snowball fight with the grown-ups at Longmeadow; Tilly Adair and Fred Luker were snowed in at a small hotel near Painswick Beacon; and Mannie Stein caught a bus running out to Brockworth Factory for a Canteen Theatre, dropped off at Barnwood to see Sibbie, and found himself stuck there with no transport back to the city.

He got hold of a girl at the Black and White Bus station on the telephone and harangued her assiduously.

'If they can run a bus out of Gloucester, they can run one back,' he anounced tightly in conclusion.

The clerk informed him that the bus in question had returned already. 'Immediately the show was over,' she enlarged. And, in case he didn't believe her, 'I can see it from where I sit, sir. Parked at the end of the line. All ready for Monday morning, weather permitting.'

He tried the taxi office without success.

'You can stay here overnight, Mannie,' Sibbie offered half-heartedly. Even without Fred's warning she was well aware that Mannie's interest in her did not really extend to all-night visits. She wasn't that keen herself.

Mannie stood looking at the telephone, for once in his life indecisive. The weather had taken things out of his hands, but there must be a way of turning his isolation to his own advantage. It was amusing as well as possibly profitable to liaise with Sibbie Luker so openly, but to stay in her house overnight was gilding the lily. She could no longer tell him anything he did not know, and her physical similarity to April, which had been so provocative at first, was now abrasive.

However as it would appear he had very little choice, he decided to milk the situation for whatever he could get from it, and, shrugging at Sibbie resignedly, he dialled his own number. He knew exactly what he would say to Bridie. 'You don't mind too much, my darling? Your stepmother will make me most welcome, I know that . . .'

There was a click and Marlene's voice came tinnily over the wire. He spoke curtly and she replied vaguely.

'Mrs Stein? Oh you mean Miss Bridget. No, she's not back yet sir. And the girls is all outside a-building the biggest snowman you ever . . what's that? Eh? I'm not entirely sure where she goes to, sir, when you're at Barnwood. Mebbe the shops. Mebbe Winterditch Lane to see Miss April. She's gen'lly back long before you sir, so she can't go far.'

He was silent for along moment, staring at the wallpaper with a concentrated frown. Then he said slowly, 'Listen carefully, Marlene. When Mrs Stein returns, will you tell her please that I am snowbound at the house of Mrs Williams. I will not be returning until tomorrow.

'Righty-oh sir. And shall she telephone you there?'

'No. And I will not telephone again, Marlene. We do not wish to be disturbed.'

'Oh.' Marlene was thick but, even so, he could practically hear her putting two and two together. 'Oh. Well. Ah.'

'Thank you, Marlene.' He hooked the receiver and immediately took it off again and dialled his office number.

'Sibbie, please go in by the fire, dear. I will be with you in a moment.' He had no wish for Sibbie to begin any additions sums; she was more intelligent than Marlene.

Monty answered the telephone; the office girls insisted on taking Saturday afternoons off.

'Good afternoon. Williams and Sons, Auctioneers. What can I do for you?'

Mannie listened hard before replying. Monty's tone

was too jocular; was there an answering giggle somewhere?

'Ah. Sorry, Gould. Interference here.' He paused again as if wrestling with Sibbie. Then he said, 'Just to let you know I'm stuck at Barnwood. Won't be back till tomorrow. I've left a message with Marlene, but you might let my wife know I won't be ringing again. Too busy.

Another pause, probably while Monty worked out what lay behind his words. Then he said, 'Er . . . do you wish me to telephone your wife, Mr Stein.'

Mannie smiled, certain now that Bridie was standing right behind Monty.

'If you wouldn't mind, Gould.'

He re-hung the receiver, glanced at the door and tore the wire out of its socket on the skirting board. Then he took his coat and hat from the hall stand and went into the small sitting-room which Sibbie now called her 'salon'.

She looked up from her armchair.

'You can use Edward's pyjamas if you like, Mannie. And sleep in the spare room.'

He was momentarily surprised; then pushed Sibbie out of his mind. 'I won't need either, thank you, my dear. I intend to walk back home immediately.' He began to shrug into his long black overcoat. Sibbie was astonished.

'It's nearly four miles, Mannie! And in this snow it will take the rest of the afternoon!'

He dusted his hat on the sleeve of his coat.

'I've got the rest of the afternoon, Sibyl. And the evening too.'

'Mannie Stein . . . you're up to something!' She got out of the armchair and tried to sound arch, but there was anxiety in her blue eyes.

'I don't want to outstay my welcome here. And I have work to do at the office.' He took her hand and bowed over it perfunctorily. 'Thank you for a pleasant lunch and some interesting conversation.'

She hung on to his hand. 'And other things too, Mannie.' Her voice lapsed into practised coquetry; instinct told her to keep him here.

But he had very definite plans.

'Goodbye, my dear.'

He released himself and was out of the front door before she could think of another ploy. In any case inclination warred with instinct; she had a good novel and a box of black market chocolates, and Mannie Stein was not really her cup of tea.

She watched him negotiate the drive and disappear down the lane before she picked up the phone. She'd ring Monty and tell him what the old goat had said. It was the least she could do and just might put Monty — and therefore May — in her debt. When she found that he had ripped out the telephone connection she knew her instinct had been right and she should have kept him with her at all costs. For a long moment she considered running after him. But it was so damned cold; and she owed neither Bridget, Monty, nor any of them, a damned thing.

She went back to the fire and found her novel under a cushion.

Elizabeth, still anxious to make up for her remark of the day before, stood at Albert's right side and tried to be his hand.

Victor shouted, 'Come on old man, no relying on your wife. Pile the snow around his feet otherwise he'll be top-heavy!'

Elizabeth panted, 'I'll do it this side darling, you do it the other.'

Unexpectedly Albert became stubborn.

'You're getting in my way, Lizzie. Let me have space!'

She looked at him, startled and hurt. It was what she'd wanted to hear for over a year, and it had to come in response to a tactless remark from his cousin. She moved sharply away from the grotesque snowman and Albert, scooping snow with his left glove, toppled to his right and collapsed into the small drift against the icy box hedge. She rushed forward, conscience-stricken, but Victor was convulsed with laughter.

'Leave him, Lizzie! He's like this thing, not a broad enough base!'

Albert scrambled to his feet and advanced on his cousin with a quickly gathered snowball. The next moment the two were grappling like grizzly bears, bulky in overcoats and scarves, helpless with stupid schoolboy sniggers.

Elizabeth called, 'Oh Tommy — oh darling — be careful. You'll fall again!'

Victor shoved him and he did indeed fall; Victor stood over him, crowing triumph.

'At last! After all these years!' Albert had always been the physically stronger of the two and had stood over Victor very often. Victor waved his arms. 'Victor the victorious! It took a world war to do it but—'

Elizabeth was aghast at this further tactlessness, amounting to brutality. Then Albert grabbed Victor's ankle and he came down on top of him with a sickening thud. She rushed forward and tugged at him. Albert looked up.

'For goodness sake, Lizzie! Do stop fussing, woman.'

Again she stared. Albert was still laughing, snow in his hair and on his eyebrows, his left hand flailing madly at Victor's head. The two of them got to their feet somehow, Albert without help from anyone. He staggered about the trodden snow trying to find his balance.

Victor spluttered, 'Spread your feet, you idiot! What's the matter with you? You've got to compensate for being lighter on one side!' He pushed his cousin and sent him sprawling again. 'Come on — come on — my God, it's too easy —' he danced about, shadow-boxing now. Elizabeth turned away.

'I'll get some tea,' she called over her shoulder. She should be glad — she should be very glad, she told herself fiercely as she went into the warmth of the kitchen. But the intense cold had made her eyes smart almost as if she were weeping.

The office was very quiet after Monty replaced his telephone. In the corner the iron Courtier stove creaked as it expanded in its own heat, and the smell of old books was throat-tickling. Bridget took her hand away from her mouth and closed her eyes for a moment.

'D'you think he knew I was here?' she breathed.

'No. Definitely not. He simply wanted to make absolutely sure you would know he was with Sibbie. He's a nasty piece of work, Bridie.'

'Yes.' Bridie opened her eyes wide and they filled with tears. 'You are the only one who understands — who believes me.' She shuddered. 'Not that I've told anyone else. He'd find a way of getting at me if I did.'

Monty stood up with much scraping of his chair to cover his emotion and went to the window. As he passed Bridget's chair he put a hand on her shoulder. It was sharp beneath the botany wool of her twin-set.

He said, 'Is there nothing I can do, Bridie?'

'Can you think of anything?' She swivelled her chair to look at his back. She was so fond of Monty Gould, so terribly fond. He was like the brother she'd never had. She sighed. 'He won't leave me, Monty. And what should I do if I left him? Where should I go?' She went to stand by him. Outside the snow blanket lay softly over King Street and its adjacent square. An army lorry, heavily chained, grated slowly beneath the window and turned into Eastgate Street; otherwise there was no traffic to be seen, and few people. She murmured, 'It's so quiet, so peaceful. I don't want to go back to Nash and Beattie and Lana and Catherine and Barty.'

'Well, you don't have to go for ages yet. You could come home with me for some tea and have a chat with May while I put Gretta to bed.'

'He'll ring the house at tea-time.'

'He said he wouldn't.'

'I know. I heard. But he will.'

'Oh Bridie. It's so ghastly. We've got to do *something*.'

'No we haven't. You've not told May, have you, darling? Because so long as I toe the line, it's not too bad at all. Honestly. He's marvellous to me so long as I let him have his own way. And now that I can keep an eye on things here I don't feel completely powerless.'

Monty took her hand. 'You know I'll tell you if there's anything happening on this front. But how can you go on and on with him?'

'It won't be forever, Monty. He's much older than I am and he has trouble with his liver.' She grinned wickedly, suddenly the old Bridie again. 'I absolutely ply him with drink, darling. He gets as much as he likes from some chappie in London and I'm simply marvellous at keeping his glass topped up.'

Monty grinned back at her, easily reassured. Since Bridie's clandestine visits to the office, he had been much less bored with his job. A little excitement made all the difference.

He put her hand to his mouth and nibbled the knuckles. 'Dear brave Bridie. You can always resort to arsenic if it gets too bad.'

'Will you supply it, Monty?'

'What? Oh, the arsenic! I thought . . .' he nibbled harder, and they both started to laugh.

It was a couple of hours later, after he had looked at her back where very faint markings were supposed to be the left-over of her last beating, that they gave up all pretence at working and sat on the floor in front of the Courtier. Her twin-set was back in position, but she looked ruffled and flushed. She put her head on Monty's shoulder and they both gazed sentimentally into the fire and talked of old times, and she was about to stand up and go home, when a draught swept like cold water around her waist and they both twisted around to see Mannie Stein standing in the open doorway, surveying them with a small smile on his dark face.

It took May some time to believe that Monty had actually been sacked.

'What on earth are you talking about, darling?'

As Victor had gone to see Albert, May had taken Gretta up to Longmeadow for the day and wanted to tell Monty about the snowball fight in the garden, the three girls bombarding the women. Even Aunt Sylv had joined in, swathed in bits of blanket and one of David's old raincoats. Then David had come home from the shop and they'd toasted pikelets in front of the fire, and it had been such fun. But Monty had this peculiar cock and bull story about Mannie Stein sacking him and had no ears for anything else.

'What's it got to do with Mannie?' she queried, her voice rising a register as Gretta started to whine about there being no fire. 'Sibbie is your boss now. And knowing what we know about Sibbie, you've got a job for life there!'

'You don't under*stand*, May! You simply do not understand!' Monty seemed distraught. He paced up and down the kitchen, ignoring poor Gretta and making no attempt to fetch any coal from the cellar. 'I'm not too concerned about myself. It's poor Bridie! My God, he'll kill her! I don't know what to do, darling. What can I do?'

But when he made her understand the full position, she was unusually unsympathetic. She insisted on him sitting down, certainly, but then she dumped the child on his lap and marched out of the kitchen with the empty coal hod. And when she returned she made the fire up as if her life depended on it, then undressed Gretta in front of it without her usual bedtime badinage.

Monty reverted to their old baby talk.

'Mummy, Monty's scared. Bridie's got weals on her back now from his . . .' he glanced at the avid Gretta, '. . . ministrations. It's obvious he tricked her into thinking he was going to spend the night with Sibbie—'

May reached for a facecloth from the sink and wiped Gretta's hands with unnecessary vigour.

'How do you know she's got weals on her back, Monty?'

'Darling . . . Mummy darling . . . she told me, of course.'

'And you believed her?'

'Well of course. Why would she lie about a terrible thing like that?'

'Because she's Bridie Williams and hasn't changed in the last forty years.'

'Oh really, May—'

'No-one can have wheels on their back anyway, Daddy,' Gretta said reasonably. 'On their feet like roller skates. But not on their backs.'

'It's past your bedtime, Gretta,' Monty snapped.

'She was hoping to tell you about her afternoon,' May said. 'But of course as you've been so busy—'

'My God, May. I'm now without a job. And you've got the gall to go all sarky on me. It's too bad.'

'You just said you weren't concerned about yourself, dear. Only Bridie. In fact you seem to be more worried about poor old Bridie that you are about me or Gretta.'

'May . . . Mummy darling. Monty doesn't know which way to turn and needs his girlies.' He tried to encircle both of them with his arms, but Gretta was bulky in her dressing-gown and May had not taken off her topcoat yet.

'Excuse me, Monty.' She made heavy weather of standing up with the child in *her* arms. 'I'm going to take Gretta up to bed now. Perhaps you'd be kind enough to do her hot-water bottle and bring it up. And then you can make some tea. *If* you don't mind.'

It was only when she had got upstairs and was listening to Gretta's prayers, that the full awfulness of Monty's tale hit her. They were used to a good salary now; they were used to the prestige of the job; they were used to Monty being practically his own boss. What on earth were they going to *do*?

In the event, Fred turned up trumps.

'You need an outlet for your acting talents, old man,' he

said when Monty broke the news the next time they met in the Lamb and Flag. 'You'd have stayed there for ever, mouldering away. Look on this as a gift from heaven.'

Monty was surprised. He had expected support from May and a turned-down mouth from brother-in-law Fred.

'All very well, Fred,' he said gloomily. 'I'm too old to go back to music hall. I suppose one day I might manage Davie, but until then it'll have to be the munitions factory like everyone else.'

'Rubbish. You're going to sell cars for me, Monty.'

'Sell cars? In wartime?'

'Quite. No-one else could do it. But you will. You're a confidence man. Have been all your life. Snow to Eskimos — all that sort of thing. Now admit it and go into selling.'

'I don't know the first thing about cars, Fred. It's bloody good of you and maybe when there's some petrol about again . . .'

'Listen, old man. I've got the Austin agency in Gloucester, as you know. Up at Winterditch camp there's an officer's mess bursting at the seams with gents from all over the world — Yanks, Poles, Free bloody French . . . they can get petrol, Monty. And they need cars so that they can have natty little Waaf drivers to take them all over the countryside.'

Monty used old Will Rising's favourite oath. 'Christa-mighty, Fred . . .'

'Quite so,' Fred agreed again. 'What do you say, brother-in-law?'

Monty grinned enormously. He knew only too well that Fred had a pretty low opinion of him on the whole; it was good for his morale that in one thing at least Fred's opinion was very high indeed. He winked across the bar at the landlord.

'And one for yourself,' he said.

They'd already had their quota for the evening — beer arrived weekly and was rationed out arbitrarily by all landlords — but their Coronation mugs were slid behind the bar and refilled immediately.

It was Fred's turn to grin.

'I knew you could do it, Monty,' he said

Bridie spent the next week incarcerated in her room with a heavy cold. She was nursed by her devoted husband and when Natasha brought her the early snowdrops from the garden, the bedroom was darkened.

'Mother has such a headache, darling,' Bridie whispered from the bed.

She was terribly tempted to ask Natasha for writing paper and her fountain pen — all removed from her handbag by Mannie — but knew that Mannie would somehow thwart all her efforts. And in any case, to whom would she write, and what would she say? Although there was nothing *really* between Monty and herself, her husband had caught her in a very compromising position, and had acted as many husbands would. And afterwards he even pretended contrition.

'I should not have left you alone so much, my darling,' he said that first night. 'Because I have been with Sibbie you found it necessary to console yourself with Monty Gould.' He completely ignored other aspects of her presence in the office. Apparently she had gone there simply and solely to seduce poor Monty. 'I shall not leave you for so long again. We will stay up here together. Always together, my Birdy.'

His attitude veered deliberately from smothering kindness to stern condemnation. He would revile her for a whore and a jezebel one minute, and then make passionate love to her the next. It was completely exhausting.

Monty wrote to her. Mannie actually brought the letter upstairs to her unopened, but then he opened it himself and read it aloud to her in mincing tones.

'. . . I cannot apologise enough, Bridie dear. If there is anything I can do — explain to your husband — or see Sibbie or anything at all, please get in touch.'

Mannie smiled as he tore the letter into shreds and let

them fall into the waste-paper basket.

'I see. It was his doing, my darling. How could I have doubted you. My poor Birdy. Come to me.'

She sobbed real tears in is arms. She felt so peculiar and weak and when he was good to her he was so very, very good. She felt it no longer mattered about her father's business; after all, Mannie was running it on her behalf. Everything he did, he did for her.

He took off her nightdress tenderly. 'Everything I do, I do for you, my darling girl,' he whispered, echoing her thoughts. 'Even Sibbie . . . you know that is only so that one day the firm of Williams and Sons will be yours and Barty's. Yours and Barty's alone.' He kissed and caressed her. 'You are trembling, darling. Tell me you love me. Tell me.'

'I love you, Mannie. Oh darling, I do love you.'

'That is my good girl. My own sweet Birdy. My wife. Mine . . .'

Fourteen

MARCH got back to her flat just as dawn lightened the sky. The big semi-detached house off Kilburn High Road had seen better days. Its neighbour, number seventeen, owned by a doctor and his family, sported a shaven lawn front and back, polished door-knocker and windows, tubs of crocuses waving fragilely on either side of the red tiled porch. Number nineteen needed paint on all its woodwork; its porch was crammed with Mrs O'Flaherty's pram and two scooters belonging to her brood. In the wilderness of couch and nettles at the back could be found a rusted bedstead, gas masks and a broken Aladdin oil heater. It was an unlikely home for fastidious March, yet home it was. As she let herself into her ground-floor bed-setting room, she felt a sense of peace she had rarely felt elsewhere. Flat one, number nineteen Chestnut Road, Kilburn, was not only hers alone, it held no memories, no responsibilities, no ties whatever. She could leave it tomorrow without a qualm and with no financial loss. But while she paid her seventeen and six a week rent, it offered rest without a single string attached.

She pulled off her cap and left it on a table just inside the door, her coat lay where it fell with her handbag. She was bone-tired in a way she recognized and liked. It meant she would collapse on to the bed and sleep the day away without any of the dreams which sometimes haunted her. She had been in London for more than a year now, part of a Rescue Unit working north of the river, and in that time she had seen some gory and harrowing sights. Once when a beam had fallen across the bonnet of the ambulance, she had lost control for a vital two seconds, pushed the gear into reverse and revved back so violently she had pinned a woman against a wall. Stan Potter, the warden, a man of March's own age, who treated his team like his own family, assured her that the woman was already dead when the ambulance struck her. March had never believed that, and she saw her in dreams quite regularly; sometimes the woman and Fred were together. Once they had been dancing in the Cadena ballroom and the woman had left a trail of blood on the dance floor.

But today she would sleep without dreams. Last night had been long and tedious. An unexploded land mine had been reported before midnight in Maida Vale. She had sat in the ambulance smoking endless cigarettes, while the bomb squad had dealt with it. Occasionally she had climbed into the back and made tea and taken it to the sergeant on guard. He'd accepted the bunch of Bakelite cups gratefully, but always said the same thing: 'Get back, miss. If this thing goes off unexpected it won't be no joke.'

So she sat it out and at five-thirty a captain, younger than Albert, came to tell her he had defused the bomb and she could go home. He produced a small silver flask of brandy, took a swig and offered it to her. She did not drink, and she was awash with tea, but she took the flask and upended it against her closed lips. It was a gesture; like a salute. She knew if she had been twenty-five years younger he would have kissed her.

She sat on the edge of her bed and kicked off her shoes, wriggled out of trousers, and pulled on what Mr Churchill called a siren suit. It was cold in the unheated room, but she did not stop to prepare a hot-water bottle. As she drew the clothes to her chin she felt sleep draining her head and body. Blissfully she gave herself to it.

It was two hours later that Mrs O'Flaherty called her by

the simple expedient of banging on her redundant cast iron radiator. In the good old days the furnace in the cellar had been stoked to provide these monstrosities with heat; now they were handy as a means of communication. The one next to March's bed reverberated sonorously and she sat up and reached automatically for her gas mask before she realized what it was. Then she looked at the clock and saw it was not yet nine.

'If it's just the post I'll kill you, Mrs O'Flaherty,' she promised, dragging herself to the door with difficulty. One of her legs was ribbed with varicose veins and invariably woke after the other. She opened the door, bellowing 'All *right!*' as she did so, and there . . . there was Bridie Williams. Or Bridie Hall. Or Bridie Stein — whatever she called herself these days.

March stared stupidly. Bridie was thinner than she remembered and very pale. Not surprisingly: if she'd come up from Gloucester she must have started at the crack of dawn.

Bridie confirmed this immediately. 'I came on the milk train, March. I've been in the waiting-room at Paddington since five. I couldn't stay there any longer. She—' a jerked chin in the direction of upstairs. 'She told me you'd be sleeping, but . . . I couldn't wait any longer.'

'You'd better come in.'

Bridie did so just as Mrs O'Flaherty panted downstairs. March said curtly. 'It's all right, Mrs O'Flaherty. Thank you for letting me know,' and started to close the door.

Mrs O'Flaherty squeaked, 'There's a coupla letters for you, Mrs Luker. Which you might as well have now seeing as how—'

March almost snatched the proffered letters. One was in April's handwriting. She closed the door and leaned against it.

Bridie had collapsed on the bed and looked up apprehensively.

'You won't turn me out?'

'Don't be absurd, Bridie. Why on earth should I?'

261

'I've run away. I've got to stay somewhere.'

'Oh Bridie . . . what about the girls? What about Barty?'

'I shall go back, of course. But I have to . . . there's something I have to do first.' She stood up and went to the French windows that looked over the back wilderness. 'March, I need your help desperately. You're the only one. The only one. He'll never find me here, he'll never dream . . .'

March felt her old irritation with Bridie stir beneath her tiredness.

'This is all I've got, Bridie. Just this one room with that sink and cooker. That's it.'

'I thought . . . I thought there was some talk of you putting Davie up. If she had a singing engagement in London or something. I heard them discussing it.' Bridie turned; her face was desperate.

March said wearily, 'If Davie wanted to stay for any length of time, I should move.' She collapsed into a chair. 'Don't look like that, Bridie. You can stay here for a while. I sleep in the day. You can have the bed at night.'

'Haven't you got a bathroom?'

'Good God, woman . . . people are homeless up here. They sleep in the Underground . . . yes, I share one with the old chap on the other side of the hall. What does that matter?'

'Well, it might matter quite a lot. Oh God, March. You don't know. How could you know?'

'Obviously I can't unless you tell me.' March yawned mightily. 'Put the kettle on, Bridie. Let's have a cup of tea.'

They sat either side of the enamel-topped table, while Bridie tried to describe the events of the past year. Even to her own ears they sounded fantastic: products of a fevered imagination. Except Olga's death. That wasn't imagination.

'It was a year ago today, March.' She began to cry into her tea cup. 'Tolly's favourite. She was torn to pieces, absolutely torn to pieces. She was the reason Tolly married me, you know. Did you know that? I was pregnant before—'

262

'I guessed it,' March said brusquely. Then she put out a hand to Bridie's. 'Look, my dear, all this — it's delayed shock. I've seen it happen over and over again. People take terrible tragedies on the chin at the time — April told me you were wonderful when Olga was killed. Then it all catches up. It's a recognized medical condition, Bridie. Nothing to be ashamed of. Stay with me by all means, but don't feel you've burned your boats. I'll get in touch with your husband and explain you're having a little break and—'

Bridie started up, her eyes enormous and terrified.

'You mustn't contact Mannie, March! Please — please — don't do that! I cannot stand against him, you see. He will come up and collect me and look after me and never let me think or feel for myself again. And when he knows . . . when he knows what has happened . . . I shall be completely in his power. Please, March. You must promise me here and now that you won't get in touch with Mannie.'

March was startled out of her exhaustion.

'All right. I promise. Now sit down and try to tell me again what has happened. I think you're quite wrong to think that May and April have ostracised you. You know very well that April has always disliked your husband, so it makes it very difficult for her to continue the friendship. And as for May . . . well, if what you say is true, I can understand her feelings too. She is very possessive where Monty is concerned, Bridie. You should know that by now. You have been almost brazen at times, my dear. I'm sorry, but it's true.' March sipped her tea and thought about Mannie Stein. She didn't care for him at all, but in all honesty it sounded as if he had acted fairly . . . properly . . . all along. It was typical of Bridie to come running up to London just because she'd put her foot in it one more time. March softened her words with a smile. 'You know Bridie, some husbands would have beaten you and kept you on bread and water for flirting with one of their employees. I don't approve of such things, but they do happen.'

263

Bridie gave a sob, struggled out of her coat and wriggled her jumper around her ears. Between the straps of her petticoat were three lines of scabbed skin.

'They were from last month. More recent ones are on my bottom. He did this to Olga too. All in the name of love.' She pulled her clothes down and stared at March. 'I haven't been out of the house since that day, March.'

March was appalled.

'Surely the girls . . . why hasn't April been round to see you? Or Monty — it's his fault, after all!'

'The girls are allowed in. The room is dark but they can see I am all right — pretty nightie, chocolates even, hothouse flowers. April has not been near the house since she called after Olga's death.'

'Oh my God,' March breathed.

'Please help me, March. You've lived here for ages now. You must know the ropes. You can tell me where to go and you've got money. I'll pay you back eventually, March — you know that. But Mannie keeps account of every penny now and I had to borrow from Marlene to buy a train ticket.'

'Of course — you know you're welcome—'

'And can you tell me where to go, March?'

'Where is it you want to go, my dear?'

'Anywhere.' Bridie straightened in her chair. 'Anywhere they don't ask questions. I'm two months so it's early days and shouldn't be difficult. I'll go wherever you think, March.'

March said slowly, 'You're pregnant again.'

'Oh God. Didn't I say? That was the idea, you see. To make me pregnant so that I would be completely in his power. Oh March, I'm forty-two. It used to be so easy with Tolly.' She began to weep. 'My darling Tolly . . . oh March.'

March whispered, 'I can't believe this.'

'I know. It was night after night. Day after day. I can't tell you how awful . . .'

'Oh my God.'

Bridie was sobbing helplessly now. 'He uses me, March. It's so difficult to explain. I hate him and I'm afraid of him, yet when he keeps kissing me and asking me if I love him, I say yes. I think I'm going mad.'

'No, dear. It's him — he's mad. Mad as a hatter. You'll have to leave him.'

'I can't. That's what is so awful, March. He's got the firm tied up so that I can't touch a penny. He's got Sibbie just where he wants her. And there's Barty and the girls. Oh March, I can't desert them. I betrayed Olga, I can't do it again!'

She put her head on the table and March automatically stroked the short brown hair that had always resembled April's. April's bright gold had faded, this had darkened.

She tried to inject some energy into her voice.

'First we'll see about an abortion. And then we'll decide what to do about Mr Stein. I don't want you to worry any more, Bridie. Everything is going to be all right. I promise.'

She thought: Fred will know what to do . . . Fred will deal with this. And with the thought came a great thankfulness.

She suffered Bridie's intense gratitude. She made tea and tried to turn the awful room into some kind of refuge. Her tiredness went away for a while and she smiled grimly when Bridie told her how good Natasha was, making certain she saw her mother every day, bringing her thin bread and butter and asking if she needed anything.

And March thought that however hard she tried, she could not escape from Gloucester and its entanglements. When she left it, it sent her its messengers to pull her back.

Mannie Stein told no-one that Bridie had disappeared. At first he thought it was a short-lived burst of her old defiance and he imagined how easy it would be to bring her back to heel; and indeed how enjoyable. But then after twenty-four hours, the secrecy became difficult. He announced at breakfast table that she had yet another of her spring colds and in an effort to isolate the germs he would take her food to her. 'My little Bird and I will eat together,' he said, ensuring that none of the girls would venture upstairs for fear of seeing something embarrassing. But when he came home from the office at midday he discovered that Marlene had no such inhibitions. He was met at the door by upflung arms and a very white face.

'Oh sir, I'm glad and thankful to see you!' She shook her head as he handed her his homburg. 'You'll 'ave to go straight out agen, sir. She en't nowhere in the 'ouse. I took 'er up a nice glass o' lemon barley just 'alf an hour ago, and she weren't in 'er room. So I went everywhere. Everywhere, sir. "Miss Bridie!" I called. "Miss Bridie" upstairs, "Miss Bridie" in the—'

With enormous restraint he hung up his own hat and coat and smiled. He was suddenly so angry that he wanted to kill her. . . but more than that, he wanted to kill Bridget.

'She came out with me this morning, Marlene. Didn't you see her? I thought a little fresh air would be good for her. She's gone visiting now and I will fetch her home in time for tea.'

Marlene only had the capacity for one emotion at a time, and relief prevailed over bewilderment.

'O-o-o-h *sir!* I bin that worried.'

'Well, do not worry any longer, Marlene. You may take the rest of the day off and go to see your mother.'

'But sir, I've got some kidneys off ration and they'm a' braising nicely for all of us tonight.'

'Then I will serve them. What could be easier? Off you go, child. That is an order.'

After she'd left he too scoured the house, this time for a note. There was none. That ruled out suicide; she would have written a note for Natasha definitely. Besides he knew his Birdy; she would never kill herself.

But she had gone somewhere. April? Yes, April was the

most likely. Or May. But May blamed Bridie for Monty's dismissal. Still . . . Bridie might have contacted Monty and told him where she was going. He stood in the middle of the sitting-room, head bent, thinking. Then he went downstairs, locked the house carefully, donned hat and coat and left by the back door. First of all he would go to the cemetery.

It wasn't exactly the end of the world when Davie failed her 'mock Cambridge'. Miss Miller was careful to tell her that the whole idea of doing a mock examination was to alert the pupil to her own shortcomings. Now if they could look at the marks together, Davie could see for herself that her weak subjects were maths and languages. She had time — just enough time — to work hard and pull up on those subjects. There must be no more performances during term time, in fact none during the Easter holidays either.

Davie said dully, 'I'm not going to do it, Miss Miller. I'm not going to get the Certificate.'

'Nonsense, child. What defeatism. My goodness, if we'd taken that attitude two years ago when France fell, where should we be now? You can do it, Davina. You can show them!'

But Davie felt that it was the end of one particular world. The world of school was almost over. She had felt it in her bones all this year, and since Victor had told her about Albert and Elizabeth, she had been certain that events were gently but inexorably turning her in another direction. Something was glimmering ahead of her. She could not identify the light, but she knew it was at the end of the tunnel.

The last period of that day was games: hockey on a soggy pitch without proper boots or pads. She went to the lavatories and sat uncomfortably on the pan until everyone had cleared out of the cloakroom. Then she sneaked out, rolled her raincoat and beret into a ball inside her shoe bag and, swinging it nonchalantly as if on the way to the hockey field, she went to the cycle sheds. When she was down Worcester Street, she got off her bike and donned her coat and beret. Then she remounted and cycled on towards the cemetery. She often went there if she had a free period. Grandma and Grandad Rising were buried near the brook, and halfway between them and Uncle Teddy's tiny grave, there was a seat. Then on the way back to the cemetery gates, she could stand for just a minute by Olga's marble angel and tell her that she was going to make it all right. She said the same words each time: 'Don't worry, Olga, I'm going to make it all right. Somehow.' Today she left off the 'somehow'. The light at the tunnel seemed brighter and much more definite.

'I'm going to make it all right, Olga.' She nodded at the simpering angel, pleased herself with this new decisive quality. Then she sighed. 'Daddy is going to be hurt about the mock. And Mummy too. You'd have got through with distinctions in everything, Olga.' Then she brightened. 'But that would mean staying on at school and doing Higher, then trying to get a scholarship to university. Flo can do all that. I've got to get on with things. There might not be time if I hang about.' She nodded again at the angel and turned to leave. And there was Olga's stepfather, Emmanuel Stein, come to pay his respects. She hoped so much that Olga knew . . .

For many years Mannie had deluded himself into believing that April returned his demonic desire for her. He might almost have believed himself the lie he put about regarding Davie's birth. But when David Daker had convinced him some years ago that April actually loathed him, all his desire had erupted into a hatred fiercer than anything he had known. Many of his actions since had been directed towards punishing her for her loathing. Now, faced with her daughter, who possessed the same elusive qualities of being not-quite-beautiful, not-quite sexual, not-quite developed, he was seized with a sudden desire to kill her where she stood. Right next to Olga's grave, and within shouting distance of her ridiculous grandparents and the apocryphal Teddy. Davina Daker, named for the man he hated most in the world, the man married to the woman he hated most in the world. Yes, it would be right and just to kill the girl-child where she stood now. It would finish the awful obsession gnawing at his vitals. It would vindicate Olga's death and Bridie's disappearance . . . everything.

The girl said, 'Good afternoon, Mr Stein. It's turned out nicely now, hasn't it?'

He could not speak. He stared at her, feeling his eyes burn in their sockets. She took a step backwards and he forced his gaze away and down to the grave. It was smothered in daffodils.

He said hoarsely, 'She's been here then? Where is she now?'

The girl said, 'Aunt Bridie? I expect she has, yes. It was the anniversary of Olga's . . . it's good of you to come, Mr Stein. You mustn't be upset. Really.'

He said, 'She brought flowers. Yesterday. She must have gone into town to buy flowers. Then she came here. You saw her. She is with your mother. Tell me the truth.'

The girl said doubtfully. 'I don't think Aunt Bridie is at home. I'm not sure. I haven't been home myself yet. And actually she didn't bring the daffs. Winnie and Gillian and Flo and me brought them.'

'You're lying!'

The girl looked shocked. She took another step back and then bent and picked up some of the flowers.

'No. Really, Mr Stein. Look — we wrote a message—'

He snatched the dripping daffodils from her and threw them behind him.

'You're lying. Just like your mother lied to me all those years ago! Sweet talk. Sweet smiles. They meant nothing. Worse than nothing because they were meant to taunt me!' The girl turned and started away and he grabbed at her raincoat and forced her round to face him. 'I knew what she wanted, you see! I knew I could give her what she wanted — and I knew that sop of a husband of hers couldn't give her anything. Anything! D'you hear me — d'you hear me, little April? Do you? Answer!'

'I hear you —' the girl was sobbing with fright but he wanted her to cry and beg for mercy. He shook her hard and she suddenly screamed into his face, 'I hear you — now let me go! Do *you* hear that?'

He almost did; and through the madness there welled a bubble of admiration for this offspring of April Rising. Then, like another bubble, a bubble from the past, he felt her shudder. It was exactly how April had shuddered once before; it was a manifestation of disgust.

She had to die. Only by killing her could he rid himself of that digust, that loathing. She was a tall girl but he was taller. And he knew how to deal with women. He paused now and then to shout at her — 'Tell me you're sorry — beg me for mercy —' but she went on clawing at his hands and refused to speak or shed a tear.

Bridie felt wonderful; drowsy and wonderful. She opened her eyes and saw March sitting by the bed. March looked different; older certainly, but not unattractively so. She looked like someone very important.

Bridie whispered, 'Is it over?'

'Yes.'

'It's a lovely place, March. It must be costing the earth. Shall I get up and come home now?'

For a moment Bridie could have sworn there were tears in the clear tea-brown eyes, except that March never wept.

'No, not yet. I've booked you in for tonight. Tomorrow we're going to an hotel at Maidenhead. And then we'll decide what to do next.'

'I want to go home, March. The girls . . .'

'Then you shall go home. I'll take you home. And I'll tell Mannie Stein — and everyone else — that you had arranged to have a holiday with me some time ago. Everything will be all right again, dear. He will know that I know and he will be . . . more careful.'

270

Bridie felt herself drifting into sleep. The sheets smelled of antiseptic and everything was white and clean and beautiful.

She said weakly, 'What about your work?'

'I've got back leave. There will be no difficulty.'

Bridie whispered, 'You're so good, March. Thank you for not telling anyone about me killing Teddy.' She heard her own words with faint surprise. She hadn't thought of that for years now. Anyway it hadn't been her fault that Teddy had got diphtheria after his tonsils operation. There had been that tin thermometer she put in his mouth, but that couldn't have killed him. Surely?

March stared at her, dry-eyed, her tears gone. It was strange that Bridie blamed herself for Teddy's death. Strange, because March herself had always felt responsible.

Fred Luker paced the length of the office above the garage in London Road, in a physical effort to bring his mental powers to bear on the matter in hand. It was unlike him. Usually he could wrap himself in a waiting stillness, feeling his way around a problem much as he felt his way around the engine of a car. He had learned grim patience at a P.O.W. camp in Silesia; and before that stoicism had been the order of the day during his harsh childhood. He must be getting old. He was missing March so much it was like constantly nagging toothache.

David, sitting at the enormous desk behind which Fred had hoped to see his son one day, spoke up. 'Look, old man, it's an exercise, that's all. We're going to be all right now, what with the Yanks and the Russians and good old Monty cracking away at El Alamein. The Jerries aren't going to be pouring landing craft up the Bristol Channel and down to Gloucester.'

'I know all that, David. Exercise or not, we're stuck with it. And I want us to win.'

'Be realistic. No-one can win. There's only one thing we can do. We get all our barges, line them up where the river narrows here —' the desk was covered by an enormous map of the river, from the docks down to Cardiff. 'Then when the South Gloucesters come up from Berkeley — here — they simply find they're blocked into a bottleneck . . . here. Few thunderflashes. Someone gets ducked. Loud cheers. Home to tea.'

'Exactly. Boy scouts.'

'What else d'you expect? If it *was* the Hun they'd strafe us out of the water anyway. This has got nothing to do with the real thing.'

'There's a purpose to exercises, David.' Fred got on well with both his brothers-in-law, but occasionally David's special brand of cynicism was strangely annoying. 'It's supposed to keep the men on their toes. Morale high. If they realize from the outset that it's a few thunderflashes before tea, where does that get them?'

David smiled slightly. 'Fred, you've changed. You've changed completely. Before the war you would have been the first to see this exercise as no more than a weekend picnic.'

'Exactly. Before the war. The war . . . changed things.'

But Fred knew that it hadn't been the war. The war was a useful excuse for this gradual change in his personality. Christamighty, was he getting stupid? There was something inside him at the moment that wanted to rout the South Gloucesters. Ambush them before they even reached the barges. Sink their boats, give 'em all a ducking in the Severn. What was it? Was it really because he was taking the exercise too seriously, as David obviously thought? Or was it because he was trying to prove to himself that his old aggressions were still alive and kicking?

He quickened his pace across the genuine Wilton off-cut from Kidderminster. In the old days he had never indulged in introspection, and he hated himself now for questioning his every motive now.

He said, 'We could go in the night before. Under cover of darkness. Get behind enemy lines.'

David said, 'The exercise begins officially at midday on April the twelfth, Fred. You're just spoiling for a fight.'

Gladys' head come round the door. She wore a high-necked blouse to hide her goitre and she looked much better.

'Someone looking for Monty. Any ideas?' She asked briefly.

'He's probably up at the Winterditch camp, propping up the officers' bar,' Fred said. Gladys made to leave and he gestured impatiently. 'Don't pass that on, for Chrissake. Who is it?

She shrugged indifferently, but David craning sideways to look out of the window, said slowly, 'It's Mannie Stein.'

'Mannie *Stein?* What the hell does he want?'

Gladys said, 'He wants Monty.'

'Yes, yes. All right. Monty's probably kept the bloody keys to his office desk at Williams' or something. Tell him to come back tomorrow.'

David said, 'Hang on a minute, Gladys.' He looked at Fred. 'He's changed all the locks if I know Mannie. This is something else. He wouldn't come looking for Monty unless it was damned important. Important to Mannie, that is. It's something to do with Bridie. Or one of the children. You'd better try to find out, Fred.'

'*I'd* better try to find out? This business between Monty and Bridget leaves me cold, David. I'm not getting involved.'

'Well, I can't. He won't say anything to me. You might be able to worm something out of him.'

'I'm damned if I'll—'

David forced a grin. 'Come on, Fred. This is just up your street. You haven't really intrigued for years now. Take him on, why don't you?'

Fred stared for a moment, then grinned too, and just as unwillingly. 'You think if I spar with Mannie Stein I might be willing to settle for a weekend picnic instead of a proper exercise? Oh . . . lead on, Gladys. Let's see what

Mr Stein wants with poor old Monty.'

Mannie Stein did not take off his hat. He looked like an undertaker, especially as he was holding a bunch of dripping daffs in one hand. Fred suppressed a smile and led him through the showroom to the sales office. Let him see the kind of cars on sale now, why not? Petrol rationing wouldn't last for ever, and he was a potential customer whether April disliked him or not. For better or worse, probably worse, Stein was married to Bridie now and would doubtless take over her half of the oldest established business in the city. He wouldn't get Sibbie's half; of that Fred was certain. Even so he would be around in the future, and April — everyone — would have to accept him.

'Did you want to buy a car?' he asked, flipping open Monty's appointment book and seeing that he would be back here by four-thirty to take Group Captain Lennox for a test-drive.

He kept his finger in the page and flipped on.

'Not at present. Though, perhaps in the future I might have need of one.' Mannie Stein usually wore an enigmatic smile beneath that homburg. Today there was none and Fred sensed his nervousness. He was deliberately silent, staring down at Monty's engagements for next week.

Stein said at last impatiently, 'Well? When may I see Mr Gould?'

Fred closed the book. 'He doesn't come in every day of course. The position here is a new one and he has to build it up gradually.' He met the dark, sloe eyes. 'You need not concern yourself, Mr Stein. Mr and Mrs Gould are perfectly well and happy.'

As he spoke, he felt a sense of closing family ranks against this invader. One of the reasons he'd eventually married March was to protect the Risings; take over where poor old Will had left off.

Mannie seemed to have lost some of his finesse. He said

bluntly, 'I wish to see Mr Gould. When would it be possible to—'

Fred felt his hackles rise. 'I thought I had made it clear. Mr Gould does not wish to see you. That . . . rather unfortunate episode . . . is now closed and finished with. There is no sense in further recriminations.'

'It is not for recriminations I wish to see him. But it is about my wife. Yes.'

Fred said curtly, 'Monty has not seen your wife since the day you dismissed him from your employ.'

'My wife is ill, Mr Luker.'

'That has nothing to do with Monty. And if you hope to embroil him emotionally again, I must warn you to keep away. In fact kindly keep away from my whole family. None of us wish to have anything to do with you.'

Mannie breathed quickly. 'That is not quite true. One member of your family has been talking to me with great civility. Just an hour ago as a matter of fact. She gave me these daffodils. She spoke kindly. She—'

'And which . . . member . . . was that?' Fred was suddenly alert. If Mannie had got April under his thumb in some way . . . he remembered her terror years before. She had an obsession about the man that had nothing to do with logic or reason. If Mannie had discovered the truth about Davie's birth and was blackmailing April into meeting him clandestinely, he would kill him. Here and now he would kill him.

Stein looked at the flowers and shook his head, not so much in negation but as if clearing it.

'Mr Luker, I have come here about my wife. She is ill. Maybe a little — temporarily — deranged—'

'Deranged? Bridget Hall?' Fred used her old name deliberately. He laughed. 'Never. Unless you have driven her mad.' He moved closer. 'Who gave you those blasted daffodils, Stein? Come on. You're going to tell me.'

Mannie backed off, his colour darkening to navy-blue. 'I am not here to talk about flowers! I have reason to think that Gould knows where my wife has gone!'

275

'Gone? She's deserted you!' Fred gave a single contemptuous snort of laughter, then sobered frowningly. 'If you think — for one moment — that she has gone off with Monty—'

'No!' the word was pitched high. 'She is mine! My wife—' Suddenly the gloved hands reached forward and took Fred by the lapels. The wet daffodils were pushed into his face. 'If this is a conspiracy, you must tell me! Where is she, Luker? You have no reason to protect Monty Gould! If he has her you must speak! Now!'

Fred dashed the flowers away and they fell to the ground. He grabbed at the scrawny neck under the homburg. The two men swayed back and forth like dancers. Once before Fred had tackled Mannie Stein. Then he had wanted some information about Albert, and he had chosen to beat it out of him. A threat would have been sufficient, but Fred had found blessed relief in hitting him. It was the same now. He wrestled with him, even when Mannie's hold on his jacket was simply to avoid slipping on the fallen flowers.

Then Mannie choked, 'You'd hide her — I know you would. When I told April that Albert Tomm⁊ was your son, I knew you'd try to get at me! It's you ⅃l the time, isn't it? You've got her!'

Fred drew back momentarily. 'You told April . . .' He stared into the black face with real hate now. 'You filthy swine!' He thought of April knowing that Albert and Davie were brother and sister. He shut his eyes. 'Christ. You swine, you underhand, filthy—'

'She can't have gone there — she can't have gone to Winterditch Lane!' The voice was panting for breath now. 'Davina would have said something — given it away somehow.'

'Davina?' Fred's fingers tightened and the sloe eyes, so close to his, bulged. 'You've been talking to Davina? And did she give you the flowers? What did you say — tell me — tell me now — what did you say to that child?' He shook Mannie as a dog shakes a rat.

276

And then a terrible thing happened. Mannie started to laugh. The laugh emerged as a gargling sound between Fred's hands, but it was recognisably a macabre chuckle of sheer delight. The acoustics of the garage amplified it and it had reached a piercing maniacal climax when David and Gladys came running. Mannie saw David and stopped laughing to point a trembling finger.

'I've killed her. I've finished it for good. I've sent little April to join the others. They're all down there. In the cemetery. All of them.'

Fred bore him down; first to his knees and then sideways into a mash of daffodils. David and Gladys tore him away from his prey just in time. Mannie lay unconscious but breathing.

It was Gladys who took control.

'I'll see to this. He can go straight to Coney Hill in the ambulance. You two get into one of the cars and drive down to the cemetery. It'll have happened by Olga's grave, I expect. That's not far from the gates on the left side of the path. Go now.'

They went.

This crisis bound them so close they looked like twins as they roared through the city; one dark, one fair, but both white and set in rigid lines of desperation. Neither of them remembered that drive afterwards; they could not even recall who drove. As the car bucked over the ancient, fallen-in tombstones, making a completely straight line for the newer section by the brook, they flung open both doors and leapt out at the same moment. They took parallel routes between obelisks and family tombs, coming on Olga's angel at the same moment.

Davina lay, muddy and discarded, beneath the blind eyes. She was breathing visibly, and though her neck and lower jaw were purple with bruises, her gaberdine raincoat was still neatly belted and buttoned and her school beret in place.

She opened her eyes as David propped her against him,

277

saw her father and began to cry immediately. Fred was beside himself.

'I should have finished him off. He's not fit to live — Christamighty —'

David said, 'It's good that she can cry. Weep away, my little apple. My precious little apple. It was a nightmare but you're awake now.'

'He'll be put away for good and all now,' Fred told her. 'He's as mad as a hatter. You've done everyone a good turn, Davie. He'll be put away for this. I'll make bloody sure he never comes out again, too!'

She hiccoughed on her sobs and looked up at him as he stood next to the angel. Olga's angel. And for once, she smiled right at her Uncle Fred. She tried to speak and could not. Her throat was much too sore. But it would get better, she had no doubt of that.

Uncle Fred smiled right back at her, pleased as Punch. And just for a silly moment, she thought perhaps the angel smiled. As if the light at the end of the tunnel had blazed into the here-and-now, and it really was all right for Olga.

Fifteen

BEFORE the hue and cry for Bridie could really get under way, she and March arrived home. The general relief was euphoric. Davie had not even been kept in hospital; she lay in state in the sitting-room at Longmeadow with Aunt Sylv knitting up old lisle stockings into slip mats opposite her and telling her tales about Newent and Kempley that were slanderously fascinating.

Bridie arrived on the scene, also a semi-invalid, and cast herself on her knees in front of Davie's armchair with tears in her eyes.

'Darling, I am so sorry. So very, very sorry. After all you've done for us — and for Olga—'

Davie, who seemed to be very relaxed, almost light-hearted, said, 'Golly. It wasn't your fault, Aunt Bridie. It sounds as if you've been having a simply ghastly time for ages now. And now it's over. I mean we're all frightfully sorry that . . . he . . . has gone criminally insane, or whatever that solicitor man called it. But Daddy says it's a good job really because otherwise Uncle Fred would have killed him and then Uncle Fred would have had to go to prison.'

'Oh my God . . . my God . . .' wept Bridie. And March, in her new role of protector, lugged her into an armchair in the special way she'd been taught at First Aid and rolled her eyes at Davie.

'Come along now, Bridie. You're flooding the place out.

279

Let's just say that all's well that ends well, shall we?'

Flo wheeled in the tea trolley at this moment and caught her end words. She looked so pleased with life that she was nearly smug. It could have been because her Easter report from the Girls' High School concluded with the words in Doc Moore's scrawl: 'Flora is highly intelligent, hard working and imaginative. The latter quality needs certain control. Otherwise she is truly a pupil to be proud of.' Her parents and Davie had read this with barely concealed smiles, and when her father's only comment was, 'Huh. She's ended with a preposition,' Flo had known just how tremendously pleased he was.

She said now, 'Yes and Uncle Fred and Davie are friends now, Aunt March, did you know?'

'No.' March glanced at Davie. 'Oh . . . that's good. Uncle Fred has always had a special feeling for you, darling.'

Aunt Sylv suddenly gripped April's arm quite painfully and said, ''Tisn't as bad as the last time, my maid. 'Twere only poor Will then to look after the lot of us and 'twere too much for 'im.'

The others thought she was rambling again, but April kissed the reptilian skin and said, 'I know, I know, my dear.'

Aunt Sylv muttered, 'We need Fred as well as David, my maid. And Albert's safe in that there farm. And Victor 'ull be 'ome. We should be thankful.'

'I know.' April almost wept herself because for a terrible moment she had thought Aunt Sylv might be going to blurt out everything she knew.

Bridie whispered, 'We are thankful, Aunt Sylv. Oh we are so thankful. I feel as if I deliberately threw away everything most dear to me, and God has given it back. Almost all of it. Almost . . .' She sobbed anew and March patted her back and said it was reaction and perfectly natural in the circumstances.

Then David arrived. Mrs Porchester had been listening to the wireless in the cutting-room and had heard that there had been a successful commando raid on St Nazaire harbour. They got out maps, spreading them all over the floor and went over the whole amazing venture.

Bridie sighed. 'I know it's wicked to say this at such a time . . . but, oh, it's such fun to be here and doing this and to know I'll go home in a minute and get the tea with Marlene.'

It was not quite so easy for March. She had been away from home for well over a year and though she had gone for very laudable reasons, there had still been an element of desertion in her long absence. She had not exactly enjoyed her work in London, but she had enjoyed being needed, being capable of such an arduous job; above all she had enjoyed not having to think, not having to justify her place on earth.

For over a week now she had been so closely involved with Bridie, she hadn't stopped to wonder whether she might be coming home for good. As far as Stan Potter was concerned she was on three weeks well-deserved leave and she was due back on 19th April which was a Sunday. She could return before then, of course. And then there would be no shame in 'working out her notice' and coming back home. There was plenty of war work she could do in Gloucester. But no-one who actually needed her . . . not desperately, at any rate.

She told herself she would stay for April's birthday on the seventh. The weather had improved slightly and Gloucester was fluttering with daffodils as if there was no war anywhere; she could feel it tugging at her roots almost physically. But she could not settle anywhere. Chattie ran Bedford Close like clockwork; she could have started spring cleaning. But she didn't feel any sense of urgency about housework. She visited Bridie every day and helped to get Brunswick Road back into its old relaxed workings again. She had bought a beautiful length of silk from Liberty's at the outrageous price of five shillings and sixpence a yard, and she packed it and took it to April for her fortieth birthday. She even took Gretta for a walk around the park, though she considered the child was spoiled worse than Victor had been, if that was possible.

When she got back to Bedford Close that afternoon she paced the house, smoking incessantly, cupping her elbow in her other hand and exhaling towards the ceiling as she went from room to room.

Fred came in at five and found her circling the piano in the sitting-room.

'Are you looking for anything special?' he asked, standing by the door and watching her carefully. Since her return he had had her 'under surveillance' yet still knew nothing of her thoughts and feelings, let alone her intentions for the future. He was confused himself. Apart from that silly session with Tilly Adair after poor Olga Hall's funeral, he had been faithful to March and should be desperately keen for her to stay at home now, but there was still that curious weariness in his attitude. He remembered telling Sibbie he was tired of fighting March; was that why he was doing nothing now to encourage her to stay?

She did not reply to his question and after a while he said irritably, 'Well?'

She glanced at him, faintly surprised. 'I'm just thinking. That's all.'

'I see. Can you tell me what about?'

'I . . . don't know.'

He frowned, wondering whether she was stone-walling him in her old aggressive way. Then she went on walking, and he knew she wasn't. She was sorting something out in her mind and she could not give it voice; the awful thing was he was doing exactly the same thing. A voice from the past — his old schoolteacher, Miss Pettinger's — echoed in his head: 'parallel lines never meet'. Was that how it would be for March and him?

He went to the mantelpiece and took a cigarette from the box there, lit a taper at the fire, and drew on the flame. Then he sat down and tried to look relaxed and at

282

home. Dammit, he was at home. And so was she . . . or so she should be. She was prowling around as if she'd never been in the place before. She started for the door.

He said, 'March, please sit down. I realize you find it hard to be in the same room with me, but it need not be for long. Sit down until Chattie brings in the tea. Please.'

She looked at him, again with that slight surprise. But she obeyed him, sitting on the edge of a chair and puffing away like an engine. He felt his nerves tighten.

'D'you realize this is only the second time you've been home for over a year?'

'Well of course.' She drew hard on her cigarette. 'The blitzkrieg does not stop for weekends or Bank holidays.'

'I wasn't reproaching you, Marcie. God forbid. You're doing a wonderful job, I know that.' He leaned forward involuntarily, as if pulled by an invisible string. 'I'm proud of you, girl. I would not have thought you could have done it. And stuck it too.'

She shrugged. 'The days go by in bed. And the nights . . . go by. There are others who . . . our warden is a wonderful man. His name is Stan Potter. Potter's the name of Albert's landlady in Birmingham.'

'Yes.' Was she needling him? He was very aware of that invisible connecting string. 'Have you been in touch with Albert?'

'No.' She stubbed out her cigarette. 'I've hardly thought of him actually. There's been no time to . . . think.'

'No. Work is . . . useful like that.' He searched for something else to say. 'Tell me about your warden.'

'Stan? He carries concentrated blackcurrant juice around with him. In a Thermos. He makes us drink it. He really cares about us. The living as well as the dead.'

He said quietly, 'Marcie, are you in love with him?' There was a sudden emptiness inside him, the forerunner of nausea.

But she laughed. 'In love? With Stan Potter?' She lit up again, inhaled and let smoke trickle through her nostrils. 'You see that as the only reason I would stay away from my home comforts for so long, do you, Fred?' She laughed again. 'Stan has a sixteen-stone wife and three married daughters all living at home. He's never looked at another woman in his life. No, I'm not in love with Stan. But I do love him. And he loves me. He has saved my life more than once.'

Chattie opened the door and wheeled in the tea trolley. There were pikelets and jam tarts she'd made. She wouldn't let March pour; she wouldn't let her move. A small table was loaded right by her side with tea and food.

'You're that thin, Mrs Luker. And you look perished. Let me bring down another cardigan. We hardly use this room now and it feels damp to me.'

'Rubbish, Chattie. To all of that. *You're* much thinner than you were, anyway. Everyone is. I was shocked at Bridie.'

Chattie wrinkled her small nose. 'It weren't *all* that 'orrible Mr Stein. More likely Marlene. She's hopeless.She can't make the rations go round and they have twice as much as anyone else what with all them kids *and* Mr Stein being in the black market.' She pulled a face. 'None of that now of course. What will happen to him, I wonder?'

Fred said, 'Broadmoor, I should think.'

Chattie shuddered. 'When I think of our Miss Davie — and right by Miss Olga's graveside too.' She departed, shaking her head. There was a long silence. Fred no longer looked at March; he stared into the fire and wondered what the hell he would have done if Davie had been dead that day . . .

It was March this time who made an effort to return to normality.

'All's well that ends well,' she said again, unwittingly echoing Stan Potter's tone of bracing reassurance. 'Let's forget all that now. Drink your tea and have something to eat.'

She did so herself, biting appreciatively into a buttery pikelet.

'Chattie is a wonder. Real butter?'

'How should I know? She hoards food like mad during the week then dishes up everything at the weekend.' He watched her eating. 'She's right, you're as thin as a lath. You don't bother to eat, I suppose?'

'Of course I eat. There's a British Restaurant just round the corner from the bed-sit.'

He made a face. 'Snoek. Whale steaks.'

'Nothing wrong with either.'

She did not enlarge and he continued to watch her covertly as she ate her tea. There was something different about her. Was it her independence? She had always been so dependent on people . . . her parents, himself, Albert. And she had been frightened, too. She was not frightened any more. He wished she would stay. It was no more than curiosity; there was no burning desire in him. But he would like to discover this new March.

She finished her tea, dabbed at her fingers and mouth with a napkin, then began to get up. He practically flung himself in front of her.

'Have a cigarette, Marcie. Relax. The six o'clock news will be on in a minute. We ought to hear the latest on St Nazaire.'

She leaned towards his lighter. Her narrow face was very like her mother's; she looked her years, but her bone structure was still fine.

She said, 'The oddest thing. I was listening to the one o'clock at May's. Apparently a man has found five farthings in the ruins of St Clement Dane's.'

He was baffled for a moment, then repeated the old nursery rhyme: 'Oranges and lemons says the bells of St Clement's, I owe you five farthings . . .'

March said, 'All those lovely old churches are gone. It's a miracle St Paul's is still there. I wish you could see it. Everything around is flat, and there it stands . . . a bit like the spire at Coventry.'

'Would you really like me to come and see it? I could do. I could come up one weekend and see where you live and perhaps you could show me some of the places . . . you know.'

She stared at him through her cigarette smoke, seriously considering the proposal.

At last she said, 'I . . . don't know, Fred. If you really want to, there's no reason why not.'

He did want to. He could go no further than that, but he did want to see her other life. Not necessarily to be a part of it again. Just to see it.

'Well then, if you've no objection.'

'No. I've no objection.'

He smiled at her, then went to the wireless and fiddled with the knobs. Lord Haw-Haw's voice invaded the quiet room and he twiddled again. Mr Middleton's homely tones came over, giving advice about digging up tennis courts and planting potatoes.

March said, 'We should do that.'

It was the first time she had said 'we' in connection with herself and Fred for a long time.

Fred said, 'How long can you stay, March?'

'I have to go back on the nineteenth. But I ought really to go back before then.'

'Don't. Please don't. Stay until after next Sunday. I'd like you to be here when I get back from Exercise Bulldog.'

She did not answer. The measured tones of Stewart Hibberd recounted the final collapse of Java. They both listened with bowed heads. Terrible things were happening in Hong Kong: British soldiers bound together and bayoneted to death. At the end Fred stood up and switched off and they were silent again.

Then she said quietly, 'That is why I have to go back, Fred.'

He bowed his head. 'Yes. I know.' Then he looked at her. 'But not for good, Marcie. That's all I want to know. Sometime we'll live together again, won't we?'

'If you want us to.' There was still no enthusiasm in her voice. The string which he could feel between them was

286

one way only.

He said, 'I want us to.'

She put out a long forefinger and touched the china teapot. He thought it might be a sign that she was coming back . . . coming back to all her possessions.

She said, 'I quite thought that by now . . . after so long . . . you would have found someone else. Maybe Tilly again.'

'Don't be a damned fool, March.' His voice was rough.

She lifted the teapot lid and peered inside.

'There's still another cup left in here. Will you have it?'

'Half each. How about it?' he asked.

She put the lid back on with great care.

'Yes. All right,' she said, and picking up the pot, she began to pour.

The siege of Tobruk seemed to Victor to be a contradiction in terms. As a boy he and Albert had played endless games of besieged fortresses from mediaeval times to Beau Geste, and always the part of the besieged was static. They could scurry about behind their fortifications preparing boiling oil and dummy defenders, but it was the attackers who roamed freely outside, chasing off reinforcements and bringing up strange-looking siege-breaking machines.

In Libya things were different. Certainly inside Tobruk were the defenders and outside were the attackers, but the defenders were outside too. Skirmishes and pitched battles took place every day miles from the city. And the Army Photographic Unit roamed more freely than friend or foe, recording everything on film for the Intelligence people or the general public in the cinemas back home. And freedom was the word within the Unit itself; sometimes a photographer would be gone for days, apparently missing believed captured. As often as not he would turn up thin and brown, but unharmed and gloating over the pictures he had managed to take.

Victor and Joe Benton had drifted together as soon as

287

they met at the Benghazi headquarters. Benton had made tea and swept up film at Pinewood Studios before the war, and the Unit was his chance to get behind a camera. Victor had the same single-mindedness about everything visual. More than that, they came from the same background. Joe Benton's pub in his London suburb was called the Flag of Truce; Victor's the Lamb and Flag. Joe's mother had worked as a dressmaker, Victor's as a hairdresser; Joe's brother was a car mechanic; so was Victor's cousin. They laughed at the same things. When the C.O's lens was neatly removed by a piece of shrapnel in the middle of filming a Stuka raid on a petrol dump, they found themselves spluttering helplessly while the C.O. stamped with rage and shook his fist at the offending aircraft. And they had both served a European 'apprenticeship' — Victor in Greece and Crete, Joe in Jugoslavia. They had seen similar horrors and heroisms and dealt with them similarly: Victor by sketching for his war paintings, Joe by planning a movie that would shake the world. When they snipped at their film before packaging it for London, Joe did not throw away his cuttings any more; they would make the skeleton on which he would hang the flesh of his epic.

On a morning in early April they heard of an attack brewing up on the Gazala line. There was no jeep available so they commandeered a Simca and set out as the sun came up over the desert. They took it in turns to drive and when it was Joe's turn, Victor stood on the passenger seat and stuck his head through the sunshine roof to watch out for tell-tale signs of mining on the trail ahead. Already he had his camera running; the string of Red Cross vehicles passing them on their way back to the base field hospital south of Tobruk, told their own tale. This area was not called the Cauldron for nothing. At times it seethed with the roar of tanks, and the bubbles of explosions popped too often for comfort. As Victor lowered his camera, he spotted the barely concealed dustbin lid of a mine on the left.

'Keep well right Joe,' he shouted into the dust which enshrouded them like a travelling cloud. Benton replied with a forecast about the fate of the Simca car. 'Never mind the bloody springs,' Victor bawled. 'We can always walk back if we've still got bloody legs!' They both laughed.

The ambulances disappeared behind them and Victor sat down abruptly and unslung his camera. Joe groaned and stopped the car with a jerk as Victor undid the lightproof door and pulled the exposed film out. He threaded in a new one, blowing hard on the gate to get rid of the ever-present sand, then they were off again.

About midday in the blistering heat, they ground up a ridge to find a Sherman tank firing on a German convoy passing below it. It was the perfect scenario. Victor and Joe leapt out, hanging on to their tin hats, and belly-crawled to the lip of the ridge, well left and right of the tank, where they could film both friend and foe. The convoy were taking heavy losses; one truck was blazing, and three were skewed into the sand, obviously out of commission. It was too good to last. The convoy's escort lumbered over the horizon, three tanks armed with shells designed to take the Sherman apart. A tactical retreat seemed the only answer. As the Sherman bucked down the ridge, Joe and Victor ran for the car. Joe slid behind the wheel chortling.

'The best shots yet. Perfect. Absolutely bloody perfect. They might have set it up just for us.'

'Keep your hat on, those shells are going to get our range any minute now. Drive west for Chrissake. Get going!'

But the Simca, mishandled ever since it had been left behind in the Italian retreat, decided enough was enough. Joe pulled frantically at the self-starter and nothing happened. Shouting oaths, Victor leapt out with the starting handle and rammed it home. He turned and tugged and capered like a lunatic. The Simca was not going to move again.

The German tanks, all three of them, lumbered over the ridge and bore down on them. Victor turned and put his hands in the air. After a volley of atrocious language, Joe got out of the car and did likewise.

'I've put my camera under the back seat, Goldie. I'm a Warco, you're my photographer. There's just a chance . . . I'll kill myself if they destroy all that film.'

'Don't worry about it, old chap. They'll probably save you the trouble.'

But it seemed that the young Oberleutnant of the Afrika Corps could hardly be bothered with the two War Correspondents, though he was interested in the camera. Smiling gently he took it from Victor, and, ignoring his protests, wrote out and handed over a receipt for it. Then, just as gently, he opened the gate and pulled out the film, letting it fall into a dried-milk can at his feet.

'I could have — er — projected it and discovered perhaps your British secrets?' He gave a shrug more typical of the Gall than the Hun. 'I do you good turn, ja?'

Victor shrugged back. 'If you had wanted to know how many Red Cross vehicles are operating in the area . . .'

The German laughed. 'And how many trucks were in our convoy. It would be of use to the British. Not to us I think.' He tilted his canvas chair and gazed at the two of them. 'Now I have to consider what to do with you. You may be able to tell our Intelligence Officer very much information.'

'But under the Geneva Convention—' Joe began feverishly.

'On the other side . . . hand . . . if you return to London and report good treatment by Germans, then it might be the better purchase.'

'Bargain,' murmured Victor.

'Definitely the better bargain,' Joe nodded enthusiastically. 'It might take us another year to win the war and you'll have to give us food and water—'

'Or you might be shot by a sniper while returning to

base. Who knows? It is, as you say, perhaps.'

'Hypothetical,' Victor said, stepping hard on Joe's foot.

The German smiled again. 'You will be shown where your Eighth Army are. Then you may go.'

'What about Goldie's camera, sir?'

Victor pulled Joe to the waiting guard who led them from the small headquarters and back to the sandy waste. They trudged off, feeling ludicrous in all that empty space, and incredulous of their good fortune.

'Don't jump about till we're out of sight, for God's sake.' Victor could barely contain himself. 'I thought you'd done for us with all that mouth—'

'I can't believe it. Christ, Goldie, we're *free!* I thought the Jerries were supposed to shoot on sight? Or string you up by your balls or something?'

'Well, he wasn't exactly brought up on *Mein Kampf*, was he? God, we're lucky. He couldn't wait to get rid of us. Obviously couldn't be bothered.'

'Still an' all . . .'

They dropped into a wadi and paused to relieve themselves.

'There has to be a few decent ones around,' Joe expounded, eyes closed blissfully. 'I mean, not all the poor buggers are Nazis. I know old Adolf did his best to weed 'em out, but stands to reason he missed a few. Just here and there like.'

'I had an uncle. He went to the Berlin Olympics and helped get some of the Jews out of the country. Real cloak and dagger stuff. He saw some sights, I'm telling you.'

'Yeah.' Joe buttoned his flies and threw himself down to rest. 'There was a chap in Belgrade like that. He'd got King Peter proclaimed just before the country was invaded.' He grinned reminiscently. 'He'd had a go at Hitler himself just before the war started. Quiet sort of a bloke, wouldn't say boo to a goose. He was supposed to be the third most wanted bloke on the Gestapo list.'

'Pimpernel stuff, eh?' Victor walked up the other side of the wadi and looked around the horizon. 'Come on then

Joe. Best foot forward.'

'Not that way Goldie — west, for God's sake. We've got to get back to the car.'

'Some other damned fool can pick up that camera, Joe. Let's go back to the base and eat. We've done enough for one day.'

Joe looked at his watch. 'It's not four o'clock yet. Come on, old man. We'll pick up a lift with a Red Cross truck. I've got to get that camera. My life's work's inside it.'

Victor hesitated, then grinned, and they started down the wadi. 'You and your bloody epic,' he grumbled.

Joe gave his schoolboy laugh. 'It was meant to be, though, eh Goldie? When I think — we were actually taken prisoner—' Both of them started to laugh again almost hysterically. It was a tale to be told in the mess. They began to rehearse it.

'He might have been Rommel himself,' Victor declaimed, striking a pose in mid-stride. 'He looked a cunning fox all right. If he'd been about fifteen years older—'

'And a bit more weight on him. No, I reckon it was Hitler in disguise. Suppose Adolf wanted to know what the Afrika Korps was up to, and he came out incognito—'

'You're going too far, Joe.'

Joe laughed, acknowledging the fact. They stumbled on, climbing out of the wadi and taking a compass bearing before striking across the scrub.

'Funny thing is . . .' Joe stopped to tug at his socks. 'That chap I was telling you about. He was the spitting image of old Adolf. He didn't have that crazy look to him and his hair wasn't greased down over his forehead or anything, but his build . . . he thought that was how he'd got so close to him in the assassination attempt.'

'I'm surprised he lived to tell the tale.'

'That was it. He wore the S.S. uniform and in the bedlam afterwards the guards thought he was the Führer. Funny chap.' He glanced at Victor. 'He sounded a bit like you, Goldie.'

'Thank God. There's the ridge. I thought we were going to wander around all bloody night!'

They struggled to the top, and beyond, looking toy-like, was the Simca.

'Lord be praised!' Joe incanted, salaaming theatrically. 'My life's work, preserved for posterity!'

They began to run down the other side of the ridge.

'How d'you mean? He sounded like me,' Victor panted.

'Your accent, old man. Gloucestershire. It's unmistakable.'

Victor slowed, then stopped.

Joe yelled, 'Come on! I might even get the damned thing started now!'

'Hang on. A Gloucestershire accent? And he was slight and dark and quiet?'

'Yeh. Come on, Goldie.'

'Christamighty.'

'What?' Joe had reached the car and was tugging on the door.

'It was Tolly. My Uncle Tolly. It must have been . . . my God, he's *alive!*'

As he spoke, the booby-trap inside the car was detonated by Joe sitting heavily on the driver's seat. Victor had a tiny fraction of a second to see him reach behind him for his precious film, then the car and Joe Benton were made one by a giant sheet of flame. The very next part of that second brought the explosion to his ears, but before that happened he had thrown himself flat on the sand to take the blast.

He knew now why the young Oberleutnant had let them go. Joe and his epic were not for posterity.

The Civil Defence exercise, named Bulldog, was what Monty called 'a turn-up for the books'. Scheduled to begin at midday on 12th April, it was actually started by the Gloucester Home Guard at midnight on 11th April, when a platoon led by Captain Luker and heavily camouflaged — 'by their wives, dammitall' accused the

Commanding Officer of the South Gloucesters, implying that the men wore make-up — swam gently along the ice-cold Severn, letting the current float them as close to the bank as possible, and holed the craft which the 'enemy' intended to use to storm Gloucester Docks. What might have been an enjoyable Sunday spent letting off smoke bombs and firing blank shells at each other in a deadlock situation, was a complete non-starter. At two o'clock on the 12th, when the enemy were frantically trying to plug their craft, the Gloucester platoon arrived, tipped them all into the water with long barge-poles, captured their standard and took it back to the Pilot Inn in the docks with much jubilation. Fred was called various names. A 'bloody outsider' was the least offensive. Some Gloucestrians who should have been on his side were more curt.

'He's always been a bloody cheat,' fumed Charles Adair from the Observer Corps base in Northgate Mansions. 'Every damned thing he does is crooked.' He thought of Tilly with renewed bitterness. Fred had let him believe that he would wean Tilly from her bloody Polish count and in due course he had made a start on the project, only to drop her like a hot cake again. The Polish count was now practically a resident at the derelict house in Quedgeley. Because of the Bulldog fiasco Charles was going to be home much earlier than expected; it probably meant he'd catch the two of them in bed together which would embarrass him and the count a bloody sight more than it would embarrass Tilly. She'd just laugh like a hyena. He picked up the telephone resignedly and dialled his home number. The Pole, whatever his bloody name was, answered, so Tilly was probably in the bloody bathroom. Charles pinched his nose.

'I wish to inform you,' he said nasally, 'that in five minutes there will be a police raid on Quedgeley House. Any aliens, friendly or not, found there will be immediately interned for the duration.'

He put down the phone, smiling a little more happily.

That would put paid to their shenanigans. He hoped poor old Stanislav would have time to put on his trousers! Even so, Fred Luker was still a bloody cheat.

March planned to spend that day sorting out Albert's things. Since Albert had left home in 1937, Fred had used his room more often than not, but had continued to keep his clothes in the big front bedroom with March's. Then when Albert went to Spain, there had been no forwarding address until they knew his whereabouts at Tangmere. Even then he had asked for nothing, and nothing had been sent. Now March decided the time had come to make up a parcel and send it to Dorset. She took up newspapers and some boxes and began to pack handkerchiefs, ties and shirts. She thought she was doing it all very calmly and matter-of-factly, but when she went upstairs into the attic and saw his train layout, dusted and cleaned as if he was still at home himself, tears caught in her throat unexpectedly, and she hurried back to his room and clutched one of his school jumpers to her face.

Fred, home hours before she expected, found her sobbing on Albert's bed, and gathered her to him. She did not resist. He held her very carefully, his eyes closed above her head. She rarely wept, and when she did it was usually in temper.

He said at last, 'What was it? His school sweater?'

She shook her head. 'Everything is so clean and neat. As if he's coming back. Chattie must dust and launder everything regularly.'

'Yes.'

'And the train set. She's polished the engines and put them all in the shed.'

'No, I did that. She wanted to do it and I was afraid she might not leave it quite . . . Besides, I wanted to do it myself.'

She wept again.

'I don't know what's happening, Fred. I'm . . . hurting. Really hurting.'

'Numbed limbs always hurt when you warm them back to life, Marcie.'

She drew away and blew her nose on one of Albert's beautifully folded handkerchiefs.

'But I wasn't numb, Fred. I didn't drown myself in work at Kilburn or anything.'

'Not just Kilburn. You haven't let yourself think of Albert — really think of him, for so long now, Marcie. First for my sake, then for your own.'

'Perhaps that's it.' She seemed to recollect herself, blew her nose again and moved further away on the bed. 'I — I don't want you to think I'm going to pieces, Fred. It was just seeing his things. Then that damned train set.'

He smiled, making no attempt to touch her again.

'D'you remember how he'd let Davie and Flo have a station each?'

'Yes.' She looked at him. 'Fred, I wouldn't want you to feel . . . you had to be . . . kind to me.'

'I don't feel that. But if I did — well, you were "kind" to me when I was knocked sideways four years ago. You got me on my feet again.'

'Yes, but this is different. That's what I mean.' She gripped the handkerchief tightly. 'I've found my feet, you see. For the very first time in my life I am truly standing on my own feet. And I like that.'

'Yes.' He swallowed. 'So do I.'

'You don't mind that I am independent?'

He said steadily, 'Surely it means that if you come back home, it will be because you really want to. Not because you need to, or because I'm ill, or because . . . anything. But simply because you want to.'

She said, 'Thank you, Fred.'

He looked at her for a long moment, then turned to go out. She put the handkerchief down suddenly, and followed him. 'Chattie's gone to see her sister. I'll make us some tea and you can tell me about the Bulldog Exercise. I take it you won?'

'How did you guess?'

She smiled. 'You would never have surrendered after only two hours. I know that. Not even if they'd started using live ammo!'

Fred had already arranged to take the next day off from work and saw no reason to change his plans. It was a fresh windy day with showers and sunshine chasing each other at regular intervals. After breakfast he suggested that they drive out to Newent and see if the gypsies had left any daffodils. His face opened with pleasure when March said gravely, 'That would be nice, Fred. April is spending the day with Bridie so she will be all right.'

It was delightful to drive over the Causeway and along the Huntley road. Almond trees leaned over the wall of the Court, heavy with blossom, then came the apple orchards. March wound down the car window and took deep breaths of the country air. 'Straight off the Welsh mountains,' she said, just as Pa had always said. 'As pure as the snow.'

Most of the Newent fields were stripped bare, but in a special meadow behind Kempley church there was an untouched drift protected by the ancient red stone church and the huddle of cottages around it.

'Let's take some for April and May,' March said, gathering as if her life depended on it. 'Pa always said April was our special daffodil with her yellow hair and loud trumpeting!'

'You were all three called the daffodil girls,' Fred reminded her. 'I've still got that old *Citizen* picture somewhere of the three of you under that caption.'

'Have you, Fred?' March tied another bunch with her scarf and looked at him curiously. 'It's strange, isn't it — our lives I mean. How closely they twist and twine. It was only May who married someone from outside.'

He paused in his picking then said deliberately, 'And Albert, of course.'

'Yes.' She stood gazing over the field. 'Yes. I think, probably, it's good. Don't you? Too much twisting and twining could strangle all of us.'

'Oh, Marcie.' He remembered having a similar thought, but coming from her it seemed a revelation. He straightened his back painfully. 'You really have changed.'

She smiled. 'Yes. I've only just realized. I haven't had time to think about Albert — honestly. And now . . . I'm not bitter any more. Sad and regretful that he wasn't man enough to take his parentage in his stride. But not bitter.'

Fred turned away and walked back towards the car. After a while she followed him, and they laid the daffodil bunches on the back seat and settled themselves for the drive back home. Then it was that she said, 'Fred, you don't have to tell me what it is, but was there another reason for Albert's flight to Spain?'

He did not answer immediately. When he did his voice was strong. 'No. Hatred of me. That was all.'

She looked at her hands folded in her lap; he waited but she said nothing else so he started up the car and they bumped back to the road and past old Grampa Rising's cottage.

'This sun is really warm,' he commented.

'Fred, I'm sorry. I shouldn't have asked. And he shouldn't have hated you. He shouldn't have hated either of us.'

'Not you, certainly. I can understand how he felt — feels — about me.' He cleared his throat. 'But there *was* something else. I'm sorry, Marcie, but it was me who advised him to find a girl and get married.'

She took a deep breath. 'So you blame yourself for that too? Oh Fred, he wouldn't have taken that advice if he could possibly help it! His marriage to Elizabeth Doswell was in spite of you, not because of you!' She gave a little laugh. 'In that respect, I can assure you I know Albert! He was as stubborn as — as — his father!'

Fred too laughed at that, a laugh of pure gratitude. He was suddenly sure she was right; it would mean he could look at Davie again without feeling guilty.

He told her about Operation Bulldog and why he was going to be rather unpopular in Gloucester for a while.

'Well, you're used to that,' she said philosophically. 'And at least this time you'll have quite a popularity vote as well — surely your platoon think you're a hero?'

'Some of them, I suppose. But most of them thought they were getting away from their wives for a whole day and possibly a night as well.' He chuckled suddenly. 'I can imagine Charles Adair's reaction. He told me he'd managed to get in a crate of beer, Observer Corps For the Use Of.'

They both laughed as they recrossed the Causeway and chugged up Westgate Street. The cathedral was a black silhouette against the pearly April sky. March said contentedly, 'It will be nice to have tea by the fire, it's getting colder now.'

And Fred said, 'March . . . maybe I'm going to mess everything up now. But I want you to know — I want to be open for once. My dear, I'm sorry, but there was once — with Tilly Adair—'

She said calmly, 'Yes. I know.'

'You *know*?'

'She'd left some hankies in my top drawer. I found them yesterday when I started that spring clean.'

'Oh my God. March . . . is that why you were crying?'

'I don't know.'

'Oh my God,' he repeated. She had never seen him so devastated since he'd 'lost' Albert. He said, 'Is that the end? Will you leave me?'

'No.' It was strange that suddenly she could answer with certainty. 'No. I'll have to finish what I've started in Kilburn. But I shall come home, Fred.'

She thought for a moment he was going to weep. His face crumpled and sagged and he looked an old man. He took the left turn at the Cross very wide and roared down Northgate Street in second. When they drew level with the Bon Marché he choked, 'Thank you. Thank you, my dear. I couldn't have taken that . . . I couldn't . . .'

She put up a hand and touched his shoulder lightly.

'Thank *you*, Fred, for telling me. You see, it proves that

299

you really trust me now. You believed that I could take the truth. I never could before, could I? You had to lie to me so often, Fred. I blamed everything on to you — made you carry my guilt for me — cheat for me. I think I'm strong enough to take my share of blame now. Thank you, Fred.'

He could not answer. He drove with great care past Chichester Street and up the Pitch, then down the other side to Barnwood Road. It was as if he'd never taken this route before.

They drove into the garage and both leaned over to pick up the daffodils. Their hands touched. They paused and looked at each other. Then very slowly, they leaned together and kissed.

The kitchen door flew open and Chattie ran down the path towards them.

'We bombed the bloomin' Eyeties last night!' she exclaimed excitedly. 'And guess what? They didn't have no blackout, so our planes could see 'em as plain as plain!' She held on to the bonnet of the Wolseley, laughing. 'I bet that old Mussolini won't 'alf give 'em a wigging!' She stuck out her chest and babbled some improvised Italian and March collapsed against Fred's shoulder in a paroxysm of giggles.

Daffodils spilled everywhere.

Sixteen

THE siege of Tobruk lasted until June, when the Axis powers took it. Victor was one of three cameramen shipped to a prison in Italy.

May wept copiously when she heard the news. She clutched Gretta to her as if she expected the child to be snatched away to join Victor.

'Darling, don't cry,' she sobbed into the golden curls. 'At least Victor is safely out of the war. At least he'll be all right now.'

But Gretta was crying because her mother was crying. And Monty was crying with sheer relief. Since he'd worked for Fred, life had been sweet; he was being paid to do the things he enjoyed most, meeting new people, eating in restaurants, socialising generally. The danger which Victor was in day and night had been the only fly in the ointment. Monty had felt from the beginning of the war that his son was vindicating his own abstinence in 'the last lot' — not even May knew how those white feathers had hurt. But there should be a limit to how much Victor must pay for his father's safety. It looked as if the limit had been reached. Victor was in no more danger than anyone else, and the debt to fate was cleared.

He said, 'Mummy is quite right, Gretta darling. Victor will be safe now.'

And Daddy could enjoy his 'buckshee' life to the full. It was the word of the moment, and applied particularly to

Monty. There was buckshee petrol through Group Captain Lennox; there was buckshee butter from the fat little A.T.S. in the cookhouse; and now that the Yanks had arrived there was buckshee candy for Gretta and — best of all — buckshee stockings, called nylons, for May.

Yes, this war wasn't like the last. He could relax now that Victor was all right. He could even enjoy it.

In August 1942 just after the Commando raid on Dieppe, the results of the Cambridge School Leaving Certificate were announced. Davina Daker's name did not appear on the notice board.

She had been very depressed by her failure with the mock exams and expected to feel much worse at this second result, but strangely she did not. The terrible business with Mr Stein had left them all with an enormous sense of thankfulness; an evil force had gone out of their lives and whatever happened now must eventually be for good.

As David said, 'Look, little apple, you worked hard and did your best. Obviously you're not going to need that certificate. So don't waste time regretting it.'

Aunt Bridie actually laughed about it.

'I got mine, darling, and toddled off to teachers' training college thinking I was something special. It didn't do me much good, did it?'

When Flo mourned, 'Oh Davie, I feel so awful about my reports now. You don't mind too much, do you?' Davie realized how little academic success really meant to her. She hugged her sister. 'Dearest Flo — I'm so proud of you. And pleased too because it will be nice for Mummy and Daddy to have someone clever in the family. But I'm not worried — honestly. Ever since Olga died I've known I was going to "sing for my supper" and this makes it easier. I mean no-one expects me to do anything else really, do they?'

That autumn and winter she got in as many charity shows as she could and began to learn how to perform.

Her singing teacher taught her a few chords on the mandolin and when she came to the edge of a stage, wearing her blue American dress and holding the mandolin by its slender neck, she soon discovered that most audiences would become very quiet and attentive and she could sing without the aid of a microphone.

At the beginning of 1943 when the Germans surrendered at Stalingrad, Mr Biggins got her a 'spot' in a Workers' Playtime being broadcast from Brockworth Aircraft factory just outside Gloucester. These daytime shows were put on at factories all over the country and were broadcast on the Home Service. The canteen at Brockworth was a barn of a place, the ceiling criss-crossed by iron girders, the concrete floor like a sounding board. The workers crowded in noisily, thrilled with this variation in their routine. There was no hope of intimacy; in any case the microphone was a necessity.

Davina was terrified. Jack Train himself was on the bill, and the killingly funny Frenchwoman Jeanne de Cassilis. There were two crooners with deep, throaty voices, and a band with four saxophone players and a crazy drummer

Uncle Monty advised, 'Choose the simplest song you can possibly think of. Get close to the mike and close your eyes. This time you're not singing to the people in front of you — don't worry if they pelt you with fag-ends — you're singing to the eight million out there —' he gestured largely, '— your song is being sung in little living-rooms and air raid shelters. Think of that and you'll be all right.'

Mr Biggins wrote: 'Have you still got your school gym-slip? If so, wear it. I want you to look as much like a schoolgirl as possible. Something else might be coming up . . .'

Aunt March, home at last after two years of blitz, had to admit she was scared. 'You're wonderful, Davie. I'd rather face old Adolf himself than those aircraft workers.'

And April said stoutly, 'Well, I'm not a bit worried. I just know Davie can do it.' But as she hugged her hard,

Davie could feel her mother's arms shaking as if with cold.

Everyone was so nice. Mr Train took off Professor Joad of the Brains Trust to absolute perfection. 'Nervous? Well, it depends what you mean by nerves . . .' They were all nervous, even the enormous audience. During the 'warm-up' when they were told what to do, some wag chirped up, 'Can you 'ear me Muther — Gawd, I 'ope not!' And the BBC producer said over the mike, 'Well, actually old man, she can. So let's give her a bit of a thrill, shall we? Let her know we're all having a good time. Everyone who's enjoying themselves say Aye!'

When it was her turn the master of ceremonies held up his hand for what he called 'Utter 'ush' and said very solemnly, 'Yes, fellow workers. I really do want utter 'ush now for someone very young and very new to this business. Gloucester's very own Singing Schoolgirl, known to you but not to the country . . . as yet. Will you please give a welcome to Miss Davie Daker!'

She waited for the applause to die down, then took Uncle Monty's advice and got very close to the microphone. She didn't close her eyes, but she looked above the audience at the girders over the canteen serving-hatches, and tried to imagine the kitchen at home with Aunt Sylv sitting very close to the wireless and the table laid ready for tea.

'I'd like to sing something my grandmother taught me a long time ago,' she said in her high clear voice. 'It's very short so I won't keep you long.' A ripple of laughter passed through the crowd. She smiled blindly. Suddenly, sitting next to Aunt Sylv in the kitchen, she could see Grandma Rising, her lovely dark hair so like Flo's, her long, thin face and gentle expression. She could see her so clearly. She began to sing.

'Aunties know all about fairies
Uncles know all about guns
Mothers and Fathers think all the day long
Of keeping their children happy and strong

304

Even the littlest ones.'

She waited a few minutes, then brought up her mandolin and struck a chord and sang the verse again, with pizzicato accompaniment. Then she stepped back and bowed low.

No-one could believe she had finished until that bow. The amazing simplicity of the tiny songlet took them by storm. They looked at each other, smiling, the women wanting to cry. The applause was as deafening as that given to the stars of the show. The MC had to hold up his hands again and demand 'further 'ush' for the toast of the Free French, Madame Jeanne De Cassilis!

Two months later Davie auditioned for a new show to be broadcast weekly from London, on the lines of Tommy Handley's 'It's That Man Again'. Mortimer and Maisie Dennis, an elderly duo from music-hall days, enacted a flimsy story built around their ancient house overlooking a children's recreation ground. There was a resident 'char' of course, and the rest of the action concerned various very cheeky children making Mort and Maisie's domestic bliss a little less blissful. Davina was billed as the 'Singing Schoolgirl' and her songs ranged from provocative to sentimental. She got the part with ease, and so began fifteen months of regular work. The show went out on Thursday evenings; she arrived in London on Tuesday and rehearsed all afternoon and evening, recorded it on Wednesday and returned home in the late afternoon.

The first time she was very nervous. The show was called 'Swing that Seesaw' and just the title made her feel seasick. On Sunday 16th May, there was a Review of the Home Guard in Hyde Park. Uncle Fred led the Gloucester platoon, so he and Aunt March took rooms in a nice boarding-house near Paddington for the whole week, and Davie stayed with them. They came with her to Kingsway and everyone ran round them as if they were the King and Queen. It helped her very much.

The studio was after all just a room, divided in two by

plate glass. One half was littered with tea cups and biscuit crumbs, the other was dominated by a large eight-sided microphone on a stand. There was someone crouching before it adjusting its height, and someone else with a row of odd-looking sound effects. Behind the plate glass was a lot of recording machinery and someone wearing headphones. That was all. Davie was quick to realize that all the reasons for 'nerves' had gone in this situation.

That evening they gathered in the lounge of Mrs Venables' boarding-house and listened to a recording of Mr Churchill's speech about the Home Guard Review. He reminded them that three years before the Home Guard had had only their fists with which to fight, yet they had been prepared to guard their country to the last man.

Davie said, 'Oh Uncle Fred, you must be so proud. It makes this afternoon seem rather silly to me.'

He was genuinely astonished. 'Why? What did we actually do except keep morale high? And that is exactly what you are doing, young lady. And don't you forget it. When you stand in front of that mike next time and sing a song, just remember you are doing important war work!'

Davie smiled gratefully at him and wondered why on earth she had disliked and mistrusted him so heartily for so long.

Seventeen

IT was in May of the following year that the situation between Elizabeth and Albert came to a head. They had been married for almost four years, and, in spite of her optimistic announcement on her wedding night, Elizabeth had to admit that their marriage had never been properly consummated. She knew it wasn't Tommy's fault, but it certainly wasn't hers. She hated the way he had given in to circumstances; there was nothing admirable in his acceptance, it was too much like resignation. What really hurt was that each time he did make some sort of effort, it was nothing to do with her. It was usually connected with his cousin Victor Gould, or some unknown member of his mysterious family. And why purport to hate them, why refuse to see them, yet at the same time be so tied to them? More than tied — tethered. Manacled.

So she sat, this warm May day, at the desk in the Sister's office of the military hospital just outside Dorchester, writing up her notes and definitely not looking forward to her weekend at home with her family.

Elizabeth Tomms at twenty-five was very conscious that her youth was over. It did not seem to have lasted very long; one minute she had been a Guider, organising summer camps for the Brownies; the next she was a pseudo-wife, a kind of companion and friend to a man she did not know very well even after four years of marriage. It was small wonder that she found relief in her work at the hospital. Like her mother-in-law, she knew she was not needed at home; here she very definitely was. Because of her brisk and stimulating encouragement, there were men who said she had made them walk again. There were other men who came in and sat staring at the walls for hours on end, saying nothing; after a few weeks of her persistent 'Good mornings' they began looking for her. She was plumply pretty and capable. A perfect combination of mother and girl-friend figure. They usually completed their various cures by falling in love with her, some more seriously than others. She had always managed to hang on to her nurse's objectivity. Until now. Captain Jack Mallory reminded her of her brother Jack; he had a way of grinning at her suddenly and then turning away as if she'd answered him. She knew that when he left here to convalesce, he was going to ask her to go with him. It had happened before. But before, she had never been tempted.

She finished writing and closed the book. It was mid-afternoon and though the sun was still bright a big bank of cloud had appeared in the direction of Weymouth and seemed to be moving in. She peered through the window at it, wondering whether she should round up the walking wounded who were taking the air in the grounds. Tea and slab cake would be served on the terrace for them in half an hour if the weather held. She thought of tomorrow and her mother laying an enormous tea in the farmhouse kitchen and fussing around Tommy. The days of moving over to their 'honeymoon cottage' had long gone. Tommy did all sorts of things around the farm now, he had even taught himself to drive the tractor. But it was nothing to do with her, of course.

She sighed and pushed tomorrow ahead of her out of sight; 'Sufficient unto the day' she murmured as she left the office and walked along the corridor to the garden doors. That was the bliss of hospital work, there was never any time for anticipating anything.

'Have you come to get us in?'

308

It was Jack Mallory, trying to look like a small boy called in from play. He really was so like brother Jack. Not for the first time she felt a physical pang of longing to see Jack again and be the girl she had been.

'I don't think so. Not yet anyway. It's quite warm.'

She went to the balustrade and watched a game of croquet played from wheelchairs. 'What do you think of Sergeant Aires? Is he coming out of his shell?'

It was her practice to encourage the men to share an interest in whatever progress was being made. She had even coined a phrase for it: self-help.

Jack Mallory joined her and leaned gratefully on the grey stone.

'I shouldn't think so. Not yet.'

She looked up, surprised. 'Why do you say that?'

'Well . . . he hasn't had time. You've got to live through what's in the shell first before you can come out of it.'

She went on looking at him. 'You're wiser than I thought, Captain Mallory.'

'For one so young?' He grinned at her. 'You always treat me like a kid, Sister. I'm twenty-three, you know.'

'Yes, I do know.'

'Of course. You know more about me than I know about myself probably.' His grin faded. 'How old are you, Sister?'

'None of your business, Captain.' She looked at her fob watch. 'Time for tea, I think.'

As if summoned by her voice, the trolleys rattled through the garden door, and the men began to converge on to the terrace.

The padre gave her a lift as far as the White Horse Inn at Coker, and her father met her there with Judy and the trap. The rain which had threatened yesterday was coming down steadily, and George looked laughable beneath a big golfing umbrella, his knees covered with an Edwardian mackintosh wrap. Elizabeth grinned as she thanked the padre and he lifted surprised brows. Sister

Tomms seemed to take life very seriously as a rule.

'Daddy, you look marvellous. Squire Doswell himself. Where's Tommy?'

'Bit of a cold. Your mother has him in front of a fire with rugs around him.'

'Rugs! It's the hottest May for years.'

'Well . . . the rain. And you know your mother.'

'Yes. And I know Tommy.'

She climbed in beside him and hugged his arm.

'It's good to see you at any rate.'

He did not reply. George Doswell was in the unenviable position of seeing the game and not being able to participate even to assist the injured. He flopped the reins gently on to Judy's back and she ambled out of the yard of the White Horse and broke into a trot along the empty country lane. The rain dimpled her fat back and she flipped her ears occasionally against it.

'Everything all right?' Elizabeth asked, just to break the silence. She'd never had to do that before; she and her father could spend hours on the farm together in perfect harmony without exchanging a word. She knew everything was all right because otherwise he would have been clearing his throat and leading up to it with ham-handed tact long before now.

'Fine. Nothing to report. And you?'

'Fine. Captain Mallory leaves at the end of the week.'

'That's the chap who was paralysed from the waist down?'

'Yes.' She smiled into the rain. 'Not any more.'

'The operation was successful then?'

'Oh yes. Though not at first. He wouldn't go to physio . . . wouldn't eat . . . you can imagine.'

George was silent again, then as they drove into the barn he said, 'Lizzie, when one of the other nurses has . . . I don't know what to call . . . a success? Like you've obviously had with Captain Mallory — are you as pleased?'

'How do you mean?'

310

'You're so obviously delighted about Captain Mallory. I can tell without you actually saying so. He's done all those things — got himself on his feet again — because of you, hasn't he?'

She jumped down from the trap and began to unhitch Judy from the shafts.

'I don't know about *that*, Daddy. He's been one of my specials though. Yes. So I suppose I am extra pleased about his progress.

'And would you have been just as pleased if someone else — what's the other Sister's name — Jocelyn Lennard — if he'd been *her* special?'

She was wiping Judy with a handful of hay and stopped to look at him in surprise.

'Daddy, what is all this? You don't think I've got a thing about Jack Mallory, do you? Is that what you're getting at? Daddy, you know me better than that.'

He pulled her case out of the trap and hung the open umbrella from a beam to drip.

'I don't know what I mean, Lizzie. I worry about you sometimes. I wonder if the people at the hospital might seem more real than we do. Mummy and me. And Tommy.'

'Dear Daddy. I love coming home, you know that. For one thing you and Mummy make sure I have a good rest, and you can't imagine how lovely that is.'

George took the hay from her and sighed. He was no good at diplomacy. 'Here, let me do that. You go on in and see Tommy.' He looked at her as she picked up her case. 'And Lizzie, don't begrudge your mother her bit of nursing. If there had been children it would have been different. But she needs to look after Tommy. Like you need to look after your patients.'

She stared at him for a long moment. Then she went out into the rain and ran across to the kitchen door.

The rain effectively put an end to a lot of the outdoor work at the farm. George and his cowman milked twice a day and led the cows to the drained pastures on the higher land around Tyler's Tump. Ellen was occupied as always, and perhaps warned by George, seemed to fuss around Tommy a little less this time. Elizabeth found herself wondering how long it could all go on. And what exactly did she mean by 'all'? Was it her marriage, or the life at Doswells', or what? She had always been completely frank and open with her family; she realized now that since her marriage that part of her had changed. She could talk to no-one about her husband's apparent impotence, least of all her husband. And now she could not talk about Jack Mallory. Her father had been trying to tell her several things; she knew that. Probably neither of them knew specifically what those things were, but they both knew that life at the moment was . . . difficult.

Of course everything was difficult with the war; people expected it to be. But the war wouldn't last forever. Elizabeth thought that she could go on living as she was at present until the war was over. Then what?

The only person who seem unchanged at the farm was Tommy. She went to the seldom-used sitting-room as soon as she arrived. He sat swathed in rugs, a jar of glycerine, lemon and honey on a table next to him, a fire in the hearth, surrounded by reading matter.

She made a determined effort.

'Hello darling. Daddy says you've got a cold.'

He looked up smiling, genuinely pleased to see her.

'It's nothing. Not really. Ellen insisted on taking my temperature, and when it started to rain, that was it!'

He bundled up some envelopes and forms and patted the arm of his chair.

'Come and sit down. How are you? How's the hospital? Are you still going to get a summer leave?'

'I'm fine, the hospital is fine, and yes.' She attempted to laugh, but just the thought of a whole fortnight at the farm was pretty dreadful. She sat opposite him, ignoring his invitation to share the chair, and stretched her legs luxuriously, feigning relaxation.

He leaned down and picked up some letters.

'Surprise.'

'Letter from Aunt May?'

She knew the structure of his family now: Aunt May had written when Victor was taken prisoner, and kept tenuously in touch ever since. There was Aunt April, Davina her daughter who had a part in a show called 'Swing that Seesaw', and other shadowy children and uncles. On the outskirts of the family was someone called Aunt Bridie; Tommy had been in Spain with her first husband. Tommy was always interested in news of her; when her second husband had been packed off to an insane asylum, he had stared into space for along time, thinking his own private thoughts.

He nodded in answer to her question.

'Well, yes actually. But that's not the surprise. The surprise is that I've decided to apply for an artificial arm.'

'Oh. Really?' She wasn't that surprised. After Victor had visited them last in that bitter Janury of '42, Tommy had taught himself to write with his left hand. When the letter had come from May telling of Victor's capture, he had driven the tractor, jamming his abdomen against the steering wheel in order to change gear. Last year when Tunisia had been taken by the Allies, he had said, 'That'll please old Victor if he hears about it,' and he had started to help George out with the milking.

He said now, 'I thought you'd be pleased. You've mentioned it so many times.'

'Of course I'm pleased. What made you decide to go ahead? Anything particular?'

'No. Aunt May says Gloucester is plastered with painted slogans. Under London Road bridge, the post office walls — everywhere — saying "Open Second Front Now". Makes me realize that we're winning this damned war. When you come home for good Lizzie, I don't want to be a bloody nuisance.'

Her heart melted; it was as much a physical sensation as yesterday's pang of depression had been. As usual this effort was stimulated by news from home, but if finally he was doing it for her, surely there was something special in his feeling for her — something besides companionship?

She got up and sat on the arm of his chair.

'Dear Tommy. Tell me about it.'

'Well, there's nothing much to tell. You fill in a lot of forms. Then they send you an appointment. Here's mine. Look. June the first. At the Woolwich Hospital. I suppose they measure you and things. Then they fit it. Then you have to go each day for a week and do exercises. But the evenings will be free. We could do a show, darling. What do you say?'

'It might be quite fun.'

'In the day you and Ellen could go shopping and treat yourselves to a lunch—'

'Mother? She won't want to come, Tommy. She hates London and she's always so busy here in the summer.'

'She suggested it actually, Lizzie.'

'Oh. Did she? Well, there'll be no need for her to come if I'm there. I'll tell her now.' She sprang off the arm of his chair as if it had become red-hot.

Albert watched her leave. He frowned and shook his head. She needed a break. She was as tense as a coiled spring.

That night she made another effort.

'Dear Tommy, I think it's marvellous about the arm. Really.' She moved over in the bed and took his head on her shoulder. He lay on her left side so he could quite easily have encircled her with his left arm, but he did not. Sometimes she had to remind herself of how he'd been when she knew him first. She had to force herself to imagine him going after the killer Stuka and avenging Jack's death. She had to remember the grim determination on his face when he'd convalesced at the farm; the way he had leaned on her shoulder; his unexpected pride in his medal. For so long now he had been in this awful state of . . . of surrender. Even before he lost his arm he'd given in. The night of their wedding, in fact. Sometimes she had wondered whether that final crash could have been avoided; she wondered whether he had hoped to finish everything that day.

She touched his forehead with her lips.

'I think it shows that you're . . . coming back.'

'Coming back? What d'you mean, Lizzie? It's you who is away. I am here all the time.'

She listened for bitterness in his voice; there was none. He'd never been bitter; he'd been resigned. She could have fought bitterness as she'd fought it for so many men. To fight for Albert was like punching a pillow.

She said, 'No, Tommy. *You*'ve been away. Somewhere right inside yourself.'

He laughed. 'Oh Lizzie. All this psychology stuff isn't you. You're practical and down-to-earth.'

'Yes, I am.' She moved her mouth down to his eyes. 'Could we . . . try again, darling?'

'If you like.' The arm came round her waist at last and he lifted his face like a dutiful small boy. 'It won't be any good, Lizzie. I know I'm hopeless. Please don't get upset.'

It wasn't any good. And she did get upset. His lack of passion, his lack of anguish, not only cut her to the quick, it made her own sudden, flaring desire into something rather disgusting. She thought, not for the first time, 'I'll never ask him again — never demean myself —' Then, unbidden, Jack Mallory's face appeared against her hot, closed lids.

She said, 'I'll have to go to the bathroom.'

And Tommy said, 'Lizzie, I'm sorry. Come back. Let me—'

She almost shouted at him. 'No! And stop being *kind* to me!'

The next day, as if to put her further in the wrong, his temperature was 101 and he confessed to aching all over.

Ellen wanted to call the doctor.

'It's this summer flu and it can be nasty, Lizzie,' she protested over the washing-up. 'I don't dispute you're a very good nurse, darling, but you don't see as much of Tommy as I do.'

'True, very true.'

'And I've seen him like this before. Dr Barnes gave him some of this new medicine, penny something, the last time he was like this and it cleared it up in no time.'

'Do what you like, Mother.'

'Well if you really don't mind—'

'For God's sake. Why should I mind? Why don't you ask Tommy if he minds?'

'He never does. He's so good and patient. A lesson to us all.' Ellen's mouth tightened. 'And I'd prefer you not to swear in this house please, Lizzie.'

'My God. It used to be our house. D'you remember? I was your daughter. Albert Tomms was a stranger.'

'Don't be silly, dear. You're overworking. It's just that sometimes you seem a little hard on Tommy. But then, I know nurses have to be hard.'

With an enormous effort, Lizzie stopped herself from responding to that. She remembered her father's words and knew he was right. Ellen needed to look after Tommy. Her mother left the washing-up and came over to hug Elizabeth.

'Darling girl. Everything will be all right after the war, you'll see. And I'm so glad you and Tommy are going to have a second honeymoon in London next month. I didn't want to come at all really, you know. But I thought I'd be helping Tommy.'

Elizabeth forced a smile and drifted into the sitting-room to pick up some books for Tommy. And that was when she read Aunt May's letter.

It was the usual stuff. Aunt May dotted her i's with a circle, and used lots of capital letters, which made it tricky to read, but Elizabeth gathered that Gretta was a little darling and Uncle Monty practically running the garage these days, and wasn't it simply marvellous about Davie?

'I've not mentioned that you will be in London at the beginning of June dear Boy, but as it happens your mother is taking Davie up for her broadcast that week. They have a permanent room at a nice place in Sussex Gardens and Davie has been asked to sing at a charity Forces do on Saturday the 3rd which means staying an extra couple of nights. So March volunteered to take her and she will visit her old warden and his family while she is there. Now dear Boy, how about Forgetting the Past and calling on them, Albie? Your mother seems very Happy and Settled these days, but I know what it would mean to her to see You again, and surely after being happily married to your Elizabeth for almost Four Years, you can bury the Hatchet. I never understood any of it, but then as you know, the Goulds never harbour Grudges . . . Aren't we doing well in Italy? I have Great Hopes that Victor will be Home again soon . . .'

Elizabeth folded the letter and replaced it in its envelope.

It was an enormous relief to get back to the hospital and become immediately involved with the small enclosed world of segregated men and women. She had been away less than forty-eight hours, yet the rhododendrons lining the drive were almost out, and the enormous horse chestnut on the main lawn looked borne down with its weight of blossom. She went into the sister's office to take over from the night staff and there was Jocelyn Lennard looking tired but content. Perhaps not content . . . fulfilled perhaps? In this life you went to bed exhausted, and righteously so. Elizabeth smiled at her own thoughts and Jocelyn said, 'Glad to be back?'

'Oh yes.'

'Don't let him get too important!'

'Who?' But Elizabeth knew only too well and was slightly bothered that Jocelyn did too.

317

'Jack Mallory of course. He's been pining for you — that's to be expected. But you're not allowed to pine for him.'

'Oh stop it, Joss. I'm a married woman.'

'Not very often.'

It was not meant as a gibe. The plain fact was that Elizabeth was one of the very few married nurses with a husband at home.

She said slowly, 'I don't really fit in any more. It's just good to be back where I do fit in. That's all.'

'That's enough. And it's bad.'

But Joss was tired and wanted to go to bed, and intimate discussions were not in their line anyway. Most of the psychology lectures were based on sound common sense, and others regarding such things as 'deviancy' and 'complexities' were too long-term for a military hospital. 'Patch 'em up and get 'em out' was the old maxim for such establishments, and things hadn't changed that much.

She went ahead of the breakfast trolley, making her own personal check on her patients. Later there would be a formal round with the matron. Then there were doctors' rounds, and in between there would be blanket baths, dressings, special diets, exercise for the walking, lunch, tea on the terrace . . .

'Good morning, Sister. Did you enjoy your leave?'

Captain Mallory was already dressed and making for the glass verandah where a breakfast table was laid. She couldn't help smiling warmly at him. His operation had been very tricky; fragments of shell had been perilously near the spine and the chance of him being permanently paralysed had been very high indeed. Yet he had fought, and won. She remembered Tommy, lying in bed, surrounded by the paraphernalia of an old man's sick-room. She was a nurse and shouldn't mind; but she did. What could it mean? Didn't she love him any more?

She could not brush Jack Mallory's question aside with a formal answer. She replied ruefully, 'Not very much. It

318

rained all the time.'

'I know,' he said fervently.

Her smile turned to laughter at his expression, and he glanced at her, surprised, then laughed too. They they both stopped laughing. After a moment she remarked, 'I do believe it will be fine today anyway. We'll be able to go outside later on.'

'Yes. We need some f.esh air,' he said, peering through the windows.

She delayed no longer. Today or tomorrow or the next day, Jack Mallory would broach the subject of her leave coinciding with his convalescence. She did not know how she would respond. They both knew the dangers of the nurse-patient relationship. Perhaps he needed to see her in mufti to kill his feeling for her stone-dead.

But she realized that did not matter. It had nothing to do with her problem at home. She had to write to Tommy before he went to London. She had to tell him she had no intention of going with him. She would have liked to beg him to go to see his mother as Aunt May had suggested; try to come to terms with whatever had soured his life so thoroughly. But something stopped her from mentioning the fact that she had read Aunt May's letter; it might seem to Albert like plain unvarnished jealousy on her part. And it was so much more than that.

So she wrote to him that night and told him she was going to spend her leave with Jack Mallory. He would understand that; it was the sort of protest any wife would make in her situation. The letter was more difficult to compose than she had imagined. She kept staring out of the window at the huge sky over Chesil Beach and wondering if brother Jack was up there somewhere, still laughing at his sister and his best friend.

Eighteen

ALBERT was thankful that the nurses at the hospital were mostly male. On the train coming up to London, he had tried to work out a line of small talk he could use on them when they fitted his artificial arm. It had stopped him thinking about Lizzie's letter and going crazy with jealousy at the thought of another man seeing those gently rounded limbs. He had to bring down a shutter on those thoughts. Though Ellen had said to him, 'Now don't think about the arm at all, Tommy. Just hand yourself over to them like a parcel — remember they're experts,' he deliberately made himself think about it in all its horrors simply because it could temporarily block out the image of Lizzie's face . . . Lizzie's shoulders . . . Lizzie . . .

He tried to imagine Victor's reaction to an artificial arm; *he* wouldn't try to pretend it was a thing of beauty, or a mechanical miracle; he'd probably find some ghastly name for it and refer to it constantly as a kind of alter ego. When the nurse came towards him bearing it . . . whatever it was . . . Victor would size her up and if she were pretty enough, he'd say something like, 'D'you think you could fall for Frankenstein, Nurse? Because he's going to be rather attached to me you see, so if you want to go on seeing him . . .'

In the event, the military hospital at Woolwich was staffed by medical orderlies, marching around the wards as if they were on parade, and 'Frankenstein' was suspended fairly innocuously on a sort of parachute harness. It looked pretty ghastly, of course: an aluminium skeleton, its hand permanently covered by a leather glove, wires going to pulleys in the 'elbow joint', but the thick pad which pressed against his stump was painless; the harness would chafe, they warned him, but that could be dealt with fairly easily.

The first time they fitted it beneath his shirt and jacket, they did so in front of a cheval mirror. It was like trying on a new suit. They stepped back and let him look at himself. He had avoided mirrors like the plague since he lost his arm; the occasional glimpse of the empty pinned sleeve always caused him to feel repelled by his own body. Now, suddenly, he knew how a woman must feel with a new hair-do. He remembered Aunt May saying in the old days, 'I can do more for anyone's morale with scissors and curling tongs, than any doctor.' And this was more permanent than a hair-do.

He thought: 'Christamighty, I could learn to knock a man out with this thing. I could get it round Lizzie and clamp her to me so that she'd never move again!' Then he remembered that he had no right to Lizzie. No right at all. By loving his own sister, he had forfeited the right to love any other woman.

He put up at the Overseas League Club in Piccadilly and travelled daily to the hospital. By the fourth day he could climb in and out of the harness without any help. He could walk with gently swinging arm, and avoid hitting other people. He was still inclined to turn his body and leave his arm behind, and it would catch up with him with an action that hurt his shoulder, then caught him in the abdomen. The doctor told him not to worry, all that control would come with time and practice. For now he should keep the gloved hand hooked lightly in his jacket pocket; think of it as a tool and take it out only when needed. It was handy for holding a cigarette, for instance; that now meant he could light his own. Yesterday he had used it to pick up a cup of tea and get it to his mouth. He had then had to throw his whole body back in order to tip the cup, but that was another knack that would come with time.

Today he emerged from the tube at Piccadilly and went into Fortnum and Mason's for tea. He ordered some cakes and looked with dismay at the fork that came with them. Slowly he put Frankenstein on the table by the side of his plate, fitted the fork between the gloved fingers, and bore down on the cake. When it reached his mouth, he looked up and met the eyes of an elderly man at a nearby table. The man's eyes flickered and he was about to look away. Albert forced himself to grin. The man lifted his tea cup and inclined his head in silent congratulation. It was Albert's first public exhibition. He forgot Elizabeth and Jack Mallory; he felt a surge of excited hopefulness that was somehow familiar. He hadn't felt like this for years. He hadn't felt like this since what he always called in his mind 'Davina Days'.

He left Fortnums and walked on to Green Park. A newspaper-seller was blabbing that Rome had fallen, and he wondered whether Victor would come home now. The fitful sun came out and gave the illusion of a perfect June day. Everything smelled fresh after such a wet May. He kept walking, hardly knowing where he was going, yet knowing he had a destination somewhere in mind. Hyde Park was interminable; the Serpentine a vast river. He made himself pause to watch the rowers and ducks. A boatload of sailors weren't feathering their oars; it struck him that probably feathering was not needed on the Atlantic. His neck was aching and he realized he had been swinging Frankenstein. He took time to put the gloved fingers in his pocket, then went on again.

The boarding-house was easily found from Aunt May's directions. He stood still, leaning against the pillar-box outside, looking at it, and wondering whether even now he should turn and go back to the Club. He wondered what Tolly would say if he were here right now. Tolly, his wise mentor from long ago. Yes, Tolly had also run from an impossible situation. What would he do now about going back? He summoned up the thin ascetic face, the dark idealistic eyes; he could almost hear the diffident voice too, because of course he knew exactly what Tolly would say. 'Do what you have to do, Albert. Really, there's no way out of that.'

A sprightly elderly lady answered the bell. She wore a pre-war crepe de Chine dress with a bow at the back and a lot of smocking at the waist. The dress might have been navy or purple or grey; it had washed to a curious mixture of all three, and the hem dipped above cuban-heeled shoes.

'Mrs Luker? Yes, she is here at the moment with her niece, the singer, you know. We are listening to the News in the lounge, if you would care to . . .' She led the way down a long passage to the back of the house. Stewart Hibbard's voice echoed nasally from behind a door. The fall of Rome was official.

'It will be nice for Mrs Luker to see a relative. Miss Daker has so many callers, of course.'

Shy Davina? He'd heard her on Workers' Playtime back in the spring, but it had never occurred to him that she would have a following. What a fool he was coming here, one of many.

The landlady flung open the door, disclosing a pleasant room with armchairs grouped around open French windows. Heads turned and looked at him, then politely turned back. Except two. Davina and his mother stared at him as if he were a ghost, and he probably did look rather wraith-like these days, straight after one of his feverish colds. They too had changed, though of course he would have known them anywhere. His mother was almost entirely grey and her face was bone-thin in the way Grandma Rising's had been. But she looked better than formerly, in some indefinable way. Not exactly joyful, but happy . . . with herself. Again like Grandma Rising had been.

Davie's face above the back of her armchair was almost

shocking in its beauty. She was more like a flower than ever; her shoulder-length hair swung bell-like as she turned to look at him, and he was transported to the daffodil fields at Newent when a breeze swept through the flowers, threatening to snap them. They always sprang back. They were delicate and strong at the same time; they had unending resilience.

He saw his mother's mouth open and her lips form his name. 'Albert!' And he saw Davie's shock turn to pleased surprise, then almost immediately to doubt. She glanced sideways at her aunt and put a protective hand on her arm.

And Albert knew that she was no longer his.

They went upstairs to talk privately. It was not easy. There was a time when Davie would have thrown her arms around her cousin, or at least stared at him with shining eyes. That time had gone and her concern was for March. She sat close to her aunt on one of the twin beds and appeared to see herself as a kind of umpire. If it hadn't been so fraught, Albert might even have been amused by her.

But the situation *was* fraught. March had leapt up from her chair in the lounge as if it had become red-hot. She had almost cannoned into the colourless crepe de Chine as she rushed to the door, and it was obvious that she expected Albert to have brought tragic news.

'What has happened?' she breathed when she reached him. 'Is it Fred?'

Her question told him so much and he hardly knew how to answer her. She was as smart as paint in a good tweed suit with pearls showing between the lapels. Davie, following, wore a cream blouse and a green skirt and a sort of alice band thing on her hair.

He stammered, 'No. Nothing has happened like that. I thought . . . Aunt May wrote and —' he tried to laugh. 'I've just had this thing fitted and when I heard you were in London too—'

Davie said in a low voice, 'It's all right, Aunt March. Nothing dreadful has happened. Let's go upstairs, shall we?'

So they were here; the two women on one bed and Albert facing them on the other. The window was heavy with crisscrossed tape, and there were ominous cracks in the ceiling, otherwise the room was pleasant enough with a Belgian carpet square on the floor and an elegant non-Utility dressing-table. He had to explain why he had come, and he did not know himself. He wondered if he'd intended saying, 'I cannot sleep with my wife. I love her like a sister. And I love my sister like a wife. And my wife is sleeping with a man who has the same name as her brother.'

He cleared his throat. 'I was coming to London to have this fitted —' he tapped Frankenstein with his left hand. 'Aunt May had sent me your address and asked me to call.'

March said, 'I see.'

Davie linked her arm through her aunt's. 'Well. That's rather nice. Isn't it, Aunt March?' She smiled brightly and insincerely and when there was no reply, she went on, 'We've been at the studio all day. And after dinner we're going to a Forces concert. At Woolwich. So I expect Aunt March is rather tired.'

Albert suddenly felt tired himself. Unbearably tired. He should have gone back to the Club and rested as he usually did. He should never have come here. He shifted on the bed.

'Yes of course. I'll go now, then—'

March put out her free hand. 'No. Don't go yet.' She seemed to make an enormous effort. 'I know it's difficult, Albert. After all, it's been seven years. But don't go until we've . . . had a few words.'

Davie said, 'Establish a bridgehead? Is that what you're trying to do, Albie?'

'I don't know.' Why couldn't he be honest and tell them that he'd run to them for help? 'I really don't know. I just started walking this afternoon and . . . arrived here!'

He gave a helpless inverted smile and March smiled back at him. 'Never mind reasons. You're here, that's what counts.' She patted the back of Davie's hand reassuringly. 'How are you getting on with the arm?'

'Frankenstein?' He smiled properly at Davie's look. 'It occurred to me that that was what Victor would call it. Frankenstein.'

Her expression softened, became genuine.

'Yes. So he would. Funny how he can say things like that and it's all right.'

'He makes everything all right. He always has.'

She smiled at him for the first time; not in the old adoring way, but with love and even gratitude.

'Yes. You're right,' she said.

March said grudgingly, 'Well, for such a spoiled child I have to admit he hasn't turned out badly!'

Albert laughed with Davie at that, knowing his mother had said it deliberately to turn their laughter on her. And then he told them about Frankenstein and gave them a demonstration. It was like doing a 'party piece' and he'd always been hopeless at parties. He sat back down on the bed, sweating profusely.

Davie said, 'Look. Why don't I go and ask Mrs Venables if she can stretch dinner for Albert. Then he could come with us to the concert.'

But to his surprise his mother vetoed this suggestion. 'You're looking tired, Albert. Davie's got a special taxi man. He'll come and take you back to wherever you're staying.' She smiled to take the sting out of her rejection. 'I think the bridgehead is established. That *was* all you wanted, wasn't it?' She stood up. 'Davie, would you pop downstairs and phone the taxi, dear? And while it's coming Mrs Venables will make Albert a cup of tea.'

She stood aside and let Davie go ahead, then she turned to him again.

'Albert, thank you for coming. I'll write. And I expect Davie will write too. But, she is happy now. She wasn't always happy — it took a long time. You understand what I am saying?'

'You're telling me to keep away from her.'

'I suppose I am. For two or three more years at any rate.'

He was amazed at her calmness. The March he knew would have flushed angrily, accused him of ruining her life and Davie's.

He said weakly, 'We were so close. Has that gone for good?'

'No, of course not. But any romantic attachment is obviously out of the question now. I think she understands that — I think she understood it from the moment I told her that Fred was your father.'

'You told her that?'

'She deserved to know. She thought you were rejecting her. Just her. I had to tell her that it was really me you were rejecting.'

He swallowed. 'I didn't think you had it in you, Mother.'

'What? Martyrdom?' She laughed. 'You don't know much about me actually, Albert. And I don't know much about you either. Yet we were all in all to each other when you were a child.'

'I know,' he said a low voice.

She spoke briskly again. 'I'll write. And you can write back. We'll get to know each other. It will be interesting. And good practice for Frankestein!' She looked at him smilingly, and after a while he managed to smile back.

There seemed nothing else to say. He longed to tell her about Elizabeth, he longed to lay before her every detail of his life and hear every detail of hers. She seemed to understand this.

'Don't try to rush anything, Albert.' She walked ahead of him to the landing and waited for him to catch up. 'Those sort of reconciliations — you know, all is forgiven and forgotten in two minutes flat — rarely last. We're two different people now. And we've got plenty of time.'

He nodded slowly, even though he was disappointed.

'One thing, Mother. All this frightful business with Aunt Bridie — which seems incidentally to have brought you all closer than ever — I think I ought to tell you in the strictest confidence, that as far as I know Uncle Tolly is still alive.'

That did stop her in her tracks. She held on to the newel post at the top of the stairs and looked at him, literally open-mouthed.

'I have to admit that I've not heard from him since before the war, but he told me that he intended to go underground. When Fred asked me about him back in '39, I didn't give him an answer. Tolly had sworn me to secrecy. You see, he had some crazy plan for assassinating Hitler.'

March breathed, 'He must have been mad. The selfishness of the man leaves me stunned. Quiet Tolly Hall plotting and planning . . .and leaving his wife and family to that ghastly Mannie Stein—'

'He couldn't know that Bridie would marry Stein, Mother — be fair. And of course I could be wrong, he could have been killed before he left Spain. But I know he planned to plant his papers elsewhere so that he would be declared dead, and then to make his way to Germany. He was anything but crazy.'

March was silent for a long time. Below them Davie could be heard telephoning.

March said slowly, 'He wouldn't have been crazy if it had worked, I suppose. I remember him saying that he had caught Herr Hitler's eye through his binoculars at the Berlin Games. It made a great impression on Tolly, I think.'

Albert nodded. 'They were similar in looks and bearing. He thought he might gain admittance on the strength of that. He felt he had a mission.' He shrugged. 'He was willing to give his own life. And — as I say — he might well have done. Who knows? But I thought someone close to Bridie should know that there is a possibility he is still alive. And Aunt May tells me that you keep an eye on the family now.'

'Bridie came to me in London after that awful man had ill-treated her. Yes, I do feel a certain responsibility for all of them.' She touched his good arm. 'Thank you, Albert. I'm glad you told me.'

Davie called up the stairs. 'He's coming right away, Albert. No time for tea I'm afraid.'

'That's all right. I'll have some back at the Club.'

They waited with him on the steps until the taxi arrived. Neither of them suggested another meeting, but at least his mother had said she would write. He waved to them until they were out of sight.

He couldn't leave it at that. He was all at sea; his mother had been wonderful, magnificent even. He felt all the old love and admiration for her regenerating. And he welcomed it; he had hated hating her. But Davie, how the hell did he feel now about Davie? Had he expected — had he wanted — her to love him passionately, as he loved her? Because he knew he did. Her beauty had amazed and delighted him all over again; everything about her, her voice, her mannerisms, everything had thrilled through him like a series of electric shocks. He felt alive again and realized he had not felt like this since he was nineteen. It would have been wonderful and marvellous if she had felt the same. It was so obvious she had not. And . . . thank God she did not. His mother was right about that; he wanted her happiness more than his own and she could never be happy being in love with him. But he could not walk away from her now without a backward glance. If he really did have to bury his love for good and all, there must be some kind of funeral. So after dinner at the Club, he walked slowly to the Underground and started on the now-familiar journey to Woolwich.

At first he didn't think he would get in; it was Forces only. He showed his identification, but it was the tin arm that did it. The soldier on the door bumped against it as he reached out, and immediately jerked his head at the blackout curtains shielding the hall. 'Go on in then.' He grinned. 'I dunno 'ow you'll get on trying to clap with that thing. Better stamp your feet instead.'

The hall was packed with men, with just a sprinkling of A.T.S. and W.A.A.F.s in the front seats. It was the usual E.N.S.A. concert; Albert had seen variations of it before. A magician, a stand-up comic, a singing duo, a few sketches. Davina came immediately after the comic. For a moment he thought it was April standing there; April as he remembered her from his childhood. Then he recalled that April's hair had been shingled, and a deeper gold anyway. And April had sung ragtime and had Charlestoned while she did it. There was a quality of stillness about Davie which was all her own. She came to the front of the platform and settled herself on a chair, her mandolin in her lap. And she waited calmly while the audience realized that they had to listen to her and settled down into complete silence. She was, after all, only half April. The other half was . . . Albert took a deep breath and sat up very straight. The other half was *his* half: his Luker half. It was the April half that made her anxious for her Aunt March this afternoon; it was the Luker half that had enabled her to be objective about it and take on the role of umpire.

She strummed once, then again, on her mandolin, and leaned over it as she began to sing. Her hair swung forward. Her lashes lay long and crescent-shaped on her cheekbones. Her legs, emerging from the plain green skirt which she had worn that afternoon, were very long and very shapely. Just like April she could combine a provocative beauty with schoolgirl innocence.

She sang a song from the First War, a song he had heard May sing very often, sickly-sweet and haunting. 'Roses are blooming in Picardy.' She sang very softly, almost as if she were singing to herself. There was no microphone, and the acoustics of the body-packed hall were not good, yet because she was commanding such an intense, listening silence, she could be heard perfectly. Albert felt himself breathing shallowly as if afraid to break the atmosphere of intimacy and at the same time standing back, as it were, objective and uninvolved, full of amused admiration at the way the Luker side of her could hold this cynical audience in the palm of her hand and manipulate them exactly as her true father had done in the past. The mandolin tinkled just ahead of the words and then was silent while she sang the final line with a slight catch in her voice: 'But there's one rose that blooms not in Picardy, That's the rose that still blooms in my heart.'

Under cover of the raving applause, Albert looked around him. He saw what he had expected to see: the tight, buttoned faces, beneath the cloud of cigarette smoke, were relaxed almost to tears. They needed the nostalgia, the sentimentality that she had given them and they could not afford it themselves. They dared not relax the stiff upper lip. This tall, leggy schoolgirl had done it for them. They clapped and frantically demanded more.

He looked back at the stage. She was standing, her mandolin in one hand at her side, her head bowed in humility. Suddenly and unexpectedly, he wanted to laugh. He was the only one here who knew her — really knew her. Better than she knew herself. Better than April or even Fred knew her. He thought with amazing clarity: of course I can go on loving her . . . God, she's my *sister!* There's no misery in that — there can be — Christamighty — there can be pride and joy and . . . fun!

He wanted to leap up on the stage and tell her it was all right, that there need be no funeral, no sadness any more. He wanted to tell her that he knew how she did it; he knew how she moved all these people with her simple childish voice. He wanted, desperately, to tell her that they were brother and sister and that the love they had would always be theirs.

And he could not.

She began to sing again; a song Rita Hayworth had made popular in a recent film. A different mood settled

331

around him; she swayed with the music, and the audience began to sway too. On the final chorus she held out her free hand and they joined in with her. Her voice was drowned and she stopped singing and revolved slowly and dreamily across the stage in foxtrot rhythm. She allowed them to think that they were in charge now; she allowed them to manipulate her.

Again Albert could not applaud, even with his feet; he was motionless with admiration for her mastery. He was so proud of her he could only stare.

He did not stop for the finale. He was exhausted after such a day and hardly knew how to get himself out of the hall and back to Piccadilly. It was still light and people roamed the streets freely as if the war was already over. A group of American G.I.s, tunics open, were laughing at the latest daub — 'Open Second Front Now' — in the Underground. One of them spotted Frankenstein and lurched drunkenly up to Albert. 'Don't you worry, bud. It won't be for nuthin! If the weather had been okay we'd a' bin there a'ready. Any minute now — any minute now, friend!' Albert grinned and went on; he knew he would sleep tonight. And tomorrow was the last day at the hospital. He could go home and do something about Elizabeth. He didn't know what, but he knew he could. It was as if Frankenstein had made him whole again. Frankenstein and Davie between them. He'd get all their stuff into the cottage and fill the place with flowers, then he'd go and fetch her. By force if necessary. He worked out the date. It would be June the sixth. The date he started fighting again.

Victor did not come home. The Red Cross informed them that he was in a camp south of the Harz mountains. May wrote to him that summer.

'Darling Boy. You will not recognize Gretta in her school uniform. We have sent her to the kindergarten at Denmark Road so that Flo can keep an eye on her. After all dearest, we managed to send you to a private school and feel we must do the same for her. We talk about you all the time so that she will never forget you. We miss you Victor my Son. I was reminding your Father of your Birth the other day. I expect I have told you before that you were conceived on Victory Night in 1918 and that is why we called you Victor. It will be another Victory for us when you come home my Darling. You will probably not recognize any of us! I am no thinner in spite of Rations, and your Father is no fatter in spite of all the free drinks he has up at Winterditch Camp. But when you saw us last we were very much the Also Rans of Gloucester. Now my Dearest, we have Gone Up in the World. Your father is talking of moving somewhere more Salubrious. But I have made him promise to wait until you can come Home and sort out all the Work in the attic. We really are very Comfortably Off Dearest. Uncle Fred pays us a good Salary and excellent commission. And of course your Father has many Contacts.'

March wrote soon after.

'Dear Victor, I know you will be pleased about my renewed contact with Albert. I think it probable that the way was paved by you a long time ago. I thank you for this and pray daily that you will soon come home and enjoy our family life again. I know it means a great deal to you, Victor. Davina speaks of you often, as does Flo, and it has become clear to me that you have been a mainstay to them both as well as to Albert in our troubled times."

The Dakers sent what they called a 'family budget'. David hoped Victor could get hold of some paper and charcoal. April broke the news to him that Aunt Sylv's mind sometimes slipped back fifty years and she would go out at night to meet people long dead or forgotten. Flo told him not to worry about that as the weather was warm and Aunt Sylv was so happy and if only she could skip up ten years or so and meet Uncle Dick again she'd have her heart's desire. She enclosed a stanza from a long narrative pastoral poem she was writing based on Aunt Sylv's life. 'In the greenwood I have waited, hair a-tangle, breath a-bated, till my love and I were mated, oh so long ago.' Davina wrote about her singing. 'My songs used to be for Olga. Now they are all for you. Be safe, Victor. Come home. It is all we ask.'

In the early spring of '45 Davie sent off another letter into the void where Victor might be.

'The war is nearly over, Victor. I no longer go to London for the radio show because of the buzzbombs and the rockets. Last week I did a broadcast from Cardiff. Next week it is to be Bristol. Beryl Langham came to see me yesterday. She is to be married to an American officer and after the war she will go to live in Vermont. She is terribly excited about it, but sad too. She said she felt a skunk marrying someone else when you were a prisoner. That's an American expression actually so she is already getting acclimatised. I told her you wouldn't mind and you would wish her every happiness. You would, wouldn't you? I can't bear it if your heart is broken. By the way you do know mine is mended, I hope. It's been mended for ages now, but I really knew all the scars were gone when we saw Albie in London last summer. I knew I could never have married him even if he'd asked me! I worshipped him like a brother, and now that I can see him properly I feel quite annoyed with him for creating all that fuss and bother just because Uncle Fred told him he was illegitimate. I mean all that nonsense went out of the window when the Yanks arrived here! It was all a bit dramatic wasn't it, going off to Spain and then refusing to see Aunt March and me properly at Haslemere. I was worried for Aunt March, but she took the whole thing like a real trouper and writes to Albie regularly now. Really, Victor, men are so funny. Not you of course. There's one who keeps sending me a black-edged card with the words "dying with love for you". I think it's rather bad taste in the circs, don't you? I'm thankful you've got your painting and I've got my singing. We're supposed to be the temperamental ones, but it doesn't work like that does it? The singing and the painting keep us sane. At least that's what I think.'

March's letters to Albert, and his in reply, were very unemotional but in their inimitable way they forged that first link between the Doswells and the Lukers.

She told him she was driving for the Red Cross in Gloucester now, using the old Wolseley and ferrying day patients into hospitals all over the county. She mentioned that Bridie had started to leave the house occasionally and seemed much stronger now. She said that Barty was growing fast and took his position of solitary male in the big household very seriously. She reported Natasha's first engagement to a Free French captain; then her second to a Canadian pilot; then her third which seemed The One, to the eldest Peplow boy home from the disastrous Arnhem raid.

Albert replied with news from the farm: the cows and their yield, the heavy plum crop, the V1 that went astray and made a crater as big as a lake just beyond Tyler's Tump.

In December when the Germans tried to stand in the Ardennes, he wrote, 'Lizzie has left the hospital and we now live permanently in the cottage. She is going to keep chickens.'

March knew nothing of his domestic arrangements, but from then on she addressed her letters to 'Mr and Mrs Tomms, The Cottage, Doswell's Farm, Coker, Dorset' and started each one, 'Dear Albert and Elizabeth.'

It was also that December that Bridie received an official letter from the War Office. It was addressed to 'Mrs Bartholomew Hall' and heavily sealed with red wax. Bridie had never received an official notification of Tolly's death, and when this arrived, she opened it in the privacy of her room, convinced that was what it was. She was

prepared for a further sense of her own uselessness in the
scheme of things, for a resurgence of all the old painful
memories associated with her husband . . . his mother . . .
his favourite daughter, Olga. When she read the contents
she could not believe them. She needed no further proof
of Mannie's perfidy of course, certainly none of Tolly's
courage and enterprise. But the fact that he was still alive
after the failure of the assassination plot of last July was
almost too much to contemplate. That day had been set
aside for her and Marlene to wash every curtain in the
house in time for Christmas. In the event she gave
Marlene the day off and did it all herself, soaking the
heavy damask in the bath and lugging each waterlogged
curtain down to the garden. In between trips she would
read the letter again.

'. . . pleased to be able to inform you that your husband
has been engaged on secret and honourable war work . . .'

It did not surprise her at all; she was more surprised
that she hadn't realized it for herself. Of course —
obviously — Tolly would be in the thick of things
wherever they were.

'. . . anonymity essential for undercover activities . . .
regretfully decided that it would be dangerous for you to
be informed of the true state of affairs . . .'

And that was typical of him too. What better
anonymity than to be dead? What a wonderful ally
Mannie had unknowingly proved to be. As she had
herself. Her pain, her humiliation had not after all been for
nothing.

'. . . at the moment receiving medical treatment after his
escape last July . . . final discharge on the 30th of this
month . . . family solicitors have been informed . . .'

She eventually folded the letter and put it away in her
handkerchief drawer. She studied her face in the
dressing-table mirror. She had never been beautiful, but
she had been attractive and had known it. Now she knew
the attraction had gone. The facile charm and
sophistication had gone too. What was there left for Tolly

336

to come home to?

She turned away and went back to her curtains. It was enough that he was alive and would one day want to see the girls again. She must be content with that. She had cheated and betrayed him; there was no reason for him to come back to her.

A final letter was sent in that spate of correspondence. It was written by Elizabeth Tomms and addressed to Mr and Mrs Luker, It began, incredibly, 'Dear Mother and Father-in-law' and ended, 'your affectionate daughter-in-law Elizabeth'. It stated very simply that they would be grandparents in early June and hoped they would be as delighted as she and Tommy were.

March could not wait to share the news. Neither April nor May were on the telephone, so she rang Bridie. For once Bridie was out. March had begged her to make the most of the spring weather, but contrarily she felt cheated that she had done so at this time.

She said to Marlene, 'Put Nash on the phone then, can you?'

'No. That I can't, Mrs Luker. Miss Nash is spending the week with young Mr Peplow. Him what's a commander.'

'A commando, Marlene. Command-oh. And I suppose the other girls are at school — Barty too?'

'Yes 'm.' There was a little pause while Marlene cleared her throat or blew her nose or something. Then her voice hissed in March's ear. 'But I en't on me own, Mrs Luker. There's a gent 'ere. A-waitin'.'

'Oh my God.' March still saw Bridie as perilously vulnerable. Was this a vengeful cohort of Mannie's? She said carefully, 'Now listen, Marlene. I know you can't say much so answer my questions yes or no. Does he look like Mr Stein in any way?'

'Ummmm. No. Not really. That is, he's dark.'

'Does he sound foreign?'

'Oh no mum. Glawster I'd say.'

March was silent for a moment, frowning into the hall

337

mirror. She adjusted the pearls on her twin set then said, 'Is he there in the hall with you, dear?'

'No.'

'Upstairs in the sitting-room?'

'Yes.'

March exploded. 'Then why all the whispering? He can't hear you, surely?'

'Shouldn't think so, Mrs Luker. But you said to say yes or no. An' if 'e were a German spy 'e might be standing at the top of the stairs a-listening.'

'Well, look around, girl. Is he?'

'No.'

March took a deep breath. 'Listen Marlene. Does he seem to know his way around the house? Because if so, he might be Mr Hall come back home.'

Marlene laughed a little shrilly.

'Come back from the dead d'you mean, mum?'

'Shut up Marlene. If it is Mr Hall, Miss Bridie is going to need a little warning. I'll go and look for her. And in case I don't find her, you are to take her into the kitchen when she comes back, and tell her there is a gentleman who looks like Mr Hall in the sitting-room. Otherwise she is likely to have a heart attack or something.'

'Oh Mrs Luker.'

'Do as I say, Marlene.'

'Yes 'm.'

March replaced the phone and went for her coat.

Ever since the War Office letter, Bridie had taken to walking to the cemetery at least twice a week. She had never bothered greatly with God, but as a child she had prayed often to Teddy Rising, and now she divided her time between Olga's and Kitty's graves, certain that if there was anything in this business of an afterlife, they would have gained it and be willing to intercede for her, although she had behaved so badly and really deserved all the terrible things that had happened to her. That day in spite of the bright sunshine, winter was still in the air.

There was a smell of it that took her right back to November; a typical Gloucester smell of river fog and age. She stared at Olga's marble angel with its spread protective wings, and felt the usual terrible regret at the young wasted life and the horror the girl had gone through before the end.

She whispered, 'Olga, I'm sorry. So sorry, darling. I could have run away from him before I did — I could have run the day he found Monty and me in the office. One of the reasons I stayed was because I felt I ought to be punished. Can you understand that, Olga? Part of me wanted to go through what you had gone through. But it didn't make it better for you, did it? Oh darling, why did you go down to Derby Road that day? Why — why?'

The angel did not even meet her eyes. There was some green mould on its feet and in the folds of its robe. Bridie fetched one of the watering cans and scrubbed at it with her handkerchief, and when she crouched before it she could see that it was blind. She took the can back to the tap and paused by Will and Flo. Their grave sported a very simple headstone in Cornish granite bearing their names and the dates of their life spans. She lingered there, surprised by the sudden sense of comfort she got from the thought of them. After all, their marriage had been no better than hers in a way. How had they managed to represent solidity and security when Will was making an absolute ass of himself with Sibbie? Was it all due to the saintly Florence, as March and May believed? April was not so certain; Bridie remembered her saying once, 'Mother couldn't have borne it like she did if she hadn't known beyond doubt that Daddy loved her and needed her above everything and everyone else. Aunt Sylv always said she was his star. He reached for her always.'

Bridie's eyes filled with tears. She had been a fool, there was no doubt about that, but Tolly had always been her star. Was he so unforgiving that he could never see her again? Would he not remember Florence Rising, the woman he had admired so much? Florence had lived in a state of forgiveness for most of her life; could he not try to emulate her?

She replaced the can and started on the long walk home. The poplar trees lining Cemetery Road were absolutely still, and Barton Street was almost somnolent in the unseasonal sunshine. On an impulse she cut down Faulkner Street so that she could go past her old Dame School in Midland Road. The Misses Midwinter were long gone, but the playground was full of children in vests and navy-blue knickers, bending and stretching under the eagle eye of a young teacher. She went under the railway subway which was already full of the winter's laurel leaves from the hedges in the park. She remembered the times March had collected April, Teddy and herself to take them back to Chichester Street for tea. There was a sweet poignancy to everything, a feeling of past, present and future, uniting, a feeling of acceptance.

She emerged from the subway and crossed into the park. Some very small children were playing on the shelters, climbing them laboriously and running down into the arms of their mothers. She watched them for a while, smiling, because somehow children transcended timescales; there were always children and they were always the same.

Her own clarity of thought alarmed her. She wondered whether she herself was about to die, so near did eternity seem, so simple did it seem. She looked round, startled, as a train shunted over the road to the docks. Perhaps she should have delayed crossing just there to coincide with the train? Ought that to have been her fate — had her hour really come — was there something else waiting for her between here and Brunswick Road to end it all? She shivered, mortally afraid in spite of her moment of epiphany. She thought in sudden agony: not yet — please God not yet. The children are still so young and Marlene has got pikelets for tea!

And she took to her heels and ran across the park as fast as she could.

As a boy of sixteen, Tolly Hall had joined other high-minded schoolboys who had bought and equipped an ambulance and gone to France. In the maelstrom of the Great War's aftermath, he had seen terrible things with a sense of terrible futility. The war had finished and there was no more reason for pain and anguish; the word 'honour' was suddenly ridiculous. He had come home with a deep inner conviction that only Communism could solve the frightful problems which the war had not touched. Gradually, during his unlikely marriage to Bridget Williams, further disenchantment had set in. He could not take a wide view as David Daker did. David had long since given up what he called his 'ideals' and saw personal and world salvation as synonymous. His own pleasure in his family and his home and his work was sufficient for him. Quite simply he thought that if everyone worked for personal contentment it would eventually follow that the world would be content. Tolly called this 'sitting on the fence' and had saved from his salary to finance a trip to Berlin during the Olympic Games when he hoped to rescue some of the imprisoned Communists there. Again he was foiled, yet again he returned home a reluctant hero. Mannie Stein had schemed and plotted to rescue some of his fellow Jews, and Tolly had been roped into that enterprise instead.

And then Bridie had betrayed him. Too late he knew that David was right and his family life was everything.

He sat now in the familiar sitting-room in Brunswick Road, and wondered why he had come back. If Olga had been alive, or his mother, they would have provided reason enough. But Natasha was practically engaged to one of the Peplow boys, and the others would hardly remember him. He did not know whether he could face young Barty.

It was obvious they were managing perfectly well now; they had reconstructed their lives since Stein was removed; the house contained no memory of him, and the girl in the kitchen, though not intelligent like Chattie,

341

seemed loyal and loving and proud of them all. It was cruel in a way to come back and force them to adjust again to a stranger. Because that was what he was, a stranger. A displaced person. No more use to the war machine, his cover well and truly blown and his nerve with it, nowhere to go.

As his thoughts reached this stage, he stood up — a physical reaction of self-disgust — and being up, he walked to the oriel and looked out. He told himself it was a preliminary to leaving. He would stare out at the quiet of Brunswick Road, the library opposite, the Co-op restaurant below. He would imprint it again on his memory. And then he would go. Perhaps he would walk to the cathedral before returning to the station. Perhaps he would look at Daker's, where he'd spent so many hours talking to David and April. But then he would leave Gloucester for good.

He knelt on the oriel and leaned his head against the glass. His mouth felt dusty with his own sense of futility, his whole body ached with tiredness. He wondered whether he had outlived his own destiny. Should he have been caught and shot last July during the Night of the Generals? Or before that in Jugoslavia? What was he doing here, still alive and useless?

Then he saw Bridie turn from Eastgate Street into Brunswick Road. There was no missing her because she was the only human being in sight, and though she had changed almost beyond ordinary recognition, Tolly saw her with an inner vision that had known her since her childhood. His gaze locked on her with an intensity that used all his strength and kept him from moving. If he was to leave without meeting her, it would have to be within the next three seconds. Yet five seconds passed and he was still there.

She was thin and she had been plump; her hair was no longer bright, it lay flat across her scalp and was peppered with grey; she had always been exquisitely dressed, now she wore a cotton frock printed with blue daisies — he

342

recognized it, it had belonged to March a long time before the war. It was as if he were seeing the real Bridie, the girl he had always known lurked behind the brash, outrageous flapper of the twenties. A Bridie who had been honed in some way . . . refined in some way.

She stopped where she was on the pavement, as if she had dropped something. There was an uncertainty about her; she seemed frightened of something or someone. She turned and looked over her shoulder towards Clarence Street, and then across the road at a soldier who was emerging from the restaurant. And then she lifted her head, and her eyes met his.

For a long moment she stayed where she was, looking. Then he saw that tears were dripping from the end of her chin. He did not know what to do. He should have gone. She was still so terribly aware of him. She had known of his presence without any physical warning. Would it be the same as before? The demands, the wanting, her voracious appetite for his very soul?

And then she lifted her hands towards the oriel window. She stood still, her hands upheld, pleading, welcoming, saying so much; but she did not move. He could still go. He knew what she was telling him; she would always want him, but he was free to go now if he did not want her.

He did not remember leaving the sitting-room. There was a glimpse of Marlene's startled face by the telephone, and a consciousness that the wonky handle on the front door had not been fixed. Then it was open and he was in the tiny front garden. She was still there, waiting. She made no move towards him. He swept her into his arms and held her as if he would never let her go. And he thought clearly and consciously: thank God to be needed and wanted . . . thank God for a place in this frightful world.

She sobbed into his neck. 'Oh Tolly, my own dear Tolly. It's like a resurrection. I've died and I'm living again.'

She hadn't changed. Not really. She had always loved

343

melodrama and she still did. He bent his head to press his face against hers because kissing wasn't enough. He thanked God that she hadn't changed. He wanted her faults as well as her graces. Oh, he wanted them so much . . .

Nineteen

AUNT Sylv waited until her favourite flower was well out before dying. Her brother Will had gone to rest amid a bower of daffodils, and she wanted to do the same. She had been ready for over six months. When the doodles and the rockets had wrought such terrible havoc in London and the 'safe areas' had been flooded all over again with evacuees, she had gently put back the clock and returned to an era which had been just as cruel but which was warm with familiarity and kindred spirits. She hoped she could hang about for Victor to come back home and for Albert to bring news of his baby, but it was understood at Longmeadow that when Dick, her husband, came to fetch her, nothing would hold her back. The day Bridie Hall brought Tolly to see her, Aunt Sylv took to her bed and did not get up again. Nobody would ever know whether she realized that Victor was with her as she took her last lumbering stride from this world to the next.

Victor's final P.O.W. camp was south of Remagen and was liberated by the Americans on 5th March. With customary transatlantic efficiency, Victor was despatchd in a lorry to the nearest airfield, given an enormous meal, a bath, delousing procedures and some money, and because his unit was unknown to the Americans he was immediately offered a lift in a Flying Fortress returning to a base in Cambridgeshire. So, just a week after liberation, he found himself on a train to London, clutching the papers given back to him by the Germans the day before the Yanks arrived. He was completely disorientated. Whatever had happened to him in the past, he had been with fellow soldiers. Now, his isolation was complete. He felt he was moving around in a block of crystal from which there was no escape.

He had had another American meal at the air base and on the journey he unwrapped the 'rations' they had given him and gorged those. His starved stomach churned uneasily and begged for real English tea. There was none on the train and the queues at the various refreshment rooms were too long for him to join.

The trains into London were almost empty and he was shocked when he arrived at Kings Cross to find enormous queues of people waiting for trains to get out of the city. He went straight to Whitehall, moving like an automaton, and was directed to the HQ of the Army Photographic Unit, where he stamped to attention in an outer office and gave his name and number and was shocked again when the Lance corporal behind the desk stood up and shook his hand and said, 'My God . . . you're one of the desert lot. Welcome home. How the devil did you get here so fast?'

An officer with colonel's pips came out of the inner office and it was old boys together. He made his report and they couldn't get over it.

'Stroke of luck for you, corporal,' the colonel congratulated him. 'You could have been hanging about for ages. It's a bit of a muddle out there what between the three of us trying to get to Berlin first.'

Victor looked around him. 'The three of us, sir?'

'Churchill, Stalin and Roosevelt!'

They laughed, so Victor laughed too.

He was told that over a million people had left London since the doodlebugs and rockets had made life almost insupportable.

'The situation is peculiar to say the least.' The colonel

was signing papers now, the lance corporal totting up his back-pay which would be sizeable. 'We're winning the damned war, but till we can get to Holland we're still being bombarded like sitting ducks here.' He looked up. 'If I were you, corporal, I'd get into one of the queues at Paddington and board the first train going to Gloucester. I know some of you chaps are tempted to sample the high life for a few days when you get back to Blighty, but those damed rockets can just as soon fall on the Windmill as anywhere else.'

'I'm not tempted, sir.'

Victor took his papers and a chit for the Paymaster's Office, and joined a queue there. London was all queues. On the way back to the station there were queues in all the shops for quite ordinary things like apples and kippers. The queue at Paddington was a quarter of a mile long; the previous month they'd closed the station for two hours while they let people on to the trains in small batches. The man in front of him said proudly, 'Well, there's one thing. We've never had to queue for bread.' So when Victor had got his precious ticket he found a baker's and bought a national loaf and ate it as soon as he got on his train. It was like sawdust and coated his stomach lining for a while.

He slept for nearly three days and three nights. On the fourth day when he came downstairs for a cup of wonderful English tea, he found his mother still tearful with relief. He sat at the kitchen table while she talked. He could not quite hear everything she said, and he did not know how to answer her. She wanted to know everything that had happened in the last three years in two or three sentences.

She said, 'Darling, when I went to the door and there you were . . . thought I should faint or have a stroke or something . . . let us know, if only you'd let us know . . . didn't speak to me . . . death warmed-up and not very well warmed at that . . . just tell me, was it terrible, was it terrible, darling?'

He found he was holding a cup of tea in both hands to warm them, though they were not cold.

He said, 'No. Boring.'

He looked at her through tea-steam. He remembered how passionately he had loved her when he was a little boy. He had been jealous of poor old Monty. Sometimes when Monty had been on tour with some show, Victor had crept into bed with his mother and it had been bliss when she circled him with her plump white arms and held him close. They had been able to talk endlessly then, a sort of meaningless chatter of communication, a verbal tickling that usually ended up in laughter.

He said, 'Look at the sun shining through the steam, mother. How on earth is anyone expected to paint steam?'

She gave a sort of sob and came round the table to hold his head to her. He put his cup down and held her too, pressing himself hard to her abdomen as if he wanted to get back into the womb. But there was no comfort there any more.

After his years of near-starvation, he had eaten too much too quickly and for another week he was in bed with what May called stoutly a 'good old-fashioned bilious attack'. Dr Green prescribed a diet of fresh fruit, and as luck would have it, a consignment of oranges arrived in the city that very day. Monty haunted the cookhouse at Winterditch and got three, April queued at Fearis' and got two, Davie, Flo and Gretta split up in the queue at the market and got one each. Gloating, they assembled the eight oranges in the kitchen at Chichester Street, and May got down the lemon squeezer with triumphant ceremony. The trouble was that so much love and care and fruit seemed too much for Victor to take. His dark eyes became darker and bigger in his white face, and his hands picked at the sheets as if they were rough prison blankets.

After ten heart-rending days of this, Monty approached Fred in his garage.

'Could you have a quiet word with him, old man? May's slaving herself to death to cook little meals and he doesn't touch a thing.'

Fred said, 'Victor's never thought much of me, Monty, you know that. David's the one.'

'David drops in every afternoon when the shop closes. Victor looks forward to seeing him, but when he's gone there's no change.' Monty sighed deeply. 'We're all too nice to him, Fred. We pussyfoot around treating him like an invalid, so he is one. I thought you might . . . you know, snap him out of it.'

'I'm the only one in the family who is not nice?' But Fred grinned, not ill-pleased.

'It's not that. But you were in prison camp during the last lot.'

'Only a year of it. Victor's had nearly three years. It's no wonder he's finding it difficult to settle in.'

'Still, you know what it's like. Please, Fred.'

'Of course I'll have a go. But I don't think I can do much good.'

Fred presented himself that afternoon. Victor had a book open on his knees but was not reading.

'Good book, old son?'

Victor tried to summon his old grin. 'Not really. One of Uncle David's. About Edda Mussolini — the most dangerous woman in Europe.'

'Not my cup of tea.'

'Nor mine. I don't want to think about it.'

'Don't blame you. I was the same when I got back. Better things to think about, eh?'

'I don't want to think about anything, actually.'

'Natural enough. Tired out, I should think. You'll soon be back on your feet.'

Victor made a hideous face and leaned on his pillows, closing his eyes.

Fred frowned, recalling his own precipitous return from Germany in 1918. Obviously there had been no mollycoddling over at number nineteen; his mother might have given him a dose of caster oil, but fruit juice was unknown in the Luker household. What had made Fred move so very fast on his return home? Two things, the need for money and his love for March.

He said, 'I suppose you'll have to think about getting some sort of work soon? I take it your demob will come through as soon as the war finishes. Weren't you keen on painting scenery for some rep company?'

'Was I? I can't remember.'

Fred smothered one of his old impatient urges to take Victor by his skeletal shoulders and shake the ennui out of him. He said instead, 'What about Beryl Langham? Wasn't she somewhere in the picture in the old days? You could try thinking about her.'

Victor opened his eyes and looked at Fred with a trace of amusement.

'That one won't wash, Uncle. Beryl's got herself a nice rich Yank. She was afraid — or perhaps she hoped — it would break my heart, but it didn't.'

Fred dropped his efforts at diplomacy and laughed.

'Well, I don't know what to suggest you think about, old man. When I got back from Silesia I went straight to Bath to get your Aunt March back from her elderly uncle. Did you know about that?'

'Sort of.'

'Ah yes. You and Albert were always close.'

Victor said, 'All that fretting and fuming and striving. It sounds hard work. And all a bit pointless in the end.'

'I don't think so.'

'You enjoyed it.'

'I don't know. I had to do it.'

'Yes.' Victor lay back again and after a while he said, 'Sorry Uncle. I know Dad asked you to have a go at me. I'm a hopeless case at the moment.'

'No you're not.' Fred stood up. 'You know that my way and David's way are no good for you. That's a start.' He went to the window and stared down at Chichester Street.

'I thought you might be more like me than David. He sat in that little shop in Barton Street and tried to drink it all away. April saved him from that.' He laughed. 'I just went on fighting my war. I'm probably still fighting it.' He turned and went to the door. 'You'll find your way, Victor. Don't worry about it.'

'Okay.' Victor did not open his eyes.

Davie brought him a cup of tea and a banana sandwich at four o'clock. He watched her putting it on the bedside table and shaking out a napkin, and it was as if she was in another dimension, another world altogether, quite divorced from him. No . . . he was the one in another dimension.

She said, 'Aunt March had to do a Red Cross trip to Bristol and there was a banana boat in. Isn't it marvellous?'

She was so beautiful, so precious. He wondered what it would be like to live in her world and love her and be with her always. Physical beauty was strange; so transient and unreal and unimportant. It was a joke really to try to love it and possess it.

She said, 'Put your head forward so that I can tie this round your neck. It'll slip otherwise.'

He poked his head obediently and felt her fingers cool on his nape. Supposing they slipped round and held his face and she leaned down and kissed him . . . would it provoke any feeling in him?

She cut a sliver of sandwich and held it to his mouth. 'Come on. Eat.' She moved the food between his lips and sat back on the bed. 'I want to talk to you and if you're eating you can't tell me to shut up and you can't go to sleep. D'you realize every time I try to say anything to you, you go to sleep.?'

He smiled and shook his head. She cut more bread and fed him determinedly.

'I've got three things on the agenda. One is long-term, so I'll tell you that first. You know that Albert and

Elizabeth are having a baby in June? Well, I want all of us to go there to the christening. I'm quite determined that there's going to be a family reconciliation. I expect it will be about August, so keep your mind on it and back me up when I suggest it.'

He was mildly tickled by her bossiness. Presumably it was the Luker side of her emerging at last.

'D'you thing it's a good idea?' That was the Rising side, suddenly diffident.

'I don't know. Nice to see Albert again though. And you'll like Lizzie.'

'Really?'

'Really. Next item.'

She cut more food and presented it.

'I'm surprised you have to ask.' She took his hand and held it between hers. 'Your painting. You've got to get started on your war paintings again, Victor.' She shook her head as he snatched his hand away. 'Don't be silly. I'm not suggesting you go into the attic and work. But you've got to begin thinking about it. You could have a sketch block and—'

He swallowed a lump of banana whole and said, 'Cut it out, Davie. I'm not interested.'

She looked angry. 'What the hell d'you mean, you're not interested?'

'I mean what I say. I don't care about painting any more.'

'Such rubbish!' She thumped the eiderdown with her clenched fist. 'I know it's not easy, but you've got to do it, Victor. It's what your life is all about — you remember we talked about it before. You can start to plan in your mind—'

'Davie.' His voice was flat. 'Listen to me. I dare not think. Uncle Fred told me to think. Uncle David brings me books to help me to think. I must not think. Can't you understand that? There is so much — so much — my head would blow off my shoulders if I let one thought creep in. Now be a good girl and go away.'

352

She was silent, staring at him. He closed his eyes so that he would not have to look at that golden loveliness.

At last she said, 'There's one more thing on the agenda, Victor.'

'Go on,' he said wearily.

'I want you to get up tomorrow and come to see Aunt Sylv.'

'Go away, Davie.'

'I mean it, Victor.'

'I'm not capable of getting out of this bed except to go to the lavatory.'

'Yes you are. I know that is heartless, dear Victor. I know you are as weak as a kitten. But you could do it. And I want you to do it.'

'Well I'm not going to.'

'Aunt Sylv is dying, Victor. She is the last of the Risings. She is waiting for something . . . someone. You must come.' She thumped the eiderdown again, this time gently, then she stood up. 'Uncle Fred will come to fetch you at eleven tomorrow morning. You have been sent home safely to us at this time for a special reason, Victor. You have got to come to say goodbye to Aunt Sylv.'

He opened his eyes. 'You really *are* heartless, Davie.'

'No I'm not. If I were heartless I wouldn't know that my heart is breaking. Right now.'

She turned and left the bedroom.

He never knew why he did it. Nothing was said. His mother brought up his breakfast as usual and Gretta came to kiss him goodbye before she went to school. Monty brought in the papers at ten to nine and pointed out that the British had at last crossed the Rhine; at a place called Weasel or Wesel or something. 'Once they can get to Holland and stop those bloody rockets we shall be happier. Nothing in the paper about them, but they were saying at the Lamb and Flag that one dropped at Speakers' Corner.'

'Really?' Victor put the paper down unopened on the

eiderdown and picked up his tea cup. He couldn't get enough tea. He loved the way the fragrant steam filled his eyes and poured into the tubes behind his face.

As soon as his mother collected the tray, he began to get ready. The walk along the landing to the bathroom seemed endless, and he sat on the mahogany lavatory seat wondering how he was going to wash and shave himself and then dress. When the gas geyser blew back — as it always did — he shook and felt his heart thumping against his ribcage, and when his pyjama cord knotted inextricably his eyes filled with tears of sheer frustration.

By ten to eleven he was ready. He went to the top of the stairs and there was his mother, waiting for him, her face stretched with anxiety.

'It's all right, Ma.' He negotiated the stairs carefully; he didn't want a ricked ankle at this stage. 'This isn't going to bother me, you know. If Davie thinks it'll jog me back to life or some such romantic notion, she's got another think coming. It's just one more chore.'

'Then don't do it,' May said, suddenly exasperated. 'I can assure you Aunt Sylv won't know you. So if you're not going to get anything out of it, just go back to bed.'

But he plodded on down, just as Uncle Fred knocked on the door.

It had been dark when he arrived home from London and he hadn't been registering much anyway. Now, after over a week in bed, he saw things with that strange clarity which comes with illness. As they swept out of Chichester Street into London Road, he caught a glimpse of Luker and Rising, the garage Uncle Fred had bought with Albert in mind. It looked prosperous considering petrol shortgages. Then they were going past the second-hand shop with its horse's head mounted on the door. How vididly coloured was the bath of junk outside . . . the mangle . . . the boxes of old books. And on the other side of the road the almshouses with their air of dignity and peace, their gardens full of blowing daffodils and flimsy crocuses. Everything was clamouring to be seen; everything was hurting his retinas.

He closed his eyes and smothered an exclamation of pain, and Fred said, 'Nearly there, old man. Round the roundabout and down Oxstalls Lane . . .' They were at the Winterditch crossroads far too quickly. The red telephone kiosk was sill there, the tall fir trees around the village shop, a child whipping a spinning top on the pavement. Fred drew up to cross the road and through the windows came the country smell of cow dung and grass. Then they chugged down the lane and suddenly arrived at Longmeadow.

The front door opened and David came out to meet them. He smiled congratulations at Victor, but his eyes were grave.

'You are just in time I think, old son, but I'm afraid she won't know you. I'm sorry. Poor Sylv. She doesn't recognize any of us. She's back in her own time.'

Victor got out of the car and clung to the gate for a second to control the shaking in his limbs. David's words hung in his mind; he could see them suspended in a crescent like a talisman. 'Her own time.' That was what Aunt Sylv had, her own time. A slice of eternity specially hers, into which nothing else could enter.

He followed Fred and his mother up the familiar stairs. The carpet was threadbare in places but it didn't matter because he could remember the pattern very well; it had been of red squares and overlapping triangles on a grey ground. Part of his time. He would always have that carpet in his time.

They crowded on to the landing, no-one wanting to open the bedroom door and go in first. David joined them, raised his eyebrows, then turned the handle.

April and her daughters were one side of the bed, March the other. May gave a little twittering sob and joined her. Aunt Sylv was propped right up in the sagging old bed she'd shared with her mother for so many years. Her hair was practically non-existent now, but one or two wisps sprang fluffily around her ears. The flesh around her jaw hung like elephants' ears. Her eyes were closed. Her resemblance to Mr Churchill was uncanny.

Victor went to the foot of the bed and grasped the brass rail. He looked and looked. He felt mildly surprised at his own stupidity in imagining that human beauty was transient. It could survive anything. Torture, age, death. He remembered Gladys, the ATS driver who had been shot in the liberty boat at Dunkirk. Only then had he seen her beauty. Thank God he had always known of Davie's and Aunt Sylv's. Thank God he could still look, he could still see.

Aunt Sylv raised heavy lids and her lizard eyes flicked to the chest of drawers.

'Daffs,' she muttered. 'Good.'

And then her gaze flicked to Victor and stayed there. She drew in a long, shuddering breath and reached out her hands. April caught one arm, March the other; she pulled herself straight.

'Dick!' she said hoarsely. 'Oh. My man.' Then she smiled and her voice became proud. 'My 'usband.'

Her breath went. They laid her on the pillow. Her eyes closed. Flo began to weep.

Albert brought Lizzie down for the funeral, so Davie had her family reconciliation sooner than she had planned. It was strange to see Victor hug Elizabeth and realize that he knew her quite well. It was stranger to sense that Elizabeth was frightened of them all; she stood very close to Albert, one hand on her abdomen as if trying to protect her family from invaders. She obviously wasn't prepared for Aunt March's tall, aristocratic figure, and Aunt March wasn't very good at being informal and oridnary. She looked at poor Uncle Fred as if he might pull a gun at any minute; and of course Aunt May and Mother were too sad to do much about her.

Sometimes it seemed to Davie that funerals were far more important occasions than weddings or christenings.

Aunt March's wedding had almost faded from her memory, but she did recall a lot of work and worry and many misgivings. Gillian Smith's sister's wedding had been nerve-wracking because she herself had had to sing during the 'signing', but apart from that it hadn't been very earth-shattering. And Gretta's christening had been just noisy. Whereas although she had been too young to attend, she would never forget Victor's account of Granddad Rising's funeral with the black-plumed horses stepping sedately down Barton Street. Grandma Rising's had been very sad, but the sadness had been for all of them, not for Grandma who had badly wanted to join Granddad. She remembered Victor hugging a distraught Aunt May and saying 'Come on Mummy-darling. She's done everything she wanted to. She's seen everything she wants to. Don't hold her back.'

Then there had been Olga's funeral. Olga had not done or seen enough. How terrible that had been. But it had been good to stand in the ancient church on the Cross and lift her voice publicly. An offering, even a sacrifice.

Davie looked across the modern pews of Winterditch church at Victor standing next to Elizabeth and Albert. He was so thin; a skeleton hung with clothes. Had he felt dreadful when Aunt Sylv mistook him for Uncle Dick? She hoped not. He really should know it was an honour. If he went into another gloom and thought he should be dead with all his friends back in that awful prison, she would shake him! She felt tears in her eyes. He was so precious and he'd been saved so that he could record all that had happened. She would have to make him see that somehow. He needed her; for the first time in his life he needed someone. She prayed urgently; 'Aunt Sylv, I'm not a bit sad at your going, you've done everything and seen everything just like Grandma. But please, please . . ' She could not end the prayer because she hardly knew what it was. Aunt Sylv might know.

There was a shuffling at the door of the church and everyone stood up.

'I am the resurrection and the life saith the Lord . . .' the vicar intoned.

April leaned across so that her mouth was next to Davie's ear. 'Don't cry, darling. Aunt Sylv wouldn't want it.'

The funeral meats were served at Bedford Close because March's house was big enough to accommodate all of them plus Tolly's large family. It was almost like pre-war days; the sun was warm enough for the French windows to be propped open for an hour or so; Chattie wheeled the trolley back and forth loaded with food which she had obtained by fair and foul means, and after the first subdued half-hour, the party broke into little groups and chattered away uninhibitedly, confident — as they kept saying — that Aunt Sylv would want it that way.

Albert wanted to show Elizabeth his old home; he was suddenly proud of it, suddenly proud of all his relatives who welcomed her and made a fuss of her.

'This is Chattie who has looked after us for years now.'

Chattie beamed approval. 'Oh I can see why Master Albert chose you, miss. You remind me of Jessie Matthews before the war. Now when that baby is born you must spend lots of time here. We've kept all Master Albert's things.'

'This is my cousin, Flo.'

'Oh Albie, it's so *lovely* to see you! Oh do say everything is all right now and you can come to see us often. Elizabeth, make him bring you to see us.'

'This is my Aunt April.' He wondered why he had felt such repugnance for April when Fred had told him about Davie. Since last summer he seemed to understand so much. He smiled at the thin face. 'I was in love with Aunt April for years. Before I met you of course, Lizzie.'

'Oh Albie . . . you wretch!' April kissed Elizabeth. 'My dear, I do wish you could have known our Aunt Sylvia. You won't think us hard-hearted for enjoying all this? She loved a good funeral, she really did. And she would be delighted that you've come to hers.'

'And here is Aunt Bridie. Oh and Uncle Tolly with Gretta. It's wonderful to see you back together.' He looked at them both and Bridie blushed faintly. Albert hurried on, 'Tolly and I shared a great deal in Spain, Lizzie.'

'Welcome to Gloucester.' Tolly pumped Elizabeth's hand and said to Albert, 'We must have a talk before you go. You kept your promise very well.'

Albert grimaced. 'I thought of it when the vicar spoke that text — "I held my tongue and said nothing, I kept silence." It must have made you very unhappy, Aunt Bridie.'

'No unhappier than Tolly. In a way I shared in his work. That is the way I like to think of those years.'

'What a wonderful woman,' Elizabeth murmured as they moved towards May and Monty.

'Bridie?' Albert was going to deny it firmly, then he paused. 'Perhaps. In a way.' He hugged her. 'Let's just say hello to the Goulds, then I want you to see my train set.'

'Train set?'

'Yes. Mother tells me that Fred has kept it cleaned and oiled.'

'What for?'

'Don't you mean "for whom"?' He glinted down at her and, in a gesture, reminiscent of Monty when May was pregnant, rested his hand lightly on the front of her smock. 'You know very well for whom.'

March said, 'You know Freddie, that girl has done wonders for Albie. Look at the way he's showing her off. He's so proud of her.'

'So he should be. I liked the way she wrote to you herself about the baby. She's got character.'

'Yes.' March took his arm. 'Oh Fred. Albie has forgiven me, I think. I wish he could forgive you too.'

'That's . . .' Fred patted her hand. 'That's a little more

difficult, my darling.' He saw her expression and added jauntily, 'Wait until the baby is born. He won't be able to resist me then. I'm going to be very good at the granddad business.'

Gretta passed them, pulling Tolly who was looking exhausted. 'Let me show you.' Fred grabbed the child and sat her on his shoulders. 'Here comes the galloping Major!' he called up to her and jogged into the hall.

Davie trailed Victor at a safe distance. He said hello to the people he hadn't seen since his return: Bridie and Tolly, Natasha's latest young man, Simon Peplow, and the other Hall children. Then he went into the kitchen and kissed Chattie and collected a plate of sandwiches and a tall jug of very hot tea; then he sneaked out of the kitchen door and went down to the air raid shelter. Almost immediately he emerged with a deckchair, set it up beneath a tree bursting with apple blossom, and settled himself down for a solitary picnic. Davie watched him lift the tea jug to his face and inhale the steam with closed eyes. She wondered whether he had a cold.

When he began on his sandwiches, she walked casually down the garden path. He watched her coming. He did not smile a welcome or stop his gentle mastication. When she sat on the grass in front of him, his concentration appeared to intensify as if he were registering how her legs folded at ankle, knee and hip; the way she pulled her navy-blue skirt between herself and the damp grass; the swathe of hair that fell over one side of her face.

She smiled. 'We can thank Aunt Sylv for that, anyway.'

'What are you talking about?'

'You. Looking. You've got that cold analytical expression which means you're trying to remember the way colours run into each other and exactly where an arm finishes and a hand begins.'

'Ha!' He leaned back and swigged more tea. 'Wrong. completely wrong. Oh, I'm looking again all right. But just at that moment I was thinking of Aunt Sylv in her coffin under all that earth.'

She was appalled. 'Victor! So morbid!'

'Wrong again. There was a Russian in the camp for a time. He could draw. So we were able to communicate. I drew Monty and May. He drew his mother. She was dead, but apparently they have glass lids to their coffins so he could still see her when she was lowered into her grave.' He bit into another sandwich. 'There are some things we shouldn't see. I used to think I wanted to see everything in the world. But I know better now. It's a question of privacy.'

He leaned forward. 'She didn't make a mistake you know, Davie. Mother thinks she mistook me for Uncle Dick. But she didn't. She knew it was me.'

Davie looked at him doubtfully. 'Perhaps she saw Uncle Dick just beyond you, Victor.'

'No. I *was* Uncle Dick.' He laughed at her expression. 'I know I'm half out of my mind, darling, but I'm as sane as you are when I say that.' His thin face became animated. 'Listen Davie, I'm no good at explaining so if this doesn't make sense, we'll have to forget it. But in that second of time, Aunt Sylv . . . *spanned* the past and the future. She knew I was her great-nephew, but I was part of the . . . the . . . romance. The eternal romance. So I was Dick. We're all part of it, Davie. This business of loving our parents and our children, our sisters and our brothers, our lovers and our husbands. That's what I have to record, my darling. Not horrors. But love.' He laughed again. 'Albert told me once that I loved everything — that I painted with love. I'd forgotten that. Aunt Sylv reminded me. And she reminded me that I couldn't just look. I had to feel. I had to be.' He put the jug carefully on to the grass and touched her hair. 'Oh Davie, I do love you so.'

She closed her eyes and felt the tears again. Aunt Sylv had answered her prayer before she asked it.

She said huskily, 'I know. I love you too. Why haven't we always known?'

'I expect we did. You don't always know what you know.'

'Oh Victor.'

He stroked her hair gently. 'It's pretty hopeless really, darling. Half of you still belongs to Albert. And I'm all at sea. Not even demobbed yet. And when I am it'll be ages before I can earn a living. I'm practically potty because everyone I know is dead. I'm an old man of twenty-six and you're a young girl of nineteen who is already famous as a singer.'

She said strongly, 'I can see it'll work very well. You see, my lovely beautiful Victor, I don't belong to Albert any more than I belong to Flo —' she heard his indrawn breath but did not pause — 'and you've always been so damned preoccupied with your painting you haven't had time to fall in love. So being potty is a boon — it's given you that time. And . . .' her voice rose. 'And, darling, you need me. I'm not dead. I'm alive. Not that that matters much. Aunt Sylv showed you there's not that much difference anyway — it's only that we can't see the others.' She turned and knelt suddenly and put her hands on his knees. He felt her energy pour into him. 'But it's lucky that I am alive because you couldn't marry me if I was dead. And if I was dead I couldn't earn enough money to look after us while you get yourself ready to be the most famous painter that ever was!' She stared into his face. 'You won't mind that, will you, darling? You see I've never been much use to anyone. It would be so good for me to know I can pull my weight. It will make my singing really worthwhile.'

He nearly wept for love of her. He tried to tell her that he knew all about her and she was a wonderful girl, but she put a finger on his mouth.

'You don't have to say things, Victor. Keep the lid on the coffin.'

He laughed through his own tears at that. And then they stood up and put their arms around each other and held on tightly.

May said, 'The really strange thing about losing Aunt Sylv, is that we're now the older generation. There's 'no-one between us and the everlasting.'

April leaned against the open window and gazed down the garden. March had planted her bulbs in the grass, and daffodils were everywhere. In the lee of the air raid shelter Victor and Davie sat quietly, talking. She wondered how Davie felt about seeing Albert and Elizabeth.

She said, 'They were a marvellous lot, weren't they? That old pair grubbing a living in a tied cottage and bringing up Vi and Sylv, Wallie and Jack—

'Not to mention Sylv's and Vi's little accidents,' May giggled.

March said, 'Our Albert loved them. He loved their closeness to the earth and the animals.'

'Like Albert Frederick. Our Albert must have passed that on to your son, March,' May said sentimentally.

'Yes.' March spoke with quiet satisfaction. 'Yes. Albert is very happy. Thank God.'

'And those old Risings,' April reminded her. 'They passed their love of the land down. Don't forget them.'

They were silent, March stacking crockery on to trays, May sitting back with her legs on a hassock admiring her still-slim ankles, April gazing at her daughter. Monty and David came into the room.

'Time we got our invalid back home, Mummy darling?' Monty asked fondly.

'He's not an invalid any more, Monty,' May said, not moving. 'Since he went to see Aunt Sylv last week he's been all right.'

'I don't think we can hope for his recovery to be quite so instantaneous, dearest.' Monty was trying to avoid a tête-a-tête with Tolly. He certainly did not want to explain why he was no longer working at Williams and Sons. 'Besides Gretta is getting fractious. She has punched Barty twice and if she does it a third time he'll forget he's a little gentleman and murder her.'

May started to laugh and March said, 'We all spoil that child. It's not fair to her.'

David was standing with his arm around April, gazing

down the garden. She turned and looked at him and said breathlessly, 'D'you suppose . . .?'

He nodded 'I would think so by the looks of things. I've often wondered if they would. They're ideally suited.'

May stood up and looked too. 'Well! Well . . . wouldn't that be *marvellous!*'

March said, 'It would make everything complete somehow.'

Fred crossed their line of vision, carrying Gretta on his shoulders. He waved to them, then turned and followed the direction of their concerted gaze. For a long moment he stared as Victor and Davie hugged each other and kissed, and hugged each other again. Then he looked back at the group in the sitting-room and his eyes sought out April. She stared back at him while Gretta thumped on the pale hair that was so like Davie's own. Then she smiled and lifted her hand in a small salute.

'Be the galloping major, Uncle Fred! Gretta shouted.

He went into action, cavorting ridiculously to show his pleasure.

'Diddly, diddly, diddly, dump, as proud as an Indian rajah!'

'One thing about being the older generation,' March commented happily, 'is that it will be so restful to sit in the wings and watch someone else do the acting.'

She stepped out of the French windows to join Fred and encourage Gretta to dismount and go home. May and Monty went for their coats. David put his arm around his wife very tightly.

'All right now, Primrose?' he asked, looking at her face searchingly.

'Yes. Oh yes, David.' She had so often wondered in terror how much David knew. Now it did not seem to matter. She said, 'I'm so pleased . . . I do hope it will work out.'

'And you'll let the dead bury their dead?'

She drew away and returned his search look.

'That always sounds so . . . harsh, darling. What do you mean?'

'I mean, will you let go of the past, Primrose?'

'But darling, I never want to forget what has happened. We *are* our past.'

'But you mustn't let it haunt you. It has its place in time. That is enough.' He cupped her face and kissed her gently. 'Listen, Primrose. In a few weeks now the war will be over. We won't forget it. But we're jolly well looking forward to peace, aren't we?'

She nodded and smiled suddenly, understanding.

'It must smell sweet, never rank,' she whispered. Then she quoted, 'Here's rosemary for remembrance.'

He whispered, 'That's it. That's it exactly.'

And they held on to each other in deep thankfulness for all their rosemary.

THE END

A SCATTERING OF DAISIES
by Susan Sallis

Will Rising had dragged himself from humble beginnings to his own small tailoring business in Gloucester — and on the way he'd fallen violently in love with Florence, refined, delicate, and wanting something better for her children.

March was the eldest girl, the least loved, the plain, unattractive one who, as the family grew, became more and more the household drudge. But March, a strange, intelligent, unhappy child, had inherited some of her mother's dreams. March Rising was determined to break out of the round of poverty and hard work, to find wealth, and love, and happiness.

0 552 12375 7

THE DAFFODILS OF NEWENT
by Susan Sallis

They were called the Daffodil Girls, spirited and bright, enduring, loving and dancing their way through the gay and desperate twenties.

APRIL   who married the tortured and sexually suspect David Daker, convinced she could blot out his memories of the trenches.

MAY   pregnant by her handsome music hall star husband who didn't want to settle down.

MARCH   loved and betrayed by the man who had fathered her child, and who still wanted her.

The Daffodils of Newent — three wonderful girls whose story began in A SCATTERING OF DAISIES.

0 552 12579 2